Michael

10/23

CHILDREN'S CLASSICS

Treasure Island

Robert Louis Stevenson

Treasure Island

PARRAGON

Treasure Island
A Parragon Classic

This is a Siena Book
Siena is an imprint of Parragon

First published in 1883

This edition published in 1999 by
Parragon
13 Whiteladies Road
Clifton
Bristol BS8 1PB

Printed and bound in the UK

To
S. L. O.,
an American gentleman,
in accordance with whose classic taste
the following narrative has been designed,
it is now, in return for numerous delightful hours
and with the kindest wishes,
dedicated by his affectionate friend,
THE AUTHOR

TO THE HESITATING PURCHASER

If sailor tales to sailor tunes,
Storm and adventure, heat and cold,
If schooners, islands, and maroons
  And Buccaneers and buried Gold,
And all the old romance, retold
  Exactly in the ancient way,
Can please, as me they pleased of old,
  The wiser youngsters of today:

—So be it, and fall on! If not,
  If studious youth no longer crave,
His ancient appetites forgot,
  Kingston, or Ballantyne the brave,
Or Cooper of the wood and wave:
  So be it, also! And may I
And all my pirates share the grave
  Where these and their creations lie!

PART I

THE OLD BUCCANEER

1. THE OLD SEA DOG AT THE "ADMIRAL BENBOW"

Squire Trelawney, Dr. Livesey, and the rest of these gentlemen having asked me to write down the whole particulars about Treasure Island, from the beginning to the end, keeping nothing back but the bearings of the island, and that only because there is still treasure not yet lifted, I take up my pen in the year of grace 17—, and go back to the time when my father kept the "Admiral Benbow" inn, and the brown old seaman, with the sabre cut, first took up his lodging under our roof.

I remember him as if it were yesterday, as he came plodding to the inn door, his sea-chest following behind him in a hand-barrow; a tall, strong, heavy, nut-brown man; his tarry pigtail falling over the shoulders of his soiled blue coat; his hands ragged and scarred, with black, broken nails; and the sabre cut across one cheek, a dirty, livid white. I remember him looking round the cove and whistling to himself as he did so, and then breaking out in that old sea-song that he sang so often afterwards:

"Fifteen men on the dead man's chest—
Yo-ho-ho, and a bottle of rum!"

in the high, old tottering voice that seemed to have been tuned and broken at the capstan bars. Then he rapped on the door with a bit of stick like a handspike that he carried, and when my father appeared, called roughly for a glass of rum. This, when it was brought to him, he drank slowly, like a connoisseur, lingering on the taste, and still looking about him at the cliffs and up at our sign-board.

"This is a handy cove," says he, at length; "and a pleasant sittyated grog-shop. Much company, mate?"

My father told him no, very little company, the more was the pity.

"Well, then," said he, this is the berth for me. Here you, matey," he cried to the man who trundled the barrow; "bring up alongside and help up my chest. I'll stay here a bit," he continued. "I'm a plain man; rum and bacon and eggs is what I want, and that head up there for to watch ships off. What you mought call me? You mought call me captain. Oh, I see what you're at—there;" and he threw down three or four gold pieces on the threshold. "You can tell me when I've worked through that," says he, looking as fierce as a commander.

And, indeed, bad as his clothes were, and coarsely as he spoke, he had none of the appearance of a man who sailed before the mast; but seemed like a mate or skipper, accustomed to be obeyed or to strike. The man who came with the barrow told us the mail had set him down the morning before at the "Royal George"; that he had inquired what inns there were along the coast, and hearing ours well spoken of, I suppose, and described as lonely, had chosen it from the others for his place of residence. And that was all we could learn of our guest.

He was a very silent man by custom. All day he hung round the cove, or upon the cliffs, with a brass telescope; all evening he sat in a corner of the parlour next the fire, and drank rum and water very strong. Mostly he would not speak when spoken to; only look up sudden and fierce, and blow through his nose like a fog-horn; and we and the people who came about our house soon learned to let him be. Every day, when he came back from his stroll, he would ask if any seafaring men had gone by along the road. At first we thought it was the want of company of his own kind that made him ask this question; but at last we began to see he was desirous to avoid them. When a seaman put up at the "Admiral Benbow" (as now and then some did, making by the coast road for Bristol), he would look in at him through the curtained door before he entered the parlour; and he was always sure to be as silent as a mouse when any such was present. For me, at least, there was no secret about the matter; for I was, in a way, a sharer in his alarms. He had taken me aside one day, and promised me a silver fourpenny on the first of every month if I would only keep my "weather-eye open for a seafaring man with one leg", and let him know the moment he appeared. Often enough, when the first of the month came round, and I applied to him for my wage, he would only blow through his nose at me, and stare me down; but before the week was out he was sure to think better of it, bring me my fourpenny piece, and repeat his orders to look out for "the seafaring man with one leg".

How that personage haunted my dreams, I need scarcely tell you. On stormy nights, when the wind shook the four corners of the house, and the surf roared along the cove and up the cliffs, I would see him in a thousand forms, and with a thousand diabolical expressions. Now the leg would be cut off at the knee, now at the hip; now he was a monstrous kind of a creature who had never had but the one leg, and that in the middle of his body. To see him leap and run and pursue me over hedge and ditch was the worst of nightmares. And altogether I paid pretty dear for my monthly fourpenny piece, in the shape of these abominable fancies.

But though I was so terrified by the idea of the seafaring man with one leg, I was far less afraid of the captain himself than anybody else who knew him. There were nights when he took a deal more rum and water than his head would carry; and then he would sometimes sit and sing his wicked, old, wild sea-songs, minding nobody; but sometimes he would call for glasses round, and force all the trembling company to listen to his stories or bear a chorus to his singing. Often I have heard the house shaking with "Yo-ho-ho, and a bottle of rum", all the neighbours joining in for dear life, with the fear of death upon them, and each singing louder than the other, to avoid remark. For in these fits he was the most over-riding companion ever known; he would slap his hand on the table for silence all round; he would fly up in a passion of anger at a question, or sometimes because none was put, and so he judged the company was not following his story. Nor would he allow anyone to leave the inn till he had drunk himself sleepy and reeled off to bed.

His stories were what frightened people worst of all. Dreadful stories they were; about hanging, and walking the plank, and storms at sea, and the Dry Tortugas, and wild deeds and places on the Spanish Main. By his own account he must have lived his life among some of the wickedest men that God ever allowed upon the sea; and the language in which he told these stories shocked our plain country people almost as much as the crimes that he described. My father was always saying the inn would be ruined, for people would soon cease coming there to be tyrannized over and put down, and sent shivering to their beds; but I really believe his presence did us good. People were frightened at the time, but on looking back they rather liked it; it was a fine excitement in a quiet country life; and there was even a party of the younger men who pretended to admire him, calling him a "true sea-dog", and "a real old salt", and such-like names, and saying there was the sort of man that made England terrible at sea.

In one way, indeed, he bade fair to ruin us; for he kept on staying week after week, and at last month after month, so that all the money had been long exhausted, and still my father never plucked up the heart to insist on having more. If ever he mentioned it, the captain blew through his nose so loudly, that you might say he roared, and stared my poor father out of the room. I have seen him wringing his hands after such a rebuff, and I am sure the annoyance and the terror he lived in must have greatly hastened his early and unhappy death.

All the time he lived with us the captain made no change whatever in his dress but to buy some stockings from a hawker. One of the cocks of his hat having fallen down, he let it hang from that day forth, though it was a great annoyance when it blew. I remember the appearance of his coat, which he patched himself upstairs in his room, and which, before the end, was nothing but patches. He never wrote or received a letter, and he never spoke with any but the neighbours, and with these, for the most part, only when drunk on rum. The great sea-chest none of us had ever seen open.

He was only once crossed, and that was towards the end, when my poor father was far gone in a decline that took him off. Dr. Livesey came late one afternoon to see the patient, took a bit of dinner from my mother, and went into the parlour to smoke a pipe until his horse should come down from the hamlet, for we had no stabling at the old "Benbow", I followed him in, and I remember observing the contrast the neat, bright doctor, with his powder as white as snow, and his bright, black eyes and pleasant manners, made with the coltish country folk, and above all, with that filthy, heavy, bleared scarecrow of a pirate of ours, sitting far gone in rum, with his arms on the table. Suddenly he—the captain, that is—began to pipe up his eternal song:

"Fifteen men on the dead man's chest—
  Yo-ho-ho, and a bottle of rum!
Drink and the devil had done for the rest—
  Yo-ho-ho, and a bottle of rum! "

At first I had supposed "the dead man's chest" to be that identical big box of his upstairs in the front room, and the thought had been mingled in my nightmares with that of the one-legged seafaring man. But by this time we had all long ceased to pay any particular notice to the song; it was new, that night, to nobody but Dr. Livesey, and on him I observed it did not produce an agreeable effect, for he looked up for a moment quite angrily before he went on with his talk to old Taylor, the gardener, on a new cure for the rheumatics. In the meantime, the captain gradually brightened up at his own music, and at last clapped his hand upon the table before him in a way we all knew to mean—silence. The voices stopped at once, all but Dr. Livesey's; he went on as before, speaking clear and kind, and drawing briskly at his pipe between every word or two. The captain glared at him for a while, flapped his hand again, glared still harder, and at last broke out with a villainous, low oath: "Silence, there, between decks!"

"Were you addressing me, sir?" says the doctor; and when the ruffian had told him, with another oath, that this was so,

"I have only one thing to say to you, sir," replies the doctor, "that if you keep on drinking rum, the world will soon be quit of a very dirty scoundrel!"

The old fellow's fury was awful. He sprang to his feet, drew and opened a sailor's clasp-knife, and, balancing it open on the palm of his hand, threatened to pin the doctor to the wall.

The doctor never so much as moved. He spoke to him, as before, over his shoulder, and in the same tone of voice; rather high, so that all the room might hear, but perfectly calm and steady: "If you do not put that knife this instant in your pocket, I promise, upon my honour, you shall hang at next assizes."

Then followed a battle of looks between them; but the captain soon knuckled under, put up his weapon, and resumed his seat, grumbling like a beaten dog.

"And now, sir," continued the doctor, "since I now know there's such a fellow in my district, you may count I'll have an eye upon you day and night. I'm not a doctor only; I'm a magistrate; and if I catch a breath of complaint against you, if it's only for a piece of incivility like tonight's, I'll take effectual means to have you hunted down and routed out of this. Let that suffice."

Soon after Dr. Livesey's horse came to the door, and he rode away; but the captain held his peace that evening, and for many evenings to come.

2. BLACK DOG APPEARS AND DISAPPEARS

It was not very long after this that there occurred the first of the mysterious events that rid us at last of the captain, though not, as you will see, of his affairs.

It was a bitter cold winter, with long, hard frosts and heavy gales; and it was plain from the first that my poor father was little likely to see the spring. He sank daily, and my mother and I had all the inn upon our hands; and were kept busy enough, without paying much regard to our unpleasant guest.

It was one January morning, very early—a pinching, frosty

morning—the cove all grey with hoar-frost, the ripple lapping softly on the stones, the sun still low and only touching the hilltops and shining far to seaward. The captain had risen earlier than usual, and set out down the beach, his cutlass swinging under the broad skirts of the old blue coat, his brass telescope under his arm, his hat tilted back upon his head. I remember his breath hanging like smoke in his wake as he strode off, and the last sound I heard of him, as he turned the big rock, was a loud snort of indignation, as though his mind was still running upon Dr. Livesey.

Well, mother was upstairs with father; and I was laying the breakfast-table against the captain's return, when the parlour door opened, and a man stepped in on whom I had never set my eyes before. He was a pale, tallowy creature, wanting two fingers of the left hand; and, though he wore a cutlass, he did not look much like a fighter. I had always my eye open for seafaring men, with one leg or two, and I remember this one puzzled me. He was not sailorly, and yet he had a smack of the sea about him too.

I asked him what was for his service, and he said he would take rum; but as I was going out of the room to fetch it he sat down upon a table and motioned me to draw near. I paused where I was with my napkin in my hand.

"Come here, sonny," say he, "Come nearer here."

I took a step nearer.

"Is this here table for my mate Bill?" he asked, with a kind of leer.

I told him I did not know his mate Bill and this was for a person who stayed in our house, whom we called the captain.

"Well," said he, "my mate Bill would be called the captain, as like as not. He has a cut on one cheek, and a mighty pleasant way with him, particularly in drink, has my mate Bill. We'll put it, for argument like, that your captain has a cut on one cheek—and we'll put it, if you like, that that cheek's the right one. Ah, well! I told you. Now, is my mate Bill in this here house?"

I told him he was out walking.

"Which way, sonny? Which way is he gone?"

And when I had pointed out the rock and told him how the captain was likely to return, and how soon, and answered a few other questions, "Ah," said he, "this'll be as good as drink to my mate Bill."

The expression of his face as he said these words was not at all pleasant, and I had my own reasons for thinking that the stranger was mistaken, even supposing he meant what he said. But it was no affair of mine, I thought; and, besides, it was difficult to know what to do. The stranger kept hanging about just outside the inn door, peering round the corner like a cat waiting for a mouse. Once I stepped out myself into the road, but he immediately called me back, and, as I did not obey quick enough for his fancy, a most horrible change came over his tallowy face, and he ordered me in, with an oath that made me jump. As soon as I was back again he returned to his former manner, half fawning, half sneering, patted me on the shoulder, told me I was a good boy, and he had taken quite a fancy to me. "I have a son of my own," said he, "as like you as two blocks, and he's all the pride of my 'art. But the great thing for boys is discipline, sonny—discipline. Now, if you had sailed along of Bill, you wouldn't have stood there to be spoke to twice—not you. That was never Bill's way, nor the way of sich as sailed with him. And here, sure enough, is my mate Bill, with a spy-glass under his arm, bless his old 'art to be sure. You and me'll just go back into the parlour, sonny, and get behind the door, and we'll give Bill a little surprise—bless his 'art, I say again."

So saying, the stranger backed along with me into the parlour, and put me behind him in the corner, so that we were both hidden by the open door. I was very uneasy and alarmed, as you may fancy, and it rather added to my fears to observe that the stranger was certainly frightened himself. He cleared the hilt of his cutlass and loosened the blade in the sheath; and all the time we were waiting there he kept swallowing as if he felt what we used to call a lump in the throat.

At last in strode the captain, slammed the door behind him, without looking to the right or left, and marched straight across the room to where his breakfast awaited him.

"Bill," said the stranger, in a voice that I thought he had tried to make bold and big. The captain spun round on his heel and fronted us; all the brown had gone out of his face, and even his nose was blue; he had the look of a man who sees a ghost, or the evil one, or something worse, if anything can be; and, upon my word, I felt sorry to see him, all in a moment, turn so old and sick.

"Come, Bill, you know me; you know an old shipmate, Bill, surely," said the stranger.

The captain made a sort of gasp.

"Black Dog!" said he.

"And who else?" returned the other, getting more at his ease. "Black Dog as ever was, come for to see his old ship-mate Billy, at the 'Admiral Benbow' inn. Ah, Bill, Bill, we have seen a sight of times, us two, since I lost them two talons," holding up his mutilated hand.

"Now, look here," said the captain; "you've run me down; here I am; well, then, speak up: what is it?"

"That's you, Bill," returned Black Dog, "you're in the right of it, Billy. I'll have a glass of rum from this dear child here, as I've took such a liking to; and we'll sit down, if you please, and talk square, like old shipmates."

When I returned with the rum, they were already seated on either side of the captain's breakfast table—Black Dog next to the door, and sitting sideways, so as to have one eye on his old shipmate, and one, as I thought, on his retreat.

He bade me go, and leave the door wide open. "None of your keyholes for me, sonny," he said; and I left them together, and retired into the bar.

For a long time, though I certainly did my best to listen, I could hear nothing but a low gabbling; but at last the voices began to grow higher, and I could pick up a word or two, mostly oaths, from the captain.

"No, no, no, no; and an end of it!" he cried once. And again, "If it comes to swinging, swing all, say I."

Then all of a sudden there was a tremendous explosion of oaths and other noises—the chair and table went over in a lump, a clash of steel followed, and then a cry of pain, and the next instant I saw Black Dog in full flight, and the captain hotly pursuing, both with drawn cutlasses, and the former streaming blood from the left shoulder. Just at the door, the. captain aimed at the fugitive one last tremendous cut, which would certainly have split him to the chine had it not been intercepted by our big sign-board of Admiral Benbow. You may see the notch on the lower side of the frame to this day.

That blow was the last of the battle. Once out upon the road, Black Dog, in spite of his wound, showed a wonderful clean pair of heels, and disappeared over the edge of the hill in half a minute. The captain, for his part, stood staring at the sign-board like a bewildered man. Then he passed his hand over his eyes several times, and at last turned back into the house.

"Jim," says he, "rum"; and as he spoke, he reeled a little, and caught himself with one hand against the wall.

"Are you hurt?" cried I.

"Rum," he repeated. "I must get away from here. Rum! rum!"

I ran to fetch it; but I was quite unsteadied by all that had fallen out, and I broke one glass and fouled the tap, and while I was still getting in my own way, I heard a loud fall in the parlour, and, running in, beheld the captain lying full length upon the floor. At the same instant my mother, alarmed by the cries and fighting, came running downstairs to help me. Between us we raised his head. He was breathing very loud and hard; but his eyes were closed, and his face a horrible colour.

"Dear, deary me," cried my mother, "what a disgrace upon the house! And your poor father sick!"

In the meantime, we had no idea what to do to help the captain, nor any other thought but that he had got his death-hurt in the scuffle with the stranger. I got the rum, to be sure, and tried to put it down his throat; but his teeth were tightly shut, and his jaws as strong as iron. It was a happy relief for us when the door opened and Doctor Livesey came in, on his visit to my father.

"Oh, doctor," we cried, "what shall we do? Where is he wounded?"

"Wounded? A fiddle-stick's end!" said the doctor. "No more wounded than you or I. The man has had a stroke, as I warned him. Now, Mrs. Hawkins, just you run upstairs to your husband, and tell him, if possible, nothing about it. For my part, I must do my best to save this fellow's trebly worthless life; and Jim here will get me a basin."

When I got back with the basin, the doctor had already ripped up the captain's sleeve, and exposed his great sinewy arm. It was tattooed in several places. "Here's luck." "A fair wind," and "Billy Bones his fancy," were very neatly and clearly executed on the forearm; and up near the shoulder there was a sketch of a gallows and a man hanging from it—done, as I thought, with great spirit.

"Prophetic," said the doctor, touching this picture with his finger. "And now, Master Billy Bones, if that be your name, we'll have a look at the colour of your blood. Jim," he said, "are you afraid of blood?"

"No, sir," said I.

"Well, then," said he, "you hold the basin"; and with that he took his lancet and opened a vein.

A great deal of blood was taken before the captain opened his eyes and looked mistily about him. First he recognized the doctor with an unmistakable frown; then his glance fell upon me, and he looked relieved. But suddenly his colour changed, and he tried to raise himself, crying:

"Where's Black Dog?"

"There is no Black Dog here," said the doctor, "except what you have on your own back. You have been drinking rum; you have had a stroke, precisely as I told you; and I have just, very much against my own will, dragged you head-foremost out of the grave. Now, Mr. Bones—"

"That's not my name," he interrupted.

"Much I care," returned the doctor. "It's the name of a buccaneer of my acquaintance; and I call you by it for the sake of shortness, and what I have to say to you is this: one glass of rum won't kill you, but if you take one you'll take another and another, and I stake my wig if you don't break off short, you'll die—do you understand that?—die, and go to your own place, like the men in the Bible. Come, now, make an effort. I'll help you to your bed for once."

Between us, with much trouble, we managed to hoist him upstairs, and laid him on his bed, where his head fell back on the pillow, as if he were almost fainting.

"Now, mind you," said the doctor, "I clear my conscience — the name of rum for you is death."

And with that he went off to see my father, taking me with him by the arm.

"This is nothing," he said, as soon as he had closed the door. "I have drawn blood enough to keep him quiet a while; he should lie for a week where he is—that is the best thing for him and you; but another stroke would settle him."

3. THE BLACK SPOT

About noon I stopped at the captain's door with some cooling drinks and medicines. He was lying very much as we had left him, only a little higher, and he seemed both weak and excited.

"Jim," he said, "you're the only one here that's worth anything; and you know I've been always good to you. Never a month but I've given you a silver fourpenny for yourself. And now you see, mate, I'm pretty low, and deserted by all; and, Jim, you'll bring me one noggin of rum, now, won't you, matey?"

"The doctor—" I began.

But he broke in cursing the doctor, in a feeble voice, but heartily. "Doctors is all swabs," he said; "and that doctor there, why, what do he know about seafaring men? I been in places hot as pitch, and mates dropping round with Yellow Jack, and the blessed land a-heaving like the sea with earthquakes—what do the doctor know of lands like that?—and I lived on rum, I tell you. It's been meat and drink, and man and wife, to me; and if I'm not to have my rum now I'm a poor old hulk on a lee shore, my blood'll be on you, Jim, and that doctor swab"; and he ran on again for a while with curses. "Look, Jim, how my fingers fidget," he continued, in the pleading tone. "I can't keep 'em still, not I. I haven't had a drop this blessed day. That doctor's a fool, I tell you. If I don't have a drain o' rum, Jim, I'll have the horrors; I seen some on 'em already. I seen old Flint in the corner there, behind you; as plain as print, I seen him; and if I get horrors, I'm a man that has lived rough, and I'll raise Cain. Your doctor hisself said one glass wouldn't hurt me. I'll give you a golden guinea for a noggin, Jim."

He was growing more and more excited, and this alarmed me for my father, who was very low that day, and needed quiet; besides, I was reassured by the doctor's words, now quoted to me, and rather offended by the offer of a bribe.

"I want none of your money," said I, "but what you owe my father. I'll get you one glass, and no more."

When I brought it to him, he seized it greedily, and drank it out.

"Ah, ay," said he, "that's some better, sure enough. And now, matey, did that doctor say how long I was to lie here in this old berth?"

"A week at least," said I.

"Thunder!" he cried. "A week! I can't do that: they'd have the black spot on me by then. The lubbers is going about to get the wind of me this blessed moment; lubbers as couldn't keep what they got, and want to nail what is another's. Is that seamanly behaviour, now, I want to know? But I'm a saving soul. I never wasted good money of mine, nor lost it neither; and I'll trick 'em again. I'm not afraid on 'em. I'll shake out another reef, matey, and daddle 'em again."

As he was thus speaking, he had risen from bed with great difficulty, holding to my shoulder with a grip that almost made me cry out, and moving his legs like so much dead weight. His words, spirited as they were in meaning, contrasted sadly with the weakness of the voice in which they were uttered. He paused when he had got into a sitting position on the edge.

"That doctor's done me," he murmured. "My ears is singing. Lay me back."

Before I could do much to help him he had fallen back again to his former place, where he lay for a while silent.

"Jim," he said, at length, "you saw that seafaring man today?"

"Black Dog?" I asked.

"Ah! Black Dog," says he. "*He's* a bad 'un; but there's worse than put him on. Now, if I can't get away nohow, and they tip me the black spot, mind you, it's my old sea-chest they're after; you get on a horse—you can, can't you? Well, then, you get on a horse, and go to—well, yes, I will!—to that eternal doctor swab, and tell him to pipe all hands—magistrates and sich—and he'll lay 'em aboard at the 'Admiral Benbow'—all old Flint's crew, man and boy, all on 'em that's left. I was first mate, I was, old Flint's first mate, and I'm the on'y one as knows the place. He gave it me to Savannah, when he lay a-dying, like as if I was to now, you see. But you won't peach unless they get the black spot on me, or unless you see that Black Dog again, or a sea-faring man with one leg, Jim—him above all."

"But what is the black spot, captain?" I asked.

"That's a summons, mate. I'll tell you if they get that. But keep your weather-eye open, Jim, and I'll share with you equals, upon my honour."

He wandered a little longer, his voice growing weaker; but soon after I had given him his medicine, which he took like a child, with the remark, "If ever a seaman wanted drugs, it's me," he fell at last into a heavy swoon-like sleep, in which I left him. What I should have done had all gone well I do not know. Probably I should have told the whole story to the doctor; for I was in mortal fear lest the captain should repent of his confessions and make an end of me. But as things fell out, my poor father died quite suddenly that evening, which put all other matters on one side. Our natural distress, the visits of the neighbours, the arranging of the funeral, and all the work of the inn to be carried on in the meanwhile, kept me so busy that I had scarcely time to think of the captain, far less to be afraid of him.

He got downstairs next morning, to be sure, and had his

meals as usual, though he ate little, and had more, I am afraid, than this usual supply of rum, for he helped himself out of the bar, scowling and blowing through his nose, and no one dared to cross him. On the night before the funeral he was as drunk as ever; and it was shocking, in that house of mourning, to hear him singing away at his ugly old sea-song; but, weak as he was, we were all in the fear of death for him, and the doctor was suddenly taken up with a case many miles away, and was never near the house after my father's death. I have said the captain was weak; and indeed he seemed rather to grow weaker than regain his strength. He clambered up and down stairs, and went from the parlour to the bar and back again, and sometimes put his nose out of doors to smell the sea, holding on to the walls as he went for support, and breathing hard and fast like a man on a steep mountain. He never particularly addressed me, and it is my belief he had as good as forgotten his confidences; but his temper was more flighty, and, allowing for his bodily weakness, more violent than ever. He had an alarming way now when he was drunk of drawing his cutlass and laying it bare before him on the table. But, with all that, he minded people less, and seemed shut up in his own thoughts and rather wandering. Once, for instance, to our extreme wonder, he piped up to a different air, a kind of country love-song, that he must have learned in his youth before he had begun to follow the sea.

So things passed until, the day after the funeral, and about three o'clock of a bitter, foggy, frosty afternoon, I was standing at the door for a moment, full of sad thoughts about my father, when I saw someone drawing slowly near along the road. He was plainly blind, for he tapped before him with a stick, and wore a great green shade over his eyes and nose; and he was hunched, as if with age or weakness, and wore a huge old tattered sea-cloak with a hood, that made him appear positively deformed. I never saw in my life a more dreadful looking figure. He stopped a little from the inn, and, raising his voice in an old sing-song, addressed the air in front of him:

"Will any kind friend inform a poor blind man, who has lost the precious sight of his eyes in the gracious defence of his native country, England, and God bless King George!—where or in what part of this country he may now be?"

"You are at the 'Admiral Benbow', Black Hill Cove, my good man," said I.

"I hear a voice", said he—"a young voice. Will you give me your hand, my kind young friend, and lead me in?"

I held out my hand, and the horrible, soft-spoken, eyeless creature gripped it in a moment like a vice. I was so much startled that I struggled to withdraw; but the blind man pulled me close up to him with a single action of his arm.

"Now, boy," he said, "take me in to the captain."

"Sir," said I, "upon my word I dare not."

"Oh," he sneered, "that's it! Take me in straight, or I'll break your arm."

And he gave it, as he spoke, a wrench that made me cry out.

"Sir," I said, "it is for yourself I mean. The captain is not what he used to be. He sits with a drawn cutlass. Another gentleman—"

"Come, now, march," interrupted he; and I never heard a voice so cruel, and cold, and ugly as that blind man's. It cowed me more than the pain; and I began to obey him at once, walking straight in at the door and towards the parlour, where our sick old buccaneer was sitting, dazed with rum. The blind man clung close to me, holding me in one iron fist, and leaning almost more of his weight on me than I could carry. "Lead me straight up to him, and when I'm in view, cry out, 'Here's a friend for you, Bill.' If you don't, I'll do this"; and with that he gave me a twitch that I thought would have made me faint. Between this and that, I was so utterly terrified of the blind beggar that I forgot my terror of the captain, and as I opened the parlour door, cried out the words he had ordered in a trembling voice.

The poor captain raised his eyes, and at one look the rum went out of him, and left him staring sober. The expression of his face was not so much of terror as of mortal sickness. He made a movement to rise, but I do not believe he had enough force left in his body.

"Now, Bill, sit where you are," said the beggar. "If I can't see, I can hear a finger stirring. Business is business. Hold out your left hand. Boy, take his left hand by the wrist, and bring it near to my right."

We both obeyed him to the letter, and I saw him pass something from the hollow of the hand that held his stick into the palm of the captain's, which closed upon it instantly.

"And now that's done," said the blind man; and at the words he suddenly left hold of me, and, with incredible accuracy and nimbleness, skipped out of the parlour and into the road, where, as I still stood motionless, I could hear his stick go tap-tap-tapping into the distance.

It was some time before either I or the captain seemed to gather our senses; but at length, and about at the same moment, I released his wrist, which I was still holding, and he drew in his hand and looked sharply into the palm.

"Ten o'clock!" he cried. "Six hours. We'll do them yet"; and he sprang to his feet.

Even as he did so, he reeled, put his hand to his throat, stood swaying for a moment, and then, with a peculiar sound, fell from his whole height face foremost to the floor.

I ran to him at once, calling my mother. But haste was all in vain. The captain had been struck dead by thundering apoplexy. It is a curious thing to understand, for I had certainly never liked the man, though of late I had begun to pity him, but as soon as I saw that he was dead, I burst into a flood of tears. It was the second death I had known, and the sorrow of the first was still fresh in my heart.

4. THE SEA-CHEST

I lost no time, of course, in telling my mother all that I knew, and perhaps should have told her long before, and we saw ourselves at once in a difficult and dangerous position. Some of the man's money—if he had any—was certainly due to us; but it was not likely that our captain's shipmates, above all the two specimens seen by me, Black Dog, and the blind beggar, would be inclined to give up their booty in payment of the dead man's debts. The captain's order to mount at once and ride for Doctor Livesey would have left my mother alone and unprotected, which was not to be thought of. Indeed, it seemed impossible for either of us to remain much longer in the house: the fall of coals in the kitchen grate, the very ticking of the clock, filled us with alarms. The neighbourhood, to our ears, seemed haunted by approaching footsteps; and what between the dead body of the captain on the parlour floor, and the thought of that detestable blind beggar hovering near at hand, and ready to return, there were moments when, as the saying goes, I jumped in my skin for terror. Something must speedily be resolved upon; and it occurred to us at last to go forth together and seek help in the neighbouring hamlet. No sooner said than done. Bare-headed as we were, we ran out at once in the gathering evening and the frosty fog.

The hamlet lay not many hundred yards away though out of view, on the other side of the next cove; and what greatly encouraged me, it was in an opposite direction from that whence the blind man had made his appearance, and whither he had presumably returned. We were not many minutes on the road, though we sometimes stopped to lay hold of each other and hearken. But there was no unusual sound—nothing but the low wash of the ripple and the croaking of the crows in the wood.

It was already candle-light when we reached the hamlet, and I shall never forget how much I was cheered to see the yellow shine in doors and windows; but that, as it proved, was the best of the help we were likely to get in that quarter. For—you would have thought men would have been ashamed of themselves—no soul would consent to return with us to the "Admiral Benbow". The more we told of our troubles, the more—man, woman, and child—they clung to the shelter of their houses. The name of Captain Flint, though it was strange to me, was well enough known to some there, and carried a great weight of terror. Some of the men who had been to field-work on the far side of the "Admiral Benbow" remembered, besides, to have seen several strangers on the road, and, taking them to be smugglers, to have bolted away; and one at least had seen a little lugger in what we called Kitt's Hole. For that matter, anyone who was a comrade of the captain's was enough to frighten them to death. And the short and the long of the matter was, that while we could get several who were willing enough to ride to Dr. Livesey's, which lay in another direction, not one would help us to defend the inn.

They say cowardice is infectious; but then argument is, on the other hand, a great emboldener; and so when each had said his say, my mother made them a speech. She would not, she declared, lose money that belonged to her fatherless boy; "if none of the rest of you dare," she said, "Jim and I dare. Back we will go, the way we came, and small thanks to you big, hulking, chicken-hearted men. We'll have that chest open, if we die for it. And I'll thank you for that bag, Mrs. Crossley, to bring back our lawful money in."

Of course, I said I would go with my mother; and of course they all cried out at our fool hardiness; but even then not a man would go along with us. All they would do was to give me a loaded pistol, lest we were attacked; and to promise to have horses ready saddled, in case we were pursued on our return; while one lad was to ride forward to the doctor's in search of armed assistance.

My heart was beating finely when we two set forth in the cold night upon this dangerous venture. A full moon was beginning to rise and peered readily through the upper edges of the fog, and this increased our haste, for it was plain, before we came forth again, that all would be as bright as day, and our departure exposed to the eyes of any watchers. We slipped along the hedges, noiseless and swift, nor did we see or hear anything to increase our terrors, till, to our huge relief, the door of the "Admiral Benbow" had closed behind us.

I slipped the bolt at once, and we stood and panted for a moment in the dark, alone in the house with the dead captain's body. Then my mother got a candle in the bar, and, holding each other's hands, we advanced into the parlour. He lay as we had left him, on his back, with his eyes open, and one arm stretched out.

"Draw down the blind, Jim, " whispered my mother, "they

might come and watch outside. And now," said she, when I had done so, "we have to get the key off *that*; and who's to touch it, I should like to know!" and she gave a kind of sob as she said the words.

I went down on my knees at once. On the floor close to his hand there was a little round of paper, blackened on the one side. I could not doubt that this was the *black spot*; and taking it up, I found written on the other side, in a very good, clear hand, this short message: "You have till ten tonight."

"He had till ten, mother," said I; and just as I said it, our old clock began striking. This sudden noise startled us shockingly; but the news was good, for it was only six.

"Now, Jim," she said, "that key."

I felt in his pockets, one after another. A few small coins, a thimble, and some thread and big needles, a piece of pigtail tobacco bitten away at the end, his gully with the crooked handle, a pocket compass, and a tinder box, were all that they contained, and I began to despair.

"Perhaps it's round his neck," suggested my mother.

Overcoming a strong repugnance, I tore open his shirt at the neck, and there, sure enough, hanging to a bit of tarry string, which I cut with his own gully, we found the key. At this triumph we were filled with hope, and hurried upstairs, without delay, to the little room where he had slept so long, and where his box had stood since the day of his arrival.

It was like any other seaman's chest on the outside, the initial "B" burned on the top of it with a hot iron, and the corners somewhat smashed and broken as by long, rough usage.

"Give me the key," said my mother; and though the lock was very stiff, she had turned it and thrown back the lid in a twinkling.

A strong smell of tobacco and tar rose from the interior, but nothing was to be seen on the top except a suit of very good clothes, carefully brushed and folded. They had never been worn, my mother said. Under that, the miscellany began—a quadrant, a tin canikin, several sticks of tobacco, two brace of very handsome pistols, a piece of bar silver, an old Spanish watch and some other trinkets of little value and mostly of foreign make, a pair of compasses mounted with brass, and five or six curious West Indian shells. It has often set me thinking since that he should have carried about these shells with him in his wandering, guilty, and hunted life.

In the meantime, we had found nothing of any value but the silver and the trinkets, and neither of these were in our way. Underneath there was an old boat-cloak whitened with sea-salt on many a harbour-bar. My mother pulled it up with impatience, and there lay before us, the last things in the chest, a bundle tied up in oilcloth, and looking like papers, and a canvas bag, that gave forth, at a touch, the jingle of gold.

"I'll show these rogues that I'm an honest woman," said my mother. "I'll have my dues, and not a farthing over. Hold Mrs. Crossley's bag." And she began to count over the amount of the captain's score from the sailor's bag into the one that I was holding.

It was a long, difficult business, for the coins were of all countries and sizes—doubloons, and louis-d'ors, and guineas, and pieces of eight, and I know not what besides, all shaken together at random. The guineas, too, were about the scarcest, and it was with these only that my mother knew how to make her count.

When we were about half way through, I suddenly put my hand upon her arm; for I had heard in the silent, frosty air, a sound that brought my heart into my mouth—the tap-tapping of the blind man's stick upon the frozen road. It drew nearer and nearer, while we sat holding our breath. Then it struck sharp on the inn door, and then we could hear the handle being turned, and the bolt rattling as the wretched being tried to enter; and then there was a long time of silence both within and without. At last the tapping recommenced, and, to our indescribable joy and gratitude, died slowly away again until it ceased to be heard.

"Mother," said I, "take the whole and let's be going"; for I was sure the bolted door must have seemed suspicious, and would bring the whole hornet's nest about our ears; though how thankful I was that I had bolted it, none could tell who had never met that terrible blind man.

But my mother, frightened as she was, would not consent to take a fraction more than was due to her, and was obstinately unwilling to be content with less. It was not yet seven, she said, by a long way; she knew her rights and she would have them; and she was still arguing with me, when a little low whistle sounded a good way off upon the hill. That was enough, and more than enough, for both of us.

"I'll take what I have," she said, jumping to her feet.

"And I'll take this to square the count," said I, picking up the oilskin packet.

Next moment, we were both groping downstairs, leaving the candle by the empty chest; and the next we had opened the door and were in full retreat. We had not started a moment too soon. The fog was rapidly dispersing; already the moon shone quite clear on the high ground on either side; and it was only in the exact bottom of the dell and round the tavern door that a thin veil still hung unbroken to conceal the first steps of our escape. Far less than half-way to the hamlet, very little beyond the bottom of the hill, we must come forth into the moonlight. Nor was this all; for the sound of several footsteps running came already to our ears, and as we looked back in their direction, a light tossing to and fro and still rapidly advancing, showed that one of the new-comers carried a lantern.

"My dear," said my mother suddenly, "take the money and run on. I am going to faint."

This was certainly the end for both of us, I thought. How I cursed the cowardice of the neighbours; how I blamed my poor mother for her honesty and her greed, for her past foolhardiness and present weakness! We were just at the little bridge, by good fortune; and I helped her, tottering as she was, to the edge of the bank, where, sure enough, she gave a sigh and fell on my shoulder. I do not know how I found the strength to do it all, and I am afraid it was roughly done; but I managed to drag her down the bank and a little way under the arch. Farther I could not move her, for the bridge was too low to let me do more than crawl below it. So there we had to stay—my mother almost entirely exposed, and both of us within earshot of the inn.

5. THE LAST OF THE BLIND MAN

My curiosity, in a sense, was stronger than my fear; for I could not remain where I was, but crept back to the bank again, whence, sheltering my head behind a bush of broom, I might command the road before our door. I was scarcely in position ere my enemies began to arrive, seven or eight of them, running hard, their feet beating out of time along the road, and the man with the lantern some paces in front. Three men ran together, hand in hand; and I made out, even through the mist, that the middle man of this trio was the blind beggar. The next moment his voice showed me that I was right.

"Down with the door!" he cried.

"Ay, ay, sir!" answered two or three; and a rush was made upon the "Admiral Benbow", the lantern-bearer following; and then I could see them pause, and hear speeches passed in a lower key, as if they were surprised to find the door open. But the pause was brief, for the blind man again issued his commands. His voice sounded louder and higher, as if he was afire with eagerness and rage.

"In, in, in!" he shouted, and cursed them for their delay.

Four or five of them obeyed at once, two remaining on the road with the formidable beggar. There was a pause, then a cry of surprise, and then a voice shouting from the house:

"Bill's dead!"

But the blind man swore at them again for their delay.

"Search him, some of you shirking lubbers, and the rest of you aloft and get the chest," he cried.

I could hear their feet rattling up our old stairs, so that the house must have shook with it. Promptly afterwards, fresh sounds of astonishment arose; the window of the captain's room was thrown open with a slam and a jingle of broken glass; and a man leaned out into the moonlight, head and shoulders, and addressed the blind beggar on the road below him.

"Pew," he cried, "they've been before us. Someone's turned the chest out alow and aloft."

"Is it there?" roared Pew.

"The money's there."

The blind man cursed the money.

"Flint's fist, I mean," he cried.

"We don't see it here, nohow," returned the man.

"Here, you below there, is it on Bill?" cried the blind man again.

At that, another fellow, probably him who had remained below to search the captain's body, came to the door of the inn. "Bill's been overhauled a'ready," said he, "nothin' left."

"It's these people of the inn—it's that boy. I wish I had put his eyes out!" cried the blind man, Pew. "They were here no time ago—they had the door bolted when I tried it. Scatter, lads, and find 'em."

"Sure enough, they left their glim here," said the fellow from the window.

"Scatter and find 'em! Rout the house out!" reiterated Pew, striking with his stick upon the road.

Then there followed a great to-do through all our old inn, heavy feet pounding to and fro, furniture thrown over, doors kicked in, until the very rocks re-echoed, and the men came out again, one after another, on the road, and declared that we were nowhere to be found. And just then the same whistle that had alarmed my mother and myself over the dead captain's money was once more clearly audible through the night, but this time twice repeated. I had thought it to be the blind man's trumpet, so to speak, summoning his crew to the assault; but I now found that it was a signal from the hillside towards the hamlet, and, from its effect upon the buccaneers, a signal to warn them of approaching danger.

"There's Dirk again," said one. "Twice! We'll have to budge, mates."

"Budge, you skulk!" cried Pew. "Dirk was a fool and a coward from the first—you wouldn't mind him. They must be close by; they can't be far; you have your hands on it. Scatter and look for them, dogs! Oh, shiver my soul," he cried, "if I had eyes!"

This appeal seemed to produce some effect, for two of the fellows began to look here and there among the lumber, but half-heartedly, I thought, and with half an eye to their own danger all the time, while the rest stood irresolute on the road.

"You have your hands on thousands, you fools, and you hang a leg! You'd be as rich as kings if you could find it, and you know it's here, and you stand there malingering. There wasn't one of you dared face Bill, and I did it—a blind man! And I'm to lose my chance for you! I'm to be a poor, crawling beggar, sponging for rum, when I might be rolling in a coach! If you had the pluck of a weevil in a biscuit you would catch them still."

"Hang it, Pew, we've got the doubloons!" grumbled one. "They might have hid the blessed thing," said another. "Take the Georges, Pew, and don't stand here squalling."

Squalling was the word for it, Pew's anger rose so high at these objections; till at last, his passion completely taking the upper hand, he struck at them right and left in his blindness, and his stick sounded heavily on more than one.

These, in their turn, cursed back at the blind miscreant, threatened him in horrid terms, and tried in vain to catch the stick and wrest it from his grasp.

This quarrel was the saving of us; for while it was still raging, another sound came from the top of the hill on the side of the hamlet—the tramp of horses galloping. Almost at the same time a pistol-shot, flash, and report, came from the hedge-side. And that was plainly the last signal of danger; for the buccaneers turned at once and ran, separating in every direction, one seaward along the cove, one slant across the hill, and so on, so that in half a minute not a sign of them remained but Pew. Him they had deserted, whether in sheer panic or out of revenge for his ill words and blows, I know not; but there he remained behind, tapping up and down the road in a frenzy, and groping and calling for his comrades. Finally he took the wrong turn, and ran a few steps past me, towards the hamlet, crying:

"Johnny, Black Dog, Dirk," and other names, "you won't, leave old Pew, mates—not old Pew!"

Just then the noise of horses topping the rise, and four or five riders came in sight in the moonlight, and swept at full gallop down the slope.

At this Pew saw his error, turned with a scream, and ran straight for the ditch, into which he rolled. But he was on his feet again in a second, and made another dash, now utterly bewildered, right under the nearest of the coming horses.

The rider tried to save him, but in vain. Down went Pew with a cry that rang high into the night; and the four hoofs trampled and spurned him and passed by. He fell on his side, then gently collapsed upon his face, and moved no more.

I leaped to my feet and hailed the riders. They were pulling up, at any rate, horrified at the accident; and I soon saw what they were. One, tailing out behind the rest, was a lad that had gone from the hamlet to Dr. Livesey's; the rest were revenue officers, whom he had met by the way, and with whom he had had the intelligence to return at once. Some news of the lugger in Kitt's Hole had found its way to Supervisor Dance, and set him forth that night in our direction, and to that circumstance my mother and I owed our preservation from death.

Pew was dead, stone dead. As for my mother, when we had carried her up to the hamlet, a little cold water and salts and that soon brought her back again, and she was none the worse for her terror, though she still continued to deplore the balance of the money. In the meantime the supervisor rode on, as fast as he could, to Kitt's Hole; but his men had to dismount and grope down the dingle, leading, and sometimes supporting, their horses, and in continual fear of ambushes; so it was no great matter for surprise that when they got down to the Hole the lugger was already under way, though still close in. He hailed her. A voice replied, telling him to keep out of the moonlight, or he would get some lead in him, and at the same time a bullet whistled close by his arm. Soon after, the lugger doubled the point and disappeared. Mr. Dance stood there, as he said, "like a fish out of water", and all he could do was to despatch a man to B—to warn the cutter. "And that," said he, "is just about as good as nothing. They've got off clean, and there's an end. Only," he added, "I'm glad I trod on Master Pew's corns"; for by this time he had heard my story.

I went back with him to the "Admiral Benbow", and you cannot imagine a house in such a state of smash; the very clock had been thrown down by these fellows in their furious hunt after my mother and myself; and though nothing had actually been taken away except the captain's money-bag and a little silver from the till, I could see at once that we were ruined. Mr. Dance could make nothing of the scene.

"They got the money, you say? Well, then, Hawkins, what in fortune were they after? More money, I suppose?"

"No, sir: not money, I think," replied I. "In fact, sir, I believe I have the thing in my breast-pocket; and, to tell you the truth, I should like to get it put in safety."

"To be sure, boy; quite right," said he. "I'll take it, if you like."

"I thought, perhaps, Dr. Livesey—" I began.

"Perfectly right," he interrupted,very cheerily, "perfectly right—a gentleman and a magistrate. And, now I come to think of it, I might as well ride round there myself and report to him or squire. Master Pew's dead, when all's done; not that I regret it, but he's dead, you see, and people will make it out against an officer of his Majesty's revenue, if make it out they can. Now, I'll tell you, Hawkins: if you like, I'll take you along."

I thanked him heartily for the offer, and we walked back to the hamlet where the horses were. By the time I had told mother of my purpose they were all in the saddle.

"Dogger," said Mr. Dance, "you have a good horse; take up this lad behind you."

As soon as I was mounted, holding on to Dogger's belt, the supervisor gave the word, and the party struck out at a bouncing trot on the road to Dr. Livesey's house.

6. THE CAPTAIN'S PAPERS

We rode hard all the way, till we drew up before Dr. Livesey's door. The house was all dark to the front.

Mr. Dance told me to jump down and knock, and Dogger gave me a stirrup to descend by. The door was opened almost at once by a maid.

"Is Dr. Livesey in?" I asked.

"No, she said; he had come home in the afternoon, but had gone up to the Hall to dine and pass the evening with the squire.

"So there we go, boys," said Mr. Dance.

This time, as the distance was short, I did not mount, but ran with Dogger's stirrup-leather to the lodge gates, and up the long, leafless, moonlit avenue to where the white line of the Hall buildings looked on either hand on great old gardens. Here Mr. Dance dismounted, and, taking me along with him, was admitted at a word into the house.

The servant led us down a matted passage, and showed us at the end into a great library, all lined with bookcases and busts upon the top of them, where the squire and Dr. Livesey sat, pipe in hand, on either side of a bright fire.

I had never seen the squire so near at hand. He was a tall man, over six feet high, and broad in proportion, and he had a bluff, rough-and-ready face, all roughened and reddened and lined in his long travels. His eyebrows were very black, and moved readily, and this gave him a look of some temper, not bad, you would say, but quick and high.

"Come in, Mr. Dance," says he, very stately and condescending.

"Good evening, Dance," says the doctor, with a nod. "And good evening to you, friend Jim. What good wind brings you here?"

The supervisor stood up straight and stiff, and told his story like a lesson; and you should have seen how the two gentlemen leaned forward and looked at each other, and forgot to smoke in their surprise and interest. When they heard how my mother went back to the inn, Dr. Livesey fairly slapped his thigh, and the squire cried "Bravo!" and broke his long pipe against the grate.

Long before it was done, Mr. Trelawney (that, you will remember, was the squire's name) had got up from his seat, and was striding about the room, and the doctor, as if to hear the better, had taken off his powdered wig, and sat there, looking very strange indeed with his own close-cropped, black poll.

At last Mr. Dance finished the story.

"Mr. Dance," said the squire, "you are a very noble fellow. And as for riding down that black, atrocious miscreant, I regard it as an act of virtue, sir, like stamping on a cockroach. This lad Hawkins is a trump, I perceive. Hawkins, will you ring that bell? Mr. Dance must have some ale."

"And so, Jim," said the doctor, "you have the thing that they were after, have you?"

"Here it is, sir," said I, and gave him the oilskin packet.

The doctor looked it all over, as if his fingers were itching to open it; but, instead of doing that, he put it quietly in the pocket of his coat.

"Squire," said he, "when Dance has had his ale he must, of course, be off on his Majesty's service; but I mean to keep Jim Hawkins here to sleep at my house, and, with your permission, I propose we should have up the cold pie, and let him sup."

"As you will, Livesey," said the squire; "Hawkins has earned better than cold pie."

So a big pigeon pie was brought in and put on a side-table, and I made a hearty supper, for I was as hungry as a hawk, while Mr. Dance was further complimented, and at last dismissed.

"And now, squire," said the doctor.

"And now, Livesey," said the squire, in the same breath.

"One at a time, one at a time," laughed Dr. Livesey. "You have heard of this Flint, I suppose?"

"Heard of him!" cried the squire. "Heard of him, you say! He was the bloodthirstiest buccaneer that sailed. Black-beard was a child to Flint. The Spaniards were so prodigiously afraid of him, that, I tell you, sir, I was sometimes proud he was an Englishman. I've seen his top-sails with these eyes, off Trinidad, and the cowardly son of a rum-puncheon that I sailed with put back—put back, sir, into Port of Spain."

"Well, I've heard of him myself, in England," said the doctor. "But the point is, had he money?"

"Money!" cried the squire. "Have you heard the story? What were these villains after but money? What do they care for but money? For what would they risk their rascal carcasses but money?"

"That we shall soon know," replied the doctor. "But you are so confoundedly hot-headed and exclamatory that I cannot get a word in. What I want to know is this: supposing that I have here in my pocket some clue to where Flint buried his treasure, will that treasure amount to much?"

"Amount, sir!" cried the squire. "It will amount to this; if we have the clue you talk about, I fit out a ship in Bristol dock, and take you and Hawkins here along, and I'll have that treasure if I search a year."

"Very well," said the doctor. "Now, then, if Jim is agreeable, we'll open the packet"; and he laid it before him on the table.

The bundle was sewn together, and the doctor had to get out his instrument-case, and cut the stitches with his medical scissors. It contained two things—a book and a sealed paper.

"First of all we'll try the book," observed the doctor.

The squire and I were both peering over his shoulder as he opened it, for Dr. Livesey had kindly motioned me to come round from the side-table, where I had been eating, to enjoy the sport of the search. On the first page there were only some scraps of writing, such as a man with a pen in his hand might make for idleness or practice. One was the same as the tattoo mark, "Billy Bones his fancy"; then there was "Mr. W. Bones, mate". "No more rum." "Off Palm Key he got itt"; and some other snatches, mostly single words and unintelligible. I could not help wondering who it was that had "got itt", and what "itt" was that he got. A knife in his back as like as not.

"Not much instruction there," said Dr. Livesey, as he passed on.

The next ten or twelve pages were filled with a curious series of entries. There was a date at one end of the line and at the other a sum of money, as in common account books; but instead of explanatory writing, only a varying number of crosses between the two. On the 12th of June, 1745, for instance, a sum of seventy pounds had plainly become due to someone, and there was nothing but six crosses to explain the cause. In a few cases, to be sure, the name of a place would be added, as "Offe Caraccas"; or a mere entry of latitude and longitude, as "62° 17' 20", 10° 2' 40"".

The record lasted over nearly twenty years, the amount of the separate entries growing larger as time went on, and at the end a grand total had been made out after five or six wrong additions, and these words appended, "Bones, his pile".

"I can't make head or tail of this," said Dr. Livesey.

"The thing is as clear as noonday," cried the squire. "This is the black-hearted hound's account-book. These crosses stand for the names of ships or towns that they sank or plundered. The sums are the scoundrel's share, and where he feared an ambiguity, you see he added something clearer. 'Offe Caraccas', now; you see, here was some unhappy vessel boarded off that coast. God help the poor souls that manned her—coral long ago."

"Right!" said the doctor. "See what it is to be a traveller. Right! And the amounts increase, you see, as he rose in rank."

There was little else in the volume but a few bearings of places noted in the blank leaves towards the end, and a table for reducing French, English, and Spanish moneys to a common value.

"Thrifty man!" cried the doctor. "He wasn't the one to be cheated."

"And now," said the squire, "for the other."

The paper had been sealed in several places with a thimble by way of seal; the very thimble, perhaps, that I had found in the captain's pocket. The doctor opened the seals with great care, and there fell out the map of an island, with latitude and longitude, soundings, names of hills, and bays and inlets, and every particular that would be needed to bring a ship to a safe anchorage upon its shores. It was about nine miles long and five across, shaped, you might say, like a fat dragon standing up, and had two fine land-locked harbours, and a hill in the centre part marked "The Spy-glass". There were several additions of a later date; but, above all, three crosses of red ink—two on the north part of the island, one in the south-west, and beside this last, in the same red ink, and in a small, neat hand, very different from the captain's tottery characters, these words: "Bulk of treasure here."

Over on the back the same hand had written this further information:

"Tall tree, Spy-glass shoulder, bearing a point to the N. of NNE.

"Skeleton Island ESE and by E.

"Ten feet."

"The bar silver is in the north cache; you can find it by the trend of the east hummock, ten fathoms south of the black crag with the face on it.

"The arms are easy found, in the sand hill, N. point of north inlet cape, bearing E. and a quarter N."

"J. F."

That was all; but brief as it was, and, to me, incomprehensible, it filled the squire and Dr. Livesey with delight.

"Livesey," said the squire, "you will give up this wretched practice at once. Tomorrow I start for Bristol. In three weeks' time—three weeks!—two weeks—ten days—we'll have the best ship, sir, and the choicest crew in England. Hawkins shall come as cabin-boy. You'll make a famous cabin-boy, Hawkins. You, Livesey, are ship's doctor; I am admiral. We'll take Redruth, Joyce, and Hunter. We'll have favourable winds, a quick passage, and not the least difficulty in finding the spot, and money to eat—to roll in—to play duck and drake with ever after."

"Trelawney," said the doctor, "I'll go with you; and, I'll go bail for it, so will Jim, and be a credit to the undertaking. There's only one man I'm afraid of."

"And who's that?" cried the squire. "Name the dog, sir!"

"You," replied the doctor; "for you cannot hold your tongue. We are not the only men who know of this paper. These fellows who attacked the inn tonight—bold, desperate blades, for sure—and the rest who stayed aboard that lugger, and more, I dare say, not far off, are, one and all, through thick and thin, bound that they'll get that money. We must none of us go alone till we get to sea. Jim and I shall stick together in the meanwhile; you'll take Joyce and Hunter when you ride to Bristol, and, from first to last, not one of us must breath a word of what we've found."

"Livesey," returned the squire, "you are always in the right of it. I'll be as silent as the grave."

PART II

THE SEA COOK

7. I GO TO BRISTOL

It was longer than the squire imagined ere we were ready for the sea, and none of our first plans—not even Dr. Livesey's, of keeping me beside him—could be carried out as we intended. The doctor had to go to London for a physician to take charge of his practice; the squire was hard at work at Bristol; and I lived on at the Hall under the charge of old Redruth, the gamekeeper, almost a prisoner, but full of sea-dreams and the most charming anticipations of strange islands and adventures. I brooded by the hour together over the map, all the details of which I well remembered. Sitting by the fire in the housekeeper's room, I approached that island in my fancy, from every possible direction; I explored every acre of its surface; I climbed a thousand times to that tall hill they call the Spyglass, and from the top enjoyed the most wonderful and changing prospects. Sometimes the isle was thick with savages, with whom we fought; sometimes full of dangerous animals that hunted us; but in all my fancies nothing occurred to me so strange and tragic as our actual adventures.

So the weeks passed on, till one fine day there came a letter addressed to Dr. Livesey, with this addition, "To be opened, in the case of his absence, by Tom Redruth, or young Hawkins". Obeying this order, we found, or rather I found—

for the game-keeper was a poor hand at reading anything but print—the following important news:

"Old Anchor Inn, Bristol, March 1, 17—.

"DEAR LIVESEY.—As I do not know whether you are at the Hall or still in London, I send this in double to both places.

"The ship is bought and fitted. She lies at anchor, ready for sea. You never imagined a sweeter schooner—a child might sail her— two hundred tons; name, *Hispaniola.*

"I got her through my old friend, Blandly, who has proved himself throughout the most surprising trump. The admirable fellow literally slaved in my interest, and so, I may say, did everyone in Bristol, as soon as they got wind of the port we sailed for—treasure, I mean."

"Redruth," said I, interrupting the letter, "Doctor Livesey will not like that. The squire has been talking, after all."

"Well, who's a better right?" growled the game-keeper. "A pretty rum go if squire ain't to talk for Doctor Livesey. I should think."

At that I gave up all attempt at commentary, and read straight on:

"Blandly himself found the *Hispaniola,* and by the most admirable management got her for the merest trifle. There is a class of men in Bristol monstrously prejudiced against Blandly. They go the length of declaring that this honest creature would do anything for money, that the *Hispaniola* belonged to him, and that he sold it me absurdly high—the most transparent calumnies. None of them dare, however, to deny the merits of the ship.

"So far there was not a hitch. The work people, to be sure—riggers and what not—were most annoyingly slow; but time cured that. It was the crew that troubled me.

"I wished a round score of men—in case of natives, buccaneers, or the odious French—and I had the worry of the deuce itself to find so much as half a dozen, till the most remarkable stroke of fortune brought me the very man that I required.

"I was standing on the dock, when, by the merest accident, I fell in talk with him. I found he was an old sailor, kept a public house, knew all the seafaring men in Bristol, had lost his health ashore, and wanted a good berth as cook to get to sea again. He had hobbled down there that morning, he said, to get a smell of the salt.

"I was monstrously touched—so would you have been—and, out of pure pity, I engaged him on the spot to be ship's cook. Long John Silver, he is called, and has lost a leg; but that I regarded as a recommendation, since he lost it in his country's service under the immortal Hawke. He has no pension, Livesey. Imagine the abominable age we live in!

"Well, sir, I thought I had only found a cook, but it was a crew I had discovered. Between Silver and myself we got together in a few days a company of the toughest old salts imaginable—not pretty to look at, but fellows, by their faces, of the most indomitable spirit. I declare we could fight a frigate.

"Long John even got rid of two out of the six or seven I had already engaged. He showed me in a moment that they were just the sort of fresh-water swabs we had to fear in an adventure of importance.

"I am in the most magnificent health and spirits, eating like a bull, sleeping like a tree, yet I shall not enjoy a moment till I hear my old tarpaulins tramping round the capstan. Seaward ho! Hang the treasure! It's the glory of the sea that has turned my head. So now, Livesey, come post; do not lose an hour, if you respect me.

"Let young Hawkins go at once to see his mother, with Redruth for a guard; and then both come full speed to Bristol.

"JOHN TRELAWNEY.

"*Postscript.*—I did not tell you that Blandly, who, by the way, is to send a consort after us if we don't turn up by the end of August, had found an admirable fellow for sailing master—a stiff man, which I regret, but, in all other respects, a treasure. Long John Silver unearthed a very competent man for a mate, a man named Arrow. I have a boatswain who pipes, Livesey; so things shall go man-o'-war fashion on board the good ship *Hispaniola.*

"I forgot to tell you that Silver is a man of substance; I know of my own knowledge that he has a banker's account, which has never been overdrawn. He leaves his wife to manage the inn; and as she is a woman of colour, a pair of old bachelors like you and I may be excused for guessing that it is the wife, quite as much as the health, that sends him back to roving.

"J. T."

"P.P.S.—Hawkins may stay one night with his mother.

"J. T."

You can fancy the excitement into which that letter put me. I was half beside myself with glee; and if ever I despised a man, it was old Tom Redruth, who could do nothing but grumble and lament. Any of the under-game-keepers would gladly have changed places with him; but such was not the squire's pleasure, and the squire's pleasure was like law among them all. Nobody but old Redruth would have dared so much as even to grumble.

The next morning he and I set out on foot for the "Admiral Benbow", and there I found my mother in good health and spirits. The captain, who had so long been a cause of so much discomfort, was gone where the wicked cease from troubling. The squire had had everything repainted, and the public rooms and the sign repainted, and had added some furniture—above all, a beautiful arm-chair for mother in the bar. He had found her a boy as an apprentice also, so that she should not want help while I was gone.

It was on seeing that boy that I understood, for the first time, my situation. I had thought up to that moment of the adventures before me, not at all of the home that I was leaving; and now at sight of this clumsy stranger, who was to stay here in my place beside my mother, I had my first attack of tears. I am afraid I led that boy a dog's life; for as he was new to the work, I had a hundred opportunities of setting him right and putting him down, and I was not slow to profit by them.

The night passed, and the next day, after dinner, Redruth and I were afoot again, and on the road. I said goodbye to mother and the cove where I had lived since I was born, and the dear old "Admiral Benbow"—since he was repainted, no longer quite so dear. One of my last thoughts was of the captain, who had so often strode along the beach with his cocked hat, his sabre-cut cheek, and his old brass telescope. Next moment we had turned the corner, and my home was out of sight.

The mail picked us up about dusk at the "Royal George" on the heath. I was wedged in between Redruth and a stout old gentleman, and in spite of the swift motion and the cold night air, I must have dozed a great deal from the very first, and then slept like a log up hill and down dale through stage after stage; for when I was awakened at last, it was by a punch in the ribs, and I opened my eyes, to find that we were standing still before a large building in a city street, and that the day had already broken a long time.

"Where are we?" I asked.

"Bristol," said Tom. "Get down."

Mr. Trelawney had taken up his residence at an inn far down the docks, to superintend the work upon the schooner. Thither we had now to walk, and our way, to my great delight, lay along the quays and beside the great multitude of ships of all sizes and rigs and nations. In one, sailors were singing at their work; in another, there were men aloft, high over my head, hanging to threads that seemed no thicker than a spider's. Though I had lived by the shore all my life, I seemed never to have been near the sea till then. The smell of tar and salt was something new. I saw the most wonderful figure-heads, that had all been far over the ocean. I saw, besides, many old sailors, with rings in their ears, and whiskers curled in ringlets, and tarry pigtails, and their swaggering, clumsy sea-walk; and if I had seen as many kings or archbishops I could not have been more delighted.

And I was going to sea myself; to sea in a schooner, with a piping boatswain, and pigtailed singing seamen; to sea, bound for an unknown island, and to seek for buried treasures!

While I was still in this delightful dream, we came suddenly in front of a large inn, and met Squire Trelawney, all dressed out like a sea-officer, in stout blue cloth, coming out of the door with a smile on his face, and a capital imitation of a sailor's walk.

"Here you are," he said, "and the doctor came last night from London. Bravo! the ship's company complete!"

"Oh, sir," cried I, "when do we sail?"

"Sail!" says he. "We sail tomorrow!"

8. AT THE SIGN OF THE "SPY-GLASS"

When I had done breakfasting the squire gave me a note addressed to John Silver, at the sign of the "Spy-glass", and told me I should easily find the place by following the line of the docks, and keeping a bright look-out for a little tavern with a large brass telescope for sign. I set off, overjoyed at this opportunity to see some more of the ships and seamen, and picked my way among a great crowd of people and carts and bales, for the dock was now at its busiest, until I found the tavern in question.

It was a bright enough little place of entertainment. The sign was newly painted; the windows had neat red curtains; the floor was cleanly sanded. There was a street on either side, and an open door on both, which made the large, low room pretty clear to see in, in spite of clouds of tobacco smoke.

The customers were mostly seafaring men; and they talked so loudly that I hung at the door, almost afraid to enter.

As I was waiting, a man came out of a side room, and, at a glance, I was sure he must be Long John. His left leg was cut off close by the hip, and under the left shoulder he carried a crutch, which he managed with wonderful dexterity, hopping about upon it like a bird. He was very tall and strong, with a face as big as a ham—plain and pale, but intelligent and smiling. Indeed, he seemed in the most cheerful spirits, whistling as he moved about among the tables, with a merry word and a slap on the shoulder for the more favoured of his guests.

Now, to tell you the truth, from the very first mention of Long John in Squire Trelawney's letter, I had taken a fear in my mind that he might prove to be the very one-legged sailor whom I had watched for so long at the old "Benbow". But one look at the man before me was enough. I had seen the captain, and Black Dog, and the blind man Pew, and I thought I knew what a buccaneer was like—a very different creature, according to me, from this clean and pleasant-tempered landlord.

I plucked up courage at once, crossed the threshold, and walked right up to the man where he stood, propped on his crutch, talking to a customer.

"Mr. Silver, sir?" I asked, holding out the note.

"Yes, my lad," said he; "such is my name, to be sure. And who may you be?"

And then as he saw the squire's letter, he seemed to me to give something almost like a start.

"Oh!" said he, quite loud, and offering his hand, "I see. You are our new cabin-boy; pleased I am to see you."

And he took my hand in his large firm grasp.

Just then one of the customers at the far side rose suddenly and made for the door. It was close by him, and he was out in the street in a moment. But his hurry had attracted my notice, and I recognized him at a glance. It was the tallow faced man, wanting two fingers, who had come first to the "Admiral Benbow".

"Oh," I cried, "stop him! it's Black Dog!"

"I don't care two coppers who he is," cried Silver. "But he hasn't paid his score. Harry, run and catch him."

One of the others who was nearest the door leaped up, and started in pursuit.

"If he were Admiral Hawke he shall pay his score," cried Silver; and then, relinquishing my hand—"Who did you say he was?" he asked. "Black what?"

"Dog, sir," said I. "Has Mr. Trelawney not told you of the buccaneers? He was one of them."

"So?" cried Silver. "In my house! Ben, run and help Harry. One of those swabs, was he? Was that you drinking with him, Morgan? Step up here."

The man whom he called Morgan—an old, grey-haired, mahogany-faced sailor—came forward pretty sheepishly, rolling his quid.

"Now, Morgan," said Long John, very sternly; "you never clapped your eyes on that Black—Black Dog before, did you, now?"

"Not I, sir," said Morgan, with a salute.

"You didn't know his name, did you?"

"No, sir."

"By the powers, Tom Morgan, it's as good for you!" exclaimed the landlord. "If you had been mixed up with the like of that, you would never have put another foot in my house, you may lay to that. And what was he saying to you?"

"I don't rightly know, sir," answered Morgan.

"Do you call that a head on your shoulders, or a blessed dead-eye?" cried Long John. "Don't rightly know, don't you! Perhaps you don't happen to rightly know who you was speaking to, perhaps? Come, now, what was he jawing—v'yages, cap'ns, ships? Pipe up! What was it?"

"We were a-talkin' of keel-hauling," answered Morgan.

"Keel-hauling, was you? and a mighty suitable thing, too, and you may lay to that. Get back to your place for a lubber, Tom."

And then, as Morgan rolled back to his seat, Silver added to me in a confidential whisper, that was very flattering, as I thought:

"He's quite an honest man, Tom Morgan, on'y stupid. And now," he ran on again aloud, "let's see—Black Dog? No, I don't know the name, not I. Yet I kind of think I've —yes, I've seen the swab. He used to come here with a blind beggar, he used."

"That he did, you may be sure," said I. "I knew that blind man, too. His name was Pew."

"It was!" cried Silver, now quite excited. "Pew! That were his name for certain. Ah, he looked a shark, he did! If we run down this Black Dog, now, there'll be news for Cap'n Trelawney! Ben's a good runner; few seamen run better than Ben. He should run him down, hand over hand, by the powers! He talked o' keel-hauling, did he? *I'll* keel-haul him!"

All the time he was jerking out these phrases he was stumping up and down the tavern on his crutch, slapping tables with his hand, and giving such a show of excitement as would have convinced an Old Bailey judge or a Bow Street runner. My suspicions had been thoroughly reawakened on finding Black Dog at the "Spy-glass," and I watched the cook narrowly. But he was too deep, and too ready, and too clever for me, and by the time the two men had come back out of breath, and confessed that they had lost the track in a crowd, and been scolded like thieves, I would have gone bail for the innocence of Long John Silver.

"See here, now, Hawkins," said he, "here's a blessed hard thing on a man like me, now, ain't it? There's Cap'n

Trelawney—what's he to think? Here I have this confounded son of a Dutchman sitting in my own house, drinking of my own rum! Here you comes and tells me of it plain; and here I let him give us all the slip before my blessed dead-lights! Now, Hawkins, you do me justice with the cap'n. You're a lad, you are, but you're as smart as paint. I see that when you first came in. Now, here it is: What could I do, with this old timber I hobble on? When I was an AB master mariner I'd have come up alongside of him, hand over hand, and broached him to in a brace of old shakes, I would; but now—"

And then, all of a sudden, he stopped, and his jaw dropped as though he had remembered something.

"The score!" he burst out. "Three goes o' rum! Why, shiver my timbers, if I hadn't forgotten my score!"

And, falling on a bench, he laughed until the tears ran down his cheeks. I could not help joining; and we laughed together, peal after peal, until the tavern rang again.

"Why, what a precious old sea-calf I am!" he said, at last, wiping his cheeks. "You and me should get on well, Hawkins, for I'll take my davy I should be rated ship's boy. But, come, now, stand by to go about. This won't do. Dooty is dooty, messmates. I'll put on my old cocked hat, and step along of you to Cap'n Trelawney, and report this here affair. For, mind you, it's serious, young Hawkins; and neither you nor me's come out of it with what I should make so bold as to call credit. Nor you neither, says you; not smart—none of the pair of us smart. But dash my buttons! that was a good 'un about my score."

And he began to laugh again, and that so heartily, that though I did not see the joke as he did, I was again obliged to join him in his mirth.

On our little walk along the quays, he made himself the most interesting companion, telling me about the different ships that we passed by, their rig, tonnage, and nationality, explaining the work that was going forward—how one was discharging, another taking in cargo, and a third making ready for sea; and every now and then telling me some little anecdote of ships or seamen, or repeating a nautical phrase till I had learned it perfectly. I began to see that here was one of the best possible shipmates.

When we got to the inn, the squire and Dr. Livesey were seated together, finishing a quart of ale with a toast in it, before they should go aboard the schooner on a visit of inspection.

Long John told the story from first to last, with a great deal of spirit and the most perfect truth. "That was how it were, now, weren't it, Hawkins?" he would say, now and again, and I could always bear him entirely out.

The two gentlemen regretted that Black Dog had got away; but we all agreed there was nothing to be done, and after he had been complimented, Long John took up his crutch and departed.

"All hands aboard by four this afternoon," shouted the squire after him.

"Ay, ay, sir," cried the cook, in the passage.

"Well, squire," said Dr. Livesey, "I don't put much faith in your discoveries, as a general thing; but I will say this, John Silver suits me."

"The man's a perfect trump," declared the squire.

"And now," added the doctor. "Jim may come on board with us, may he not?"

"To be sure he may," says squire. "Take your hat, Hawkins, and we'll see the ship."

9. POWDER AND ARMS

The *Hispaniola* lay some way out, and we went under the figureheads and round the sterns of many other ships, and their cables sometimes grated underneath our keel, and sometimes swung above us. At last, however, we got alongside, and were met and saluted as we stepped aboard by the mate, Mr. Arrow, a brown old sailor, with earrings in his ears and a squint. He and the squire were very thick and friendly, but I soon observed that things were not the same between Mr. Trelawney and the captain.

This last was a sharp-looking man, who seemed angry with

everything on board, and was soon to tell us why, for we had hardly got down into the cabin when a sailor followed us.

"Captain Smollett, sir, axing to speak with you," said he.

"I am always at the captain's orders. Show him in," said the squire.

The captain, who was close behind his messenger, entered at once, and shut the door behind him.

"Well, Captain Smollet, what have you to say? All well, I hope; all shipshape and seaworthy?"

"Well, sir," said the captain, "better speak plain, I believe, even at the risk of offence. I don't like this cruise; I don't like the men; and I don't like my officer. That's short and sweet."

"Perhaps, sir, you don't like the ship?" inquired the squire, very angry, as I could see.

"I can't speak as to that, sir not having seen her tried," said the captain. "She seems a clever craft; more I can't say."

"Possibly, sir, you may not like your employer, either?" says the squire.

But here Dr. Livesey cut in.

"Stay a bit," said he, "stay a bit. No use of such questions as that but to produce ill-feeling. The captain has said too much or he has said too little, and I'm bound to say that I require an explanation of his words. You don't, you say, like this cruise. Now, why?"

"I was engaged, sir, on what we call sealed orders, to sail this ship for that gentleman where he should bid me," said the captain. "So far so good. But now I find that every man before the mast knows more than I do. I don't call that fair, now, do you?"

"No," said Dr. Livesey, "I don't."

"Next," said the captain, "I learn we are going after treasure—hear it from my own hands, mind you. Now, treasure is ticklish work; I don't like treasure voyages on any account; and I don't like them, above all, when they are secret, and when (begging your pardon, Mr. Trelawney) the secret has been told to the parrot."

"Silver's parrot?" asked the squire.

"It's a way of speaking," said the captain. "Blabbed, I mean.

It's my belief neither of you gentlemen know what you are about; but I'll tell you my way of it—life or death, and a close run."

"That is all clear, and, I daresay, true enough," replied Dr. Livesey. "We take the risk; but we are not so ignorant as you believe us. Next, you say you don't like the crew. Are they not good seamen?"

"I don't like them, sir," returned Captain Smollett. "And I think I should have had the choosing of my own hands, if you go to that."

"Perhaps you should," replied the doctor. "My friend should, perhaps, have taken you along with him; but the slight, if there be one, was unintentional. And you don't like Mr. Arrow?"

"I don't, sir. I believe he's a good seaman; but he's too free with the crew to be a good officer. A mate should keep himself to himself—shouldn't drink with the men before the mast!"

"Do you mean he drinks?" cried the squire.

"No, sir," replied the captain; "only that he's too familiar."

"Well, now, and the short and long of it, captain?" asked the doctor. "Tell us what you want."

"Well, gentlemen, are you determined to go on this cruise?"

"Like iron," answered the squire.

"Very good," said the captain. "Then, as you've heard me very patiently, saying things that I could not prove, hear me a few words more. They are putting the powder and the arms in the fore-hold. Now, you have a good place under the cabin; why not put them there?—first point. Then you are bringing four of your own people with you, and they tell me some of them are to be berthed forward. Why not give them the berths here beside the cabin?—second point."

"Any more?" asked Mr. Trelawney.

"One more," said the captain. "There's been too much blabbing already."

"Far too much," agreed the doctor.

"I'll tell you what I've heard myself," continued Captain Smollet: "that you have a map of an island; that there's crosses on the map to show where treasure is; and that the island lies—" And then he named the latitude and longitude exactly.

"I never told that," cried the squire, "to a soul!"

"The hands know it, sir," returned the captain.

"Livesey, that must have been you or Hawkins," cried the squire.

"It doesn't much matter who it was," replied the doctor. And I could see that neither he nor the captain paid much regard to Mr. Trelawney's protestations. Neither did I, to be sure, he was so loose a talker; yet in this case I believe he was really right, and that nobody had told the situation of the island.

"Well, gentlemen," continued the captain, "I don't know who has this map; but I make it a point, it shall be kept secret even from me and Mr. Arrow. Otherwise I would ask you to let me resign."

"I see," said the doctor. "You wish us to keep this matter dark, and to make a garrison of the stern part of the ship, manned with my friend's own people, and provided with all the arms and powder on board. In other words, you fear a mutiny."

"Sir," said Captain Smollet, "with no intention to take offence, I deny your right to put words into my mouth. No captain, sir, would be justified in going to sea at all if he had ground enough to say that. As for Mr. Arrow, I believe him thoroughly honest; some of the men are the same; all may be for what I know. But I am responsible for the ship's safety and the life of every man Jack aboard of her. I see things going, as I think, not quite right. And I ask you to take certain precautions, or let me resign my berth. And that's all."

"Captain Smollet," began the doctor, with a smile, "did ever you hear the fable of the mountain and the mouse? You'll excuse me, I daresay. but you remind me of that fable. When you came in here I'll stake my wig you meant more than this."

"Doctor," said the captain, "you are smart. When I came in here I meant to get discharged. I had no thought that Mr. Trelawney would hear a word."

"No more I would," cried the squire. "Had Livesey not been here I should have seen you to the deuce. As it is, I have heard you. I still do as you desire; but I think the worse of you."

"That's as you please, sir," said the captain. "You'll find I do my duty."

And with that he took his leave.

"Trelawney," said the doctor, "contrary to all my notions, I believe you have managed to get two honest men on board with you—that man and John Silver."

"Silver, if you like," cried the squire; "but as for that intolerable humbug, I declare I think his conduct unmanly, unsailorly, and downright un-English."

"Well," says the doctor, "we shall see."

When we came on deck, the men had begun already to take out the arms and powder, yo-ho-ing at their work, while the captain and Mr. Arrow stood by superintending.

The new arrangement was quite to my liking. The whole schooner had been overhauled; six berths had been made astern, out of what had been the after-part of the main hold, and this set of cabins was only joined to the galley and forecastle by a sparred passage on the port side; It had been originally meant that the captain, Mr. Arrow, Hunter, Joyce, the doctor, and the squire, were to occupy these six berths. Now, Redruth and I were to get two of them, and Mr. Arrow and the captain were to sleep on deck in the companion, which had been enlarged on each side till you might almost have called it a round-house. Very low it was still, of course; but there was room to swing two hammocks, and even the mate seemed pleased with the arrangement. Even he, perhaps, had been doubtful as to the crew, but that is only guess; for, as you shall hear, we had not long the benefit of his opinion.

We were all hard at work, changing the powder and the berths, when the last man or two, and Long John along with them, came off in a shore-boat. The cook came up the side like a monkey for cleverness, and, as soon as he saw what was doing, "So ho, mates!" says he, "what's this?"

"We're a-changing of the powder, Jack," answers one.

"Why, by the powers," cried Long John, "if we do, we'll miss the morning tide!"

"My orders!" said the captain shortly. "You may go below, my man. Hands will want supper."

"Ay, ay, sir," answered the cook; and, touching his fore-lock, he disappeared at once in the direction of his galley.

"That's a good man, captain," said the doctor.

"Very likely, sir," replied Captain Smollett. "Easy with that, men—easy," he ran on, to the fellows who were shifting the powder; and then suddenly observing me examining the swivel gun we carried amidships, a long brass nine—"Here, you ship's boy," he cried, "out o' that! Off with you to the cook and get some work."

And then as I was hurrying off I heard him say, quite loudly, to the doctor:

"I'll have no favourites on my ship."

I assure you I was quite of the squire's way of thinking, and hated the captain deeply.

10. THE VOYAGE

All that night we were in a great bustle getting things stowed in their place, and boatfuls of the squire's friends, Mr. Blandly and the like, coming off to wish him a good voyage and a safe return. We never had a night at the "Admiral Benbow" when I had half the work; and I was dog tired when, a little before dawn, the boatswain sounded his pipe, and the crew began to man the capstan-bars. I might have been twice as weary, yet I would not have left the deck; all was so new and interesting to me—the brief commands, the shrill note of the whistle, the men bustling to their places in the glimmer of the ship's lanterns.

"Now, Barbecue, tip us a stave," cried one voice.

"The old one," cried another.

"Ay, ay, mates," said Long John, who was standing by, with his crutch under his arm, and at once broke out in the air and words I knew so well:

"Fifteen men on the dead man's chest"—

And then the whole crew bore chorus:

"Yo-ho-ho, and a bottle of rum!"

And at the third "ho!" drove the bars before them with a will.

Even at that exciting moment it carried me back to the old "Admiral Benbow" in a second; and I seemed to hear the voice of the captain piping in the chorus. But soon the anchor was short up; soon it was hanging dripping at the bows; soon the sails began to draw, and the land and shipping to flit by on either side; and before I could lie down to snatch an hour of slumber the *Hispaniola* had begun her voyage to the Isle of Treasure.

I am not going to relate that voyage in detail. It was fairly prosperous. The ship proved to be a good ship, the crew were capable seamen, and the captain thoroughly understood his business. But before we came the length of Treasure Island, two or three things had happened which require to be known.

Mr. Arrow, first of all, turned out even worse than the captain had feared. He had no command among the men, and people did what they pleased with him. But that was by no means the worst of it; for after a day or two at sea he began to appear on deck with hazy eye, red cheeks, stuttering tongue, and other marks of drunkenness. Time after time he was ordered below in disgrace. Sometimes he fell and cut himself; sometimes he lay all day long in his little bunk at one side of the companion; sometimes for a day or two he would be almost sober and attend to his work at least passably.

In the meantime, we could never make out where he got the drink. That was the ship's mystery. Watch him as we pleased we could do nothing to solve it; and when we asked him to his face, he would only laugh, if he were drunk, and if he were sober, deny solemnly that he ever tasted anything but water.

He was not only useless as an officer, and a bad influence amongst the men, but it was plain that at this rate he must soon kill himself outright; so nobody was much surprised, nor very sorry, when one dark night, with a head sea, he disappeared entirely and was seen no more.

"Overboard!" said the captain. "Well, gentlemen, that saves the trouble of putting him in irons."

But there we were, without a mate; and it was necessary, of

course, to advance one of the men. The boatswain, Job Anderson, was the likeliest man aboard, and, though he kept his old title, he served in a way as mate. Mr. Trelawney had followed the sea, and his knowledge made him very useful, for he often took a watch himself in easy weather. And the coxswain, Israel Hands, was a careful, wily, old, experienced seaman, who could be trusted at a pinch with almost anything. He was a great confidant of Long John Silver, and so the mention of his name leads me on to speak of our ship's cook, Barbecue, as the men called him.

Aboard ship he carried his crutch by a lanyard round his neck, to have both hands as free as possible. It was something to see him wedge the foot of the crutch against a bulk-head, and, propped against it, yielding to every movement of the ship, get on with his cooking like someone safe ashore. Still more strange was it to see him in the heaviest of weather cross the deck. He had a line or two rigged up to help him across the widest spaces—Long John's earrings, they were called; and he would hand himself from one place to another, now using the crutch, now trailing it alongside by the lanyard, as quickly as another man could walk. Yet some of the men who had sailed with him before expressed their pity to see him so reduced.

"He's no common man, Barbecue," said the coxswain to me. "He had good schooling in his young days, and can speak like a book when so minded; and brave—a lion's nothing alongside of Long John! I seen him grapple four, and knock their heads together—him unarmed."

All the crew respected and even obeyed him. He had a way of talking to each and doing everybody some particular service.

To me he was unweariedly kind; and always glad to see me in the galley, which he kept as clean as a new pin; the dishes hanging up burnished, and his parrot in a cage in one corner.

"Come away, Hawkins," he would say; "come and have a yarn with John. Nobody more welcome than yourself, my son. Sit you down and hear the news. Here's Cap'n Flint—I calls my parrot Cap'n Flint, after the famous buccaneer—here's

Cap'n Flint predicting success to our v'yage. Wasn't you, cap'n?"

And the parrot would say, with great rapidity, "Pieces of eight! pieces of eight! pieces of eight!" till you wondered that it was not out of breath, or till John threw his handkerchief over the cage.

"Now, that bird," he would say, "is, may be, two hundred years old, Hawkins—they lives for ever mostly; and if any body's seen more wickedness, it must be the devil himself. She's sailed with England, the great Cap'n England, the pirate. She's been at Madagascar, and at Malabar, the Surinam, and Providence, and Portobello. She was at the fishing up of the wrecked Plate ships. It's there she learned 'Pieces of eight,' and little wonder; three hundred and fifty thousand of 'em Hawkins! She was at the boarding of the Viceroy of the Indies out at Goa, she was; and to look at her you would think she was a babby. But you smelt powder—didn't you, cap'n?"

"Stand by to go about," the parrot would scream.

"Ah, she's a handsome craft, she is," the cook would say, and give her sugar from his pocket, and then the bird would peck at the bars and swear straight on, passing belief for wickedness. "There," John would add, "you can't touch pitch and not be mucked, lad. Here's this poor old innocent bird o' mine swearing blue fire, and none the wiser, you may lay to that. She would swear the same, in a manner of speaking, before chaplain." And John would touch his forelock with a solemn way he had, that made me think he was the best of men.

In the meantime, squire and Captain Smollett were still on pretty distant terms with one another. The squire made no bones about the matter; he despised the captain. The captain, on his part, never spoke but when he was spoken to, and then sharp and short and dry, and not a word wasted. He owned, when driven into a corner, that he seemed to have been wrong about the crew, that some of them were as brisk as he wanted to see, and all had behaved fairly well. As for the ship, he had taken a downright fancy to her. "She'll lie a point nearer the wind than a man has a right to expect of his own married wife, sir. But," he would add, "all I say is we're not home again, and I don't like the cruise."

The squire, at this, would turn away and march up and down the deck, chin in air.

"A trifle more of that man," he would say, "and I should explode."

We had some heavy weather, which only proved the qualities of the *Hispaniola*. Every man on board seemed well content, and they must have been hard to please if they had been otherwise; for it is my belief there was never a ship's company so spoiled since Noah put to sea. Double grog was going on the least excuse; there was duff on odd days, as, for instance, if the squire heard it was any man's birthday; and always a barrel of apples standing broached in the waist, for anyone to help himself that had a fancy.

"Never knew good come of it yet," the captain said to Dr. Livesey. "Spoil foc's'le hands, make devils. That's my belief."

But good did come of the apple barrel, as you shall hear; for if it had not been for that, we should have had no note of warning, and might all have perished by the hand of treachery.

This was how it came about.

We had run up the trades to get the wind of the island we were after—I am not allowed to be more plain—and now we were running down for it with a bright look-out day and night. It was about the last day of our outward voyage, by the largest computation; some time that night, or, at latest, before noon of the morrow, we should sight the Treasure Island. We were heading SSW., and had a steady breeze abeam and a quiet sea. The *Hispaniola* rolled steadily, dipping her bowsprit now and then with a whiff of spray. All was drawing alow and aloft; everyone was in the bravest spirits, because we were now so near an end of the first part of our adventure.

Now, just after sundown, when all my work was over, and I was on my way to my berth, it occurred to me that I should like an apple. I ran on deck. The watch was all forward looking out for the island. The man at the helm was watching the luff of the sail, and whistling away gently to himself; and that was the only sound excepting the swish of the sea against the bows and around the sides of the ship.

In I got bodily into the apple barrel, and found there was scarce an apple left; but, sitting down there in the dark, what with the sound of the waters and the rocking movement of the ship, I had either fallen asleep, or was on the point of doing so, when a heavy man sat down with rather a clash close by. The barrel shook as he leaned his shoulders against it, and I was just about to jump up when the man began to speak. It was Silver's voice, and, before I had heard a dozen words, I would not have shown myself for all the world, but lay there, trembling and listening, in the extreme of fear and curiosity; for from these dozen words I understood that the lives of all the honest men aboard depended upon me alone.

11. WHAT I HEARD IN THE APPLE BARREL

"No, not I," said Silver. "Flint was cap'n; I was quarter-master, along of my timber leg. The same broadside I lost my leg, old Pew lost his daylights. It was a master surgeon, him that ampytated me—out of college and all—Latin by the bucket, and what not; but he was hanged like a dog, and sun-dried like the rest, at Corso Castle. That was Roberts' men, that was, and comed of changing names of their ships—*Royal Fortune* and so on. Now, what a ship was christened, so let her stay, I says. So it was with the *Cassandra,* as brought us all safe home from Malabar, after England took the Viceroy of the Indies; so it was with the old *Walrus,* Flint's old ship, as I've seen a'muck with the red blood and fit to sink with gold."

"Ah!" cried another voice, that of the youngest hand on board, and evidently full of admiration, "he was the flower of the flock, was Flint!"

"Davis was a man, too, by all accounts," said Silver. "I never sailed along of him; first with England, then with Flint, that's my story; and now here on my own account, in a manner of speaking. I laid by nine hundred safe, from England, and two thousand after Flint. That ain't bad for a man before the mast—all safe in bank. 'Tain't earning now, it's saving does it, you may lay to that. Where's all England's men now? I dunno. Where's Flint's? Why, most on 'em aboard here, and glad to get the duff—been begging before that, some on 'em. Old Pew, as had lost his sight, and might have thought shame, spends twelve hundred pounds in a year, like a lord in Parliament. Where is he now? Well, he's dead now and under hatches; but for two year before that, shiver my timbers! the man was starving. He begged, and he stole, and he cut throats, and starved at that, by the powers!"

"Well, it ain't much use, after all," said the young seaman.

"'Tain't much use for fools, you may lay to it—that, nor nothing," cried Silver. "But now, you look here: you're young, you are, but you're as smart as paint. I see that when I set my eyes on you, and I'll talk to you like a man."

You may imagine how I felt when I heard this abominable old rogue addressing another in the very same words of flattery as he had used to myself. I think, if I had been able, that I would have killed him through the barrel. Meantime, he ran on, little supposing he was overheard.

"Here it is about gentlemen of fortune. They lives rough, and they risk swinging, but they eat and drink like fighting-cocks, and when a cruise is done, why it's hundreds of pounds instead of hundreds of farthings in their pockets. Now, the most goes for rum and a good fling, and to sea again in their shirts. But that's not the course I lay. I puts it all away, some here, some there, and none too much anywheres, by reason of suspicion. I'm fifty, mark you; once back from this cruise, I set up gentleman in earnest. Time enough, too, says you. Ah, but I've lived easy in the mean-time; never denied myself o' nothing heart desires, and slep' soft and ate dainty all my days, but when at sea. And how did I begin? Before the mast, like you!"

"Well," said the other, "but all the other money's gone now, ain't it? You daren't show face in Bristol after this."

"Why, where might you suppose it was?" asked Silver, derisively.

"At Bristol, in banks and places," answered his companion.

"It were," said the cook; "it were when we weighed anchor. But my old missis has it all by now. And the 'Spy-glass' is sold, lease and goodwill and rigging; and the old girl's off to meet me. I would tell you where, for I trust you; but it 'ud make jealousy among the mates."

"And can you trust your missis?" asked the other.

"Gentlemen of fortune," returned the cook, "usually trust little among themselves, and right they are, you may lay to it. But I have a way with me, I have. When a mate brings a slip on his cable—one as knows me, I mean—it won't be in the same world with old John. There was some that was feared of Pew, and some that was feared of Flint; but Flint his own self was feared of me. Feared he was, and proud. They was the roughest crew afloat, was Flint's; the devil himself would have been feared to go to sea with them. Well, now, I tell you, I'm not a boasting man, and you seen yourself how easy I keep company; but when I was quarter-master, *lambs* wasn't the word for Flint's old buccaneers. Ah, you may be sure of yourself in old John's ship."

"Well, I tell you now," replied the lad, "I didn't half a quarter like the job till I had this talk with you, John; but there's my hand on it now."

"And a brave lad you were, and smart, too," answered Silver, shaking hands so heartily that all the barrel shook, "and a finer figurehead for a gentleman of fortune I never clapped my eyes on." By this time I had begun to understand the meaning of their terms. By a "gentleman of fortune" they plainly meant neither more nor less than a common pirate, and the little scene that I had overheard was the last act in the corruption of one of the honest hands—perhaps of the last one left aboard. But on this point I was soon to be relieved, for Silver giving a little whistle, a third man strolled up and sat down by the party.

"Dick's square," said Silver.

"Oh, I know'd Dick was square," returned the voice of the coxswain, Israel Hands. "He's no fool, is Dick." And he turned his quid and spat. "But, look here," he went on, "here's what

I want to know, Barbecue: how long are we a-going to stand off and on like a blessed bumboat? I've had a'most enough o' Cap'n Smollett; he's hazed me long enough, by thunder! I want to go into that cabin, I do. I want their pickles and wines, and that."

"Israel," said Silver, "your head ain't much account, nor ever was. But you're able to hear, I reckon; leastways, your ears is big enough. Now, here's what I say: you'll berth forward, and you'll lie hard, and you'll speak soft, and you'll keep sober, till I give the word; and you may lay to that, old son."

"Well, I don't say no, do I?" growled the coxswain. "What I say is, when? That's what I say."

"When! by the powers!" cried Silver. "Well, now, if you want to know. I'll tell you when. The-last-moment I can manage; and that's when. Here's a first-rate seaman, Cap'n Smollett, sails the blessed ship for us. Here's this squire and doctor with a map and such—I don't know where it is, do I? No more do you, says you. Well, then, I mean this squire and doctor shall find the stuff, and help us to get it aboard, by the powers. Then we'll see. If I was sure of you all, sons of double Dutchmen, I'd have Cap'n Smollett navigate us half-way back again before I struck."

"Why, we're all seamen aboard here, I should think," said the lad Dick.

"We're all foc's'le hands, you mean," snapped Silver. "We can steer a course, but who's to set one? That's what all you gentlemen split on, first and last. If I had my way, I'd have Cap'n Smollett work us back into the trades at least; then we'd have no blessed miscalculations and a spoonful of water a day. But I know the sort you are. I'll finish with 'em at the island, as soon's the blunt's on board, and a pity it is. But you're never happy till you're drunk. Split my sides, I've a sick heart to sail with the likes of you!"

"Easy all, Long John," cried Israel. "Who's a-crossin' of you?"

"Why, how many tall ships, think ye, now, have I seen laid aboard? and how many brisk lads drying in the sun at Execution Dock?" cried Silver, "and all for this same hurry and hurry and hurry. You hear me? I seen a thing or two at sea, I have. If you would on'y lay your course, and a p'int to windward, you would ride in carriages, you would. But not you! I know you. You'll have your mouthful of rum tomorrow, and go hang."

"Everybody know'd you was a kind of a chapling, John; but there's others as could hand and steer as well as you," said Israel. "They liked a bit of fun, they did. They wasn't so high and dry, nohow, but took their fling, like jolly companions every one."

"So?" says Silver. "Well, and where are they now? Pew was that sort, and he died a beggar-man. Flint was, and he died of rum at Savannah. Ah, they was a sweet crew, they was! on'y, where are they?"

"But," asked Dick, "when we do lay 'em athwart, what are we to do with 'em, anyhow?"

"There's the man for me!" cried the cook, admiringly. "That's what I call business. Well, what would you think? Put 'em ashore like maroons? That would have been England's way. Or cut 'em down like that much pork? That would have been Flint's or Billy Bones's."

"Billy was the man for that," said Israel. "'Dead men don't bite,' says he. Well, he's dead now hisself; he knows the long and short of it now; and if ever a rough hand come to port, it was Billy."

"Right you are," said Silver, "rough and ready. But mark you here: I'm an easy man—I'm quite the gentleman, says you; but this time it's serious. Dooty is dooty, mates. I give my vote—death. When I'm in Parlyment, and riding in my coach, I don't want none of these sea-lawyers in the cabin a-coming home, unlooked for, like the devil at prayers. Wait is what I say; but when the time comes, why let her rip!"

"John," cries the coxswain, "you're a man!"

"You'll say so, Israel, when you see," said Silver. "Only one thing I claim—I claim Trelawney. I'LL wring his calf's head off his body with these hands. Dick!" he added, breaking off, "you just jump up, like a sweet lad, and get me an apple, to wet my pipe like."

You may fancy the terror I was in! I should have leaped out and run for it, if I had found the strength, but my limbs and heart alike misgave me. I heard Dick begin to rise, and then someone seemingly stopped him, and the voice of Hands exclaimed: "Oh, stow that! Don't you get sucking of that bilge, John. Lets have a go of the rum."

"Dick," said Silver, "I trust you. I've a gauge on the keg, mind. There's the key; you fill a pannikin and bring it up."

Terrified as I was, I could not help thinking to myself that this must have been how Mr. Arrow got the strong waters that destroyed him.

Dick was gone but a little while, and during his absence Israel spoke straight on in the cook's ear. It was but a word or two that I could catch, and yet I gathered some important news; for, besides other scraps that tended to the same purpose, this whole clause was audible: "Not another man of them'll jine." Hence there were still faithful men on board.

When Dick returned, one after another of the trio took the panniking and drank—one "To luck"; another with a "Here's to old Flint"; and Silver himself saying, in a kind of song. "Here's to ourselves, and hold your luff, plenty of prizes and plenty of duff."

Just then a sort of brightness fell upon me in the barrel, and, looking up, I found the moon had risen, and was silvering the mizzen-top and shining white on the luff of the foresail; and almost at the same time the voice of the look-out shouted "Land ho!"

12. COUNCIL OF WAR

There was a great rush of feet across the deck. I could hear people tumbling up from the cabin and the foc's'le; and, slipping in an instant outside my barrel, I dived behind the fore-sail, made a double towards the stern, and came out upon the open deck in time to join Hunter and Dr. Livesey in the rush for the weather bow.

There all hands were already congregated. A belt of fog had lifted almost simultaneously with the appearance of the moon. Away to the south-west of us we saw two low hills, about a couple of miles apart, and rising behind one of them a third and higher hill, whose peak was still buried in the fog. All three seemed sharp and conical in figure.

So much I saw, almost in a dream, for I had not yet recovered from my horrid fear of a minute or two before. And then I heard the voice of Captain Smollett issuing orders. The *Hispaniola* was laid a couple of points nearer the wind, and now sailed a course that would just clear the island on the east.

"And now, men," said the captain, when all was sheeted home, "has any one of you ever seen that land ahead?"

"I have, sir," said Silver. "I've watered there with a trader I was cook in."

"The anchorage is on the south, behind an islet, I fancy?" asked the captain.

"Yes, sir; Skeleton Island they calls it. It were a main place for pirates once, and a hand we had on board knowed all their names for it. That hill to the nor'ard they calls the Fore-mast Hill; there are three hills in a row running south'ard—fore, main, and mizzen, sir. But the main—that's the big 'un with the cloud on it—they usually calls the Spy-glass, by reason of a look-out they kept when they was in the anchorage cleaning; for it's there they cleaned their ships sir, asking your pardon."

"I have a chart here," says Captain Smollet. "See if that's the place."

Long John's eyes burned in his head as he took the chart; but, by the fresh look of the paper, I knew he was doomed to disappointment. This was not the map we found in Billy Bones's chest, but an accurate copy, complete in all things—names and heights and soundings—with the single exception of the red crosses and the written notes.

Sharp as must have been his annoyance, Silver had the strength of mind to hide it.

"Yes, sir," said he, "this is the spot to be sure; and very prettily drawed out. Who might have done that, I wonder? The pirates were too ignorant, I reckon. Ay, here it is: 'Capt. Kidd's

Anchorage'—just the name my shipmate called it. There's a strong current runs along the south, and then away nor'ard up the west coast. Right you was, sir," says he, "to haul your wind and keep the weather of the island. Leastways, if such was your intention as to enter and careen, and there ain't no better place for that in these waters."

"Thank you, my man," says Captain Smollett. "I'll ask you, later on, to give us a help. You may go."

I was surprised at the coolness with which John avowed his knowledge of the island; and I own I was half frightened when I saw him drawing nearer to myself. He did not know to be sure, that I had overheard his council from the apple barrel, and yet I had, by this time, taken such a horror of his cruelty, duplicity, and power, that I could scarce conceal a shudder when he laid his hand upon my arm.

"Ah," says he, "this here is a sweet spot, this island—a sweet spot for a lad to get ashore on. You'll bathe, and you'll climb trees, and you'll hunt goats, you will; and you'll get aloft on them hills like a goat yourself. Why, it makes me young again. I was going to forget my timber leg, I was. It's a pleasant thing to be young, and have ten toes, and you may lay to that. When you want to go a bit of exploring, you just ask old John, and he'll put up a snack for you to take along."

And clapping me in the friendliest way upon the shoulder, he hobbled off forward and went below.

Captain Smollett, the squire, and Dr. Livesey were talking together on the quarter-deck, and, anxious as I was to tell them my story, I durst not interrupt them openly. While I was still casting about in my thoughts to find some probable excuse, Dr. Livesey called me to his side. He had left his pipe below, and being a slave to tobacco, had meant that I should fetch it; but as soon as I was near enough to speak and not be overheard, I broke out immediately: "Doctor, let me speak. Get the captain and squire down to the cabin, and then make some pretence to send for me. I have terrible news."

The doctor changed countenance a little, but next moment he was master of himself.

"Thank you, Jim," said he, quite loudly, "that was all I wanted to know," as if he had asked me a question.

And with that he turned on his heel and rejoined the other two.

They spoke together for a little, and though none of them started, or raised his voice, or so much as whistled, it was plain enough that Dr. Livesey had communicated my request; for the next thing that I heard was the captain giving an order to Job Anderson, and all hands were piped on deck.

"My lads," said Captain Smollett, "I've a word to say to you. This land that we have sighted is the place we have been sailing to. Mr. Trelawney, being a very open-handed gentleman, as we all know, has just asked me a word or two, and as I was able to tell him that every man on board had done his duty, alow and aloft, as I never ask to see it done better, why, he and I and the doctor are going below to the cabin to drink *your* health and luck, and you'll have grog served out for you to drink *our* health and luck. I'll tell you what I think of this: I think it handsome. And if you think as I do, you'll give a good sea cheer for the gentleman that does it."

The cheer followed—that was a matter of course; but it rang out so full and hearty, that I confess I could hardly believe these same men were plotting for our blood.

"One more cheer for Cap'n Smollett," cried Long John, when the first had subsided.

And this also was given with a will.

On the top of that the three gentlemen went below, and not long after, word was sent forward that Jim Hawkins was wanted in the cabin.

I found them all three seated round the table, a bottle of Spanish wine and some raisins before them, and the doctor smoking away, with his wig on his lap, and that, I knew, was a sign that he was agitated. The stern window was open, for it was a warm night, and you could see the moon shining behind on the ship's wake.

"Now, Hawkins," said the squire, "you have something to say. Speak up."

I did as I was bid, and, as short as I could make it, told the whole details of Silver's conversation. Nobody interrupted me till I was done, nor did any one of the three of them make so much as a movement, but they kept their eyes upon my face from first to last.

"Jim," said Dr. Livesey, "take a seat."

And they made me sit down at table beside there, poured me out a glass of wine, filled my hands with raisins, and all three, one after the other, and each with a bow, drank my good health, and their service to me, for my luck and courage.

"Now, captain," said the squire, "you were right, and I was wrong. I own myself an ass, and I await your orders."

"No more an ass than I, sir," returned the captain, "I never heard of a crew that meant to mutiny but what showed signs before, for any man that had an eye in his head to see the mischief and take steps according. But this crew," he added, "beats me."

"Captain," said the doctor, "with your permission, that's Silver. A very remarkable man."

"He'd look remarkably well from a yard-arm, sir," returned the captain. "But this is talk; this don't lead to anything. I see three or four points, and with Mr. Trelawney's permission, I'll name them."

"You, sir, are the captain. It is for you to speak," says Mr. Trelawney, grandly.

"First point," began Mr. Smollett. "We must go on, because we can't turn back. If I gave the word to go about, they would rise at once. Second point, we have time before us—at least, until this treasure's found. Third point, there are faithful hands. Now, sir, it's got to come to blows sooner or later; and what I propose is, to take time by the forelock, as the saying is, and come to blows some fine day when they least expect it. We can count, I take it, on your own home servants, Mr. Trelawney?"

"As upon myself," declared the squire.

"Three," reckoned the captain, "ourselves make seven, counting Hawkins, here. Now, about the honest hands?"

"Most likely Trelawney's own men," said the doctor; "those he had picked up for himself, before he lit on Silver."

"Nay," replied the squire. "Hands was one of mine."

"I did think I could have trusted Hands," added the captain.

"And to think that they're all Englishmen!" broke out the squire. "Sir, I could find it in my heart to blow the ship up."

"Well, gentlemen," said the captain, "the best that I can say is not much. We must lay to, if you please, and keep a bright look out. It's trying on a man, I know. It would be pleasanter to come to blows. But there's no help for it till we know our men. Lay to, and whistle for a wind, that's my view."

"Jim here," said the doctor, "can help us more than anyone. The men are not shy with him, and Jim is a noticing lad."

"Hawkins, I put prodigious faith in you," added the squire.

I began to feel pretty desperate at this, for I felt altogether helpless; and yet, by an odd train of circumstances, it was indeed through me that safety came. In the meantime, talk as we pleased, there were only seven out of the twenty-six on whom we could rely; and out of these seven one was a boy, so that the grown men on our side were six to their nineteen.

PART III

MY SHORE ADVENTURE

13. HOW I BEGAN MY SHORE ADVENTURE

The appearance of the island when I came on deck next morning was altogether changed. Although the breeze had now utterly failed, we had made a great deal of way during the night, and were now lying becalmed about half a mile to the south-east of the low eastern coast. Grey-coloured woods covered a large part of the surface. This even tint was indeed broken up by streaks of yellow sandbreak in the lower lands, and by many tall trees of the pine family, out-topping the others—some singly, some in clumps; but the general colouring was uniform and sad.

The hills ran up clear above the vegetation in spires of naked rock. All were strangely shaped, and the Spy-glass, which was by three or four hundred feet the tallest on the island, was likewise the strangest in configuration, running up sheer from almost every side, and then suddenly cut off at the top like a pedestal to put a statue on.

The *Hispaniola* was rolling scuppers under in the ocean swell. The booms were tearing at the blocks, the rudder was banging to and fro, and the whole ship creaking, groaning, and jumping like a manufactory. I had to cling tight to the backstay, and the world turned giddily before my eyes; for though I was a good enough sailor when there was way on, this standing still and being rolled about like a bottle was a thing I never learned to stand without a qualm or so, above all in the morning, on an empty stomach.

Perhaps it was this—perhaps it was the look of the island with its grey, melancholy woods, and wild stone spires, and the surf that we could both see and hear foaming and thundering on the steep beach—at least, although the sun shone bright and hot, and the shore birds were fishing and crying all around us, and you would have thought anyone would have been glad to get to land after being so long at sea, my heart sank, as the saying is, into my boots; and from that first look onward, I hated the very thought of Treasure Island.

We had a dreary morning's work before us, for there was no sign of any wind, and the boats had to be got out and manned, and the ship warped three or four miles round the corner of the island, and up the narrow passage to the haven behind Skeleton Island. I volunteered for one of the boats, where I had, of course, no business. The heat was sweltering, and the men grumbled fiercely over their work. Anderson was in command of my boat, and instead of keeping the crew in order, he grumbled as loud as the worst.

"Well," he said, with an oath, "it's not for ever."

I thought this was a very bad sign; for, up to that day, the men had gone briskly and willingly about their business; but the very sight of the island had relaxed the cords of discipline.

All the way in, Long John stood by the steersman and conned the ship. He knew the passage like the palm of his hand; and though the man in the chains got everywhere more water than was down in the chart, John never hesitated once.

"There's a strong scour with the ebb," he said, "and this here passage has been dug out, in a manner of speaking, with a spade."

We brought up just where the anchor was in the chart, about a third of a mile from either shore, the mainland on one side, and Skeleton Island on the other. The bottom was clean sand. The plunge of our anchor sent up clouds of birds wheeling and crying over the woods; but in less than a minute they were down again, and all was once more silent.

The place was entirely land-locked, buried in woods, the trees coming right down to high-water mark, the shores mostly flat, and the hill-tops standing round at a distance in a sort of amphitheatre, one here, one there. Two little rivers, or, rather, two swamps, emptied out into this pond, as you might call it; and the foliage round that part of the shore had a kind of poisonous brightness. From the ship, we could see nothing of the house or stockade, for they were quite buried among trees; and if it had not been for the chart on the companion, we might have been the first that had ever anchored there since the island arose out of the seas.

There was not a breath of air moving, nor a sound but that of the surf booming half a mile away along the beaches and against the rocks outside. A peculiar stagnant smell hung over the anchorage—a smell of sodden leaves and rotting tree trunks. I observed the doctor sniffing and sniffing, like someone tasting a bad egg.

"I don't know about treasure," he said, "but I'll stake my wig there's fever here."

If the conduct of the men had been alarming in the boat, it became truly threatening when they had come aboard. They lay about the deck growling together in talk. The slightest order was received with a black look, and grudgingly and carelessly obeyed. Even the honest hands must have caught the infection, for there was not one man aboard to mend another. Mutiny, it was plain, hung over us like a thunder-cloud.

And it was not only we of the cabin party who perceived the danger. Long John was hard at work going from group to group, spending himself in good advice, and as for example no man could have shown a better. He fairly outstripped himself in willingness and civility; he was all smiles to every-one. If an order were given, John would be on his crutch in an instant, with the cheeriest "Ay, ay, sir!" in the world; and when there was nothing else to do, he kept up one song after another, as if to conceal the discontent of the rest.

Of all the gloomy features of that gloomy afternoon, this obvious anxiety on the part of Long John appeared the worst.

We held a council in the cabin.

"Sir," said the captain, "if I risk another order, the whole ship'll come about our ears by the run. You see, sir, here it is. I get a rough answer, do I not? Well, if I speak back, pikes will be going in two shakes; if I don't, Silver will see there's something under that, and the game's up. Now, we've only one man to rely on."

"And who is that?" asked the squire.

"Silver, sir," returned the captain; "he's as anxious as you and I to smother things up. This is a tiff; he'd soon talk 'em out of it if he had the chance, and what I propose to do is to give him the chance. Let's allow the men an afternoon ashore. If they all go, why, we'll fight the ship. If they none of them go, well, then, we hold the cabin, and God defend the right. If some go, you mark my words, sir, Silver'll bring 'em aboard again as mild as lambs."

It was so decided; loaded pistols were served out to all the sure men; Hunter, Joyce, and Redruth were taken into our confidence, and received the news with less surprise and a better spirit than we had looked for, and then the captain went on deck and addressed the crew.

"My lads," said he, "we've had a hot day, and are all tired and out of sorts. A turn ashore'll hurt nobody—the boats are still in the water; you can take the gigs, and as many as please can go ashore for the afternoon. I'll fire a gun half an hour before sundown."

I believe the silly fellows must have thought they would break their shins over treasure as soon as they were landed; for they all came out of their sulks in a moment, and gave a cheer that started the echo in a far-away hill, and sent the birds once more flying and squalling round the anchorage.

The captain was too bright to be in the way. He whipped out of sight in a moment, leaving Silver to arrange the party; and I fancy it was as well he did so. Had he been on deck, he could no longer so much as have pretended not to understand the situation. It was as plain as day. Silver was the captain, and a mighty rebellious crew he had of it. The honest hands—and I was soon to see it proved that there were such on board—must have been very stupid fellows. Or rather, I suppose the truth was this, that all hands were disaffected by the example of the ringleaders—only some more, some less; and a few, being good fellows in the main, could neither be led nor driven any further. It is one thing to be idle and skulk, and quite another to take a ship and murder a number of innocent men.

At last, however, the party was made up. Six fellows were to stay on board, and the remaining thirteen, including Silver, began to embark.

Then it was that there came into my head the first of the mad notions that contributed so much to save our lives. If six men were left by Silver, it was plain our party could not take and fight the ship; and since only six were left, it was equally plain that the cabin party had no present need of my assistance. It occurred to me at once to go ashore. In a jiffy I had slipped over the side, and curled up in the fore-sheets of the nearest boat, and almost at the same moment she shoved off.

No one took notice of me, only the bow oar saying, "Is that you, Jim? Keep your head down." But Silver, from the other boat, looked sharply over and called out to know if that were me; and from that moment I began to regret what I had done.

The crews raced for the beach; but the boat I was in, having some start, and being at once the lighter and the better manned, shot far ahead of her consort, and the bow had struck among the shore-side trees, and I had caught a branch and swung myself out, and plunged into the nearest thicket, while Silver and the rest were still a hundred yards behind.

"Jim, Jim!" I heard him shouting.

But you may suppose I paid no heed; jumping, ducking, and breaking through, I ran straight before my nose, till I could run no longer.

14. THE FIRST BLOW

I was so pleased at having given the slip to Long John, that I began to enjoy myself and look around me with some interest on the strange land that I was in.

I had crossed a marshy tract full of willows, bulrushes, and odd, outlandish, swampy trees; and I had now come out upon the skirts of an open piece of undulating, sandy country, about a mile long, dotted with a few pines, and a great number of contorted trees, not unlike the oak in growth, but pale in the foliage, like willows. On the far side of the open stood one of the hills, with two quaint, craggy peaks, shining vividly in the sun.

I now felt for the first time the joy of exploration. The isle was uninhabited; my shipmates I had left behind, and nothing lived in front of me. but dumb brutes and fowls. I turned hither and thither among the trees. Here and there were flowering plants, unknown to me; here and there I saw snakes, and one raised his head from a ledge of rock and hissed at me with a noise not unlike the spinning of a top. Little did I suppose that he was a deadly enemy, and that the noise was the famous rattle.

Then I came to a long thicket of these oak-like trees—live, or evergreen, oaks, I heard afterwards they should be called—which grew low along the sand like brambles, the boughs curiously twisted, the foliage compact, like thatch. The thicket stretched down from the top of one of the sandy knolls, spreading and growing taller as it went, until it reached the margin of the broad, reedy fen, through which the nearest of the little rivers soaked its way into the anchorage. The marsh was steaming in the strong sun, and the outline of the Spy-glass trembled through the haze.

All at once there began to be a sort of bustle among the bulrushes; a wild duck flew up with a quack, another followed, and soon over the whole surface of the marsh a great cloud of birds hung screaming and circling in the air. I judged at once that some of my shipmates must be drawing near along the borders of the fen. Nor was I deceived; for soon I heard the very distant and low tones of a human voice, which, as I continued to give ear, grew steadily louder and nearer.

This put me in a great fear, and I crawled under cover of the nearest live-oak, and squatted there, hearkening, as silent as a mouse.

Another voice answered; and then the first voice, which I now recognized to be Silver's, once more took up the story, and ran on for a long while in a stream, only now and again interrupted by the other. By the sound they must have been talking earnestly, and almost fiercely; but no distinct word came to my hearing.

At last the speakers seemed to have paused, and perhaps to have sat down; for not only did they cease to draw any nearer, but the birds themselves began to grow more quiet, and to settle again to their places in the swamp.

And now I began to feel that I was neglecting my business; that since I had been so foolhardy as to come ashore with these desperadoes, the least I could do was to overhear them at their councils; and that my plain and obvious duty was to draw as close as I could manage, under the favourable ambush of the crouching trees.

I could tell the direction of the speakers pretty exactly, not only by the sound of their voices, but by the behaviour of the few birds that still hung in alarm above the heads of the intruders.

Crawling on all-fours, I made steadily but slowly towards them; till at last, raising my head to an aperture among the leaves, I could see clear down into a little green dell beside the marsh, and closely set about with trees, where Long John Silver and another of the crew stood face to face in conversation.

The sun beat full upon them. Silver had thrown his hat beside him on the ground, and his great, smooth, blond face, all shining with heat, was lifted to the other man's in a kind of appeal.

"Mate," he was saying, "it's because I thinks gold dust of you—gold dust, and you may lay to that! If I hadn't took to you like pitch, do you think I'd have been here a-warning of you? All's up—you can't make or mend; it's to save your neck that I'm a-speaking, and if one of the wild 'uns knew it, where 'ud I be, Tom—now, tell me, where 'ud I be?"

"Silver," said the other man—and I observed he was not only red in the face, but spoke as hoarse as a crow, and his voice shook, too, like a taut rope—"Silver," says he, "you're old, and you're honest, or has the name for it; and you've money, too, which lots of poor sailors hasn't; and you're brave, or I'm mistook. And ill you tell me you'll let yourself be led away with that kind of a mess of swabs? not you! As sure as God sees me, I'd sooner lose my hand. If I turn agin my dooty—"

And then all of a sudden he was interrupted by a noise. I had found one of the honest hands—well, here, at that same moment, came news of another. Far away out in the marsh there arose, all of a sudden, a sound like the cry of anger, then another on the back of it; and then one horrid, long-drawn scream. The rocks of the Spy-glass re-echoed it a score of times; the whole troop of marsh-birds rose again, darkening heaven, with a simultaneous whirr; and long after that death-yell was still ringing in my brain silence had re-established its empire, and only the rustle of the descending birds and the boom of the distant surges disturbed the languor of the afternoon.

Tom had leaped at the sound, like a horse at the spur; but Silver had not winked an eye. He stood where he was, resting lightly on his crutch, watching his companion like a snake about to spring.

"John!" said the sailor, stretching out his hand.

"Hands off!" cried Silver, leaping back a yard, as it seemed to me, with the speed and security of a trained gymnast.

"Hands off, if you like, John Silver," said the other. "It's a black conscience that can make you feared of me. But, in heaven's name, tell me what was that?"

"That?" returned Silver, smiling away, but warier than ever, his eye a mere pin-point in his face, but gleaming like a crumb of glass. "That? Oh, I reckon that'll be Alan."

And at this poor Tom flashed out like a hero.

"Alan!" he cried. "Then rest his soul for a true seaman! And as for you, John Silver, long you've been a mate of mine, but you're mate of mine no more. If I die like a dog, I'll die in my dooty. You've killed Alan, have you? Kill me, too, if you can. But I defies you."

And with that, this brave fellow turned his back directly on the cook, and set off walking for the beach. But he was not destined to go far. With a cry, John seized the branch of a tree, whipped the crutch out of his armpit, and sent that uncouth missile hurtling through the air. It struck poor Tom, point foremost, and with stunning violence, right between the shoulders in the middle of his back. His hands flew up, he gave a sort of gasp and fell.

Whether he were injured much or little, none could ever tell. Like enough, to judge from the sound, his back was broken on the spot. But he had no time given him to recover. Silver, agile as a monkey, even without leg or crutch, was on the top of him next moment, and had twice buried his knife up to the hilt in that defenceless body. From my place of ambush, I could hear him pant aloud as he struck the blows.

I do not know what it rightly is to faint, but I do know that for the next little while the whole world swam away from before me in a whirling mist; Silver and the birds, and the tall Spy-glass hill-top, going round and round and topsy-turvy before my eyes, and all manner of bells ringing and distant voices shouting in my ears.

When I came again to myself, the monster had pulled himself together, his crutch under his arm, his hat upon his head. Just before him Tom lay motionless upon the sward; but the murderer minded him not a whit, cleansing his blood-stained knife the while upon a wisp of grass. Everything else was unchanged, the sun still shining mercilessly on the steaming marsh and the tall pinnacle of the mountain, and I could scarce persuade myself that murder had been actually done, and a human life cruelly cut short a moment since, before my eyes.

But now John put his hand into his pocket, brought out a whistle, and blew upon it several modulated blasts, that rang far across the heated air. I could not tell, of course, the meaning of the signal; but it instantly awoke my fears. More men would be coming. I might be discovered. They had already slain two of the honest people; after Tom and Alan, might not I come next?

Instantly I began to extricate myself and crawl back again, with what speed and silence I could manage, to the more open portion of the wood. As I did so, I could hear hails coming and going between the old buccaneer and his comrades, and this sound of danger lent me wings.

As soon as I was clear of the thicket, I ran as I never ran before, scarce minding the direction of my flight, so long as it led me from the murderers; and as I ran, fear grew and grew upon me, until it turned into a kind of frenzy.

Indeed, could anyone be more entirely lost than I? When the gun fired, how should I dare to go down to the boats among those fiends, still smoking from their crime? Would not the first of them who saw me wring my neck like a snipe's? Would not my absence itself be an evidence to them of my alarm, and therefore of my fatal knowledge? It was all over, I thought. Goodbye to the *Hispaniola*; good-bye to the squire, the doctor, and the captain! There was nothing left for me but death by starvation, or death by the hands of the mutineers.

All this while, as I say, I was still running, and, without taking any notice, I had drawn near to the foot of the little hill with the two peaks, and had got into a part of the island where the live-oaks grew more widely apart, and seemed more like forest trees in their bearing and dimensions. Mingled with these were a few scattered pines, some fifty, some nearer seventy, feet high. The air, too, smelt more freshly than down beside the marsh.

And here a fresh alarm brought me to a standstill with a thumping heart.

15. THE MAN OF THE ISLAND

From the side of the hill, which was here steep and stony, a spout of gravel was dislodged, and fell rattling and bounding through the trees. My eyes turned instinctively in that direction, and I saw a figure leap with great rapidity behind the trunk of a pine. What it was, whether bear or man or monkey, I could in no wise tell. It seemed dark and shaggy; more I knew not. But the terror of this new apparition brought me to a stand.

I was now, it seemed, cut off upon both sides; behind me the murderers, before me this lurking nondescript. And immediately I began to prefer the dangers that I knew to those I knew not. Silver himself appeared less terrible in contrast with this creature of the woods, and I turned on my heel, and, looking sharply behind me over my shoulder, began to retrace my steps in the direction of the boats.

Instantly the figure reappeared, and, making a wide circuit, began to head me of. I was tired, at any rate; but had I been as fresh as when I rose, I could see it was in vain for me to contend in speed with such an adversary. From trunk to trunk the creature flitted like a deer, running manlike on two legs, but unlike any man that I had ever seen, stooping almost double as it ran. Yet a man it was, I could no longer be in doubt about that.

I began to recall what I had heard of cannibals. I was within an ace of calling for help. But the mere fact that he was a man, however wild, had somewhat reassured me, and my fear of Silver began to revive in proportion. I stood still, therefore, and cast about for some method of escape; and as I was so thinking, the recollection of my pistol flashed into my mind. As soon as I remembered I was not defenceless, courage glowed again in my heart; and I set my face resolutely for this man of the island, and walked briskly towards him.

He was concealed by this time, behind another tree trunk; but he must have been watching me closely, for as soon as I began to move in his direction he reappeared and took a step to meet me. Then he hesitated, drew back, came forward again, and at last, to my wonder and confusion, threw himself on his knees and held out his clasped hands in supplication.

At that I once more stopped.

"Who are you?" I asked.

"Ben Gunn," he answered, and his voice sounded hoarse and awkward, like a rusty lock. "I'm poor Ben Gunn, I am; and I haven't spoke with a Christian these three years."

I could now see that he was a white man like myself, and that his features were even pleasing. His skin, wherever it was exposed, was burnt by the sun; even his lips were black; and his fair eyes looked quite startling in so dark a face.

Of all the beggar-men that I had seen or fancied, he was the chief for raggedness. He was clothed with tatters of old ship's canvas and old sea cloth; and this extraordinary patchwork was all held together by a system of the most various and incongruous fastenings, brass buttons, bits of stick, and loops of tarry gaskin. About his waist he wore an old brass-buckled leather belt, which was the one thing solid in his whole accoutrement.

"Three years!" I cried. "Were you shipwrecked?"

"Nay, mate," said he— "marooned."

I had heard the word, and I knew it stood for a horrible kind of punishment common enough among the buccaneers, in which the offender is put ashore with a little powder and shot, and left behind on some desolate and distant island.

"Marooned three years agone," he continued, "and lived on goats since then, and berries, and oysters. Wherever a man is, says I, a man can do for himself. But, mate, my heart is sore for Christian diet. You mightn't happen to have a piece of cheese about you, now? No? Well, many's the long night I've dreamed of cheese—toasted, mostly—and woke up again, and here I were."

"If ever I can get aboard again," said I, "you shall have cheese by the stone."

All this time he had been feeling the stuff of my jacket, smoothing my hands, looking at my boots, and generally, in the intervals of his speech, showing a childish pleasure in the presence of a fellow-creature. But at my last words he perked up into a kind of startled slyness.

"If ever you can get aboard again, says you?" he repeated. "Why, now, who's to hinder you?"

"Not you, I know," was my reply.

"And right you was," he cried. "Now you—what do you call yourself, mate?"

"Jim," I told him.

"Jim, Jim," says he, quite pleased apparently. "Well, now, Jim, I've lived that rough as you'd be ashamed to hear of. Now, for instance, you wouldn't think I had had a pious mother—to look at me?" he asked.

"Why, no, not in particular," I answered.

"Ah, well," said he, "but I had—*re*markable pious. And I was a civil, pious boy; and could rattle off my catechism that fast, as you couldn't tell one word from another. And here's what it come to, Jim, and it begun with chuckfarthen on the blessed grave-stones! That's what it begun with, but it went further'n that; and so my mother told me, and predicked the whole, she did, the pious woman! But it were Providence that put me here. I've thought it all out in this here lonely island, and I'm back on piety. You don't catch me tasting rum so much; but just a thimbleful for luck, of course, the first chance I have. I'm bound I'll be good, and I see the way to. And, Jim"—looking all round him, and lowering his voice to a whisper—"I'm rich."

I now felt that the poor fellow had gone crazy in his solitude, and I suppose I must have shown the feeling in my face; for he repeated the statement hotly:

"Rich! rich! I says. And I'll tell you what: I'll make a man of you, Jim. Ah, Jim, you'll bless your stars, you will, you was the first that found me!"

And at this there came suddenly a lowering shadow over

his face, and he tightened his grasp upon my hand, and raised a forefinger threateningly before my eyes. "Now, Jim, you tell me true; that ain't Flint's ship?" he asked.

At this I had a happy inspiration. I began to believe that I had found an ally, and I answered him at once.

"It's not Flint's ship, and Flint is dead; but I'll tell you true, as you ask me—there are some of Flint's hands aboard; worse luck for the rest of us."

"Not a man—with one—leg?" he gasped.

"Silver?" I asked.

"Ah, Silver!" says he; "that were his name."

"He's the cook; and the ringleader, too."

He was still holding me by the wrist, and at that he gave it quite a wring.

"If you was sent by Long John," he said, "I'm as good as pork, and I know it. But where was you, do you suppose?"

I had made my mind up in a moment, and by way of answer told him the whole story of our voyage, and the predicament in which we found ourselves. He heard me with the keenest interest, and when I had done he patted me on the head. "You're a good lad, Jim," he said, "and you're all in a clove hitch, ain't you? Well, you just put your trust in Ben Gunn—Ben Gunn's the man to do it. Would you think it likely, now, that your squire would prove a liberal-minded one in case of help—him being in a clove hitch, as you remark?"

I told him the squire was the most liberal of men.

"Ay, but you see," returned Ben Gunn, "I didn't mean giving me a gate to keep, and a suit of livery clothes, and such; that's not my mark, Jim. What I mean is, would he be likely to come down to the toon of, say, one thousand pounds out of money that's as good as a man's own already?"

"I am sure he would," said I. "As it was, all hands were to share."

"*And* a passage home?" he added, with a look of great shrewdness.

"Why," I cried, "the squire's a gentleman. And, besides, if we got rid of the others, we should want you to help work the vessel home."

"Ah," said he, "so you would." And he seemed very much relieved.

"Now, I'll tell you what," he went on. "So much I'll tell you, and no more. I were in Flint's ship when he buried the treasure; he and six along—six strong seamen. They was ashore nigh on a week, and us standing off and on in the old *Walrus*. One fine day up went the signal, and here come Flint by himself in a little boat, and his head done up in a blue scarf. The sun was getting up, and mortal white he looked about the cutwater. But, there he was, you mind, and the six all dead—dead and buried. How he done it, not a man aboard us could make out. It was battle, murder, and sudden death, leastways—him against six. Billy Bones was the mate; Long John, he was quartermaster; and they asked him where the treasure was. 'Ah,' says he, 'you can go ashore, if you like, and stay,' he says; 'but as for the ship she'll beat up for more, by thunder!' That's what he said.

"Well, I was in another ship three years back, and we sighted this island. 'Boys,' said I, 'here's Flint's treasure; let's land and find it.' The cap'n was displeased at that; but my messmates were all of a mind, and landed. Twelve days they looked for it, and every day they had the worse word for me, until one fine morning all hands went aboard. 'As for you, Benjamin Gunn,' says they, 'here's a musket,' they says, 'and a spade, and pickaxe. You can stay here, and find Flint's money for yourself,' they says.

"Well, Jim, three years have I been here, and not a bite of Christian diet from that day to this. But now, you look here; look at me. Do I look like a man before the mast? No, says you. Nor I weren't, neither, I says." With that he winked and pinched me hard.

"Just you mention them words to your squire, Jim," he went on: "Nor he weren't, neither—that's the words. Three years he were the man of this island, light and dark, fair and rain; and sometimes he would, maybe, think upon a prayer (says you), and sometimes he would, maybe, think of his old mother, so be as she's alive (you'll say); but the most part of Gunn's time (this is what you'll say)—the most part of his time was took up with another matter. And then you'll give him a nip, like I do."

And he pinched me again in the most confidential manner.

"Then," he continued—"then you'll up, and you'll say this:—Gunn is a good man (you'll say), and he puts a precious sight more confidence—a precious sight, mind that—in a gen'leman born than in these gen'lemen of fortune, having been one hisself."

"Well," I said, "I don't understand one word that you've been saying. But that's neither here nor there; for how am I to get on board?"

"Ah," said he, "that's the hitch, for sure. Well, there's my boat, that I made with my two hands. I keep her under the white rock. If the worst come to the worst, we might try that after dark. Hi!" he broke out, "what's that?"

For just then, although the sun had still an hour or two to run, all the echoes of the island awoke and bellowed to the thunder of a cannon.

"They have begun to fight!" I cried. "Follow me."

And I began to run towards the anchorage, my terrors all forgotten; while, close at my side, the marooned man in his goatskins trotted easily and lightly.

"Left, left," says he; "keep to your left hand, mate Jim! Under the trees with you! Theer's where I killed my first goat. They don't come down here now; they're all mast-headed on them mountings for the fear of Benjamin Gunn. Ah! and there's the cetemery"—cemetery, he must have meant. "You see the mounds? I come here and prayed, nows and thens, when I thought maybe a Sunday would be about doo. It weren't quite a chapel, but it seemed more solemn like; and then, says you, Ben Gunn was shorthanded—no chapling, nor so much as a Bible and a flag, you says."

So he kept talking as I ran, neither expecting nor receiving any answer.

The cannon-shot was followed, after a considerable interval, by a volley of small arms.

Another pause, and then, not a quarter of a mile in front of me, I beheld the Union Jack flutter in the air above a wood.

Part IV

THE STOCKADE

16. NARRATIVE CONTINUED BY THE DOCTOR: HOW THE SHIP WAS ABANDONED

It was about half past one—three bells in the sea phrase— that the two boats went ashore from the *Hispaniola*. The captain, the squire, and I were talking matters over in the cabin. Had there been a breath of wind we should have fallen on the six mutineers who were left aboard with us, slipped our cable, and away to sea. But the wind was wanting; and, to complete our helplessness, down came Hunter with the news that Jim Hawkins had slipped into a boat and was gone ashore with the rest.

It never occurred to us to doubt Jim Hawkins; but we were alarmed for his safety. With the men in the temper they were in, it seemed an even chance if we should see the lad again. We ran on deck. The pitch was bubbling in the seams; the nasty stench of the place turned me sick; if ever a man smelt fever and dysentery, it was in that abominable anchorage. The six scoundrels were sitting grumbling under a sail in the forecastle; ashore we could see the gigs made fast, and a man sitting in each, hard by where the river runs in. One of them was whistling "Lillibullero."

Waiting was a strain; and it was decided that Hunter and I should go ashore with the jolly-boat, in quest of information. The gigs had leaned to their right; but Hunter and I pulled straight in, in the direction of the stockade upon the chart. The two who were left guarding their boats seemed in a bustle at our appearance; "Lillibullero" stopped off, and I could see the pair discussing what they ought to do. Had they gone and told Silver, all might have turned out differently; but they had their orders, I suppose, and decided to sit quietly where they were and hark back again to "Lillibullero."

There was a slight bend in the coast, and I steered so as to put it between us; even before we landed we had thus lost sight of the gigs. I jumped out, and came as near running as I durst, with a big silk handkerchief under my hat for coolness sake, and a brace of pistols ready primed for safety.

I had not gone a hundred yards when I came on the stockade.

This was how it was: a spring of clear water rose almost at the top of a knoll. Well, on the knoll, and enclosing the spring, they had clapped a stout log-house, fit to hold two score people on a pinch, and loopholed for musketry on every side. All round this they had cleared a wide space, and then the thing was completed by a paling six feet high, without door or opening, too strong to pull down without time and labour, and too open to shelter the besiegers. The people in the log-house had them in every way; they stood quiet in shelter and shot the others like partridges. All they wanted was a good watch and food; for, short of a complete surprise, they might have held the place against a regiment.

What particularly took my fancy was the spring. For, though we had a good enough place of it in the cabin of the *Hispaniola,* with plenty of arms and ammunition, and things to eat, and excellent wines, there had been one thing over looked—we had no water. I was thinking this over, when there came ringing over the island the cry of a man at the point of death. I was not new to violent death—I have served his Royal Highness the Duke of Cumberland, and got a wound myself at Fontenoy—but I know my pulse went dot and carry one. "Jim Hawkins is gone," was my first thought.

It is something to have been an old soldier, but more still to have been a doctor. There is no time to dilly-dally in our work. And so now I made up my mind instantly, and with no time lost returned to the shore, and jumped on board the jolly-boat.

By good fortune Hunter pulled a good oar. We made the

water fly; and the boat was soon alongside, and I aboard the schooner.

I found them all shaken, as was natural. The squire was sitting down, as white as a sheet, thinking of the harm he had led us to, the good soul! and one of the six forecastle hands was little better.

"There's a man," says Captain Smollett, nodding towards him, "new to this work. He came nigh-hand fainting, doctor, when he heard the cry. Another touch of the rudder and that man would join us."

I told my plan to the captain, and between us we settled on the details of its accomplishment.

We put old Redruth in the gallery between the cabin and the forecastle, with three or four loaded muskets and a mattress for protection. Hunter brought the boat round under the stern-port, and Joyce and I set to work loading her with powder tins, muskets, bags of biscuits, kegs of pork, a cask of cognac, and my invaluable medicine chest.

In the meantime, the squire and the captain stayed on deck, and the latter hailed the coxswain, who was the principal man aboard.

"Mr. Hands," he said, "here are two of us with a brace of pistols each. If any one of you six make a signal of any description, that man's dead."

They were a good deal taken aback; and, after a little consultation, one and all tumbled down the fore companion, thinking, no doubt, to take us on the rear. But when they saw Redruth waiting for them in the sparred gallery, they went about ship at once, and a head popped out again on deck.

"Down, dog!" cried the captain.

And the head popped back again; and we heard no more, for the time, of these six very faint-hearted seamen.

By this time, tumbling things in as they came, we had the jolly-boat loaded as much as we dared. Joyce and I got out through the stern-port, and we made for shore again, as fast as oars could take us.

This second trip fairly aroused the watchers by the shore. "Lillibullero" was dropped again; and just before we lost sight of them behind the little point, one of them whipped ashore and disappeared. I had half a mind to change my plan and destroy their boats, but I feared that Silver and the others might be close at hand, and all might very well be lost by trying for too much.

We had soon touched land in the same place as before, and set to provision the block-house. All three made the first journey, heavily laden, and tossed our stores over the palisade. Then, leaving Joyce to guard them—one man, to be sure, but with half a dozen muskets—Hunter and I returned to the jolly-boat, and loaded ourselves once more. So we proceeded without pausing to take breath, till the whole cargo was bestowed, when the two servants took up their position in the block-house, and I, with all my power, sculled back to the *Hispaniola*.

That we should have risked a second boatload seems more daring than it really was. They had the advantage of numbers, of course, but we had the advantage of arms. Not one of the men ashore had a musket, and before they could get within range for pistol shooting, we flattered ourselves we should be able to give a good account of a half-dozen at least.

The squire was waiting for me at the stern window, all his faintness gone from him. He caught the painter and made it fast, and we fell to loading the boat for our very lives. Pork, powder, and biscuit was the cargo, with only a musket and a cutlass apiece for squire and me and Redruth and the captain. The rest of the arms and powder we dropped overboard in two fathoms and a half of water, so that we could see the bright steel shining far below us in the sun, on the clean, sandy bottom.

By this time the tide was beginning to ebb, and the ship was swinging round to her anchor. Voices were heard faintly halloaing in the direction of the two gigs; and though this reassured us for Joyce and Hunter, who were well to the eastward, it warned our party to be off.

Redruth retreated from his place in the gallery, and dropped into the boat, which we then brought round to the ship's counter, to be handier for Captain Smollett.

"Now, men," said he, "do you hear me?"

There was no answer from the forecastle.

"It's to you, Abraham Gray—it's to you I am speaking."

Still no reply.

"Gray," resumed Mr. Smollett, a little louder, "I am leaving this ship, and I order you to follow your captain. I know you are a good man at bottom, and I daresay not one of the lot of you's as bad as he makes out. I have my watch here in my hand; I give you thirty seconds to join me in."

There was a pause.

"Come, my fine fellow," continued the captain, "don't hang so long in stays. I'm risking my life, and the lives of these good gentlemen, every second."

There was a sudden scuffle, a sound of blows, and out burst Abraham Gray with a knife-cut on the side of the cheek, and came running to the captain, like a dog to the whistle.

"I'm with you, sir," said he. And the next moment he and the captain had dropped aboard of us, and we had shoved off and given way.

We were clear out of the ship; but not yet ashore in our stockade.

17. NARRATIVE CONTINUED BY THE DOCTOR: THE JOLLY BOAT'S LAST TRIP

This fifth trip was quite different from any of the others. In the first place, the little gallipot of a boat that we were in was gravely overloaded. Five grown men, and three of them—Trelawney, Redruth, and the captain—over six feet high, was already more than she was meant to carry. Add to that the powder, pork, and bread-bags. The gunwale was lipping astern. Several times we shipped a little water, and my breeches and the tails of my coat were all soaking wet before we had gone a hundred yards.

The captain made us trim the boat, and we got her to lie a little more evenly. All the same, we were afraid to breathe.

In the second place the ebb was now making—a strong

rippling current running westward through the basin, and then south'ard and seaward down the straits by which we had entered in the morning.

Even the ripples were a danger to our overloaded craft; but the worst of it was that we were swept out of our true course, and away from our proper landing-place behind the point. If we let the current have its way we should come ashore beside the gigs, where the pirates might appear at any moment.

"I cannot keep her head for the stockade, sir," said I to the captain. I was steering, while he and Redruth, two fresh men, were at the oars. "The tide keeps washing her down. Could you pull a little stronger?"

"Not without swamping the boat," said he, "You must bear up, sir, if you please—bear up until you see you're gaining."

I tried, and found by experiment that the tide kept sweeping us westward until I had laid her head due east, or just about right angles to the way we ought to go.

"We'll never get ashore at this rate," said I.

"If it's the only course that we can lie, sir, we must even lie it," returned the captain. "We must keep upstream. You see, sir," he went on, "if once we dropped to leeward of the landing-place, it's hard to say where we should get ashore, besides the chance of being boarded by the gigs; whereas, the way we go the current must slacken, and then we can dodge back along the shore."

"The current's less a'eady, sir," said the man Gray, who was sitting in the fore-sheets; "you can ease her off a bit."

"Thank you, my man," said I, quite as if nothing had happened; for we had all quietly made up our mind to treat him like one of ourselves.

Suddenly the captain spoke up again, and I thought his voice was a little changed.

"The gun!" said he.

"I have thought of that," said I, for I made sure he was thinking of a bombardment of the fort. "They could never get the gun ashore, and if they did, they could never haul it through the woods."

"Look astern, doctor," replied the captain.

We had entirely forgotten the long nine; and there, to our horror, were the five rogues busy about her, getting off her jacket, as they called the stout tarpaulin cover under which she sailed. Not only that, but it flashed into my mind at the same moment that the round-shot and the powder for the gun had been left behind, and a stroke with an axe would put it all into the possession of the evil ones aboard.

"Israel was Flint's gunner," said Gray, hoarsely.

At any risk, we put the boat's head direct for the landing-place. By this time we had got so far out of the run of the current that we kept steerage way even at our necessarily gentle rate of rowing, and I could keep her steady for the goal. But the worst of it was, that with the course I now held, we turned our broadside instead of our stern to the *Hispaniola,* and offered a target like a barn door.

I could hear, as well as see, that brandy-faced rascal, Israel Hands, plumping down a round-shot on the deck.

"Who's the best shot?" asked the captain.

"Mr. Trelawney, out and away," said I.

"Mr. Trelawney, will you please pick me off one of these men, sir? Hands, if possible," said the captain.

Trelawney was as cool as steel. He looked to the priming of his gun.

"Now," cried the captain, "easy with that gun, sir, or you'll swamp the boat. All hands stand by to trim her when he aims."

The squire raised his gun, the rowing ceased, and we leaned over to the other side to keep the balance, and all was so nicely contrived that we did not ship a drop.

They had the gun, by this time, slewed round upon the swivel, and Hands, who was at the muzzle with the rammer, was, in consequence, the most exposed. However, we had no luck; for just as Trelawney fired, down he stooped, the ball whistled over him, and it was one of the other four who fell. The cry he gave was echoed, not only by his companions on board, but by a great number of voices from the shore, and looking in that direction I saw the other pirates trooping out from among the trees and tumbling into their places in the boats.

"Here come the gigs, sir," said I.

"Give way then," cried the captain. "We mustn't mind if we swamp her now. If we can't get ashore, all's up."

"Only one of the gigs is being manned sir," I added, "the crew of the other most likely going round by shore to cut us off."

"They'll have a hot run, sir," returned the captain. "Jack ashore, you know. It's not them I mind; it's the roundshot. Carpet bowls! My lady's maid couldn't miss. Tell us, squire, when you see the match, and we'll hold water."

In the meanwhile we had been making headway at a good pace for a boat so overloaded, and we had shipped but little water in the process.

We were now close in; thirty or forty strokes and we should beach her; for the ebb had already disclosed a narrow belt of sand below the clustering trees. The gig was no longer to be feared; the little point had already concealed it from our eyes. The ebb-tide, which had so cruelly delayed us, was now making reparation, and delaying our assailants. The one source of danger was the gun.

"If I durst," said the captain, "I'd stop and pick off another man."

But it was plain that they meant nothing should delay their shot. They had never so much as looked at their fallen comrade, though he was not dead, and I could see him trying to crawl away.

"Ready!" cried the squire.

"Hold!" cried the captain, quick as an echo.

And he and Redruth backed with a great heave that sent her stern bodily under water. The report fell in at the same instant of time. This was the first that Jim heard, the sound of the squire's shot not having reached him. Where the ball passed, not one of us precisely knew; but I fancy it must have been over our heads, and that the wind of it may have contributed to our disaster.

At any rate, the boat sank by the stern, quite gently, in three feet of water, leaving the captain and myself, facing each other, on our feet. The other three took complete headers, and came up again, drenched and bubbling.

So far there was no great harm. No lives were lost, and we could wade ashore in safety. But there were all our stores at the bottom, and, to make things worse, only two guns out of five remained in a state of service. Mine I had snatched from my knees and held over my head, by a sort of instinct. As for the captain, he had carried his over his shoulder by a bandoleer, and, like a wise man, lock uppermost. The other three had gone down with the boat.

To add to our concern we heard voices already drawing near us in the woods along shore; and we had not only the danger of being cut off from the stockade in our half-crippled state, but the fear before us whether, if Hunter and Joyce were attacked by half a dozen, they would have the sense and conduct to stand firm. Hunter was steady, that we knew; Joyce was a doubtful case—a pleasant, polite man for a valet, and to brush one's clothes, but not entirely fitted for a man of war.

With all this in our minds, we waded ashore as fast as we could, leaving behind us the poor jolly-boat, and a good half of all our powder and provisions.

18. NARRATIVE CONTINUED BY THE DOCTOR: END OF THE FIRST DAY'S FIGHTING

We made our best speed across the strip of wood that now divided us from the stockade; and at every step we took the voices of the buccaneers rang nearer. Soon we could hear their footfalls as they ran, and the crashing of the branches as they breasted across a bit of thicket.

I began to see we should have a brush for it in earnest, and looked to my priming.

"Captain," said I, "Trelawney is the dead shot. Give him your gun; his own is useless."

They exchanged guns, and Trelawney, silent and cool as he had been since the beginning of the bustle, hung a moment on his heel to see that all was fit for service. At the same time, observing Gray to be unarmed, I handed him my cutlass. It did all our hearts good to see him spit in his hand, knit his brows, and make the blade sing through the air. It was plain from every line of his body that our new hand was worth his salt.

Forty paces farther we came to the edge of the wood and saw the stockade in front of us. We struck the enclosure about the middle of the south side, and, almost at the same time, seven mutineers—Job Anderson, the boatswain, at their head—appeared in full cry at the south-western corner.

They paused, as if taken aback; and before they recovered, not only the squire and I, but Hunter and Joyce from the block-house, had time to fire. The four shots came in after a scattering volley; but they did the business; one of the enemy actually fell, and the rest, without hesitation, turned and plunged into the trees.

After reloading, we walked down the outside of the palisade to see to the fallen enemy. He was stone dead—shot through the heart.

We began to rejoice over our good success, when just at that moment a pistol cracked in the bush, a ball whistled close past my ear, and poor Tom Redruth stumbled and fell his length on the ground. Both the squire and I returned the shot; but as we had nothing to aim at, it is probable we only wasted powder. Then we reloaded, and turned our attention to poor Tom.

The captain and Gray were already examining him; and I saw with half an eye that all was over.

I believe the readiness of our return volley had scattered the mutineers once more, for we were suffered without further molestation to get the poor old gamekeeper hoisted over the stockade, and carried, groaning and bleeding, into the log-house. Poor old fellow, he had not uttered one word of surprise, complaint, fear, or even acquiescence, from the very beginning of our troubles till now, when we had laid him down in the log-house to die. He had lain like a Trojan behind his mattress in the gallery; he had followed every order silently, doggedly, and well; he was the oldest of our party by a score of years; and now, sullen, old, serviceable servant, it was he that was to die.

The squire dropped down beside him on his knees and kissed his hand, crying like a child.

"Be I going, doctor?" he asked.

"Tom, my man," said I, "you're going home."

"I wish I had had a lick at them with the gun first," he replied.

"Tom," said the squire, "say you forgive me, won't you?"

"Would that be respectful like, from me to you, squire?" was the answer. "Howsoever, so be it, amen!"

After a little while of silence, he said he thought somebody might read a prayer. "It's the custom, sir," he added, apologetically. And not long after, without another word, he passed away.

In the meantime the captain, whom I had observed to be wonderfully swollen about the chest and pockets, had turned out at great man various stores—the British colours, a Bible, a coil of stoutish rope, pen, ink, the log-book, and pounds of tobacco. He had found a longish fir-tree lying felled and cleared in the enclosure, and with the help of Hunter, he had set it up at the corner of the log-house where the trunks crossed and made an angle. Then, climbing on the roof, he had with his own hand bent and run up the colours.

This seemed mightily to relieve him. He re-entered the log-house, and set about counting up the stores, as if nothing else existed. But he had an eye on Tom's passage for all that; and as soon as all was over, came forward with another flag, and reverently spread it on the body.

"Don't you take on, sir," he said, shaking the squire's hand. "All's well with him; no fear for a hand that's been shot down in his duty to captain and owner. It mayn't be good divinity, but it's a fact."

Then he pulled me aside.

"Dr. Livesey," he said, "in how many weeks do you and squire expect the consort?"

I told him it was a question, not of weeks, but of months; that if we were not back by the end of August, Blandly was to send to find us; but neither sooner nor later. "You can calculate for yourself," I said.

"Why, yes," returned the captain, scratching his head, "and making a large allowance, sir, for all the gifts of Providence, I should say we were pretty close hauled."

"How do you mean?" I asked.

"It's a pity, sir, we lost that second load. That's what I mean," replied the captain. "As for powder and shot, we'll do. But the rations are short, very short—so short, Dr. Livesey, that we're perhaps as well without that extra mouth."

And he pointed to the dead body under the flag.

Just then, with a roar and a whistle, a round-shot passed high above the roof of the log-house and plumped far beyond us in the wood.

"Oho!" cried the captain. "Blaze away! You've little enough powder already, my lads."

At the second trial, the aim was better, and the ball descended inside the stockade, scattering a cloud of sand, but doing no further damage.

"Captain," said the squire, "the house is quite invisible from the ship. It would be the flag they are aiming at. Would it not be wiser to take it in?"

"Strike my colours!" cried the captain. "No, sir, not I"; and, as soon as he had said the words, I think we all agreed with him. For it was not only a piece of stout, seamanly, good feeling; it was good policy besides, and showed our enemies that we despised their cannonade.

All through the evening they kept thundering away. Ball after ball flew or fell short, or kicked up the sand in the enclosure; but they had to fire so high that the shot fell dead and buried itself in the soft sand. We had no ricochet to fear; and though one popped in through the roof of the log-house and out again through the floor, we soon got used to that sort of horse-play, and minded it no more than cricket.

"There is one thing good about all this," observed the captain; "the wood in front of us is likely clear. The ebb has made a good while; our stores should be uncovered. Volunteers to go and bring in pork."

Gray and Hunter were the first to come forward. Well armed, they stole out of the stockade; but it proved a useless mission. The mutineers were bolder than we fancied, or they put more trust in Israel's gunnery. For four or five of them were busy carrying off our stores, and wading out with them to one of the gigs that lay close by, pulling an oar or so to hold her steady against the current. Silver was in the stern-sheets in command; and every man of them was now provided with a musket from some secret magazine of their own.

The captain sat down to his log, and here is the beginning of the entry:

"Alexander Smollet, master; David Livesey, ship's doctor; Abraham Gray, carpenter's mate; John Trelawney, owner; John Hunter and Richard Joyce, owner's servants, landsmen—being all that is left faithful of the ship's company—with stores for ten days at short rations, came ashore this day, and flew British colours on the log-house in Treasure Island. Thomas Redruth, owner's servant, landsman, shot by the mutineers; James Hawkins, cabinboy—"

And at the same time I was wondering over poor Jim Hawkins's fate.

A hail on the land side.

"Somebody hailing us," said Hunter, who was on guard.

"Doctor! squire! captain! Hullo, Hunter, is that you?" came the cries.

And I ran to the door in time to see Jim Hawkins, safe and sound, come climbing over the stockade.

19. NARRATIVE RESUMED BY JIM HAWKINS: THE GARRISON IN THE STOCKADE

As soon as Ben Gunn saw the colours he came to a halt, stopped me by the arm, and sat down.

"Now," said he, "there's your friends, sure enough."

"Far more likely it's the mutineers," I answered.

"That!" he cried "Why, in a place like this, where nobody puts in but gen'lemen of fortune, Silver would fly the Jolly Roger, you don't make no doubt of that. No; that's your friends. There's been blows, too, and I reckon your friends has had the best of it, and here they are ashore in the old stockade, as was made years and years ago by Flint. Ah, he was the man to have a headpiece, was Flint! Barring rum, his match were never seen. He were afraid of none, not he; on'y Silver—Silver was that genteel."

"Well," said I, "that may be so, and so be it; all the more reason that I should hurry on and join my friends."

"Nay, mate," returned Ben, "not you. You're a good boy, or I'm mistook; but you're on'y a boy, all told. Now, Ben Gunn is fly. Rum wouldn't bring me there, where you're going—not rum wouldn't, till I see your born gen'leman, and gets it on his word of honour. And you won't forget my words: 'A precious sight (that's what you'll say), a precious sight more confidence'—and then nips him."

And he pinched me the third time with the same air of cleverness.

"And when Ben Gunn is wanted, you know where to find him, Jim. Just where you found him today. And him that comes is to have a white thing in his hand; and he's to come alone. Oh! and you'll say this: 'Ben Gunn,' says you, 'has reasons of his own.'"

"Well," said I, "I believe I understand, You have something to propose, and you wish to see the squire or the doctor; and you're to be found where I found you. Is that all?"

"And when? says you," he added. "Why, from about noon observation to about six bells."

"Good," said I, "and now may I go?"

"You won't forget?" he inquired, anxiously. "Precious sight, and reasons of his own, says you. Reasons of his own; that's the mainstay; as between man and man. Well, then"—still holding me—"I reckon you can go, Jim. And, Jim, if you was to see Silver, you wouldn't go for to sell Ben Gunn? wild horses wouldn't draw it from you? No, says you. And if them pirates camp ashore, Jim, what would you say but there'd be widders in the morning?"

Here he was interrupted by a loud report, and a cannon-ball came tearing through the trees and pitched in the sand, not a hundred yards from where we two were talking. The next moment each of us had taken to his heels in a different direction.

For a good hour to come frequent reports shook the island, and balls kept crashing through the woods. I moved from hiding-place to hiding-place, always pursued, or so it seemed to me, by these terrifying missiles. But towards the end of the bombardment, though still I durst not venture in the direction of the stockade, where the balls fell oftenest, I had begun, in a manner, to pluck up my heart again; and after a long detour to the east, crept down among the shore-side trees. The sun had just set, the sea breeze, was rustling and tumbling in the woods, and ruffling the grey surface of the anchorage; the tide, too, was far out, and great tracts of sand lay uncovered; the air, after the heat of the day, chilled me through my jacket.

The *Hispaniola* still lay where she had anchored; but, sure enough, there was the Jolly Roger—the black flag of piracy—flying from her peak. Even as I looked, there came another red flash and another report, that sent the echoes clattering, and one more round-shot whistled through the air. It was the last of the cannonade.

I lay for some time, watching the bustle which succeeded the attack. Men were demolishing something with axes on the beach near the stockade; the poor jolly-boat, I afterwards discovered. Away, near the mouth of the river, a great fire was glowing among the trees, and between that point and the ship one of the gigs kept coming and going, the men, whom I had seen so gloomy, shouting at the oars like children. But there was a sound in their voices which suggested rum.

At length I thought I might return towards the stockade. I was pretty far down on the low, sandy spit that encloses the anchorage to the east, and is joined at half-water to Skeleton Island; and now, as I rose to my feet, I saw, some distance further down the spit, and rising from among low bushes, an isolated rock, pretty high, and peculiarly white in colour. It occurred to me that this might be the white rock of which Ben Gunn had spoken, and that some day or other a boat might be wanted, and I should know where to look for one.

Then I skirted among the woods until I had regained the rear, or shoreward side, of the stockade, and was soon welcomed by the faithful party.

I had soon told my story, and began to look about me. The log-house was made of unsquared trunks of pine—roof, walls, and floor. The latter stood in several places as much as a foot or a foot and a half above the surface of the sand. There was a porch at the door, and under this porch the little spring welled up into an artificial basin of a rather odd kind—no other than a great ship's kettle of iron, with the bottom knocked out, and sunk "to her bearings", as the captain said, among the sand.

Little had been left beside the framework of the house; but in one corner there was a stone slab laid down by way of hearth, and an old rusty iron basket to contain the fire.

The slopes of the knoll and all the inside of the stockade had been cleared of timber to build the house, and we could see by the stumps what a fine and lofty grove had been destroyed. Most of the soil had been washed away or buried in drift after the removal of the trees; only where the streamlet ran down from the kettle a thick bed of moss and some ferns and little creeping bushes were still green among the sand. Very close around the stockade—too close for defence, they said—the wood still flourished high and dense, all of fir on the land side, but towards the sea with a large admixture of live-oaks.

The cold evening breeze, of which I have spoken, whistled through every chink of the rude building, and sprinkled the floor with a continual rain of fine sand. There was sand in our eyes, sand in our teeth, sand in our suppers, sand dancing in the spring at the bottom of the kettle, for all the world like porridge beginning to boil. Our chimney was a square hole in the roof: it was but a little part of the smoke that found its way out, and the rest eddied about the house, and kept us coughing and piping the eye.

Add to this that Gray, the new man, had his face tied up in

a bandage for a cut he had got in breaking away from the mutineers; and that poor old Tom Redruth, still unburied, lay along the wall, stiff and stark, under the Union Jack.

If we had been allowed to sit idle, we should all have fallen in the blues, but Captain Smollett was never the man for that. All hands were called up before him, and he divided us into watches. The doctor, and Gray, and I, for one; the squire, Hunter, and Joyce upon the other. Tired as we all were, two were sent out for firewood; two more were set to dig a grave for Redruth; the doctor was named cook; I was put sentry at the door; and the captain himself went from one to another, keeping up our spirits, and lending a hand wherever it was wanted.

From time to time the doctor came to the door for a little air and to rest his eyes, which were almost smoked out of his head; and whenever he did so, he had a word for me.

"That man Smollett," he said once, "is a better man than I am. And when I say that it means a deal, Jim."

Another time he came and was silent for a while. Then he put his head on one side, and looked at me.

'"Is this Ben Gunn a man?" he asked.

"I do not know, sir," said I. "I am not very sure whether he's sane."

"If there's any doubt about the matter, he is," returned the doctor. "A man who has been three years biting his nails on a desert island, Jim, can't expect to appear as sane as you or me. It doesn't lie in human nature. Was it cheese you said he had a fancy for?"

"Yes, sir, cheese," I answered.

"Well, Jim," says he, "just see the good that comes of being dainty in your food. You've seen my snuff-box, haven't you? And you never saw me take snuff; the reason being that in my snuff-box I carry a piece of Parmesan cheese—a cheese made in Italy, very nutritious. Well, that's for Ben Gunn!"

Before supper was eaten we buried old Tom in the sand, and stood round him for a while bare-headed in the breeze. A good deal of firewood had been got in, but not enough for the captain's fancy; and he shook his head over it, and told us we "must get back to this tomorrow rather livelier". Then, when we had eaten our pork, and each had a good stiff glass of brandy grog, the three chiefs got together in a corner to discuss our prospects.

It appears they were at their wits' end what to do, the stores being so low that we must have been starved into surrender long before help came. But our best hope, it was decided, was to kill off the buccaneers until they either hauled down their flag or ran away with the *Hispaniola*. From nineteen they were already reduced to fifteen, two others were wounded, and one, at least—the man shot beside the gun—severely wounded, if he were not dead. Every time we had a crack at them, we were to take it, saving our own lives, with the extremest care. And, besides that, we had two able allies—rum and the climate.

As for the first, though we were about half a mile away, we could hear them roaring and singing late into the night; and as for the second, the doctor staked his wig that, camped where they were in the marsh and unprovided with remedies, the half of them would be on their backs before a week. "So," he added, "if we are not all shot down first, they'll be glad to be packing in the schooner. It's always a ship, and they can get to buccaneering again, I suppose."

"First ship that ever I lost," said Captain Smollett.

I was dead tired, as you may fancy; and when I got to sleep, which was not till after a great deal of tossing, I slept like a log of firewood.

The rest had long been up, and had already breakfasted and increased the pile of firewood by about half as much again, when I was awakened by a bustle and the sound of voices.

"Flag of truce!" I heard someone say; and then, immediately after, with a cry of surprise, "Silver himself!"

And, at that, up I jumped, and, rubbing my eyes, ran to a loophole in the wall.

20. SILVER'S EMBASSY

Sure enough, there were two men just outside the stockade, one of them waving a white cloth; the other, no less a person than Silver himself, standing placidly by.

It was still quite early, and the coldest morning that I think I ever was abroad in; a chill that pierced into the marrow. The sky was bright and cloudless overhead, and the tops of the trees shone rosily in the sun. But where Silver stood with his lieutenant all was still in shadow, and they waded knee deep in a low, white vapour, that had crawled during the night out of the morass. The chill and the vapour taken together told a poor tale of the island. It was plainly a damp, feverish, unhealthy spot.

"Keep indoors, men," said the captain. "Ten to one this is a trick."

Then he hailed the buccaneer.

"Who goes? Stand, or we fire."

"Flag of truce," cried Silver.

The captain was in the porch, keeping himself carefully out of the way of a treacherous shot should any be intended. He turned and spoke to us:

"Doctor's watch on the look out. Dr. Livesey, take the north side, if you please; Jim, the east; Gray, west. The watch below, all hands to load muskets. Lively, men, and careful."

And then he turned again to the mutineers.

"And what do you want with your flag of truce?" he cried.

This time it was the other man who replied.

"Cap'n Silver, sir, to come on board and make terms," he shouted.

"Cap'n Silver! Don't know him. Who's he?" cried the captain. And we could hear him adding to himself: "Cap'n, is it? My heart, and here's promotion!"

Long John answered for himself.

"Me, sir. These poor lads have chosen me cap'n, after your desertion, sir"—laying a particular emphasis upon the word 'desertion'. "We're willing to submit, if we can come to terms, and no bones about it. All I ask is your word, Cap'n Smollett, to let me safe and sound out of this here stockade, and one minute to get out o' shot before a gun is fired."

"My man," said Captain Smollett, "I have not the slightest desire to talk to you. If you wish to talk to me, you can come, that's all. If there's any treachery, it'll be on your side, and the Lord help you."

"That's enough, cap'n," shouted Long John, cheerily. "A word from you's enough. I know a gentleman, and you may lay to that."

We could see the man who carried the flag of truce attempting to hold Silver back. Nor was that wonderful, seeing how cavalier had been the captain's answer. But Silver laughed at him aloud, and slapped him on the back, as if the idea of alarm had been absurd. Then he advanced to the stockade, threw over his crutch, got a leg up, and with great vigour and skill succeeded in surmounting the fence and dropping safely to the other side. I will confess that I was far too much taken up with what was going on to be of the slightest use as sentry; indeed, I had already deserted my eastern loophole, and crept up behind the captain, who had now seated himself on the threshold, with his elbows on his knees, his head in his hands, and his eyes fixed on the water, as it bubbled out of the old iron kettle in the sand. He was whistling to himself, "Come Lasses and Lads".

Silver had terrible hard work getting up the knoll. What with the steepness of the incline, the thick tree-stumps, and the soft sand, he and his crutch were as helpless as a ship in stays. But he stuck to it like a man in silence, and at last arrived before the captain, whom he saluted in the handsomest style. He was tricked out in his best; an immense blue coat, thick with brass buttons, hung as low as to his knees, and a fine laced hat was set on the back of his head.

"Here you are, my man," said the captain, raising his head. "You had better sit down."

"You ain't a-going to let me inside, cap'n?" complained Long John. "It's a main cold morning, to be sure, sir, to sit outside upon the sand."

"Why, Silver," said the captain, "if you had pleased to be an honest man, you might have been sitting in your galley. It's your own doing. You're either my ship's cook—and then you were treated handsome—or Cap'n Silver, a common mutineer and pirate, and then you can go hang!"

"Well, well, cap'n," returned the sea cook, sitting down as he was bidden on the sand, "you'll have to give me a hand up again, that's all. A sweet pretty place you have of it here. Ah, there's Jim! The top of the morning to you, Jim. Doctor, here's my service. Why, there you all are together like a happy family, in a manner of speaking."

"If you have anything to say, my man, better say it," said the captain.

"Right you were, Cap'n Smollett," replied Silver. "Dooty is dooty, to be sure. Well, now, you look here, that was a good lay of yours last night. I don't deny it was a good lay. Some of you pretty handy with a handspike-end. And I'll not deny neither but what some of my people was shook—maybe all was shook; maybe I was shook myself; maybe that's why I'm here for terms. But you mark me, cap'n, it won't do twice, by thunder! We'll have to do sentry-go, and ease off a point or so on the rum. Maybe you think we were all in a sheet in the wind's eye. But I'll tell you I was sober; I was on'y dog tired; and if I'd awoke a second sooner I'd a' caught you at the act, I would. He wasn't dead when I got round to him, not he."

"Well?" says Captain Smollett, as cool as can be.

All that Silver said was a riddle to him, but you would never have guessed it from his tone. As for me, I began to have an inkling. Ben Gunn's last words came back to my mind. I began to suppose that he had paid the buccaneers a visit while they all lay drunk together round their fire, and I reckoned up with glee that we had only fourteen enemies to deal with.

"Well, here it is," said Silver. "We want that treasure, and we'll have it—that's our point! You would just as soon save your lives, I reckon; and that's yours. You have a chart, haven't you?"

"That's as may be," replied the captain.

"Oh, well, you have, I know that," returned Long John. "You needn't be so husky with a man; there ain't a particle of service in that, and you may lay to it. What I mean is, we want your chart. Now, I never meant you no harm, myself."

"That won't do with me, my man," interrupted the captain. "We know exactly what you mean to do, and we don't care; for now, you see, you can't do it."

And the captain looked at him calmly, and proceeded to fill a pipe.

"If Abe Gray— " Silver broke out.

"Avast there!" cried Mr. Smollett. "Gray told me nothing, and I asked him nothing: and what's more I would see you and him and this whole island blown clean out of the water into blazes first. So there's my mind for you, my man, on that."

This little whiff of temper seemed to cool Silver down. He had been growing nettled before, but now he pulled himself together.

"Like enough," said he. "I would set no limits to what gentlemen might consider shipshape, or might not, as the case were. And, seein' as how you are about to take a pipe, cap'n, I'll make so free as do likewise."

And he filled a pipe and lighted it; and the two men sat silently smoking for quite a while, now looking each other in the face, now stopping their tobacco, now leaning forward to spit. It was as good as the play to see them.

"Now," resumed Silver, "here it is. You give us the chart to get the treasure by, and drop shooting poor seamen, and stoving of their heads in while asleep. You do that, and we'll offer you a choice. Either you come aboard along of us, once the treasure's shipped, and then I'll give you my affydavy, upon my word of honour, to clap you somewhere safe ashore. Or, if that ain't to your fancy, some of my hands being rough, and having old scores, on account of hazing, then you can stay here, you can. We'll divide stores with you, man for man; and I'll give my affy-davy, as before, to speak the first ship I sight, and send 'em here to pick you up."

"Now you'll own that's talking. Handsomer you couldn't look to get, not you. And I hope"—raising his voice—"that all hands in this here block-house will overhaul my words, for what is spoke to one is spoke to all."

Captain Smollett rose from his seat, and knocked out the ashes of his pipe in the palm of his left hand.

"It that all?" he asked.

"Every last word, by thunder!" answered John. "Refuse that, and you've seen the last of me but musket-balls."

"Very good," said the captain. "Now you'll hear me. If you'll come up one by one, unarmed, I'll engage to clap you all in irons, and take you home to a fair trial in England. If you won't, my name is Alexander Smollett, I've flown my sovereign's colours, and I'll see you all to Davy Jones. You can't find the treasure. You can't sail the ship—there's not a man among you fit to sail the ship. You can't fight us—Gray, there, got away from five of you. Your ship's in irons, Master Silver; you're on a lee shore, and so you'll find. I stand here and tell you so; and they're the last good words you'll get from me; for, in the name of heaven, I'll put a bullet in your back when next I meet you. Tramp, my lad. Bundle out of this, please, hand over hand, and double quick."

Silver's face was a picture; his eyes started in his head with wrath. He shook the fire out of his pipe.

"Give me a hand up!" he cried.

"Not I," returned the captain.

"Who'll give me a hand up?" he roared.

Not a man among us moved. Growling the foulest imprecations, he crawled along the sand till he got hold of the porch and could hoist himself again upon his crutch. Then he spat into the ground.

"There," he cried, "that's what I think of ye. Before an hour's out, I'll stove in your old block-house like a rum puncheon. Laugh, by thunder, laugh! Before an hour's out, ye'll laugh upon the other side. Them that die'll be the lucky ones."

And with a dreadful oath he stumbled off, ploughed down the sand, was helped across the stockade, after four or five failures, by the man with the flag of truce, and disappeared in an instant afterwards among the trees.

21. THE ATTACK

As soon as Silver disappeared, the captain, who had been closely watching him, turned towards the interior of the house, and found not a man of us at his post but Gray. It was the first time we had ever seen him angry.

"Quarters!" he roared. And then, as we all slunk back to our places, "Gray," he said, "I'll put your name in the log; you've stood by your duty like a seaman. Mr. Trelawney, I'm surprised at you, sir. Doctor, I thought you had worn the king's coat! If that was how you served at Fontenoy, sir, you'd have been better in your berth."

The doctor's watch were all back at their loopholes, the rest were busy loading the spare muskets, and every one with a red face, you may be certain, and a flea in his ear, as the saying is.

The captain looked on for a while in silence. Then he spoke.

"My lads," said he, "I've given Silver a broadside. I pitched it in red-hot on purpose; and before the hour's out, as he said, we shall be boarded. We're outnumbered, I needn't tell you that, but we fight in shelter; and, a minute ago, I should have said we fought with discipline. I've no manner of doubt that we can drub them, if you choose."

Then he went the rounds, and saw, as he said, that all was clear.

On the two short sides of the house, east and west, there were only two loopholes; on the south side where the porch was, two again; and on the north side, five. There was a round score of muskets for the seven of us; the firewood had been built into four piles—tables, you might say—one about the middle of each side, and on each of these tables some ammunition and four loaded muskets were laid ready to the hand of the defenders. In the middle, the cutlasses lay ranged.

"Toss out the fire," said the captain; "the chill is past, and we mustn't have smoke in our eyes."

The iron fire basket was carried bodily out by Mr. Trelawney, and the embers smothered among sand.

"Hawkins hasn't had his breakfast. Hawkins, help yourself, and back to your post to eat it," continued Captain Smollett. "Lively, now, my lad; you'll want it before you've done. Hunter, serve out a round of brandy to all hands."

And while this was going on, the captain completed, in his own mind, the plan of the defence.

"Doctor, you will take the door," he resumed. "See, and don't expose yourself; keep within, and fire through the porch. Hunter, take the east side, there. Joyce, you stand by the west, my man. Mr. Trelawney, you are the best shot—you and Gray will take this long north side, with the five loopholes; it's there the danger is. If they can get up to it, and fire in upon us through our own ports, things would begin to look dirty. Hawkins, neither you nor I are much account at the shooting; we'll stand by to load and bear a hand."

As the captain had said, the chill was past. As soon as the sun had climbed above our girdle of trees, it fell with all its force upon the clearing, and drank up the vapours at a draught. Soon the sand was baking, and the resin melting in the logs of the block-house. Jackets and coats were flung aside; shirts thrown open at the neck, and rolled up to the shoulders; and we stood there, each to his post, in a fever of heat and anxiety.

An hour passed away.

"Hang them!" said the captain. "This is as dull as the doldrums. Gray, whistle for a wind."

And just at that moment came the first news of the attack.

"If you please, sir," said Joyce, "if I see anyone am I to fire?"

"I told you so!" cried the captain.

"Thank you, sir," returned Joyce, with the same quiet civility.

Nothing followed for a time; but the remark had set us all on the alert, straining ears and eyes—the musketeers with their pieces balanced in their hands, the captain out in the middle of the block-house, with his mouth very tight and a frown on his face.

So some seconds passed, till suddenly Joyce whipped up his musket and fired. The report had scarcely died away ere it was repeated and repeated from without in a scattering volley, shot behind shot, like a string of geese, from every side of the enclosure. Several bullets struck the log-house, but not one entered; and, as the smoke cleared away and vanished, the stockade and the woods around it looked as quiet and empty as before. Not a bough waved, not the gleam of a musket-barrel betrayed the presence of our foes.

"Did you hit your man?" asked the captain.

"No, sir," replied Joyce. "I believe not, sir."

"Next best thing to tell the truth," muttered Captain Smollett. "Load his gun, Hawkins. How many should you say there were on your side, doctor?"

"I know precisely," said Dr. Livesey. "Three shots were fired on this side. I saw the three flashes—two close together—one farther to the west."

"Three!" repeated the captain. "And how many on yours, Mr. Trelawney?"

But this was not so easily answered. There had come many from the north—seven, by the squire's computation; eight or nine, according to Gray. From the east and west only a single shot had been fired. It was plain, therefore, that the attack would be developed from the north, and that on the other three sides we were only to be annoyed by a show of hostilities.

But Captain Smollet made no change in his arrangements. If the mutineers succeeded in crossing the stockade, he argued, they would take possession of any unprotected loop-hole, and shoot us down like rats in our own stronghold.

Nor had we much time left to us for thought. Suddenly, with a loud huzza, a little cloud of pirates leaped from the woods on the north side, and ran straight on the stockade. At the same moment, the fire was once more opened from the woods, and a rifle-ball sang through the doorway, and knocked the doctor's musket into bits.

The boarders swarmed over the fence like monkeys. Squire and Gray fired again and yet again; three men fell, one forwards into the enclosure two back on the outside. But of these, one was evidently more frightened than hurt, for he was on his feet again in a crack, and instantly disappeared among the trees.

Two had bit the dust, one had fled, four had made good their footing inside our defences; while from the shelter of the woods seven or eight men, each evidently supplied with several muskets, kept up a hot though useless fire on the loghouse.

The four who had boarded made straight before them for the building, shouting as they ran, and the men among the trees shouted back to encourage them. Several shots were fired; but, such was the hurry of the marksmen, that not one appeared to have taken effect. In a moment, the four pirates had swarmed up the mound and were upon us.

The head of Job Anderson, the boatswain, appeared at the middle loophole.

"At 'em, all hands—all hands!" he roared, in a voice of thunder.

At the same moment, another pirate grasped Hunter's musket by the muzzle, wrenched it from his hands, plucked it through the loophole, and, with one stunning blow, laid the poor fellow senseless on the floor. Meanwhile a third, running unharmed all round the house, appeared suddenly in the doorway, and fell with his cutlass on the doctor.

Our position was utterly reversed. A moment since we were firing under cover, at an exposed enemy; now it was we who lay uncovered, and could not return a blow.

The log-house was full of smoke, to which we owed our comparative safety. Cries and confusion, the flashes and reports of pistol shots, and one loud groan, rang in my ears.

"Out lads, out, and fight 'em in the open! Cutlasses!" cried the captain. I snatched a cutlass from the pile, and someone, at the same time, snatching another, gave me a cut across the knuckles which I hardly felt. I dashed out of the door into the clear sunlight. Someone was close behind, I knew not who. Right in front, the doctor was pursuing his assailant down the hill, and sent him sprawling on his back, with a great slash across the face.

"Round the house, lads! round the house!" cried the captain; and even in the hurly-burly I perceived a change in his voice.

Mechanically I obeyed, turned eastwards, and with my cutlass raised, ran round the corner of the house. Next moment I was face to face with Anderson. He roared aloud, and his hanger went up above his head, flashing in the sunlight. I had not time to be afraid, but, as the blow still hung impending, leaped in a trice upon one side, and missing my foot in the soft sand, rolled headlong down the slope.

When I had first sallied from the door, the other mutineers

had been already swarming up the palisade to make an end of us. One man, in a red night-cap, with his cutlass in his mouth, had even got upon the top and thrown a leg across. Well, so short had been the interval, that when I found my feet again all was in the same posture, the fellow with the red night-cap still half-way over, another still just showing his head above the top of the stockade. And yet, in this breath of time, the fight was over, and the victory was ours.

Gray, following close behind me, had cut down the big boatswain ere he had time to recover from his lost blow. Another had been shot at a loophole in the very act of firing into the house, and now lay in agony; the pistol still smoking in his hand. A third, as I had seen, the doctor disposed of at a blow. Of the four who had scaled the palisade, one only remained unaccounted for, and he, having left his cutlass on the field, was now clambering out again with the fear of death upon him.

"Fire—fire from the house!" cried the doctor. "And you, lads, back into cover."

But his words were unheeded, no shot was fired, and the last boarder made good his escape, and disappeared with the rest into the wood. In three seconds nothing remained of the attacking party but the five who had fallen, four on the inside, and one on the outside, of the palisade.

The doctor and Gray and I ran full speed for shelter. The survivors would soon be back where they had left their muskets, and at any moment the fire might recommence.

The house was by this time somewhat cleared of smoke, and we saw at a glance the price we had paid for victory. Hunter lay beside his loophole, stunned; Joyce by his, shot through the head, never to move again; while right in the centre, the squire was supporting the captain, one as pale as the other.

"The captain's wounded", said Mr. Trelawney.

"Have they run?" asked Mr. Smollett.

"All that could, you may be bound," returned the doctor; "but there's five of them will never run again."

"Five!" cried the captain. "Come, that's better. Five against three leaves us four to nine. That's better odds than we had at starting. We were seven to nineteen then, or thought we were, and that's as bad to bear."*

PART V

MY SEA ADVENTURE

22. HOW I BEGAN MY SEA ADVENTURE

There was no return of the mutineers—not so much as another shot out of the woods. They had "got their rations for that day", as the captain put it, and we had the place to ourselves and a quiet time to overhaul the wounded and get dinner. Squire and I cooked outside in spite of the danger, and even outside we could hardly tell what we were at, for horror of the loud groans that reached us from the doctor's patients.

Out of the eight men who had fallen in the action, only three still breathed—that one of the pirates who had been shot at the loophole, Hunter, and Captain Smollett; and of these the first two were as good as dead; the mutineer, indeed, died under the doctor's knife, and Hunter, do what we could, never recovered consciousness in this world. He lingered all day, breathing loudly like the old buccaneer at home in his apoplectic fit; but the bones of his chest had been crushed by the blow and his skull fractured in falling, and some time in the following night, without sign or sound, he went to his Maker.

*The mutineers were soon only eight in number, for the man shot by Mr Trelawney on board the schooner died that same evening of his wound. But this was, of course, not known till after by the faithful party.

As for the captain, his wounds were grievous indeed, but not dangerous. No organ was fatally injured. Anderson's ball—for it was Job that shot him first—had broken his shoulderblade and touched the lung, not badly; the second had only torn and displaced some muscles in the calf. He was sure to recover, the doctor said, but, in the meantime and for weeks to come, he must not walk nor move his arm, nor so much as speak when he could help it.

My own accidental cut across the knuckles was a flea-bite. Dr. Livesey patched it up with plaster, and pulled my ears for me into the bargain.

After dinner the squire and the doctor sat by the captain's side a while in consultation; and when they had talked to their heart's content, it being then a little past noon, the doctor took up his hat and pistols, girt on a cutlass, put the chart in his pocket, and with a musket over his shoulder, crossed the palisade on the north side, and set off briskly through the trees.

Gray and I were sitting together at the far end of the blockhouse, to be out of earshot of our officers consulting; and Gray took his pipe out of his mouth and fairly forgot to put it back again, so thunderstruck he was at this occurrence.

"Why, in the name of Davy Jones," said he, "is Dr. Livesey mad?"

"Why, no," says I. "He's about the last of his crew for that, I take it!"

"Well, shipmate," said Gray, "mad he may not be; but if *he's* not, you mark my words, *I* am."

"I take it," replied I, "the doctor has his idea; and if I am right, he's going now to see Ben Gunn."

I was right, as appeared later; but, in the meantime, the house being stifling hot, and the little patch of sand inside the palisade ablaze with midday sun, I began to get another thought into my head, which was not by any means so right. What I began to do was to envy the doctor, walking in the cool shadow of the woods, with the birds about him, and the pleasant smell of the pines, while I sat grilling, with my clothes stuck to the hot resin, and so much blood about me, and so many poor dead bodies lying all around, that I took a disgust of the place that was almost as strong as fear.

All the time I was washing out the block-house, and then washing up the things from dinner, this disgust and envy kept growing stronger and stronger, till at last, being near a bread-bag, and no one then observing me, I took the first step towards my escapade, and filled both pockets of my coat with biscuit.

I was a fool, if you like, and certainly I was going to do a foolish, over-bold act; but I was determined to do it with all the precautions in my power. These biscuits, should any thing befall me, would keep me, at least, from starving till far on in the next day.

The next thing I laid hold of was a brace of pistols, and as I already had a powder-horn and bullets, I felt myself well supplied with arms.

As for the scheme I had in my head, it was not a bad one in itself. I was to go down the sandy spit that divides the anchorage on the east from the open sea, find the white rock I had observed last evening, and ascertain whether it was there or not that Ben Gunn had hidden his boat; a thing quite worth doing, as I still believe. But as I was certain I should not be allowed to leave the enclosure, my only plan was to take French leave, and slip out when nobody was watching; and that was so bad a way of doing it as made the thing itself wrong. But I was only a boy, and I had made my mind up.

Well, as things at last fell out, I found an admirable opportunity. The squire and Gray were busy helping the captain with his bandages; the coast was clear; I made a bolt for it over the stockade and into the thickest of the trees, and before my absence was observed I was out of cry of my companions.

This was my second folly, far worse than my first, as I left but two sound men to guard the house; but like the first, it was a help towards saving all of us.

I took my way straight for the east coast of the island, for I was determined to go down the sea side of the spit to avoid all chance of observation from the anchorage. It was already late in the afternoon, although still warm and sunny. As I continued to thread the tall woods I could hear from far before me not only the continuous thunder of the surf, but a certain tossing of foliage and grinding of boughs which showed me the sea breeze had set in higher than usual. Soon cool draughts of air began to reach me; and a few steps farther I came forth into the open borders of the grove, and saw the sea lying blue and sunny to the horizon, and the surf tumbling and tossing its foam along the beach.

I have never seen the sea quiet around Treasure Island. The sun might blaze overhead, the air be without a breath, the surface smooth and blue, but still these great rollers would be running along all the external coast, thundering and thundering by day and night; and I scarce believe there is one spot in the island where a man would be out of earshot of their noise.

I walked along beside the surf with great enjoyment till, thinking I was now gone far enough to the south, I took the cover of some thick bushes, and crept warily up to the ridge of the spit.

Behind me was the sea, in front the anchorage. The sea breeze, as though it had the sooner blown itself out by its unusual violence, was already at an end; it had been succeeded by light, variable airs from the south and south-east, carrying great banks of fog; and the anchorage, under lee of Skeleton Island, lay still and leaden as when first we entered it. The *Hispaniola,* in that unbroken mirror, was exactly portrayed from the truck to the water-line, the Jolly Roger hanging from her peak.

Alongside lay one of the gigs, Silver in the stern-sheets—him I could always recognize—while a couple of men were leaning over the stern bulwarks, one of them with a red cap—the very rogue that I had seen some hours before stride-legs upon the palisade. Apparently they were talking and laughing, though at that distance—upwards of a mile—I could, of course, hear no word of what was said. All at once, there began the most horrid, unearthly screaming, which at first startled me badly, though I had soon remembered the voice of Captain Flint, and even thought I could make out the bird by her bright plumage as she sat perched upon her master's wrist.

Soon after the jolly-boat shoved off and pulled for shore and the man with the red cap and his comrade went below by the cabin companion.

Just about the same time the sun had gone down behind the Spy-glass, and as the fog was collecting rapidly, it began to grow dark in earnest. I saw I must lose no time if I were to find the boat that evening.

The white rock, visible enough above the brush, was still some eighth of a mile farther down the spit, and it took me a goodish while to get up with it, crawling, often on all fours, among the scrub. Night had almost come when I laid my hands on its rough sides. Right below it there was an exceedingly small hollow of green turf, hidden by banks and a thick underwood about knee-deep, that grew there very plentifully; and in the centre of the dell, sure enough, a little tent of goat-skins, like what the gipsies carry about with them in England.

I dropped into the hollow, lifted the side of the tent, and there was Ben Gunn's boat—home-made if ever anything was home-made; a rude, lop-sided framework of tough wood, and stretched upon that a covering of goat-skin, with the hair inside. The thing was extremely small, even for me, and I can hardly imagine that it could have floated with a full-sized man. There was one thwart set as low as possible, a kind of stretcher in the bows, and a double paddle for propulsion.

I had not then seen a coracle, such as the ancient Britons made, but I have seen one since, and I can give you no fairer idea of Ben Gunn's boat than by saying it was like the first and the worst coracle ever made by man. But the great advantage of the coracle it certainly possessed, for it was exceedingly light and portable.

Well, now that I had found the boat, you would have thought I had had enough of truantry for once; but, in the meantime, I had taken another notion, and become so obstinately fond of it, that I would have carried it out, I believe, in the teeth of Captain Smollett himself. This was to slip out under cover of the night, cut the *Hispaniola* adrift, and let her go ashore where she fancied. I had quite made up my mind that the mutineers, after their repulse of the morning, had nothing nearer their hearts than to up anchor and away to sea; this, I thought, it would be a fine thing to prevent; and now that I had seen how they left their watchmen unprovided with a boat, I thought it might be done with little risk.

Down I sat to wait for darkness, and made a hearty meal of biscuit. It was a night out of ten thousand for my purpose. The fog had now buried all heaven. As the last rays of daylight dwindled and disappeared, absolute blackness settled down on Treasure Island. And when, at last, I shouldered the coracle, and groped my way stumblingly out of the hollow where I had supped, there were but two points visible on the whole anchorage.

One was the great fire on shore, by which the defeated pirates lay carousing in the swamp. The other, a mere blur of light upon the darkness, indicated the position of the anchored ship. She had swung round to the ebb—her bow was now towards me—the only lights on board were in the cabin; and what I saw was merely a reflection on the fog of the strong rays that flowed from the stern window.

The ebb had already run some time, and I had to wade through a long belt of swampy sand, where I sank several times above the ankle, before I came to the edge of the retreating water, and wading a little way in, with some strength and dexterity, set my coracle, keel downwards, on the surface.

23. THE EBB-TIDE RUNS

The coracle—as I had ample reason to know before I was done with her—was a very safe boat for a person of my height and weight, both buoyant and clever in a seaway; but she was the most cross-grained, lop-sided craft to manage. Do as you please, she always made more leeway than anything else, and turning round and round was the manoeuvre she was best at. Even Ben Gunn himself has admitted that she was "queer to handle till you knew her way".

Certainly I did not know her way. She turned in every direction but the one I was bound to go; the most part of the time we were broadside on, and I am very sure I never should have made the ship at all but for the tide. By good fortune, paddle as I pleased, the tide was still sweeping me down; and there lay the *Hispaniola* right in the fairway, hardly to be missed.

First she loomed before me like a blot of something yet blacker than darkness, then her spars and hull began to take shape, and the next moment, as it seemed (for the further I went, the brisker grew the current of the ebb), I was along-side of her hawser, and had laid hold.

The hawser was as taut as a bowstring—so strong she pulled upon her anchor. All round the hull, in the blackness, the rippling current bubbled and chattered like a little mountain stream. One cut with my sea-gully, and the *Hispaniola* would go humming down the tide.

So far so good; but it next occurred to my recollection that a taut hawser, suddenly cut, is a thing as dangerous as a kicking horse. Ten to one, if I were so foolhardy as to cut the *Hispaniola* from her anchor, I and the coracle, would be knocked clean out of the water.

This brought me to a full stop, and if fortune had not again particularly favoured me, I should have had to abandon my design. But the light airs which had begun blowing from the south-east and south had hauled round after nightfall into the south-west. Just while I was meditating, a puff came, caught the *Hispaniola*, and forced her up into the current; and to my great joy, I felt the hawser slacken in my grasp, and the hand by which I held it dip for a second under water.

With that I made my mind up, took out my gully, opened it with my teeth, and cut one strand after another, till the vessel only swung by two. Then I lay quiet, waiting to sever these last when the strain should be even more lightened by a breath of wind.

All this time I had heard the sound of loud voices from the cabin; but, to say truth, my mind had been so entirely taken up with other thoughts that I had scarcely given ear. Now, however, when I had nothing else to do, I began to pay more heed.

One I recognized for the coxswain's, Israel Hands, that had been Flint's gunner in former days. The other was, of course, my friend of the red night-cap. Both men were plainly the worse for drink, and they were still drinking; for, even while I was listening, one of them, with a drunken cry, opened the stern window and threw out something, which I divined to be an empty bottle. But they were not only tipsy; it was plain that they were furiously angry. Oaths flew like hailstones, and every now and then there came forth such an explosion as I thought was sure to end in blows. But each time the quarrel passed off, and the voices grumbled lower for a while, until the next crisis came, and, in its turn, passed away without result.

On shore, I could see the glow of the great camp fire burning warmly through the shore-side trees. Someone was singing, a dull, old, droning sailor's song, with a droop and a quaver at the end of every verse, and seemingly no end to it all but the patience of the singer. I had heard it on the voyage more than once, and remembered these words:

"But one man of her crew alive
What put to sea with seventy-five."

And I thought it was a ditty rather too dolefully appropriate for a company that had met such cruel losses in the morning. But, indeed, from what I saw, all these buccaneers were as callous as the sea they sailed on.

At last the breeze came; the schooner sidled and drew nearer in the dark; I felt the hawser slacken once more, and with a good, tough effort, cut the last fibres through.

The breeze had but little action on the coracle, and I was almost instantly swept against the bows of the *Hispaniola*. At the same time the schooner began to turn upon her heel, spinning-slowly, end for end, across the current.

I wrought like a fiend, for I expected every moment to be swamped; and since I found I could not push the coracle directly off, I now shoved straight astern. At length I was clear of my dangerous neighbour; and just as I gave the last impulsion, my hands came across a light cord that was trailing overboard across the stern bulwarks. Instantly I grasped it.

Why I should have done so I can hardly say. It was at first mere instinct; but once I had it in my hands and found it fast, curiosity began to get the upper hand, and I determined I should have one look through the cabin window.

I pulled in hand over hand on the cord, and, when I judged myself near enough, rose at infinite risk to about half my height, and thus commanded the roof and a slice of the interior of the cabin.

By this time the schooner and her little consort were gliding pretty swiftly through the water; indeed, we had already fetched up level with the camp fire. The ship was talking, as sailors say, loudly, treading the innumerable ripples with an incessant weltering splash; and until I got my eye above the window-sill I could not comprehend why the watchmen had taken no alarm. One glance, however, was sufficient; and it was only one glance that I durst take from that unsteady skiff. It showed me Hands and his companion locked together in deadly wrestle, each with a hand upon the other's throat.

I dropped upon the thwart again, none too soon, for I was near overboard. I could see nothing for the moment but these two furious, encrimsoned faces, swaying together under the smoky lamp; and I shut my eyes to let them grow once more familiar with the darkness.

The endless ballad had come to an end at last, and the whole diminished company about the camp fire had broken into the chorus I had heard so often:

"Fifteen men on the dead man's chest—
  Yo-ho-ho, and a bottle of rum!
Drink and the devil had done for the rest—
  Yo-ho-ho, and a bottle of rum!"

I was just thinking how busy drink and the devil were at that very moment in the cabin of the *Hispaniola,* when I was surprised by a sudden lurch of the coracle. At the same moment she yawed sharply and seemed to change her course. The speed in the meantime had strangely increased.

I opened my eyes at once. All round me were little ripples, coming over with a sharp, bristling sound and slightly phosphorescent. The *Hispaniola* herself, a few yards in whose wake I was still being whirled along, seemed to stagger in her course, and I saw her spars toss a little against the blackness of the night; nay, as I looked longer, I made sure she also was wheeling to the southward.

I glanced over my shoulder, and my heart jumped against my ribs. There, right behind me, was the glow of the camp fire. The current had turned at right angles, sweeping round along with it the tall schooner and the little dancing coracle; ever quickening, ever bubbling higher, ever muttering louder, it went spinning through the narrows for the open sea.

Suddenly the schooner in front of me gave a violent yaw, turning, perhaps, through twenty degrees; and almost at the same moment one shout followed another from on board; I could hear feet pounding on the companion ladder; and I knew that the two drunkards had at last been interrupted in their quarrel and awakened to a sense of their disaster.

I lay down flat in the bottom of that wretched skiff, and devoutly recommended my spirit to its Maker. At the end of the straits, I made sure we must fall into some bar of raging breakers, where all my troubles would be ended speedily, and though I could, perhaps, bear to die, I could not bear to look upon my fate as it approached.

So I must have lain for hours, continually beaten to and fro upon the billows, now and again wetted with flying sprays, and never ceasing to expect death at the next plunge. Gradually weariness grew upon me; a numbness, an occasional stupor, fell upon my mind even in the midst of my terrors; until sleep at last supervened, and in my sea-tossed coracle I lay and dreamed of home and the old "Admiral Benbow".

24. THE CRUISE OF THE CORACLE

It was broad day when I awoke, and found myself tossing at the south-west end of Treasure Island. The sun was up, but was still hid from me behind the great bulk of the Spy-glass, which on this side descended almost to the sea in formidable cliffs.

Haulbowline Head and Mizzen-mast Hill were at my elbow; the hill bare and dark, the head bound with cliffs forty or fifty feet high, and fringed with great masses of fallen rock. I was scarce a quarter of a mile to seaward, and it was my first thought to paddle in and land.

That notion was soon given over. Among the fallen rocks the breakers spouted and bellowed; loud reverberations, heavy sprays flying and falling, succeeded one another from second to second; and I saw myself, if I ventured nearer, dashed to death upon the rough shore, or spending my strength in vain to scale the beetling crags.

Nor was that all; for crawling together on flat tables of rock, or letting themselves drop into the sea with loud reports, I beheld huge slimy monsters—soft snails, as it were, of incredible bigness—two or three score of them together, making the rocks to echo with their barkings.

I have understood since that they were sea-lions, and entirely harmless. But the look of them, added to the difficulty of the shore and the high running of the surf, was more than enough to disgust me with that landing-place. I felt willing rather to starve at sea than to confront such perils.

In the meantime I had a better chance, as I supposed, before me. North of Haulbowline Head, the land runs in a long way, leaving, at low tide, a long stretch of yellow sand. To the north of that, again, there comes another cape—Cape of the Woods, at it was marked upon the chart—buried in tall green pines, which descended to the margin of the sea.

I remembered what Silver had said about the current that sets northward along the whole west coast of Treasure Island; and seeing from my position that I was already under its influence, I preferred to leave Haulbowline Head behind me, and reserve my strength for an attempt to land upon the kindlier-looking Cape of the Woods.

There was a great, smooth swell upon the sea. The wind blowing steady and gentle from the south, there was no contrariety between that and the current, and the billows rose and fell unbroken.

Had it been otherwise, I must long ago have perished; but as it was, it is surprising how easily and securely my little and light boat could ride. Often, as I still lay at the bottom, and kept no more than an eye above the gunwale, I would see a big blue summit heaving close above me; yet the coracle would but bounce a little, dance as if on springs, and subside on the other side into the trough as lightly as a bird.

I began after a little to grow very bold, and sat up to try my skill at paddling. But even a small change in the disposition of the weight will produce violent changes in the behaviour of a coracle. And I had hardly moved before the boat, giving up at once her gentle dancing movement, ran straight down a slope of water so steep that it made me giddy, and struck her nose, with a spout of spray, deep into the side of the next wave.

I was drenched and terrified, and fell instantly back into my old position, whereupon the coracle seemed to find her head again, and led me as softly as before among the billows. It was plain she was not to be interfered with, and at any rate, since I could in no way influence her course, what hope had I left of reaching land?

I began to be horribly frightened, but I kept my head, for all that. First, moving with all care, I gradually baled out the coracle with my sea-cap; then getting my eye once more above the gunwale, I set myself to study how it was she managed to slip so quietly through the rollers.

I found each wave, instead of the big, smooth glossy mountain it looks from shore, or from a vessel's deck, was for all the world like any range of hills on the dry land, full of peaks and smooth places and valleys. The coracle, left to herself, turning from side to side, threaded, so to speak, her way through these lower parts, and avoided the steep slopes and higher, toppling summits of the wave.

"Well, now," thought I to myself, "it is plain I must lie where I am, and not disturb the balance; but it is plain, also, that I can put the paddle over the side, and from time to time, in smooth places, give her a shove or two towards land." No sooner thought upon than done. There I lay on my elbows, in the most trying attitude, and every now and again gave a weak stroke or two to turn her head to shore.

It was very tiring and slow work, yet I did visibly gain ground; and, as we drew near the Cape of the Woods, though

I saw I must infallibly miss that point, I had still made some hundred yards of easting. I was, indeed, close in. I could see the cool green tree-tops swaying together in the breeze, and I felt sure I should make the next promontory without fail.

It was high time, for I now began to be tortured with thirst. The glow of the sun from above, its thousandfold reflection from the waves, the sea-water that fell and dried upon me, caking my very lips with salt, combined to make my throat burn and my brain ache. The sight of the trees so near at hand had almost made me sick with longing; but the current had soon carried me past the point; and, as the next reach of sea opened out, I beheld a sight that changed the nature of my thoughts.

Right in front of me, not half a mile away, I beheld the *Hispaniola* under sail. I made sure, of course, that I should be taken; but I was so distressed for want of water, that I scarce knew whether to be glad or sorry at the thought; and, long before I had come to a conclusion, surprise had taken entire possession of my mind, and I could do nothing but stare and wonder.

The *Hispaniola* was under her main-sail and two jibs, and the beautiful white canvas shone in the sun like snow or silver. When I first sighted her, all her sails were drawing; she was lying a course about north-west; and I presumed the men on board were going round the island on their way back to the anchorage. Presently she began to fetch more and more to the westward, so that I thought they had sighted me and were going about to chase. At last, however, she fell right into the wind's eye, was taken dead aback, and stood there a while helpless, with her sails shivering.

"Clumsy fellows," said I; "they must still be drunk as owls." And I thought how Captain Smollett would have set them skipping.

Meanwhile, the schooner gradually fell off, and filled again upon another tack, sailed swiftly for a minute or so, and brought up once more dead in the wind's eye. Again and again was this repeated. To and fro, up and down, north, south, east, and west, the *Hispaniola* sailed by swoops and dashes, and at each repetition ended as she had begun, with idly-flapping canvas. It became plain to me that nobody was steering. And, if so, where were the men? Either they were dead drunk, or had deserted her, I thought, and perhaps if I could get on board, I might return the vessel to her captain.

The current was bearing coracle and schooner southward at an equal rate. As for the latter's sailing, it was so wild and intermittent, and she hung each time so long in irons, that she certainly gained nothing, if she did not even lose. If only I dared to sit up and paddle, I made sure that I could overhaul her. The scheme had an air of adventure that inspired me, and the thought of the water-breaker beside the fore companion doubled my growing courage.

Up I got, was welcomed almost instantly by another cloud of spray, but this time stuck to my purpose; and set myself, with all my strength and caution, to paddle after the unsteered *Hispaniola*. Once I shipped a sea so heavy that I had to stop and bale, with my heart fluttering like a bird; but gradually I got into the way of the thing, and guided my coracle among the waves, with only now and then a blow upon her bows and a dash of foam in my face.

I was now gaining rapidly on the schooner; I could see the brass glisten on the tiller as it banged about; and still no soul appeared upon her decks. I could not choose but suppose she was deserted. If not, the men were lying drunk below, where I might batten them down, perhaps, and do what I chose with the ship.

For some time she had been doing the worst thing possible for me—standing still. She headed nearly due south, yawing, of course, all the time, Each time she fell off her sails partly filled, and these brought her, in a moment, right to the wind again. I have said this was the worst thing possible for me; for helpless as she looked in this situation, with the canvas cracking like cannon, and the blocks trundling and banging on the deck, she still continued to run away from me, not only with the speed of the current, but by the whole amount of her leeway, which was naturally great.

But now, at last, I had my chance. The breeze fell, for some seconds, very low, and the current gradually turning her, the *Hispaniola* revolved slowly round her centre, and at last presented me her stern, with the cabin window still gaping open, and the lamp over the table still burning on into the day. The main-sail hung drooped like a banner. She was stock-still, but for the current.

For the last little while I had even lost; but now redoubling my efforts, I began once more to overhaul the chase.

I was not a hundred yards from her when the wind came again in a clap; she filled on the port tack, and was off again, stooping and skimming like a swallow.

My first impulse was one of despair, but my second was towards joy. Round she came, till she was broadside on to me—round still till she had covered a half, and then two-thirds, and then three-quarters of the distance that separated us. I could see the waves boiling white under her forefoot. Immensely tall she looked to me from my low station in the coracle.

And then, of a sudden, I began to comprehend. I had scarce time to think—scarce time to act and save myself. I was on the summit of one swell when the schooner came swooping over the next. The bowsprit was over my head. I sprang to my feet, and leaped, stamping the coracle under water. With one hand I caught the jib-boom, while my foot was lodged between the stay and the brace; and as I still clung there panting a dull blow told me that the schooner had charged down upon and struck the coracle, and that I was left without retreat on the *Hispaniola*.

25. I STRIKE THE JOLLY ROGER

I had scarce gained a position on the bowsprit, when the flying jib flapped and filled upon the other tack, with a report like a gun. The schooner trembled to her keel under the reverse; but next moment, the other sails still drawing, the jib flapped back again, and hung idle.

This had nearly tossed me off into the sea; and now I lost

no time, crawled back along the bowsprit, and tumbled head foremost on the deck.

I was on the lee side of the forecastle, and the mainsail, which was still drawing, concealed from me a certain portion of the after-deck. Not a soul was to be seen. The planks, which had not been swabbed since the mutiny, bore the print of many feet; and an empty bottle, broken by the neck, tumbled to and fro like a live thing in the scuppers.

Suddenly the *Hispaniola* came right into the wind. The jibs behind me cracked aloud; the rudder slammed to; the whole ship gave a sickening heave and shudder, and at the same moment the main-boom swung inboard, the sheet groaning in the blocks, and showed me the lee after-deck.

There were the two watchmen, sure enough: red-cap on his back, as stiff as a handspike, with his arms stretched out like those of a crucifix, and his teeth showing through his open lips; Israel Hands propped against the bulwarks, his chin on his chest, his hands lying open before him on the deck, his face as white, under its tan, as a tallow candle.

For a while the ship kept bucking and sidling like a vicious horse, the sails filling, now on one tack, now on another, and the boom swinging to and fro till the mast groaned aloud under the strain. Now and again, too, there would come a cloud of light sprays over the bulwark, and a heavy blow of the ship's bows against the swell; so much heavier weather was made of it by this great rigged ship than by my homemade, lop-sided coracle, now gone to the bottom of the sea.

At every jump of the schooner, red-cap slipped to and fro; but—what was ghastly to behold—neither his attitude nor his fixed teeth-disclosing grin was anyway disturbed by this rough usage. At every jump, too, Hands appeared still more to sink into himself and settle down upon the deck, his feet sliding ever the farther out, and the whole body canting towards the stern, so that his face became, little by little, hid from me; and at last I could see nothing beyond his ear and the frayed ringlet of one whisker.

At the same time, I observed, around both of them, splashes

of dark blood upon the planks, and began to feel sure that they had killed each other in their drunken wrath.

While I was thus looking and wondering, in a calm moment, when the ship was still, Israel Hands turned partly round, and, with a low moan, writhed himself back to the position in which I had seen him first. The moan, which told of pain and deadly weakness, and the way in which his jaw hung open, went right to my heart. But when I remembered the talk I had overheard from the apple barrel, all pity left me.

I walked aft until I reached the main-mast.

"Come aboard, Mr. Hands," I said ironically.

He rolled his eyes round heavily; but he was too far gone to express surprise. All he could do was to utter one word, "Brandy".

It occurred to me there was no time to lose; and, dodging the boom as it once more lurched across the deck, I slipped aft, and down the companion-stairs into the cabin.

It was such a scene of confusion as you can hardly fancy. All the lock-fast places had been broken open in quest of the chart. The floor was thick with mud, where ruffians had sat down to drink or consult after wading in the marshes round their camp. The bulkheads, all painted in clear white, and beaded round with gilt, bore a pattern of dirty hands. Dozens of empty bottles clinked together in corners to the rolling of the ship. One of the doctor's medical books lay open on the table, half of the leaves gutted out, I suppose, for pipelights. In the midst of all this the lamp still cast a smoky glow, obscure and brown as umber.

I went into the cellar; all the barrels were gone, and of the bottles a most surprising number had been drunk out and thrown away. Certainly, since the mutiny began, not a man of them could ever have been sober.

Foraging about, I found a bottle with some brandy left, for Hands; and for myself I routed out some biscuit, some pickled fruits, a great bunch of raisins, and a piece of cheese. With these I came on deck, put down my own stock behind the rudder-head, and well out of the coxswain's reach, went forward to the water-breaker, and had a good, deep drink of water, and then, and not till then, gave Hands the brandy.

He must have drunk a gill before he took the bottle from his mouth.

"Aye," said he, "by thunder, but I wanted some o' that!"

I had sat down already in my own corner and begun to eat.

"Much hurt?" I asked him.

He grunted, or rather I might say, he barked.

"If that doctor was aboard," he said, "I'd be right enough in a couple of turns; but I don't have no manner of luck, you see, and that's what's the matter with me. As for that swab, he's good and dead, he is," he added, indicating the man with the red cap. "He warn't no seaman, anyhow. And where mought you have come from?"

"Well," said I, "I've come aboard to take possession of this ship, Mr. Hands; and you'll please regard me as your captain until further notice."

He looked at me sourly enough, but said nothing. Some of the colour had come back into his cheeks, though he still looked very sick, and still continued to slip out and settle down as the ship banged about.

"By-the-bye," I continued, "I can't have these colours, Mr. Hands; and, by your leave, I'll strike 'em. Better none than these."

And, again dodging the boom, I ran to the colour lines, handed down their cursed black flag, and chucked it overboard.

"God save the King!" said I waving my cap; "and there's an end to Captain Silver!"

He watched me keenly and slyly, his chin all the while on his breast.

"I reckon," he said at last—"I reckon, Cap'n Hawkins, you'll kind of want to get ashore, now. S'pose we talks."

"Why, yes," says I, "with all my heart, Mr. Hands. Say on." And I went back to my meal with a good appetite.

"This man," he began, nodding feebly at the corpse—"O'Brien were his name—a rank Irelander—this man and me got the canvas on her, meaning for to sail her back. Well, *he's* dead now, he is—as dead as bilge; and who's to sail this ship, I don't see. Without I gives you a hint, you ain't that man, as far's I can tell. Now, look here, you gives me food and drink, and a old scarf or ankecher to tie my wound up, you do; and I'll tell you how to sail her; and that's about square all round, I take it."

"I'll tell you one thing," says I: "I'm not going back to Captain Kidd's anchorage. I mean to get into North Inlet, and beach her quietly there."

"To be sure you does," he cried. "Why, I ain't sich an infernal lubber, after all. I can see, can't I? I've tried my fling, I have, and I've lost, and it's you has the wind of me. North Inlet? Why, I haven't no ch'ice, not I! I'd help you sail her up to Execution Dock, by thunder! so I would."

Well, as it seemed to me, there was some sense in this. We struck our bargain on the spot. In three minutes I had the *Hispaniola* sailing easily before the wind along the coast of Treasure Island, with good hopes of turning the northern point ere noon, and beating down again as far as North Inlet before high water, when we might beach her safely, and wait till the subsiding tide permitted us to land.

Then I lashed the tiller and went below to my own chest, where I got a soft silk handkerchief of my mother's. With this, and with my aid, Hands bound up the great bleeding stab he had received in the thigh, and after he had eaten a little and had a swallow or two more of the brandy, he began to pick up visibly, sat straighter up, spoke louder and clearer, and looked in every way another man.

The breeze served us admirably. We skimmed before it like a bird, the coast of the island flashing by, and the view changing every minute. Soon we were past the high lands and bowling beside low, sandy country, sparsely dotted with dwarf pines, and soon we were beyond that again, and had turned the corner of the rocky hill that ends the island on the north.

I was greatly elated with my new command, and pleased with the bright, sunshiny weather and these different prospects of the coast. I had now plenty of water and good things to eat, and my conscience, which had smitten me hard for my desertion, was quieted by the great conquest I had made. I should, I think, have had nothing left me to desire, but for the eyes of the coxswain as they followed me derisively about the deck, and the odd smile that appeared continually on his face. It was a smile that had in it something both of pain and weakness—a haggard, old man's smile; but there was, besides that, a grain of derision, a shadow of treachery, in his expression as he craftily watched, and watched, and watched me at my work.

26. ISRAEL HANDS

The wind, serving us to a desire, now hauled into the west. We could run so much the easier from the north-east corner of the island to the mouth of the North Inlet. Only, as we had no power to anchor, and dared not beach her till the tide had flowed a good deal farther, time hung on our hands. The coxswain told me how to lay the ship to; after a good many trials I succeeded, and we both sat in silence, over another meal.

"Cap'n," said he, at length, with that same uncomfortable smile, "here's my old shipmate, O'Brien; s'pose you was to heave him overboard. I ain't partic'lar as a rule, and I don't take no blame for settling his hash; but I don't reckon him ornamental, now, do you?"

"I'm not strong enough, and I don't like the job; and there he lies, for me," said I.

"This here's an unlucky ship—this *Hispaniola,* Jim," he went on, blinking. "There's a power of men been killed in this *Hispaniola*—a sight o' poor seamen dead and gone since you and me took ship to Bristol. I never seen sich dirty luck, not I. There was this here O'Brien, now—he's dead, ain't he? Well, now, I'm no scholar, and you're a lad as can read and figure; and to put it straight, do you take it as a dead man is dead for good, or do he come alive again?"

"You can kill the body, Mr. Hands, but not the spirit; you

must know that already," I replied. "O'Brien there is in another world, and maybe watching us."

"Ah!" says he. "Well, that's unfort'nate—appears as if killing parties was a waste of time. Howsomever, sperrits don't reckon for much, by what I've seen. I'll chance it with the sperrits, Jim. And now, you've spoke up free, and I'll take it kind if you'd step down into that there cabin and get me a—well, a—shiver my timbers! I can't hit the name on't; well, you get me a bottle of wine, Jim—this here brandy's too strong for my head."

Now, the coxswain's hesitation seemed to be unnatural; and as for the notion of his preferring wine to brandy, I entirely disbelieved it. The whole story was a pretext. He wanted me to leave the deck—so much was plain; but with what purpose I could in no way imagine. His eyes never met mine; they kept wandering to and fro, up and down, now with a look to the sky, now with a flitting glance upon the dead O'Brien. All the time he kept smiling, and putting his tongue out in the most guilty, embarrassed manner, so that a child could have told that he was bent on some deception. I was prompt with my answer, however, for I saw where my advantage lay; and that with a fellow so densely stupid I could easily conceal my suspicions to the end.

"Some wine?" I said. "Far better. Will you have white or red?"

"Well, I reckon it's about the blessed same to me, shipmate," he replied; "so it's strong, and plenty of it, what's the odds?"

"All right," I answered. "I'll bring you port, Mr. Hands. But I'll have to dig for it."

With that I scuttled down the companion with all the noise I could, slipped off my shoes, ran quietly along the sparred gallery, mounted the forecastle ladder, and popped my head out of the fore companion. I knew he would not expect to see me there; yet I took every precaution possible; and certainly the worst of my suspicions proved too true.

He had risen from his position to his hands and knees; and, though his leg obviously hurt him pretty sharply when he moved—for I could hear him stifle a groan—yet it was at a good, rattling rate that he trailed himself across the deck. In half a minute he had reached the port scuppers, and picked, out of a coil of rope, a long knife, or rather a short dirk, discoloured to the hilt with blood. He looked upon it for a moment, thrusting forth his under jaw, tried the point upon his hand, and then, hastily concealing it in the bosom of his jacket, trundled back again into his old place against the bulwark.

This was all that I required to know. Israel could move about; he was now armed; and if he had been at so much trouble to get rid of me, it was plain that I was meant to be the victim. What he would do afterwards—whether he would try to crawl right across the island from North Inlet to the camp among the swamps, or whether he would fire Long Tom, trusting that his own comrades might come first to help him, was, of course, more than I could say.

Yet I felt sure that I could trust him in one point, since in that our interests jumped together, and that was in the disposition of the schooner.

We both desired to have her stranded safe enough, in a sheltered place, and so that, when the time came, she could be got out again with as little labour and danger as might be; and until that was done I considered that my life would certainly be spared.

While I was thus turning the business over in my mind, I had not been idle with my body. I had stolen back to the cabin, slipped once more into my shoes, and laid my hand at random on a bottle of wine, and now, with this for an excuse, I made my reappearance on the deck.

Hands lay as I had left him, all fallen together in a bundle, and with his eyelids lowered, as though he were too weak to bear the light. He looked up, however, at my coming, knocked the neck off the bottle, like a man who had done the same thing often, and took a good swig, with his favourite toast of "Here's luck!" Then he lay quiet for a little, and then, pulling out a stick of tobacco, begged me to cut him a quid.

"Cut me a junk o' that," says he, "for I haven't no knife, and hardly strength enough, so be as I had. Ah, Jim, Jim, I reckon I've missed stays! Cut me a quid, as'll likely be the last, lad; for I'm for my long home, and no mistake."

"Well," said I, "I'll cut you some tobacco; but if I was you and thought myself so badly, I would go to my prayers, like a Christian man."

"Why?" said he. "Now, you tell me why."

"Why?" I cried. "You were asking me just now about the dead. You've broken your trust; you've lived in sin and lies and blood; there's a man you killed lying at your feet this moment; and you ask me why! For God's mercy, Mr. Hands, that's why." I spoke with a little heat, thinking of the bloody dirk he had hidden in his pocket, and designed, in his ill thoughts, to end me with. He, for his part, took a great draught of the wine, and spoke with the most unusual solemnity.

"For thirty years," he said, "I've sailed the seas, and seen good and bad, better and worse, fair weather and foul, provisions running out, knives going, and what not. Well, now I tell you, I never seen good come o' goodness yet. Him as strikes first is my fancy; dead men don't bite; them's my views—amen, so be it. And now, you look here," he added, suddenly changing his tone, "we've had about enough of this foolery. The tide's made good enough by now. You just take my orders, Cap'n Hawkins, and we'll sail slap in and be done with it."

All told, we had scarce two miles to run; but the navigation was delicate, the entrance to this northern anchorage was not only narrow and shoal, but lay east and west, so that the schooner must be nicely handled to be got in. I think I was a good, prompt subaltern, and I am very sure that Hands was an excellent pilot; for we went about and about, and dodged in, shaving the banks, with a certainty and a neatness that were a pleasure to behold.

Scarcely had we passed the heads before the land closed around us. The shores of North Inlet were as thickly wooded as those of the southern anchorage; but the space was longer and narrower, and more like, what in truth it was, the estuary of a river. Right before us, at the southern end, we saw the wreck of a ship in the last stages of dilapidation. It had been a great vessel of three masts, but had lain so long exposed to the injuries of the weather, that it was hung about with great webs of dripping seaweed, and on the deck of it shore bushes had taken root, and now flourished thick with flowers. It was a sad sight, but it showed us that the anchorage was calm.

"Now," said Hands, "look there; there's a pet bit to beach a ship in. Fine flat sand, never a catspaw, trees all around of it, and flowers a-blowing like a garding on that old ship."

"And once beached," I inquired, "how shall we get her off again?"

"Why, so," he replied; "you take a line ashore there on the other side at low water: take a turn about one o' them big pines; bring it back, take a turn round the capstan, and lie to for the tide. Come high water, all hands take a pull upon the line, and off she comes as sweet as natur'. And now, boy, you stand by. We're near the bit now, and she's too much way on her. Starboard a little—so—steady—starboard—larboard a little—steady—steady!"

So he issued his commands, while I breathlessly obeyed; till, all of a sudden, he cried, "Now, my hearty, luff!" And I put the helm hard up, and the *Hispaniola* swung round rapidly, and ran stem on for the low wooded shore.

The excitement of these last manoeuvres had somewhat interfered with the watch I had kept hitherto, sharply enough, upon the coxswain. Even then I was still so much interested, waiting for the ship to touch, that I had quite forgot the peril that hung over my head, and stood craning over the starboard bulwarks and watching the ripples spreading wide before the bows. I might have fallen without a struggle for my life, had not a sudden disquietude seized upon me, and made me turn my head. Perhaps I had heard a creak, or seen his shadow moving with the tail of my eye; perhaps it was an instinct like a cat's; but, sure enough, when I looked around, there was Hands, already half-way towards me, with the dirk in his right hand.

We must both have cried out aloud when our eyes met; but while mine was the shrill cry of terror, his was a roar of fury like a charging bull's. At the same instant he threw himself forward, and I leapt sideways towards the bows. As I did so, I left hold of the tiller, which sprang sharp to leeward; and I think this saved my life, for it struck Hands across the chest, and stopped him, for the moment, dead.

Before he could recover, I was safe out of the corner where he had me trapped, with all the deck to dodge about. Just forward of the mainmast I stopped, drew a pistol from my pocket, took a cool aim, though he had already turned and was once more coming directly after me, and drew the trigger. The hammer fell, but there followed neither flash nor sound; the priming was useless with sea water. I cursed myself for my neglect. Why had not I, long before, reprimed and reloaded my only weapons? Then I should not have been, as now, a mere fleeing sheep before this butcher.

Wounded as he was, it was wonderful how fast he could move, his grizzled hair tumbling over his face, and his face itself as red as a red ensign with his haste and fury. I had no time to try my other pistol, nor, indeed, much inclination, for I was sure it would be useless. One thing I saw plainly: I must not simply retreat before him, or he would speedily hold me boxed into the bows, as a moment since he had so nearly boxed me in the stern. Once so caught, and nine or ten inches of the blood-stained dirk would be my last experience on this side of eternity. I placed my palms against the mainmast, which was of a goodish bigness, and waited, every nerve upon the stretch.

Seeing that I meant to dodge, he also paused; and a moment or two passed in feints on his part, and corresponding movements upon mine. It was such a game as I had often played at home about the rocks of Black Hill Cove; but never before, you may be sure, with such a wildly beating heart as now. Still, as I say, it was a boy's game, and I thought I could hold my own at it, against an elderly seaman with a wounded thigh. Indeed, my courage had begun to rise so high, that I allowed myself a few darting thoughts on what would be the end of the affair; and while I saw certainly that I could spin it out for long, I saw no hope of any ultimate escape.

Well, while things stood thus, suddenly the *Hispaniola* struck, staggered, ground for an instant in the sand, and then, swift as a blow, canted over to the port side, till the deck stood at an angle of forty-five degrees, and about a puncheon of water splashed into the scupper-holes, and lay, in a pool, between the deck and bulwark.

We were both of us capsized in a second, and both of us rolled, almost together, into the scuppers; the dead red-cap, with his arms still spread out, tumbling stiffly after us.

So near were we, indeed, that my head came against the coxswain's foot with a crack that made my teeth rattle. Blow and all, I was the first afoot again; for Hands had got involved with the dead body. The sudden canting of the ship had made the deck no place for running on; I had to find some new way of escape, and that upon the instant, for my foe was almost touching me. Quick as thought I sprang into the mizzen shrouds, rattled up hand over hand, and did not draw a breath till I was seated on the cross-trees.

I had been saved by being prompt; the dirk had struck not half a foot below me, as I pursued my upward flight; and there stood Israel Hands with his mouth open and his face upturned to mine, a perfect statue of surprise and disappointment.

Now that I had a moment to myself I lost no time in changing the priming of my pistol, and then, having one ready for service, and to make assurance doubly sure, I proceeded to draw the load of the other, and recharge it afresh from the beginning.

My new employment struck Hands all of a heap; he began to see the dice going against him; and after an obvious hesitation, he also hauled himself heavily into the shrouds, and, with the dirk in his teeth, began slowly and painfully to mount. It cost him no end of time and groans to haul his wounded leg behind him; and I had quietly finished my arrangements before he was much more than a third of the way up. Then, with a pistol in either hand, I addressed him.

"One more step, Mr. Hands," said I, "and I'll blow your brains out! Dead men don't bite, you know," I added, with a chuckle. He stopped instantly. I could see by the working of his face that he was trying to think, and the process was so slow and laborious that, in my new-found security, I laughed aloud. At last, with a swallow or two, he spoke, his face still wearing the same expression of extreme perplexity. In order to speak he had to take the dagger from his mouth, but, in all else, he remained unmoved.

"Jim," says he, "I reckon we're fouled, you and me, and we'll have to sign articles. I'd have had you but for that there lurch; but I don't have no luck, not I; and I reckon I'll have to strike, which comes hard, you see, for a master mariner to a ship's younker like you, Jim."

I was drinking in his words and smiling away, as conceited as a cock upon a wall, when, all in a breath, back went his right hand over his shoulder. Something sang like an arrow through the air; I felt a blow and then a sharp pang, and there I was pinned by the shoulder to the mast. In the horrid pain and surprise of the moment—I scarce can say it was by my own volition, and I am sure it was without a conscious aim—both my pistols went off, and both escaped out of my hands. They did not fall alone; with a choked cry, the coxswain loosed his grasp upon the shrouds, and plunged head first into the water.

27. "PIECES OF EIGHT"

Owing to the cant of the vessel, the masts hung far out over the water, and from my perch on the cross-trees I had nothing below me but the surface of the bay. Hands, who was not so far up, was, in consequence, nearer to the ship, and fell between me and the bulwarks. He rose once to the surface in a lather of foam and blood, and then sank again for good. As the water settled I could see him lying huddled together on the clean, bright sand in the shadow of the vessel's sides. A fish or two whipped past his body. Sometimes, by the quivering of the water, he appeared to move a little, as if he were trying to rise. But he was dead enough, for all that, being both shot and drowned, and was food for fish in the very place where he had designed my slaughter.

I was no sooner certain of this than I began to feel sick, faint, and terrified. The hot blood was running over my back and chest. The dirk, where it had pinned my shoulder to the mast, seemed to burn like a hot iron; yet it was not so much these real sufferings that distressed me, for these, it seemed to me, I could bear without a murmur; it was the horror I had upon my mind of falling from the cross-trees into that still green water, beside the body of the coxswain.

I clung with both hands till my nails ached, and I shut my eyes as if to cover up the peril. Gradually my mind came back again, my pulses quieted down to a more natural time, and I was once more in possession of myself.

It was my first thought to pluck forth the dirk; but either it stuck too hard or my nerve failed me; and I desisted with a violent shudder. Oddly enough, that very shudder did the business. The knife, in fact, had come the nearest in the world to missing me altogether; it held me by a mere pinch of skin, and this the shudder tore away. The blood ran down the faster, to be sure; but I was my own master again, and only tacked to the mast by my coat and shirt.

These last I broke through with a sudden jerk, and then regained the deck by the starboard shrouds. For nothing in the world would I have again ventured, shaken as I was, upon the overhanging port shrouds, from which Israel had so lately fallen.

I went below, and did what I could for my wound; it pained me a good deal, and still bled freely; but it was neither deep nor dangerous, nor did it greatly gall me when I used my arm. Then I looked around me, and as the ship was now, in a sense, my own, I began to think of clearing it from its last passenger—the dead man, O'Brien.

He had pitched, as I have said, against the bulwarks, where he lay like some horrible, ungainly sort of puppet; life-sized, indeed, but how different from life's colour or life's comeliness! In that position, I could easily have my way with him; and as the habit of tragical adventures had worn off almost all my terror for the dead, I took him by the waist as if he had been a sack of bran, and, with one good heave, tumbled him overboard. He went in with a sounding plunge; the red cap came off, and remained floating on the surface; and as soon as the splash subsided, I could see him and Israel lying side by side, both wavering with the tremulous movement of the water. O'Brien, though still quite a young man, was very bald. There he lay, with that bald head across the knees of the man who had killed him, and the quick fishes steering to and fro over both.

I was now alone upon the ship; the tide had just turned. The sun was within so few degrees of setting that already the shadow of the pines upon the western shore began to reach right across the anchorage, and fall in patterns on the deck. The evening breeze had sprung up, and though it was well-warded off by the hill with the two peaks upon the east, the cordage had begun to sing a little softly to itself and the idle sails to rattle to and fro.

I began to see a danger to the ship. The jibs I speedily doused and brought tumbling to the deck; but the main-sail was a harder matter. Of course, when the schooner canted over, the boom had swung out-board, and the cap of it and a foot or two of sail hung even under water. I thought this made it still more dangerous; yet the strain was so heavy that I half feared to meddle. At last, I got my knife and cut the halyards. The peak dropped instantly, a great belly of loose canvas floated broad upon the water; and since, pull as I liked, I could not budge the down-haul, that was the extent of what I could accomplish. For the rest, the *Hispaniola* must trust to luck, like myself.

By this time the whole anchorage had fallen into shadow — the last rays, I remember, falling through a glade of the wood, and shining bright as jewels, on the flowery mantle of the wreck. It began to be chill; the tide was rapidly fleeting seaward, the schooner settling more and more on her beam-ends.

I scrambled forward and looked over. It seemed shallow enough, and holding the cut hawser in both hands for a last security, I let myself drop softly overboard. The water scarcely reached my waist; the sand was firm and covered with ripple marks, and I waded ashore in great spirits, leaving the *Hispaniola* on her side, with her main-sail trailing wide upon the surface of the bay. About the same time the sun went fairly down, and the breeze whistled low in the dusk among the tossing pines.

At least, and at last, I was off the sea, nor had I returned thence empty-handed. There lay the schooner, clear at last from buccaneers and ready for our own men to board and get to sea again. I had nothing nearer my fancy than to get home to the stockade and boast of my achievements. Possibly I might be blamed a bit for my truantry, but the recapture of the *Hispaniola* was a clenching answer, and I hoped that even Captain Smollett would confess I had not lost my time.

So thinking, and in famous spirits, I began to set my face homeward for the block-house and my companions. I remembered that the most easterly of the rivers which drain into Captain Kidd's anchorage ran from the two peaked hill upon my left; and I bent my course in that direction that I might pass the stream while it was small. The wood was pretty open, and keeping along the lower spurs, I had soon turned the corner of that hill, and not long after waded to the mid-calf across the watercourse.

This brought me near to where I had encountered Ben Gunn, the maroon; and I walked more circumspectly, keeping an eye on every side. The dusk had come nigh-hand completely, and, as I opened out the cleft between the two peaks, I became aware of a wavering glow against the sky, where, as I judged, the man of the island was cooking his supper before a roaring fire. And yet I wondered, in my heart, that he should show himself so careless. For if I could see his radiance, might it not reach the eyes of Silver himself where he camped upon the shore among the marshes?

Gradually the night fell blacker; it was all I could do to guide myself even roughly towards my destination; the double hill behind me and the Spy-glass on my right hand loomed faint and fainter; the stars were few and pale; and in the low ground where I wandered I kept tripping among bushes and rolling into sandy pits.

Suddenly a kind of brightness fell about me. I looked up; a pale glimmer of moonbeams had alighted on the summit of the Spy-glass, and soon after I saw something broad and silvery moving low down behind the trees, and knew the moon had risen.

With this to help me, I passed rapidly over what remained to me of my journey; and, sometimes walking, sometimes running, impatiently drew near to the stockade. Yet, as I began to thread the grove that lies before it, I was not so thoughtless but that I slacked my pace and went a trifle warily. It would have been a poor end of my adventures to get shot down by my own party in mistake.

The moon was climbing higher and higher; its light began to fall here and there in masses through the more open districts of the wood; and right in front of me a glow of a different colour appeared among the trees. It was red and hot, and now and again it was a little darkened—as it were the embers of a bonfire smouldering.

For the life of me, I could not think what it might be.

At last I came right down upon the borders of the clearing. The western end was already steeped in moonshine; the rest, and the block-house itself, still lay in a black shadow, chequered with long, silvery streaks of light. On the other side of the house an immense fire had burned itself into clear embers and shed a steady, red reverberation, contrasted strongly with the mellow paleness of the moon. There was not a soul stirring, nor a sound beside the noises of the breeze.

I stopped, with much wonder in my heart, and perhaps a little terror also. It had not been our way to build great fires; we were, indeed, by the captain's orders, somewhat niggardly of firewood; and I began to fear that something had gone wrong while I was absent.

I stole round by the eastern end, keeping close in shadow, and at a convenient place, where the darkness was thickest, crossed the palisade.

To make assurance surer, I got upon my hands and knees, and crawled, without a sound, towards the corner of the house. As I drew nearer, my heart was suddenly and greatly lightened. It is not a pleasant noise in itself, and I have often complained of it at other times; but just then it was like music to hear my friends snoring together so loud and peaceful in their sleep. The sea cry of the watch, that beautiful "All's well", never fell more reassuringly on my ear.

In the meantime, there was no doubt of one thing; they kept an infamous bad watch. If it had been Silver and his lads that were now creeping in on them, not a soul would have seen daybreak. That was what it was, thought I, to have the captain wounded; and again I blamed myself sharply for leaving them in that danger with so few to mount guard.

By this time I had got to the door and stood up. All was dark within, so that I could distinguish nothing by the eye. As for sounds, there was the steady drone of the snorers, and a small occasional noise, a lickering or pecking that I could in no way account for.

With my arms before me I walked steadily in. I should lie down in my own place (I thought, with a silent chuckle) and enjoy their faces when they found me in the morning.

My foot struck something yielding—it was a sleeper's leg; and he turned and groaned, but without awaking.

And then, all of a sudden, a shrill voice broke forth out of the darkness:

"Pieces of eight! pieces of eight! pieces of eight! pieces of eight! pieces of eight!" and so forth, without pause or change, like the clacking of a tiny mill.

Silver's green parrot, Captain Flint! It was she whom I had heard pecking at a piece of bark; it was she, keeping better watch than any human being, who thus announced my arrival with her wearisome refrain.

I had no time left me to recover. At the sharp, clipping tone of the parrot, the sleepers awoke and sprang up; and with a mighty oath, the voice of Silver cried:

"Who goes?"

I turned to run, struck violently against one person, recoiled, and ran full into the arms of a second, who, for his part, closed upon and held me tight.

"Bring a torch, Dick," said Silver, when my capture was thus assured.

And one of the men left the log-house and presently returned with a lighted brand.

Part VI

CAPTAIN SILVER

28. IN THE ENEMY'S CAMP

The red glare of the torch, lighting up the interior of the block-house, showed me the worst of my apprehensions realized. The pirates were in possession of the house and stores; there was the cask of cognac, there were the pork and bread, as before; and, what tenfold increased my horror, not a sign of any prisoner. I could only judge that all had perished, and my heart smote me sorely that I had not been there to perish with them.

There were six of the buccaneers, all told; not another man was left alive. Five of them were on their feet, flushed and swollen, suddenly called out of the first sleep of drunkenness. The sixth had only risen upon his elbow: he was deadly pale, and the blood-stained bandage round his head told that he had recently been wounded, and still more recently dressed. I remembered the man who had been shot and had run back among the woods in the great attack, and doubted not that this was he.

The parrot sat, preening her plumage, on Long John's shoulder. He himself, I thought, looked somewhat paler and more stern than I was used to. He still wore the fine broad-cloth suit in which he had fulfilled his mission, but it was bitterly the worse for wear, daubed with clay and torn with the sharp briers of the wood.

"So," said he, "here's Jim Hawkins, shiver my timbers! dropped in, like, eh? Well, come, I take that friendly!"

And thereupon he sat down across the brandy cask, and began to fill a pipe.

"Give me a loan of the link, Dick," said he; and then, when he had a good light, "That'll do, lad," he added, "stick the link in the wood heap; and you, gentlemen, bring yourselves to!—you needn't stand up for Mr. Hawkins; *he'll* excuse you, you may lay to that. And so, Jim"—stopping the tobacco—"here you were, and quite a pleasant surprise for poor old John. I see you were smart when first I set my eyes on you; but this here gets away from me clean, it do."

To all this, as may be well supposed, I made no answer.

They had set me with my back against the wall; and I stood there, looking Silver in the face, pluckily enough, I hope, to all outward appearance, but with black despair in my heart.

Silver took a whiff or two of his pipe with great composure, and then ran on again.

"Now you see, Jim, so be as you *are* here," says he, "I'll give you a piece of my mind. I've always liked you, I have, for a lad of spirit, and the picter of my own self when I was young and handsome. I always wanted you to jine and take your share, and die a gentleman, and now, my cock, you've got to. Cap'n Smollett's a fine seaman, as I'll own up to any day, but stiff on discipline. 'Dooty is dooty,' says he, and right he is. Just you keep clear of the cap'n. The doctor himself is gone dead again you—'ungrateful scamp' was what he said; and the short and the long of the whole story is about here: you can't go back to your own lot, for they won't have you; and without you start a third ship's company all by yourself, which might be lonely, you'll have to jine with Cap'n Silver."

So far so good. My friends, then, were still alive, and though I partly believed the truth of Silver's statement, that the cabin party were incensed at me for my desertion, I was more relieved than distressed by what I heard.

"I don't say nothing as to your being in our hands," continued Silver, "though there you are, and you may lay to it. I'm all for argyment; I never seen good come out o' threatening. If you like the service, well, you'll jine; and if you don't, Jim, why you're free to answer no—free and welcome, shipmate; and if fairer can be said by mortal seaman, shiver my sides!"

"Am I to answer, then?" I asked, with a very tremulous voice. Through all this sneering talk, I was made to feel the threat of death that overhung me, and my cheeks burned and my heart beat painfully in my breast.

"Lad," said Silver, "no one's a-pressing of you. Take your bearings. None of us won't hurry you, mate; time goes so pleasant in your company, you see."

"Well," says I, growing a bit bolder, "if I'm to choose, I declare I have a right to know what's what, and why you're here, and where my friends are."

"Wot's wot?" repeated one of the buccaneers, in a deep growl. "Ah, he'd be a lucky one as knowed that!"

"You'll perhaps batten down your hatches till you're spoke to, my friend," cried Silver truculently to this speaker: And then, in his first gracious tones, he replied to me. "Yesterday morning, Mr. Hawkins," said he, "in the dog-watch, down came Doctor Livesey with a flag of truce. Says he, 'Cap'n Silver, you're sold out. Ship's gone.' Well, maybe we'd been taking a glass, and a song to help it round. I won't say no. Leastways none of us had looked out. We looked out, and, by thunder! the old ship was gone. I never seen a pack o' fools look fishier; and you may lay to that, if I tells you that looked the fishiest. 'Well,' says the doctor, 'let's bargain.' We bargained, him and I, and here we are: stores, brandy, block-house, the firewood you was thoughtful enough to cut, and in a manner of speaking, the whole blessed boat, from cross-trees to kelson. As for them, they've tramped; I don't know where's they are."

He drew again quietly at his pipe.

"And lest you should take it into that head of yours," he went on, "that you was included in the treaty, here's the last word that was said: 'How many are you,' says I, 'to leave?'

'Four,' says he—'four, and one of us wounded. As for that boy, I don't know where he is, confound him,' says he, 'nor I don't much care. We're about sick of him.' These was his words."

"Is that all?" I asked.

"Well, it's all that you're to hear, my son," returned Silver.

"And now I am to choose?"

"And now you are to choose, and you may lay to that," said Silver.

"Well," said I, "I am not such a fool but I know pretty well what I have to look for. Let the worst come to the worst, it's little I care. I've seen too many die since I fell in with you. But there's a thing or two I have to tell you," I said, and by this time I was quite excited; "and the first is this: here you are, in a bad way: ship lost, treasure lost, men lost; your whole business gone to wreck; and if you want to know who did it—it was I! I was in the apple barrel the night we sighted land, and I heard you, John, and you, Dick Johnson, and Hands, who is now at the bottom of the sea, and told every word you said before the hour was out. And as for the schooner, it was I who cut her cable, and it was I that killed the men you had aboard of her, and it was I who brought her where you'll never see her more, not one of you. The laugh's on my side; I've had the top of this business from the first; I no more fear you than I fear a fly. Kill me, if you please, or spare me. But one thing I'll say, and no more; if you spare me, bygones are bygones, and when you fellows are in court for piracy, I'll save you all I can. It is for you to choose. Kill another and do yourselves no good, or spare me and keep a witness to save you from the gallows."

I stopped, for, I tell you, I was out of breath, and, to my wonder, not a man of them moved, but all sat staring at me like as many sheep. And while they were still staring, I broke out again:

"And now, Mr. Silver," I said, "I believe you're the best man here, and if things go the worst, I'll take it kind of you to let the doctor know the way I took it."

"I'll bear it in mind," said Silver, with an accent so curious that I could not, for the life of me, decide whether he were laughing at my request, or had been favourably affected by my courage.

"I'll put one to that," cried the old mahogany-faced seaman—Morgan by name—whom I had seen in Long John's public-house upon the quays of Bristol. "It was him that knowed Black Dog."

"Well, and see here," added the sea cook. "I'll put another again to that, by thunder! for it was this same boy that faked the chart from Billy Bones. First and last, we've split upon Jim Hawkins!"

"Then here goes!" said Morgan, with an oath.

And he sprang up, drawing his knife as if he had been twenty.

"Avast there!" cried Silver. "Who are you, Tom Morgan? Maybe you thought you was cap'n here, perhaps. By the powers, but I'll teach you better! Cross me, and you'll go where many a good man's gone before you, first and last, these thirty years back—some to the yard-arm, shiver my sides! and some by the board, and all to feed the fishes. There's never a man looked me between the eyes and seen a good day a'terwards, Tom Morgan, you may lay to that."

Morgan paused; but a hoarse murmur rose from the others.

"Tom's right," said one.

"I stood hazing long enough from one," added another. "I'll be hanged if I'll be hazed by you, John Silver."

"Did any of you gentlemen want to have it out with *me*?" roared Silver, bending far forward from his position on the keg, with his pipe still glowing in his right hand. "Put a name on what you're at; you ain't dumb, I reckon. Him that wants shall get it. Have I lived this many years, and a son of a rum puncheon cock his hat athwart my hawse at the latter end of it? You know the way; you're all gentlemen o' fortune, by your account. Well, I'm ready. Take a cutlass, him that dares, and I'll see the colour of his inside, crutch and all, before that pipe's empty."

Not a man stirred; not a man answered.

"That's your sort, is it?" he added, returning his pipe to his mouth. "Well, you're a gay lot to look at, anyway. Not much worth to fight, you ain't. P'r'aps you can understand King George's English. I'm cap'n here by 'lection. I'm cap'n here because I'm the best man by a long sea-mile. You won't fight as gentlemen o' fortune should; then, by thunder, you'll obey, and you may lay to it! I like that boy, now; I never seen a better boy than that. He's more a man than any pair of rats of you in this here house, and what I say is this: let me see him that'll lay a hand on him—that's what I say, and you may lay to it."

There was a long pause after this. I stood straight up against the wall, my heart still going like a sledge-hammer, but with a ray of hope now shining in my bosom. Silver leant back against the wall, his arms crossed, his pipe in the corner of his mouth, as calm as though he had been in church; yet his eye kept wandering furtively, and he kept the tail of it on his unruly followers. They, on their part, drew gradually together towards the far end of the block-house, and the low hiss of their whispering sounded in my ear continuously like a stream. One after another they would look up, and the red light of the torch would fall for a second on their nervous faces; but it was not towards me, it was towards Silver that they turned their eyes.

"You seem to have a lot to say," remarked Silver, spitting far into the air. "Pipe up and let me hear it, or lay to."

"Ax your pardon, sir," returned one of the men; "you're pretty free with some of the rules; maybe you'll kindly keep an eye upon the rest. This crew's dissatisfied; this crew don't vally bullying a marlin-spike; this crew has its rights like other crews, I'll make so free as that; and by your own rules, I take it we can talk together. I ax your pardon, sir, acknowledging you for to be capting at this present; but I claim my right, and steps outside for a council."

And with an elaborate sea-salute, this fellow, a long ill-looking, yellow-eyed man of five-and-thirty, stepped coolly towards the door and disappeared out of the house. One after another, the rest followed his example; each making a salute as he passed; each adding some apology. "According to rules," said one. "Fo'c's'le council," said Morgan. And so with one remark or another, all marched out, and left Silver and me alone with the torch.

The sea cook instantly removed his pipe.

"Now, look you here, Jim Hawkins," he said, in a steady whisper, that was no more than audible, "you're within half a plank of death, and, what's a long sight worse, of torture. They're going to throw me off. But, you mark, I stand by you through thick and thin. I didn't mean to; no, not till you spoke up. I was about desperate to lose that much blunt, and be hanged into the bargain. But I see you was right sort. I says to myself: You stand by Hawkins, John, and Hawkins'll stand by you. You're his last card, and, by the living thunder, John, he's yours! Back to back, says I. You save your witness, and he'll save your neck!"

I began dimly to understand.

"You mean all's lost?" I asked.

"Ay, by gum, I do!" he answered. "Ship gone, neck gone — that's the size of it. Once I looked into that bay, Jim Hawkins, and seen no schooner—well, I'm tough, but I gave out. As for that lot and their council, mark me, they're outright fools and cowards. I'll save your life—if so be as I can—from them. But, see here, Jim—tit for tat—you save Long John from swinging."

I was bewildered; it seemed a thing so hopeless he was asking—he, the old buccaneer, the ringleader throughout.

"What I can do, that I'll do," I said.

"It's a bargain!" cried Long John. "You speak up plucky, and, by thunder! I've a chance."

He hobbled to the torch, where it stood propped among the firewood, and took a fresh light to his pipe.

"Understand me, Jim," he said, returning. "I've a head on my shoulders, I have. I'm on squire's side now. I know you've got that ship safe somewheres. How you done it, I don't know, but safe it is. I guess Hands and O'Brien turned soft. I never much believed in neither of *them*. Now you mark me. I ask no questions, nor I won't let others. I know when a game's up, I do; and I know a lad that's staunch. Ah, you that's young—you and me might have done a power of good together!"

He drew some cognac from the cask into a tin cannikin.

"Will you taste, messmate?" he asked; and when I had refused: "Well, I'll take a drain myself, Jim," said he. "I need a caulker, for there's trouble on hand. And, talking o' trouble, why did that doctor give me the chart, Jim?"

My face expressed a wonder so unaffected that he saw the needlesness of further questions.

"Ah, well, he did, though," said he. "And there's something under that, no doubt—something, surely, under that, Jim—bad or good."

And he took another swallow of the brandy, shaking his great fair head like a man who looks forward to the worst.

29. THE BLACK SPOT AGAIN

The council of the buccaneers had lasted some time when one of them re-entered the house, and with a repetition of the same salute, which had in my eyes an ironical air, begged for a moment's loan of the torch. Silver briefly agreed; and this emissary retired again, leaving us together in the dark.

"There's a breeze coming, Jim," said Silver, who had, by this time, adopted quite a friendly and familiar tone.

I turned to the loophole nearest me and looked out. The embers of the great fire had so far burned themselves out, and now glowed so low and duskily, that I understood why these conspirators desired a torch. About half way down the slope to the stockade, they were collected in a group; one held the light; another was on his knees in their midst, and I saw the blade of an open knife shine in his hand with varying colours, in the moon and torchlight. The rest were all somewhat stooping, as though watching the manoeuvres of this last. I could just make out that he had a book as well as a knife in his hand; and was still wondering how anything so incongruous had come in their possession, when the kneeling figure rose once more to his feet, and the whole party began to move together towards the house.

"Here they come," said I; and I returned to my former position, for it seemed beneath my dignity that they should find me watching them.

"Well, let 'em come, lad—let 'em come," said Silver, cheerily. "I've still a shot in my locker."

The door opened, and the five men, standing huddled together just inside, pushed one of their number forward. In any other circumstances it would have been comical to see his slow advance, hesitating as he set down each foot, but holding his closed right hand in front of him.

"Step up, lad," cried Silver. "I won't eat you. Hand it over, lubber. I know the rules, I do; I won't hurt a depytation."

Thus encouraged, the buccaneer stepped forth more briskly, and having passed something to Silver, from hand to hand, slipped yet more smartly back again to his companions.

The sea cook looked at what had been given him.

"The black spot! I thought so," he observed. "Where might you have got the paper? Why, hillo! look here, now: this ain't lucky! You've gone and cut this out of a Bible. What fool's cut a Bible?"

"Ah, there!" said Morgan—"there! Wot did I say? No good'll come o' that, I said."

"Well, you've about fixed it now, among you," continued Silver. "You'll all swing now, I reckon. What soft-hearted lubber had a Bible?"

"It was Dick," said one.

"Dick, was it? Then Dick can get to prayers," said Silver. "He's seen his slice of luck, has Dick, and you may lay to that."

But here the long man with the yellow eyes struck in.

"Belay that talk, John Silver," he said. "This crew has tipped you the black spot in full council, as in dooty bound; just you turn it over, as in dooty bound, and see what's wrote there. Then you can talk."

"Thanky, George," replied the sea cook. "You always was brisk for business, and has the rules by heart, George, as I'm pleased to see. Well, what is it, anyway? Ah! 'Deposed'—that's it, is it? Very pretty wrote, to be sure; like print, I swear. Your hand o' write, George? Why, you was gettin' quite a leadin' man in this here crew. You'll be cap'n next, I shouldn't wonder. Just oblige me with that torch again, will you? this pipe don't draw."

"Come, now," said George, "you don't fool this crew no more. You're a funny man, by your account; but you're over now, and you'll maybe step down off that barrel, and help vote."

"I thought you said you knowed the rules" returned Silver, contemptuously. "Leastways, if you don't, I do; and I wait here—and I'm still your cap'n, mind—till you outs with your grievances, and I reply; in the meantime, your black spot ain't worth a biscuit. After all, we'll see."

"Oh," replied George, "you don't be under no kind of apprehension; *we're* all square, we are. First, you've made a hash of this cruise—you'll be a bold man to say no to that. Second, you let the enemy out o' this here trap for nothing. Why did they want out? I dunno; but it's pretty plain they wanted it. Third, you wouldn't let us go at them upon the march. Oh, we see through you, John Silver; you want to play booty, that's what's wrong with you. And then, fourth, there's this here boy."

"Is that all?" asked Silver quietly.

"Enough, too," retorted George. "We'll all swing and sundry for your bungling."

"Well, now, look here, I'll answer these four p'ints; one after another I'll answer 'em. I made a hash o' this cruise, did I? Well, now, you all know what I wanted: and you all know, if that had been done, that we'd 'a' been aboard the *Hispaniola* this night as ever was, every man of us alive, and fit, and full of good plum-duff, and the treasure in the hold of her, by thunder! Well, who crossed me? Who forced my hand, as was the lawful cap'n? Who tipped me the black spot the day we landed, and began this dance? Ah, it's a fine dance—I'm with you there—and looks mighty like a hornpipe in a rope's end at Execution Dock by London town, it does. But who done it? Why, it was Anderson, and Hands, and you, George Merry! And you're the last above board of that same meddling crew; and you have the Davy Jones's insolence to up and stand for cap'n over me—you, that sank the lot of us! By the powers! but this tops the stiffest yarn to nothing."

Silver paused, and I could see by the faces of George and his late comrades that these words had not been said in vain.

"That's for number one," cried the accused, wiping the sweat from his brow, for he had been talking with a vehemence that shook the house. "Why, I give you my word, I'm sick to speak to you. You've neither sense or memory, and I leave it to fancy where your mothers was that let you come to sea. Sea! Gentlemen o' fortune! I reckon tailors is your trade."

"Go on, John," said Morgan. "Speak up to the others."

"Ah, the others!" returned John. "They're a nice lot, ain't they? You say this cruise is bungled. Ah! by gum, if you could understand how bad it's bungled, you would see! We're that near the gibbet that my neck's stiff with thinking on it. You've seen 'em, maybe, hanged in chains, birds about 'em, seamen p'inting 'em out as they go down with the tide. 'Who's that?' says one. 'That! Why, that's John Silver. I knowed him well,' says another. And you can hear the chains a-jangle as you go about and reach for the other buoy. Now, that's about where we are, every mother's son of us, thanks to him, and Hands, and Anderson, and other ruination fools of you. And if you want to know about number four, and that boy, why, shiver my timbers! isn't he a hostage? Are we a-going to waste a hostage? No, not us; he might be our last chance, and I shouldn't wonder. Kill that boy? not me, mates! And number three? Ah, well, there's a deal to say to number three. Maybe you don't count it nothing to have a real college doctor come to see you every day—you, John, with your head broke—or you, George Merry, that had the ague shakes upon you not six hours agone, and has your eyes the colour of lemon peel to this same moment on the clock? And maybe, perhaps, you didn't know there was a consort coming, either? But there is; and not so long till then; and we'll see who'll be glad to have a hostage when it comes to that. And as for number two, and why I made a bargain—well, you came crawling on your knees to me to make it—on your knees you came, you was that down-hearted—and you'd have starved, too, if I hadn't—but that's a trifle! You look here—that's why!"

And he cast down upon the floor a paper that I instantly recognized—none other than the chart on yellow paper, with the three red crosses, that I had found in the oilcloth at the bottom of the captain's chest. Why the doctor had given it to him was more than I could fancy.

But if it were inexplicable to me, the appearance of the chart was incredible to the surviving mutineers. They leaped upon it like cats upon a mouse. It went from hand to hand, one tearing it from another; and by the oaths and the cries and the childish laughter with which they accompanied their examination, you would have thought, not only they were fingering the very gold, but were at sea with it, besides, in safety.

"Yes," said one, "that's Flint, sure enough. J. F., and a score below, with a clove hitch to it; so he done ever."

"Mighty pretty," said George. "But how are we to get away with it, and us no ship?"

Silver suddenly sprang up, and supporting himself with a hand against the wall: "Now I give you warning, George," he cried. "One more word of your sauce, and I'll call you down and fight you. How? Why, how do I know? You had ought to tell me that—you and the rest, that lost me my schooner, with your interference, burn you! But not you, you can't; you hain't got the invention of a cockroach. But civil you can speak, and shall, George Merry, you may lay to that."

"That's fair enow," said the old man Morgan.

"Fair! I reckon so, said the sea cook. "You lost the ship; I found the treasure. Who's the better man at that? And now I resign, by thunder! Elect whom you please to be your cap'n now; I'm done with it."

"Silver!" they cried. "Barbecue for ever! Barbecue for cap'n!"

"So that's the toon, is it?" cried the cook. "George, I reckon you'll have to wait another turn, friend; and lucky for you as I'm not a revengeful man. But that was never my way. And now, shipmates, this black spot? 'Tain't much good, now is it? Dick's crossed his luck and spoiled his Bible, and that's about all."

"It'll do to kiss the book on still, won't it?" growled Dick, who was evidently uneasy at the curse he had brought upon himself.

"A Bible with a bit cut out!" returned Silver derisively. "Not it. It don't bind no more'n a ballad-book."

"Don't it, though?" cried Dick, with a sort of joy. "Well, I reckon that's worth having, too."

"Here, Jim—here's a cur'osity for you," said Silver; and he tossed me the paper.

It was a round about the size of a crown piece. One side was blank, for it had been the last leaf; the other contained a verse or two of Revelation—these words among the rest, which struck sharply home upon my mind: "Without are dogs and murderers." The printed side had been blackened with wood ash, which already began to come off and soil my fingers; on the blank side had been written with the same material the one word "Depposed". I have that curiosity beside me at this moment; but not a trace of writing now remains beyond a single scratch, such as a man might make with his thumb-nail.

That was the end of the night's business. Soon after, with a drink all round, we lay down to sleep, and the outside of Silver's vengeance was to put George Merry up for sentinel, and threaten him with death if he should prove unfaithful.

It was long ere I could close an eye, and Heaven knows I had matter enough for thought in the man whom I had slain that afternoon, in my own most perilous position, and, above all, in the remarkable game that I saw Silver now engaged upon—keeping the mutineers together with one hand, and grasping, with the other, after every means, possible and impossible, to make his peace and save his miserable life. He himself slept peacefully, and snored aloud; yet my heart was sore for him, wicked as he was, to think on the dark perils that environed, and the shameful gibbet that awaited him.

30. ON PAROLE

I was wakened—indeed, we were all wakened, for I could see even the sentinel shake himself together from where he had fallen against the door-post—by a clear, hearty voice hailing us from the margin of the wood:

"Block-house, ahoy!" it cried. "Here's the doctor."

And the doctor it was. Although I was glad to hear the

sound, yet my gladness was not without admixture. I remembered with confusion my insubordinate and stealthy conduct; and when I saw where it had brought me—among what companions and surrounded by what dangers—I felt ashamed to look him in the face.

He must have risen in the dark, for the day had hardly come; and when I ran to a loophole and looked out, I saw him standing, like Silver once before, up to the midleg in creeping vapour.

"You, doctor! Top o' the morning to you, sir!" cried Silver, broad awake and beaming with good nature in a moment. "Bright and early, to be sure; and it's the early bird, as the saying goes, that gets the rations. George, shake up your timbers, son, and help Dr. Livesey over the ship's side. All a-doin' well, your patients was—all well and merry."

So he pattered on, standing on the hill-top, with his crutch under his elbow, and one hand upon the side of the log-house—quite the old John in voice, manner, and expression.

"We've quite a surprise for you, too, sir," he continued. "We've a little stranger here—he! he! A noo boarder and lodger, sir, and looking fit and taut as a fiddler; slep' like a supercargo, he did, right alongside of John—stem to stem we was, all night."

Dr. Livesey was by this time across the stockade and pretty near the cook; and I could hear the alteration in his voice as he said:

"Not Jim?"

"The very same Jim as ever was," says Silver.

The doctor stopped outright, although he did not speak, and it was some seconds before he seemed able to move on.

"Well, well," he said, at last, "duty first and pleasure afterwards, as you might have said yourself, Silver. Let us overhaul these patients of yours."

A moment afterwards he had entered the block-house, and, with one grim nod to me, proceeded with his work among the sick. He seemed under no apprehension, though he must have known that his life, among these treacherous demons, depended on a hair; and he rattled on to his patients as if he were paying an ordinary professional visit in a quiet English family. His manner, I suppose, reacted on the men; for they behaved to him as if nothing had occurred—as if he were still ship's doctor, and they still faithful hands before the mast.

"You're doing well, my friend," he said to the fellow with the bandaged head; "and if ever any person had a close shave, it was you; your head must be as hard as iron. Well, George, how goes it? You're a pretty colour, certainly; why, your liver, man, is upside down. Did you take that medicine? Did he take that medicine, men?"

"Ay, ay, sir, he took it, sure enough," returned Morgan.

"Because, you see, since I am mutineers' doctor, or prison doctor, as I prefer to call it", says Dr. Livesey, in his pleasantest way, "I make it a point of honour not to lose a man for King George (God bless him!) and the gallows."

The rogues looked at each other, but swallowed the home-thrust in silence.

"Dick don't feel well, sir," said one.

"Don't he?" replied the doctor. "Well, step up here, Dick, and let me see your tongue. No, I should be surprised if he did! the man's tongue is fit to frighten the French. Another fever."

"Ah, there," said Morgan, "that comed of sp'iling Bibles."

"That comed—as you call it—of being arrant asses," retorted the doctor, "and not having sense enough to know honest air from poison, and the dry land from a vile, pestiferous slough. I think it most probable—though, of course, it's only an opinion—that you'll all have the deuce to pay before you get that malaria out of your systems. Camp in a bog, would you? Silver, I'm surprised at you. You're less of a fool than many, take you all round; but you don't appear to me to have the rudiments of a notion of the rules of health."

"Well," he added, after he had dosed them round, and they had taken his prescriptions, with really laughable humility, more like charity school-children than bloodguilty mutineers and pirates—"well, that's done for today. And now I should wish to have a talk with that boy, please."

And he nodded his head in my direction carelessly.

George Merry was at the door, spitting and spluttering over some bad-tasted medicine; but at the first word of the doctor's proposal he swung round with a deep flush, and cried "No!" and swore.

Silver struck the barrel with his open hand.

"Si-lence!" he roared, and looked about him positively like a lion. "Doctor," he went on, in his usual tones, "I was a-thinking of that, knowing as how you had a fancy for the boy. We're all humbly grateful for your kindness, and, as you see, puts faith in you, and takes the drugs down like that much grog. And I take it, I've found a way as'll suit all. Hawkins, will you give me your word of honour as a young gentleman—for a young gentleman you are, although poor born—your word of honour not to slip your cable?"

I readily gave the pledge required.

"Then, doctor," said Silver, "you just step outside o' that stockade, and once you're there, I'll bring the boy down on the inside, and I reckon you can yarn through the spars. Good day to you, sir, and all our dooties to the squire and Cap'n Smollett."

The explosion of disapproval, which nothing but Silver's black looks had restrained, broke out immediately the doctor had left the house. Silver was roundly accused of playing double—of trying to make a separate peace for himself— of sacrificing the interests of his accomplices and victims; and, in one word, of the identical, exact thing that he was doing. It seemed to me so obvious, in this case, that I could not imagine how he was to turn their anger. But he was twice the man the rest were; and his last night's victory had given him a huge preponderance on their minds. He called them all the fools and dolts you can imagine, said it was necessary I should talk to the doctor, fluttered the chart in their faces, asked them if they could afford to break the treaty the very day they were bound a-treasure-hunting.

"No, by thunder!" he cried, "it's us must break the treaty when the time comes; and till then I'll gammon that doctor, if I have to ile his boots with brandy."

And then he bade them get the fire lit, and stalked out upon his crutch, with his hand on my shoulder, leaving them in a disarray, and silenced by his volubility rather than convinced.

"Slow, lad, slow," he said. "They might round upon us in a twinkle of an eye, if we was seen to hurry."

Very deliberately, then, did we advance across the sand to where the doctor awaited us on the other side of the stockade, and as soon as we were within easy speaking distance, Silver stopped.

"You'll make a note of this here also, doctor," says he, "and the boy'll tell you how I saved his life, and were deposed for it, too, and you may lay to that. Doctor. when a man's steering as near the wind as me—playing chuck-farthing with the last breath in his body, like—you wouldn't think it too much, mayhap, to give him one good word? You'll please bear in mind it's not my life only now—it's that boy's into the bargain; and you'll speak me fair, doctor, and give me a bit o' hope to go on, for the sake of mercy."

Silver was a changed man, once he was out there and had his back to his friends and the block-house; his cheeks seemed to have fallen in, his voice trembled; never was a soul more dead in earnest.

"Why, John, you're not afraid?" asked Dr. Livesey.

"Doctor, I'm no coward! no, not I—not *so* much!" and he snapped his fingers. "If I was I wouldn't say it. But I'll own up fairly, I've the shakes upon me for the gallows. You're a good man and a true; I never seen a better man! And you'll not forget what I done good, not any more than you'll forget the bad, I know. And I step aside—see here— and leave you and Jim alone. And you'll put that down for me, too, for it's a long stretch is that!"

So saying, he stepped back a little way, till he was out of earshot, and there sat down upon a tree-stump and began to whistle; spinning round now and again upon his seat so as to command a sight, sometimes of me and the doctor, and sometimes of his unruly ruffians as they went to and fro in the sand, between the fire—which they were busy rekindling — and the house, from which they brought forth pork and bread to make the breakfast.

"So, Jim," said the doctor sadly, "here you are. As you have brewed, so shall you drink, my boy. Heaven knows, I cannot find it in my heart to blame you; but this much I will say, be it kind or unkind: when Captain Smollett was well, you dared not have gone off; and when he was ill, and couldn't help it, by George, it was downright cowardly!"

I will own that I here began to weep. "Doctor," I said, "you might spare me. I have blamed myself enough; my life's forfeit anyway, and I should have been dead by now, if Silver hadn't stood for me; and, doctor, believe this, I can die—and I daresay I deserve it—but what I fear is torture. If they come to torture me—"

"Jim," the doctor interrupted, and his voice was quite changed, "Jim, I can't have this. Whip over, and we'll run for it."

"Doctor," said I, "I passed my word."

"I know. I know," he cried. "We can't help that, Jim, now. I'll take it on my shoulders, holus bolus, blame and shame, my boy; but stay here, I cannot let you. Jump! One jump, and you're out, and we'll run for it like antelopes."

"No," replied, "you know right well you wouldn't do the thing yourself; neither you, nor squire, nor captain; and no more will I. Silver trusted me; I passed my word, and back I go. But, doctor, you did not let me finish. If they come to torture me, I might let slip a word of where the ship is; for I got the ship, part by luck and part by risking, and she lies in North Inlet, on the southern beach, and just below high water. At half-tide she must be high and dry."

"The ship!" exclaimed the doctor.

Rapidly I described to him my adventures, and he heard me out in silence.

"There is a kind of fate in this," he observed, when I had done. "Every step, it's you that saves our lives; and do you suppose by any chance that we are going to let you lose yours? That would be a poor return, my boy. You found out the plot; you found Ben Gunn—the best deed that ever you did, or will do, though you live to ninety. Oh, by Jupiter, and talking of Ben Gunn! why, this is the mischief in person. Silver!" he cried,

"Silver!—I'll give you a piece of advice," he continued as the cook drew near again; "don't you be in any great hurry after that treasure."

"Why, sir, I do my possible, which that ain't," said Silver. "I can only, asking your pardon, save my life and the boy's by seeking for that treasure; and you may lay to that."

"Well, Silver," replied the doctor, "if that is so, I'll go one step further: look out for squalls when you find it."

"Sir," said Silver, "as between man and man, that's too much and too little. What you're after, why you left the block-house, why you given me that there chart, I don't know, now, do I? and yet I done your bidding with my eyes shut and never a word of hope! But, no, this here's too much. If you won't tell me what you mean plain out, just say so, and I'll leave the helm."

"No," said the doctor, musingly, "I've no right to say more; it's not my secret, you see, Silver, or, I give you my word, I'd tell it you. But I'll go as far with you as I dare go, and a step beyond; for I'll have my wig sorted by the captain or I'm mistaken! And, first, I'll give you a bit of hope: Silver, if we both get alive out of this wolf-trap, I'll do my best to save you, short of perjury."

Silver's face was radiant. "You couldn't say more, I'm sure, sir, not if you was my mother," he cried.

"Well, that's my first concession," added the doctor. "My second is a piece of advice: Keep the boy close beside you, and when you need help, halloo. I'm off to seek it for you, and that itself will show you if I speak at random. Goodbye, Jim." And Dr. Livesey shook hands with me through the stockade, nodded to Silver, and set off at a brisk pace into the wood.

31. THE TREASURE HUNT—FLINT'S POINTER

"Jim," said Silver, when we were alone, "if I saved your life, you saved mine; and I'll not forget it. I seen the doctor waving you to run for it—with the tail of my eye, I did; and I seen you say no, as plain as hearing. Jim, that's one to you. This is the first glint of hope I had since the attack failed, and I owe it to you. And now, Jim, we're to go in for this here treasure hunting, with sealed orders, too, and I don't like it; and you and me must stick close, back to back like, and we'll save our necks in spite of fate and fortune."

Just then a man hailed us from the fire that breakfast was ready, and we were soon seated here and there about the sand over biscuit and fried junk. They had lit a fire fit to roast an ox; and it was now grown so hot that they could only approach it from the windward, and even there not without precaution. In the same wasteful spirit, they had cooked, I suppose, three times more than we could eat; and one of them, with an empty laugh, threw what was left into the fire, which blazed and roared again over this unusual fuel. I never in my life saw men so careless of the morrow; hand to mouth is the only word that can describe their way of doing; and what with wasted food and sleeping sentries, though they were bold enough for a brush and be done with it, I could see their entire unfitness for anything like a prolonged campaign.

Even Silver, eating away, with Captain Flint upon his shoulder, had not a word of blame for their recklessness. And this the more surprised me, for I thought he had never shown himself so cunning as he did then.

"Ay, mates," said he, "it's lucky you have Barbecue to think for you with this here head. I got what I wanted, I did. Sure enough, they have the ship. Where they have it, I don't know yet; but once we hit the treasure, we'll have to jump about and find out. And then, mates, us that has the boats, I reckon, has the upper hand."

Thus he kept running on, with his mouth full of the hot bacon: thus he restored their hope and confidence, and, I more than suspect, repaired his own at the same time.

"As for hostage," he continued, "that's his last talk, I guess, with them he loves so dear. I've got my piece o' news, and thanky to him for that; but it's over and done. I'll take him in a line when we go treasure-hunting, for we'll keep him like so much gold, in case of accidents, you mark, and in the meantime. Once we got the ship and treasure both, and off to sea like jolly companions, why, then, we'll talk Mr. Hawkins over, we will, and we'll give him his share, to be sure, for all his kindness."

It was no wonder the men were in a good humour now. For my part, I was horribly cast down. Should the scheme he had now sketched prove feasible, Silver, already doubly a traitor, would not hesitate to adopt it. He had still a foot in either camp, and there was no doubt he would prefer wealth and freedom with the pirates to a bare escape from hanging, which was the best he had to hope on our side.

Nay, and even if things so fell out that he was forced to keep his faith with Dr. Livesey, even then what danger lay before us! What a moment that would be when the suspicions of his followers turned to certainty, and he and I should have to fight for dear life—he, a cripple, and I, a boy—against five strong and active seamen!

Add to this double apprehension, the mystery that still hung over the behaviour of my friends; their unexplained desertion of the stockade; their inexplicable cession of the chart; or, harder still to understand, the doctor's last warning to Silver, "Look out for squalls when you find it"; and you will readily believe how little taste I found in my breakfast, and with how uneasy a heart I set forth behind my captors on the quest for treasure.

We made a curious figure, had anyone been there to see us; all in soiled sailor clothes, and all but me armed to the teeth. Silver had two guns slung about him—one before and one behind—besides the great cutlass at his waist, and a pistol in each pocket of his square-tailed coat. To complete his strange appearance, Captain Flint sat perched upon his shoulder and gabbling odds and ends of purposeless sea-talk. I had a line about my waist, and followed obediently after the sea cook, who held the loose end of the rope, now in his free hand, now between his powerful teeth. For all the world, I was led like a dancing bear.

The other men were variously burthened; some carrying picks and shovels—for that had been the very first necessary they brought ashore from the *Hispaniola*—others laden with pork, bread, and brandy for the midday meal. All the stores, I observed, came from our stock; and I could see the truth of Silver's words the night before. Had he not struck a bargain with the doctor, he and his mutineers, deserted by the ship, must have been driven to subsist on clear water and the proceeds of their hunting. Water would have been little to their taste; a sailor is not usually a good shot; and besides all that, when they were so short of eatables, it was not likely they would be very flush of powder.

Well, thus equipped, we all set out—even the fellow with the broken head, who should certainly have kept in shadow and straggled, one after another, to the beach, where the two gigs awaited us. Even these bore trace of the drunken folly of the pirates, one in a broken thwart, and both in their muddled and unbaled condition. Both were to be carried along with us, for the sake of safety; and so, with our numbers divided between them, we set forth upon the bosom of the anchorage.

As we pulled over, there was some discussion on the chart. The red cross was, of course, far too large to be a guide; and the terms of the note on the back, as you will hear, admitted of some ambiguity. They ran, the reader may remember, thus:

"Tall tree, Spy-glass shoulder, bearing a point to the N. of NNE.
"Skeleton Island ESE. and by E.
"Ten feet."

A tall tree was thus the principal mark. Now, right before us, the anchorage was bounded by a plateau from two to three hundred feet high, adjoining on the north the sloping southern shoulder of the Spy-glass, and rising again towards the south into the rough cliffy eminence called the Mizzen-mast Hill. The top of the plateau was dotted thickly with pine trees of varying height. Every here and there, one of a different species rose forty or fifty feet clear above its neighbours, and which of these was the particular "tall tree" of Captain Flint could only be decided on the spot, and by the readings of the compass.

Yet, although that was the case, every man on board the boats had picked a favourite of his own ere we were half way over, Long John alone shrugging his shoulders and bidding them wait till they were there.

We pulled easily, by Silver's directions, not to weary the hands prematurely; and, after quite a long passage, landed at the mouth of the second river—that which runs down a woody cleft of the Spy-glass. Thence, bending to our left, we began to ascend the slope towards the plateau.

At the first onset, heavy, miry ground and a matted, marish vegetation, greatly delayed our progress; but by little and little the hill began to steepen and become stony under foot, and the wood to change its character and to grow in a more open order. It was, indeed, a most pleasant portion of the island that we were now approaching. A heavy-scented broom and many flowering shrubs had almost taken the place of grass. Thickets of green nutmeg trees were dotted here and there with the red columns and the broad shadow of the pines; and the first mingled their spice with the aroma of the others. The air, besides, was fresh and stirring, and this, under the sheer sunbeams, was a wonderful refreshment to our senses.

The party spread itself abroad, in a fan shape, shouting and leaping to and fro. About the centre, and a good way behind the rest, Silver and I followed—I tethered by my rope, he ploughing, with deep pants, among the sliding gravel. From time to time, indeed, I had to lend him a hand, or he must have missed his footing and fallen backward down the hill.

We had thus proceeded for about half a mile, and were approaching the brow of the plateau, when the man upon the farthest left began to cry aloud, as if in terror. Shout after shout came from him, and the others began to run in his direction.

"He can't 'a' found the treasure," said old Morgan, hurrying past us from the right, "for that's clean a-top."

Indeed, as we found when we also reached the spot, it was something very different. At the foot of a pretty big pine, and involved in a green creeper, which had even partly lifted some of the smaller bones, a human skeleton lay, with a few shreds of clothing, on the ground. I believe a chill struck for a moment to every heart.

"He was a seaman," said George Merry, who, bolder than the rest, had gone up close, and was examining the rags of clothing. "Leastways, this is good sea-cloth."

"Ay, ay," said Silver, "like enough; you wouldn't look to find a bishop here, I reckon. But what sort of a way is that for bones to lie? 'Tain't in natur'."

Indeed, on a second glance, it seemed impossible to fancy that the body was in a natural position. But for some disarray (the work, perhaps, of the birds that had fed upon him, or of the slow-growing creeper that had gradually enveloped his remains) the man lay perfectly straight—his feet pointing in one direction, his hands, raised above his head like a diver's, pointing directly in the opposite.

"I've taken a notion into my old numskull," observed Silver. "Here's the compass; there's the tip-top p'int o' Skeleton Island, stickin' out like a tooth. Just take a bearing, will you, along the line of them bones."

It was done. The body pointed straight in the direction of the island, and the compass read duly ESE. and by E.

"I thought so," cried the cook; "this here is a p'inter. Right up there is our line for the Pole Star and the jolly dollars. But, by thunder! if it don't make me cold inside to think of Flint. This is one of *his* jokes, and no mistake. Him and these six was alone here; he killed 'em, every man; and this one he hauled here and laid down by compass, shiver my timbers! They're long bones, and the hair's been yellow. Ay, that would be Allardyce. You mind Allardyce, Tom Morgan?"

"Ay, ay," returned Morgan, "I mind him; he owed me money, he did, and took my knife ashore with him."

"Speaking of knives," said another, "why don't we find his'n lying round? Flint warn't the man to pick a seaman's pocket; and the birds, I guess, would leave it be."

"By the powers, and that's true!" cried Silver.

"There ain't a thing left here," said Merry, still feeling round among the bones, "not a copper doit nor a baccy box. It don't look nat'ral to me."

"No, by gum, it don't," agreed Silver; "not nat'ral, nor not nice, says you. Great guns! messmates, but if Flint was living, this would be a hot spot for you and me. Six they were, and six are we; and bones is what they are now."

"I saw him dead with these here deadlights," said Morgan. "Billy took me in. There he laid, with penny-pieces on his eyes."

"Dead—ay, sure enough he's dead and gone below," said the fellow with the bandage; "but if ever sperrit walked, it would be Flint's. Dear heart, but he died bad, did Flint!"

"Ay, that he did," observed another; "now he raged, and now he hollered for the rum, and now he sang. 'Fifteen Men' were his only song, mates; and I tell you true, I never rightly liked to hear it since. It was main hot, and the windy was open, and I hear that old song comin' out as clear as clear—and the death-haul on the man already."

"Come, come," said Silver, "stow this talk. He's dead, and he don't walk, that I know; leastways, he won't walk by day, and you may lay to that. Care killed a cat. Fetch ahead for the doubloons."

We started, certainly; but in spite of the hot sun and the staring daylight, the pirates no longer ran separate and shouting through the wood, but kept side by side and spoke with bated breath. The terror of the dead buccaneer had fallen on their spirits.

32. THE TREASURE HUNT—THE VOICE AMONG THE TREES

Partly from the damping influence of this alarm, partly to rest Silver and the sick folk, the whole party sat down as soon as they had gained the brow of the ascent.

The plateau being somewhat tilted towards the west, this spot on which we had paused commanded a wide prospect on either hand. Before us, over the tree-tops, we beheld the Cape of the Woods fringed with surf; behind, we not only looked down upon the anchorage and Skeleton Island, but saw—clear across the spit and the eastern lowlands—a great field of open sea upon the east. Sheer above us rose the Spy-glass, here dotted with single pines, there black with precipices.

There was no sound but that of the distant breakers, mounting from all round, and the chirp of countless insects in the brush. Not a man, not a sail upon the sea; the very largeness of the view increased the sense of solitude.

Silver, as he sat, took certain bearings with his compass.

"There are three 'tall trees'," said he, "about in the right line from Skeleton Island. 'Spy-glass Shoulder,' I take it, means that lower p'int there. It's child play to find the stuff now. I've half a mind to dine first."

"I don't feel sharp," growled Morgan. "Thinkin' o' Flint —I think it were—'as done me."

"Ah, well, my son, you praise your stars he's dead," said Silver.

"He was an ugly devil," cried a third pirate, with a shudder! "that blue in the face, too!"

"That was how the rum took him," added Merry. "Blue! well, I reckon he was blue. That's a true word!"

Ever since they had found the skeleton and got upon this train of thought, they had spoken lower and lower, and they had almost got to whispering by now, so that the sound of their talk hardly interrupted the silence of the wood. All of a sudden, out of the middle of the trees in front of us, a thin, high, trembling voice struck up the well-known air and words:

"Fifteen men on the dead man's chest—
Yo-ho-ho, and a bottle of rum!"

I never have seen men more dreadfully affected than the pirates. The colour went from their six faces like enchantment; some leaped to their feet, some clawed hold of others; Morgan grovelled on the ground.

"It's Flint, by—!" cried Merry.

The song had stopped as suddenly as it began—broken off, you would have said, in the middle of a note, as though someone had laid his hand upon the singer's mouth.

Coming so far through the clear, sunny atmosphere among the green tree-tops, I thought it had sounded airily and sweetly; and the effect on my companions was the stranger.

"Come," said Silver, struggling with his ashen lips to get the word out, "this won't do. Stand by to go about. This is a rum start, and I can't name the voice: but it's someone skylarking—someone that's flesh and blood, and you may lay to that." His courage had come back as he spoke, and some of the colour to his face along with it. Already the others had begun to lend an ear to his encouragement, and were coming a little to themselves, when the same voice broke out again—not this time singing, but in a faint distant hail, that echoed yet fainter among the clefts of the Spy-glass.

"Darby M'Graw," it wailed—for that is the word that best describes the sound—"Darby M'Graw! Darby M'Graw!" again and again and again; and then rising a little higher, and with an oath that I leave out, "Fetch aft the rum, Darby!"

The buccaneers remained rooted to the ground, their eyes starting from their heads. Long after the voice had died away they still stared in silence, dreadfully, before them.

"That fixes it!" gasped one. "Let's go."

"They was his last words," moaned Morgan, "his last words above board."

Dick had his Bible out, and was praying volubly. He had been well brought up, had Dick, before he came to sea and fell among bad companions.

Still, Silver was unconquered. I could hear his teeth rattle in his head; but he had not yet surrendered.

"Nobody in this here island ever heard of Darby," he muttered, "not one but us that's here." And then, making a great effort, "Shipmates," he cried, "I'm here to get that stuff, and I'll not be beat by man nor devil. I never was feared of Flint in his life, and, by the powers, I'll face him dead. There's seven hundred thousand pound not a quarter of a mile from here. When did ever a gentleman o' fortune show his stern to that much dollars, for a boozy old seaman with a blue mug—and him dead, too?"

But there was no sign of re-awakening courage in his

followers; rather, indeed, of growing terror at the irreverence of his words.

"Belay there, John!" said Merry. "Don't you cross a sperrit."

And the rest were all too terrified to reply. They would have run away severally had they dared; but fear kept them together, and kept them close by John, as if his daring helped them. He, on his part, had pretty well fought his weakness down.

"Sperrit? Well, maybe," he said. "But there's one thing not clear to me. There was an echo. Now, no man ever seen a sperrit with a shadow; well, then, what's he doing with an echo to him, I should like to know? That ain't in natur', surely?"

This argument seemed weak enough to me. But you can never tell what will affect the superstitious, and, to my wonder, George Merry was greatly relieved.

"Well, that's so," he said. "You've a head upon your shoulders, John, and no mistake. 'Bout ship, mates! this here crew is on a wrong tack, I do believe. And come to think on it, it was like Flint's voice, I grant you, but not just so clearaway like it, after all. It was liker somebody else's voice, now—it was liker—"

"By the powers, Ben Gunn!" roared Silver.

"Ay, and so it were," cried Morgan, springing on to his knees. "Ben Gunn it were!"

"It don't make much odds, do it now?" asked Dick. "Ben Gunn's not here in the body, any more'n Flint."

But the older hands greeted this remark with scorn.

"Why, nobody minds Ben Gunn," cried Merry; "dead or alive, nobody minds him."

It was extraordinary how their spirits had returned, and how the natural colour had revived in their faces. Soon they were chatting together, with intervals of listening; and not long after, hearing no further sound, they shouldered the tools and set forth again, Merry walking first with Silver's compass to keep them on the right line with Skeleton Island. He had said the truth: dead or alive, nobody minded Ben Gunn.

Dick alone still held his Bible, and looked around him as he went, with fearful glances; but he found no sympathy, and Silver even joked him on his precautions.

"I told you," said he—"I told you you had sp'iled your Bible. If it ain't no good to swear by, what do you suppose a sperrit would give for it? Not that!" and he snapped his big fingers, halting a moment on his crutch.

But Dick was not to be comforted; indeed, it was soon plain to me that the lad was falling sick; hastened by heat, exhaustion, and the shock of his alarm, the fever, predicted by Doctor Livesey, was evidently growing swiftly higher.

It was fine open walking here, upon the summit; our way lay a little downhill, for, as I have said, the plateau tilted towards the west. The pines, great and small, grew wide apart; and even between the clumps of nutmeg and azalea, wide open spaces baked in the hot sunshine. Striking, as we did, pretty near north-west across the island, we drew, on the one hand, ever nearer under the shoulders of the Spy-glass, and on the other, looked ever wider over the western bay where I had once tossed and trembled in the coracle.

The first of the tall trees was reached, and by the bearing, proved the wrong one. So with the second. The third rose nearly two hundred feet into the air above a clump of underwood; a giant of a vegetable, with a red column as big as a cottage, and a wide shadow around it in which a company could have manoeuvred. It was conspicuous far to sea both to the east and west, and might have been entered as a sailing mark upon the chart.

But it was not its size that now impressed my companions; it was the knowledge that seven hundred thousand pounds in gold lay somewhere buried below its spreading shadow. The thought of the money, as they drew nearer, swallowed up their previous terrors. Their eyes burned in their heads; their feet grew speedier and lighter; their whole soul was bound up in that fortune, that whole lifetime of extravagance and pleasure, that lay waiting there for each of them.

Silver hobbled, grunting, on his crutch; his nostrils stood out and quivered; he cursed like a madman when the flies settled on his hot and shiny countenance; he plucked furiously at the line that held me to him, and, from time to time, turned his eyes upon me with a deadly look. Certainly he took no pains to hide his thoughts; and certainly I read them like print. In the immediate nearness of the gold, all else had been forgotten; his promise and the doctor's warning were both things of the past; and I could not doubt that he hoped to seize upon the treasure, find and board the *Hispaniola* under cover of night, cut every honest throat about that island, and sail away as he had at first intended, laden with crimes and riches.

Shaken as I was with these alarms, it was hard for me to keep up with the rapid pace of the treasure-hunters. Now and again I stumbled; and it was then that Silver plucked so roughly at the rope and launched at me his murderous glances. Dick, who had dropped behind us, and now brought up the rear, was babbling to himself both prayers and curses, as his fever kept rising. This also added to my wretchedness, and, to crown all, I was haunted by the thought of the tragedy that had once been acted on that plateau, when that ungodly buccaneer with the blue face—he who died at Savannah, singing and shouting for drink—had there, with his own hand, cut down his six accomplices. This grove, that was now so peaceful, must have rung with cries, I thought; and even with the thought I could believe I heard it ringing still.

We were now at the margin of the thicket.

"Huzza, mates, all together!" shouted Merry; and the foremost broke into a run.

And suddenly, not ten yards further, we beheld them stop. A low cry arose. Silver doubled his pace, digging away with the foot of his crutch like one possessed; and next moment he and I had come also to a dead halt.

Before us was a great excavation, not very recent, for the sides had fallen in and grass had sprouted on the bottom. In this were the shaft of a pick broken in two and the boards of several packing-cases strewn around. On one of these boards I saw, branded with a hot iron, the name *Walrus*—the name of Flint's ship.

All was clear to probation. The *cache* had been found and rifled; the seven hundred thousand pounds were gone!

33. THE FALL OF A CHIEFTAIN

There never was such an overturn in this world. Each of these six men was as though he had been struck. But with Silver the blow passed almost instantly. Every thought of his soul had been set full-stretch, like a racer, on that money; well, he was brought up in a single second, dead; and he kept his head, found his temper, and changed his plan before the others had had time to realise the disappointment.

"Jim," he whispered, "take that, and stand by for trouble."

And he passed me a double-barrelled pistol.

At the same time he began quietly moving northward, and in a few steps had put the hollow between us two and the other five. Then he looked at me and nodded, as much as to say, "Here is a narrow corner," as, indeed, I thought it was. His looks were now quite friendly; and I was so revolted at these constant changes, that I could not forbear whispering, "So you've changed sides again."

There was no time left for him to answer in. The buccaneers, with oaths and cries', began to leap, one after another, into the pit, and to dig with their fingers, throwing the boards aside as they did so. Morgan found a piece of gold. He held it up with a perfect spout of oaths. It was a two-guinea piece, and it went from hand to hand among them for a quarter of a minute.

"Two guineas!" roared Merry, shaking it at Silver. "That's your seven hundred thousand pounds, is it? You're the man for bargains, ain't you? You're him that never bungled nothing, you wooden-headed lubber!"

"Dig away, boys," said Silver, with the coolest insolence; "you'll find some pig-nuts and I shouldn't wonder."

"Pig-nuts!" repeated Merry, in a scream. "Mates, do you hear that? I tell you, now, that man there knew it all along. Look in the face of him, and you'll see it wrote there."

"Ah, Merry," remarked Silver, "standing for cap'n again? You're a pushing lad, to be sure."

But this time everyone was entirely in Merry's favour. They began to scramble out of the excavation, darting furious glances behind them. One thing I observed, which looked well for us: they all got out upon the opposite side from Silver.

Well, there we stood, two on one side, five on the other, the pit between us, and nobody screwed up high enough to offer the first blow. Silver never moved; he watched them, very upright on his crutch, and looked as cool as ever I saw him. He was brave, and no mistake.

At last, Merry seemed to think a speech might help matters.

"Mates," says he, "there's two of them alone there; one's the old cripple that brought us all here and blundered us down to this; the other's that cub that I mean to have the heart of. Now, mates—"

He was raising his arm and his voice, and plainly meant to lead a charge. But just then—crack! crack! crack!—three musket-shots flashed out of the thicket. Merry tumbled head foremost into the excavation; the man with the bandage spun round like a teetotum, and fell all his length upon his side, where he lay dead, but still twitching; and the other three turned and ran for it with all their might.

Before you could wink, Long John had fired two barrels of a pistol into the struggling Merry; and as the man rolled up his eyes at him in the last agony, "George," said he, "I reckon I settled you."

At the same moment the doctor, Gray, and Ben Gunn joined us, with smoking muskets, from among the nutmeg trees.

"Forward!" cried the doctor. "Double quick, my lads. We must head 'em off the boats."

And we set off, at a great pace, sometimes plunging through the bushes to the chest.

I tell you, but Silver was anxious to keep up with us. The work that man went through, leaping on his crutch till the muscles of his chest were fit to burst, was work no sound man ever equalled; and so thinks the doctor. As it was, he was already thirty yards behind us, and on the verge of strangling, when we reached the brow of the slope.

"Doctor," he hailed, "see there! no hurry!"

Sure enough there was no hurry. In a more open part of the plateau, we could see the three survivors still running in the same direction as they had started, right for Mizzen-mast Hill. We were already between them and the boats; and so we four sat down to breathe, while Long John, mopping his face, came slowly up with us.

"Thank ye kindly, doctor," says he. "You came in in about the nick, I guess, for me and Hawkins. And so it's you, Ben Gunn!" he added. "Well, you're a nice one to be sure."

"I'm Ben Gunn, I am," replied the maroon, wriggling like an eel in his embarrassment, "And," he added, after a long pause, "how do, Mr. Silver? Pretty well, I thank ye, says you."

"Ben, Ben," murmured Silver, "to think as you've done me!"

The doctor sent back Gray for one of the pickaxes, deserted, in their flight, by the mutineers; and then as we proceeded leisurely downhill to where the boats were lying, related, in a few words, what had taken place. It was a story that profoundly interested Silver; and Ben Gunn, the half-idiot maroon, was the hero from beginning to end.

Ben, in his long, lonely wanderings about the island, had found the skeleton—it was he that had rifled it; he had found the treasure; he had dug it up (it was the shaft of his pickaxe that lay broken in the excavation); he had carried it on his back, in many weary journeys, from the foot of the tall pine to a cave he had on the two-pointed hill at the north-east angle of the island, and there it had lain stored in safety since two months before the arrival of the *Hispaniola*.

When the doctor had wormed this secret from him, on the afternoon of the attack, and when, next morning, he saw the anchorage deserted, he had gone to Silver, given him the chart, which was now useless—given him the stores, for Ben Gunn's cave was well supplied with goat's meat salted by himself—given anything and everything to get a chance of moving in safety from the stockade to the two-pointed hill, there to be clear of malaria and keep a guard upon the money.

"As for you, Jim," he said, "it went against my heart, but I did what I thought best for those who had stood by their duty; and if you were not one of these, whose fault was it?"

That morning, finding that I was to be involved in the horrid disappointment he had prepared for the mutineers, he had run all the way to the cave, and, leaving squire to guard the captain, had taken Gray and the maroon, and started, making the diagonal across the island, to be at hand beside the pine. Soon, however, he saw that our party had the start of him; and Ben Gunn, being fleet of foot, had been despatched in front to do his best alone. Then it had occurred to him to work upon the superstitions of his former shipmates; and he was so far successful that Grey and the doctor had come up and were already ambushed before the arrival of the treasure-hunters.

"Ah," said Silver, "it were fortunate for me that I had Hawkins here. You would have let old John be cut to bits, and never given it a thought, doctor."

"Not a thought," replied Doctor Livesey, cheerily.

And by this time we had reached the gigs. The doctor, with the pickaxe, demolished one of them, and then we all got aboard the other and set out to go round by sea for North Inlet.

This was a run of eight or nine miles. Silver, though he was almost killed already with fatigue, was set to an oar, like the rest of us, and we were soon skimming swiftly over a smooth sea. Soon we passed out of the straits and doubled the south-east corner of the island, round which, four days ago, we had towed the *Hispaniola.*

As we passed the two-pointed hill, we could see the black mouth of Ben Gunn's cave, and a figure standing by it, leaning on a musket. It was the squire; and we waved a handkerchief and gave him three cheers, in which the voice of Silver joined as heartily as any.

Three miles farther, just inside the mouth of North Inlet, what should we meet but the *Hispaniola,* cruising by herself! The last flood had lifted her; and had there been much wind, or a strong current, as in the southern anchorage, we should never have found her more, or found her stranded beyond help. As it was, there was little amiss, beyond the wreck of the mainsail. Another anchor was got ready, and dropped in a fathom and a half of water. We all pulled round again to Rum Cove, the nearest point for Ben Gunn's treasure-house; and then Gray, single-handed, returned with the gig to the *Hispaniola,* where he was to pass the night on guard.

A gentle slope ran up from the beach to the entrance of the cave. At the top, the squire met us. To me he was cordial and kind, saying nothing of my escapade, either in the way of blame or praise. At Silver's polite salute he somewhat flushed.

"John Silver," he said, "you're a prodigious villain and impostor—a monstrous impostor, sir. I am told I am not to prosecute you. Well, then, I will not. But the dead men, sir, hang about your neck like millstones."

"Thank you kindly, sir," replied Long John, again saluting.

"I dare you to thank me!" cried the squire. "It is a gross dereliction of my duty. Stand back."

And thereupon we all entered the cave. It was a large, airy place, with a little spring and a pool of clear water, overhung with ferns. The floor was sand. Before a big fire lay Captain Smollett; and in a far corner, only duskily flickered over by the blaze, I beheld great heaps of coin and quadrilaterals built of bars of gold. That was Flint's treasure that we had come so far to seek, and that had cost already the lives of seventeen men from the *Hispaniola.* How many it had cost in the amassing, what blood and sorrow, what good ships scuttled on the deep, what brave men walking the plank blindfold, what shot of cannon, what shame and lies and cruelty, perhaps no man alive could tell. Yet there were still three upon that island—Silver, and old Morgan, and Ben Gunn—who had each taken his share in these crimes, as each had hoped in vain to share in the reward.

"Come in, Jim," said the Captain. "You're a good boy in your line, Jim; but I don't think you and me'll go to sea again. You're too much of the born favourite for me. Is that you, John Silver? What brings you here, man?"

"Come back to my dooty, sir," returned Silver.

"Ah!" said the captain; and that was all he said.

What a supper I had of it that night, with all my friends around me; and what a meal it was, with Ben Gunn's salted goat, and some delicacies and a bottle of old wine from the *Hispaniola.* Never, I am sure, were people gayer or happier. And there was Silver, sitting back almost out of the firelight, but eating heartily, prompt to spring forward when anything was wanted, even joining quietly in our laughter—the same bland, polite, obsequious seaman of the voyage out.

34. AND LAST

The next morning we fell early to work, for the transportation of this great mass of gold near a mile by land to the beach, and thence three miles by boat to the *Hispaniola,* was a considerable task for so small a number of workmen. The three fellows still abroad upon the island did not greatly trouble us; a single sentry on the shoulder of the hill was sufficient to ensure us against any sudden onslaught, and we thought, besides, they had had more than enough of fighting.

Therefore the work was pushed on briskly. Gray and Ben Gunn came and went with the boat, while the rest, during their absences, piled treasure on the beach. Two of the bars, slung in a rope's-end, made a good load for a grown man— one that he was glad to walk slowly with. For my part, as I was not much use at carrying, I was kept busy all day in the cave, packing the minted money into bread-bags.

It was a strange collection, like Billy Bones's hoard for the diversity of coinage, but so much larger and so much more varied that I think I never had more pleasure than in sorting them. English, French, Spanish, Portuguese, Georges, and Louises, doubloons and double guineas and moidores and sequins, the pictures of all the kings of Europe for the last hundred years, strange Oriental pieces stamped with what looked like wisps of string or bits of spider's web, round pieces and square pieces, and pieces bored through the middle, as if to wear them round your neck—nearly every variety of money in the world must, I think, have found a place in that collection; and for number, I am sure they were like autumn leaves, so that my back ached with stooping and my fingers with sorting them out.

Day after day this work went on; by every evening a fortune had been stowed aboard, but there was another fortune waiting for the morrow; and all this time we heard nothing of the three surviving mutineers.

At last—I think it was on the third night—the doctor and I were strolling on the shoulder of the hill where it overlooks the lowlands of the isle, when, from out the thick darkness below, the wind brought us a noise between shrieking and singing. It was only a snatch that reached our ears, followed by the former silence.

"Heaven forgive them," said the doctor; "'tis the mutineers!"

"All drunk, sir," struck in the voice of Silver from behind us.

Silver, I should say, was allowed his entire liberty, and, in spite of daily rebuffs, seemed to regard himself once more as quite a privileged and friendly dependant. Indeed, it was remarkable how well he bore these slights, and with what unwearying politeness he kept on trying to ingratiate himself with all. Yet, I think, none treated him better than a dog; unless it was Ben Gunn, who was still terribly afraid of his old quartermaster, or myself, who had really something to thank him for; although for that matter, I suppose, I had reason to think even worse of him than anybody else, for I had seen him meditating a fresh treachery upon the plateau. Accordingly, it was pretty gruffly that the doctor answered him.

"Drunk or raving," said he.

"Right you were, sir," replied Silver; "and precious little odds which, to you and me."

"I suppose you would hardly ask me to call you a humane man," returned the doctor with a sneer, "and so my feelings may surprise you, Master Silver. But if I were sure they were raving—as I am morally certain one, at least, of them is down with fever—I should leave this camp, and, at whatever risk to my own carcase, take them the assistance of my skill."

"Ask your pardon, sir, you would be very wrong," quoth Silver. "You would lose your precious life, and you may lay to that. I'm on your side now, hand and glove; and I shouldn't wish for to see the party weakened, let alone yourself, seeing as I know what I owes you. But these men down there, they couldn't keep their word—no, not supposing they wished to; and what's more, they couldn't believe as you could."

"No," said the doctor. "You're the man to keep your word, we know that."

Well, that was about the last news we had of the three pirates. Only once we heard a gunshot a great way off, and supposed them to be hunting. A council was held, and it was decided that we must desert them on the island—to the huge glee, I must say, of Ben Gunn, and with the strong approval of Gray. We left a good stock of powder and shot, the bulk of the salt goat, a few medicines, and some other necessaries, tools, clothing, a spare sail, a fathom or two of rope, and, by the particular desire of the doctor, a handsome present of tobacco.

That was about our last doing on the island. Before that, we had got the treasure stowed, and had shipped enough water and the remainder of the goat meat in case of any distress; and at last, one fine morning, we weighed anchor, which was about all that we could manage, and stood out of North Inlet, the same colours flying that the captain had flown and fought under at the palisade.

The three fellows must have been watching us closer than we thought, as we soon had proved. For, coming through the narrows, we had to lie very near the southern point, and there we saw all three of them kneeling together on a spit of sand, with their arms raised in supplication. It went to all our hearts, I think, to leave them in that wretched state; but we could not risk another mutiny; and to take them home for the gibbet would have been a cruel sort of kindness. The doctor hailed them and told them of the stores we had left, and where they were to find them. But they continued to call us by name, and appeal to us, for God's sake, to be merciful, and not to leave them to die in such a place.

At last, seeing the ship still bore on her course, and was now swiftly drawing out of earshot, one of them—I know not which it was—leapt to his feet with a hoarse cry, whipped his musket to his shoulder, and sent a shot whistling over Silver's head and through the mainsail.

After that, we kept under cover of the bulwarks, and when next I looked out they had disappeared from the spit, and the spit itself had almost melted out of sight in the growing distance. That was, at least, the end of that; and before noon, to my inexpressible joy, the highest rock of Treasure Island had sunk into the blue round of sea.

We were so short of men that everyone on board had to bear a hand—only the captain lying on a mattress in the stern and giving his orders; for, though greatly recovered, he was still in want of quiet. We laid her head for the nearest port in Spanish America, for we could not risk the voyage home without fresh hands; and as it was, what with baffling winds and a couple of fresh gales, we were all worn out before we reached it.

It was just at sundown when we cast anchor in a most beautiful land-locked gulf, and were immediately surrounded by shore boats full of Negroes, and Mexican Indians, and half-bloods, selling fruits and vegetables, and offering to dive for bits of money. The sight of so many goodhumoured faces (especially the blacks), the taste of the tropical fruits, and above all, the lights that began to shine in the town, made a most charming contrast to our dark and bloody sojourn on the island; and the doctor and the squire, taking me along with them, went ashore to pass the early part of the night. Here they met the captain of an English man-of-war, fell in talk with him, went on board his ship, and, in short, had so agreeable a time, that day was breaking when we came alongside the *Hispaniola*.

Ben Gunn was on deck alone, and, as soon as we came on board, he began, with wonderful contortions, to make us a confession. Silver was gone. The maroon had connived at his escape in a shore boat some hours ago, and he now assured us he had only done so to preserve our lives, which would certainly have been forfeit if "that man with the one leg had stayed aboard". But this was not all. The sea cook had not gone empty-handed. He had cut through a bulk-head unobserved, and had removed one of the sacks of coin, worth, perhaps, three or four hundred guineas, to help him on his further wanderings.

I think we were all pleased to be so cheaply quit of him.

Well, to make a long story short, we got a few hands on board, made a good cruise home, and the *Hispaniola* reached Bristol just as Mr. Blandly was beginning to think of fitting out her consort. Five men only of those who had sailed returned with her. "Drink and the devil had done for the rest", with a vengeance; although, to be sure, we were not quite in so bad a case as that other ship they sang about:

"With one man of her crew alive,
What put to sea with seventy-five."

All of us had an ample share of the treasure, and used it wisely or foolishly, according to our nature. Captain Smollett is now retired from the sea. Gray not only saved his money, but, being suddenly smit with a desire to rise, also studied his profession; and he is now mate and part owner of a fine full-rigged ship; married besides, and the father of a family. As for Ben Gunn, he got a thousand pounds, which he spent or lost in three weeks, or, to be exact, in nineteen days, for he was back begging on the twentieth. Then he was given a lodge to keep, exactly as he had feared upon the island; and he still lives, a great favourite, though something of a butt, with the country boys, and a notable singer in church on Sundays and saint's days.

Of Silver we have heard no more. That formidable sea-faring man with one leg has at last gone clean out of my life; but I daresay he met his old Negress, and perhaps still lives in comfort with her and Captain Flint. It is to be hoped so, I suppose, for his chances of comfort in another world are very small.

The bar silver and the arms still lie, for all that I know, where Flint buried them; and certainly they shall lie there for me. Oxen and wain-ropes would not bring me back again to that accursed island; and the worst dreams that ever I have are when I hear the surf booming about its coasts, or start upright in bed, with the sharp voice of Captain Flint still ringing in my ears: "Pieces of eight! pieces of eight!"

CHILDREN'S CLASSICS

Kidnapped

ROBERT LOUIS STEVENSON

Kidnapped

PARRAGON

Kidnapped
A Parragon Classic

This is a Siena Book
Siena is an imprint of Parragon

This edition published in 1999 by
Parragon
13 Whiteladies Road
Clifton
Bristol BS8 1PB

Printed and bound in the UK

DEDICATION

MY DEAR CHARLES BAXTER,

If you ever read this tale, you will likely ask yourself more questions than I should care to answer: as for instance how the Appin murder has come to fall in the year 1751, how the Torran rocks have crept so near to Earraid, or why the printed trial is silent as to all that touches David Balfour. These are nuts beyond my ability to crack. But if you tried me on the point of Alan's guilt or innocence, I think I could defend the reading of the text. To this day you will find the tradition of Appin clear in Alan's favour. If you inquire, you may even hear that the descendants of "the other man" who fired the shot are in the country to this day. But that other man's name, inquire as you please, you shall not hear; for the Highlander values a secret for itself and for the congenial exercise of keeping it. I might go on for long to justify one point and own another indefensible; it is more honest to confess at once how little I am touched by the desire of accuracy. This is no furniture for the scholar's library, but a book for the winter evening school-room when the tasks are over and the hour for bed draws near; and honest Alan, who was a grim old fire-eater in his day, has in this new avatar no more desperate purpose than to steal some young gentleman's attention from his Ovid, carry him awhile into the Highlands and the last century, and pack him to bed with some engaging images to mingle with his dreams.

As for you, my dear Charles, I do not even ask you to like the tale. But perhaps when he is older, your son will; he may then be pleased to find his father's name on the fly-leaf; and in the meanwhile it pleases me to set it there in memory of many days that were happy and some (now perhaps as pleasant to remember) that were sad. If it is strange for me to look back from a distance both in time and space on these bygone adventures of our youth, it must be stranger for you who tread the same streets—who may tomorrow open the door of the old Speculative, where we begin to rank with Scott and Robert Emmet and the beloved and inglorious Macbean—or may pass the corner of the close where that great society, the L.J.R., held its meetings and drank its beer, sitting in the seats of Burns and his companions. I think I see you, moving there by plain daylight, beholding with your natural eyes those places that have now become for your companion a part of the scenery of dreams. How, in the intervals of present business, the past must echo in your memory! Let it not echo often without some kind thoughts of your friend.

R. L. S.

Skerryvore,
Bournemouth

CHAPTER 1

I SET OFF UPON MY JOURNEY TO THE HOUSE OF SHAWS

I will begin the story of my adventures with a certain morning early in the month of June, the year of grace 171— when I took the key for the last time out of the door of my father's house. The sun began to shine upon the summit of the hills as I went down the road; and by the time I had come as far as the manse, the blackbirds were whistling in the garden lilacs, and the mist that hung around the valley in the time of the dawn was beginning to arise and die away.

Mr Campbell, the minister of Essendean, was waiting for me by the garden gate, good man! He asked me if I had breakfasted; and hearing that I lacked for nothing, he took my hand in both of his and clapped it kindly under his arm.

"Well, Davie, lad," said he, "I will go with you as far as the ford, to set you on the way."

And we began to walk forward in silence.

"Are ye sorry to leave Essendean?" said he, after a while.

"Why, sir," said I, "If I knew where I was going or what was likely to become of me, I would tell you candidly. Essendean is a good place indeed, and I have been very happy there; but then I have never been anywhere else. My father and mother, since they are both dead, I shall be no nearer to in Essendean than in the Kingdom of Hungary; and, to speak truth, if I thought I had a chance to better myself where I was going, I would go with a good will."

"Ay?" said Mr Campbell. "Very well, Davie. Then it behoves me to tell your fortune; or so far as I may. When your mother was gone, and your father (the worthy, Christian man) began to sicken for his end, he gave me in charge a certain letter, which he said was your inheritance. 'So soon,' says he, 'as I am gone, and the house is redd up and the gear disposed of' (all which, Davie, hath been done) 'give my boy this letter into his hand, and start him off to the house of Shaws, not far from Cramond. That is the place I came from,' he said, 'and it's where it befits that my boy should return. He is a steady lad,' your father said, 'and a canny goer;

and I doubt not he will come safe, and be well liked where he goes.' "

"The house of Shaws!" I cried. "What had my poor father to do with the house of Shaws?"

"Nay," said Mr Campbell, "who can tell that for a surety? But the name of that family, Davie boy, is the name you bear—Balfours of Shaws: an ancient, honest, reputable house, peradventure in these latter days decayed. Your father, too, was a man of learning as befitted his position; no man more plausibly conducted school; nor had he the manner nor yet the speech of a common dominie; but (as ye will yourself remember) I took aye a pleasure to have him to the manse to meet the gentry; and those of my own house, Campbell of Kilrennet, Campbell of Dunswire, Campbell of Minch, and many others, all well-kenned gentlemen, had pleasure in his society. Lastly, to put all the elements of this affair before you, here is the testamentary letter itself, superscribed by the own hand of our departed brother."

He gave me the letter, which was addressed in these words: "To the hands of Ebenezer Balfour, Esquire, of Shaws, in his house of Shaws, these will be delivered by my son, David Balfour." My heart was beating hard at this great prospect now suddenly opening before a lad of sixteen years of age, the son of a poor country dominie in the Forest of Ettrick.

"Mr Campbell," I stammered, "and if you were in my shoes, would you go?"

"Of a surety," said the minister, "that would I, and without pause. A pretty lad like you should get to Cramond (which is near in by Edinburgh) in two days of walk. If the worst came to the worst, and your high relations (as I cannot but suppose them to be somewhat of your blood) should put you to the door, ye can but walk the two days back again and rap at the manse door. But I would rather hope that ye shall be well received, as your poor father forecast for you, and for anything that I ken, come to be a great man in time. And here, Davie, laddie," he resumed, "it lies near upon my conscience to improve this parting, and set you on the right guard against the dangers of the world."

Here he cast about for a comfortable seat, lighted on a big boulder under a birch by the trackside, sat down upon it with a very long, serious upper lip, and, the sun now shining in upon us between two peaks, put his pocket-handkerchief over his cocked hat to shelter him. There, then, with uplifted forefinger, he first put me on my guard against a considerable number of heresies, to which I had no temptation, and there he urged upon me to be instant in my prayers and reading of the Bible. That done, he drew a picture of the great house that I was bound to, and how I should conduct myself with its inhabitants.

"Be soople, Davie, in things immaterial," said he. "Bear ye this in mind, that, though gentle born, ye have had a country rearing. Dinnae shame us, Davie, dinnae shame us! In yon great, muckle house, with all these domestics, upper and under, show yourself as nice, as circumspect, as quick at the conception, and as slow of speech as any. As for the laird—remember he's the laird; I say no more: honour to whom honour. It's pleasure to obey a laird; or should be, to the young."

"Well, sir," said I, "it may be; and I'll promise you I'll try to make it so."

"Why, very well said," replied Mr Campbell, heartily. "And now to come to the material, or (to make a quibble) to the immaterial. I have here a little packet which contains four things." He tugged it, as he spoke, and with some difficulty, from the skirt pocket of his coat. "Of these four things, the first is your legal due: the little pickle money for your father's books and plenishing, which I have bought (as I have explained from the first) in the design of re-selling at a profit to the incoming dominie. The other three are gifties that Mrs Campbell and myself would be blithe of your acceptance. The first, which is round, will likely please ye best at the first off-go; but, O Davie, laddie, it's but a drop of water in the sea; it'll help you but a step, and vanish like the morning. The second, which is flat and square and written upon, will stand by you through life, like a good staff for the road, and a good pillow to your head in sickness. And as for the last, which is cubical, that'll see you, it's my prayerful wish, into a better land."

With that he got upon his feet, took off his hat, and prayed a little while aloud, and in affecting terms, for a young man setting out into the world; then suddenly took me in his arms and embraced me very hard; then held me at arm's length, looking at me with his face all working with sorrow; and then whipped about, and crying goodbye to me, set off backward by the way that we had come at a sort of jogging run. It might have been laughable to another; but I was in no mind to laugh. I watched him as long as he was in sight; and he never stopped hurrying, nor once looked back. Then it came in upon my mind that this was all his sorrow at my departure; and my conscience smote me hard and fast, because I, for my part, was overjoyed to get away out of that quiet countryside, and go to a great, busy house, among rich and respected gentlefolk of my own name and blood.

"Davie, Davie," I thought, "was ever seen such black ingratitude? Can you forget old favours and old friends at the mere whistle of a name? Fie, fie; think shame!"

And I sat down on the boulder the good man had just left, and opened the parcel to see the nature of my gifts. That which he had called cubical, I had never had much doubt of; sure enough it was a little Bible, to carry in a plaid-neuk. That which he had called round, I found to be a shilling piece; and the third, which was to help me so wonderfully both in health and sickness all the days of my life, was a little piece of coarse yellow paper, written upon thus in red ink:

To Make Lilly of the Valley Water.—Take the flowers of lilly of the valley and distil them in sack, and drink a spooneful or two as there is occasion. It restores speech to those that have the dumb palsey. It is good against the Gout; it comforts the heart and strengthens the memory; and the flowers, put into a Glasse, close stopt, and set into ane hill of ants for a month, then take it out, and you will find a liquor which comes from the flowers, which keep in a vial; it is good, ill or well, and whether man or woman.

And then, in the minister's own hand, was added:

Likewise for sprains, rub it in; and for the cholic, a great spooneful in the hour.

To be sure, I laughed over this; but it was rather tremulous laughter; and I was glad to get my bundle on my staffs end and set out over the ford and up the hill upon the farther side; till, just as I came on the green drove-road running wide through the heather, I took my last look of Kirk Essendean, the trees about the manse, and the big rowans in the kirkyard where my father and my mother lay.

Chapter 2

I COME TO MY JOURNEY'S END

On the forenoon of the second day, coming to the top of a hill, I saw the country fall away before me down to the sea; and in the midst of this descent, on a long ridge, the city of Edinburgh smoking like a kiln. There was a flag upon the castle, and ships moving or lying anchored in the firth; both of which, for as far away as they were, I could distinguish clearly; and both brought my country heart into my mouth.

Presently after, I came by a house where a shepherd lived, and got a rough direction for the neighbourhood of Cramond; and so, from one to another, worked my way to the westward of the capital by Colinton, till I came out upon the Glasgow road. And there, to my great pleasure and wonder, I beheld a regiment marching to the fifes, every foot in time; an old red-faced general on a grey horse at the one end, and at the other the company of Grenadiers, with their Pope's-hats. The pride of life seemed to mount into my brain at the sight of the red-coats and the hearing of that merry music.

A little farther on, and I was told I was in Cramond parish, and began to substitute in my inquiries the name of the house of Shaws. It was a word that seemed to surprise those of whom I sought my way. At first I thought the plainness of my appearance, in my country habit, and that all dusty from the road, consorted ill with the greatness of the place to which I was bound. But after two, or maybe three, had given me the same look and the same answer, I began to take it in my head there was something strange about the Shaws itself.

The better to set this fear at rest, I changed the form of my inquiries; and spying an honest fellow coming along a lane on the shaft of his cart, I asked him if he had ever heard tell of a house they called the house of Shaws.

He stopped his cart and looked at me, like the others.

"Ay," said he. "What for?"

"It's a great house?" I asked.

"Doubtless," says he."The house is a big, muckle house."

"Ah," said I, "but the folk that are in it?"

"Folk?" cried he. "Are ye daft? There's nae folk there—to call folk."

"What?" says I; "not Mr Ebenezer?"

"Oh, ay," says the man, "there's the laird, to be sure, if it's him you're wanting. What'll like be your business, mannie?"

"I was led to think that I would get a situation," I said, looking as modest as I could.

"What?" cries the carter, in so sharp a note that his very horse started; and then, "Well, mannie," he added,"it's nane of my affairs; but ye seem a decent-spoken lad; and if ye'll take a word from me, ye'll keep clear of the Shaws."

The next person I came across was a dapper little man in a beautiful white wig, whom I saw to be a barber on his rounds; and knowing well that barbers were great gossips, I asked him plainly what sort of a man was Mr Balfour of the Shaws.

"Hoot, hoot, hoot," said the barber, "nae kind of a man, nae kind of a man at all"; and began to ask me very shrewdly what my business was; but I was more than a match for him at that, and he went on to his next customer no wiser than he came.

I cannot well describe the blow this dealt to my illusions. The more indistinct the accusations were, the less I liked them, for they left the wider field to fancy. What kind of a great house was this, that all the parish should start and stare to be asked the way to it? Or what sort of a gentleman, that his ill-fame should be thus current on the wayside? If an hour's walking would have brought me back to Essendean, I had left my adventure then and there, and returned to Mr Campbell's. But when I had come so far a way already, mere shame would not suffer me to desist till I had put the matter to the touch of proof; I was bound, out of mere self-respect, to carry it through; and little as I liked the sound of what I heard, and slow as I began to travel, I still kept asking my way and still kept advancing.

It was drawing on to sundown when I met a stout, dark, sour looking woman coming trudging down a hill; and she, when I had put my usual question, turned sharp about, accompanied me back to the summit she had just left, and pointed to a great bulk of building standing very bare upon a green in the bottom of the next valley. The country was pleasant round about, running in low hills, pleasantly watered and wooded, and the crops, to my eyes, wonderfully good; but the house itself appeared to be a kind of ruin; no road led up to it; no smoke arose from any of the chimneys; nor was there any semblance of a garden. My heart sank. "That!" I cried.

The woman's face lit up with a malignant anger. "That is the house of Shaws!" she cried. "Blood built it; blood stopped the building of it; blood shall bring it down. See here!" she cried again—"I spit upon the ground, and crack my thumb at it! Black be its fall! If ye see the laird, tell him what ye hear; tell him this makes the twelve hunner and nineteen time that Jennet Clouston has called down the curse on him and his house, byre, and stable, man, guest, and master, wife, miss, or bairn—black, black be their fall!"

And the woman, whose voice had risen to a kind of eldritch singsong, turned with a skip, and was gone. I stood where she left me, with my hair on end. In those days folk still believed in witches and trembled at a curse; and this one, falling so pat, like a wayside omen, to arrest me ere I carried out my purpose, took the pith out of my legs.

I sat me down and stared at the house of Shaws. The more I looked, the pleasanter that countryside appeared; being all set with hawthorn bushes full of flowers; the fields dotted with grazing sheep; a fine flight of rooks in the sky; and every sign of a kind soil and climate; and yet the barrack in the midst of it went sore against my fancy.

Country folk went by from the fields as I sat there on the side of the ditch, but I lacked the spirit to give them a good-e'en. At last the sun went down, and then, right up against the yellow sky, I saw a scroll of smoke go mounting, not much thicker, as it seemed to me, than the smoke of a candle; but still there it was, and meant a fire, and warmth, and cookery, and some living inhabitant that must have lit it; and this comforted my heart wonderfully—more, I feel sure, than a whole flask of the lily of the valley water that Mrs Campbell set so great a store by.

So I set forward by a little faint track in the grass that led in my direction. It was very faint indeed to be the only way to a place of habitation; yet I saw no other. Presently it brought me to stone uprights, with an unroofed lodge beside them, and coats of arms upon the top. A main entrance, it was plainly meant to be, but never finished; instead of gates of wrought iron, a pair of hurdles were tied across with a straw rope; and as there were no park walls, nor any sign of avenue, the track that I was following passed on the right hand of the pillars, and went wandering on toward the house.

The nearer I got to that, the drearier it appeared. It seemed like the one wing of a house that had never been finished. What should have been the inner end stood open on the upper floors, and showed against the sky with steps and stairs of uncompleted masonry. Many of the windows were unglazed, and bats flew in and out like doves out of a dovecote.

The night had begun to fall as I got close; and in three of the lower windows, which were very high up, and narrow, and well barred, the changing light of a little fire began to glimmer.

Was this the palace I had been coming to? Was it within these walls that I was to seek new friends and begin great fortunes? Why, in my father's house on Essen-Waterside, the fire and the bright lights would show a mile away, and the door open to a beggar's knock.

I came forward cautiously, and giving ear as I came, heard someone rattling with dishes, and a little dry, eager cough that came in fits; but there was no sound of speech, and not a dog barked.

The door, as well as I could see it in the dim light, was a great piece of wood all studded with nails; and I lifted my hand with a faint heart under my jacket, and knocked once. Then I stood and waited. The house had fallen into a dead silence; a whole minute passed away, and nothing stirred but the bats overhead. I knocked again, and hearkened again. By this time my ears had grown so accustomed to the quiet, that I could hear the ticking of the clock inside as it slowly counted out the seconds; but whoever was in that house kept deadly still, and must have held his breath.

I was in two minds whether to run away; but anger got the upper hand, and I began instead to rain kicks and buffets on the door, and to shout out aloud for Mr Balfour. I was in full career, when I heard the cough right overhead, and jumping back and looking up, beheld a man's head in a tall nightcap, and the bell mouth of a blunderbuss, at one of the first storey windows.

"It's loaded," said a voice.

"I have come here with a letter," I said, "to Mr Ebenezer Balfour of Shaws. Is he here?"

"From whom is it?" asked the man with the blunderbuss.

"That is neither here nor there," said I, for I was growing very wroth.

"Well," was the reply, "ye can put it down upon the doorstep, and be off with ye."

"I will do no such thing," I cried. "I will deliver it into Mr Balfour's hands, as it was meant I should. It is a letter of introduction."

"A what?" cried the voice sharply.

I repeated what I had said.

"Who are ye, yourself?" was the next question, after a considerable pause.

"I am not ashamed of my name," said I. "They call me David Balfour."

At that, I made sure the man started, for I heard the blunderbuss rattle on the window-sill; and it was after quite a long pause, and with a curious change of voice, that the next question followed:

"Is your father dead?"

I was so much surprised at this, that I could find no voice to answer, but stood staring.

"Ay," the man resumed, "he'll be dead, no doubt; and that'll be what brings ye chapping to my door." Another pause, and then, defiantly, "Well, man," he said, "I'll let ye in"; and he disappeared from the window.

Chapter 3

I MAKE ACQUAINTANCE OF MY UNCLE

Presently there came a great rattling of chains and bolts, and the door was cautiously opened, and shut to again behind me as soon as I had passed.

"Go into the kitchen and touch naething," said the voice; and while the person of the house set himself to replacing the defences of the door, I groped my way forward and entered the kitchen.

The fire had burned up fairly bright, and showed me the barest room I think I ever put my eyes on. Half-a-dozen dishes stood upon the shelves; the table was laid for supper with a bowl of porridge, a horn spoon, and a cup of small beer. Besides what I have named, there was not another thing in that great, stone-vaulted, empty chamber but lockfast chests arranged along the wall and a corner cupboard with a padlock.

As soon as the last chain was up, the man rejoined me. He was a mean, stooping, narrow-shouldered, clay-faced creature; and his age might have been anything between fifty and seventy. His nightcap was of flannel and so was the nightgown that he wore, instead of coat and waistcoat, over his ragged shirt. He was long unshaved; but what most distressed and even daunted me, he would neither take his eyes away from me nor look me fairly in the face. What he was, whether by trade or birth, was more than I could fathom; but he seemed most like an old, unprofitable serving-man, who should have been left in charge of that big house upon board wages.

"Are ye sharp-set?" he asked, glancing at about the level of my knee. "Ye can eat that drop parritch."

I said I feared it was his own supper.

"Oh," said he, "I can do fine wanting it. I'll take the ale, though, for it slockens my cough." He drank the cup about half out, still keeping an eye upon me as he drank; and then suddenly held out his hand. "Let's see the letter," said he.

I told him the letter was for Mr Balfour; not for him.

"And who do you think I am?" says he. "Give me Alexander's letter!"

"You know my father's name?"

"It would be strange if I didnae," he returned, "for he was my born brother; and little as ye seem to like either me or my house, or my good parritch, I'm your born uncle, Davie, my man, and you my born nephew. So give us the letter, and sit down and fill your kyte."

If I had been some years younger, what with shame, weariness, and disappointment, I believe I had burst into tears. As it was, I could find no words, neither black nor white, but handed him the letter, and sat down to the porridge with as little appetite for meat as ever a young man had.

Meanwhile, my uncle, stooping over the fire, turned the letter over and over in his hands.

"Do ye ken what's in it?" he asked, suddenly.

"You see for yourself, sir," said I, "the seal's not been broken."

"Ay," said he, "but what brought you here?"

"To give the letter," said I.

"No," says he, cunningly, "but ye'll have had some hopes, nae doubt?"

"I confess, sir," said I, "when I was told that I had kinsfolk well-to-do, I did indeed indulge the hope that they might help me in my life. But I am no beggar; I look for no favours at your hands, and I want none that are not freely given. For as poor as I appear, I have friends of my own that will be blithe to help me."

"Hoot-toot," said Uncle Ebenezer, "dinnae fly up in the snuff at me. We'll agree fine yet. And, Davie, my man, if you're done with that bit parritch, I could just take a sup of it myself. Ay," he continued, as soon as he had ousted me from the stool and spoon, "they're fie, halesome food—they're grand food, parritch." He murmured a little grace to himself and fell to. "Your father was very fond of his meat, I mind; he was a hearty, if not a great eater; but as for me, I could never do mair than pyke at food." He took a pull at the small beer, which probably reminded him of hospitable duties; for his next speech ran thus: "If ye're dry, ye'll find water behind the door."

To this I returned no answer, standing stiffly on my two feet, and looking down upon my uncle with a mighty angry heart. He, on his part, continued to eat like a man under some pressure of time, and to throw out little darting glances now at my shoes and now at my home-spun stockings. Once only, when he had ventured to look a little higher, our eyes met; and no thief taken with a hand in a man's pocket could have shown more lively signals of distress. This set me in a muse, whether his timidity arose from too long a disuse of any human company; and whether perhaps, upon a little trial, it might pass off, and my uncle change into an altogether different man. From this I was awakened by his sharp voice.

"Your father's been long dead?" he asked.

"Three weeks, sir," said I.

"He was a secret man, Alexander—a secret, silent man," he continued. "He never said muckle when he was young. He'll never have spoken muckle of me?"

"I never knew, sir, till you told it me, that he had any brother."

"Dear me!" said Ebenezer. "Nor yet of Shaws, I dare say?"

"Not so much as the name, sir," said I.

"To think o' that!" said he. "A strange nature of a man! For all that, he seemed singularly satisfied, but whether with himself, or me, or with this conduct of my father's, was more than I could read. Certainly, however, he seemed to be outgrowing that distaste, or ill-will, that he had conceived at first against my person; for presently he jumped up, came across the room behind me, and hit me a smack upon the shoulder. We'll agree fine yet!" he cried. I'm just as glad I let you in. And now come awa' to your bed."

To my surprise, he lit no lamp or candle, but set forth into the dark passage, groped his way, breathing deeply, up a flight of steps, and paused before a door, which he unlocked. I was close upon his heels, having stumbled after him as best I might; and he bade me go in, for that was my chamber. I did as he bid, but paused after a few steps, and begged a light to go to bed with.

"Hoot-toot!" said Uncle Ebenezer, "there's a fine moon."

"Neither moon nor star, sir, and pit-mirk," said I. "I cannae see the bed."

"Hoot-toot, hoot-toot," said he. "Lights in a house is a thing I dinnae agree with. I'm unco feared of fires. Good night to ye, Davie, my man."

And before I had time to add a further protest, he pulled the door to, and I heard him lock me in from the outside.

I did not know whether to laugh or cry. The room was as cold as a well, and the bed when I had found my way to it, as damp as a peat-hag; but by good fortune I had caught up my bundle and my plaid, and rolling myself in the latter, I lay down upon the floor under the lee of the big bedstead, and fell speedily asleep.

With the first peep of day I opened my eyes, to find myself in a great chamber, hung with stamped leather, furnished with fine embroidered furniture, and lit by three fair windows. Ten years ago, or perhaps twenty, it must have been as pleasant a room to lie down or to awake in, as a man could wish; but damp, dirt, disuse, and the mice and spiders had done their worst since then. Many of the window-panes, besides, were broken; and indeed this was so common a feature in that house, that I believe my uncle must at some time have stood a siege from his indignant neighbours—perhaps with Jennet Clouston at their head.

Meanwhile the sun was shining outside; and being very cold in that miserable room, I knocked and shouted till my gaoler came and let me out. He carried me to the back of the house, where was a draw-well, and told me to "wash my face there, if I wanted"; and when that was done, I made the best of my own way back to the kitchen, where he had lit the fire and was making the porridge. The table was laid with two bowls and two horn spoons, but the same single measure of small beer. Perhaps my eye rested on this particular with some surprise, and perhaps my uncle observed it; for he spoke up as if in answer to my thought, asking me if I would like to drink ale—for so he called it.

I told him such was my habit, but not to put himself about.

"Na, na," said he; "I'll deny you nothing in reason."

He fetched another cup from the shelf; and then, to my great surprise, instead of drawing more beer, he poured an accurate half from one cup to the other. There was a kind of nobleness in this that took my breath away; if my uncle was certainly a miser, he was one of that thorough breed that goes near to make the vice respectable.

When we had made an end of our meal, my uncle Ebenezer unlocked a drawer, and drew out of it a clay pipe and a lump of tobacco, from which he cut one fill before he locked it up again. Then he sat down in the sun at one of the windows and silently smoked. From time to time his eyes came coasting round to me, and he shot out one of his questions. Once it was, "And your mother?" And when I had told him that she, too, was dead, "Ay, she was a bonnie lassie!" Then, after another long pause, "Whae were these friends o' yours?"

I told him they were different gentlemen of the name of Campbell; though, indeed, there was only one, and that the minister, that had ever taken the least note of me; but I began to think my uncle made too light of my position, and finding myself all alone with him, I did not wish him to suppose me helpless.

He seemed to turn this over in his mind; and then, "Davie, my man," said he, "ye've come to the right bit when ye came to your Uncle Ebenezer. I've a great notion of the family, and I mean to do the right by you; but while I'm taking a bit think to mysel' of what's the best thing to put you to—whether the law, or the meenistry, or maybe the army, whilk is what boys are fondest of—I wouldnae like the Balfours to be humbled before a wheen Hieland Campbells, and I'll ask you to keep your tongue within your teeth. Nae letters; nae messages; no kind of word to onybody; or else—there's my door."

"Uncle Ebenezer," said I, "I've no manner of reason to suppose you mean anything but well by me. For all that, I would have you to know that I have a pride of my own. It was by no will of mine that I came seeking you; and if you show me your door again, I'll take you at the word."

He seemed grievously put out. "Hoots-toots," said he, "ca' cannie, man—ca' cannie! Bide a day or two. I'm nae warlock, to find a fortune for you in the bottom of a parritch bowl; but just you give me a day or two, and say naething to naebody, and as sure as sure, I'll do the right by you."

"Very well," said I, "enough said. If you want to help me,

there's no doubt but I'll be glad of it, and none but I'll be grateful."

It seemed to me (too soon, I daresay) that I was getting the upper hand of my uncle; and I began next to say that I must have the bed and bedclothes aired and put to sun-dry; for nothing would make me sleep in such a pickle.

"Is this my house or yours?" said he, in his keen voice, and then all of a sudden broke off. "Na, na," said he, "I dinnae mean that. What's mine is yours, Davie, my man, and what's yours is mine. Blood's thicker than water; and there's naebody but you and me that ought the name." And then on he rambled about the family, and its ancient greatness, and his father that began to enlarge the house, and himself that stopped the building as a sinful waste; and this put it in my head to give him Jennet Clouston's message.

"The limmer" he cried. "Twelve hunner and nineteen—that's every day since I had the limmer rowpit! Dod, David, I'll have her roasted on red peats before I'm by with it! A witch—a proclaimed witch! I'll aff and see the session clerk."

And with that he opened a chest, and got out a very old and well-preserved blue coat and waistcoat, and a good enough beaver hat, both without lace. These he threw on anyway, and taking a staff from the cupboard, locked all up again, and was for setting out, when a thought arrested him.

"I cannae leave you by yoursel' in the house," said he. "I'll have to lock you out."

The blood came into my face. "If you lock me out," I said, "it'll be the last you see of me in friendship."

He turned very pale, and sucked his mouth in. "This is no the way," said he, looking wickedly at a corner of the floor, "this is no the way to win my favour, David."

"Sir," says I, "with a proper reverence for your age and our common blood, I do not value your favour at a boddle's purchase. I was brought up to have a good conceit of myself; and if you were all the uncle, and all the family, I had in the world ten times over, I wouldn't buy your liking at such prices."

Uncle Ebenezer went and looked out of the window for a while. I could see him all trembling and twitching, like a man with palsy. But when he turned round, he had a smile upon his face.

"Well, well," said he, "awe must bear and forbear. I'll no go; that's all that's to be said of it."

"Uncle Ebenezer," I said, "I can make nothing out of this. You use me like a thief; you hate to have me in this house; you let me see it, every word and every minute; it's not possible that you can like me; and as for me, I've spoken to you as I never thought to speak to any man. Why do you seek to help me, then? Let me gang back to Essendean—let me gang back to the friends I have, and that like me!"

"Na, na; na, na," he said, very earnestly. "I like you fine; we'll agree fine yet; and for the honour of the house I couldnae let you leave the way ye came. Bide here quiet, there's a good lad; just you bide here quiet a bittie, and ye'll find that we agree."

"Well, sir," said I, after I had thought the matter out in silence, "I'll stay a while. It's more just I should be helped by my own blood than strangers; and if we don't agree, I'll do my best it shall be through no fault of mine."

CHAPTER 4

I RUN A GREAT DANGER IN THE HOUSE OF SHAWS

For a day that was begun so ill, the day passed fairly well. We had the porridge cold again at noon, and hot porridge at night; porridge and small beer was my uncle's diet. He spoke but little, and that in the same way as before, shooting a question at me after a long silence; and when I sought to lead him in talk about my future, slipped out of it again. In a room next door to the kitchen, where he suffered me to go, I found a great number of books, both Latin and English, in which I took great pleasure all the afternoon. Indeed the time passed so lightly in this good company, that I began to be almost reconciled to my residence at Shaws; and nothing but the sight of my uncle, and his eyes playing hide and seek with mine, revived the force of my distrust.

One thing I discovered, which put me in some doubt. This was an entry on the fly-leaf of a chapbook (one of Patrick Walker's) plainly written in my father's hand and thus conceived:"To my brother Ebenezer on his fifth birthday." Now, what puzzled me was this: That as my father was of course the younger brother, he must either have made some strange error, or he must have written, before he was yet five, an excellent, clear, manly hand of writing.

I tried to get this out of my head; but though I took down many interesting authors, old and new, history, poetry, and story-book, this notion of my father's hand of writing stuck to me; and when at length I went back into the kitchen, and sat down once more to porridge and small beer, the first thing I said to Uncle Ebenezer was to ask him if my father had not been very quick at his book.

"Alexander? No him!" was the reply. "I was far quicker myself; I was a clever chappie when I was young. Why, I could read as soon as he could."

This puzzled me yet more: and a thought coming into my head, I asked if he and my father had been twins.

He jumped upon his stool, and the horn spoon fell out of his hand upon the door, "What gars ye ask that?" he said, and caught me by the breast of the jacket, and looked this time straight into my eyes; his own, which were little and light, and bright like a bird's, blinking and winking strangely.

"What do you mean?" I asked, very calmly, for I was far stronger than he, and not easily frightened. "Take your hand from my jacket. This is no way to behave."

My uncle seemed to make a great effort upon himself. "Dod, man David," he said, "ye shouldnae speak to me about your father. That's where the mistake is." He sat a while and shook, blinking in his plate; "He was all the brother that ever I had," he added, but with no heart in his voice; and then he caught his spoon and fell to supper again, but still shaking.

Now this last passage, this laying of hands upon my person and sudden profession of love for my dead father, went so clean beyond my comprehension that it put me into both fear and hope. On the one hand, I began to think my uncle was perhaps insane and might be dangerous; on the other, there came up into my mind (quite unbidden by me and even discouraged) a story like some ballad I had heard folk singing, of a poor lad that was a rightful heir and a wicked kinsman that tried to keep him from his own. For why should my uncle play a part with a relative that came, almost a beggar, to his door, unless in his heart he had some cause to fear him?

With this notion, all unacknowledged, but nevertheless getting firmly settled in my head, I now began to imitate his covert looks; so that we sat at table like a cat and a mouse, each stealthily observing the other. Not another word had he to say to me, black or white, but was busy turning something secretly over in his mind; and the longer we sat and the more I looked at him, the more certain I became that the something was unfriendly to myself.

When he had cleared the platter, he got out a single pipeful of tobacco, just as in the morning, turned round a stool into the chimney corner, and sat a while smoking, with his back to me.

"Davie," he said at length, "I've been thinking"; then he paused, and said it again. "There's a wee bit siller that I half promised ye before ye were born," he continued; "promised it to your father. Oh, naething legal, ye understand; just gentlemen daffing at their wine. Well, I keepit that bit money separate—it was a great expense, but a promise is a promise—and it has grown by now to be a maitter of just precisely just exactly"—and here he paused and stumbled— "of just exactly forty pounds!" This last he rapped out with a sidelong glance over his shoulder; and the next moment added, almost with a scream, "Scots!"

The pound Scots being the same thing as an English shilling, the difference made by this second thought was considerable; I could see, besides, that the whole story was a lie, invented with some end which it puzzled me to guess; and I made no attempt to conceal the tone of raillery in which I answered—

"Oh, think again, sir! Pounds sterling, I believe!"

"That's what I said," returned my uncle; "pounds sterling! And if you'll step out-by to the door a minute, just to see what kind of a night it is, I'll git it out to ye and call ye in again."

I did his will, smiling to myself in my contempt that he should think I was so easily to be deceived. It was a dark night, with a few stars low down; and as I stood just outside the door, I heard a hollow moaning of wind far off among the hills. I said to myself there was something thundery and changeful in the weather, and little knew of what a vast importance that should prove to me before the evening passed.

When I was called in again, my uncle counted out into my hand seven and thirty golden guinea pieces; the rest was in his hand, in small gold and silver; but his heart failed him there, and he crammed the change into his pocket.

"There," said he, "that'll show you! I'm a queer man, and strange wi' strangers; but my word is my bond, and here's the proof o' it."

Now, my uncle seemed so miserly that I was struck dumb by

this sudden generosity, and could find no words in which to thank him.

"No a word!" said he. "Nae thanks: I want nae thanks. I do my duty; I'm no saying that everybody would have done it; but for my part (though I'm a careful body, too) it's a pleasure to me to do the right by my brother's son; and it's a pleasure to me to think that now we'll agree as such near friends should."

I spoke him in return as handsomely as I was able; but all the while I was wondering what would come next, and why he had parted with his precious guineas; for as to the reason he had given, a baby would have refused it.

Presently, he looked towards me sideways.

"And see here," says he, "tit for tat."

I told him I was ready to prove my gratitude in any reasonable degree, and then waited, looking for some monstrous demand. And yet, when at last he plucked up courage to speak, it was only to tell me (very properly, as I thought) that he was growing old and a little broken, and that he would expect me to help him with the house and the bit garden.

I answered, and expressed my readiness to serve.

"Well," he said, "let's begin." He pulled out of his pocket a rusty key. "There," says he, "there's the key of the stair-tower at the far end of the house. Ye can only win into it from the outside, for that part of the house is no finished. Gang ye in there, and up the stairs, and bring me down the chest that's at the top. There's papers in't," he added.

"Can I have a light, sir?" said I.

"Nae?" said he, very cunningly, "Nae lights in my house."

"Very well, sir," said I. "Are the stairs good?"

"They're grand," said he; and then as I was going, "Keep to the wall," he added; "there's nae banisters. But the stairs are grand under foot."

Out I went into the night. The wind was still moaning in the distance, though never a breath of it came near the house of Shaws. It had fallen blacker than ever; and I was glad to feel along the wall till I came the length of the stair-tower door at the far end of the unfinished wing. I had got the key into the keyhole and had just turned it, when all upon a sudden, without sound of wind or thunder, the whole sky lighted up with wild fire and went black again. I had to put my hand over my eyes to get back to the colour of the darkness; and indeed I was already half blinded when I stepped into the tower.

It was so dark inside, it seemed a body could scarce breathe; but I pushed out with foot and hand, and presently struck the wall with the one, and the lowermost round of the stair with the other. The wall, by the touch, was of fine hewn stone; the steps too, though somewhat steep and narrow, were of polished masonwork, and regular and solid under foot. Minding my uncle's word about the banisters, I kept close to the tower side, and felt my way in the pitch darkness with a beating heart.

The house of Shaws stood some five full storeys high, not counting lofts. Well, as I advanced, it seemed to me the stair grew airier and a thought more lightsome; and I was wondering what might be the cause of this change, when a second blink of the summer lightning came and went. If I did not cry out, it was because fear had me by the throat; and if I did not fall, it was more by Heaven's mercy than my own strength. It was not only that the flash shone in on every side through breaches in the wall, so that I seemed to be clambering aloft upon an open scaffold, but the same passing brightness showed me the steps were of unequal length, and that one of my feet rested that moment within two inches of the well.

This was the grand stair! I thought; and with the thought, a gust of a kind of angry courage came into my heart. My uncle had sent me here, certainly to run great risks, perhaps to die. I swore I would settle that "perhaps", if I should break my neck for it; got me down upon my hands and knees; and as slowly as a snail, feeling before me every inch, and testing the solidity of every stone, I continued to ascend the stair. The darkness, by contrast with the flash, appeared to have redoubled; nor was that all, for my ears were now troubled and my mind confounded by a great stir of bats in the top part of the tower, and the foul beasts, flying downwards, sometimes beat about my face and body.

The tower, I should have said, was square; and in every corner the step was made of a great stone of a different shape, to join the flights. Well, I had come close to one of these turns, when, feeling forward as usual, my hand slipped upon an edge and found nothing but emptiness beyond it. The stair had been carried no higher: to set a stranger mounting it in the darkness was to send him straight to his death; and (although, thanks to the lightning and my own precautions, I was safe enough) the mere thought of the peril in which I might have stood, and the dreadful height I might have fallen, brought out the sweat upon my body and relaxed my joints.

But I knew what I wanted now, and turned and groped my way down again, with a wonderful anger in my heart. About half-way down, the wind sprang up in a clap and shook the tower, and died again; the rain followed; and before I had reached the ground level it fell in buckets. I put out my head into the storm, and looked along towards the kitchen. The door, which I had shut behind me when I left, now stood open, and shed a little, glimmer of light; and I thought I could see a figure standing in the rain, quite still, like a man hearkening. And then there came a blinding flash, which showed me my uncle plainly, just where I had fancied him to stand; and hard upon the heels of it, a great tow-row of thunder.

Now, whether my uncle thought the crash to be the sound of my fall, or whether he heard in it God's voice denouncing murder, I will leave you to guess. Certain it is, at least, that he was seized on by a kind of panic fear, and that he ran into the house and left the door open behind him. I followed as softly as I could, and coming unheard into the kitchen, stood and watched him.

He had found time to open the corner cupboard and bring out a great case bottle of aqua vitae, and now sat with his back towards me at the table. Ever and again he would be seized with a fit of deadly shuddering and groan aloud, and carrying the bottle to his lips, drink down the raw spirits by the mouthful.

I stepped forward, came close behind him where he sat, and suddenly clapping my two hands down upon his shoulders—"Ah!" cried I.

My uncle gave a kind of broken cry like a sheep's bleat, flung up his arms, and tumbled to the floor like a dead man. I was somewhat shocked at this; but I had myself to look to first of all, and did not hesitate to let him lie as he had fallen. The keys were hanging in the cupboard; and it was my design to furnish myself with arms before my uncle should come again to his senses and the power of devising evil: In the cupboard were a few bottles, some apparently of medicine; a great many bills and other papers, which I should willingly enough have rummaged, had I had the time; and a few necessaries, that were nothing to my purpose. Thence I turned to the chests. The first was full of meal; the second of money-bags and papers tied into sheaves; in the third, with many other things (and these for the most part clothes), I found a rusty, ugly-looking Highland dirk without the scabbard. This, then, I concealed inside my waistcoat, and turned to my uncle.

He lay as he had fallen, all huddled, with one knee up and one arm sprawling abroad; his face had a strange colour of blue, and he seemed to have ceased breathing. Fear came on me that he was dead; then I got water and dashed it in his face; and with that he seemed to come a little to himself, working his mouth and fluttering his eyelids. At last he looked up and saw me, and there came into his eyes a terror that was not of this world.

"Come, come," said I, "sit up."

"Are ye alive?" he sobbed. "O man, are ye alive?"

"That am I," said I. "Small thanks to you!"

He had begun to seek for his breath with deep sighs. The blue phial, said he—"in the aumry—the blue phial." His breath came slower still.

I ran to the cupboard, and, sure enough, found there a blue phial of medicine, with the dose written on it on a paper, and this I administered to him with what speed I might.

"It's the trouble," said he, reviving a little; "I have a trouble, Davie. It's my heart."

I set him on a chair and looked at him. It is true I felt some pity for a man that looked so sick, but I was full besides of righteous anger; and I numbered over before him the points on which I wanted explanation: why he lied to me at every word; why he feared that I should leave him; why he disliked it to be hinted that he and my father were twins—"Is that because it is true?" I asked; why he had given me money to which I was convinced I had no claim; and, last of all, why he had tried to kill me. He heard me all through in silence; and then, in a broken voice, begged me to let him go to bed.

"I'll tell ye the morn," he said; "as sure as death I will."

And so weak was he that I could do nothing but consent. I locked him into his room, however, and pocketed the key; and then returning to the kitchen, made up such a blaze as had not shone there for many a long year, and wrapping myself in my plaid, lay down upon the chests and fell asleep.

Chapter 5

I GO TO THE QUEEN'S FERRY

Much rain fell in the night; and the next morning there blew a bitter wintry wind out of the north-west, driving scattered clouds.

For all that, and before the sun began to peep or the last of the stars had vanished, I made my way to the side of the burn, and had a plunge in a deep whirling pool. All aglow from my bath, I sat down once more beside the fire, which I replenished, and began gravely to consider my position.

There was now no doubt about my uncle's enmity; there was no doubt I carried my life in my hand, and he would leave no stone unturned that he might compass my destruction. But I was young and spirited, and like most lads that have been country-bred, I had a great opinion of my shrewdness. I had come to his door no better than a beggar and little more than a child; he had met me with treachery and violence; it would be a fine consummation to take the upper hand, and drive him like a herd of sheep.

I sat there nursing my knee and smiling at the fire; and I saw myself in fancy smell out his secrets one after another, and grow to be that man's king and ruler. The warlock of Essendean, they say, had made a mirror in which men could read the future; it must have been of other stuff than burning coal; for in all the shapes and pictures that I sat and gazed at, there was never a ship, never a seaman with a hairy cap, never a big bludgeon for my silly head, or the least sign of all those tribulations that were ripe to fall on me.

Presently, all swollen with conceit, I went upstairs and gave my prisoner his liberty. He gave me good morning civilly; and I gave the same to him, smiling down upon him from the heights of my sufficiency. Soon we were set to breakfast, as it might have been the day before. "Well, sir," said I, with a jeering tone, "have you nothing more to say to me?" And then, as he made no articulate reply, "It will be time, I think, to understand each other," I continued. "You took me for a country Johnnie Raw, with no more mother-wit or courage than a porridge-stick. I took you for a good man, or no worse than others at the least. It seems we were both wrong. What cause you have to fear me, to cheat me, and to attempt my life—"

He murmured something about a jest, and that he liked a bit of fun; and then, seeing me smile, changed his tone, and assured me he would make all clear as soon as we had breakfasted. I saw by his face that he had no lie ready for me, though he was hard at work preparing one; and I think I was about to tell him so, when we were interrupted by a knocking at the door.

Bidding my uncle sit where he was, I went to open it, and found on the doorstep a half-grown boy in sea-clothes. He had no sooner seen me that he began to dance some steps of the sea-hornpipe (which I had never before heard of, far less seen), snapping his fingers in the air and footing it right cleverly. For all that, he was blue with the cold; and there was something in his face, a look between tears and laughter, that was highly pathetic and consisted ill with this gaity of manner. "What cheer, mate?" says he, with a cracked voice.

I asked him soberly to name his business.

"Oh, pleasure!" says he; and then began to sing:

"For it's my delight, of a shiny night,
In the season of the year."

"Well," said I, "If you have no business at all, I will even be so unmannerly as to shut you out."

"Stay, brother!" he cried. "Have you no fun about you? or do you want to get me thrashed? I've brought a letter from old Heasyoasy to Mr Belflower." He showed me a letter as he spoke. "And I say, mate," he added, "I'm mortal hungry."

"Well," said I, "come into the house, and you shall have a bite if I go empty for it."

With that I brought him in and set him down to my own place, where he fell-to greedily on the remains of breakfast, winking to me between whiles, and making many faces, which I think the poor soul considered manly.

Meanwhile, my uncle had read the letter and sat thinking; then, suddenly, he got to his feet with a great air of liveliness, and pulled me apart into the farthest corner of the room.

"Read that," said he, and put the letter in my hand.

Here it is, lying before me as I write:

The Hawes Inn, at the Queen's Ferry.

SIR.—I lie here with my hawser up and down, and send my cabin-boy to informe. If you have any further commands for over-seas, to-day will be the last occasion, as the wind will serve us well out of the firth. I will not seek to deny that I have had crosses with your doer, Mr Rankeillor; of which, if not speedily redd up, you may looke to see some losses follow. I have drawn a bill upon you, as per margin, and am, sir, your most obedt, humble servant,

Elias Hoseason

"You see, Davie," resumed my uncle, as soon as he saw that I had done,"I have a venture with this man Hoseason, the captain of a trading brig, the *Covenant*, of Dysart. Now, if you and me was to walk over with yon lad, I could see the captain at the Hawes, or maybe on board the *Covenant*, if there was papers to be signed; and so far from a loss of time, we can jog on to the lawyer, Mr Rankeillor's. After a' that's come and gone, ye would be swier to believe me upon my naked word; but ye'll believe Rankeillor. He's factor to half the gentry in these parts; an auld man, forby: highly respeckit; and he kenned your father."

I stood awhile and thought. I was going to some place of shipping, which was doubtless populous, and where my uncle durst attempt no violence, and, indeed, even the society of the cabin-boy so far protected me. Once there, I believed I could force on the visit to the lawyer, even if my uncle were now insincere in proposing it; and perhaps, in the bottom of my heart, I wished a nearer view of the sea and ships. You are to remember I had lived all my life in the inland hills, and just two days before had my first sight of the firth lying like a blue door, and the sailed ships moving on the face of it, no bigger than toys. One thing with another, I made up my mind.

"Very well," says I, "let us go to the Ferry."

My uncle got into his hat and coat, and buckled an old rusty cutlass on; and then we trod the fire out, locked the door, and set forth upon our walk.

The wind, being in that cold quarter, the north-west, blew nearly in our faces as we went. It was the month of June; the grass was all white with daisies and the trees with blossom; but, to judge by our blue nails and aching wrists, the time might have been winter and the whiteness a December frost.

Uncle Ebenezer trudged in the ditch, jogging from side to side like an old ploughman coming home from work. He never said a word the whole way; and I was thrown for talk on the cabin-boy. He told me his name was Ransome, and that he had followed the sea since he was nine, but could not say how old he was, as he had lost his reckoning. He showed me tattoo marks, baring his breast in the teeth of the wind and in spite of my remonstrances, for I thought it was enough to kill him; he swore horribly whenever he remembered, but more like a silly schoolboy than a man; and boasted of many wild and bad things that he had done: stealthy thefts, false accusations, ay, and even murder; but all with such a dearth of likelihood in the details, and such a weak and crazy swagger in the delivery, as disposed me rather to pity than to believe him.

I asked him of the brig (which he declared was the finest ship that sailed and of Captain Hoseason, in whose praise he was equally loud. Heasy-oasy (for so he still named the skipper) was a man, by his account, that minded for nothing either in heaven or earth; one that, as people said, would "crack on all sail into the day of judgement; rough, fierce, unscrupulous, and brutal;" and all this my poor cabin-boy had taught himself to admire as something seamanlike and manly. He would only admit one flaw in his idol."He ain't no seaman," he admitted. "That's Mr Shuan that navigates the brig; he's the finest seaman in the trade, only for drink; and I tell you I believe it! Why, look 'ere"; and turning down his stocking, he showed me a great, raw, red wound that made my blood run cold."He done that—Mr Shuan done it," he said, with an air of pride.

"What!" I cried, "do you take such savage usage at his hands? Why, you are no slave, to be so handled!"

"No," said the poor moon-calf, changing his tune at once, "and so he'll find! See 'ere"; and he showed me a great case-knife, which he told me was stolen. "Oh," says he, "let me see him try; I dare him to; I'll do for him! Oh, he ain't the first!" And he confirmed it with a poor, silly, ugly oath.

I have never felt such pity for anyone in this wide world as I felt for that half-witted creature; and it began to come over me that the brig *Covenant* (for all her pious name) was little better than a hell upon the seas. "Have you no friends?" said I.

He said he had a father in some English seaport, I forget which. "He was a fine man, too," he said; "but he's dead."

"In Heaven's name," cried I, "can you find no reputable life on shore?"

"Oh, no," says he, winking and looking very sly; "they would put me to a trade. I know a trick worth two of that, I do!"

I asked him what trade could be so dreadful as the one he followed, where he ran the continual peril of his life, not alone from wind and sea, but the horrid cruelty of those who were his masters. He said it was very true; and then began to praise the life, and tell what a pleasure it was to get on shore with money in his pocket, and spend it like a man, and buy apples, and swagger, and surprise what he called stick-in-the-mud boys. "And then it's not all as bad as that," says he; "there's worse off than me: there's the twenty-pounders. Oh, laws! you should see them taking on. Why, I've seen a man as old as you, I dessay"—(to him I seemed old)—"ah, and he had a beard too,—well, and as soon as we cleared out of the river, and he had the drug out of his head—my how he cried and carried on I made a fine fool of hun, I tell you! And then there's little uns,-too; oh, little by me! I tell you, I keep them in order. When we carry little uns, I have a rope's end of my own to wollop 'em." And so he ran on, until it came in on me that what he meant by twenty-pounders were those unhappy criminals who were sent over-seas to slavery in North America, or the still more unhappy innocents who were kidnapped or trepanned (as the word went) for private interest or vengeance.

Just then we came to the top of the hill, and looked down on the Ferry and the Hope. The Firth of Forth (as is very well known) narrows at this point to the width of a good-sized river, which makes a convenient ferry going north, and turns the upper reach into a land-locked haven for all manner of ships. Right in the midst of the narrows lies an islet with some ruins; on the south shore they have built a pier for the service of the Ferry; and at the end of the pier, on the other side of the road, and backed against a pretty garden of holly-trees and hawthorns, I could see the building which they call the Hawes Inn.

The town of Queensferry lies farther west, and the neighbourhood of the inn looked pretty lonely at that time of day, for the boat had just gone north with passengers. A skiff, however, lay beside the pier, with some seamen sleeping on the thwarts; this, as Ransome told me, was the brig's boat waiting for the captain; and about half a mile off, and all alone in the anchorage, he showed me the *Covenant* herself. There was a sea-going bustle on board; yards were swinging into place; and as the wind blew from that quarter, I could hear the song of the sailors as they pulled upon the ropes. After all I had listened to upon the way, I looked at that ship with an extreme abhorrence; and from the bottom of my heart I pitied all poor souls that were condemned to sail in her.

We had all three pulled up on the brow of the hill; and now I marched across the road and addressed my uncle. "I think it right to tell you, sir," says I; "there's nothing that will bring me on board that *Covenant*."

He seemed to waken from a dream. "Eh?" he said. "What's that?"

I told him over again.

"Well, well," he said, "we'll have to please ye, I suppose. But what are we standing here for? It's perishing cold; and if I'm no mistaken, they're busking the *Covenant* for sea."

Chapter 6

WHAT BEFELL AT THE QUEEN'S FERRY

As soon as we came to the inn, Ransome led us up the stair to a small room, with a bed in it, and heated like an oven by a great fire of coal.

At a table hard by the chimney, a tall, dark, sober-looking man sat writing. In spite of the heat of the room, he wore a thick sea-jacket, buttoned up to the neck, and a tall hairy cap drawn down over his ears; yet I never saw any man, not even a judge upon the bench, look cooler, or more studious and self-possessed, than this ship-captain.

He got to his feet at once, and coming forward, offered his large hand to Ebenezer.

"I am proud to see you, Mr Balfour," said he, in a fine deep voice, "and glad that ye are here in time. The wind's fair, and the tide upon the turn; we'll see the old coal-bucket burning on the Isle of May before tonight."

"Captain Hoseason," returned my uncle, "you keep your room unco hot."

"It's a habit I have, Mr Balfour," said the skipper. "I'm a cold-rife man by my nature; I have a cold blood, sir. There's neither fur, nor flannel—no, sir, nor hot rum, will warm up what they call the temperature. Sir, it's the same with most men that have been carbonadoed, as they call it, in the tropic seas."

"Well, well, captain," replied my uncle, "we must all be the way we're made."

But it chanced that this fancy of the captain's had a great share in my misfortunes. For though I had promised myself not to let my kinsman out of sight, I was both so impatient for a nearer look at the sea, and so sickened by the closeness of the room, that when he told me to "run downstairs and play by myself awhile", I was fool enough to take him at his word.

Away I went, therefore, leaving the two men sitting down to a bottle and a great mass of papers; and crossing the road in front of the inn, walked down upon the beach. With the wind in that quarter, only little wavelets, not much bigger than I had seen upon a lake, beat upon the shore. But the weeds were new to me—some green, some brown and long, and some with little bladders that cracked between my fingers. Even so far up the firth, the smell of the sea water was exceedingly salt and stirring; the *Covenant*, besides, was beginning to shake out her sails, which hung upon the yards in clusters, and the spirit of all that I beheld put me in thoughts of far voyages and foreign places.

I looked, too, at the seamen with the skiff—big brown fellows, some in shirts, some with jackets, some with coloured handkerchiefs about their throats, one with a brace of pistols stuck into his pockets, two or three with knotty bludgeons, and all with their case-knives. I passed the time of day with one that looked less desperate than his fellows, and asked him of the sailing of the brig. He said they would get under way as soon as the ebb set, and expressed his gladness to be out of port where there were no taverns and fiddlers; but all with such horrifying oaths, that I made haste to get away from him.

This threw me back on Ransome, who seemed the least wicked of that gang, and who soon came out of the inn and ran to me, crying for a bowl of punch. I told him I would give him no such thing, for neither he nor I was of an age for such indulgences. "But a glass of ale you may have, and welcome," said I. He mopped and mowed at me, and called me names; but he was glad to get the ale, for all that; and presently we were set down at a table in the front room of the inn, and both eating and drinking with a good appetite.

Here it occurred to me that, as the landlord was a man of that county, I might do well to make a friend of him. I offered him a share, as was much the custom in these days; and he was far too great a man to sit with such poor customers as Ransome and myself, and he was leaving the room, when I called him back to ask if he knew Mr Rankeillor.

"Hoot, ay," says he, "and a very honest man. And, oh, by the by," says he, "was it you that came in with Ebenezer?" And when I had told him yes, "Ye'll be no friend of his?" he asked, meaning, in the Scottish way, that I would be no relative.

I told him no, none.

"I thought not," said he, "and yet ye have a kind of gliff of Mr Alexander."

I said it seemed that Ebenezer was ill-seen in the country.

"Nae doubt," said the landlord. "He's a wicked auld man, and there's many would like to see him girning in a tow: Jennet Clouston and mony mair that he has harried out of house and hame. And yet he was ance a fine young fellow, too. But that was before the sough gaed abroad about Mr Alexander; that was like the death of him."

"And what was it?" I asked.

"Ou, just that he had killed him," said the landlord. "Did ye never hear that?"

"And what would he kill him for?" said I.

"And what for, but just to get the place," said he.

"The place?" said I, "The Shaws?"

"Nae other place that I ken," said he.

"Is that so?" said I. "Was my—was Alexander the eldest son?"

"Deed was he," said the landlord. "What else would he have killed him for?"

And with that he went away, as he had wished to all along.

Of course, I had guessed it a long while ago; but it is one thing to guess, another to know; and I sat stunned with my good fortune, and could scarce grow to believe that the same poor lad who had trudged in the dust from Ettrick Forest not two days ago, was now one of the rich of the earth, and had a house and broad lands, and if he but knew how to ride, might mount his horse tomorrow. All these pleasant things, and a thousand others, crowded into my mind, as I sat staring before me out of the inn window, and paying no heed to what I saw; only I remember that my eye lighted on Captain Hoseason down on the pier among his seamen, and speaking with authority. Presently he came marching back towards the house, with no mark of a sailor's clumsiness, but carrying his fine, tall figure with a manly bearing, and still with the same sober, grave expression on his face. I wondered if it was possible that Ransome's stories could be true, and half disbelieved them; they fitted so ill with the man's looks. But indeed, he was neither so good as I supposed him, nor quite so bad as Ransome did; for, in fact, he was two men, and left the better one behind as soon as he set foot on board his vessel.

The next thing, I heard my uncle calling for me, and found the pair in the road together. It was the sea-captain who addressed me, and that with an air (very flattering to a young lad) of grave equality.

"Sir," said he, "Mr Balfour tells me great things of you; and for my own part, I like your looks. I wish I was for longer here, that we might make the better friends; but we'll make the most of what we have. Ye shall come on board my brig for half an hour, till the ebb sets, and drink a bowl with me."

Now, I longed to see the inside of a ship more than words can tell; but I was not going to put myself in jeopardy, and I told him my uncle and I had an appointment with a lawyer.

"Ay, ay," said he, "he passed me word of that. But, ye see, the boat'll set ye ashore at the town pier, and that's but a penny stone-cast from Rankeillor's house." And here he suddenly leaned down and whispered in my ear; "Take care of the old tod; he means mischief. Come aboard till I can get a word with ye." And then, passing his arm through mine, he continued aloud, as he set off towards his boat: "But come, what can I bring ye from the Carolinas? Any friend of Mr Balfour's can command. A roll of tobacco? Indian featherwork? a skin of a wild beast? a stone pipe? the mocking-bird that mews for all the world like a cat? the cardinal bird that is as red as blood?—take your pick and say your pleasure."

By this time we were at the boat-side, and he was handing me in. I did not dream of hanging back; I thought (the poor fool!) that I had found a good friend and helper, and I was rejoiced to see the ship. As soon as we were all set in our places, the boat was thrust off from the pier and began to move over the waters; and what with my pleasure in this new movement and my surprise at our low position, and the appearance of the shores, and the growing bigness of the brig as we drew near to it, I could hardly understand what the captain said, and must have answered him at random.

As soon as we were alongside (where I sat fairly gaping at the ship's height, the strong humming of the tide against its sides, and the pleasant cries of the seamen at their work) Hoseason, declaring that he and I must be the first aboard, ordered a tackle to be sent down from the mainyard. In this I was whipped into the air and set down again on the deck, where the captain stood ready waiting for me, and instantly slipped back his arm under mine. There I stood some while, a little dizzy with the unsteadiness of all around me, perhaps a little afraid, and yet vastly pleased with these strange sights; the captain meanwhile pointing out the strangest, and telling me their names and uses.

"But where is my uncle?" said I, suddenly.

"Ay," said Hoseason, with a sudden grimness, "that's the point."

I felt I was lost. With all my strength I plucked myself clear of him and ran to the bulwarks. Sure enough, there was the boat pulling for the town, with my uncle sitting in the stern. I gave a piercing cry—"Help, help! Murder!"—so that both sides of the anchorage rang with it, and my uncle turned round where he was sitting, and showed me a face full of cruelty and terror.

It was the last I saw. Already strong hands had been plucking me back from the ship's side; and now a thunderbolt seemed to strike me; I saw a great flash of fire, and fell senseless.

CHAPTER 7

I GO TO SEA IN THE BRIG *COVENANT* OF DYSART

I came to myself in darkness, in great pain, bound hand and foot, and deafened by many unfamiliar noises. There sounded in my ears a roaring of water as of a huge milldam; the thrashing of heavy sprays, the thundering of the sails, and the shrill cries of seamen. The whole world now heaved giddily up, and now rushed giddily downward; and so sick and hurt was I in body, and my mind so much confounded, that it took me a long while, chasing my thoughts up and down, and ever stunned again by a fresh stab of pain, to realize that I must be lying somewhere bound in the belly of that unlucky ship, and that the wind must have strengthened to a gale. With the clear perception of my plight, there fell upon, me a blackness of despair, a horror of remorse at my own folly, and a passion of anger at my uncle, that once more bereft me of my senses.

When I returned again to life, the same uproar, the same confused and violent movements, shook and deafened me; and presently, to my other pains and distresses, there was added the sickness of an unused landsman on the sea. In that time of my adventurous youth, I suffered many hardships; but none that was so crushing to my mind and body, or lit by so few hopes, as these first hours on board the brig.

I heard a gun fire, and supposed the storm had proved too strong for us, and we were firing signals of distress. The thought of deliverance, even by death in the deep sea, was welcome to me. Yet it was no such matter; but (as I was afterwards told) a common habit of the captain's, which I here set down to show that even the worst man may have his kindlier sides. We were then passing, it appeared, within some miles of Dysart, where the brig was built, and where old Mrs Hoseason, the captain's mother, had come some years before to live; and whether outward or inward bound, the *Covenant;* was never suffered to go by that place by day without a gun fired and colours shown.

I had no measure of time; day and night were alike in that ill-smelling cavern of the ship's bowels where I lay; and the misery of my situation drew out the hours to double. How long, therefore, I lay waiting to hear the ship split upon some rock, or to feel her reel head foremost into the depths of the sea, I have not the means of computation. But sleep at length stole from me the consciousness of sorrow.

I was awakened by the light of a hand-lantern shining in my face. A small man of about thirty, with green eyes and a tangle of fair hair, stood looking down at me.

"Well," said he, "how goes it?"

I answered by a sob; and my visitor then felt my pulse and temples, and set himself to wash and dress the wound upon my scalp.

"Ay," said he, "a sore dunt. What, man? Cheer up! The world's no done; you've made a bad start of it, but you'll make a better. Have you had any meat?"

I said I could not look at it; and thereupon he gave me some brandy and water in a tin pannikin, and left me once more to myself.

The next time he came to see me, I was lying betwixt sleep and waking, my eyes wide open in the darkness, the sickness quite departed, but succeeded by a horrid giddiness and swimming that was almost worse to bear. I ached, besides, in every limb, and the cords that bound me seemed to be on fire. The smell of the hole in which I lay seemed to have become a part of me; and during the long interval since his last visit I had suffered tortures of fear, now from the scurrying of the ship's rats, that sometimes pattered on my very face, and now from the dismal imaginings that haunt the bed of fever.

The glimmer of the lantern, as a trap opened, shone in like the heaven's sunlight; and though it only showed me the strong, dark beams of the ship that was my prison, I could have cried aloud for gladness.

The man with the green eyes was the first to descend the ladder, and I noticed that he came somewhat unsteadily. He was followed by the captain. Neither said a word; but the first set to and examined me, and dressed my wound as before, while Hoseason looked me in my face with an odd, black look.

"Now, sir, you see for yourself," said the first: "a high fever, no appetite, no light, no meat, you see for yourself precisely what that means."

"I am no conjurer, Mr Riach," said the captain.

"Give me leave, sir," said Riach; "you've a good head upon your shoulders, and a good Scotch tongue to ask with; but I will leave you no manner of excuse; I want that boy taken out of this hole and put in the forecastle."

"What ye may want, sir, is a matter of concern to nobody but yoursel'," returned the captain; "but I can tell ye that which is to be. Here he is; here he shall bide."

"Admitting that you have been paid in a proportion," said the other, "I will crave leave humbly to say that I have not. Paid I am, and none too much, to be the second officer of this old tub; and you ken very well if I do my best to earn it. But I was paid for nothing more."

"If ye could hold back your hand from the tin-pan, Mr Riach, I would have no complaint to make of ye," returned the skipper; "and instead of asking riddles, I make bold to say that ye would keep your breath to cool your porridge. We'll be required on deck," he added, in a sharper note, and set one foot upon the ladder.

But Mr Riach caught him by the sleeve.

"Admitting that you have been paid to do a murder—" he began.

Hoseason turned upon him with a flash.

"What's that?" he cried. What kind of talk is that?"

"It seems it is the talk that you can understand," said Mr Riach, looking him steadily in the face.

"Mr Riach, I have sailed with ye three cruises," replied the captain. "In all that time, sir, ye should have learned to know me;

I'm a stiff man, and a dour man; but for what ye say now—fie, fie—it comes from a bad heart and a black conscience. If ye say the lad will die—"

"Ay, will he!" said Mr Riach.

"Well, sir, is not that enough?" said Hoseason. "Flit him where ye please! "

Thereupon the captain ascended the ladder; and I, who had lain silent throughout this strange conversation, beheld Mr Riach turn after him and bow as low as to his knees in what was plainly a spirit of derision. Even in my then state of sickness, I perceived two things; that the mate was touched with liquor, as the captain hinted, and that (drunk or sober) he was like to prove a valuable friend.

Five minutes afterwards my bonds were cut, I was hoisted on a man's back, carried up to the forecastle, and laid in a bunk on some sea-blankets; where the first thing that I did was to lose my senses.

It was a blessed thing indeed to open my eyes again upon the daylight, and to find myself in the society of men. The forecastle was a roomy place enough, set all about with berths, in which the men of the watch below were seated smoking, or lying down asleep. The day being calm and the wind fair, the scuttle was open, and not only the good daylight, but from time to time (as the ship rolled) a dusty beam of sunlight shone in, and dazzled and delighted me. I had no sooner moved, moreover, than one of the men brought me a drink of something healing which Mr Riach had prepared, and bade me lie still and I should soon be well again. There were no bones broken, he explained: "A clout on the head was naething. Man," said he, "it was me that gave it ye!"

Here I lay for the space of many days a close prisoner, and not only got my health again, but came to know my companions. They were a rough lot indeed, as sailors mostly are; being men rooted out of all the kindly parts of life, and condemned to toss together on the rough seas, with masters no less cruel. There were some among them that had sailed with the pirates and seen things it would be a shame even to speak of; some were men that had run from the king's ships, and went with a halter round their necks, of which they made no secret; and all, as the saying goes, were "at a word and a blow" with their best friends. Yet I had not been many days shut up with them before I began to be ashamed of my first judgement, when I had drawn away from them at the Ferry pier, as though they had been unclean beasts.

No class of man is altogether bad; but each has its own faults and virtues; and these shipmates of mine were no exception to the rule. Rough they were, sure enough; and bad, I suppose; but they had many virtues. They were kind when it occurred to them, simple even beyond the simplicity of a country lad like me, and had some glimmerings of honesty.

There was one man of maybe forty, that would sit on my berth-side for hours, and tell me of his wife and child. He was a fisher that had lost his boat, and thus been driven to the deep-sea voyaging. Well, it is years ago now: but I have never forgotten him. His wife (who was "young by him", as he often told me) waited in vain to see her man return; he would never again make the fire for her in the morning, nor yet keep the bairn when she was sick. Indeed, many of these poor fellows (as the event proved) were upon their last cruise; the deep seas and cannibal fish received them; and it is a thankless business to speak ill of the dead.

Among other good deeds that they did, they returned my money, which had been shared among them; and though it was about a third short, I was very glad to get it, and hoped great good from it in the land I was going to. The ship was bound for the Carolinas; and you must not suppose that I was going to that place merely as an exile. The trade was even then much depressed; since that, and with the rebellion of the colonies and the formation of the United States, it has, of course, come to an end; but in these days of my youth, white men were still sold into slavery on the plantations, and that was the destiny to which my wicked uncle had condemned me.

The cabin-boy Ransome (from whom I had first heard of these atrocities) came in at times from the round-house, where he berthed and served, now nursing a bruised limb in silent agony, now raving against the cruelty of Mr Shuan. It made my heart bleed; but the men had a great respect for the chief mate, who was, as they said, "the only seaman of the whole jing-bang, and none such a bad man when he was sober." Indeed, I found there was a strange peculiarity about our two mates: that Mr Riach was sullen, unkind, and harsh when he was sober, and Mr Shuan would not hurt a fly except when he was drinking. I asked about the captain: but I was told drink made no difference upon that man of iron.

I did my best in the small time allowed me to make something like a man, or rather I should say something like a boy, of the poor creature, Ransome. But his mind was scarce truly human. He could remember nothing of the time before he came to sea; only that his father had made docks, and had a starling in the parlour, which could whistle "The North Countrie"; all else had been blotted out in these years of hardship and cruelties. He had a strange notion of the dry land, picked up from sailors' stories: that it was a place where lads were put to some kind of slavery called a trade, and where apprentices were continually lashed and clapped into foul prisons. In a town, he thought every second person a decoy, and every third house a place in which seamen would be drugged and murdered. To be sure, I could tell him how kindly I had myself been used upon that dry land he was so much afraid of, and how well fed and carefully taught both by my friends and my parents: and if he had been recently hurt, he would weep bitterly and swear to run away; but if he was in his usual crackbrain humour or (still more) if he had had a glass of spirits in the round-house, he would deride the notion.

It was Mr Riach (Heaven forgive him!) who gave the boy drink; and it was, doubtless, kindly meant; but besides that it was ruin to his health, it was the pitifullest thing in life to see this unhappy, unfriended creature staggering, and dancing, and talking he knew not what. Some of the men laughed, but not all; others would grow as black as thunder (thinking, perhaps, of their own childhood or their own children) and bid him stop that nonsense, and think what he was doing. As for me, I felt ashamed to look at him, and the poor child still comes about me in my dreams.

All this time, you should know, the *Covenant* was meeting continuous head-winds and tumbling up and down against head-seas, so that the scuttle was almost constantly shut, and the forecastle lighted only by a swinging lantern on a beam. There was constant labour for all hands; the sails had to be made and shortened every hour; the strain told on the men's temper; there was a growl of quarrelling all day long from berth to berth; and as I was never allowed to set my foot on deck, you can picture to yourselves how weary of my life I grew to be, and how impatient for a change.

And a change I was to get, as you shall hear; but I must first tell of a conversation I had with Mr Riach, which put a little heart in me to bear my troubles. Getting him in a favourable stage of drink (for indeed he never looked near me when he was sober) I pledged him to secrecy, and told him my whole story.

He declared it was like a ballad; that he would do his best to help me; that I should have paper, pen, and ink, and write one line to Mr Campbell and another to Mr Rankeillor; and that if I told the truth, ten to one he would be able (with their help) to pull me through and set me in my rights.

"And in the meantime", says he, "keep your heart up. You're not the only one, I'll tell you that. There's many a man hoeing tobacco over-seas that should be mounting his horse at his own door at home; many and many! And life is all a variorum, at the best. Look at me: I'm a laird's son and more than half a doctor, and here I am, man-Jack to Hoseason!"

I thought it would be civil to ask him for his story.

He whistled loud.

"Never had one," said he. "I liked fun, that's all." And he skipped out of the forecastle.

Chapter 8

THE ROUND-HOUSE

One night, about nine o'clock, a man of Mr Riach's watch (which was on deck) came down for his jacket; and instantly there began to go a whisper about the forecastle that "Shuan had done for him at last".

There was no need to give the name; we all knew who was meant; but we had scarce time to get the idea rightly in our heads, far less to speak of it, when the scuttle was again flung wide open, and Captain Hoseason came down the ladder. He looked sharply round the bunks in the tossing light of the lantern; and then, walking straight up to me, he addressed me, to my great surprise, in tones of some kindness.

"My man," said he, "we want ye to serve in the round-house. You and Ransome are to change berths. Run away aft with ye."

Even as he spoke, two seamen appeared in the scuttle, carrying Ransome in their arms; and the ship at that moment giving a great sheer into the sea, and the lantern swinging, the light fell direct on the boy's face. It was as white as wax, and had a look upon it like a dreadful smile.The blood in me ran cold, and I drew in my breath as if I had been struck.

"Run away aft; run away aft with ye!" cried Hoseason.

And at that I brushed by the sailors and the boy (who neither spoke nor moved), and ran up the ladder on deck.

The brig was sheering swiftly and giddily through a long, cresting swell. She was on the starboard tack, and on the left hand, under the arched foot of the foresail, I could see the sunset still quite bright. This, at such an hour of the night, surprised me greatly; but I was too ignorant to draw the true conclusion—that we were going north-about round Scotland, and were now on the high sea between the Orkney and the Shetland Islands, having avoided the dangerous currents of the Pentland Firth. For my part, who had been so long shut in the dark and knew nothing of head-winds, I thought we might be half-way or more across the Atlantic. And indeed (beyond that I wondered a little at the lateness of the sunset light) I gave no heed to it, and pushed on across the decks, running between the seas, catching at ropes, and only saved from going overboard by one of the hands on deck, who had been always kind to me.

The round-house, for which I was bound, and where I was now to sleep and serve, stood some six feet above the decks, and considering the size of the brig, was of good dimensions. Inside were a fixed table and bench, and two berths, one for the captain and the other for the two mates, turn and turn about. It was all fitted with lockers from top to bottom, so as to stow away the officers' belongings and a part of the ship's stores; there was a second storeroom underneath, which you entered by a hatchway in the middle of the deck; indeed, all the best of the meat and drink and the whole of the powder were collected in this place; and all the firearms, except the two pieces of brass ordnance, were set in a rack in the aftermost wall of the round-house. The most of the cutlasses were in another place.

A small window with a shutter on each side, and a skylight in the roof, gave it light by day; and after dark, there was a lamp always burning. It was burning when I entered, not brightly, but enough to show Mr Shuan sitting at the table, with the brandy bottle and a tin pannikin in front of him. He was a tall man, strongly made and very black; and he stared before him on the wooden table like one dazed and stupid.

He took no notice of my coming in; nor did he move when the captain followed and leant on the berth beside me, looking darkly at the mate.

I stood in great fear of Hoseason, and had my reasons for it;

but something told me I need not be afraid of him just then; and I whispered in his ear, "How is he?"

He shook his dark head like one that does not know and does not wish to think, and his face was grim and very stern in the lamplight.

Presently Mr Riach came in. He gave the captain a glance that meant the boy was dead as plain as speaking, and took his place like the rest of us; so that we all three stood without a word, staring down at Mr Shuan, and Mr Shuan (on his side) sat without a word, looking hard upon the table.

All of a sudden he put out his hand to take the bottle; and at that Mr Riach started forward and caught it away from him, rather by surprise than violence, crying out, with an oath, that there had been too much of this work altogether, and that a judgement would fall upon the ship. And as he spoke (the weather sliding-doors standing open) he tossed the bottle into the sea.

Mr Shuan was on his feet in a trice; he still looked dazed, but he meant murder, ay, and would have done it, for the second time that night, had not the captain stepped in between him and his victim.

"Sit down!" roars the captain. "Ye sot and swine, do ye know what ye've done? Ye've murdered the boy!"

Mr Shuan seemed to understand; for he sat down again and put up his hand to his brow.

"Well," he said, "he brought me a dirty pannikin!"

At that word, the captain and I and Mr Riach all looked at each other for a second with a kind of frightened look; and then Hoseason walked up to his chief officer, took him by the shoulder, led him across to his bunk, and bade him lie down and go to sleep, as you might speak to a bad child. The murderer cried a little, but he took off his sea-boots and obeyed.

"Ah!" cried Mr Riach, with a dreadful voice, "ye should have interfered long syne. It's too late now."

"Mr Riach," said the captain, "this night's work must never be kennt in Dysart. The boy went overboard, sir; that's what the story is; and I would give five pounds out of my pocket it was true!" He turned to the table. "What made ye throw the good bottle away?" he added. "There was nae sense in that, sir. Here, David, draw me another. They're in the bottom locker"; and he tossed me a key. "Ye'll need a glass yourself, sir," he added, to Riach. "Yon was an ugly thing to see."

So the pair sat down and hob-a-nobbed; and while they did so, the murderer, who had been lying and whimpering in his berth, raised himself upon his elbow and looked at them and at me.

That was the first night of my new duties; and in the course of the next day I had got well into the run of them. I had to serve at the meals, which the captain took at regular hours, sitting down with the officer who was off duty; all the day through I would be running with a dram to one or other of my three masters; and at night I slept on a blanket thrown on the deck boards at the aftermost end of the round-house, and right in the draught of the two doors. It was a hard and a cold bed; nor was I suffered to sleep without interruption; for some one would be always coming in from deck to get a dram, and when a fresh watch was to be set, two and sometimes all three would sit down and brew a bowl together. How they kept their health, I know not, any more than how I kept my own.

And yet in other ways it was an easy service. There was no cloth to lay; the meals were either of oatmeal porridge or salt junk, except twice a week, when there was duff; and though I was clumsy enough and (not being firm on my sea-legs) sometimes fell with what I was bringing them, both Mr Riach and the captain were singularly patient. I could not but fancy they were making up lee-way with their consciences, and that they would scarce have been so good with me if they had not been worse with Ransome.

As for Mr Shuan, the drink, or his crime, or the two together, had certainly troubled his mind. I cannot say I ever saw him in his proper wits. He never grew used to my being there, stared at me continually (sometimes, I could have thought, with terror) and more than once drew back from my hand when I was serving him. I was pretty sure from the first that he had no clear mind of what he had done, and on my second day in the round-house I had proof of it. We were alone, and he had been staring at me a long time, when, all at once, up he got, as pale as death, and came close up to me, to my great terror. But I had no cause to be afraid of him.

"You were not here before?" he asked.

"No sir," said I.

"There was another boy?" he asked again; and when I had answered him, "Ah!" says he, "I thought that," and went and sat down, without another word, except to call for brandy.

You may think it strange, but for all the horror I had, I was still sorry for him. He was a married man, with a wife in Leith; but whether or no he had a family, I have now forgotten; I hope not.

Altogether it was no very hard life for the time it lasted, which (as you are to hear) was not long. I was as well fed as the best of them; even their pickles, which were the great dainty, I was allowed my share of; and had I liked, I might have been drunk from morning to night, like Mr Shuan. I had company, too, and good company of its sort. Mr Riach, who had been to the college, spoke to me like a friend when he was not sulking, and told me many curious things, and some that were informing; and even the captain, though he kept me at the stick's end the most part of the time, would sometimes unbuckle a bit, and tell me of the fine countries he had visited.

The shadow of poor Ransome, to be sure, lay on all four of us, and on me and Mr Shuan, in particular, most heavily. And then I had another trouble of my own. Here I was, doing dirty work for three men that I looked down upon, and one of whom, at least, should have hung upon a gallows; that was for the present; and as for the future, I could only see myself slaving alongside of negroes in the tobacco field. Mr Riach, perhaps from caution, would never suffer me to say another word about my story; the captain, whom I tried to approach, rebuffed me like a dog and would not hear a word; and as the days came and went, my heart sank lower and lower, till I was even glad of the work which kept me from thinking.

CHAPTER 9

THE MAN WITH THE BELT OF GOLD

More than a week went by, in which the ill-luck that had pursued the *Covenant* upon this voyage grew yet more strongly marked. Some days she made a little way; others, she was even driven back. At last we were beaten so far to the south that we tossed and tacked to and fro the whole of the ninth day, within sight of Cape Wrath and the wild, rocky coast on either hand of it. There followed a council of officers, and some decision which I did not understand, seeing only the result: that we had made a fair wind of a foul one and were running south. The tenth afternoon, there was a falling swell and a thick, wet, white fog that hid one end of the brig from the other. All afternoon, when I went on deck, I saw men and officers listening hard over the bulwarks—"for breakers", they said; and though I did not understand the word, I felt danger in the air, and was excited.

Maybe about ten at night, I was serving Mr Riach and the captain at their supper, when the ship struck something with a great sound, and we heard voices singing out. My two masters leaped to their feet.

"She's struck," said Mr Riach.

"No, sir," said the captain. "We've only run a boat down".

And they hurried out.

The captain was in the right of it. We had run down a boat in the fog, and she had parted in the midst and gone to the bottom with all her crew, but one. This man (as I heard afterwards) had been sitting in the stern as a passenger, while the rest were on the benches rowing.

At the moment of the blow, the stern had been thrown into the air, and the man (having his hands free, and for all he was encumbered with a frieze overcoat that came below his knees) had leaped up and caught hold of the brig's bowsprit. It showed he had luck and much agility and unusual strength, that he should have thus saved himself from such a pass.

And yet, when the captain brought the man into the round-house, and I set eyes on him for the first time, he looked as cool and undaunted as I did.

He was smallish in stature, but well set and as nimble as a goat; his face was of a good open expression, but sunburnt very dark, and heavily freckled and pitted with the smallpox; his eyes were unusually light and had a kind of dancing madness in them, that was both engaging and alarming; and when he took off his great-coat, he laid a pair of fine, silver-mounted pistols on the table, and I saw that he was belted with a great sword.

His manners, besides, were elegant, and he pledged the captain very handsomely. Altogether I thought of him, at the first sight, that here was a man I would far rather call my friend than my enemy.

The captain, too, was taking his observations, but rather of the man's clothes than his person.

And to be sure, as soon as he had taken off the great-coat, he showed forth mighty fine for the round-house of a merchant brig; having a hat with feathers, a red waistcoat, breeches of black plush, and a blue coat with silver buttons and handsome silver lace; costly clothes, though somewhat spoiled with the fog and with being slept in.

"I'm vexed, sir, about the boat," says the captain.

"There are some pretty men gone to the bottom," said the stranger, "that I 'd rather see on dry land again than half a score of boats."

"Friends of yours?" said Hoseason.

"You have none such friends in your country," was the reply. "They would have died for me like dogs."

"Well, sir," said the captain, still watching him, "there are more men in the world than boats to put them in."

"And that's true too," cried the other, "and ye seem to be a gentleman of great penetration."

"I have been in France, sir," says the captain, so that it was plain he meant more by the words than showed upon the face of them.

"Well, sir," says the other, "and so has many a pretty man, for the matter of that."

"No doubt, sir," says the captain, "and fine coats."

"Oho!" says the stranger, "is that how the wind sets?" And he laid his hand quickly on his pistols.

"Don't be hasty," said the captain. "Don't do a mischief, before ye see the need for it. Ye've a French soldier's coat upon your back and a Scotch tongue in your head, to be sure; but so has many an honest fellow in these days, and I dare say none the worse of it."

"So?" said the gentleman in the fine coat: "are ye of the honest party?" (meaning; Was he a Jacobite? for each side, in these sort of civil broils, takes the name of honesty for its own).

"Why, sir," replied the captain, "I am a true-blue Protestant, and I thank God for it." (It was the first word of any religion I had ever heard from him, but I learnt afterwards he was a great churchgoer while on shore.) "But, for all that," says he, "I can be sorry to see another man with his back to the wall."

"Can ye so, indeed?" asked the Jacobite. "Well, sir, to be quite plain with ye, I am one of those honest gentlemen that were in trouble about the years forty-five and six; and (to be still quite plain with ye) if I got into the hands of any of the red-coated gentry, it's like it would go hard with me. Now, sir, I was for France; and there was a French ship cruising here to pick me up; but she gave us the go-by in the fog—as I wish from the heart that ye had done yoursel'! And the best that I can say is this: If ye can set me ashore where I was going, I have that upon me will reward you highly for your trouble."

"In France?" says the captain. "No, sir; that I cannot do. But where ye come from—we might talk of that."

And then, unhappily, he observed me standing in my corner, and packed me off to the galley to get supper for the gentleman. I lost no time, I promise you; and when I came back into the round-house, I found the gentleman had taken a money-belt from about his waist, and poured out a guinea or two upon the table. The captain was looking at the guineas, and then at the belt, and then at the gentleman's face; and I thought he seemed excited.

"Half of it," he cried, "and I'm your man!"

The other swept back the guineas into the belt, and put it on again under his waistcoat. "I have told ye, sir," said he, "that not one doit of it belongs to me. It belongs to my chieftain"—and here he touched his hat—"and while I would be but a silly messenger to grudge some of it that the rest might come safe, I should show myself a hound indeed if I bought my own carcase any too dear. Thirty guineas on the seaside, or sixty if ye set me on the Linnhe loch. Take it, if ye will; if not, ye can do your worst."

"Ay," said Hoseason. "And if I give ye over to the soldiers?"

"Ye would make a fool's bargain," said the other. "My chief, let me tell you, sir, is forfeited, like every honest man in Scotland. His estate is in the hands of the man they call King George; and it is his officers that collect the rents, or try to collect them. But for the honour of Scotland, the poor tenant bodies take a thought upon their chief lying in exile; and this money is a part of that very rent for which King George is looking. Now, sir, ye seem to me to be a man that understands things: bring his money within the reach of Government, and how much of it'll come to you?"

"Little enough, to be sure," said Hoseason; and then, "If they knew," he added, dryly. "But I think, if I was to try, that I could hold my tongue about it."

"Ah, but I'll begowk ye there!" cried the gentleman. "Play me false, and I'll play you cunning. If a hand's laid upon me, they shall ken what money it is."

"Well," returned the captain, "what must be must. Sixty guineas, and done. Here's my hand upon it."

"And here's mine," said the other.

And thereupon the captain went out (rather hurriedly, I thought), and left me alone in the round-house with the stranger.

At that period (so soon after the forty-five) there were many exiled gentlemen coming back at the peril of their lives, either to see their friends or to collect a little money; and as for the Highland chiefs that had been forfeited, it was a common matter of talk how their tenants would stint themselves to send them money, and their clansmen outface the soldiery to get it in, and run the gauntlet of our great navy to carry it across. All this I had, of course, heard tell of; and now I had a man under my eyes whose life was forfeit on all these counts and upon one more; for he was not only a rebel and a smuggler of rents, but had taken service with King Louis of France. And as if all this were not enough, he had a belt full of golden guineas round his loins. Whatever my opinions, I could not look on such a man without a lively interest.

"And so you're a Jacobite?" said I, as I set meat before him.

"Ay," said he, beginning to eat. "And you, by your long face, should be a Whig?"†

"Betwixt and between," said I, not to annoy him; for indeed I was as good a Whig as Mr Campbell could make me.

"And that's naething," said he. "But I'm saying, Mr Betwixt-and-Between," he added, "this bottle of yours is dry; and it's hard if I'm to pay sixty guineas and be grudged a dram upon the back of it."

"I'll go and ask for the key," said I, and stepped on deck.

The fog was as close as ever, but the swell almost down. They had laid the brig to, not knowing precisely where they were, and the wind (what little there was of it) not serving well for their true course. Some of the hands were still hearkening for breakers; but the captain and the two officers were in the waist with their heads together. It struck me, I don't know why, that they were after no good; and the first word I heard, as I drew softly near, more than confirmed me.

It was Mr Riach, crying out as if upon a sudden thought:

"Couldn't we wile him out of the round-house?"

"He's better where he is," returned Hoseason; "he hasn't room to use his sword."

"Well, that's true," said Riach; "but he's hard to come at."

"Hoot!" said Hoseason. "We can get the man in talk, one upon each side, and pin him by the two arms; or if that'll not hold, sir,

†Whig or Whigamore was the cant name for those who were loyal to King George.

we can make a run by both the doors and get him under hand before he has the time to draw."

At this hearing, I was seized with both fear and anger at these treacherous greedy, bloody men that I sailed with. My first mind was to run away; my second was bolder.

"Captain," said I, "the gentleman is seeking a dram, and the bottle's out. Will you give me the key?"

They all started and turned about.

"Why, here's our chance to get the firearms! " Riach cried, and then to me: "Hark ye, David," he said, "do ye ken where the pistols are?"

"Ah, ay," put in Hoseason. "David kens; David's a good lad. Ye see, David my man, yon wild Hielandman is a danger to the ship, besides being a rank foe to King George, God bless him!"

I had never been so be-Davided since I came on board; but I said yes, as if all I heard were quite natural.

"The trouble is," resumed the captain, "that all our firelocks, great and little, are in the round-house under this man's nose; likewise the powder. Now if I, or one of the officers, was to go in and take them, he would fall to thinking. But a lad like you, David, might snap up a horn and a pistol or two without remark. And if ye can do it cleverly, I'll bear in mind when it'll be good for you to have friends; and that's when we came to Carolina."

Here Mr Riach whispered him a little.

"Very right sir," said the captain; and then to myself: "And see here, David, yon man has a beltful of gold, and I give you my word that you shall have your fingers in it."

I told him I would do as he wished, though indeed I had scarce breath to speak with; and upon that he gave me the key of the spirit locker, and I began to go slowly back to the round-house. What was I to do? They were dogs and thieves; they had stolen me from my own country; they had killed poor Ransome; and was I to hold the candle to another murder? But then, upon the other hand, there was the fear of death very plain before me; for what could a boy and a man do, if they were as brave as lions, against a whole ship's company?

I was still arguing it back and forth, and getting no great clearness, when I came into the round-house and saw the Jacobite eating his supper under the lamp; and at that my mind was made up all in a moment. I have no credit by it; it was by no choice of mine, but as if by compulsion, that I walked right up to the table and put my hand on his shoulder.

"Do you want to be killed?" said I.

He sprang to his feet, and looked a question at me as clear as if he had spoken.

"Oh!" cried I, "they're all murderers here; it's a ship full of them! They've murdered a boy already. Now it's you."

"Ay, ay," said he; "but they haven't got me yet." And then looking at me steadfastly and with some curiousity, Will ye stand with me?"

"That will I!" said I, "I am no thief, nor yet murderer. I'll stand by you."

"Why, then," said he, "what's your name?"

"David Balfour," said I; and then thinking that a man with so fine a coat must like fine people, I added for the first time "of Shaws."

It never occurred to him to doubt me, for a Highlander is used to see great gentlefolk in great poverty; but as he had no estate of his own, my words nettled a very childish vanity he had.

"My name is Stewart," he said, drawing himself up. "Alan Breck, they call me. A king's name is good enough for me, though I bear it plain and have the name of no farm-midden to clap to the hindend of it."

And having administered this rebuke, as though it were something of a chief importance, (which to him it was), he turned to examine our defences.

The round-house was built very strong, to support the breaching of the seas. Of its five apertures, only the skylight and the two doors were large enough for the passage of a man. The doors, besides, could be drawn close: they were of stout oak, and ran in grooves, and were fitted with hooks to keep them either shut or open, as the need arose. The one that was already shut, I secured in this fashion; but when I was proceeding to slide to the other, Alan stopped me.

"David," said he—"for I cannae bring to mind the name of your landed estate, and so will make so bold as to call you David—that door, being open, is the best part of my defences."

"It would be yet better shut," says I.

"Not so, David," says he, "Ye see, I have but one face; but so long as that door is open and my face to it, the best part of my enemies will be in front of me, where I would aye wish to find them."

Then he gave me from the rack a cutlass (of which there were a few besides the firearms), choosing it with great care, shaking his head and saying he had never in all his life seen poorer weapons; and next he set me down to the table with a powder-horn, a bag of bullets, and all the pistols, which he bade me charge.

"And that will be better work, let me tell you," said he, "for a gentleman of decent birth, than scraping plates and raxing drams to a wheen tarry sailors."

Then he stood up in the midst with his face to the door, and drawing his great sword, made trial of the room he had to wield it in.

"I must stick to the point," he said, shaking his head; "and that's a pity, too. It doesn't set my genius, which is all for the upper guard. And now," said he, "do you keep on charging the pistols, and give heed to me."

I told him I would listen closely. My chest was tight, my mouth dry, the light dark to my eyes; the thought of the numbers that were soon to leap in upon us kept my heart in a flutter; and the sea, which I heard washing round the brig, and where I thought my dead body would be cast ere morning, ran in my mind strangely.

"First of all," said he, "how many are against us?"

I reckoned them up; and such was the hurry of my mind, I had to cast the numbers twice, "Fifteen," said I.

Alan whistled. "Well," said he, "that can't be cured. And now follow me. It is my part to keep this door, where I look for the main battle. In that, ye have no hand. And mind and dinnae fire to this side unless they get me down; for I would rather have ten foes in front of me than one friend like you cracking pistols at my back."

I told him, indeed I was no great shot.

"And that's very bravely said," he cried, in a great admiration of my candour. "There's many a pretty gentleman that wouldnae dare to say it."

"But then, sir," said I, "there is the door behind you, which they may perhaps break in."

"Ay," said he, "and that is a part of your work. No sooner the pistols charged, then ye must climb up into yon bed where ye're handy at the window; and if they lift hand against the door, ye're to shoot. But that's not all. Let's make a bit of a soldier of ye, David. What else have ye to guard?"

"There's the skylight," said I. "But indeed, Mr Stewart, I would need to have eyes upon both sides to keep the two of them; for when my face is at the one, my back is to the other."

"And that's very true," said Alan. "But have ye no ears to your head?"

"To be sure!" cried I. "I must hear the bursting of the glass!"
"Ye have some rudiments of sense," said Alan, grimly.

CHAPTER 10

THE SIEGE OF THE ROUND-HOUSE

But now our time of truce was come to an end. Those on deck had waited for my coming till they grew impatient; and scarce had Alan spoken, when the captain showed face in the open door.

"Stand!" cried Alan, and pointed his sword at him.

The captain stood, indeed; but he neither winced nor drew back a foot.

"A naked sword?" says he. "This is a strange return for hospitality."

"Do ye see me?" said Alan. "I am come of kings; I bear a king's name. My badge is the oak. Do ye see my sword? It has slashed the heads off mair Whigamores than you have toes upon your feet. Call up your vermin to your back! sir, and fall on! The sooner the clash begins, the sooner ye'll taste this steel throughout your vitals."

The captain said nothing to Alan, but he looked over at me with an ugly look. "David," said he, "I'll mind this"; and the sound of his voice went through me with a jar.

Next moment he was gone.

"And now," said Alan, "let your hand keep your head, for the grip is coming."

Alan drew a dirk, which he held in his left hand in case they should run in under his sword. I, on my part, clambered up into the berth with an armful of pistols and something of a heavy heart, and set open the window where I was to watch. It was a small part of the deck that I could overlook, but enough for our purpose. The sea had gone down, and the wind was steady and kept the sails quiet; so that there was a great stillness in the ship, in which I made sure I heard the sound of muttering voices. A little after, and there came a clash of steel upon the deck, by which

I knew they were dealing out the cutlasses and one had been let fall; and after that, silence again.

I do not know if I was what you call afraid; but my heart beat like a bird's, both quick and little; and there was a dimness came before my eyes which I continually rubbed away, and which continually returned. As for hope, I had none; but only a darkness of despair and a sort of anger against all the world that made me long to sell my life as dear as I was able. I tried to pray, I remember, but that same hurry of my mind, like a man running, would not suffer me to think upon the words, and my chief wish was to have the thing begin and be done with it.

It came all of a sudden when it did, with a rush of feet and a roar, and then a shout from Alan, and a sound of blows and someone crying out as if hurt. I looked back over my shoulder, and saw Mr Shuan in the doorway, crossing blades with Alan.

"That's him that killed the boy!" I cried.

"Look to your window!" said Alan; and as I turned back to my place, I saw him pass his sword through the mate's body. It was none too soon for me to look to my own part; for my head was scarce back at the window, before five men carrying a spare yard for a battering-ram, ran past me and took post to drive the door in. I had never fired with a pistol in my life, and not often with a gun; far less against a fellow-creature. But it was now or never; and just as they swung the yard, I cried out, "Take that!" and shot into their midst.

I must have hit one of them, for he sang out and gave back a step, and the rest stopped as if a little disconcerted. Before they had time to recover, I sent another ball over their heads; and at my third shot (which went as wide as the second) the whole party threw down the yard and ran for it.

Then I looked round again into the deck-house. The whole place was full of the smoke of my own firing, just as my ears seemed to be burst with the noise of the shots. But there was Alan, standing as before; only now his sword was running blood to the hilt, and himself swelled with triumph and fallen into so fine an attitude, that he looked to be invincible. Right before him on the floor was Mr Shuan, on his hands and knees; the blood was pouring from his mouth, and he was sinking slowly lower, with a terrible, white face, and just as I looked, some of those from behind caught hold of him by the heels and dragged him bodily out of the round-house. I believe he died as they were doing it.

"There's one of your Whigs for ye!" cried Alan; and then turning to me, he asked if I had done much execution.

I told him I had winged one, and thought it was the captain.

"And I've settled two," says he. "No, there's not enough blood let; they'll be back again. To your watch, David. This was but a dram before meat."

I settled back to my place, re-charging the three pistols I had fired, and keeping watch with both eye and ear. Our enemies were disputing not far off upon the deck, and that so loudly that I could hear a word or two above the washing of the seas.

"It was Shuan bauchled it," I heard one say.

And another answered with, "Wheesht, man! He's paid the piper."

After that the voices fell again into the same muttering as before. Only now, one person spoke most of the time, as though laying down a plan, and first one and then another answered him briefly, like men taking orders. By this, I made sure they were coming on again, and told Alan.

"It's what we have to pray for," said he. "Unless we can give them a good distaste of us, and done with it, there'll be nae sleep for either you or me. But this time, mind, they'll be in earnest."

By this, my pistols were ready, and there was nothing to do but listen and wait. While the brush lasted, I had not the time to think if I was frightened; but now, when all was still again, my mind ran upon nothing else. The thought of the sharp swords and the cold steel was strong in me; and presently, when I began to hear stealthy steps and a brushing of men's clothes against the round-house wall, and knew they were taking their places in the dark, I could have found it in my mind to cry out aloud. All this was upon Alan's side; and I had begun to think my share of the fight was at an end, when I heard someone drop softly on the roof above me.

Then there came a single call on the sea-pipe, and that was the signal. A knot of them made one rush of it, cutlass in hand, against the door; and at the same moment, the glass of the skylight was dashed in a thousand pieces, and a man leaped through and landed on the floor. Before he got his feet, I had clapped a pistol to his back, and might have shot him, too; only at the touch of him (and him alive) my whole flesh misgave me, and I could no more pull the trigger than I could have flown.

He had dropped his cutlass as he jumped, and when he felt the pistol, whipped straight round and laid hold of me, roaring out an oath; and at that either my courage came again, or I grew so much afraid as came to the same thing; for I gave a shriek and shot him in the midst of the body. He gave the most horrible, ugly groan and fell to the floor.

The foot of a second fellow, whose legs were dangling through the skylight, struck me at the same time upon the head; and at that I snatched another pistol and shot this one through the thigh, so that he slipped through and tumbled in a lump on his companion's body. There was no talk of missing, any more than there was time to aim; I clapped the muzzle to the very place and fired. I might have stood and stared at them for long, but I heard Alan shout as if for help, and that brought me to my senses. He had kept the door so long; but one of the seamen, while he was engaged with others, had run in under his guard and caught him about the body. Alan was dirking him with his left hand, but the fellow clung like a leech. Another had broken in and had his cutlass raised. The door was thronged with their faces. I thought we were lost, and catching up my cutlass, fell on them in flank.

But I had not time to be of help. The wrestler dropped at last; and Alan, leaping back to get his distance, ran upon the others like a bull, roaring as he went. They broke before him like water, turning, and running, and falling one against another in their haste. The sword in his hands flashed like quicksilver into the huddle of our fleeing enemies; and at every flash there came the scream of a man hurt. I was still thinking we were lost, when lo! they were all gone, and Alan was driving them along the deck as a sheepdog chases sheep.

Yet he was no sooner out than he was back again, being as cautious as he was brave; and meanwhile the seamen continued running and crying out as if he was still behind them; and we heard them tumble one upon another into the forecastle, and clap-to the hatch.

The round-house was like a shambles; three were dead inside, another lay in his death agony across the threshold; and there were Alan and I victorious and unhurt.

He came to me with open arms. "Come to my arms!" he cried, and embraced and kissed me hard upon both cheeks. "David," said he, "I love you like a brother. And oh, man," he cried in a kind of ecstasy, "am I no a bonny fighter?"

Thereupon he turned to the four enemies, passed his sword clean through each of them, and tumbled them out of doors one after the other. As he did so, he kept humming and singing and whistling to himself, like a man trying to recall an air; only what *he* was trying, was to make one. All the while, the flush was in his face, and his eyes were as bright as a five-year-old child's with a new toy. And presently he sat down upon the table, sword in hand; the air that he was making all the time began to run a little clearer, and then clearer still; and then out he burst with a great voice into a Gaelic song.

I have translated it here, not in verse (of which I have no skill) but at least in the king's English. He sang it often afterwards, and the thing became popular; so that I have heard it, and had it explained to me, many's the time.

This is the song of the sword of Alan:
The smith made it,
The fire set it;
Now it shines in the hand of Alan Breck.

Their eyes were many and bright,
Swift were they to behold,
Many the hands they guided:
The sword was alone.

The dun deer troop over the hill,
They are many, the hill is one;
The dun deer vanish,
The hill remains.

Come to me from the hills of heather,
Come from the isles of the sea.
O far-beholding eagles,
Here is your meat.

Now this song which he made (both words and music) in the hour of our victory, is something less than just to me, who stood beside him in the tussle. Mr Shuan and five more were either killed outright or thoroughly disabled; but of these, two fell by my hand, the two that came by the skylight. Four more were hurt, and of that number, one (and he not the least important) got his hurt from me. So that, altogether, I did my fair share both of the killing, and the wounding, and might have claimed a place in Alan's verses. But poets (as a very wise man once told me) have to think upon their rhymes; and in good prose talk, Alan always did me more than justice. In the meanwhile, I was innocent of any wrong being done me. For not only I knew no word of the Gaelic; but what with the long suspense of the waiting, and the scurry and strain of our two spirits of fighting, and, more than all, the horror

I had of some of my own share in it, the thing was no sooner over than I was glad to stagger to a seat. There was that tightness on my chest that I could hardly breathe; the thought of the two men I had shot sat upon me like a nightmare; and all upon a sudden, before I had a guess of what was coming, I began to sob and cry like any child. Alan clapped my shoulder, and said I was a brave lad and wanted nothing but a sleep.

"I'll take the first watch," said he. "Ye've done well by me, David, first and last; and I wouldn't lose you for all Appin—no, nor for Breadalbane."

So he made up my bed on the floor, and took the first spell, pistol in hand and sword on knee; three hours by the captain's watch upon the wall. Then he roused me up, and I took my turn of three hours; before the end of which it was broad day, and a very quiet morning, with a smooth, rolling sea that tossed the ship and made the blood run to and fro on the round-house floor, and a heavy rain that drummed on the roof. All my watch there was nothing stirring; and by the banging of the helm, I knew they had no one at the tiller. Indeed (as I learned afterwards) they were so many of them hurt or dead, and the rest in so ill a temper, that Mr Riach and the captain had to take turn and turn like Alan and me, or the brig might have gone ashore and nobody the wiser. It was a mercy the night had fallen still, for the wind had gone down as soon as the rain began. Even as it was, I judged by the wailing of a great number of gulls crying and fishing round the ship, that she must have drifted near pretty the coast or one of the islands of the Hebrides; and at last, looking out of the door of the round-house, I saw the great stone hills of Skye on the right hand, and, a little more astern, the strange isle of Rum.

Chapter 11

THE CAPTAIN KNUCKLES UNDER

Alan and I sat down to breakfast about six of the clock. The floor was covered with broken glass and in a horrid mess of blood, which took away my hunger.

In all other ways we were in a situation not only agreeable but merry; having ousted the officers from their own cabin, and having at command all the drink in the ship—both wine and spirits and all the dainty part of what was eatable, such as the pickles and the fine sort of biscuit. This, of itself, was enough to set us in good humour; but the richest part of it was this, that the two thirstiest men that ever came out of Scotland (Mr Shuan being dead) were now shut in the forepart of the ship and condemned to what they hated most—cold water.

"And depend upon it," Alan said, "we shall hear more of them ere long. Ye may keep a man from the fighting but never from his bottle."

We made good company for each other. Alan, indeed, expressed himself most lovingly; and taking a knife from the table, cut me off one of the silver buttons from his coat.

"I had them," says he, "from my father, Duncan Stewart; and now give ye one of them to be a keepsake for last night's work. And wherever ye go and show that button, the friends of Alan Breck will come around you."

He said this as if he had been Charlemagne, and commanded armies; and indeed, much as I admired his courage, I was always in danger of smiling at his vanity: in danger, I say, for had I not kept my countenance, I would be afraid to think what a quarrel might have followed.

As soon as we were through with our meal, he rummaged in the captain's locker till he found a clothes-brush; and then taking off his coat, began to visit his suit and brush away the stains, with such care and labour as I supposed to have been only usual with women. To be sure, he had no other; and, besides (as he said) it belonged to a King and so behoved to be royally looked after.

For all that, when I saw what care he took to pluck out the threads where the button had been cut away, I put a higher value on his gift.

He was still so engaged, when we were hailed by Mr Riach from the deck, asking for a parley; and I, climbing through the skylight and sitting on the edge of it, pistol in hand and with a bold front, though inwardly in fear of broken glass, hailed him back again and bade him speak out. He came to the edge of the round-house, and stood on a coil of rope, so that his chin was on a level with the roof; and we looked at each other a while in silence. Mr Riach, as I do not think he had been very forward in the battle, so he had got off with nothing worse than a blow upon the cheek; but he looked out of heart and very weary, having been all night afoot, either standing watch or doctoring the wounded.

"This is a bad job," said he at last, shaking his head.

"It was none of our choosing," said I.

"The captain," says he, "would like to speak with our friend. They might speak at the window."

"And how do we know what treachery he means?" cried I.

"He means none, David," returned Mr Riach soberly; "and if he did, I'll tell ye the honest truth, we couldnae get the men to follow."

"Is that so?" said I.

"I'll tell ye more than that," said he. It's not only the men; it's me. I'm frigh'ened, Davie." And he smiled across at me. "No," he continued, "what we want is to be shut of him."

Thereupon I consulted with Alan, and the parley was agreed to and parole given upon either side; but this was not the whole of Mr Riach's business, and he now begged me for a dram with such instancy and such reminders of his former kindness, that at last I handed him a pannikin with about a gill of brandy. He drank a part, and then carried the rest down upon the deck, to share it (I suppose) with his superior.

A little after, the captain came (as was agreed) to one of the windows, and stood there in the rain, with his arm in a sling, and looking stern and pale, and so old that my heart smote me for having fired upon him.

Alan at once held a pistol in his face.

"Put that thing up!" said the captain. "Have I not passed my word, sir? Or do ye seek to affront me?"

"Captain," says Alan, "I doubt your word is a breakable. Last night ye haggled and argle-bargled like an apple-wife; and then passed me your word, and gave me your hand to back it; and ye ken very well what was the upshot. Be damned to your word!" says he.

"Well, well, sir," said the captain, "ye'll get little good by swearing." (And truly that was a fault of which the captain was quite free.) "But we have other things to speak," he continued, bitterly. "Ye've made a sore hash of my brig; I haven't hands enough left to work her; and my first officer (whom I could ill spare) has got your sword through his vitals, and passed without speech. There is nothing left me, sir, but to put back into the port of Glasgow after hands; and there (by your leave) ye will find them that are better able to talk to ye."

"Ay?" said Alan; "and faith, "I'll have a talk with them mysel'! Unless there's naebody speaks English in that town, I have a bonny tale for them. Fifteen tarry sailors upon the one side, and a man and a halfling boy upon the other! Oh, man, it's peetiful!"

Hoseason flushed red.

"No," continued Alan, "that'll no do. Ye'll just have to set me ashore as we agreed."

"Ay," said Hoseason, "but my first officer is dead—ye ken best how. There's none of the rest of us acquaint with this coast, sir; and it's one very dangerous to ships."

"I give ye your choice," says Alan. "Set me on dry ground in Appin, or Ardgour, or in Morven, or Arisaig, or Morar; or, in brief where ye please, within thirty miles of my own country; except in a country of the Campbells. That's a broad target. If ye miss that, ye must be as feckless at the sailoring as I have found ye at the fighting. Why, my poor country people in their bit cobles pass from island to island in all weathers, ay, and by night too, for the matter of that."

"A coble's not a ship, sir," said the captain. It has nae draught of water."

"Well, then, to Glasgow if ye list," says Alan. "We'll have the laugh of ye at the least."

"My mind runs little upon laughing," said the captain. "But all this will cost money, sir."

"Well, sir," says Alan, "I am nae weathercock. Thirty guineas, if ye land me on the sea-side; and sixty, if ye put me in the Linnhe loch."

"But see, sir, where we lie, we are but a few hours' sail from Ardnamurchan," said Hoseason. "Give me sixty, and I'll set ye there."

"And I'm to wear my brogues and run jeopardy of the red coats to please you?" cries Alan. "No, sir, if ye want sixty guineas, earn them, and set me in my own country."

"It's to risk the brig, sir," said the captain, "and your own lives along with her."

"Take it or want it," says Alan.

"Could ye pilot us at all," asked the captain, who was frowning to himself.

"Well, it's doubtful," said Alan. "I'm more of a fighting man (as ye have seen for yoursel') taken a sailorman. But I have been often enough picked up and set down upon this coast, and should ken something of the lie of it."

The captain shook his head, still frowning.

"If I had lost less money on this unchancy cruise," says he, "I would see you in a rope's-end before I risked my brig, sir. But be it as ye will. As soon as I get a slant of wind (and there's some coming, or I'm the more mistaken) I'll put it in hand. But there's one thing more. We may meet in with a king's ship and she may lay us aboard, sir, with no blame of mine; they keep the cruisers thick upon this coast, ye ken who for. Now, sir, if that was to befall, ye might leave the money."

"Captain," says Alan, "if ye see a pennant, it shall be your part to run away. And now, as I hear you're a little short of brandy in the forepart, I'll offer ye a change: a bottle of brandy against two buckets of water."

That was the last clause of the treaty, and was duly executed on both sides; so that Alan and I could at last wash out the round-house and be rid of the memorials of those whom we had slain, and the captain and Mr Riach could be happy again in their own way, the name of which was drink.

Chapter 12

I HEAR OF THE RED FOX

Before we had done cleaning out the round-house, a breeze sprang up from a little to the east of north. This blew off the rain and brought out the sun.

And here I must explain; and the reader would do well to look at a map. On the day when the fog fell and we ran down Alan's boat, we had been running through the Little Minch. At dawn after the battle, we lay becalmed to the east of the Isle of Canna or between that and the Isle Eriska in the chain of the Long Islands. Now to get from there to the Linnhe Loch, the straight course was through the narrows of the Sound of Mull. But the captain had no chart; he was afraid to trust his brig so deep among the islands; and the wind serving well, he preferred to go by west of Tiree and come up under the southern coast of the great Isle of Mull. All day the breeze held in the same point, and rather freshened than died down; and towards afternoon, a swell began to set in from round the outer Hebrides. Our course, to go round about the inner isles, was to the west of south, so that at first we had this swell upon our beam, and were much rolled about. But after nightfall, when we had turned the end of Tiree and began to head more to the east, the sea came right astern.

Meanwhile, the early part of the day, before the swell came up, was very pleasant; sailing, as we were, in a bright sunshine and with many mountainous islands upon different sides. Alan and I sat in the round-house with the doors open on each side (the wind being straight astern) and smoked a pipe or two of the captain's fine tobacco. It was at this time we heard each other's stories, which was the more important to me, as I gained some knowledge of that wild Highland country, on which I was so soon to land. In those days, so close on the back of the great rebellion, it was needful a man should know what he was doing when he went upon the heather.

It was I that showed the example, telling him all my misfortune; which he heard with great good nature. Only, when I came to mention that good friend of mine, Mr Campbell the minister, Alan fired up and cried out that he hated all that were of that name.

"Why," said I, "he is a man you should be proud to give your hand to."

"I know nothing I would help a Campbell to," says he, "unless it was a leaden bullet. I would hunt all of that name like blackcocks. If I lay dying, I would crawl upon my knees to my chamber window for a shot at one."

"Why, Alan," I cried, "what ails ye at the Campbells?"

"Well," says he, "ye ken very well that I am an Appin Stewart, and the Campbells have long harried and wasted those of my name; ay, and got lands of us by treachery—but never with the sword," he cried loudly, and with the word brought down his fist upon the table. But I paid the less attention to this, for I knew it was usually said by those who have the under hand. "There's more than that," he continued, "and all in the same story: lying words, lying papers, tricks fit for a peddler, and the show of what's legal over all, to make a man the more angry."

"You that are so wasteful of your buttons," said I, "I can hardly think you would be a good judge of business."

"Ah!" says he, falling again to smiling, "I got my wastefulness from the same man I got the buttons from; and that was my poor father, Duncan Stewart, grace be to him! He was the prettiest man of his kindred; and the best swordsman in the Hielands, David, and that is the same as to say, in all the world. I should ken, for it was him that taught me. He was in the Black Watch, when first it was mustered; and like other gentlemen privates, had a gillie at his back to carry his firelock for him on the march. Well, the King, it appears, was wishful to see Hieland swordsmanship; and my father and three more were chosen out and sent to London town, to let him see it at the best. So they were had into the palace and showed the whole art of the sword for two hours at a stretch, before King George and Queen Caroline, and the Butcher Cumberland, and many more of whom I havenae mind. And when they were through, the King (for all he was a rank usurper) spoke them fair and gave each man three guineas in his hand. Now, as they were going out of the palace, they had a porter's lodge to go by; and it came in on my father, as he was perhaps the first private Hieland gentleman that had ever gone by that door, it was right he should give the poor porter a proper notion of their quality. So he gives the King's three guineas into the man's hand, as if it was his common custom; the three others that came behind him did the same; and there they were on the street, never a penny the better for their pains. Some say it was one, that was the first to fee the King's porter; and some say it was another; but the truth of it is, that it was Duncan Stewart, as I am willing to prove with either sword or pistol. And that was the father that I had, God rest him!"

"I think he was not the man to leave you rich," said I.

"And that's true," said Alan. "He left me my breeks to cover me, and little besides. And that was how I came to enlist, which was a black spot upon my character at the best of times, and would still be a sore job for me if I fell among the red-coats."

"What," cried I, "were you in the English army?"

"That was I," said Alan. "But I deserted to the right side at Preston Pans—and that's some comfort."

I could scarcely share this view: holding desertion under arms for an unpardonable fault in honour. But for all I was so young, I was wiser than say my thought. "Dear, dear," says I, "the punishment is death."

"Ay," said he; "if they got hands on me, it would be a short shrift and a lang tow for Alan! But I have the King of France's commission in my pocket, which would aye be some protection."

"I misdoubt it much," said I.

"I have doubts mysel'," said Alan, drily.

"And, good heaven, man," cried I, "you that are a condemned rebel, and a deserter, and a man of the French King's—what tempts ye back into this country? It's a braving of Providence."

"Tut!" says Alan, "I have been back every year since forty-six!"

"And what brings ye, man?" cried I.

"Well, ye see, I weary for my friends and country," said he. "France is a braw place, nae doubt; but I weary for the heather and the deer. And then I have bit things that I attend to. Whiles I pick up a few lads to serve the King of France: recruits, ye see; and that's aye a little money. But the heart of the matter is the business of my chief, Ardshiel."

"I thought they called your chief Appin," said I.

"Ay, but Ardshiel is the captain of the clan," said he, which scarcely cleared my mind. "Ye see, David, he that was all his life so great a man, and come of the blood and bearing the name of kings, is now brought down to live in a French town like a poor and private person. He that had four hundred swords at his whistle, I have seen, with these eyes of mine, buying butter in the market-place, and taking it home in a kale-leaf. This is not only a pain but a disgrace to us of his family and clan. There are the bairns forby, the children and the hope of Appin, that must be learned their letters and how to hold a sword, in that far country. Now, the tenants of Appin have to pay a rent to King George; but their hearts are staunch, they are true to their chief; and what with love and a bit of pressure, and maybe a threat or two, the poor folk scrape up a second rent for Ardshiel. Well, David, I'm the hand that carries it." And he struck the belt about his body, so that the guineas rang.

"Do they pay both?" cried I.

"Ah, David, both," says he.

"What? two rents?" I repeated.

"Ay, David," said he. "I told a different tale to yon captain man; but this is the truth of it. And it's wonderful to me how little pressure is needed. But that's the handiwork of my good kinsman and my father's friend, James of the Glens; James Stewart, that is: Ardshiel's half-brother. He it is that gets the money in, and does the management."

This was the first time I heard the name of that James Stewart, who was afterwards so famous at the time of his hanging. But I took little heed at the moment, for all my mind was occupied with the generosity of these poor Highlanders.

"I call it noble," I cried. "I'm a Whig, or little better; but I call it noble."

"Ay," said he, "ye're a Whig, but ye're a gentleman; and that's what does it. Now, if ye were one of the cursed race of Campbell, ye would gnash your teeth to hear tell of it. If ye were the Red Fox." . . . And at that name, his teeth shut together, and he ceased speaking. I hae seen many a grim face, but never a grimmer than Alan's when he had named the Red Fox.

"And who is the Red Fox?" I asked, daunted, but still curious.

"Who is he?" cried Alan. "Well, and I'll tell you that. When the men of the clans were broken at Culloden, and the good cause went down, and the horses rode over the fetlocks in the best blood of the north, Ardshiel had to flee like a poor deer upon the mountains—he and his lady and his bairns. A sair job we had of it before we got him shipped; and while he still lay in the heather, the English rogues, that couldnae come at his life, were striking at his rights. They stripped him of his powers; they stripped him of his lands; they plucked the weapons from the hands of his clansmen, that had borne arms for thirty centuries; ay, and the very clothes off their backs—so that it's now a sin to wear a tartan plaid, and a man may be cast into a gaol if he has but a kilt about his legs. One thing they couldnae kill. That was the love the clansmen bore their chief. These guineas are the proof of it. And now, in there steps a man, a Campbell, red-headed Colin of Glenure—"

"Is that him you call the Red Fox?" said I.

"Will ye bring me his brush?" cries Alan, fiercely. "Ay, that's the man. In he steps, and gets papers from King George, to be so-called King's factor on the lands of Appin. And at first he sings small, and is-hail-fellow-well-met with Sheamus—that's James of the Glens, my chieftain's agent. But by and by, that came to his ears that I have just told you; how the poor commons of Appin, the farmers and the crofters and the boumen, were wringing their very plaids to get a second rent, and send it over-seas for Ardshiel and his poor bairns. What was it ye called it, when I told ye?"

"I called it noble, Alan," said I.

"And you little better than a common Whig" cries Alan. "But when it came to Colin Roy, the black Campbell blood in him ran wild. He sat gnashing his teeth at the wine table. What! should a Stewart get a bite of bread, and him not be able to prevent it? Ah! Red Fox, if ever I hold you at a gun's end, the Lord have pity upon ye!" (Alan stopped to swallow down his anger.) "Well, David, what does he do? He declares all the farms to let. And thinks he, in his black heart, I'll soon get other tenants that'll overbid these Stewarts, and Maccolls, and Macrobs (for these are all names in my clan, David), 'and then,' thinks he, 'Ardshiel will have to hold his bonnet on a French roadside.'"

"Well," said I, "what followed?"

Alan laid down his pipe, which he had long since suffered to go out, and set his hands upon his knees.

"Ay," said he, "ye'll never guess that! For these same Stewarts, and Maccolls, and Macrobs (that had two rents to pay, one to King George by stark force, and one to Ardshiel by natural kindness), offered him a better price than any Campbell in all broad Scotland; and far he sent seeking them—as far as to the sides of Clyde and the cross of Edinburgh—seeking, and fleeching, and begging them to come, where there was a Stewart to be starved and a red-headed hound of a Campbell to be pleasured!"

"Well, Alan," said I, "that is a strange story, and a fine one, too. And Whig as I may be, I am glad the man was beaten."

"Him beaten?" echoed Alan. "It's little ye ken of Campbells and less of the Red Fox. Him beaten? No: nor will be, till his blood's on the hillside! But if the day comes, David man, that I can find time and leisure for a bit of hunting, there grows not enough heather in all Scotland to hide him from my vengeance!"

"Alan, Alan," said I, "ye are neither very wise nor very Christian to blow off so many words of anger. They will do the man ye call the Fox no harm, and yourself no good. Tell me your tale plainly out. What did he next?"

"And that's a good observe, David," said Alan. "Troth and indeed, they will do him no harm; the more's the pity! And barring that about Christianity (of which my opinion is quite otherwise, or I would be nae Christian) I am much of your mind."

"Opinion here or opinion there," said I, "it's a kennt thing that Christianity forbids revenge."

"Ay," said he, "it's well seen it was a Campbell taught ye! It would be a convenient world for them and their sort, if there was no such a thing as a lad and a gun behind a heather bush! But that's nothing to the point. This is what he did."

"Ay," said I, "come to that."

"Well, David," said he, "since he couldnae be rid of the loyal commons by fair means, he swore he would be rid of them by foul. Ardshiel was to starve: that was the thing he aimed at. And since them that fed him in his exile wouldnae be bought out—right or wrong, he would drive them out. Therefore he sent for lawyers, and papers, and red-coats to stand at his back. And the kindly folk of that country must all pack and tramp, every father's son out of his father's house, and out of the place where he was bred and fed, and played when he was a callant. And who are to succeed them? Bareleggit beggars! King George is to whistle for his rents; he maun dow with less; he can spread his butter thinner: what cares Red Colin? If he can hurt Artshiel, he has his wish; if he can pluck the meat from my chieftain's table, and the bit toys out of his children's hands, he will gang hame singing to Glenure!"

"Let me have a word," said I. "Be sure, if they take less rents, be sure Government has a finger in the pie. It's not this Campbell's fault, man—it's his orders. And if ye killed this Colin tomorrow, what better would ye be? There would be another factor in his shoes, as fast as spur can drive."

"Ye're a good lad in a fight," said Alan; "but man! ye have Whig blood in ye!"

He spoke kindly enough, but there was so much anger under his contempt that I thought it was wise to change the conversation. I expressed my wonder how, with the Highlands covered with troops and guarded like a city in a siege, a man in his situation could come and go without arrest.

"It's easier than ye would think," said Alan. "A bare hillside (ye see) is like all one road; if there's a sentry at one place, ye just go by another. And then heather's a great help. And everywhere there are friends' houses and friends' byres and haystacks. And besides, when folk talk of a country covered with troops, it's but a kind of a byword at the best. A soldier covers nae mair of it than his boot-soles. I have fished a water with a sentry on the other side of the brae, and killed a fine trout; and I have sat in a heather bush within six feet of another, and learned a real bonny tune from his whistling. This was it," said he, and whistled me the air.

"And then, besides," he continued, "it's no sae bad now as it was in forty-six. The Hielands are what they call pacified. Small wonder, with never a gun or a sword left from Cantyre to Cape Wrath, but what tenty folk have hidden in their thatch! But what I would like to ken, David, is just how long? Not long, ye would think, with men like Ardshiel in exile and men like the Red Fox sitting birling the wine and oppressing the poor at home But it's a kittle thing to decide what folk'll bear, and what they will not. Or why would Red Colin be riding his horse all over my poor country of Appin, and never a pretty lad to put a bullet in him?"

And with this Alan fell into a muse, and for a long time sat very sad and silent.

I will add the rest of what I have to say about my friend, that he was skilled in all kinds of music, but principally pipe-music; was a well-considered poet in his own tongue; had read several books both in French and English; was a dead shot, a good angler, and an excellent fencer with the small sword as well as with his own particular weapon. For his faults, they were on his face, and I now knew them all. But the worst of them, his childish propensity to take offence and to pick quarrels, he greatly laid aside in my case, out of regard for the battle of the round-house. But whether it was because I had done well myself, or because I had been a witness of his own much greater prowess, is more than I can tell. For though he had a great taste for courage in other men, yet he admired it most in Alan Breck.

CHAPTER 13

THE LOSS OF THE BRIG

It was already late at night, and as dark as it ever would be at that season of the year and that is to say, it was still pretty bright, when Hoseason clapped his head into the round-house door.

"Here," said he, "come out and see if ye can pilot."

"Is this one of your tricks?" asked Alan.

"Do I look like tricks?" cried the captain. "I have other things to think of—my brig's in danger!"

By the concerned look of his face, and, above all, by the sharp tones in which he spoke of his brig, it was plain to both of us he was in deadly earnest; and so Alan and I, with no great fear of treachery, stepped on deck.

The sky was clear; it blew hard, and was bitter cold; a great deal of daylight lingered; and the moon, which was nearly full, shone brightly. The brig was close hauled, so as to round the south-west corner of the Island of Mull, the hills of which (and Ben More above them all, with a wisp of mist upon the top of it) lay full upon the starboard bow. Though it was no good point of sailing for the *Covenant*, she tore through the seas at a great rate, pitching and straining, and pursued by the westerly swell.

Altogether it was no such ill night to keep the seas in; and I had begun to wonder what it was that sat so heavily upon the captain, when the brig rising suddenly on the top of a high swell, he pointed and cried to us to look. Away on the lee bow, a thing like a fountain rose out of the moonlit sea, and immediately after we heard a low sound of roaring.

"What do ye call that?" asked the captain, gloomily.

"The sea breaking on a reef," said Alan. "And now ye ken where it is; and what better would ye have?"

"Ay," said Hoseason, "if it was the only one."

And sure enough just as he spoke there came a second fountain further to the south.

"There!" said Hoseason. "Ye see for yourself. If I had kent of these reefs, if I had had a chart, or if Shuan had been spared, it's not sixty guineas, no, nor six hundred, would have made me risk my brig in sic a stoneyard! But you, sir, that was to pilot us, have ye never a word?"

"I'm thinking," said Alan, "these'll be what they call the Torran Rocks."

"Are there many of them?" says the captain.

"Truly, sir, I am nae pilot," said Alan; "but it sticks in my mind there are ten miles of them."

Mr Riach and the captain looked at each other.

"There's a way through them, I suppose?" said the captain.

"Doubtless," said Alan; "but where? But it somehow runs in my mind once more, that it is clearer under the land."

"So?" said Hoseason. "We'll have to haul our wind then, Mr Riach; we'll have to come as near in about the end of Mull as we can take her, sir; and even then we'll have the land to keep the wind off us, and that stoneyard on our lee. Well, we're in for it now, and may as well crack on."

With that he gave an order to the steersman, and sent Riach to the foretop. There were only five men on deck, counting the officers; these were all that were fit (or, at least, both fit and willing) for their work; and two of these were hurt. So, as I say, it fell to Mr Riach to go aloft, and he sat there looking out and hailing the deck with news of all he saw.

"The sea to the south is thick," he cried; and then, after a while, "It does seem clearer in by the land."

"Well, sir," said Hoseason to Alan, "we'll try your way of it.

But I think I might as well trust to a blind fiddler. Pray God you're right."

"Pray God I am!" says Alan to me. "But where did I hear it? Well, well, it will be as it must."

As we got nearer to the turn of the land the reefs began to be sown here and there on our very path; and Mr Riach sometimes cried down to us to change the course. Sometimes, indeed, none too soon; for one reef was so close on the brig's weather board that when a sea burst upon it the lighter sprays fell upon her deck and wetted us like rain.

The brightness of the night showed us these perils as clearly as by day, which was perhaps, the more alarming. It showed me, too, the face of the captain as he stood by the steersman, now on one foot, now on the other, and sometimes blowing in his hands, but still listening and looking and as steady as steel. Neither he nor Mr Riach had shown well in the fighting; but I saw they were brave in their own trade, and admired them all the more because I found Alan very white.

"Ochone, David," says he, "this is no the kind of death I fancy."

"What, Alan! " I cried, "you're not afraid?"

"No," said he, wetting his lips, "but you'll allow yourself it's a cold ending."

By this time, now and then sheering to one side or the other to avoid a reef, but still hugging the wind and the land, we had got round Iona and begun to come alongside Mull. The tide at the tail of the land ran very strong, and threw the brig about. Two hands were put to the helm, and Hoseason himself would sometimes lend a help; and it was strange to see three strong men throw their weight upon the tiller, and it (like a living thing) struggle against and drive them back. This would have been the greater danger, had not the sea been for some while free of obstacles. Mr Riach, besides, announced from the top that he saw clear water ahead.

"Ye were right," said Hoseason to Alan. "Ye have saved the brig, sir; I'll mind that when we come to clear accounts." And I believe he not only meant what he said, but would have done it; so high a place did the *Covenant* hold in his affections.

But this is matter only for conjecture, things having gone otherwise than he forecast.

"Keep her away a point," sings out Mr Riach. "Reef to windward!"

And just at the same time the tide caught the brig, and threw the wind out of her sails. She came round into the wind like a top, and the next moment struck the reef with such a crunch as threw us all flat upon the deck, and came near to shake Mr Riach from his place upon the mast.

I was on my feet in a minute. The reef on which we had struck was close in under the south-west end of Mull, off a little isle they called Earraid, which lay low and black upon the starboard. Sometimes the swell broke clean over us; sometimes it only ground the poor brig upon the reef, so that we could hear her beat herself to pieces; and what with the great rise of the sails, and the singing of the wind, and the flying of the spray in the moonlight, and the sense of danger, I think my head must have been partly turned, for I could scarcely understand the things I saw.

Presently I observed Mr Riach and the seamen busy round the skiff; and still in the same blank, ran over to assist them; and as soon as I set my hand to work, my mind came clear again. It was no very easy task, for the skiff lay amidships and was full of hamper, and the breaking of the heavier seas continually forced us to give over and hold on; but we all wrought like horses while we could.

Meanwhile such of the wounded as could move came clambering out of the fore-scuttle and began to help; while the rest that lay helpless in their bunks harrowed me with screaming and begging to be saved.

The captain took no part. It seemed he was struck stupid. He stood holding by the shrouds, talking to himself and groaning out aloud whenever the ship hammered on the rock. His brig was like wife and child to him; he had looked on, day by day, at the mishandling of poor Ransome; but when it came to the brig, he seemed to suffer along with her.

All the time of our working at the boat, I remember only one other thing; that I asked Alan, looking across at the shore, what country it was; and he answered, it was the worst possible for him, for it was a land of the Campbells.

We had one of the wounded men told off to keep a watch upon the seas and cry us warning. Well, we had the boat about ready to be launched, when this man sang out pretty shrill: "For God's sake, hold on!" We knew by his tone that it was something more than ordinary; and sure enough, there followed a sea so huge that it lifted the brig right up and canted her over on her beam. Whether the cry came too late or my hold was too weak, I know not; but at the sudden tilting of the ship I was cast clean over the bulwarks into the sea.

I went down, and drank my fill; and then came up, and got a blink of the moon; and then down again. They say a man sinks the "third time for good." I cannot be made like other folk, then; for I would not like to write how often I went down or how often I came up again. All the while, I was being hurled along, and beaten upon and choked, and then swallowed whole; and the thing was so distracting to my wits, that I was neither sorry nor afraid.

Presently, I found I was holding to a spar, which helped me some-what. And then all of a sudden I was in quiet water, and began to come to myself.

It was the spare yard I had got hold of, and I was amazed to see how far I had travelled from the brig. I hailed her, indeed; but it was plain she was already out of cry. She was still holding together; but whether or not they had yet launched the boat, I was too far off and too low down to see.

While I was hailing the brig, I spied a tract of water lying between us, where no great waves came, but which yet boiled white all over and bristled in the moon with rings and bubbles. Sometimes the whole tract swung to one side, like the tail of a live serpent; sometimes, for a glimpse, it all would disappear and then boil up again. What it was I had no guess, which for the time increased my fear of it; but I now know it must have been the roost or tide race, which had carried me away so fast and tumbled me about so cruelly, and at last, as if tired of that play, had flung out me and the spare yard upon its landward margin.

I now lay quite becalmed, and began to feel that a man can die of cold as well as of drowning. The shores of Earraid were close in; I could see in the moonlight the dots of heather and the sparkling of the mica in the rocks.

"Well," thought I to myself, "if I cannot get as far as that, it's strange!"

I had no skill of swimming, Essen Water being small in our neighbourhood; but when I laid hold upon the yard with both arms, and kicked out with both feet, I soon began to find that I was moving. Hard work it was, and mortally slow; but in about an hour of kicking and splashing, I had got well in between the points of a sandy bay surrounded by low hills.

The sea was here quite quiet; there was no sound of any surf; the moon shone clear; and I thought in my heart I had never seen a place so desert and desolate. But it was dry land; and when at last it grew so shallow that I could leave the yard and wade ashore upon my feet, I cannot tell if I was more tired or more grateful. Both at least, I was; tired as I never was before that night; and grateful to God as I trust I have been often, though never with more cause.

Chapter 14

THE ISLET

With my stepping ashore I began the most unhappy part of my adventures. It was half past twelve in the morning, and though the wind was broken by the land, it was a cold night. I dared not sit down (for I thought I should have frozen), but took off my shoes and walked to and fro upon the sand, barefoot, and beating my breast, with infinite weariness. There was no sound of man or cattle; not a cock crew, though it was about the hour of their first waking; only the surf broke outside in the distance, which put me in mind of my perils and those of my friend. To walk by the sea at that hour of the morning, and in a place so desert-like and lonesome, struck me with a kind of fear.

As soon as the day began to break I put on my shoes and climbed a hill—the ruggedest scramble I ever undertook—falling, the whole way, between big blocks of granite or leaping from one to another. When I got to the top the dawn was come. There was no sign of the brig, which must have lifted from the reef and sunk. The boat, too, was nowhere to be seen. There was never a sail upon the ocean; and in what I could see of the land, was neither house nor man.

I was afraid to think what had befallen my shipmates, and afraid to look longer at so empty a scene. What with my wet clothes and weariness, and my belly that now began to ache with hunger, I had enough to trouble me without that. So I set off eastward along the south coast, hoping to find a house where I might warm myself, and perhaps get news of those I had lost. And at the worst, I considered the sun would soon rise and dry my clothes.

After a little, my way was stopped by a creek or inlet of the sea, which seemed to run pretty deep into the land; and as I had no means to get across, I must needs change my direction to go about the end of it.

It was still the roughest kind of walking; indeed the whole, not only of Earraid, but of the neighbouring part of Mull (which they call the Ross) is nothing but a jumble of granite rocks with heather in among. At first the creek kept narrowing as I had looked to see; but presently to my surprise it began to widen out again. At this I scratched my head, but had still no notion of the truth; until at last I came to a rising ground, and it burst upon me all in a moment that I was cast upon a little, barren isle, and cut off on every side by the salt seas.

Instead of the sun rising to dry me, it came on to rain, with a thick mist; so that my case was lamentable.

I stood in the rain, and shivered, and wondered what to do, till it occurred to me that perhaps the creek was fordable. Back I went to the narrowest point and waded in. But not three yards from shore, I plumbed in head over ears; and if ever I was heard of more it was rather by God's grace than my own prudence. I was no wetter (for that could hardly be) but I was all the colder for this mishap; and having lost another hope, was the more unhappy.

And now, all at once, the yard came in my head. What had carried me trough the roost, would surely serve me to cross this little quiet creek in safety. With that I set off, undaunted, across the top of the isle, to fetch and carry it back. It was a weary tramp in all ways, and if hope had not buoyed me up, I must have cast myself down and given up. Whether with the sea salt, or because I was growing fevered, I was distressed with thirst, and had to stop, as I went, and drink the peaty water out of the hags.

I came to the bay at last, more dead than alive; and at the first glance, I thought the yard was something further out than when I left it. In I went, for the third time, into the sea. The sand was smooth and firm and shelved gradually down; so that I could wade out till the water was almost to my neck and the little waves splashed into my face. But at that depth my feet began to leave me and I durst venture in no further. As for the yard, I saw it bobbing very quietly some twenty feet in front of me.

I had borne up well until this last disappointment; but at that I came ashore, and flung myself down upon the sands and wept.

The time I spent upon the island is still so horrible a thought to me, that I must pass it lightly over. In all the books I have read of people cast away, they had either their pockets full of tools, or a chest of things would be thrown upon the beach along with them, as if on purpose. My case was very different. I had nothing in my pockets but money and Alan's silver button; and being inland bred, I was as much short of knowledge as of means.

I knew indeed that shell-fish were counted good to eat; and among the rocks of the isle I found a great plenty of limpets, which at first I could scarcely strike from their places, not knowing quickness to be needful. There were, besides, some of the little shells that we call buckies; I think periwinkle is the English name. Of these two I made my whole diet, devouring them cold and raw as I found them; and so hungry was I, that at first they seemed to me delicious.

Perhaps they were out of season, or perhaps there was something wrong in the sea about my island. But at least I had no sooner eaten my first meal than I was seized with giddiness and retching, and lay for a long time no better than dead. A second trial of the same food (indeed I had no other) did better with me and I revived my strength. But as long as I was on the island, I never knew what to expect when I had eaten; sometimes all was well, and sometimes I was thrown into a miserable sickness; nor could I ever distinguish what particular fish it was that hurt me.

All day it streamed rain; the island ran like a sop; there was no dry spot to be found; and when I lay down that night, between two boulders that made a kind of roof, my feet were in a bog.

The second day I crossed the island to all sides. There was no one part of it better than another; it was all desolate and rocky; nothing living on it but game birds which I lacked the means to kill, and the gulls which haunted the outlying rocks in a prodigious number. But the creek, or straits, that cut off the isle from the main land of the Ross, opened out on the north into a bay, and the bay again opened into the sound of Iona; and it was the neighbourhood of this place that I chose to be my home; though if I had thought upon the very name of home in such a spot, I must have burst out weeping.

I had good reasons for my choice. There was in this part of the isle a little hut of a house like a pig's hut, where fishers used to sleep when they came there upon their business; but the turf roof of it had fallen entirely in; so that the hut was of no use to me, and gave me less shelter than my rocks. What was more important, the shell-fish on which I lived grew there in great plenty;

when the tide was out I could gather a peck at a time: and this was doubtless a convenience. But the other reason went deeper. I had become in no way used to the horrid solitude of the isle, but still looked round me on all sides (like a man that was hunted) between fear and hope that I might see some human creature coming. Now, from a little up the hillside over the bay, I could catch a sight of the great, ancient church and the roofs of the people's houses in Iona. And on the other hand, over the low country of the Ross, I saw smoke go up, morning and evening, as if from a homestead in a hollow of the land.

I used to watch this smoke, when I was wet and cold, and had my head half turned with loneliness; and think of the fireside and the company, till my heart burned. It was the same with the roofs of Iona. Altogether, this sight I had of men's homes and comfortable lives, although it put a point on my own sufferings, yet it kept hope alive, and helped me to eat my raw shell-fish (which had soon grown to be a disgust) and saved me from the sense of horror I had when ever I was quite alone with dead rocks, and fowls, and the rain, and the cold sea.

I say it kept hope alive; and indeed it seemed impossible that I should be left to die on the shores of my own country, and within view of a church tower and the smoke of men's houses. But the second day passed; and though as long as the light lasted I kept a bright look-out for boats on the Sound or men passing on the Ross, no help came near me. It still rained; and I turned in to sleep, as wet as ever and with a cruel sore throat, but a little comforted, perhaps, by having said good night to my next neighbours, the people of Iona.

Charles the Second declared a man could stay outdoors more days in the year in the climate of England than in any other. This was very like a king with a palace at his back and changes of dry clothes. But he must have had better luck on his flight from Worcester than I had on that miserable isle. It was the height of the summer; yet it rained for more than twenty-four hours, and did not clear until the afternoon of the third day.

This was the day of incidents. In the morning I saw a red deer, a buck with a fine spread of antlers, standing in the rain on the top of the island; but he had scarce seen me rise from under my rock, before he trotted off upon the other side. I supposed he must have swum the straits; though what should bring any creature to Earraid, was more than I could fancy.

A little after, as I was jumping about after my limpets, I was startled by a guinea-piece, which fell upon a rock in front of me and glanced off into the sea. When the sailors gave me my money again, they kept back not only about a third of the whole sum, but my father's leather purse; so that from that day out, I carried my gold loose in a pocket with a button. I now saw there must be a hole, and clapped my hand to the place in a great hurry. But this was to lock the stable door after the steed was stolen. I had left the shore at Queensferry with near on fifty pounds; now I found no more than two guinea-pieces and a silver shilling.

It is true I picked up a third guinea a little after, where it lay shining on a piece of turf. That made a fortune of three pounds and four shillings, English money, for a lad, the rightful heir of an estate, and now starving on an isle at the extreme end of the wild Highlands.

This state of my affairs dashed me still further; and indeed my plight on that third morning was truly pitiful. My clothes were beginning to rot; my stockings in particular were quite worn through, so that my shanks went naked; my hands had grown quite soft with the continual soaking; my throat was very sore, my strength had much abated, and my heart so turned against the horrid stuff I was condemned to eat, that the very sight of it came near to sicken me.

And yet the worst was not yet come.

There is a pretty high rock on the north-west of Earraid, which (because it had a flat top and overlooked the Sound) I was much in the habit of frequenting; not that ever I stayed in one place, save when asleep, my misery giving me no rest. Indeed I wore myself down with continual and aimless goings and comings in the rain.

As soon, however, as the sun came out, I lay down on the top of that rock to dry myself. The comfort of the sunshine is a thing I cannot tell. It set me thinking hopefully of the deliverance, of which I had begun to despair, and I scanned the sea and the Ross with a fresh interest. On the south of my rock, a part of the island jutted out and hid the open ocean, so that a boat could thus come quite near me upon that side, and I be none the wiser.

Well, all of a sudden, a coble with a brown sail and a pair of fishers aboard of it, came flying round that corner of the isle, bound for Iona. I shouted out, and then fell on my knees on the rock and reached up my hands and prayed to them. They were near enough to hear—I could even see the colour of their hair; and there was no doubt but they observed me, for they cried out in the Gaelic tongue, and laughed. But the boat never turned aside, and flew on, right before my eyes, for Iona.

I could not believe such wickedness, and ran along the shore from rock to rock, crying on them piteously; even after they were out of reach of my voice, I still cried and waved to them; and when they were quite gone, I thought my heart would have burst. All the time of my troubles I wept only twice. Once, when I could not reach the yard; and now, the second time, when these fishers turned a deaf ear to my cries. But this time I wept and roared like a wicked child, tearing up the turf with my nails and grinding my face in the earth. If a wish would kill men, those two fishers would never have seen morning, and I should likely have died upon my island.

When I was a little over my anger, I must eat again, but with such loathing of the mess as I could now scarce control. Sure enough, I should have done as well to fast, for my fishes poisoned me again. I had all my first pains; my throat was so sore I could scarce swallow; I had a fit of strong shuddering, which clucked my teeth together; and there came on me that dreadful sense of illness, which we have no name for either in Scotch or English. I thought I should have died, and made my peace with God, forgiving all men, even my uncle and the fishers; and as soon as I had thus made up my mind to the worst, clearness came upon me: I observed the night was falling dry; my clothes were dried a good deal; truly, I was in a better case than ever before, since I had landed on the isle; and so I got to sleep at last, with a thought of gratitude.

The next day (which was the fourth of this horrible life of mine) I found my bodily strength run very low. But the sun shone, the air was sweet, and what I managed to eat of the shell-fish agreed well with me and revived my courage.

I was scarce back on my rock (where I went always the first thing after I had eaten) before I observed a boat coming down the Sound, and with her head, as I thought, in my direction.

I began at once to hope and fear exceedingly; for I thought these men might have thought better of their cruelty and be coming back to my assistance. But another disappointment, such as yesterday's, was more than I could bear. I turned my back, accordingly, upon the sea, and did not look again till I had counted many hundreds. The boat was still heading for the island. The next time I counted the full thousand, as slowly as I could, my heart beating so as to hurt me. And then it was out of all question. She was coming straight to Earraid.

I could no longer hold myself back, but ran to the sea side and out, from one rock to another, as far as I could go. It is a marvel I was not drowned; for when I was brought to a stand at last, my legs shook under me, and my mouth was so dry, I must wet it with the sea-water before I was able to shout.

All this time the boat was coming on; and now I was able to perceive it was the same boat and the same two men as yesterday. This I knew by their hair, which the one had of a bright yellow and the other black. But now there was a third man along with them, who looked to be of a better class.

As soon as they were come within easy speech, they let down their sail and lay quiet. In spite of my supplications, they drew no nearer in, and what frightened me most of all, the new man tee-hee'd with laughter as he talked and looked at me.

Then he stood up in the boat and addressed me a long while, speaking fast and with many wavings of his hand. I told him I had no Gaelic; and at this he became very angry, and I began to suspect he thought he was talking English. Listening very close, I caught the word "whateffer" several times; but all the rest was Gaelic, and might have been Greek and Hebrew for me.

"Whatever," said I, to show him I had caught a word.

"Yes, yes—yes, yes," says he, and then he looked at the other men, as much as to say, "I told you I spoke English," and began again as hard as ever in the Gaelic.

This time I picked out another word, "tide". Then I had a flash of hope. I remembered he was always waving his hand towards the mainland of the Ross.

"Do you mean when the tide is out—?" I cried, and could not finish.

"Yes, yes," said he. "Tide."

At that I turned tail upon their boat (where my adviser had once more begun to tee-hee with laughter), leaped back the way I had come, from one stone to another, and set off running across the isle as I had never run before. In about half an hour I came out upon the shores of the creek; and, sure enough, it was shrunk into a little trickle of water, through which I dashed, not above my knees, and landed with a shout on the main island.

A sea-bred boy would not have stayed a day on Earraid; which is only what they call a tidal islet, and except in the bottom of the neaps, can be entered and left twice in every twenty-four hours, either dry-shod, or at the most by wading. Even I, who had the tide going out and in before me in the bay, and even watched for the ebbs, the better to get my shell-fish—even I (I say), if I had sat down to think, instead of raging at my fate, must have soon guessed the secret, and got free. It was no wonder the fishers had not understood me. The wonder was rather that they had ever guessed my pitiful illusion, and taken the trouble to come back. I had starved with cold and hunger on that island for close upon one hundred hours. But for the fishers, I might have left my bones there, in pure folly. And even as it was, I had paid for it pretty dear, not only in past sufferings, but in my present case; being clothed like a beggar-man, scarce able to walk, and in great pain of my sore throat.

I have seen wicked men and fools., a great many of both; and I believe they both get paid in the end; but the fools first.

CHAPTER 15

THE LAD WITH THE SILVER BUTTON: THROUGH THE ISLE OF MULL

The Ross of Mull, which I had now got upon, was rugged and trackless, like the isle I had just left; being all bog, and briar, and big stone. There may be roads for them that know that country well; but for many part I had no better guide than my own nose, and no other landmark than Ben More.

I aimed as well as I could for the smoke I had seen so often from the island; and with all my great weariness and the difficulty of the way, came upon the house in the bottom of a little hollow, about five or six at night. It was low and longish, roofed with turf and built of unmortared stones; and on a mound in front of it, an old gentleman sat smoking his pipe in the sun. With what little English he had, he gave me to understand that my shipmates had got safe ashore, and had broken bread in that very house on the day after.

"Was there one," I asked, "dressed like a gentleman?"

He said they all wore rough great-coats; but to be sure, the first of them, the one that came alone, wore breeches and stockings, while the rest had sailors' trousers.

"Ah," said I, "and he would have a feathered hat?"

He told me, no, that he was bare-headed like myself.

At first I thought Alan might have lost his hat; and then the rain came in my mind, and I judged it more likely he had it out of harm's way under his great coat. This set me smiling, partly because my friend was sage, partly to think of his vanity in dress.

And then the old gentleman clapped his hand to his brow, and cried out that I must be the lad with the silver button.

"Why, yes!" said I, in some wonder.

"Well, then," said the old gentleman, "I have a word for you that you are to follow your friend to his country, by Torosay."

He then asked me how I had fared, and I told him my tale. A south-country man would certainly have laughed; but this old gentleman (I call him so because of his manners, for his clothes were dropping off his back) heard me all through with nothing but gravity and pity. When I had done, he took me by the hand, led me into his hut (it was no better) and presented me before his wife, as if she had been the Queen and I a duke.

The good woman set oat-bread before me and a cold grouse, patting my shoulder and smiling to me all the time, for she had no English; and the old gentleman (not to be behind) brewed me a strong punch out of their country spirit. All the time I was eating, and after that when I was drinking the punch, I could scarce come to believe in my good fortune; and the house, though it was thick with the peat-smoke and as full of holes as a colander, seemed like a palace.

The punch threw me in a strong sweat and a deep slumber; the good people let me lie; and it was near noon of the next day before I took the road, my throat already easier and my spirits restored by good fare and good news. The old gentleman, although I pressed him hard, would take no money, and gave me an old bonnet for my head; though I am free to own I was no sooner out of view of the house, than I very jealously washed this gift of his in a wayside fountain.

Thought I to myself: "If these are the wild Highlanders, I could wish my own folk wilder."

I not only started late, but I must have wandered nearly half the time. True, I met plenty of people, grubbing in little miserable fields that would not keep a cat, or herding little kine about the bigness of asses. The Highland dress being forbidden by law since the rebellion, and the people condemned to the lowland habit, which they much disliked, it was strange to see the variety of their array. Some went bare, only for a hanging cloak or great-coat, and carried their trousers on their backs like a useless burthen; some had made an imitation of the tartan with little particoloured stripes patched together like a old wife's quilt; others, again, still wore the highland philabeg, but by putting a few stitches between the le[illegible]rmed it into a pair of trousers like a Dutchman's. [illegible]ifts were condemned and punished, for the law [illegible], in hopes to break up the clan spirit; but in [illegible] sea-bound isle, there were few to make [illegible]tell tales.

[illegible] poverty; which was no doubt natural, [illegible] down, and the chiefs kept no longer an [illegible]ds (even such a wandering, country by- [illegible]d) were infested with beggars. And here [illegible]e from my own part of the country. For d[illegible]n the gownsmen themselves, who beg b[illegible] flattering way with them, and if you g[illegible]ked change, would very civilly return y[illegible]ghland beggars stood on their dignity, as[illegible]nuff (by their account) and would give no change.

To be sure, this was no concern of mine, except in so far as it entertained me by the way. What was much more to the purpose, few had any English, and these few (unless they were of the brotherhood of beggars) not very anxious to place it at my service. I knew Torosay to be my destination, and repeated the name to them and pointed; but instead of simply pointing in reply, they would give me a screed of the Gaelic that set me foolish; so it was small wonder if I went out of my road as often as I stayed in it.

At last, about eight at night and already very weary, I came to a lone house, where I asked admittance, and was refused, until I bethought me of the power of money in so poor a country, and held up one of my guineas in my finger and thumb. Thereupon, the man of the house, who had hitherto pretended to have no English, and driven me from his door by signals, suddenly began to speak as clearly as was needful, and agreed for five shillings to give me a night's lodging and guide me the next day to Torosay.

I slept uneasily that night, fearing I should be robbed; but I might have spared myself the pain; for my host was no robber, only miserably poor and, a great cheat. He was not alone in his poverty; for the next morning, we must go five miles about to the house of what he called a rich man to have one of my guineas changed. This was perhaps a rich man for Mull; he would have scarce been thought so in the south; for it took all he had, the whole house was turned upside down, and a neighbour brought under contribution, before he could scrape together twenty shillings in silver. The odd shilling he kept for himself, protesting he could ill afford to have so great a sum of money lying "locked upon". For all that he was very courteous and well spoken, made us both sit down with his family to dinner, and brewed punch in a fine china bowl, over which my rascal guide grew so merry that he refused to start.

I was for getting angry, and appealed to the rich man (Hector Maclean was his name) who had been a witness to our bargain and to my payment of the five shillings. But Maclean had taken his share of the punch, and vowed that no gentleman should leave his table after the bowl was brewed; so there was nothing for it but to sit and hear Jacobite toasts and Gaelic songs, till all were tipsy and staggered off to bed or the barn for their night's rest.

Next day (the fourth of my travels) we were up before five upon, the clock; but my rascal guide got to the bottle at once, and it was three hours before I had him clear of the house, and then (as you shall hear) only for a worse disappointment.

As long as we went down a heathery valley that lay before Mr Maclean's house, all went well; only my guide looked constantly over his shoulder, and when I asked him the cause, only grinned at me. No sooner, however, had we crossed the back of a hill, and got out of sight of the house windows, than he told me Torosay lay right in front, and that a hill-top (which he pointed out) was my best landmark.

"I care very little for that," said I, "since you are going me."

The impudent cheat answered me in the Gaelic that he had no English.

"My fine fellow," I said "I know very well your English comes and goes. Tell me what will bring it back? Is it more money you wish?"

"Five shillings mair," said he, "and hersel' will bring ye there."

I reflected a while and then offered him two, which he accepted greedily, and insisted on having in his hands at once—"for luck", as he said, but I think it was rather for my misfortune.

The two shillings carried him not quite as many miles; at the end of which distance! he sat down upon the wayside and took off his brogues from his feet, like a man about to rest.

I was now red-hot. "Ha!" said I, "have you no more English?"

He said impudently, "no."

At that I boiled over and lifted my hand to strike him; and he, drawing a knife from his rags, squatted back and grinned at me like a wild-cat. At that, forgetting everything but my anger, I ran in upon him, put aside his knife with my left and struck him in the mouth with the right. I was a strong lad and very angry, and he but a little man; and he went down before me heavily. By good luck, his knife flew out of his hand as he fell.

I picked up both that and his brogues, wished him a good morning, set off upon my way, leaving him bare-foot and disarmed. I chuckled to myself as I went, being sure I was done with that rogue, for a variety of reasons. First, he knew he could have no more of my money; next, the brogues were worth in that country only a few pence; and lastly the knife, which was really a dagger, it was against the law for him to carry.

In about half-an-hour of walk, I overtook a great, ragged man, moving pretty fast but feeling before him with a staff. He was quite blind, and told me he was a catechist, which should have put me at my ease. But his face went against me; it seemed dark and dangerous and secret; and presently, as we began to go on alongside, I saw the steel butt of a pistol sticking from under the flap of his coat-pocket. To carry such a thing meant a fine of fifteen pounds sterling upon a first offence, and transportation to the colonies upon a second. Nor could I quite see why a religious teacher should go armed, or what a blind man could be doing with a pistol.

I told him about my guide, for I was proud of what I had done, and my vanity for once got the heels of my prudence. At the mention of the five shillings he cried out so loud that I made up my mind I should say nothing of the other two, and was glad he could not see my blushes.

"Was it too much?" I asked, a little faltering.

"Too much!" cries he. "Why, I will guide you to Torosay myself for a dram of brandy. And give you the great pleasure of my company (me that is a man of some learning) in the bargain."

I said I did not see how a blind man could be a guide; but at that he laughed aloud, and said his stick was eyes enough for an eagle.

"In the Isle of Mull, at least," says he, "where I knew every stone and heather-bush by mark of head. See, now," he said, striking right and left, as if to make sure, "down there a burn is running; and at the head of it there stands a bit of a small hill with a stone cocked upon the top of that; and it's hard at the foot of the hill, that the way runs by to Torosay; and the way here, being for droves, is plainly trodden, and will show grassy through the heather."

I had to own he was right in every feature, and told my wonder.

"Ha!" says he, "that's nothing. Would ye believe me now, that before the Act came out, and when there were weapons in this country, I could shoot? Ay, could I!" cries he, and then with a leer: "If ye had such a thing as a pistol here to try with, I would show ye how it's done."

I told him I had nothing of the sort, and gave him a wider berth. If he had known, his pistol stuck at that time quite plainly out of his pocket, and I could see the sun twinkle on the steel of the butt. But by the better luck for me, he knew nothing, thought all was covered, and lied on in the dark.

He then began to question me cunningly, where I came from, whether I was rich, whether I could change a five-shilling piece for him (which he declared he had that moment in his sporran) and all the time he kept edging up to me, and I avoiding him. We were now upon a sort of green cattle-track which crossed the hills towards Torosay, and we kept changing sides upon that like dancers in a reel. I had so plainly the upper-hand that my spirits rose, and indeed I took a pleasure in this game of blind-man's buff; but the catechist grew angrier and angrier, and at last began to swear in Gaelic and to strike for my legs with his staff.

Then I told him that, sure enough, I had a pistol in my pocket as well as he, and if he did not strike across the hill due south I would even blow his brains out.

He became at once very polite; and after trying to soften me for some time, but quite in vain, he cursed me once more in the Gaelic and took himself off. I watched him striding along, through bog and brier, tapping with his stick, until he turned the end of a hill and disappeared in the next hollow. Then I struck on again for Torosay, much better pleased to be alone than to travel with that man of learning. This was an unlucky day, and these two, of whom I had just rid myself one after the other, were the two worst men I met with in the Highlands.

At Torosay, on the Sound of Mull, and looking over to the main-land of Morven, there was an inn with an innkeeper, who was a Maclean, it appeared, of a very high family; for to keep an inn is thought even more genteel in the Highlands than it is with us, perhaps as partaking of hospitality, or perhaps because the trade is idle and drunken. He spoke good English, and finding me to be something of a scholar, tried me first in French, where he easily beat me, and then in the Latin, in which I don't now which of us did best. This pleasant rivalry put us at once upon friendly terms; and I sat up and drank punch with him (or to be more correct, sat up and watched him drink it) until he was so tipsy that he wept upon my shoulder.

I tried him, as if by accident, with a sight of Alan's button; but it was plain he had never seen or heard of it. Indeed, he bore some grudge against the family and friends of Ardshiel, and before he was drunk he read me a lampoon, in very good Latin, but with a very ill meaning, which he had made in elegiac verses upon a person of that house.

When I told him of my catechist, he shook his head, and said I was lucky to have got clear off. "That is a very dangerous man," he said; "Duncan Mackiegh is his name; he can shoot by the ear at several yards, and has been often accused of highway robberies, and once of murder."

"The cream of it is," says I, "that he called himself a catechist."

"And why should he not" says he, "when that is what he is? It was Maclean of Duart gave it to him because he was blind. But, perhaps, it was a peety," says my host, "for he is always on the road, going from one place to another to hear the young folk say their religion; and doubtless, that is a great temptation to the poor man."

At last, when my landlord could drink no more, he showed me to a bed, and I lay down in very good spirits; having travelled the greater part of that big and crooked Island of Mull, from Earraid to Torosay, fifty mile as the crow flies and (with my wanderings) much nearer a hundred, in four days and with little fatigue. Indeed I was by far in better heart and health of body at the end of that long tramp than I had been at the beginning.

Chapter 16

THE LAD WITH THE SILVER BUTTON: ACROSS MORVEN

There is a regular ferry from Torosay to Kinlochaline on the mainland. Both shores of the Sound are in the country of the strong clan of the Macleans, and the people that passed the ferry with me were almost all of that clan. The skipper of the boat, on the other hand, was called Neil Roy Macrob; and since Macrob was one of the names of Alan's clansmen, and Alan himself had sent me to that ferry, I was eager to come to private speech of Neil Roy.

In the crowded boat this was of course impossible, and the passage was a very slow affair. There was no wind, and as the boat was wretchedly equipped, we could pull but two oars on one side, and one on the other. The men gave way, however, with a good will, the passengers taking spells to help them, and the whole company giving the time in Gaelic boat-songs. And what with the songs, and the sea air, and the good nature and spirit of all concerned, and the bright weather, the passage was a pretty thing to have seen.

But there was one melancholy part. In the mouth of Loch Aline we found a great sea-going ship at anchor; and this I supposed at first to be one of the King's cruisers which were kept along that coast, both summer and winter, to prevent communication with the French. As we got a little nearer, it became plain she was a ship of merchandise; and what still more puzzled me, not only her decks, but the sea-beach also, were quite black with people, and skiffs continually plying to and fro between them. Yet nearer, and there began to come to our ears a great sound of mourning, the people on board and those on the shore crying and lamenting one to another as to pierce the heart.

Then I understood this was an emigrant ship bound for the American colonies. We put the ferry-boat alongside, and the exiles leaned over the bulwarks, weeping and reaching out their hands to my fellow-passengers, among whom they counted some near friends. How long this might have gone on I do not know, for they seemed to have no sense of time; but at last the captain of the ship, who seemed near beside himself (and no great wonder) in the midst of this crying and confusion, came to the side and begged us to depart.

Thereupon Neil sheered off; and the chief singer in our boat struck into a melancholy air, which was presently taken up both by the emigrants and their friends upon the beach, so that it sounded from all sides like a lament for the dying. I saw the tears run down the cheeks of the men and women in the boat, even as they bent at the oars; and the circumstances and the music of the song (which is one called "Lochaber no more") were highly affecting even to myself.

At Kinlochaline I got Neil Roy upon one side on the beach, and said I made sure he was one of Appin's men.

"And what for no?" said he.

"I am seeking somebody," said I; "and it comes in my mind that you will have news of him. Alan Breck Stewart is his name." And very foolishly, instead of showing him the button, I sought to pass a shilling in his hand. At this he drew back.

"I am very much affronted," he said; "and this is not the way that one shentleman should behave to another at all. The man you ask for is in France; but if he was in my sporran," says he, "and your belly full of shillings, I would not hurt a hair upon his body."

I saw I had gone the wrong way to work, and without wasting time upon apologies, showed him the button lying in the hollow of my palm.

"Aweel, aweel," said Neil; "and I think ye might have begun with that end of the stick, whatever! But if ye are the lad with the silver button, all is well, and I have the word to see that ye come safe. But if ye will pardon me to speak plainly," says he, "there is a name that you should never take into your mouth, and that is the name of Alan Breck; and there is a thing that ye would never do, and that is to offer your dirty money to a Hieland shentleman."

It was not very easy to apologize; for I could scarce tell him (what was the truth) that I had never dreamed he would set up to be a gentleman until he told me so. Neil on his part had no wish to prolong his dealings with me, only to fulfil his orders and be done with it; and he made haste to give me my route. This was to lie the night in Kinlochaline in the public inn; to cross Morven the next day to Ardgour, and lie the night in the house of one John of the Claymore, who was warned that I might come; the third day, to be set across one loch at Corran and another at Balachulish, and then ask my way to the house of James of the Glens, at Aucharn in Duror of Appin. There was a good deal of ferrying, as you hear; the sea in all this part running deep into the mountains and winding about their roots. It makes the country strong to hold and difficult to travel, but full of prodigious wild and dreadful prospects.

I had some other advice from Neil: to speak with no one by the way, to avoid Whigs, Campbells, and the "red soldiers"; to leave the road and lie in a bush, if I saw any of the latter coming "for it was never chancy to meet in with them"; and in brief, to conduct myself like a robber or a Jacobite agent, as perhaps Neil thought me.

The inn at Kinlochaline was the most beggarly vile place that ever pigs were styed in, full of smoke, vermin, and silent Highlanders. I was not only discontented with my lodging, but with myself for my mismanagement of Neil, and thought I could hardly be worse off. But very wrongly, as I was soon to see; for I had not been half an hour at the inn (standing in the door most of the time, to ease my eyes from the peat smoke) when a thunder-storm came close by, the springs broke in a little hill on which the inn stood, and one end of the house became a running water. Places of public entertainment were bad enough all over Scotland in those days; yet it was a wonder to myself, when I had to go from the fireside to the bed in which I slept, wading over the shoes.

Early in my next day's journey I overtook a little, stout, solemn man, walking very slowly with his toes turned out, sometimes reading in a book and sometimes marking the place with his finger, and dressed decently and plainly in something of a clerical style.

This I found to be another catechist, but of a different order from the blind man of Mull: being indeed one of those sent out by the Edinburgh Society for Propagating Christian Knowledge, to evangelize the more savage places of the Highlands. His name was Henderland; he spoke with the broad south-country tongue, which I was beginning to weary for the sound of; and besides common countryship, we soon found we had a more particular bond of interest. For my good friend, the minister of Essendean, had translated into the Gaelic in his by-time a number of hymns and pious books, which Henderland used in his work, and held in great esteem; it was one of these he was carrying and reading when we met.

We fell in company at once, our ways lying together as far as to Kingairloch. As we went, he stopped and spoke with all the wayfarers and workers that we met or passed; and though of course I could not tell what they discoursed about, yet I judged Mr Henderland must be well liked in the countryside, for I observed many of them to bring out their mulls and share a pinch of snuff with him.

I told him as far in my affairs as I judged wise; as far, that is, as they were none of Alan's; and gave Balachulish as the place I was travelling to, to meet a friend; for I thought Aucharn, or even Duror, would be too particular and might put him on the scent.

On his part he told me much of his work and the people he worked among, the hiding priests and Jacobites, the Disarming Act, the dress, and many other curiosities of the time and place. He seemed moderate; blaming Parliament in several points, and especially because they had framed the Act more severely against those who wore the dress than against those who carried weapons.

This moderation put it in my mind to question him of the Red Fox and the Appin tenants; questions which, I thought, would seem natural enough in the mouth of one travelling to that country.

He said it was a bad business. "It's wonderful," said he, "where the tenants find the money, for their life is mere starvation. (Ye don't carry such a thing as snuff, do ye, Mr Balfour? No. Well, I'm better wanting it.) But these tenants (as I was saying) are doubtless partly driven to it. James Stewart in Duror (that's him they call James of the Glens) is half-brother to Ardshiel, the captain of the clan; and he is a man much looked up to, and drives very hard. And then there's one they call Alan Breck—"

"Ah!" cried I, "what of him?"

"What of the wind that bloweth where it listeth?" said Henderland. "He's here and awa; here today and gone tomorrow: a fair heather-cat. He might be glowering at the two of us out of yon whinbush, and I wouldnae wonder! Ye'll no carry such a thing as snuff, will ye?"

I told him no, and that he had asked the same thing more than once.

"It's highly possible," said he sighing. "But it seems strange ye shouldnae carry it. However, as I was saying, this Alan Breck is a bold, desperate customer, and well kent to be James's right hand. His life is forfeit already; he would boogle at naething; and maybe, if a tellant-body was to hang back, he would get a dirk in his wame."

"You make a poor story of it all, Mr Henderland," said I. "If it is all fear upon both sides, I care to hear no more of it."

"Nae," said Mr Henderland, "but there's love too, and self-denial that should put the like of you and me to hame. There's something fine about it; no perhaps Christian, but humanly fine. Even Alan Breck, by all that I hear, is a chield to be respected. There's many a lying sneck-draw sits close in kirk in our own part of the country, and stands well in the world's eye, and maybe is a far worse man, Mr Balfour, than yon misguided shedder of man's blood. Ay, ay, we might take a lesson by them.—Ye'll perhaps think I've been too long in the Hielands?" he added, smiling to me.

I told him not at all; that I had seen much to admire among the Highlanders; and if he came to that, Mr Campbell himself was a Highlander.

"Ay," said he, "that's true. It's a fine blood."

"And what is the King's agent about?" I asked.

"Colin Campbell?" says Henderland. "Putting his head in a bees' byke!"

"He is to turn the tenants out by force, I hear?" said I.

"Yes," says he, "but the business has gone back and forth, as folk say. First, James of the Glens rode to Edinburgh and got some lawyer (a Stewart, nae doubt—they all hing together like bats in a steeple) and had the proceedings stayed. And then Colin Campbell cam' in again, and had the upper-hand before the Barons of Exchequer. And now they tell me the first of the tenants are to flit tomorrow. It's to begin at Duror under James's very windows, which doesnae seem wise by my humble way of it."

"Do you think they'll fight?" I asked.

"Well," says Henderland, "they're disarmed—or supposed to be—for there's still a good deal of cold iron lying by in quiet places. And then Colin Campbell has the sogers coming. But for all that, if I was his lady wife, I wouldnae be well pleased till I got him home again. They're queer customers, the Appin Stewarts."

I asked if they were worse than their neighbours.

"No they," said he. "And that's the worst part of it. For if Colin Roy can get his business in Appin, he has it all to begin again in the next country, which they call Mamore, and which is one of the countries of the Camerons. He's King's Factor upon both, and from both he has to drive out the tenant; and indeed, Mr Balfour (to be open with ye), it's my belief that if he escapes the one lot, he'll get his death by the other."

So we continued talking and walking the great part of the day; until at last, Mr Henderland, after expressing his delight in my company, and satisfaction at meeting with a friend of Mr Campbell's ("whom," says he, "I will make bold to call that sweet singer of our covenanted Zion") proposed that I should make a short stage, and lie the night in his house a little beyond Kingairloch. To say truth, I was overjoyed; for I had no great desire for John of the Claymore, and since my double misadventure, first with the guide and next with the gentleman skipper, I stood in some fear of any Highland stranger. Accordingly we shook hands upon the bargain, and came in the afternoon to a small house, standing alone by the shore of the Linnhe Loch. The sun was already gone from the desert mountains of Ardgour upon the hither side, but shone on those of Appin on the farther; the loch lay as still as a lake, only the gulls were crying round the sides of it; and the whole place seemed solemn and uncouth.

We had no sooner come to the door of Mr Henderland's dwelling, than to my great surprise (for I was now used to the politeness of Highlanders) he burst rudely past me, dashed into the room, caught up a jar and a small horn spoon, and began ladling snuff into his nose in most excessive quantities. Then he had a hearty fit of sneezing, and looked round upon me with a rather silly smile.

"It's a vow I took," says he. "I took a vow upon me that I would-nae carry it. Doubtless it's a great privation; but when I think upon the martyrs, not only to the Scottish Covenant but to other points of Christianity, I think shame to mind it."

As soon as we had eaten (and porridge and whey was the best of the good man's diet) he took a grave face and said he had a duty to perform by Mr Campbell, and that was to inquire into my state of mind towards God. I was inclined to smile at him, since the business of the snuff; but he had not spoken long before he brought the tears into my eyes. There are two things that men should never weary of, goodness and humility; we get none too much of them in this rough world among cold, proud people; but Mr Henderland had their very speech upon his tongue. And though I was a good deal puffed up with my adventures and with having come off, as the saying is, with flying colours; yet he soon had me on my knees beside a simple, poor old man, and both proud and glad to be there.

Before we went to bed he offered me sixpence to help me on my way, out of a scanty store he kept in the turf wall of his house; at which excess of goodness I knew not what to do. But at last he was so earnest with me, that I thought it there more mannerly part to let him have his way, and so left him poorer than myself.

CHAPTER 17

THE DEATH OF THE RED FOX

The next day Mr Henderland found for me a man who had a boat of his own and was to cross the Linnhe Loch that afternoon into Appin, fishing. Him he prevailed on to take me, for he was one of his flock; and in this way I saved a long day's travel and the price of the two public ferries I must otherwise have passed.

It was near noon before we set out; a dark sky, with clouds, and the sun shining upon little patches. The sea was here very deep and still, and had scarce a wave upon it; so that I must put the water to my lips before I could believe it to be truly salt. The mountains on either side were high, rough and barren, very black and gloomy in the shadow of the clouds, but all silver-laced with little watercourses where the sun shone upon them. It seemed a hard country, this of Appin, for people to care as much about as Alan did.

There was but one thing to mention. A little after we had started, the sun shone upon a little moving clump of scarlet close in along the waterside to the north. It was much of the same red as soldier's coats; every now and then, too, there came little sparks and lightnings, as though the sun had struck upon bright steel.

I asked my boatman what it should be; and he answered he supposed it was some of the red soldiers coming from Fort William into Appin, against the poor tenantry of the country. Well, it was a sad sight to me; and whether it was because of my thoughts of Alan, or from something prophetic in my bosom, although this was but the second time I had seen King George's troops, I had no good will to them.

At last we came so near the point of land at the entering in of Loch Leven that I begged to be set on shore. My boatman (who was an honest fellow and mindful of his promise to the catechist) would fain have carried me on to Balachulish; but as this was to take me farther from my secret destination, I insisted, and was set on shore at last under the wood of Lettermore (or Lettervore, for I have heard it both ways) in Alan's country of Appin.

This was a wood of birches, growing on a steep, craggy side of a mountain that overhung the loch. It had many openings and ferny dells; and a road or bridle track ran north and south through the midst of it, by the edge of which, a spring, I sat down to eat some oatbread of Mr Henderland's, and think upon my situation.

Here I was not only troubled by a cloud of stinging midges, but far more by the doubts of my mind. What I ought to do, why I was going to join myself with an outlaw and a would-be murderer like Alan, whether I should not be acting more like a man of sense to tramp back to the south country direct, by my own guidance and at my own charges, and what Mr Campbell or even Mr Henderland would think of me if they should ever learn my folly and presumption; these were the doubts that now began to come in on me stronger than ever.

As I was sitting and thinking, a sound of men and horses came to me through the wood; and presently after, at a turning of the road, I saw four travellers come into view.

The way was in this part so rough and narrow that they came in single file and led their horses by the reins. The first was a great, red-headed gentleman, of an imperious and flushed face, who carried his hat in his hand and fanned himself, for he was in a breathing heat. The second, by his decent black garb and white wig, I correctly took to be a lawyer. The third was a servant, and wore some part of his clothes in tartan, which showed that his master was of a Highland family, and either an outlaw or else in singular good odour with the Government, since the wearing of tartan was against the Act. If I had been better versed in these things, I would have known the tartan to be of the Argyle (or Campbell) colours. This servant had a good-sized portmanteau strapped on his horse, and a net of lemons (to brew punch with) hanging at the saddle-bow; as was often enough the custom with luxurious travellers in that part of the country.

As for the fourth, who brought up the tail, I had seen his like before, and knew him at once to be a sheriff's officer.

I had no sooner seen these people coming than I made up my

mind (for no reason that I can tell) to go through with my adventure; and when the first came alongside of me, I rose up from the bracken and asked him the way to Aucharn.

He stopped and looked at me, as I thought, a little oddly; and then, turning to the lawyer, "Mungo," said he, "there's many a man would think this more of a warning than two pyats. Here am I on the road to Duror on the job ye ken; and here is a young lad starts up out of the bracken, and speers if I am on the way to Aucharn."

"Glenure," said the other, "this is an ill subject for jesting."

These two had now drawn close up and were gazing at me, while the two followers had halted about a stone-cast in the rear.

"And what seek ye in Aucharn?" said Colin Roy Campbell of Glenure; him they called the Red Fox; for he it was that I had stopped.

"The man that lives there," said I.

"James of the Glens," says Glenure, musingly; and then to the lawyer: "Is he gathering his people, think ye?"

"Anyway", says the lawyer, "we shall do better to bide where we are, and let the soldiers rally us."

"If you are concerned for me," said I, "I am neither of his people nor yours, but an honest subject of King George, owing no man and fearing no man."

"Why, very well said," replies the Factor. "But if I may make so bold as ask, what does this honest man so far from his country? and why does he come seeking the brother of Ardshiel? I have power here, I must tell you. I am King's Factor upon several of these estates, and have twelve files of soldiers at my back."

"I have heard a waif word in the country," said I, a little nettled, "that you were a hard man to drive."

He still kept looking at me, as if in doubt.

"Well," said he, at last, "your tongue is bold; but I am no unfriend to plainness. If ye had asked me the way to the door of James Stewart on any other day but this, I would have set ye right and bidden ye God speed. But today—eh, Mungo?" And he turned again to look at the lawyer.

But just as he turned there came the shot of a firelock from higher up the hill; and with the very sound of it Glenure fell upon the road.

"Oh, I am dead!" he cried, several times over.

The lawyer had caught him up and held him in his arms, the servant standing over and clasping his hands. And now the wounded man looked from one to another with scared eyes, and there was a change in his voice that went to the heart.

"Take care of yourselves," says he. "I am dead."

He tried to open his clothes as if to look for the wound, but his fingers slipped on the buttons. With that he gave a great sigh, his head rolled on his shoulder, and he passed away.

The lawyer said never a word, but his face was as sharp as a pen and as white as the dead man's; the servant broke out into a great noise of crying and weeping, like a child; and I, on my side, stood staring at them in a kind of horror.

The sheriff's officer had run back along the road at the first sound of the shot, to hasten the coming of Glenure's soldiers.

At last the lawyer laid town the dead man in his blood upon the road, and got to his own feet with a kind of stagger.

I believe it was his movement that brought me to my senses, for he had no sooner done so than I began to scramble up the hill, crying out, "The murderer! the murderer!"

So little a time had elapsed, that when I got to the top of the first steepness, and could see some part of the open mountain, the murderer was still moving away at no great distance. He was a big man, in a black coat, with metal buttons, and carried a long fowling-piece.

"Here!" I cried, "I see him!"

At that the murderer gave a little, quick look over his shoulder, and began to run. The next moment he was lost in a fringe of birches; then he came out again on the upper side, where I could see him climbing like a jackanapes, for that part was again very steep; and then he dipped behind a shoulder, and I saw him no more.

All this time I had been running on my side, and had got a good way up, when a voice cried upon me to stand.

I was at the edge of the upper wood, and so now, when I halted and looked back, I saw all the open part of the hill below me.

The lawyer and the sheriff's officer were standing just above the road, crying and waving on me to come back; and on their left, the red-coats, musket in hand, were beginning to struggle singly out of the lower wood.

"Why should I come back?" I cried. "Come you on!"

"Ten pounds if ye take that lad!" cried the lawyer. "He's an accomplice. He was posted here to hold us in talk."

At that word (which I could hear quite plainly, though it was to the soldiers and not to me that he was crying it) my heart came into my mouth with quite a new kind of terror. Indeed, it is one thing to stand the danger of your life, and quite another to run the peril of both life and character. The thing, besides, had come so suddenly, like thunder out of a clear sky, that I was all amazed and helpless.

The soldiers began to spread, some of them to run, and others to put up their pieces and cover me; and still I stood.

"Jouk in here among the trees," said a voice, close by.

Indeed, I scarce knew what I was doing, but I obeyed; and as I did so, I heard the firelocks bang and the balls whistle in the birches.

Just inside the shelter of the trees I found Alan Breck standing, with a fishing-rod. He gave me no salutation; indeed it was no time for civilities; only "Come!" says he, and set off running along the side of the mountain towards Balachulish; and I, like a sheep, to follow him.

Now we ran among the birches, now stooping behind low humps upon the mountain side; now crawling on all fours among the heather. The pace was deadly; my heart seemed bursting against my ribs; and I had neither time to think nor breath to speak with. Only I remembered seeing with wonder that Alan every now and then would straighten himself to his full height and look back; and every time he did so, there came a great far-away cheering and crying of the soldiers.

Quarter of an hour later, Alan stopped, clapped down flat in the heather, and turned to me.

"Now," said he, "it's earnest. Do as I do for your life."

And at the same speed, but now with infinitely more precaution, we traced back again across the mountain side by the same way that we had come, only perhaps higher; till at last Alan threw himself down in the upper wood of Lettermore, where I had found him at first, and lay, with his face in the bracken, panting like a dog. My own sides so ached, my head so swam, my tongue so hung out of my mouth with heat and dryness, that I lay beside him like one dead.

Chapter 18

I TALK WITH ALAN IN THE WOOD OF LETTERMORE

Alan was the first to come round. He rose, went to the border of the wood, peered out a little, and then returned and sat down.

"Well," said he, "yon was a hot burst, David."

I said nothing, nor so much as lifted my face. I had seen murder done, and a great, ruddy, jovial gentleman struck out of life in a moment; the pity of that sight was still sore within me, yet that was but a part of my concern. Here was murder done upon the man Alan hated; here was Alan skulking in the trees and running from the troops; whether his was the hand that fired or only the head that ordered, signified little. By my way of it, my only friend in that wild country was blood-guilty in the first degree; I held him in horror; I could not look upon his face; I would have rather lain alone in the rain on my cold isle, than in that warm wood beside a murderer.

"Are ye still wearied?" he asked again.

"No," said I, still with my face in the bracken; "no, I am not wearied now, and I can speak. You and me must twine," I said. "I liked you very well, Alan; but your ways are not mine, and they're not God's; and the short and the long of it is just that we must twine."

"I will hardly twine from ye, David, without some kind of reason for the same, said Alan, mighty gravely. "If ye ken anything against my reputation, it's the least thing that ye should do, for old aquaintance sake, to let me hear the name of it; and if ye have only taken a distaste to my society, it will be proper for me to judge if I'm insulted."

"Alan," said I, "what is the sense of this? Ye ken very well yon Campbell-man lies in his blood upon the road."

He was silent for a little; then says he, "Did ever ye hear tell of the story of the Man and the Good People?"—by which he meant the fairies.

"No," said I, "nor do I want to hear it."

"With your permission, Mr Balfour, I will tell it you, whatever," says Alan. "The man, ye should ken, was cast upon a rock in the sea, where it appears the Good People were in use to come and rest as they went through to Ireland. The name of this rock is called the Skerryvore, and it's not far from where we suffered shipwreck. Well, it seems the man cried so sore, if he could just see his little bairn before he died, that at last the king of the Good People took peety upon him, and sent one flying that brought back the bairn in a poke and laid it down beside the man where he lay sleeping. So when the man woke, there was a poke beside him and something into the inside of it that moved. Well, it seems he was one of these gentry that think aye the worst of things; and for greater security, he stuck his dirk throughout that poke before he opened it, and there was his bairn dead. I am thinking to myself, Mr Balfour, that you and the man are very much alike."

"Do you mean you had no hand in it?" cried I, sitting up.

"I will tell you first of all, Mr Balfour of Shaws, as one friend to another," said Alan, "that if I were going to kill a gentleman, it would not be in my own country, to bring trouble on my clan; and I would not go wanting sword and gun, and with a long fishing-rod upon my back."

"Well," said I, "that's true!"

"And now," continued Alan, taking out his dirk and laying his hand upon it in a certain manner, "I swear upon the Holy Iron I had neither art nor part, act nor thought in it."

"I thank God for that! cried I, and offered him my hand.

He did not appear to see it.

"And here is a great deal of work about a Campbell!" said he. "They are not so scarce, that I ken!"

"At least," said I, "you cannot justly blame me, for you know very well what you told me in the brig. But the temptation and the act are different, I thank God again for that. We may all be tempted; but to take a life in cold blood, Alan!" And I could say no more for the moment. "And do you know who did it?" I added. "Do you know that man in the black coat?"

"I have nae clear mind about his coat," said Alan, cunningly; "but it sticks in my head that it was blue."

"Blue or black, did ye know him?" said I.

"I couldnae just conscientiously swear to him," says Alan. "He gaed very close by me, to be sure, but it's a strange thing that I should just have been tying my brogues."

"Can you swear that you don't know him, Alan?" I cried, half angered, half in a mind to laugh at his evasions.

"Not yet," says he; "but I've a grand memory for forgetting David."

"And yet there was one thing I saw clearly," said I; "and that was, that you exposed yourself and me to draw the soldiers."

"It's very likely," said Alan; "and so would any gentleman. You and me were innocent of that transaction."

"The better reason, since we were falsely suspected, that we should get clear," I cried. "The innocent should surely come before the guilty."

"Why, David," said he, "the innocent have aye a chance to get assoiled in court; but for the lad that shot the bullet, I think the best place for him will be the heather. Them that havenae dipped their hands in any little difficulty, should be very mindful of the case of them that have. And that is the good Christianity. For if it was the other way round about, and the lad whom I couldnae just clearly see had been in our shoes, and we in his (as might very well have been) I think we would be a good deal obliged to him oursel's if he would draw the soldiers."

When it came to this, I gave Alan up. But he looked so innocent all the time, and was in such clear good faith in what he said, and so ready to sacrifice himself for what he deemed his duty, that my mouth was closed.

Mr Henderland's words came back to me: that we ourselves might take a lesson by these wild Highlanders. Well, here I had taken mine. Alan's morals were all tail-first; but he was ready to give his life for them, such as they were.

"Alan," said I, "I'll not say it's the good Christianity as I understand it, but it's good enough. And here I offer ye my hand for the second time."

Whereupon he gave me both of his, saying surely I had cast a spell upon him, for he could forgive me anything. Then he grew very grave, and said we had not much time to throw away, but must both flee that country; he, because he was a deserter, and the whole Appin would now be searched like a chamber, and every one obliged to give a good account of himself; and I, because I was certainly involved in the murder.

"Oh!" says I, willing to give him a little lesson, "I have no fear of the justice of my country."

"As if this was your country!" said he. "Or as if ye would be tried here, in a country of Stewarts!"

"It's all Scotland," said I.

"Man, I whiles wonder at ye," said Alan. "This is a Campbell that's been killed. Well, it'll be tried in Inverara, the Campbells' head place; with fifteen Campbells in the jurybox, and the biggest

Campbell of all (and that's the Duke) sitting cocking on the bench. Justice, David? The same justice, by all the world, as Glenure found a while ago at the roadside."

This frightened me a little, I confess, and would have frighted me more if I had known how nearly exact were Alan's predictions; indeed it was but in one point that he exaggerated, there being but eleven Campbells on the jury; though as the other four were equally in the Duke's dependence, it mattered less than might appear. Still, I cried out that he was unjust to the Duke of Argyle who (for all he was a Whig), was yet a wise and honest nobleman.

"Hoot!" cried Alan, "the man's a Whig, nae doubt; but I would never deny he was a good chieftain to his clan. And what would the clan think if there was a Campbell shot, and naebody hanged, and their own chief the Justice General? But I have often observed," says Alan, "that you Low-country bodies have no clear idea of what's right and wrong."

At this I did at last laugh out aloud; when to my surprise, Alan joined in and laughed as merrily as myself.

"Na, na," said he, "we're in the Hielands, David; and when I tell ye to run, take my word and run. Nae doubt it's a hard thing to skulk and starve in the heather, but it's harder yet to lie shackled in a red-coat prison."

I asked him whither we should flee; and as he told me "to the Lowlands," I was a little better inclined to go with him; for indeed I was growing impatient to get back and have the upper hand of my uncle. Besides, Alan made so sure there would be no question of justice in the matter, that I began to be afraid he might be right. Of all deaths, I would truly like least to die by the gallows; and the picture of that uncanny instrument came into my head with extraordinary clearness (as I had once seen it engraved at the top of a pedlar's ballad) and took away my appetite for courts of justice.

"I'll chance it, Alan," said I. "I'll go with you."

"But mind you," said Alan, "it's no small thing. Ye maun lie bare and hard, and brook many an empty belly. Your bed shall be the moorcock's, and your life shall be like the hunted deer's, and ye shall sleep with your hand upon your weapons. Ay, man, ye shall taigle many a weary foot, or we get clear! I tell ye this at the start, for it's a life that I ken well. But if ye ask what other chance ye have, I answer: Nane. Either take to the heather with me, or else hang."

"And that's a choice very easily made," said I; and we shook hands upon it.

"And now let's take another peek at the red-coats," says Alan, and he led me to the north-eastern fringe of the wood.

Looking out between the trees, we could see a great side of mountain, running down exceeding steep into the waters of the loch. It was a rough part, all hanging stone, and heather, and bit scrags of birchwood; and away at the far end towards Balachulish, little wee red soldiers were dipping up and down over hill and browe, and growing smaller every minute. There was no cheering now, for I think they had other uses for what breath was left them; but they still stuck to the trail, and doubtless thought that we were close in front of them.

Alan watched them, smiling to himself.

"Ay," said he, "they'll be gey weary before they've got to the end of that employ! And so you and me, David, can sit down and eat a bite, and breathe a bit longer, and take a dram from my bottle. Then we'll strike for Aucharn, the house of my kinsman, James of the Glens, where I must get my clothes, and my arms, and money to carry us along; and then David, we'll cry 'Forth, Fortune!' and take a cast among the heather."

So we sat again and ate and drank, in a place whence we could see the sun going down into a field of great, wild, and houseless mountains, such as I was now condemned to wander in with my companion. Partly as we so sat, and partly afterwards, on the way to Aucharn, each of us narrated his adventures; and I shall here set down so much of Alan's as seems either curious or needful.

It appears he ran to the bulwarks as soon as the wave was passed; saw me, and lost me, and saw me again, as I tumbled in the roost; and at last had one glimpse of me clinging on the yard. It was this that put him in some hope I would maybe get to land after all, and made him leave those clues and messages which had brought me (for my sins) to that unlucky country of Appin.

In the meanwhile, those still on the brig had got the skiff launched, and one or two were on board of her already, when there came a second wave greater than the first, and heaved the brig out of her place, and would certainly have sent her to the bottom, had she not struck and caught on some projection of the reef. When she had struck first, it had been bows-on, so that the stern had hitherto been lowest. But now her stern was thrown in the air, and the bows plunged under the sea; and with that, the water began to pour into the fore-scuttle like the pouring of a mill-dam.

It took the colour out of Alan's face, even to tell what followed. For there were still two men lying impotent in their bunks; and these, seeing the water pour in and thinking the ship had foundered, began to cry out aloud, and that with such harrowing cries that all who were on deck tumbled one after another into the skiff and fell to their oars. They were not two hundred yards away, when there came a third great sea; and at that the brig lifted clean over the reef; her canvas filled for a moment, and she seemed to sail in chase of them, but settling all the while; and presently she drew down and down, as if a hand was drawing her; and the sea closed over the *Covenant* of Dysart.

Never a word they spoke as they pulled ashore, being stunned with the horror of that screaming; but they had scarce set foot upon the beach when Hoseason woke up, as if out of a muse, and bade them lay hands upon Alan. They hung back indeed, having little taste for the employment; but Hoseason was like a fiend; crying that Alan was alone, that he had a great sum about him, that he had been the means of losing the brig and drowning all their comrades, and that here was both revenge and wealth upon a single cast. It was seven against one; in that part of the shore there was no rock that Alan could set his back to; and the sailors began to spread out and come behind him.

"And then," said Alan, "the little man with the red head—I havenae mind of the name that he is called."

"Riach," said I.

"Ay," said Alan, "Riach! Well, it was him that took up the clubs for me, asked the men if they werenae feared of a judgement, and says he, 'Dod, I'll put my back to the Hielandman's mysel'.' That's none such an entirely bad little man, yon little man with the red head," said Alan. "He had some spunks of decency."

"Well," said I, "he was kind to me in his way."

"And so he was to Alan," said he; "and by my troth, I found his way a very good one! But ye see, David, the loss of the ship and the cries of these poor lads sat very ill upon the man; and I'm thinking that would be the cause of it."

"Well, I would think so," says I; "for he was as keen as any of the rest at the beginning. But how did Hoseason take it?"

"It sticks in my mind that he would take it very ill," says Alan. "But the little man cried to me to run, and indeed I thought it was a good observe, and ran. The last that I saw they were all in a knot upon the beach, like folk that were not agreeing very well together."

"What do you mean by that?" said I.

"Well, the fists were going," said Alan; "and I saw one man go down like a pair of breeks. But I thought it would be better no to wait. Ye see there's a strip of Campbells in that end of Mull, which is no good company for a gentleman like me. If it hadnae been for that I would have waited and looked for ye mysel', let alone giving a hand to the little man." (It was droll how Alan dwelt on Mr Riach's stature, for, to say the truth, the one was not much smaller than the other). "So," says he, continuing, "I set my best foot forward and whenever I met in with anyone I cried out there was a wreck ashore. Man, they didnae stop to fash with me! Ye should have seen them linking for the beach! And when they got there they found they had had the pleasure of a run, which is aye good for a Campbell. I'm thinking it was a judgement on the clan that the brig went down in the lump and didnae break. But it was a very unlucky thing for you, that; for if any wreck had come ashore they would have hunted high and low, and would soon have found ye."

CHAPTER 19

THE HOUSE OF FEAR

Night fell as we were walking, and the clouds, which had broken up in the afternoon, settled in and thickened, so that it fell, for the season of the year, extremely dark. The way we went was over rough mountain sides; and though Alan pushed on with an assured manner, I could by no means see how he directed himself.

At last, about half past ten of the clock, we came to the top of a brae, and saw lights below us. It seemed a house door stood open and let out a beam of fire and candlelight; and all round the house and steading five or six persons were moving hurriedly about, each carrying a lighted brand.

"James must have tint his wits," said Alan. "If this was the soldiers instead of you and me, he would be in a bonny mess. But I dare say he'll have a sentry on the road, and he would ken well enough no soldiers would find the way that we came."

Hereupon he whistled three times, in a particular manner. It was strange to see how, at the first sound of it, all the moving torches came to a stand, as if the bearers were affrighted; and how, at the third, the bustle began again as before.

Having thus set folks' minds at rest, we came down the brae, and were met at the yard gate (for this place was like a well-doing farm) by a tall, handsome man of more than fifty, who cried out to Alan in the Gaelic.

"James Stewart," said Alan. "I will ask ye to speak in Scotch, for here is a young gentleman with me that has nane of the other. This is him," he added, putting his arm through mine; "a young gentleman of the lowlands, and a laird in his country too, but I am thinking it will be the better for his health if we give his name the go-by."

James of the Glens turned to me for a moment, and greeted me courteously enough; the next he had turned to Alan.

"This has been a dreadful accident," he cried. "It will bring trouble on the country." And he wrung his hands.

"Hoots!" said Alan, "ye must take the sour with the sweet, man. Colin Roy is dead, and be thankful for that!"

"Ay," said James, "and by my troth, I wish he was alive again! It's all very fine to blow and boast beforehand; but now it's done, Alan; and who's to bear the wyte of it? The accident fell out in Appin—mind ye that, Alan; it's Appin that must pay; and I am a man that has a family."

While this was going on I looked about me at the servants. Some were on ladders, digging in the thatch of the house or the farm buildings, from which they brought out guns, swords, and different weapons of war; others carried them away; and by the sound of mattock blows from somewhere further down the brae, I suppose they buried them.

Though they were all so busy, there prevailed no kind of order in their efforts; men struggled together for the same gun and ran into each other with their burning torches; and James was continually turning about from his talk with Alan, to cry out orders which were apparently never understood or even heeded. The faces in the torchlight were like those of people overborne with hurry and panic; and though none spoke above his breath, their speech sounded both anxious and angry.

It was about this time that a lassie came out of the house carrying a pack or bundle; and it has often made me smile to think how Alan's instinct awoke at the mere sight of it.

"What's that the lassie has?" he asked.

"We're just setting the house in order, Alan," said James, in his frightened and somewhat fawning way. "They'll search Appin with candles, and we must have all things straight. We're digging the bit guns and swords into the moss, ye see; and these, I am thinking, will be your ain French clothes."

"Bury my French clothes!" cried Alan. "'Troth, no!" And he laid hold upon the packet and retired into the barn to shift himself, recommending me in the meanwhile to this kinsman.

James carried me accordingly into the kitchen, and sat down with me at table, smiling and talking at first in a very hospitable manner. But presently the gloom returned upon him; he sat frowning, and biting his fingers; only remembered me from time to time; and then gave me but a word or two and a poor smile, and back into his private terrors. His wife sat by the fire and wept, with her face in her hands; his eldest son was crouched upon the floor, running over a great mass of papers and now and again setting one alight and burning it to the bitter end; all the while a servant with a red face was rummaging about the room, in a blind hurry of fear, and whimpering as she went: and every now and again one of the men would thrust in his face from the yard, and cry for orders.

At last James could keep his seat no longer, and begged my permission to be so unmannerly as walk about. "I am but poor company altogether, sir," says he, "but I can think of nothing but this dreadful accident, and the trouble it is like to bring upon quite innocent persons."

A little after he observed his son burning a paper, which he thought should have been kept; and at that his excitement burst out so that it was painful to witness. He struck the lad repeatedly.

"Are you gone gyte?" he cried. "Do you wish to hang your father and forgetful of my presence, carried on at him a long time together in the Gaelic, the young man answering nothing; only the wife, at the name of hanging, throwing her apron over her face and sobbing out louder than before.

This was all wretched for a stranger like myself to hear and see; and I was right glad when Alan returned, looking like himself in his fine French clothes, though (to be sure) they were now grown almost too battered and withered to deserve the name of fine. I was then taken out in my turn by another of the sons, and given that change of clothing of which I had stood so long in need, and a pair of Highland brogues made of deer-leather, rather strange at first, but after a little practice very easy to the feet.

By the time I came back Alan must have told his story; for it seemed understood that I was to fly with him, and they were all busy upon our equipment.

They gave us each a sword and pistols, though I professed my inability to use the former; and with these weapons, and some ammunition, a bag of oatmeal, an iron pan, and a bottle of right French brandy, we were ready for the heather. Money, indeed, was sorely lacking. I had about two guineas left; Alan's belt having earlier been despatched by another hand, that trusty messenger had no more than seventeen-pence to his whole fortune; and as for James, it appears he had brought himself so low with journeys to Edinburgh and legal expenses on behalf of the tenants, that he could only scrape together three-and-five-pence-halfpenny, the most of it in coppers.

"This'll no do," said Alan.

"Ye must find a safe bit somewhere near by," said James, "and get word sent to me. Ye see, ye'll have to get this business prettily off, Alan. This is no time to be stayed for a guinea or two. They're sure to get wind of ye, sure to seek ye, and by my word of it, sure to lay on ye the wyte of this day's accident. If it falls on you, it falls on me that am your near kinsman and harboured ye while ye were in the country. And if it comes on me—" he paused, and bit his fingers, with a white face. "It would be a painful thing for our friends if I was to hang," said he.

"It would be an ill day for Appin," says Alan.

"It's a day that sticks in my throat," said James, "Oh man, man, man—man Alan! you and me have spoken like two fools!" he cried, striking his hand upon the wall so that the house rang again.

"Well, and that's true, too," said Alan; "and my friend from the lowlands here" (nodding at me) "gave me a good word upon that head, if I would only have listened to him."

"But see here," said James, returning to his former manner, "if they lay me by the heels, Alan, it's then that you'll be needing the money. For with all that I have said and that you have said, it will look very black against the two of us; do ye mark that? Well, follow me out, and ye'll see that I'll have to get a paper out against ye mysel'; I'll have to offer a reward for ye; ay, will I! It's a sore thing to de between such near friends; but if I get the dirdum of this dreadful accident, I'll have to fend for myself, man. Do ye see that?"

He spoke with a pleading earnestness, taking Alan by the coat.

"Ay," said Alan, "I see that."

"And ye'll have to be clear of the country, Alan—ay, clear of Scotland—you and your friend, too. For I'll have to paper your friend from the lowlands. Ye see that, Alan—say that ye see that!"

I thought Alan flushed a bit. "This is unco hard on me that brought him here, James," said he, throwing his head back. "It's like making me a traitor!"

"Now, Alan, man!" cried James. "Look things in the face! He'll be papered anyway; Mungo Campbell'll be sure to paper him; what matters if I paper him too? And then, Alan, I am a man that has a family." And then, after a little pause on both sides: "And, Alan, it'll be a jury of Campbells," said he.

"There's this," said Alan, musingly, "naebody kens his name."

"Nor yet they shallnae, Alan! There's my hand on that," cried James, for all the world as if he had really known my name and was forgoing some advantage. "But just the habit he was in, and what he looked like, and his age, and the like? I couldnae well do less."

"I wonder at your father's son," cried Alan. "Would ye sell the lad with a gift? would ye change his clothes and then betray him?"

"No, no, Alan," said James, "No, no: the habit he took off—the habit Mungo saw him in." But I thought he seemed crestfallen; indeed, he was clutching at every straw, and all the time, I dare say, saw the faces of his hereditary foes on the bench and in the jury-box, and the gallows in the background.

"Well, sir," says Alan, turning to me, "what say ye to that? Ye are here under the safeguard of my honour; and it's my part to see nothing done but what shall please you."

"I have but one word to say," said I; "for to all this dispute I am a perfect stranger. But the plain common sense is to set the blame where it belongs, and that is on the man that fired the shot. Paper him, as ye call it, set the hunt on him; and let honest, innocent folk show their faces in safety."

But at this both Alan and James cried out in horror; bidding me hold my tongue, for what was not to be thought of; and asking me "What the Camerons would think?" (which confirmed me, it must have been a Cameron from Mamore that did the act) and if I did not see that the lad might be caught? "Ye havenae surely thought of that?" said they, with such innocent earnestness, that my hands dropped at my side and I despaired of argument.

"Very well, then," said I, "paper me, if you please, paper Alan, paper King George! We're all three innocent, and that seems to be what's wanted! But at least, sir," said I to James, recovering from my little fit of annoyance, "I am Alan's friend, and if I can be helpful to friends of his, I will not stumble at the risk."

I thought it best to put a fair face on my consent, for I saw Alan troubled; and besides (thinks I to myself, as soon as my back is turned, they will paper me, as they call it, whether I consent or not. But in this I saw I was wrong; for I had no sooner said the words, than Mrs Stewart leaped out of her chair, came running over to us, and wept first upon my neck and then on Alan's, blessing God for our goodness to her family.

"As for you, Alan, it was no more than your bounden duty," she said. "But for this lad that has come here and seen us at our worst, and seen the good man leeching like a suitor, him that by rights should give his commands like any king—as for you, my lad," she says, "my heart is wae not to have your name, but I have your face; and as long as my heart beats under my bosom, I will keep it, and think of it, and bless it." And with that she kissed me, and burst once more into such sobbing, that I stood abashed.

"Hoot, hoot," said Alan, looking mighty silly. "The day comes unco soon in this month of July; and tomorrow there'll be a fine to-do in Appin, a fine riding of dragoons, and crying of 'Cruachan!'* and running of red-coats; and it behoves you and me to be the sooner gone."

Thereupon we said farewell, and set out again, bending somewhat eastward, in a fine mild dark night, and over much the same broken country as before.

CHAPTER 20

THE FLIGHT IN THE HEATHER: THE ROCKS

Sometimes we walked, sometimes ran; and as it drew on to morning, walked ever the less and ran the more. Though, upon

*The rallying-word of the Campbells.

its face, that country appeared to be a desert, yet there were huts and houses of the people, of which we must have passed more than twenty, hidden in quiet places of the hills. When we came to one of these, Alan would leave me in the way, and go himself and rap upon the side of the house and speak a while at the window with some sleeper awakened. This was to pass the news; which, in that country, was so much of a duty that Alan must pause to attend to it even while fleeing for his life; and so well attended to by others, that in more than half of the houses where we called they had heard already of the murder. In the others, as well as I could make out (standing back at a distance and hearing a strange tongue) the news was received with more of consternation than surprise.

For all our hurry, day began to come in while we were still far from any shelter. It found us in a prodigious valley, strewn with rocks and where ran a foaming river. Wild mountains stood around it; there grew there neither grass nor trees; and I have sometimes thought since then, that it may have been the valley called Glencoe, where the massacre was in the time of King William. But for the details of our itinerary, I am all to seek; our way lying now by short cuts, now by great detours; our pace being so hurried; our time of journeying usually by night; and the names of such places as I asked and heard, being in the Gaelic tongue and the more easily forgotten.

The first peep of morning, then, showed us this horrible place, and I could see Alan knit his brow.

"This is no fit place for you and me," he said. "This is a place they're bound to watch."

And with that he ran harder than ever down to the water side, in a part where the river was split in two among three rocks. It went through with a horrid thundering that made my belly quake; and there hung over the lynn a little mist of spray. Alan looked neither to the right nor to the left, but jumped clean upon the middle rock and fell there on his hands and knees to check himself, for that rock was small and he might have pitched over on the far side. I had scarce time to measure the distance or to understand the peril, before I had followed him, and he had caught and stopped me.

So there we stood, side by side upon a small rock slippery with spray, a far broader leap in front of us, and the river dinning upon all sides. When I saw where I was, there came on me a deadly sickness of fear, and I put my hand over my eyes. Alan took me and shook me; I saw he was speaking, but the roaring of the falls and the trouble of my mind prevented me from hearing; only I saw his face was red with anger, and that he stamped upon the rock. The same looked showed me the water raging by, and the mist hanging in the air; and with that, I covered my eyes again and shuddered.

The next minute Alan had set the brandy bottle to my lips, and forced me to drink about a gill, which sent the blood into my head again. Then, putting his hands to his mouth and his mouth to my ear, he shouted, "Hang or drown!" and turning his back upon me, leaped over the farther branch of the stream, and landed safe.

I was now alone upon the rock, which gave me the more room; the brandy was singing in my ears; I had this good example fresh before me, and just wit enough to see that if I did not leap at once, I should never leap at all. I bent low on my knees and flung myself forth, with that kind of anger of despair that has sometimes stood me in stead of courage. Sure enough, it was but my hands that reached the full length; these slipped, caught again, slipped again; and I was sliddering back into the lynn, when Alan seized me, first by the hair, then by the collar, and with a great strain dragged me into safety.

Never a word he said, but set off running again for his life, and I must stagger to my feet and run after him. I had been weary before, but now I was sick and bruised, and partly drunken, with the brandy; I kept stumbling as I ran, I had a stitch that came near to overmaster me; and when at last Alan paused under a great rock that stood there among a number of others, it was none too soon for David Balfour.

A great rock, I have said; but by rights it was two rocks leaning together at the top, both some twenty feet high, and at first sight inaccessible. Even Alan (though you may say he had as good as four hands) failed twice in an attempt to climb them; and it was only at the third trial, and then by standing on my shoulders and leaping up with such force as I thought must have broken my collar-bone, that he secured a lodgement. Once there, he let down his leathern girdle; and with the aid of that and a pair of shallow footholds in the rocks, I scrambled up beside him.

Then I saw why he had come there; for the two rocks, being both somewhat hollow on the top and sloping one to the other, made a kind of dish or saucer, where as many as three or four men might have lain hidden.

All this while Alan had not said a word, and had run and

climbed with such a savage, silent frenzy of hurry, that I knew he was in mortal fear of some miscarriage. Even now we were on the rock he said nothing, nor so much as relaxed the frowning look upon his face; but clapped flat down, and keeping only one eye above the edge of our place of shelter, scouted all round the compass. The dawn had come quite clear; we could see the stony sides of the valley, and its bottom, which was bestrewed with rocks, and the river, which went from one side to another, and made white falls; but nowhere the smoke of a house, nor any living creature but some eagles screaming round a cliff.

Then at last Alan smiled.

"Ay," said he, "now we have a chance"; and then looking at me with amusement, "Ye're no very gleg at the jumping," said he.

At this I suppose I coloured with mortification, for he added at once, "Hoots! small blame to ye! To be feared of a thing and yet to do it, is what makes the prettiest kind of a man. And then there was water there, and water's a thing that dauntons even me. No, no," said Alan, "it's no you that's to blame, it's me."

I asked him why.

"Why," said he, "I have proved myself a gomeral this night. For first of all I take a wrong road, and that in my own country of Appin; so that the day has caught us where we should never have been; and thanks to that, we lie here in some danger and mair discomfort. And next (which is the worst of the two, for a man that has been so much among the heather as myself) I have come wanting a water-bottle, and here we lie for a long summer's day with naething but neat spirit. Ye may think that a small matter; but before it comes night, David, ye'll give me news of it."

I was anxious to redeem my character, and offered, if he would pour out the brandy, to run down and fill the bottle at the river.

"I wouldnae waste the good spirit either," says he. "It's been a good friend to you this night; or in my poor opinion, ye would still be cocking on yon stone. And what's mair," says he, "ye may have observed (you that's a man of so much penetration) that Alan Breck Stewart was perhaps walking quicker than his ordinar'."

"You!" I cried, "you were running fit to burst."

"Was I so?" said he. "Well, then, ye may depend upon it, there was nae time to be lost. And now here is enough said; gang you to your sleep, lad, and I'll watch."

Accordingly, I lay down to sleep; a little peaty earth had drifted in between the top of the two rocks, and some bracken grew there, to be a bed to me; the last thing I heard was still the crying of the eagles.

I dare say it would be nine in the morning when I was roughly awakened, and found Alan's hand pressed upon my mouth.

"Wheesht!" he whispered. "Ye were snoring."

"Well," said I, surprised at his anxious and dark face, "and why not?"

He peered over the edge of the rock, and signed to me to do the like.

It was now high day, cloudless, and very hot. The valley was as clear as in a picture. About half a mile up the water was a camp of red-coats; a big fire blazed in their midst, at which some were cooking; and near by, on the top of a rock about as high as ours, there stood a sentry, with the sun sparkling on his arms. All the way down along the riverside were posted other sentries; here near together, there widelier scattered; some planted like the first, on places of command, some on the ground level and marching and counter-marching, so as to meet half way. Higher up the glen, where the ground was more open, the chain of posts was continued by horse-soldiers, whom we could see in the distance riding to and fro. Lower down, the infantry continued; but as the stream was suddenly swelled by the confluence of a considerable burn, they were more widely set, and only watched the fords and stepping-stones.

I took but one look at them, and ducked again into my place. It was strange indeed to see this valley, which had lain so solitary in the hour of dawn, bristling with arms and dotted with the red coats and breeches.

"Ye see," said Alan, "this was what I was afraid of, Davie: that they would watch the burn-side. They began to come in about two hours ago, and, man! but ye're a grand hand at the sleeping! We're in a narrow place. If they get up the sides of the hill, they could easy spy us with a glass; but if they'll only keep in the foot of the valley, we'll do yet. The posts are thinner down the water; and, come night, we'll try our hand at getting by them."

"And what are we to do till night?" I asked.

"Lie here," says he, "and birstle."

That one good Scotch word, "birstle", was indeed the most of the story of the day that we had now to pass. You are to remember that we lay on the bare top of a rock, like scones upon a griddle; the sun beat upon us cruelly; the rock grew so heated, a man could scarce endure the touch of it; and the little patch of earth and fern, which kept cooler, was only large enough for one at a time. We took turn about to lie on the naked rock, which was indeed like the position of that saint that was martyred on a gridiron; and it ran in my mind how strange it was, that in the same climate and at only a few days' distance, I should have suffered so cruelly, first from cold upon my island, and now from heat upon this rock.

All the while we had no water, only a raw brandy for a drink, which was worse than nothing; but we kept the bottle as cool as we could, burying it in the earth, and got some relief by bathing our breasts and temples.

The soldiers kept stirring all day in the bottom of the valley, now changing guard, now in patrolling parties hunting among the rocks. These lay round in so great a number, that to look for men among them was like looking for a needle in a bottle of hay; and being so hopeless a task, it was gone about with the less care. Yet we could see the soldiers pike their bayonets among the heather, which sent a cold thrill into my vitals; and they would sometimes hang about our rock, so that we scarce dared to breathe.

It was in this way that I first heard the right English speech; one fellow as he went by actually clapping his hand upon the sunny face of the rock on which we lay, and plucking it off again with an oath.

"I tell you it's 'ot," says he; and I was amazed at the clipping tones and the odd sing-song in which he spoke, and no less at that strange trick of dropping out the letter h. To be sure, I had heard Ransome; but he had taken his ways from all sorts of people, and spoke so imperfectly at the best, that I set down the most of it to childishness. My surprise was all the greater to hear that manner of speaking in the mouth of a grown man; and indeed I have never grown used to it; nor yet altogether with the English grammar, as perhaps a very critical eye might here and there spy out even in these memoirs.

The tediousness and pain of these hours upon the rock grew only the greater as the day went on; the rock getting still the hotter and the sun the fiercer. There were giddiness, and sickness, and sharp pangs like rheumatism, to be supported. I minded then, and have often minded since, on the lines in our Scotch psalm:

> The moon by night thee shall not smite,
> Nor yet the sun by day;

and indeed it was only by God's blessing that we were neither of us sun-smitten.

At last, about two, it was beyond men's bearing, and there was now temptation to resist as well as pain to thole. For the sun being now got a little into the west, there came a patch of shade on the east side of our rock, which was the side sheltered from the soldiers.

"As well one death as another," said Alan, and slipped over the edge and dropped on the ground on the shadowy side.

I followed him at once, and instantly fell all my length, so weak was I and so giddy with that long exposure. Here, then, we lay for an hour or two, aching from head to foot, as weak as water, and lying quite naked to the eye of any soldier who should have strolled that way. None came, however, all passing by on the other side; so that our rock continued to be our shield even in this new position.

Presently we began again to get a little strength; and as the soldiers were now lying closer along the riverside, Alan proposed that we should try a start. I was by this time afraid of but one thing in the world; and that was to be set back upon the rock; anything else was welcome to me; so we got ourselves at once in marching order, and began to slip from rock to rock one after the other, now crawling flat on our bellies in the shade, now making a run for it, heart in mouth.

The soldiers, having searched this side of the valley after a fashion, and being perhaps somewhat sleepy with the sultriness of the afternoon, had now laid by much of their vigilance, and stood dozing at their posts or only kept a lookout along the banks of the river; so that in this way, keeping down the valley and at the same time towards the mountains we drew steadily away from their neighbourhood. But the business was the most wearing I had ever taken part in. A man had need of a hundred eyes in every part of him, to keep concealed in that uneven country and within cry of so many and scattered sentries. When we must pass an open place, quickness was not all, but a swift judgement not only of the lie of the whole country, but of the solidity of every stone on which we must set foot; for the afternoon was now fallen so breathless that the rolling of a pebble sounded abroad like a pistol shot, and would start the echo calling among the hills and cliffs.

By sundown we had made some distance, even by our slow rate of progress, though to be sure the sentry on the rock was still plainly in our view. But now we came on something that put all fears out of season; and that was a deep rushing burn, that tore down, in that part, to join the glen river. At the sight of this we cast ourselves on the ground and plunged head and shoulders in the water; and I cannot tell which was the more pleasant, the great shock as the cool stream went over us, or the greed with which we drank of it.

We lay there (for the banks hid us), drank again and again, bathed our chests, let our wrists trail in the running water till they ached with the chill; and at last, being wonderfully renewed, we got out the meal-bag and made drammach in the iron pan. This, though it is but cold water mingled with oatmeal, yet makes a good enough dish for a hungry man; and where there are no means of making fire, or (as in our case) good reason for not making one, it is the chief stand-by of those who have taken to the heather.

As soon as the shadow of the night had fallen, we set forth again, at first with the same caution, but presently with more boldness, standing our full height and stepping out at a good pace of walking. The way was very intricate, lying up the steep sides of mountains and along the brows of cliffs; clouds had come in with the sunset, and the night was dark and cool; so that I walked without much fatigue, but in continual fear of falling and rolling down the mountains, and with no guess at our direction.

The moon rose at last and found us still on the road; it was in its last quarter and was long beset with clouds; but after a while shone out, and showed me many dark heads of mountains, and was reflected far underneath us on the narrow arm of a sea-loch.

At this sight we both paused: I struck with wonder to find myself so high and walking (as it seemed to me) upon clouds: Alan to make sure of his direction.

Seemingly he was well pleased, and he must certainly have judged us out of ear-shot of all our enemies; for throughout the rest of our night-march he beguiled the way with whistling of many tunes, warlike, merry, plaintive; reel tunes that made the foot go faster; tunes of my own south country that made me fain to be home from my adventures; and all these, on the great, dark, desert mountains, making company upon the way.

CHAPTER 21

THE FLIGHT IN THE HEATHER: THE HEUGH OF CORRYNAKIEGH

Early as day comes in the beginning of July, it was still dark when we reached our destination, a cleft in the head of a great mountain, with a water running through the midst, and upon the one hand a shallow cave in a rock. Birches grew there in a thin, pretty wood, which a little farther on was changed into a wood of pines. The burn was full of trout; the wood of cushat-doves; on the open side of the mountain beyond, whaups would be always whistling, and cuckoos were plentiful. From the mouth of the cleft we looked down upon a part of Lamore, and on the sea-loch that divides that country from Appin; and this from so great a height, as made it my continual wonder and pleasure to sit and behold them.

The name of the cleft was the Heugh of Corrynakiegh; and although from its height and being so near upon the sea, it was often beset with clouds, yet it was on the whole a pleasant place, and the five days we lived in it went happily.

We slept in the cave, making our bed of heather bushes which we cut for that purpose, and covering ourselves with Alan's great-coat. There was a low concealed place, in a turning of the glen, where we were, so bold as to make fire; so that we could warm ourselves when the clouds set in, and cook hot porridge, and grill the little trouts that we caught with our hands under the stones and overhanging banks of the burn. This was indeed our chief pleasure and business; and not only to save our meal against worse times, but with a rivalry that much amused us, we spent a great part of our days at the water side, stripped to the waist and groping about or (as they say) guddling for these fish. The largest we got might have been a quarter of a pound; but they were of good flesh and flavour, and when broiled upon the coals, lacked only a little salt to be delicious.

In any by-time Alan must teach me to use my sword, for my ignorance had much distressed him; and I think besides, as I had sometimes the upper hand of him in the fishing, he was not sorry to turn to an exercise where he had so much the upper hand of me. He made it somewhat more of a pain than need have been, for he stormed at me all through the lessons in a very violent manner of scolding, and would push me so close that I made sure he must run me through the body. I was often tempted to turn tail, but held my ground for all that, and got some profit of my lessons; if it was but to stand on guard with an assured countenance, which is often all that is required. So, though I could never in the least please my master, I was not altogether displeased with myself.

In the meantime, you are not to suppose that we neglected our chief business, which was to get away.

"It will be many a long day," Alan said to me on our first morning, "before the red-coats think upon seeking Corrynakiegh; so now we must get word sent to James, and he must find the siller for us."

"And how shall we send that word?" says I. "We are here in a desert place, which yet we dare not leave; and unless ye get the fowls of the air to be your messengers, I see not what we shall be able to do."

"Ay?" said Alan. "Ye're a man of small contrivance, David."

Thereupon he fell in a muse, looking in the embers of the fire; and presently, getting a piece of wood, he fashioned it in to a cross, the four ends of which he blackened on the coals. Then he looked at me a little shyly. "Could ye lend me my button?" says he. "It seems a strange thing to ask a gift again, but I own I am laith to cut another."

I gave him the button; whereupon he strung it on a strip of his great coat which he had used to bind the cross; and tying in a little sprig of birch and another of fir, he looked upon his work with satisfaction.

"Now," said he, "there is a little clachan" (what is called a hamlet in the English) "not very far from Corrynakiegh, and it has the name of Koalisnacoan. There, there are living many friends of mine whom I could trust with my life, and some that I am not just so sure of. Ye see, David, there will be money set upon our heads; James himsel' is to set money on them; and as for the Campbells, they would never spare siller where there was a Stewart to be hurt. If it was otherwise, I would go down to Koalisnacoan whatever, and trust my life into these people's hands as lightly as I would trust another with my glove."

"But being so?" said I.

"Being so," said he, "I would as lief they didnae see me. There's bad folk everywhere, and what's far worse, weak ones. So when it comes dark again, I will steal down into that clachan, and set this that I have been making in the window of a good friend of mine, John Breck Maccoll, a bouman of Appin's."

"With all my heart," says I; "and if he finds it, what is he to think."

"Well," says Alan, "I wish he was a man of more penetration, for by my troth I am afraid he will make little enough of it! But this is what I have in my mind. This cross is something in the nature of the crosstarrie, or fiery cross, which is the signal of gathering in our clans; yet he will know well enough the clan is not to rise, for there it is standing in his window, and no word with it. So, he will say to himsel', *The clan is not to rise, but there is something.* Then he will see my button, and that was Duncan Stewart's. And then he will say to himsel', *The son of Duncan is in the heather, and has need of me.*"

"Well," said I, "it may be. But even supposing so, there is a good deal of heather between here and the Forth."

"And that is a very true word," says Alan. "But then John Breck will see the sprig of birch and the sprig of pine; and he will say to himsel' (if he is a man of any penetration at all, which I misdoubt) *Alan will be lying in a wood which is both of pines and birches.* Then he will think to himsel', *That is not so very rife hereabout;* and then he will come and give us a look up in Corrynakiegh. And if he does not, David, the devil may fly away with him, for what I care; for he will no be worth the salt to his porridge."

"Eh, man," said I, drolling with him a little, "you're very ingenious! But would it not be simpler for you to write him a few words in black-and-white?"

"And that is an excellent observe, Mr Balfour of Shaws," says Alan, drolling with me; "and it would certainly be much simpler for me to write to him, but it would be a sore job for John Breck to read it. He would have to go to the school for two-three years; and it's possible we might be wearied waiting for him."

So that night Alan carried down his fiery cross and set it in the bouman's window. He was troubled when he came back; for the dogs had barked and the folk run out from their houses; and he thought he had heard a clatter of guns and seen a red-coat come to one of the doors. On all accounts we lay the next day in the borders of the wood and kept a close look-out; so that if it was

John Breck that came, we might be ready to guide him, and if it was the red-coats, we should have time to get away.

About noon a man was to be spied, straggling up the open side of the mountain in the sun, and looking round him as he came, from under his hand. No sooner had Alan seen him than he whistled; the man turned and came a little towards us; then Alan would give another "peep!" and the man would come still nearer; and so by the sound of whistling, he was guided to the spot where we lay.

He was a ragged, wild, bearded man, about forty, grossly disfigured with the smallpox, and looked both dull and savage. Although his English was very bad and broken, yet Alan (according to his very handsome use, whenever I was by) would suffer him to speak no Gaelic. Perhaps the strange language made him appear more backward than he really was; but I thought he had little good-will to serve us, and what he had was the child of terror.

Alan would have had him carry a message to James; but the bouman would hear of no message. "She was forget it," he said in his screaming voice; and would either have a letter or wash his hands of us.

I thought Alan would be gravelled at that, for we lacked the means of writing in that desert. But he was a man of more resources than I knew; searched the wood until he found the quill of a cushat-dove, which he shaped into a pen; made himself a kind of ink with gunpowder from his horn and water from the running stream; and tearing a corner from his French military commission (which he carried in his pocket, like a talisman to keep him from the gallows) he sat down and wrote as follows:

DEAR KINSMAN,—Please send the money by the bearer to the place he kens of.—Your affectionate cousin,

A.S.

This he entrusted to the bouman, who promised to make what manner of speed he best could, and carried it off with him down the hill.

He was three days gone, but about five in the evening of the third, we heard a whistling in the wood, which Alan answered; and presently the bouman came up the waterside, looking for us, right and left. He seemed less sulky than before, and indeed he was no doubt well pleased to have got the end of such a dangerous commission.

He gave us the news of the country; that it was alive with redcoats; that arms were being found, and poor folk brought in trouble daily; and that James and some of his servants were already clapped in prison at Fort William, under strong suspicion of complicity. It seemed, it was noised on all sides that Alan Breck had fired the shot; and there was a bill issued for both him and me, with one hundred pounds reward.

This was all as bad as could be; and the little note the bouman had carried us from Mrs Stewart was of a miserable sadness. In it she besought Alan not to let himself be captured, assuring him, if he fell in the hands of the troops, both he and James were no better than dead men. The money she had sent was all that she could beg or borrow, and she prayed heaven we could be doing with it. Lastly, she said she enclosed us one of the bills in which we were described.

This we looked upon with great curiosity and not a little fear, partly as a man may look in a mirror, partly as he might look into the barrel of an enemy's gun to judge if it be truly aimed. Alan was advertised as "a small, pock-marked, active man of thirty-five or thereby, dressed in a feathered hat, a French side-coat of blue with silver buttons and lace a great deal tarnished, a red waistcoat and breeches of black shag"; and I as "a tall strong lad of about eighteen, wearing an old blue coat, very ragged, an old Highland bonnet, a long homespun waistcoat, blue breeches; his legs bare; low-country shoes, wanting the toes; speaks like a lowlander, and has no beard."

Alan was well enough pleased to see his finery so fully remembered and set down; only when he came to the word tarnish, he looked upon his lace like one a little mortified.

As for myself, I thought I cut a miserable figure in the bill; and yet was well enough pleased too, for since I had changed these rags, the description had ceased to be a danger and become a source of safety.

"Alan," said I, "you should change your clothes."

"Na, troth!" said Alan, "I have nae others. A fine sight I would be, if I went back to France in a bonnet!"

This put a second reflection in my mind: that if I were to separate from Alan and his tell-tale clothes I should be safe against arrest, and might go openly about my business. Nor was this all; for suppose I was arrested when I was alone, there was little against me; but suppose I was taken in company with the reputed murderer, my case would begin to be grave. For generosity's sake,

I dare not speak my mind upon this head; but I thought of it none the less.

I thought of it all the more, too, when the bouman brought out a green purse with four guineas in gold, and the best part of another in small change. True, it was more than I had. But then Alan, with less than five guineas, had to get as far as France; I, with my less than two, not beyond Queensferry; so that, taking things in their proportion, Alan's society was not only a peril to my life but a burden on my purse.

But there was no thought of the sort in the honest head of my companion. He believed he was serving, helping, and protecting me. And what could I do but hold my peace, and chafe, and take my chance of it?

"It's little enough," said Alan, putting the purse in his pocket, "but it'll do my business. And now John Breck, if ye will hand me over my button, this gentleman and me will be for taking the road."

But the bouman, after feeling about in a hairy purse that hung in front of him in the Highland manner though he wore otherwise the lowland habit, (with sea-trousers) began to roll his eyes strangely, and at last said, "Her nainsel will loss it," meaning he thought he had lost it.

"What!" cried Alan, "you will lose my button, that was my father's before me? Now, I will tell you what is in my mind, John Breck: it is in my mind this is the worst day's work that ever ye did since ye were born."

And as Alan spoke, he set his hands on his knees and looked at the bouman with a smiling mouth, and that dancing light in his eyes that meant mischief to his enemies.

Perhaps the bouman was honest enough; perhaps he had meant to cheat and then, finding himself alone with two of us in a desert place, cast back to honesty as being safer; at least, and all at once, he seemed to find that button and handed it to Alan.

"Well, and it is a good thing for the honour of the Maccolls," said Alan, and then to me, "Here is my button back again, and I thank you for parting with it, which is of a piece with all your friendships to me." Then he took the warmest parting of the bouman. "For," says he, "ye have done very well by me, and set your neck at a venture, and I will always give you the name of a good man."

Lastly, the bouman took himself off one way; and Alan and I (getting our chattels together) struck into another to resume our flight.

Chapter 22

THE FLIGHT IN THE HEATHER: THE MOOR

More than eleven hours of incessant, hard travelling brought us early in the morning to the end of a range of mountains. In front of us there lay a piece of low, broken, desert land, which we must now cross. The sun was not long up, and shone straight in our eyes; a little, thin mist went up from the face of the moorland like a smoke; so that (as Alan said) there might have been twenty squadron of dragoons there and we none the wiser. We sat down, therefore, in a house of the hillside till the mist should have risen, and made ourselves a dish of drammach, and held a council of war.

"David," said Alan, "this is the kittle bit. Shall we lie here till it comes night, or shall we risk it and stave on ahead?"

"Well," said I, "I am tired indeed, but I could walk as far again, if that was all."

"Ay, but it is nae," said Alan, "nor yet the half. This is how we stand: Appin's fair death to us. To the south it's all Campbells, and no to be thought of. To the north; well, there's no muckle to be gained by going north; neither for you, that wants to get to Queensferry, nor yet for me, that wants to get to France. Well, then, we'll can strike east."

"East be it!" says I, quite cheerily; but I was thinking, in to myself: "Oh, man, if you would only take one point of the compass and let me take any other, it would be the best for both of us."

"Well, then, east, ye see, we have the muirs," said Alan. "Once there, David, it's mere pitch-and-toss. Out on yon bald, naked, flat place, where can a body turn to? Let the red-coats come over a hill, they can spy you miles away; and the sorrow's in their horses' heels, they would soon ride you down. It's no good place, David; and I'm free to say, it's worse by daylight than by dark."

"Alan," said I, "hear my way of it. Appin's death for us; we have none too much money, nor yet meal; the longer they seek, the nearer they may guess where we are; it's all a risk; and I give my word to go ahead until we drop."

Alan was delighted. "There are whiles," said he, "when ye are altogether too canny and Whiggish to be company for a gentleman like me; but there come other whiles when ye show yoursel' a mettle spark; and it's then, David; that I love ye like a brother."

The mist rose and died away, and showed us that country lying as waste as the sea; only the moorfowl and the peewees crying upon it, and far over to the east, a herd of deer, moving like dots. Much of it was red with heather; much of the rest broken up, with bogs and hags and peaty pools; some had been burnt black in a heath fire; and in another place there was quite a forest of dead firs, standing like skeleton. A wearier looking desert man never saw; but at least it was clear of troops, which was our point.

We went down accordingly into the waste, and began to make our toilsome and devious travel towards the eastern verge. There were the tops of mountains all round (you are to remember) from whence we might be spied at any moment; so it behoved us to keep in the hollow parts of the moor, and when these turned aside from our direction, to move upon its naked face with infinite care. Sometimes, for half an hour together, we must crawl from one heather bush to another, as hunters do when they are hard upon the deer. It was a clear day again, with a blazing sun; the water in the brandy bottle was soon gone; and altogether, if I had guessed what it would be to crawl half the time upon my belly and to walk much of the rest stooping nearly to the knees, I should certainly have held back from such a killing enterprise.

Toiling and resting and toiling again, we wore away the morning; and about noon lay down in a thick bush of heather to sleep. Alan took the first watch; and it seemed to me I had scarce closed my eyes before I was shaken up to take the second. We had no clock to go by; and Alan stuck a sprig of heath in the ground to serve instead; so that as soon as the shadow of the bush should fall so far to the east, I might know to rouse him. But I was by this time so weary that I could have slept twelve hours at a stretch; I had the taste of sleep in my throat; my joints slept even when my mind was waking; the hot smell of the heather, and the drone of the wild bees, were like possets to me; and every now and again I would give a jump and find I had been dozing.

The last time I woke I seemed to come back from farther away, and thought the sun had taken a great start in the heavens. I looked at the sprig of heather, and then I could have cried aloud; for I saw I had betrayed my trust. My head was nearly turned with fear and shame; and at what I saw, when I looked out around me on the moor, my heart was like dying in my body. For sure enough, a body of horse-soldiers had come during my sleep, and were drawing near to us from the south-east, spread out in the shape of a fan and riding their horses to and fro in the deep parts of the heather. When I waked Alan, he glanced first at the soldiers, then at the mark and the position of the sun, and knitted his brows with a sudden, quick look, both ugly and anxious, which was all the reproach I had of him.

"What are we to do now?" I asked.

"We'll have to play at being hares," said he. "Do ye see yon mountain?" pointing to one on the north-eastern sky.

"Ay," said I.

"Well, then," says he, "let us strike for that. Its name is Ben Alder; it is a wild, desert mountain full of hills and hollows, and if we can win to it before the morn, we may do yet."

"But, Alan," cried I, "that will take us across the very coming of the soldiers!"

"I ken that fine," said he; "but if we are driven back on Appin, we are two dead men. So now, David man, be brisk!"

With that he began to run forward on his hands and knees with an incredible quickness, as though it were his natural way of going. All the time, too, he kept winding in and out in the lower parts of the moorland where we were the best concealed. Some of these had been burned or at least scathed with fire; and there rose in our faces (which were close to the ground) a blinding, choking dust as fine as smoke. The water was long out; and this posture of running on the hands and knees brings an overmastering weakness and weariness, so that the joints ache and the wrists faint under your weight.

Now and then, indeed, where was a big bush of heather, we lay a while, and panted, and putting aside the leaves, looked back at the dragoons. They had not spied us, for they held straight on; a halftroop, I think, covering about two miles of ground, and beating it mighty thoroughly as they went. I had awakened just in time; a little later, and we must have fled in front of them, instead of escaping on one side. Even as it was, the least misfortune might betray us; and now and again, when a grouse rose out of the heather with a clap of wings, we lay as still as the dead and were afraid to breathe.

The aching and faintness of my body, the labouring of my heart, the soreness of my hands, and the smarting of my throat and eyes in the continual smoke of dust and ashes, had soon grown to be so unbearable that I would gladly have given up. Nothing but the fear of Alan lent me enough of false kind of courage to continue. As for himself (and you are to bear in mind that he was cumbered with a great-coat), he had first turned crimson, but as time went on, the redness began to be mingled with patches of white; his breath cried and whistled as it came; and his voice, when he whispered his observations in my ear during our halts, sounded like nothing human. Yet he seemed in no way dashed in spirits, nor did he at all abate in his activity; so that I was driven to marvel at the man's endurance.

At length, in the first gloaming of the night, we heard a trumpet sound, and looking back from among the heather, saw the troops beginning to collect. A little after, they had built a fire and camped for the night, about the middle of the waste.

At this I begged and besought that we might lie down and sleep.

"There shall be no sleep the night!" said Alan. "From now on, these weary dragoons of yours will keep the crown of the muirland, and none will get out of Appin but winged fowls. We got through in the nick of time, and shall we jeopard what we've gained? Na, na, when the day comes, it shall find us in a fast place on Ben Alder."

"Alan," I said, "it's not the want of will: it's strength that I want, If I could, I would; but as sure as I'm alive I cannot."

"Very well, then," said Alan. "I'll carry ye."

I looked to see if he were jesting; but no, the little man was in dead earnest; and the sight of so much resolution shamed me.

"Lead away!" said I, "I'll follow."

He gave me one look, as much as to say "Well done, David!" and off he set again at his top speed.

It grew cooler and even a little darker (but not much) with the coming of the night. The sky was cloudless; it was still early in July, and pretty far north; in the darkest part of that night, you would have needed pretty good eyes to read, but for all that, I have often seen it darker in a winter midday. Heavy dew fell and drenched the moor like rain; and this refreshed me for a while. When we stopped to breathe, and I had time to see all about me, the clearness and sweetness of the night, the shapes of the hills like things asleep, and the fire dwindling away behind us, like a bright spot in the midst of the moor, anger would come upon me in a clap that I must still drag myself in agony and eat the dust like a worm.

By what I have read in books, I think few that have held a pen were ever really wearied, or they would write of it more strongly. I had no care of my life, neither past nor future, and I scarce remembered there was such a lad as David Balfour. I did not think of myself, but just of each fresh step which I was sure would be my last, with despair—and of Alan, who was the cause of it, with hatred. Alan was in the right trade as a soldier; this is the officer's part to make men continue to do things, they know not wherefore, and when, if the choice was offered, they would lie down where they were and be killed. And I dare say I would have made a good enough private; for in these last hours, it never occurred to me that I had any choice, but just to obey as long as I was able, and die obeying.

Day began to come in, after years, I thought; and by that time we were past the greatest danger, and could walk upon our feet like men, instead of crawling like brutes. But, dear heart have mercy! what a pair we must have made, going double like old grandfathers, stumbling like babes, and as white as dead folk. Never a word passed between us; each set his mouth and kept his eyes in front of him, and lifted up his foot and set it down, like people lifting weights at a country play; all the while, with the moorfowl crying "peep!" in the heather, and the light coming slowly clearer in the east.

I say Alan did as I did. Not that ever I looked at him, for I had enough to keep my feet; but because it is plain he must have been as stupid with weariness as myself, and looked as little where we were going, or we should not have walked into an ambush like blind men. It fell in this way. We were going down a heathery brae, Alan leading and I following a pace or two behind, like a fiddler and his wife; when upon a sudden the heather gave a rustle, three or four ragged men leaped out, and the next moment we were lying on our backs, each with a dirk at his throat.

I don't think I cared; the pain of this rough handling was quite swallowed up by the pains of which I was already full; and I was too glad to have stopped walking to mind about a dirk. I lay looking up in the face of the man that held me; and I mind his face was black with the sun and his eyes very light, but I was not afraid of him. I heard Alan and another whispering in the Gaelic; and what they said was all one to me.

Then the dirks were put up, our weapons were taken away, and we were set face to face, sitting in the heather.

"They are Cluny's men," said Alan. "We couldnae have fallen

better. We're just to bide here with these, which are his outsentries, till they can get word to the chief of my arrival."

Now Cluny Macpherson, the chief of the clan Vourich, had been one of the leaders of the great rebellion six years before; there was a price on his life; and I had supposed him long ago in France, with the rest of the heads of that desperate party. Even tired as I was, the surprise of what I heard half wakened me.

"What?" I cried, "Is Cluny still here?"

"Ay is he so!" said Alan, "Still in his own country and kept by his own clan. King George can do no more."

I think I would have asked further, but Alan gave me the putoff. "I am rather wearied," he said, "and I would like fine to get a sleep". And without more words, he rolled on his face in a deep heather bush, and seemed to sleep at once.

There was no such thing possible for me. You have heard grasshoppers whirring in the grass in the summer time? Well, I had no sooner closed my eyes, than my body and above all my head, belly, and wrists, seemed to be filled with whirring grasshoppers; and I must open my eyes again at once, and tumble and toss, and sit up and lie down; and look at the sky which dazzled me, or at Cluny's wild and dirty sentries, peering out over the top of the brae and chattering to each other in the Gaelic.

That was all the rest I had, until the messenger returned; when, as it appeared that Cluny would be glad to receive us, we must get once more upon our feet and set forward. Alan was in excellent good spirits, much refreshed by his sleep, very hungry, and looking pleasantly forward to a dram and a dish of hot collops, of which, it seems, the messenger had brought him word. For my part, it made me sick to hear of eating. I had been dead-heavy before, and now I felt a kind of dreadful lightness, which would not suffer me to walk. I drifted like a gossamer; the ground seemed to me a cloud, the hills a feather-weight, the air to have a current, like a running burn, which carried me to and fro. With all that, a sort of horror of despair set on my mind, so that I could have wept at my own helplessness.

I saw Alan knitting his brows at me, and supposed it was in anger; and that gave me a pang of light-headed fear, like what a child may have. I remember, too, that I was smiling, and could not stop smiling, hard as I tried; for I thought it was out of place at such a time. But my good companion had nothing in his mind but kindness; and the next moment, two of the gillies had me by the arms, and I began to be carried forward with great swiftness (or so it appeared to me, although I dare say it was slowly enough in truth) through a labyrinth of dreary glens and hollows and into the heart of that dismal mountain of Ben Alder.

CHAPTER 23

CLUNY'S CAGE

We came at last to the foot of an exceeding steep wood, which scrambled up a craggy hillside, and was crowned by a naked precipice.

"It's here," said one of the guides, and we struck up hill.

The trees clung upon the slope, like sailors on the shrouds of a ship; and their trunks were like the rounds of a ladder, by which we mounted.

Quite at the top, and just before the rocky face of the cliff sprang above the foliage, we found that strange house which was known in the country as "Cluny's Cage". The trunks of several trees had been wattled across, the intervals strengthened with stakes, and the ground behind this barricade levelled up with earth to make the floor. A tree, which grew out from the hillside, was the living centre-beam of the roof. The walls were of wattle and covered with moss. The whole house had something of an egg shape; and it half hung, half stood in that steep, hillside thicket, like a wasps' nest in a green hawthorn.

Within, it was large enough to shelter five or six persons with some comfort. A projection of the cliff had been cunningly employed as the fireplace; and the smoke rising against the face of the rock, and being not dissimilar in colour, readily escaped notice from below.

This was but one of Cluny's hiding places; he had caves, besides, and underground chambers in several parts of his country; and following the reports of his scouts, he moved from one to another as the soldiers drew near or moved away. By this manner of living, and thanks to the affection of his clan, he had not only stayed all this time in safety, while so many others had fled or been taken and slain; but stayed four or five years longer, and only went to France at last by the express command of his master. There he soon died; and it is strange to reflect that he may have regretted his Cage upon Ben Alder.

When we came to the door he was seated by his rock chimney, watching a gillie about some cookery. He was mighty plainly habited, with a knitted nightcap drawn over his ears, and smoked a foul cutty pipe. For all that he had the manners of a king, and it was quite a sight to see him rise out of his place to welcome us.

"Well, Mr Stewart, come awa' sir!" said he, "and bring in your friend that as yet I dinna ken the name of."

"And how is yourself, Cluny?" said Alan. "I hope ye do brawly, sir. And I am proud to see ye, and to present to ye my friend the Laird of Shaws, Mr David Balfour."

Alan never referred to my estate without a touch of a sneer, when we were alone; but with strangers, he rang the words out like a herald.

"Step in by, the both of ye, gentlemen," said Cluny. "I make ye welcome to my house, which is a queer, rude place for certain, but one where I have entertained a royal personage, Mr Stewart—ye doubtless ken the personage I have in my eye. We'll take a dram for luck, and as soon as this handless man of mine has the collops ready, we'll dine and take a hand at the cartes as gentlemen should. My life is a bit driegh," says he, pouring out the brandy; "I see little company, and sit and twirl my thumbs, and mind upon a great day that is gone by, and weary for another great day that we all hope will be upon the road. And so here's a toast to ye: The Restoration!"

Thereupon we all touched glasses ad drank. I am sure I wished no ill to King George; and if he had been there himself in proper person, it's like he would have done as I did. No sooner had I taken out the dram than I felt hugely better, and could look on and listen, still a little mistily perhaps, but no longer with the same groundless horror and distress of mind.

It was certainly a strange place, and we had a strange host. In his long hiding, Cluny had grown to have all manner of precise habits, like those of an old maid. He had a particular place, where no one else must sit; the Cage was arranged in a particular way, which none must disturb; cookery was one of his chief fancies, and even while he was greeting us in, he kept an eye to the collops.

It appears, he sometimes visited or received visits from his wife and one or two of his nearest friends, under the cover of night;

but for the most part lived quite alone, and communicated only with his sentinels and the gillies that waited on him in the Cage. The first thing in the morning, one of them, who was a barber, came and shaved him, and gave him the news of the country, of which he was immoderately greedy. There was no end to his questions; he put them as earnestly as a child; and at some of the answers, laughed out of all bounds of reason, and would break out again laughing at the mere memory, hours after the barber was gone.

To be sure, there might have been a purpose in his questions; for though he was the sequestered, and like the other landed gentlemen of Scotland, stripped by the late Act of Parliament of legal powers, he still exercised a patriarcal justice in his clan. Disputes were brought to him in his hiding-hole to be decided; and the men of his country, who would have snapped their fingers at the Court of Session, laid aside revenge and paid down money at the bare word of this forfeited and hunted outlaw. When he was angered, which was often enough, he gave his commands and breathed threats of punishment like any king; and his gillies trembled and crouched away from him like children before a hasty father. With each of them, as he entered, he ceremoniously shook hand, both parties touching their bonnets at the same time in a military manner. Altogether, I had a fair chance to see some of the inner workings of a Highland clan; and this with a proscribed, fugitive chief; his country conquered; the troops riding upon all sides in quest of him, sometimes within a mile of where he lay; and when the least of the ragged fellows whom he rated and threatened, could have made a fortune by betraying him.

On that first day, as soon as the collops were ready, Cluny gave them with his own hand a squeeze of a lemon (for he was well supplied with luxuries) and bade us draw in to our meal.

"They," said he, meaning the collops, "are such as I gave His Royal Highness in this very house; bating the lemon juice, for at that time we were glad to get the meat and never fashed for kitchen. Indeed, there were mair dragoons than lemons in my country in the year forty-six."

I do not know if the collops were truly very good, but my heart rose against the sight of them, and I could eat but little. All the while Cluny entertained us with stories of Prince Charlie's stay in the Cage, giving us the very words of the speakers, and rising from his place to show us where they stood. By these, I gathered the Prince was a gracious, spirited boy, like the son of a race of polite kings, but not so wise as Solomon. I gathered, too, that while he was in the Cage, he was often drunk; so the fault that has since, by all accounts, made such a wreck of him, had even then begun to show itself.

We were no sooner done eating than Cluny brought out an old, thumbed, greasy pack of cards, such as you may find in a mean inn; and his eyes brightened in his face as he proposed that we should fall to playing.

Now this was one of the things I had been brought up to eschew like disgrace; it being held by my father neither the part of a Christian nor yet a gentleman, to set his own livelihood and fish for that of others, on the cast of painted pasteboard. To be sure, I might have pleaded my fatigue, which was excuse enough; but I thought it behoved that I should bear a testimony. I must have got very red in the face, but I spoke steadily, and told them I had no call to be a judge of others, but for my own part, it was a matter in which I had no clearness.

Cluny stopped mingling the cards. "What in devil's name is this?" says he. "What kind of Whiggish, canting talk is this, for the house of Cluny Macpherson?"

"I will put my hand in the fire for Mr Balfour," says Alan. "He is an honest and a mettle gentleman, and I would have ye bear in mind who says it. I bear a king's name," says he, cocking his hat; "and I and any that I call friend are company for the best. But the gentleman is tired, and should sleep; if he has no mind to the cartes, it will never hinder you and me. And I'm fit and willing, sir, to play ye any game that ye can name."

"Sir," says Cluny, "in this poor house of mine I would have you ken that any gentleman may follow his pleasure. If your friend would like to stand on his head, he is welcome. And if either he, or you, or any other man, is not preceesely satisfied, I will be proud to step outside with him."

I had no will that these two friends should cut their throats for my sake.

"Sir," said I, "I am very wearied, as Alan says; and what's more, as you are a man that likely has sons of your own, I may tell you it was a promise to my father."

"Say nae mair, say nae mair," said Cluny, and pointed me to a bed of heather in a corner of the Cage.

For all that he was displeased enough, looked at me askance, and grumbled when he looked. And indeed it must be owned that both my scruples and the words in which I declared them, smacked somewhat of the Covenanter, and were little in their place among wild Highland Jacobites.

What with the brandy and the venison, a strange heaviness had come over me; and I had scarce lain down upon the bed before I fell into a kind of trance, in which I continued almost the whole time of our stay in the Cage.

Sometimes I was broad awake and understood what passed; sometimes I only heard voices or men snoring, like the voice of a silly river; and the plaids upon the wall dwindled down and swelled out again, like firelight shadows on the roof.

I must sometimes have spoken or cried out, for I remember I was now and then amazed at being answered; yet I was conscious of no particular nightmare, only of a general, black, abiding horror—a horror of the place I was in, and the bed I lay in, and the plaids on the wall, and the voices, and the fire, and myself.

The barber-gillie, who was a doctor too, was called in to prescribe for me; but as he spoke in the Gaelic, I understood not a word of his opinion, and was too sick even to ask for a translation. I knew well enough I was ill, and that was all I cared about.

I paid little heed while I lay in this poor pass. But Alan and Cluny were most of the time at the cards, and I am clear that Alan must have begun by winning; for I remember sitting up, and seeing them hard at it, and a great glittering pile of as much as sixty or a hundred guineas on the table. It looked strange enough, to see all this wealth in a nest upon a cliff-side, wattled about growing trees. And even then, I thought it seemed deep water for Alan to be riding, who had no better battle-horse than a green purse and a matter of five pounds.

The luck, it seems, changed on the second day. About noon I was awakened as usual for dinner, and as usual refused to eat, and was given a dram with some bitter infusion which the barber had prescribed.

The sun was shining in at the open door of the Cage, and this dazzled and offended me.

Cluny sat at the table, biting the pack of cards. Alan had stooped over the bed, and had his face close to my eyes; to which, troubled a they were with the fever, it seemed of the most shocking bigness.

He asked me for a loan of my money.

"What for?" said I.

"Oh, just for a loan," said he.

"But why?" I repeated. "I don't see."

"Hut, David!" said Alan, "ye wouldnae grudge me a loan?"

I would though, if I had had my senses. But all I thought of then was to get his face away, and I handed him my money.

On the morning of the third day, when we had been forty-eight hours in the Cage, I awoke with a great relief of spirits, very weak and weary indeed, but seeing things of the right size and with their honest, everyday appearance. I had a mind to eat, moreover; rose from bed of my own movement; and as soon as we had breakfasted, stepped to the entry of the Cage and sat down outside in the top of the wood. It was a grey day with a cool, mild air: and I sat in a dream all morning, only disturbed by the passing by of Cluny's scouts and servants coming with provisions and reports; for as the coast was at that time clear, you might almost say he held court openly. When I returned, he and Alan had laid the cards aside, and were questioning a gillie; and the chief turned about and spoke to me in the Gaelic.

"I have no Gaelic, sir," said I.

Now since the card question, everything I said or did had the power of annoying Cluny. "Your name has more sense than yourself, then," said he, angrily; "for it's good Gaelic. But the point is this. My scout reports all clear in the south, and the question is have ye the strength to go?"

I saw cards on the table, but no gold; only a heap of little written papers, and these all on Cluny' side. Alan, besides, had an odd look, like man not very well content; and I began to have a strong misgiving.

"I do not know if I am as well as I should be," said I, looking at Alan; "but the little money we have has a long way to carry us."

Alan took his under-lip into his mouth, and looked upon the ground.

"David," says he, at last, "I've lost it; there's the naked truth."

"My money too?" said I.

"Your money too," says Alan, with a groan. "Ye shouldnae have given it me. I'm daft when I get to the cartes."

"Hoot-toot, hoot-toot," said Cluny. "It was all daffing; it's all nonsense. Of course, ye'll have your money back again, and the double of it, if ye'll make so free with me. It would be a singular thing for me to keep it. It's not to be supposed that I would be any hindrance to gentlemen in your situation; that would be a singular thing!" cries he, and began to pull gold out of his pocket, with a mighty red face.

Alan said nothing, only looked on the ground.

"Will you step to the door with me, sir?" said I.

Cluny said he would be very glad, and followed me readily enough, but he looked flustered and put out.

"And now sir," says I, "I must first acknowledge your generosity."

"Nonsensical nonsense!" cries Cluny. "Where's the generosity? This is just a most unfortunate affair; but what would ye have me do—boxed up in this bee step of a cage of mune—but just set my friends to the cartes, when I can get them? And if they lose, of course, it's not to be supposed—" And here he came to a pause.

"Yes," said I, "if they lose, you give them back their money; and if they win, they carry away yours in their pouches! I have said before that I grant your generosity; but to me, sir, it's a very painful thing to be placed in this position."

There was a little silence, in which Cluny seemed always as if he was about to speak, but said nothing. All the time he grew redder and redder in the face.

"I am a young man," said I, "and I ask your advice. Advise me as you would your son. My friend fairly lost this money, after having fairly gained a far greater sum of yours; can I accept it back again? would that be the right part for me to play? Whatever I do, you can see for yourself it must be hard upon a man of any pride."

"It's rather hard on me, too, Mr Balfour," said Cluny, "and ye give me very much the look of a man that has entrapped poor people to their hurt. I wouldnae have my friends come to any house of mine to accept affronts; no," he cried, with a sudden heat of anger, "nor yet to give them!"

"And so you see, sir," said I, "there is something to be said upon my side; and this gambling is a very poor employ for gentlefolks. But I am still waiting your opinion."

I am sure if ever Cluny hated any man it was David Balfour. He looked me all over with a warlike eye, and I saw the challenge at his lips. But either my youth disarmed him, or perhaps his own sense of justice. Certainly it was a mortifying matter for all concerned, and not least for Cluny; the more credit that he took it as he did.

"Mr Balfour," said he, "I think you are too like and covenanting, but for all that you have the spirit of a very pretty gentleman. Upon my honest word, ye may take this money—it's what I would tell my son—and here's my hand along with it."

Chapter 24

THE FLIGHT IN THE HEATHER: THE QUARREL

Alan and I were put across Loch Errocht under cloud of night, and went down its eastern shore to another hiding place near the head of Loch Rannoch, whither we were led by one of the gillies from the Cage. This fellow carried all our luggage and Alan's great-coat in the bargain, trotting along under the burden, far less than the half of which used to weigh me to the ground, like a stout hill pony with a feather; yet he was a man that, in plain contest, I could have broken on my knee.

Doubtless it was a great relief to walk disencumbered; and perhaps without that relief, and the consequent sense of liberty and lightness, I could not have walked at all. I was but new risen from a bed of sickness; and there was nothing in the state of our affairs to hearten me for much exertion; travelling, as we did, over the most dismal deserts in Scotland, under a cloudy heaven, and with divided hearts among the travellers.

For long, we said nothing; marching alongside or one behind the other, each with a set countenance; I, angry and proud, and drawing what strength I had from these two violent and sinful feelings: Alan angry and ashamed, ashamed that he had lost my money, angry that I should take it so ill.

The thought of a separation ran always the stronger in my mind; and the more I approved of it, the more ashamed I grew of my approval. It would be a fine, handsome, generous thing, indeed, for Alan to turn round and say to me: "Go, I am in the most danger, and my company only increases yours." But for me to turn to the friend who certainly loved me, and say to him:, "You are in great danger, I am in but little; your friendship is a burden; go take your risk and bear your hardships alone"—no, that was impossible; and even to think of it privily to myself, made my cheeks to burn.

And yet Alan had behaved like a child and (what is worse) a treacherous child. Wheedling my money from me while I lay half conscious, was scarce better than theft; and yet here he was trudging by my side, without a penny to his name, and by what I could see, quite blithe to sponge upon the money he had driven me to beg. True, I was ready to share it with him; but it made me rage to see him count upon my readiness.

These were the two things uppermost in my mind; and I could open my mouth upon neither without black ungenerosity. So I did the next worst, and said nothing, nor so much as looked once at my companion, save with the tail of my eye.

At last, upon the other side of Loch Errocht, going over a smooth, rushy place, where the walking was easy, he could bear it no longer, and came close to me.

"David," says he, "this is no way for two friends to take a small accident. I have to say that I'm sorry; and so that's said. And now if you have anything, ye'd better say it."

"Oh," says I, "I have nothing."

He seemed disconcerted; at which I was meanly pleased.

"No," said he, with rather a trembling voice, "but when I say I was to blame?"

"Why, of course, ye were to blame," said I, coolly; "and you will bear me out that I have never reproached you."

"Never," says he; "but ye ken very well that ye've done worse. Are we to part? Ye said so once before. Are ye to say it again? There's hills and heather enough between here and the two seas, David; and I will own I'm no very keen to stay where I'm no wanted."

This pierced me like a sword, and seemed to lay bare my private disloyalty.

"Alan Breck!" I cried; and then: "Do you think I am one to turn my back on you in your chief need? You dursn't say it to my face. My whole conduct's there to give the lie to it. It's true, I fell asleep upon the muir; but that was from weariness, and you do wrong to cast it up to me—"

"Which is what I never did," said Alan.

"But aside from that," I continued, "what have I done that you should even me to dogs by such a supposition? I never yet failed a friend, and it's not likely I'll begin with you. There are things between us that I can never forget, even if you can."

"I will only say this to ye, David," said Alan, very quietly, "that I have long been owing ye my life, and now I owe ye money. Ye should try to make that burden light for me."

This ought to have touched me, and in a manner it did, but the wrong manner. I felt I was behaving badly; and was now not only angry with Alan, but angry with myself in the bargain; and it made me the more cruel.

"You asked me to speak," said I. "Well, then, I will. You own yourself that you have done me a disservice; I have had to swallow an affront: I have never reproached you, I never named the thing till you did. And now you blame me," cried I, "because I cannae laugh and sing as if I was glad to be affronted. The next thing will be that I'm go down upon my knees and thank you for it! Ye should think more of others, Alan Breck. If ye thought more of others, ye would perhaps speak less about yourself; and when a friend that likes you very well, has passed over an offence without a word, you would be blithe to let it lie, instead of making it a stick to break his back with. By your own way of it, it was you that was to blame; then it shouldnae be you to seek the quarrel."

"Aweel," said Alan, "say nae mair."

And we fell back into our former silence; and came to our journey's end, and supped, and lay down to sleep, without another word.

The gillie put us across Loch Rannoch in the dark of the next day, and gave us his opinion as to our best route. This was to get us up at once into the tops of the mountains: to go round by a circuit, turning the heads of Glen Lyon, Glen Lochay, and Glen Dochart, and come down upon the lowlands by Kippen and the upper waters of the Forth. Alan was little pleased with a route which led us through the country of his blood-foe, the Glenorchy Campbells. He objected that by turning to the east, we should come almost at once among the Athole Stewarts, a race of his own name and lineage although following a different chief, and come besides by a far easier and swifter way to the place whither we were bound. But the gillie, who was indeed the chief man of Cluny's scouts, had good reasons to give him on all hands, naming the force of troops in every district, and alleging finally (as well as I could understand) that we should nowhere be so little troubled as in a country of the Campbells.

Alan gave way at last, but with only half a heart. "It's one of the dowiest countries in Scotland," said he. "There's naething there that I ken, but heath and crows, and Campbells. But I see that ye're a man of some penetration; and be it as ye please!"

We set forth accordingly by this itinerary; and for the best part of three nights travelled on eerie mountains and among the well-heads of wild rivers; often buried in mist, almost continually blown and rained upon, and not once cheered by any glimpse of sunshine. By day, we lay and slept in the drenching heather; by night, incessantly clambered upon breakneck hills and among rude crags. We often wandered; we were often so involved in fog, what we must lie quiet till it lightened. A fire was never to be thought of. Our only food was drammach and a portion of cold meat that we had carried from the Cage; and as for drink, Heaven knows we had no want of water.

This was a dreadful time, rendered the more dreadful by the gloom of the weather and the country. I was never warm; my teeth chattered in my head; I was troubled with a very sore throat, such as I had on the isle; I had a painful stitch in my side, which never left me; and when I slept in my wet bed, with the rain beating above and the mud oozing below me, it was to live over again in fancy the worst part of my adventures—to see the tower of Shaws lit by lightning, Ransome carried below the men's backs, Shuan dying on the round-house floor, or Colin Campbell grasping at the bosom of his coat. From such broken slumbers, I would be aroused in the gloaming, to sit up in the same puddle where I had slept, and sup cold drammach; the rain driving sharp in my face or running down my back in icy trickles; the mist enfolding us like as in a gloomy chamber—or perhaps, if the wind blew, falling suddenly apart and showing us the gulf of some dark valley where the streams were crying aloud.

The sound of an infinite number of rivers came up from all round. In this steady rain the springs of the mountain were broken up; every glen gushed water like a cistern; every stream was in high spate, and had filled and overflowed its channel. During our night tramps, it was solemn to hear the voice of them below in the valleys, now booming like thunder, now with an angry cry. I could well understand the story of the Water Kelpie, that demon of the streams, who is fabled to keep wailing and roaring at the ford until the coming of the doomed traveller. Alan, I saw, believed it, or half believed it; and when the cry of the river rose more than usually sharp, I was little surprised (though, of course, I would still be shocked) to see him cross himself in the manner of the Catholics.

During all these horrid wanderings we had no familiarity, scarcely even that of speech. The truth is that I was sickening for my grave, which is my best excuse. But besides that I was of an unforgiving disposition from my birth. slow to take offence, slower to forget it, and now incensed both against my companion and myself. For the best part of two days he was unweariedly kind; silent, indeed, but always ready to help, and always hoping (as I could very well see) that my displeasure would blow by. For the same length of time I stayed in myself, nursing my anger, roughly refusing his services, and passing him over with my eyes as if he had been a bush or a stone.

The second night, or rather the peep of the third day, found us upon a very open hill, so that we could not follow our usual plan and lie down immediately to eat and sleep. Before we had reached a place of shelter, the grey had come pretty clear, for though it still rained, the clouds ran higher; and Alan, looking in my face, showed some marks of concern.

"Ye had better let me take your pack," said he, for perhaps the ninth time since we had parted from the scout beside Loch Rannoch.

"I do very well, I thank you," said I, as cold as ice.

Alan flushed darkly. "I'll not offer it again," he said. "I'm not a patient man, David."

"I never said you were," said I, which was exactly the rude, silly speech of a boy of ten.

Alan made no answer at the time, but his conduct answered for him. Henceforth, it is to be thought, he quite forgave himself for the affair at Cluny's; cocked his hat again, walked jauntily, whistled airs, and looked at me upon one side with a provoking smile.

The third night we were to pass through the western end of the country of Balquidder. It came clear and cold, with a touch in the air like frost, and a northerly wind that blew the clouds away and made the stars bright. The streams were full, of course, and still made a great noise among the hills; but I observed that Alan thought no more upon the Kelpie, and was in high good spirits. As for me, the change of weather came too late; I had lain in the mire so long that (as the Bible has it) my very clothes "abhorred me"; I was dead weary, deadly sick, and full of pains and shiverings; the chill of the wind went through me, and the sound of it confused my ears. In this poor state I had to bear from my companion something in the nature of a persecution. He spoke a good deal, and never without a taunt. "Whig" was the best name he had to give me. "Here," he would say, "here's a dub for ye to jump, my Whiggie! I ken you're a fine jumper!" And so on; all the time with a gibing voice and face.

I knew it was my own doing, and no one else's; but I was too miserable to repent. I felt I could drag myself but little farther; pretty soon, I must lie down and die on these wet mountains like a sheep or a fox, and my bones must whiten there like the bones of a beast. My head was light, perhaps; but I began to love the prospect, I began to glory in the thought of such a death, alone in the desert, with the wild eagles besieging my last moments. Alan would repent then, I thought; he would remember, when I was dead, how much he owed me, and the remembrance would be torture. So I went like a sick, silly, and bad-hearted schoolboy, feeding my anger against a fellow-man, when I would have been better on my knees, crying on God for mercy. And at each of Alan's taunts, I hugged myself. "Ah!" thinks I to myself, "I have a better taunt in readiness; when I lie down and die, you will feel it like a buffet in your face; ah, what a revenge! ah, how you will regret your ingratitude and cruelty!"

All the while, I was growing worse and worse. Once I had fallen, my legs simply doubling under me, and this had struck Alan for the moment; but I was afoot so briskly, and set off again with such a natural manner, that he soon forgot the incident. Flushes of heat went over me, and then spasms of shuddering. The stitch in my side was hardly bearable. At last I began to feel that I could trail myself no farther; and with that, there came on me all at once the wish to have it out with Alan, let my anger blaze, and be done with my life in a more sudden manner. He had just called me "Whig". I stopped.

"Mr Stewart," said I, in a voice that quivered like a fiddlestring, "you are older than I am, and should know your manners. Do you think it either very wise or very witty to cast my politics in my teeth? I thought, where folk differed, it was the part of gentlemen to differ civility and if I did not, I may tell you I could find a better taunt than some of yours."

Alan had stopped opposite to me, his hat cocked, his hands in his breeches pockets, his head a little to one side. He listened, smiling evilly, as I could see by the starlight; and when I had done he began to whistle a Jacobite air. It was the air made in mockery of General Cope's defeat at Preston Pans:

"Hey, Jonnie Cope, are ye waukin' yet?
And are your drums a-beatin' yet?

And it came in my mind that Alan, on the day of that battle, had been engaged upon the royal side.

"Why do ye take that air, Mr Stewart?" said I. "Is that to remind me you have been beaten on both sides?"

The air stopped on Alan's lips. "David!" said he.

"But it's time these manners ceased," I continued; "and I mean you shall henceforth speak civilly of my King and my good friends the Campbells."

"I am a Stewart—" began Alan.

"Oh," says I, "I ken ye bear a king's name. But you are to remember, since I have been in the Highlands, I have seen a good many of those that bear it; and the best I can say of them is this, that they would be none the worse of washing."

"Do you know that you insult me?" said Alan, very low.

"I am sorry for that," said I, "for I am not done; and if you distaste the sermon, I doubt the pirliecue will please you as little. You have been chased in the field by the grown men of my party; it seems a poor kind of pleasure to outface a boy. Both the Campbells and the Whigs have beaten you; you have run before them like a hare. It behoves you to speak of them as of your betters."

Alan stood quite still, the tails of his great-coat clapping behind him in the wind.

"This is a pity," he said at last. "There are things said that cannot be passed over."

"I never asked you to," said I. "I am as ready as yourself."

"Ready?" said he.

"Ready," I repeated. "I am no blower and boaster like some that I could name. Come on!" And drawing my sword, I fell on guard as Alan himself had taught me.

"David!" he cried. "Are ye daft? I cannae draw upon ye, David. It's fair murder."

"That was your look-out when you insulted me," said I.

"It's the truth!" cried Alan, and he stood for a moment, wringing his mouth in his hand like a man in sore perplexity. "It's the bare truth," he said, and drew his sword. But before I could touch his blade with mine, he had thrown it from him and fallen to the ground. "Na, na," he kept saying, "na, na—I cannae, I cannae."

At this the last of my anger oozed all out of me; I found myself only sick, and sorry, and blank, and wondering at myself. I would have given the world to take back what I had said; but a word once spoken, who can recapture it? I minded all Alan's kindness and courage in the past, how he had helped and cheered and borne with me in our evil days; and recalled my own insults, and saw that I had lost for ever that doughty friend. At the same time, the sickness that hung upon me seemed to redouble, and the pang in my side was like a sword for sharpness. I thought I must have swooned where I stood.

This it was that gave me a thought. No apology could blot out what I had said; it was needless to think of one, none could cover the offence; but where an apology was vain, a mere cry for help might bring Alan back to my side. I put my pride away from me. "Alan!" I said; "if you cannae help me, I must just die here."

He started up sitting, and looked at me.

"It's true," said I. "I'm by with it. Oh, let me get into the bield of a house—I'll can die there easier." I had no need to pretend; whether I chose or not, I spoke in a weeping voice that would have melted a heart of stone.

"Can ye walk?" asked Alan.

"No," said I, "not without help. This last hour, my legs have been fainting under me; I've a stitch in my side like a red-hot iron; I cannae breathe right. If I die, ye'll can forgive me, Alan? In my heart, I liked ye fine—even when I was the angriest."

"Wheesht, wheesht!" cried Alan. "Dinnae say that! David man, ye ken—" He shut his mouth upon a sob. "Let me get my arm about ye," he continued; "that's the way! Now lean upon me hard. Gude kens where there's a house! We're in Balwhidder, too; there should be no want of houses, no, nor friends' houses here. Do ye gang easier so, Davie?"

"Ay," said I, "I can be doing this way"; and I pressed his arm with my hand. Again he came near sobbing.

"Davie," said he, "I'm no a right man at all; I have neither sense nor kindness; I couldnae remember ye were just a bairn, I couldnae see ye were dying on your feet; Davie, ye'll have to try and forgive me."

"Oh, man, let's say no more about it!" said I. "We're neither one of us to mend the other—that's the truth! We must just bear and forbear, man Alan! Oh, but my stitch is sore! Is there nae house?"

"I'll find a house to ye, David," he said, stoutly. "We'll follow down the burn, where there's bound to be houses. My poor man, will ye no be better on my back?"

"Oh, Alan," says I, "and me a good twelve inches taller?"

"Ye're no such a thing," cried Alan, with a start. "There may be a trifling matter of an inch or two; I'm no saying I'm just exactly what ye would call a tall man, whatever; and I dare say," he added, his voice trailing off in a laughable manner, "now when I come to think of it, I dare say ye'll be just about right. Ay, it'll be a foot, or near hand; or may be even mair!"

It was sweet and laughable to hear Alan eat his words up in the fear of some fresh quarrel. I could have laughed, had not my stitch caught me so hard; but if I had laughed, I think I must have wept too.

"Alan," cried I, "what makes ye so good to me? What makes ye care for such a thankless fellow?"

"Deed, and I don't know," said Alan. "For just precisely what I thought I liked about ye, was that ye never quarrelled;—and now I like ye better!"

CHAPTER 25

IN BALQUHIDDER

At the door of the first house we came to, Alan knocked, which was no very safe enterprise in such a part of the Highlands as the Braes of Balquidder. No great clan held rule there; it was filled and disputed by small septs, and broken remnants, and what they call chiefless folk, driven into the wild country about the springs of Forth and Teith by the advance of the Campbells. Here were Stewarts and Maclarens, which came to the same thing, for the Maclarens followed Alan's chief in war, and made but one clan with Appin. Here, too, were many of that old, proscribed, nameless, red-handed clan of the Macgregors. They had always been ill considered, and now worse than ever, having credit with no side or party in the whole country of Scotland. Their chief, Macgregor of Macgregor, was in exile; the more immediate leader of that part of them about Balquidder, James More, Rob Roy's eldest son, lay waiting his trial in Edinburgh Castle; they were in ill-blood with Highlander and Lowlander, with the Grahames, the Maclarens and the Stewarts; and Alan, who took up the quarrel of any friend however distant, was extremely wishful to avoid them.

Chance served us very well; for it was a household of Maclarens that we found, where Alan was not only welcome for his name's sake but known by reputation. Here then I was got to bed without delay, and a doctor fetched, who found me in a sorry plight. But whether because he was a very good doctor, or I a very young, strong man, I lay bed-ridden for no more than a week, and before a month I was able to make the road again with a good heart.

All this time Alan would not leave me; though I often pressed him, and indeed his foolhardiness in staying was a common subject of outcry with the two or three friends that were let into the secret. He hid by day in a hole of the braes under a little wood; and at night when the coast was clear, would come into the house to visit me. I need not say if I was pleased to see him; Mrs Maclaren, our hostess, thought nothing good enough for such a guest; and as Duncan Dhu (which was the name of our host) had a pair of pipes in his house and was much of a lover of music, the time of my recovery was quite a festival, and we commonly turned night into day.

The soldiers let us be; although once a party of two companies and some dragoons went by in the bottom of the valley, where I could see them through the windows as I lay in bed. What was much more astonishing, no magistrate came near me, and there was no question put of whence I came or whither I was going; and in that time of excitement, I was as free of all inquiry as though I had lain in a desert. Yet my presence was known before I left to all the people in Balquidder and the adjacent parts; many coming about the house on visits and these (after the custom of the country) spreading the news among their neighbours. The bills, too, had now been printed. There was one pinned near the foot of my bed, where I could read my own not very flattering portrait and, in larger characters, the amount of the blood money that had been set upon my life. Duncan Dhu and the rest that knew that I had come there in Alan's company, could have entertained no doubt of who I was; and many others must have had their guess. For though I had changed my clothes, I could not change my age or person; and lowland boys of eighteen were not so rife in these parts of the world, and above all about that time, that they could fail to put one thing with another and connect me with the bill. So it was, at least. Other folk keep a secret among two or three near friends, and somehow it leaks out; but among these clansmen, it is told to a whole countryside, and they will keep it for a century.

There was but one thing happened worth narrating; and that is the visit I had of Robin Oig, one of the sons of the notorious Rob Roy. He was sought upon all sides on a charge of carrying a young woman from Balfron and marrying her (as was alleged) by force; yet he stepped about Balquidder like a gentleman in his own walled policy. It was he who had shot James Maclaren at the plough stilts, a quarrel never satisfied; yet he walked into the house of his blood enemies as a rider might into a public inn. Duncan had time to pass me word of who it was; and we looked at one another in concern. You should understand, it was then close upon the time of Alan's coming; the two were little likely to agree; and yet if we sent word or sought to make a signal, it was sure to arouse suspicion in a man under so dark a cloud as the Macgregor.

He came in with a great show of civility, but like a man among inferiors; took off his bonnet to Mrs Maclaren, but clapped it on his head again to speak to Duncan; and having thus set himself (as he would have thought) in a proper light, came to my beside and bowed.

"I am given to know, sir," says he, "that your name is Balfour."

"They call me David Balfour," said I, "at your service."

"I would give ye my name in return, sir," he replied, "but it's one somewhat blown upon of late days; and it's perhaps suffice if I tell ye that I am own brother to James More Drummond or Macgregor, of whom ye will scarce have failed to hear."

"No, sir," said I, a little alarmed; "nor yet of your father, Macgregor-Campbell." And I sat up and bowed in bed; for I thought best to compliment him, in case he was proud of having had an outlaw to his father.

He bowed in return. "But what I am come to say, sir," he went on, "is this. In the year '45, my brother raised a part of the 'Gregara', and marched six companies to strike a stroke for the good side; and the surgeon that marched with our clan and cured my brother's leg when it was broken in the brush at Preston Pans, was a gentleman of the same name precisely as yourself. He was brother to Balfour of Baith; and if you are in any reasonable degree of nearness one of the gentleman's kin, I have come to put myself and my people at your command."

You are to remember that I knew no more of my descent than any cadger's dog; my uncle, to be sure, had prated of some of our high connexions, but nothing to the present purpose; and there was nothing left me but that bitter disgrace of owning that I could not tell.

Robin told me shortly he was sorry he had put himself about, turned his back upon me without a sign of salutation, and as he went towards the door, I could hear him telling Duncan that I was "only some kinless loon that didn't know his own father".

Angry as I was at these arrogant words and ashamed of my own woeful ignorance, I could scarce keep myself from smiling that a man who was under the lash of the law (and who was indeed hanged some three years later) should be so nice as to the descent of his acquaintances.

Just in the door, he met Alan coming in; and the two drew back and looked at each other like strange dogs. They were neither of them big men, but they seemed fairly to swell out with pride. Each wore a sword, and by a movement of his haunch, thrust clear the hilt of it, so that it might be the more readily grasped and the blade drawn.

"Mr Stewart, I am thinking," says Robin.

"Troth, Mr Macgregor, it's not a name to be ashamed of," answered Alan.

"I did not know ye were in my country, sir," says Robin.

"It sticks in my mind that I am in the country of my friends the Maclarens," says Alan.

"That's a kittle point," returned the other. "There may be two words to say to that. But I think I will have heard that you are a man of your sword?"

"Unless ye were born deaf, Mr Macgregor, ye will have heard a deal more than that," says Alan. "I am not the only man that can draw steel in Appin; and when my kinsman and captain, Ardshiel, had a talk with a gentleman of your name, not so many years back, I could never hear that the Macgregor had the best of it."

"Do ye mean my father, sir," says Robin.

"Well, I wouldnae wonder," said Alan. "The gentleman I have in my mind had the ill-taste to clap Campbell to his name."

"My father was an old man," returned Robin. "The match was unequal. You and me would make a better pair, sir."

"I was thinking that," said Alan.

I was half out of bed, and Duncan had been hanging at the elbow of these fighting cocks, ready to intervene upon the least occasion. But when that word was uttered, it was a case of now or never; and Duncan, with something of a white face to be sure, thrust himself between. "Gentlemen," said he, "I will have been thinking of a very different matter, whateffer. Here are my pipes, and here are you two gentlemen who are baith acclaimed pipers. It's an auld dispute which one of ye's the best. Here will be a braw chance to settle it."

"Why, sir," said Alan, still addressing Robin, from whom indeed he had not so much as shifted his eyes, nor yet Robin from him, "why, sir," says Alan, "I think I will have heard some sough of the sort. Have ye music, as folk say? Are ye a bit of a piper?"

"I can pipe like a Macrimmon!" cries Robin.

"And that is a very bold word," quoth Alan.

"I have made bolder words good before now," returned Robin, "and that against better adversaries."

"It is easy to try that," says Alan.

Duncan Dhu made haste to bring out the pair of pipes that was his principal possession, and to set before his guests a mutton-ham and a bottle of that drink which they call Athole brose, and which is made of old whiskey, strained honey, and sweet cream, slowly beaten together in the right order and proportion. The two enemies were still on the very breach of a quarrel; but down they sat, one upon each side of the peat fire, with a mighty show of politeness. Maclaren pressed them to taste his mutton-ham and "the wife's brose", reminding them the wife was out of Athole and hat a name far and wide for her skill in that confection. But Robin put aside these hospitalities as bad for the breath.

"I would have ye to remark, sir," said Alan, "that I havenae broken bread for near upon ten hours, which will be worse for the breath than any brose in Scotland."

"I will take no advantages, Mr Stewart," replied Robin. "Eat and drink; I'll follow you."

Each ate a small portion of the ham and drank a glass of the brose to Mrs Maclaren; and then after a great number of civilities, Robin took the pipes and played a little spring in a very ranting manner.

"Ay, ye can blow," said Alan; and taking the instrument from his rival, he first played the same spring in a manner identical with Robin's; and then wandered into variations, which, as he went on, he decorated with a perfect flight of grace-notes, such as pipers love, and call the "warblers".

I had been pleased with Robin's playing, Alan's ravished me.

"That's not very bad, Mr Stewart," said the rival, "but ye show a poor device in your warblers."

"Me!" cried Alan, the blood starting suddenly to his face. "I give ye the lie."

"Do ye own yourself beaten at the pipes, then," said Robin, "that ye seek to change them for the sword?"

"And that's very well said, Mr Macgregor," returned Alan; "and in the meantime" (laying a strong accent on the word) "I take back the lie. I appeal to Duncan."

"Indeed, ye need appeal to naebody," said Robin. "Ye're a far better judge than any Maclaren in Balquidder: for-it's a God's truth that you're a very creditable piper for a Stewart. Hand me the pipes."

Alan did as he asked; and Robin proceeded to imitate and correct some part of Alan's variations, which it seemed that he remembered perfectly.

"Ay, ye have music," said Alan, gloomily.

"And now be the judge yourself, Mr Stewart," said Robin; and talking up the variations from the beginning, he worked them throughout to so new a purpose, with some ingenuity and sentiment, and with so odd a fancy and so quick a knack in the grace-notes, that I was amazed to hear him.

As for Alan, his face grew dark and hot, and he sat and gnawed his fingers, like a man under some deep affront. "Enough!" he cried. "Ye can blow the pipes—make the most of that." And he made as if to rise.

But Robin only held out his hand as if to ask for silence, and struck into the slow measure of a pibroch.

It was a fine piece of music in itself, and nobly played; but it seems besides it was a piece peculiar to the Appin Stewarts and a chief favourite with Alan. The first notes were scarce out, before there came a change in his face; when the time quickened, he seemed to grow restless in his seat; and long before that piece was at an end, the last signs of his anger died from him, and he had no thought but for the music.

"Robin Oig," he said, when it was done, "ye are a great piper. I am not fit to blow in the same kingdom with ye. Body of me! ye have mair music in your sporran that I have in my head! And though it still sticks in my mind that I could maybe show ye another of it with the cold steel, I warn ye beforehand—it'll no be fair! It would go against my heart to haggle a man that can blow the pipes as you can!"

Thereupon the quarrel was made up; all night long the brose was going and the pipes changing hands; and the day had come pretty bright, and the three men were none the better for what they had been taking, before Robin as much as thought upon the road.

It was the last I saw of him, for I was in the Low Countries at the University of Leyden, when he stood his trial, and was hanged in the Grassmarket. And I have told this at so great length, partly because it was the last incident of any note that befell me on the wrong side of the Highland Line, and partly because (as the man came to be hanged) it's in a manner history.

Chapter 26

END OF THE FLIGHT: WE PASS THE FORTH

The month, as I have said, was not yet out, but it was already far through August, and beautiful warm weather, with every sign of an early and great harvest, when I was pronounced able for my journey. Our money was now run to so low an ebb that we must think first of all on speed; for if we came not soon to Mr Rankeillor's, or if when we came there he should fail to help me, we must surely starve. In Alan's view, besides, the hunt must have now greatly slackened; and the line of the Forth and even Stirling Bridge, which is the main pass over that river, would be watched with little interest.

"It's a chief principle in military affairs," said he, "to go where ye are least expected. Forth is our trouble; ye ken the saying, 'Forth bridles the wild Hielandman'. Well, if we seek to creep round about the head of that river and come down by Kippen or Balfron, it's just precisely there that they'll be looking to lay hands on us. But if we stave on straight to the auld Brig of Stirling, I'll lay my sword they let us pass unchallenged."

The first night, accordingly, we pushed to the house of a Maclaren in Strathire a friend of Duncan's, where we slept the twenty-first of the month, and whence we set forth again about the fall of night to make another easy stage. The twenty-second we lay in a heather bush on a hillside in Uam Var, within view of a herd of deer the happiest ten hours of sleep in a fine, breathing sunshine and on bone-dry ground, that I have ever tasted.

That night we struck Allan Water, and followed it down; and coming to the edge of the hills saw the whole Carse of Stirling underfoot, as flat as a pancake, with the town and castle on a hill in the midst of it, and the moon shining on the Links of Forth.

"Now," said Alan, "I kenna if ye care, but ye're in your own land again. We passed the Hieland Line in the first hour; and now if we could but pass yon crooked water, we might cast our bonnets in the air."

In Allan Water, near by where it falls into the Forth, we found a little sandy islet, overgrown with burdock, butterbur, and the like low plants, that would just cover us if we lay flat. Here it was we made our camp, within plain view of Stirling Castle, whence we could hear the drums beat as some part of the garrison paraded. Shearers worked all day in a field on one side of the river, and we could hear the stones going on the hooks and the voices and even the words of the men talking. It behoved to lie close and keep silent. But the sand of the little isle was sun-warm, the green plants gave us shelter for our heads, we had food and drink in plenty; and to crown all, we were within sight of safety.

As soon as the shearers quit their work and the dusk began to fall, we waded ashore and struck for the Bridge of Stirling, keeping to the fields and under the field fences.

The bridge is close under the castle hill, an old, high, narrow bridge with pinnacles along the parapet; and you may conceive with how much interest I looked upon it, not only as a place famous in history, but as the very doors of salvation to Alan and myself. The moon was not yet up when we came there; a few lights shone along the front of the fortress and lower down a few lighted windows in the town; but it was all mighty still, and there seemed to be no guard upon the passage. I was for pushing straight across; but Alan was more wary.

"It looks unco' quiet," said he; "but for all that we'll lie down here cannily behind a dyke, and make sure."

So we lay for about a quarter of an hour, whiles whispering, whiles lying still and hearing nothing earthly but the washing of the water on the pier.

At last there came by an old, hobbling woman with a crutch stick; who first stopped a little, close to where we lay, and bemoaned herself and the long way she had travelled; and then set forth again up the steep spring of the bridge. The woman was so little, and the night still so dark, that we soon lost sight of her;

only heard the sound of her steps, and her stick, and a cough that she had by fits, draw slowly farther away.

"She's bound to be across now," I whispered.

"Na," said Alan, "her foot still sounds boss upon the bridge."

And just then—"Who goes?" cried a voice, and we heard the butt of a musket rattle on the stones. I must suppose the sentry had been sleeping, so that had we tried, we might have passed unseen; but he was awake now, and the chance forfeited.

"This'll never do," said Alan. "This'll never, never do for us, David."

And without another word, he began to crawl away through the fields; and a little after, being well out of eyeshot, got to his feet again, and struck along a road that led to the eastward. I could not conceive what he was doing; and indeed I was so sharply cut by the disappointment, that I was little likely to be pleased with anything. A moment back, and I had seen myself knocking at Mr Rankeillor's door to claim my inheritance, like a hero in a ballad; and here was I back again, a wandering, hunted blackguard, on the wrong side of Forth.

"Well?" said I.

"Well," said Alan, "what would ye have? They're none such fools as I took them for. We have still the Forth to pass, Davie—weary fall the rains that fed and the hillsides that guided it!"

"And why go east?" said I.

"Ou, just upon the chance!" said he, "If we cannae pass the river, we'll have to see what can do for the firth."

"There are fords upon the river, and none upon the firth," said I.

"To be sure there are fords, and a bridge forby," quoth Alan: "and of what service, when they are watched?"

"Well," said I, "but a river can be swum."

"By them that have the skill of it," returned he; "but I have yet to hear that either you or me is much of a hand at that exercise; and for my own part, I swim like a stone."

"I'm not up to you in talking back, Alan," I said; "but I can see we're making bad worse. If it's hard to pass a river, it stands to reason it must be worse to pass a sea."

"But there's such a thing as a boat," says Alan, "or I'm the more deceived."

"Ay, and such a thing as money," says I. "But for us that have neither one nor other, they might just as well not have been invented."

"Ye think so?" said Alan

"I do that," said I.

"David," says he, "ye're a man of small invention and less faith. But let me set my wits upon the hone, and if I cannae beg, borrow, nor yet steal a boat, I'll make one!"

"I think I see ye!" said I. "And what's more than all that: if ye pass a bridge, it can tell no tales; but if we pass the firth, there's the boat on the wrong side—somebody must have brought it—the countryside will all be in a bizz—"

"Man!" cried Alan, "if I make a boat, I'll make a body to take it back again! So leave me with no more of your nonsense, but walk (for that's what you've got to do)—and let Alan think for ye."

All night, then, we walked through the north side of the Carse under the high line of the Ochil mountains; and by Alloa and Clackmannan and Culross, all of which we avoided; and about ten in the morning, mighty hungry and tired, came to the little clachan of Limekilns. This is a place that sits near in by the waterside, and looks across the Hope to the town of the Queensferry. Smoke went up from both of these, and from other villages and farms upon all hands.

The fields were being reaped; two ships lay anchored and boats were coming and going on the Hope. It was altogether a right pleasant sight to me; and I could not take my fill of gazing at these comfortable, green, cultivated hills and the busy people both of the field and sea.

For all that, there was Mr Rankeillor's house on the south shore, where I had no doubt wealth awaited me; and here was I upon the north, clad in poor enough attire of an outlandish fashion, with three silver shillings left to me of all my fortune, a price set upon my head, and an outlawed man for my sole company.

"O, Alan!" said I, "to think of it! Over there, there's all that heart could want waiting me; and the birds go over, and the boats go over—all that please can go, but just me only! O, man, but it's a heartbreak!"

In Limekilns we entered a small change-house, which we only knew to be a public by the wand over the door, and bought some bread and cheese from a good looking lass that was the servant. This we carried with us in a bundle, meaning to sit and eat it in a bush of wood on the seashore, that we saw some third part of a mile in front. As we went, I kept looking across the water and sighing to myself; and though I took no heed of it, Alan had fallen into a muse. At last he stopped in the way.

"Did ye take heed of the lass we bought this of?" says he, tapping on the bread and cheese.

"To be sure," said I, "and a bonny lass she was."

"Ye thought that?" cried he. "Man David, that's good news."

"In the name of all that's wonderful, why so?" says I, "What good can that do?"

"Well," said Alan, "with one of his droll looks, I was rather in hopes it would maybe get us that boat."

"If it were the other way about, it would be liker it," said I.

"That's all that you ken, ye see," said Alan. "I don't want the lass to fall in love with ye, I want her to be sorry for ye, David; to which end, there is no manner of need that she should take you for a beauty. Let me see" (looking me curiously over). "I wish ye were a wee thing paler; but apart from that ye'll do fine for my purpose—ye have a fine, hangdog, rag-and-tatter, clappermaclaw kind of a look to ye, as if ye had stolen the coat from a potato-bogle. Come; right about, and back to the change-house for that boat of ours."

I followed him laughing.

"David Balfour," said he, "ye're a very funny gentleman by your way of it, and this is a very funny employ for ye, no doubt. For all that, if ye have any affection for my neck (to say nothing of your own) ye will perhaps be kind enough to take this matter responsibly. I am going to do a bit of play-acting, the bottom ground of which-is just exactly as serious as the gallows for the pair of us. So bear it, if ye please, in mind, and conduct yourself according."

"Well, well," said I, "have it as you will."

As we got near the clachan, he made me take his arm and hang upon it like one almost helpless with weariness; and by the time he pushed open the change-house door, he seemed to be half carrying me. The maid appeared surprised (as well she might be) at our speedy return; but Alan had no words to spare for her in explanation, helped me to a chair, called for a tass of brandy with which he fed me in little sips, and then breaking up the bread and cheese helped me to eat it like a nursery-lass; the whole with that grave, concerned, affectionate countenance, that might have imposed upon a judge. It was small wonder if the maid were taken with the picture we presented, of a poor, sick, overwrought lad and his most tender comrade. She drew quite near, and stood leaning with her back on the next table.

"What's like wrong with him?" said she at last.

Alan turned upon her, to my great wonder, with a kind of fury. "Wrong?" cries he. "He's walked more hundreds of miles than he has hairs upon his chin, and slept oftener in wet heather than dry sheets. Wrong, quo' she! Wrong enough, I would think! Wrong, indeed!" and he kept grumbling to himself, as he fed me, like a man ill-pleased.

"He's young for the like of that," said the maid.

"Ower young," said Alan, with his back to her.

"He would be better riding," says she.

"And where could I get a horse to him?" cried Alan, turning on her with the same appearance of fury. "Would ye have me steal?"

I thought this roughness would have sent her off in dudgeon, as indeed it closed her mouth for the time. But my companion knew very well what he was doing; and for as simple as he was in some things of life, had a great fund of roguishness in such affairs as these.

"Ye neednae tell me," she said at last—"ye're gentry."

"Well," said Alan, softened a little (I believe against his will) by this artless comment, "and suppose we were? Did ever you hear that gentrice put money in folk's pockets?"

She sighed at this, as if she were herself some disinherited great lady. "No," says she, "that's true indeed."

I was all this while chafing at the part played, and sitting tongue-tied between shame and merriment; but somehow at this I could hold in no longer, and bade Alan let me be, for I was better already. My voice struck in my throat, for I ever hated to take part in lies; but my very embarrassment helped on the plot, for the lass no doubt set down my husky voice to sickness and fatigue.

"Has he nae friends?" said she, in a tearful voice.

"That has he so!" cried Alan, "if we could but win to them!—friends and rich friends, beds to lie in, foot to eat, doctors to see to him—and here he must tramp in the dubs and sleep in the heather like a beggarman."

"And why that?" says the lass.

"My dear," says Alan, "I cannae very safely say; but I'll tell ye what I'll do instead," says he, "I'll whistle ye a bit tune." And with that he leaned pretty far over the table, and in a mere breath of a whistle, but with a wonderful pretty sentiment, gave her a few bars of "Charlie is my darling".

"Wheesht," says she, and looked over her shoulder to the door.

"That's it," said Alan.

"And him so young!" cried the lass.

"He's old enough to—" and Alan struck his forefinger on the back part of his neck, meaning that I was old enough to lose my head.

"It would be a black shame," she cried, flushing high.

"It's what will be, though," said Alan, "unless we manage the better."

At this the lass turned and ran out of that part of the house, leaving us alone together, Alan in high good humour at the furthering of his schemes, and I in bitter dudgeon at being called a Jacobite and treated like a child.

"Alan," I cried, "I can stand no more of this."

"Ye'll have to sit it then, Davie," said he. "For if ye upset the pot now, ye may scrape your own life out of the fire, but Alan Breck is a dead man."

This was so true that I could only groan; and even my groan served Alan's purpose, for it was overheard by the lass as she came flying in again with a dish of white puddings and a bottle of strong ale.

"Poor lamb!" says she, and had no sooner set the meat before us, than she touched me on the shoulder with a little friendly touch, as much as to bid me cheer up. Then she told us to fall to, and there would be no more to pay; for the inn was her own, or at least her father's, and he was gone for the day to Pittencrieff. We waited for no second bidding, for bread and cheese is but cold comfort and the puddings smelt excellently well; and while we sat and ate, she took up that same place by the next table, looking on, and thinking, and frowning to herself, and drawing the string of her apron through her hand.

"I'm thinking ye have rather a long tongue," she said at last to Alan.

"Ay," said Alan; "but ye see I ken the folk I speak to."

"I would never betray ye," said she, "if ye mean that."

"No," said he, "ye're not that kind. But I'll tell ye what ye would do, ye would help."

"I couldnae," said she, shaking her head. "Na, I couldnae."

"No," said he, "but if ye could?"

She answered him nothing.

"Look here, my lass," said Alan, "there are boats in the kingdom of Fife, for I saw two (no less) upon the beach, as I came in by your town's end. Now if we could have the use of a boat to pass under cloud of night into Lothian, and some secret, decent kind of a man to bring that boat back again and keep his counsel, there would be two souls saved—mine to all likelihood—his to a dead surety. If we lack that boat, we have but three shillings left in this wide world; and where to go, and how to do, and what other place there is for us except the chains of a gibbet—I give you my naked word, I kenna! Shall we go wanting, lassie? Are ye to lie in your warm bed and think upon us, when the wind howls in the chimney and the rain tirls on the roof? Are ye to eat your meat by the cheeks of a red fire, and think upon this poor sick lad of mine, biting his finger ends on a blae muir for cauld and hunger? Sick or sound, he must aye be moving; with the death grapple at his throat he must aye be trailing in the rain on the lang roads; and when he gants his last on a rickle of cauld stanes, there will be nae friends near him but only me and God."

At this appeal, I could see the lass was in great trouble of mind, being tempted to help us, and yet in some fear she might be helping malefactors; and so now I determined to step in myself and to allay her scruples with a portion of the truth.

"Did ever you hear," said I, "of Mr Rankeillor of the Ferry?"

"Rankeillor the writer?" said she. "I daursay that!"

"Well," said I, "it's to his door that I am bound, so you may judge by that if I am an ill-doer; and I will tell you more, that though I am indeed, by a dreadful error, in some peril of my life, King George has no truer friend in all Scotland than myself."

Her face cleared up mightily at this, although Alan's darkened.

"That's more than I would ask," said she. "Mr Rankeillor is a kennt man."

And she bade us finish our meat, get clear of the clachan as soon as might be, and lie close in the bit wood on the sea beach. "And ye can trust me," says she, "I'll find some means to put you over."

At this we waited for no more, but shook hands with her upon the bargain, made short work of the puddings, and set forth again from Limekilns as far as to the wood. It was a small piece of perhaps a score of elders and hawthorns and a few young ashes, not thick enough to veil us from passersby upon the road or beach. Here we must lie, however, making the best of the brave warm weather and the good hopes we now had of deliverance, and planning more particularly what remained for us to do.

We had but one trouble all day; when a strolling piper came and sat in the same wood with us; a red-nosed, bleareyed, drunken dog, with a great bottle of whisky in his pocket, and a long story of wrongs that had been done him by all sorts of persons, from the Lord President of the Court of Session who had denied him justice, down to the Baillies of Inverkeithing who had given him more of it than he desired. It was impossible but he should conceive some suspicion of two men lying all day concealed in a thicket and having no business to allege. As long as he stayed there, he kept us in hot water with prying questions; and after he was gone, as he was a man not very likely to hold his tongue, we were in the greater impatience to be gone ourselves.

The day came to an end with the same brightness; the night fell quiet and clear; lights came out in houses and hamlets and then, one after another, began to be put out; but it was past eleven, and we were long since strangely tortured with anxieties, before we heard the grinding of oars upon the rowing pins. At that, we looked out and saw the lass herself coming rowing to us in a boat. She had trusted no one with our affairs, not even her sweetheart, if she had one; but as soon as her father was asleep, had left the house by a window, stolen a neighbour's boat, and come to our assistance single-handed.

I was abashed how to find expression for my thanks; but she was no less abashed at the thought of hearing them; begged us to lose no time and to hold our peace, saying (very properly) that the heart of our matter was in haste and silence; and so, what with one thing and another, she had set us on the Lothian shore not far from Carriden, had shaken hands with us, and was out again at sea and rowing for Limekilns, before there was one word said either of her service or our gratitude.

Even after she was gone, we had nothing to say, as indeed nothing was enough for such a kindness. Only Alan stood a great while upon the shore shaking his head.

"It is a very fine lass," he said at last. "David, it is a very fine lass." And a matter of an hour later, as we were lying in a den on the seashore and I had been already dozing, he broke out again in commendations of her character. For my part, I could say nothing, she was so simple a creature that my heart smote me both with remorse and fear; remorse because we had traded upon her ignorance; and fear lest we should have anyway involved her in the dangers of our situation.

CHAPTER 27

I COME TO MR RANKEILLOR

The next day it was agreed that Alan should fend for himself till sunset; but as soon as it began to grow dark, he should lie in the fields by the roadside near to Newhalls, and stir for naught until he heard me whistling. At first I proposed I should give him for a signal the "Bonnie House of Airlie", which was a favourite of mine; but he objected that as the piece was very commonly known, any ploughman might whistle it by accident; and taught me instead a little fragment of a Highland air, which has run in my head from that day to this, and will likely run in my head when I lie dying. Every time it comes to me, it takes me off to that last day of my uncertainty, with Alan sitting up in the bottom of the den, whistling and beating the measure with a finger, and the grey of the dawn coming on his face.

I was in the long street of Queensferry before the sun was up. It was a fairly built burgh, the houses of good stone, many slated; the town-hall not so fine, I thought, as that of Peebles, nor yet the street so noble; but take it altogether, it put me to shame for my foul tatters.

As the morning went on, and the fires began to be kindled, and the windows to open, and the people to appear out of the houses, my concern and despondency grew ever the blacker. I saw now that I had no ground to stand upon; and no clear proof of my rights, nor so much as of my own identity. If it was all a bubble, I was indeed sorely cheated and left in a sore pass. Even if things were as I conceived, it would in all likelihood take time to establish my contentions; and what time had I to spare with less than three shillings in my pocket, and a condemned, hunted man upon my hands to ship out of the country? Truly, if my hope broke with me, it might come to the gallows yet for both of us. And as I continued to walk up and down, and saw people looking askance at me upon the street or out of windows, and nudging or speaking one to another with smiles, I took a fresh apprehension; that it might be no easy matter even to come to speech of the lawyer, far less to convince him of my story.

For the life of me I could not muster up the courage to address any of these reputable burghers; I thought shame even to speak with them in such a pickle of rags and dirt; and if I had asked for the house of such a man as Mr Rankeillor, I supposed they would have burst out laughing in my face. So I went up and down, and through the street, and down to the harbour-side, like a dog that has lost its master, with a strange gnawing in my inwards, and every now and then a movement of despair. It grew to be high day at last, perhaps nine in the forenoon; and I was worn with these wanderings, and chanced to have stopped in front of a very good house on the land-ward side, a house with beautiful, clear glass windows, flowering knots upon the sills, the walls new-harled, and a chase-dog sitting yawning on the step like one that was at home. Well, I was even envying this dumb brute, when the door fell open and there issued forth a shrewd, ruddy, kindly, consequential man in a well-powdered wig and spectacles. I was in such a plight that no one set eyes on me once, but he looked at me again; and this gentleman, as it proved, was so much struck with my poor appearance that he came straight up to me and asked me what I did.

I told him I was come to the Queensferry on business, and taking heart of grace, asked him to direct me to the house of Mr Rankeillor.

"Why", said he, "that is his house that I have just come out of; and for a rather singular chance, I am that very man."

"Then, sir," said I, "I have to beg the favour of an interview."

"I do not know your name," said he, "nor yet your face."

"My name is David Balfour," said I.

"David Balfour?" he repeated, in rather a high tone, like one surprised. "And where have you come from, Mr David Balfour?" he asked, looking me pretty drily in the face.

"I have come from a great many strange places, sir," said I; "but think it would be as well to tell you where and how in a more private manner."

He seemed to muse awhile, holding his lip in his hand, and looking now at me and now upon the causeway of the street.

"Yes," says he, "that will be the best, no doubt." And he led me back with him into his house, cried out to someone whom I could not see that he would be engaged all morning, and brought me into a little dusty chamber full of books and documents. Here he sat down, and bade me be seated; though I thought he looked a little ruefully from his clean chair to my muddy rags. 'And now,' says he, 'if you have any business, pray be brief and come swiftly to the point. *Nec gemino bellum Trojanum orditur ab ovo*—do you understand that?' says he, with a keen look.

"I will even do as Horace says, sir," I answered, smiling, "and carry you *in medias res.*" He nodded as if he was well pleased, and indeed his scrap of Latin had been set to test me. For all that, and though I was somewhat encouraged, the blood came in my face when I added: "I have reason to believe myself some rights on the estate of Shaws."

He got a paper book out of a drawer and set it before him open. "Well?" said he.

But I had shot my bolt and sat speechless. "Come, come, Mr Balfour," said he, "you must continue. Where were you born?"

"In Essendean, sir," said I, "the year 1734, the 12th of March."

He seemed to follow this statement in his paper book; but what that meant I knew not. "Your father and mother?" said he.

"My father was Alexander Balfour, schoolmaster of that place," said I, "and my mother Grace Pitarrow; I think her people were from Angus."

"Have you any papers proving your identity?" asked Mr Rankeillor.

"No, sir," said I, "but they are in the hands of Mr Campbell, the minister, and could be readily produced. Mr Campbell, too, would give me his word; and for that matter, I do not think my uncle would deny me."

"Meaning Mr Ebenezer Balfour?" says he.

"The same," said I.

"Whom you have seen?" he asked.

"By whom I was received into his own house," I answered.

"Did you ever meet a man of the name of Hoseason?" asked Mr Rankeillor.

"I did so, sir, for my sins," said I; "for it was by his means and the procurement of my uncle, that I was kidnapped within sight of this town, carried to sea, suffered shipwreck and a hundred other hardships, and stand before you today in this poor accoutrement."

"You say you were shipwrecked," said Rankeillor; "where was that?"

"Off the south end of the Isle of Mull," said I. "The name of the isle on which I was cast up is the Island Earraid."

"Ah!" says he, smiling, "you are deeper than me in the geography. But so far, I may tell you, this agrees pretty exactly with other information that I hold. But you say you were kidnapped; in what sense?"

"In the plain meaning of the word, sir," said I. "I was on my way to your house, when I was trepanned on board the brig, cruelly struck down, thrown below, and knew no more of anything till we were far at sea. I was destined for the plantations; a fate that, in God's providence, I have escaped."

"The brig was lost on June the 27th," says he, looking in his book, "and we are now at August the 24th. Here is a considerable hiatus, Mr Balfour, of near upon two months. It has already caused a vast amount of trouble to your friends; and I own I shall not be very well contented until it is set right."

"Indeed, sir," said I, "these months are very easily filled up; but yet before I told my story, I would be glad to know that I was talking to a friend."

"This is to argue in a circle," said the lawyer. "I cannot be convinced till I have heard you. I cannot be your friend till I am properly informed. If you were more trustful, it would better befit your time of life. And you know, Mr Balfour, we have a proverb in the country that evil-doers are aye evil-dreaders."

"You are not to forget, sir," said I, "that I have already suffered by my trustfulness; and was shipped off to be a slave by the very man that (if I rightly understand) is your employer."

All this while, I had been gaining ground with Mr Rankeillor, and in proportion as I gained ground, gaining confidence. But at this sally, which I made with something of a smile myself, he fairly laughed aloud.

"No, no," said he, "it is not so bad as that. *Fui, non sum.* I was indeed your uncle's man of business; but while you *(imberbis juvenis custode remoto)* were gallivanting in the west, a good deal of water has run under the bridge; and if your ears did not sing, it was not for lack of being talked about. On the very day of your sea disaster, Mr Campbell stalked into my office, demanding you from all the winds. I had never heard of your existence; but I had known your father; and from matters in my competence (to be touched upon herafter) I was disposed to fear the worst. Mr Ebenezer admitted having seen you; declared (what seemed improbable) that he had given you considerable sums; and that you had started for the continent of Europe, intending to fulfil your education, which was probable and praiseworthy. Interrogated how you had come to send no word to Mr Campbell, he deponed that you had expressed a great desire to break with your past life. Further interrogated where you now were, protested ignorance, but believed you were in Leyden. That is a close sum of his replies. I am not exactly sure that anyone believed him," continued Mr Rankeillor with a smile; "and in particular he so much disrelished some expressions of mine that (in a word) he showed me to the door. We were then at a full stand; for whatever shrewd supicions we might entertain, we had no shadow of probation. In the very article, comes Captain Hoseason with the story of your drowning; whereupon all fell through; with no consequence but concern to Mr Campbell, injury to my pocket, and another blot upon your uncle's character, which could very ill afford it. And now, Mr Balfour," said he, "you understand the whole process of these matters, and can judge for yourself to what extent I may be trusted."

Indeed he was more pedantic than I can represent him, and placed more scraps of Latin in his speech; but it was all uttered with a fine geniality of eye and manner which went far to conquer my distrust. Moreover, I could see he now treated me as if I was myself beyond a doubt; so that first point of my identity seemed fully granted.

"Sir," said I, "if I tell you my story, I must commit a friend's life to your discretion. Pass me your word it shall be sacred; and for what touches myself, I will ask no better guarantee than just your face."

He passed me his word very seriously. "But," said he, "these are rather alarming prolocutions; and if there are in your story any little jostles to the law, I would beg you to bear in mind that I am a lawyer, and pass lightly."

Thereupon I told him my story from the first, he listening with his spectacles thrust up and his eyes closed, so that I sometimes feared he was asleep. But no such matter! he heard every word (as I found afterwards) with such quickness of hearing and precision of memory as often surprised me. Even strange, outlandish Gaelic names, heard for that time only, he remembered and would remind me of, years after. Yet when I called Alan Breck in full, we had an odd scene. The name of Alan had of course rung through Scotland, with the news of the Appin murder and the offer of the reward; and it had no sooner escaped me than the lawyer moved in his seat and opened his eyes.

"I would name no unnecessary names, Mr Balfour," said he; "above all of Highlanders, many of whom are obnoxious to the law."

"Well, it might have been better not," said I; "but since I have let it slip, I may as well continue."

"Not at all," said Mr Rankeillor. "I am somewhat dull of hearing, as you may have remarked; and I am far from sure I caught the name exactly. We will call your friend, if you please, Mr Thomson—that there may be no reflections. And in future, I would take some such way with any Highlander that you may have to mention—dead or alive."

By this, I saw he must have heard the name all too clearly and had already guessed I might be coming to the murder. If he chose to play this part of ignorance, it was no matter of mine; so I smiled, said it was no very Highland sounding name, and consented. Through all the rest of my story Alan was Mr Thomson; which amused me the more, as it was a piece of policy after his own heart. James Stewart, in like manner, was mentioned under the style of Mr Thomson's kinsman; Colin Campbell passed as a Mr Glen; and to Cluny, when I came to that part of my tale, I gave the name of "Mr Jameson, a Highland chief". It was truly the most open farce, and I wondered that the lawyer should care to keep it up; but after all it was quite in the taste of that age, when there were two parties in the state, and quiet persons, with no very high opinions of their own, sought out every cranny to avoid offence to either.

"Well, well," said the lawyer, when I had quite done, "this is a great epic, a great Odyssey of yours. You must tell it, sir, in a sound Latinity when your scholarship is riper; or in English if you please, though for my part I prefer the stronger tongue. You have rolled much; *quae regio in terris*—what parish in Scotland (to make a homely translation) has not been filled with your wanderings? You have shown, besides, a singular aptitude for getting into false positions; and, yes, upon the whole, for behaving well in them. This Mr Thomson seems to me a gentleman of some choice qualities, though perhaps a trifle bloody-minded. It would please me none the worse, if (with all his merits) he were soused in the North Sea; for the man, Mr David, is a sore embarrassment. But you are doubtless quite right to adhere to him; indubitably, he adhered to you. *It comes*—we may say—he was your true companion; nor less, *paribus curis vestigia figit*, for I dare say you would both take another thought upon the gallows. Well, well, these days are fortunately by; and I think (speaking humanly) that you are near the end of your troubles."

As he thus moralized on my adventures, he looked upon me with so much humour and benignity that I could scarce contain my satisfaction. I had been so long wandering with lawless people, and making my bed upon the hills and under the bare sky, that to sit once more in a clean, covered house, and to talk amicably with a gentle-man in broadcloth, seemed mighty elevations. Even as I thought so, my eye fell on my unseemly tatters, and I was once more plunged in confusion. But the lawyer saw and understood me. He rose, called over the stair to lay another plate, for Mr Balfour would stay to dinner, and led me into a bedroom in the upper part of the house. Here he set before me water and soap and a comb; and laid out some clothes that belonged to his son; and here, with another apposite tag, he left me to my toilet.

Chapter 28

I GO IN QUEST OF MY INHERITANCE

I made what change I could in my appearance; and blithe was I to look in the glass and find the beggar-man a thing of the past, and David Balfour come to life again.

And yet I was ashamed of the change too, and above all, of the borrowed clothes. When I had done, Mr Rankeillor caught me on the stair, made me his compliments, and had me again into the cabinet.

"Sit ye down, Mr David," said he, "and now that you are looking a little more like yourself, let me see if I can find you and news. You will be wondering, no doubt, about your father and your uncle? To be sure it is a singular tale; and the explanation is one that I blush to have to offer you. "For," says he, really with embarrassment, "the matter hinges on a love affair."

"Truly," said I, "I cannot very well join that notion with my uncle."

"But your uncle, Mr David, was not always old," replied the lawyer, "and what may perhaps surprise you more, not always ugly. He had a fine, gallant air; people stood in their doors to look after him, as he went by upon a mettle horse. I have seen it with these eyes, and I ingenuously confess, not altogether without envy; for I was a plain lad myself and a plain man's son; and in those days. it was a case of *Odi te, qui bellus es, Sabelle*."

"It sounds like a dream," said I.

"Ay, ay," said the lawyer, "that is how it is with youth and age. Nor was that all, but he had a spirit of his own that seemed to promise great things in the future. In 1715, what must he do but run away to join the rebels? It was your father that pursued him, found him in a ditch, and brought him back *multum gementem*; to the mirth of the whole country. However, *majora canamus*—the two lads fell in love, and that with the same lady. Mr Ebenezer, who was the admired and the beloved, and the spoiled one, made, no doubt, mighty certain of the victory; and when he found he had deceived himself, screamed like a peacock. The whole county heard of it; now he lay sick at home, with his silly family standing round the bed in tears; now he rode from public house to public house, and shouted his sorrows into the lug of Tom, Dick, and Harry. Your father, Mr David, was a kind gentleman; but he was weak, dolefully weak; took all this folly with a long countenance; and one day—by your leave—resigned the lady. She was no such fool, however; it's from her you must inherit your excellent good sense; and she refused to be bandied from one to another. Both got upon their knees to her; and the upshot of the matter for that while, was that she showed both of them the door. That was in August; dear me! the same year I came from college. The scene must have been highly farcical."

I thought myself it was a silly business, but I could not forget my father had a hand in it. "Surely, sir, it had some note of tragedy," said I.

"Why, no, sir, not all," returned the lawyer. "For tragedy implies some ponderable matter in dispute, some *dignus vindice nodus*; and this piece of work was all about the petulance of a young ass that had been spoiled, and wanted nothing so much as to be tied up and soundly belted. However, that was not your father's view; and the end of it was, that from concession to concession on your father's part, and from one height to another of squalling, sentimental selfishness upon your uncle's, they came at last to drive a sort of bargain, from whose ill-results you have recently been smarting. The one man took the lady, the other the estate. Now, Mr David, they talk a great deal of charity and generosity; but in this disputable state of life, I often think the happiest consequences seem to flow when a gentleman consults his lawyers and takes all the law allows him. Anyhow, this piece of quixotry upon your father's part, as it was unjust in itself, has brought forth a monstrous family of injustices. Your father and mother lived and died poor folk; you were poorly reared; and in the meanwhile, what a time it has been for the tenants on the estate of Shaws! And I might add (if it was a matter I cared much about) what a time for Mr Ebenezer!"

"And yet that is certainly the strangest part of all," said I, "that a man's nature should thus change."

"True," said Mr Rankeillor. "And yet I imagine it was natural enough. He could not think that he had played a handsome part. Those who knew the story gave him the cold shoulder; those who knew it not, seeing one brother disappear, and the other succeed in the estate, raised a cry of murder; so that upon all sides, he found himself evited. Money was all he got by his bargain; well, he came to think the more of money. He was selfish when he was young, he is selfish now that he is old; and the latter end of all these pretty manners and fine feelings, you have seen for yourself."

"Well, sir," said I, "and in all this, what is my position?"

"The estate is yours beyond a doubt," replied the lawyer. "It matters nothing what your father signed, you are the heir of entail. But your uncle is a man to fight the indefensible; and it would be likely your identity that he would call in question. A lawsuit is always expensive, and a family lawsuit always scandalous; besides which, if any of your doings with your friend Mr Thomson were to come out, we might find that we had burned our fingers. The kidnapping, to be sure, would be a court card upon our side, if we could only prove it. But it may be difficult to prove; and my advice (upon the whole) is to make a very easy bargain with your uncle, perhaps even leaving him at Shaws where he has taken root for a quarter of a century, and contenting yourself in the meanwhile with a fair provision."

I told him I was very willing to be easy, and that to carry family concerns before the public was a step from which I was naturally much averse. In the meantime (thinking to myself) I began to see the outlines of that scheme on which we afterwards acted.

"The great affair," I asked, "is to bring home to him the kidnapping?"

"Surely," said Mr Rankeillor, "and if possible, out of court. For mark you here, Mr David; we could no doubt find some men of the *Covenant* who would swear to your reclusion; but once they were in the box, we could no longer check their testimony, and some word of your friend Mr Thomson must certainly crop out. Which (from what you have let fall) I cannot think to be desirable."

"Well, sir," said I, "here is my way of it." And I opened my plot to him.

"But this would seem to involve my meeting the man Thomson?" says he, when I had done.

"I think so, indeed, sir," said I.

"Dear doctor!" cries he, rubbing his brow. "Dear doctor! No, Mr David, I am afraid your scheme is inadmissible. I say nothing against your friend Mr Thomson; I know nothing against him; and if I did— mark this, Mr David!—it would be my duty to lay hands on him. Now I put it to you: is it wise to meet? He may have matters to his charge. He may not have told you all. His name may not be even Thomson!" cries the lawyer, twinkling; "for some of these fellows will pick up names by the roadside as another would gather haws."

"You must be the judge, sir," said I.

But it was clear my plan had taken hold upon his fancy, for he kept musing to himself till we were called to dinner and the company of Mrs Rankeillor; and that lady had scarce left us again to ourselves and a bottle of wine, ere he was back harping on my proposal. When and where was I to meet my friend Mr Thomson; was I sure of Mr T's discretion; supposing we could catch the old fox tripping, would I consent to such and such a term of an agreement—these and the like questions he kept asking at long intervals, while he thoughtfully rolled his wine upon his tongue. When I had answered all of them, seemingly to his contentment, he fell into a still deeper muse, even the claret being now forgotten. Then he got a sheet of paper and a pencil, and set to work writing and weighing every word; and at last touched a bell and had his clerk into the chamber.

"Torrance," said he, "I must have this written out fair against tonight; and when it is done, you will be so kind as to put on your hat and be ready to come along with this gentleman and me, for you will probably be wanted as a witness."

"What, sir," cried I, as soon as the clerk was gone, "are you to venture it?"

"Why, so it would appear," says he, filling his glass. "But let us speak no more of business. The very sight of Torrance brings in my head a little, droll matter of some years ago, when I had made a tryst with the poor oaf at the cross of Edinburgh. Each had gone his proper errand; and when it came four o'clock, Torrance had been taking a glass and did not know his master, and I, who had forgot my spectacles, was so blind without them, that I give you my word I did not know my own clerk." And thereupon he laughed heartily.

I said it was an odd chance, and smiled out of politeness; but what held me all the afternoon in wonder, he kept returning and dwelling on this story, and telling it again with fresh details and laughter; so that I began at last to be quite put out of countenance and feel ashamed for my friend's folly.

Towards the time I had appointed with Alan, we set out from the house, Mr Rankeillor and I arm in arm, and Torrance following behind with the deed in his pocket and a covered basket in his hand. All through the town, the lawyer was bowing right and left, and continually being button-holed by gentlemen on matters of burgh or private business; and I could see he was greatly looked up to in the county. At last we were clear of the houses, and began to go along the side of the haven and towards the Hawes Inn and the ferry pier, the scene of my misfortune. I could not look upon the place without emotion, recalling how many that had been there with me that day were now no more: Ransome taken, I could hope, from the evil to come; Shuan passed where I dared not follow him; and the poor souls that had gone down with the brig in her last plunge. All these, and the brig herself, I had out-lived; and come through these hardships and fearful perils without scathe. My only thought should have been of gratitude; and yet I could not behold the place without sorrow for others and a chill of recollected fear.

I was so thinking when, upon a sudden, Mr Rankeillor cried out, clapped his hand to his pockets, and began to laugh.

"Why," he cried, "if this be not a farcical adventure! After all that I said, I have forgotten my glasses!"

At that, of course, I understood the purpose of his anecdote, and knew that if he had left his spectacles at home, it had been done on purpose, so that he might have the benefit of Alan's help without the awkwardness of recognizing him. And indeed it was well thought upon; for now (suppose things to go the very worst) how could Rankeillor swear to my friend's identity, or how be made to bear damaging evidence against myself? For all that, he had been a long while of finding out his want, and had spoken to and recognized a good few persons as we came through the town; and I had little doubt myself that he saw reasonably well.

As soon as we were past the Hawes (where I recognized the land-lord smoking his pipe in the door, and was amazed to see him look no older) Mr Rankeillor changed the order of march, walking behind with Torrance and sending me forward in the manner of a scout. I went up the hill, whistling from time to time my Gaelic air; and at length I had the pleasure to hear it answered and to see Alan rise from behind a bush. He was somewhat dashed in spirits, having passed a long day alone skulking in the country, and made but a poor meal in an alehouse near Dundas. But at the mere sight of my clothes, he began to brighten up; and as soon as I had told him in what a forward state our matters were, and the part I looked to him to play in what remained; he sprang into a new man.

"And that is a very good notion of yours," says he; "and I dare say that you could lay your hands upon no better man to put it through, than Alan Breck. It is not a thing (mark ye) that anyone could do, but takes a gentleman of penetration. But it sticks in my head your lawyer-man will be somewhat wearying to see me," says Alan.

Accordingly I cried and waved on Mr Rankeillor, who came up alone and was presented to my friend, Mr Thomson.

"Mr Thomson, I am pleased to meet you," said he. "But I have forgotten my glasses; and our friend, Mr David here" (clapping me on the shoulder) "will tell you that I am little better than blind, and that you must not be surprised if I pass you by tomorrow."

This he said, thinking that Alan would be pleased; but the Highlandman's vanity was ready to startle at a less matter than that.

"Why, sir," said he, stiffly, "I would say it mattered the less as we are met here for a particular end, to see justice done to Mr Balfour; and by what I can see, not very likely to have much else in common. But I accept your apology, which was a very proper one to make."

"And that is more than I could look for, Mr Thomson," said Rankeillor, heartily. "And now as you and I are the chief actors in this enterprise, I think we should come into a nice agreement; to which end, I propose that you should lend me your arm, for (what with the dusk and the want of my glasses) I am not very clear as to the path; and as for you, Mr David, you will find Torrance a pleasant kind of body to speak with. Only let me remind you, it's quite needless he should hear more of your adventures or those of—ahem— Mr Thomson."

Accordingly these two went on ahead in very close talk, and Torrance and I brought up the rear.

Night was quite come when we came in view of the house of Shaws. Ten had been gone some time; it was dark and mild, with a pleasant, rustling wind in the south-west that covered the sound of our approach; and as we drew near we saw no glimmer of light in any portion of the building. It seemed my uncle was already in bed, which was indeed the best thing for our arrangements. We made our last whispered consultations some fifty yards away; and then the lawyer and Torrance and I crept quietly up and crouched down beside the corner of the house; and as soon as we were in our places, Alan strode to the door without concealment and began to knock.

Chapter 29

I COME INTO MY KINGDOM

For some time Alan volleyed upon the door, and his knocking only roused the echoes of the house and neighbourhood. At last, however, I could hear the noise of a window gently thrust up, and knew that my uncle had come to his observatory.

By what light there was he would see Alan standing, like a dark shadow, still on the steps; the three witnesses were hidden quite out of his view; so that there was nothing to alarm an honest man in his own house.

For all that, Ebenezer studied his visitor awhile in deadly silence, and when at last he spoke his voice had a quaver of misgiving.

"What's this?" says he. "This is nae kind of time of night for decent folk; and I hae nae trokings wi' nighthawks. What brings ye here? I have a blunderbush."

"Is that yoursel', Mr Balfour?" returned Alan, stepping back and looking up into the darkness. "Have a care of that blunderbuss, they're nasty things to burst."

"What brings ye here? and whae are ye? says my uncle, angrily.

"I have no manner of inclination to shout out my name to the countryside," said Alan; "but what brings me here is another story, being more of your affairs than mine; and if ye're sure it's what ye would like, I'll set it to a tune and sing it to you."

"And what is't?" asked my uncle.

"David," says Alan.

"What was that?" cried my uncle, in a mighty changed voice.

"Shall I give ye the rest of the name, then?" said Alan.

There was a pause; and then, "I'm thinking I'll better let ye in," says my uncle, doubtfully.

"I dare say that," said Alan; "but the point is, Would I go? Now I will tell you what I am thinking. I am thinking that it is here upon this doorstep that we must confer upon this business; and it shall be here or nowhere at all whatever; for I would have you to understand that I am as stiffnecked as yoursel', and a gentleman of better family."

This change of note disconcerted Ebenezer; he was a little while digesting it; and then says he, "Weel, weel, what must be must," and shut the window. But it took him a long time to get downstairs, and a still longer to undo the fastenings, repenting (I dare say) and taken with fresh claps of fear at every second step and every bolt and bar. At last, however, we hear the creak of the hinges, and it seems my uncle slipped gingerly out and (seeing that Alan had stepped back a pace or two) sate him down on the top doorstep with the blunderbuss ready in his hands.

"And now," says he, "mind I have my blunderbush, and if ye take a step nearer y're as good as deid."

"And a very civil speech," said Alan, "to be sure."

"Na," says my uncle, "but this is no a very chancy kind of a proceeding, and I'm bound to be prepared. And now that we understand each other, ye'll can name your business."

"Why," says Alan, "you that are a man of so much understanding, will doubtless have perceived that I am a Hieland gentleman. My name has nae business in my story; but the county of my friends is no very far from the Isle of Mull, of which ye will have heard. It seems there was a ship lost in those parts; and the next day a gentleman of my family was seeking wreckwood for his fire among the sands, when he came upon a lad that was half drowned. Well, he brought him to; and he and some other gentlemen took and clapped him in an auld, ruined castle, where from that day to this he has been a great expense to my friends. My friends are a wee wild-like, and not so particular about the law as some that I could name; and finding that the lad owned some decent folk, and was your born nephew, Mr Balfour, they asked me to give ye a bit call and to confer upon the matter. And I may kill ye at the off-go, unless we can agree upon some terms, ye are little likely to set eyes upon him. For my friends," added Alan, simply, "are no very well off."

My uncle cleared his throat.

"I'm no very caring," says he. "He wasnae a good lad at the best of it, and I've nae call to interfere."

"Ay, ay," said Alan, "I see what ye would be at: pretending ye don't care, to make the ransom smaller."

"Na," said my uncle, "it's the mere truth. I take nae manner of interest in the lad, and I'll pay nae ransom, and ye can make a kirk and a mill of him for what I care."

"Hoot, sir," says Alan, "Blood's thicker than water, in the devil's name! Ye cannae desert your brother's son for the fair shame of it; and if ye did, and it came to be kennt, ye wouldnae be very popular in your countryside, or I'm the more deceived."

"I'm no just very popular the way it is," returned Ebenezer; "and I dinnae see how it would come to be kennt. No by me, onyway; nor by you or your friends. So that's idle talk, my buckie," says he.

"Then it'll have to be David that tells it," said Alan.

"How that?" says my uncle, sharply.

"Ou, just this way," says Alan. "My friends would doubtless keep your nephew as long as there was any likelihood of siller to be made of it, but if there was nane, I am clearly of opinion they would let him gang where he pleased, and be damned to him."

"Ay, but I'm no very caring about that either," said my uncle. "I wouldnae be muckle made up with that."

"I was thinking that," said Alan.

"And what for why?" asked Ebenezer.

"Why, Mr Balfour," replied Alan, "by all that I could hear, there were two ways of it: either ye liked David and would pay to get him back; or else ye had very good reasons for not wanting him, and would pay for us to keep him. It seems it's not the first; well then, it's the second; and blythe am I to ken it, for it should be a pretty penny in my pocket and the pockets of my friends."

"I dinnae follow ye there," said my uncle.

"No?" said Alan. "Well, see here; you dinnae want the lad back; well, what do ye want done with him, and how much will ye pay?"

My uncle made no answer, but shifted uneasily on his seat.

"Come, sir," cried Alan. "I would have ye ken that I am a gentleman; I bear a king's name; I am nae rider to kick my shanks at your hall door. Either give me an answer in civility, and that out of hand; or by the top of Glencoe, I will ram three feet of iron through your vitals."

"Eh, man," cried my uncle, scrambling to his feet, "give me a meenit! What's like wrong with ye? I'm just a plain man, and nae dancing master; and I'm trying to be as ceevil as it's morally possible. As for that wild talk, it's fair disrepitable. Vitals, says you! And where would I be with my blunderbush?" he snarled.

"Powder and your auld hands are but as the snail to the swallow against the bright steel in the hands of Alan," said the other. "Before your jottering finger could find the trigger, the hilt would dirl on your breast bane."

"Eh, man, whae's denying it?" said my uncle. "Pit it as ye please, hae't your ain way; I'll do naething to cross ye. Just tell me what like ye'll be wanting, and ye'll see that we'll can agree fine."

"Troth, sir," said Alan, "I ask for nothing but plain dealing. In two words: do ye want the lad killed or kept?"

"O, sirs!" cried Ebenezer. "O, sirs, me! that's no kind of language!"

"Killed or kept?" repeated Alan.

"Oh, keepit, keepit!" wailed my uncle. "We'll have nae bloodshed, if you please."

"Well," says Alan, "as ye please; that'll be the dearer."

"The dearer?" cries Ebenezer. "Would ye fyle your hand wi' crime?"

"Hoot!" said Alan, "they're baith crime, whatever! And the killing's easier, and quicker, and surer. Keeping the lad'll be a fashious job, a fashious, kittle business."

"I'll have him keepit, though," returned my uncle. "I never had naething to do with onything morally wrong; and I'm no gaun to begin to pleasure a wild Hielandman."

"Ye're unco' scrupulous," sneered Alan.

"I'm a man o' principle," said Ebenezer simply; "and if I have to pay for it, I'll have to pay for it. And besides," says he, "ye forget the lad's my brother's son."

"Well, well," said Alan, "and now about the price. It's no very easy for me to set a name upon it; I would first have to ken some small matters. I would have to ken, for instance, what ye gave Hoseason at the first off-go?"

"Hoseason?" cries my uncle, struck aback. "What for?"

"For kidnapping David," says Alan.

"It's a lee, it's a black lee!" cried my uncle. "He was never kidnapped. He leed in his throat that tauld ye that. Kidnapped? He never was!"

"That's no fault of mine or yet of yours," said Alan; "nor yet of Hoseason's, if he's a man that can be trusted."

"What do ye mean?" cried Ebenezer. "Did Hoseason tell ye?"

"Why, ye donnered auld runt, how else would I ken?" cried Alan. "Hoseason and I are partners; we gang shares; so ye can see for yoursel', what good ye can do leeing. And I must plainly say ye drove a fool's bargain when ye let a man like the sailor-man so far forward in your private matters. But that's past praying for; and ye must lie on your bed the way ye made it. And the point in hand is just this: what did ye pay him?"

"Has he tauld ye himsel'?," asked my uncle.

"That's my concern," said Alan.

"Weel," said my uncle, "I dinnae care what he said, he leed, and the solemn God's truth is this, that I gave him twenty pound. But I'll be perfec'ly honest with ye: forby that, he was to have the selling of the lad in Caroliny, whilk would be as muckle mair, but no from my pocket, ye see."

"Thank you, Mr Thomson. That will do excellently well," said the lawyer, stepping forward; and then mighty civilly, "Good evening, Mr Balfour," said he.

"And, Good evening, uncle Ebenezer," said I.

"And, "It's a braw nicht, Mr Balfour," added Torrance.

Never a word said my uncle, neither black nor white, but just sat where he was on the top doorstep and stared upon us like a man turned to stone. Alan filched away his blunderbuss; and the lawyer, taking him by the arm, plucked him up from the doorstep, led him into the kitchen, whither we all followed, and set him down in a chair beside the hearth, where the fire was out and only a rush-light burning.

There we all looked upon him for a while, exulting greatly in our success, but yet with a sort of pity for the man's shame.

"Come, come, Mr Ebenezer," said the lawyer, "you must not be down-hearted, for I promise you we shall make easy terms. In the meanwhile give us the cellar key, and Torrance shall draw us a bottle of your father's wine in honour of the event." Then, turning to me and taking my by the hand, "Mr David," says he, "I wish you all joy in your good fortune, which I believe to be deserved."

And then to Alan, with a spice of drollery, "Mr Thomson, I pay you my compliment; it was most artfully conducted; but in one point you somewhat outran my comprehension. Do I understand your name to be James? or Charles? or is it George perhaps?"

"And why should it be any of the three, sir?" quoth Alan, drawing himself, up like one who smelt an offence.

"Only, sir, that you mentioned a king's name," replied Rankeillor; "and as there has never yet been a King Thomson, or his fame at last has never come my way, I judged you must refer to that you had in baptism."

This was just the stab that Alan would feel keenest, and I am free to confess he took it very ill. Not a word would he answer, but stept off to the far end of the kitchen, and sat down and sulked; and it was not till I stepped after him, and gave him my hand, and thanked him by title as the chief spring of my success, that he began to smile a bit, and was at last prevailed upon to join our party.

By that time we had the fire lighted, and a bottle of wine uncorked; a good supper came out of the basket, to which Torrance and I and Alan set ourselves down; while the lawyer and my uncle passed into the next chamber to consult. They stayed there closeted about an hour; at the end of which period they had come to a good understanding, and my uncle and I set our hands to the agreement in a formal manner. By the terms of this, my uncle bound himself to satisfy Rankeillor as to his intromissions, and to pay me two clear thirds of the yearly income of Shaws.

So the beggar in the ballad had come home; and when I lay down that night on the kitchen chests, I was a man of means and had a name in the country. Alan and Torrance and Rankeillor slept and snored on their hard beds; but for me, who had lain out under heaven and upon dirt and stones, so many days and nights, and often with an empty belly; and in fear of death, this good change in my case unmanned me more than any of the former evil ones; and I lay till dawn, looking at the fire on the roof and planning the future.

CHAPTER 30

GOOD-BYE

So far as I was concerned myself, I had come to port; but I had still Alan, to whom I was so much beholden, on my hands; and I felt besides a heavy charge in the matter of the murder and James of the Glens. On both these heads I unbosomed to Rankeillor the next morning, walking to and fro about six of the clock before the house of Shaws, and with nothing in view but the fields and woods that had been my ancestors' and were now mine. Even as I spoke on these grave subjects, my eye would take a glad bit of a run over the prospect, and my heart jump with pride.

About my clear duty to my friend, the lawyer had no doubt; I must help him out of the county at whatever risk; but in the case of James, he was of different mind.

"Mr Thomson," says he, "is one thing, Mr Thomson's kinsman quite another. I know little of the facts; but I gather that a great noble (whom we will call, if you like, the D. of A.[1]) has some concern and is even supposed to feel some animosity in the matter. The D. of A. is doubtless an excellent nobleman; but, Mr David, *timeo qui nocuere deos.* If you interfere to baulk his vengeance, you should remember there is one way to shut your testimony out; and that is to put you in the dock. There, you would be in the same pickle as Mr Thomson's kinsman. You will object that you are innocent; well, but so is he. And to be tried for your life before a Highland jury, on a Highland quarrel, and with a Highland judge upon the bench, would be a brief transition to the gallows."

Now I had made all these reasonings before and found no very good reply to them; so I put on all the simplicity I could. "In that case, sir," said I, "I would just have to be hanged—would I not?"

"My dear boy," cries he, "go in God's name, and do what you think is right. It is a poor thought that at my time of life I should be advising you to choose the safe and shameful; and I take it back with an apology. Go and do your duty; and be hanged, if you must, like a gentleman. There are worse things in the world than to be hanged."

"Not many, sir," said I, smiling.

1. The Duke of Argyle

"Why, yes, yes, sir," he cried, "very many. And it would be ten times better for your uncle (to go no farther afield) if he were dangling decently upon a gibbet."

Thereupon he turned into the house (still in a great fervour of mind, so that I saw I had pleased him heartily) and there he wrote me two letters, making his comments on them as he wrote.

"This," says he, "is to my bankers, the British Linen Company, placing a credit to your name. Consult Mr Thomson; he will know of ways; and you, with this credit, can supply the means. I trust you will be a good husband of your money; but in the affairs of a friend like Mr Thomson, I would be even prodigal. Then, for his kinsman, there is no better way than that you should seek the Advocate, tell him your tale, and offer testimony; whether he may ask it or not, is quite another matter, and will turn on the D. of A. Now that you may reach the Lord Advocate well recommended, I give you here a letter to a namesake of your own, the learned Mr Balfour of Pilrig, a man whom I esteem. It will look better that you should be presented by one of your own name; and the laird of Pilrig is much looked up to in the Faculty and stands well with Lord Advocate Grant. I would not trouble him, if I were you, with any particulars; and (do you know?) I think it would be needless to refer to Mr Thomson. Form yourself upon the laird, he is a good model; when you deal with the Advocate, be discreet; and in all these matters, may the Lord guide you, Mr David!"

Thereupon he took his farewell, and set out with Torrance for the Ferry, while Alan and I turned our faces for the city in Edinburgh. As we went by the footpath and beside the gateposts and the unfinished lodge, we kept looking back at the house of my fathers. It stood there, bare and great and smokeless, like a place not lived in; only in one of the top windows, there was the peak of a nightcap bobbing up and down and back and forward, like the head of a rabbit from a burrow. I had little welcome when I came, and less kindness while I stayed; but at least I was watched as I went away.

Alan and I went slowly forward upon our way, having little heart either to walk or speak. The same thought was uppermost in both, that we were near the time of our parting; and remembrance of all the bygone days sat upon us sorely. We talked indeed of what should be done; and it was resolved that Alan should keep to the county, biding now here, now there, but coming once in the day to a particular place where I might be able to communicate with him, either in my own person or by messenger. In the meanwhile, I was to seek out a lawyer, who was an Appin Stewart, and a man therefore to be wholly trusted; and it should be his part to find a ship and to arrange for Alan's safe embarkation. No sooner was this business done, than the words seemed to leave us; and though I would seek to jest with Alan under the name of Mr Thomson, and he with me on my new clothes and my estate, you could feel very well that we were nearer tears than laughter.

We came the by-way over the hill of Corstorphine; and when we got near to the place called Rest-and-be-Thankful, and looked down on Corstorphine bogs and over to the city and the castle on the hill, we both stopped, for we both knew without a word said, that we had come to where our ways parted. Here he repeated to me once again what had been agreed upon between us; the address of the lawyer, the daily hour at which Alan might be found, and the signals that were to be made by any that came seeking him. Then I gave what money I had (a guinea or two of Rankeillor's) so that he should not starve in the meanwhile; and then we stood a space, and looked over at Edinburgh in silence.

"Well, good-bye," said Alan, and held out his left hand.

"Good-bye," said I, and gave the hand a little grasp, and went off down hill.

Neither one of us looked the other in the face, nor so long as he was in my view did I take one back glance at the friend I was leaving. But as I went on my way to the city, I felt so lost and lonesome, that I could have found it in my heart to sit down by the dyke, and cry and weep like any baby.

It was coming near noon when I passed in by the West Kirk and the Grassmarket into the streets of the capital. The huge height of the buildings, running up to ten and fifteen storeys, the narrow arched entries that continually vomited passengers, the wares of the merchants in their windows, the hubbub and endless stir, the foul smells and the fine clothes, and a hundred other particulars too small to mention, struck me into a kind of stupor of surprise, so that I let the crowd carry me to and fro; and yet all the time what I was thinking of was Alan at Rest-and-be-Thankful; and all the time (although you would think I would not choose but be delighted with these braws and novelties) there was a cold gnawing in my inside like a remorse for something wrong.

The hand of Providence brought me in my drifting to the very doors of the British Linen Company's bank.

[Just there, with his hand upon his fortune, the present editor inclines for the time to say farewell to David. How Alan escaped, and what was done about the murder, with a variety of other delectable particulars, may be some day set forth. That is a thing, however, that hinges on the public fancy. The editor has a great kindness for both Alan and David, and would gladly spend much of his life in their society; but in this he may find himself to stand alone. In the fear of which, and lest any one should complain of scurvy usage, he hastens to protest that all went well with both, in the limited and human sense of the word 'well'; that whatever befell them, it was not dishonour, and whatever failed them, they were not found wanting to themselves.]

CHILDREN'S CLASSICS

Around the World in Eighty Days

JULES VERNE

Around the World in Eighty Days

PARRAGON

Around the World in Eighty Days
A Parragon Classic

This is a Siena Book
Siena is an imprint of Parragon

This edition published in 1999 by
Parragon
13 Whiteladies Road
Clifton
Bristol BS8 1PB

Printed and bound in the UK

Chapter 1

In which Phileas Fogg and Passepartout accept each other—the one as Master, the other as Servant

In the year 1872, the house No. 7 Saville Row, Burlington Gardens—the house in which Sheridan died, in 1814—was inhabited by Phileas Fogg, Esq., one of the most singular and most noticed members of the Reform Club of London, although he seemed to take care to do nothing which might attract attention.

This Phileas Fogg, then, an enigmatic personage, of whom nothing was known but that he was a very polite man, and one of the most perfect gentlemen of good English society, succeeded one of the great orators that honour England.

An Englishman Phileas Fogg was surely, but perhaps not a Londoner. He was never seen on 'Change, at the Bank, or in any of the counting-rooms of the "City." The docks of London had never received a vessel fitted out by Phileas Fogg. This gentleman did not figure in any public body. His name had never sounded in any Inns of Court, nor in the Temple, nor Lincoln's Inn, nor Gray's Inn. He never pleaded in the Court of Chancery, nor the Queen's Bench, nor the Exchequer, nor the Ecclesiastical Courts. He was neither a manufacturer, nor a trader, nor a merchant, nor a gentleman farmer. He was not a member of the Royal Institution of Great Britain, or the London Institution, or the Artisan's Association, or the Russell Institution, or the Literary Institution of the West, or the Law Institute, or that Institute of the Arts and Sciences, placed under the direct patronage of Her Gracious Majesty. In fact, he belonged to none of the numerous societies that swarm in the capital of England, from the Harmonic to the Entomological Society, founded principally for the purpose of destroying hurtful insects.

Phileas Fogg was a member of the Reform Club, and that was all.

Should anyone be astonished that such a mysterious gentleman should be among the members of this honourable institution, we will reply that he obtained admission on the recommendation of Baring Brothers, with whom he had an open credit. Thence a certain appearance due to his cheques being regularly paid at sight by the debit of his account current, which was always to his credit.

Was this Phileas Fogg rich? Undoubtedly. But the best informed could not say how he had made his money, and Mr. Fogg was the last person to whom it would have been proper to go for information. He was by no means extravagant in anything, neither was he avaricious, for when money was needed for a noble, useful, or benevolent purpose, he gave it quietly, and even anonymously. In short, no one was less communicative than this gentleman. He talked as little as possible, and seemed much more mysterious than silent. But his life was open to the light, but what he did was always so mathematically the same thing, that the imagination, unsatisfied, sought further.

Had he travelled? It was probable, for none knew the world better than he; there was no spot so secluded that he did not appear to have a special acquaintance with it. Sometimes, in a few, brief, clear words, he would correct the thousand suppositions circulating in the Club with reference to travellers lost or strayed; he pointed out the true probabilities, and so often did events justify his predictions that he seemed as if gifted with a sort of second sight. He was a man who must have travelled everywhere, in spirit at least.

One thing was certain, that for many years Phileas Fogg had not been from London. Those who had the honour of knowing him more intimately than others, affirmed that no one could pretend to have seen him elsewhere than upon the direct route, which he traversed every day to go from his house to the Club. His only pastime was reading the papers and playing whist. He frequently won at this quiet game, so very appropriate to his nature; but his winnings never went into his purse, and made an important item in his charity fund. Besides, it must be remarked, that Mr. Fogg evidently played for the sake of playing, not to win. The game was for him a contest, a struggle against a difficulty; but a motionless, unwearying struggle, and that suited his character.

Phileas Fogg was not known to have either wife or children—which may happen to the most respectable people—neither relatives nor friends—which is more rare, truly. Phileas Fogg lived alone in his house in Saville Row, where nobody entered. There was never a question as to its interior. A single servant sufficed to serve him. Breakfasting and dining at the Club, at hours fixed with the utmost exactness, in the same hall, at the same table, not entertaining his colleagues nor inviting a stranger, he returned home only to go to bed, exactly at midnight, without ever making use of the comfortable chambers which the Reform Club puts at the disposal of its favoured members. Of the twenty-four hours he passed ten at his residence either sleeping or busying himself at his toilet. If he walked, it was invariably with a regular step in the entrance hall with its Mosaic floor, or in the circular gallery, above which rose a dome with blue-painted windows, supported by twenty Ionic columns of red porphyry. If he dined or breakfasted, the kitchens, the buttery, the pantry, the dairy of the Club furnished his table from their succulent stores; the waiters of the Club, grave personages in dress-coats and shoes with swanskin soles, served him in a special porcelain and on fine Saxon linen; the Club decanters of a lost mould contained his sherry, his port, and his claret, flavoured with orange flower water and cinnamon; and finally the ice of the Club, brought at great expense from the American lakes, kept his drinks in a satisfactory condition of freshness.

If to live in such conditions is to be eccentric, it must be granted that eccentricity has something good in it!

The mansion of Saville Row, without being sumptuous, recommended itself by its extreme comfort. Besides, with the unvarying habits of the occupants, the number of servants was reduced to one. But Phileas Fogg demanded from his only servant an extraordinary and regular punctuality. This very day, the second of October, Phileas Fogg had dismissed James Forster—this youth having incurred his displeasure by bringing him shaving-water at eighty-four degrees Fahrenheit, instead of eighty-six—and he was waiting for his successor, who was to make his appearance between eleven and half-past eleven.

Phileas Fogg, squarely seated in his armchair, his feet close together like those of a soldier on parade, his hands resting on his knees, his body straight, his head erect, was watching the hand of the clock move—a complicated mechanism which indicated the hours, the minutes, the seconds, the days, the days of the month, and the year. At the stroke of half-past eleven Mr. Fogg would, according to his daily habit, leave his house and repair to the Reform Club.

At this moment, there was a knock at the door of the small parlour in which was Phileas Fogg.

James Forster, the dismissed servant, appeared.

"The new servant," said he.

A young man, aged thirty years, came forward and bowed.

"You are a Frenchman, and your name is John?" Phileas Fogg asked him.

"Jean, if it does not displease Monsieur," replied the newcomer. "Jean Passepartout, a surname which has clung to me and which my natural aptitude for withdrawing from a business has justified. I believe, sir, that I am an honest fellow; but to be frank, I have had several trades. I have been a travelling singer; a circus rider, vaulting like Leotard, and dancing on the rope like Blondin; then I became professor of gymnastics, in order to render my talents more useful; and in the last place, I was a sergeant fireman at Paris. I have among my papers notes of remarkable fires. But five years have passed since I left France, and wishing to have a taste of family life, I have been a valet in England. Now, finding myself out of a situation, and having learned that Monsieur Phileas Fogg was the most exact and the most settled gentleman in the United Kingdom, I have presented myself to monsieur with the hope of living tranquilly with him, and of forgetting even the name of Passepartout."

"Passepartout suits me," replied the gentleman. "You are recommended to me. I have good reports concerning you. You know my conditions?"

"Yes, sir."

"Well, what time have you?"

"Twenty-two minutes after eleven," replied Passepartout, drawing from the depths of his pocket an enormous silver watch.

"You are slow," said Mr. Fogg.

"Pardon me, monsieur, but it is impossible."

"You are four minutes too slow. It does not matter. It suffices to state the difference. Then, from this moment—twenty-nine minutes after eleven o'clock a.m., this Wednesday, October 2,1872, you are in my service."

That said, Phileas Fogg rose, took his hat in his left hand, placed it upon his head with an automatic movement, and disappeared without another word.

Passepartout heard the street door close once; it was his new master going out; then a second time; it was his predecessor, James Forster, departing in his turn. Passepartout remained alone in the house in Saville Row.

Chapter 2

In which Passepartout is Convinced that he has Found his ideal

"Upon my word," said Passepartout to himself, "I have known at Madame Tussaud's good people as lively as my new master!"

It is proper to say here that Madame Tussaud's "good people'" are wax figures, much visited in London, and who, indeed, are only wanting in speech.

During the few minutes that he had interviewed Phileas Fogg, Passepartout had examined his future master, rapidly but carefully. He was a man that might be forty years old, of fine handsome face, of tall figure, which a slight corpulence did not disparage, his hair and whiskers light, his forehead compact, without appearance of wrinkles at the temples, his face rather pale than flushed, his teeth magnificent. He appeared to possess in the highest degree what physiognomists call "repose in action," a quality common to those who do more work than talking. Calm, phlegmatic, with a clear eye and immovable eyelid, he was the finished type of those cool-blooded Englishmen so frequently met in the United Kingdom, and whose somewhat academic posture Angelica Kauffman has marvellously reproduced under her pencil. Seen in the various acts of his existence, this gentleman gave the idea of a well-balanced being in all his parts, evenly hung, as perfect as a Leroy or Earnshaw chronometer. Indeed Phileas Fogg was exactness personified, which was seen clearly from "the expression of his feet and his hands," for with man, as well as with the animals, the limbs themselves are organs expressive of the passions.

Phileas Fogg was one of those mathematically exact people, who, never hurried and always ready, are economical of their steps and their motions. He never made one stride too many, always going by the shortest route. He did not give an idle look. He did not allow himself a superfluous gesture. He had never been seen moved or troubled. He was a man of the least possible haste, but he always arrived in time. However, it will be understood that he lived alone, and, so to speak, outside of every social relation. He knew that in life one must take his share of friction, and as frictions retard, he never rubbed against anyone.

As for Jean, called Passepartout, a true Parisian of Paris, he had sought vainly for a master to whom he could attach himself, in the five years that he lived in England and served as a valet in London. Passepartout was not one of those Frontins or Mascarilles, who, with high shoulders, nose high in air, a look of assurance, and staring eye, are only impudent dunces. No, Passepartout was a good fellow, of amiable physiognomy, his lips a little prominent, always ready to taste or caress, a mild and serviceable being, with one of those good round heads that we like to see on the shoulders of a friend. His eyes were blue, his complexion rosy, his face fat enough for him to see his cheek-bones, his chest broad, his form full, his muscles vigorous, and he possessed a herculean strength which his youthful exercise had splendidly developed. His brown hair was somewhat tumbled. If the ancient sculptors knew eighteen ways of arranging Minerva's hair, Passepartout knew of but one for fixing his own: three strokes of a large tooth-comb, and it was dressed.

The most meagre stock of prudence would not permit of saying that the expansive character of this young man would agree with that of Phileas Fogg. Would Passepartout be in all respects exactly the servant that his master needed? That would only be seen by using him. After having had, as we have seen, quite a wandering youth, he longed for repose. Having heard the exactness and proverbial coolness of the English gentlemen praised, he came to seek his fortune in England. But until the present, Fate had treated him badly. He had not been able to take root anywhere. He had served in ten different houses. In every one the people were capricious and irregular, running after adventures or about the country—which no longer suited Passepartout. His last master, young Lord Longsferry, Member of Parliament, after having passed his nights in the Haymarket oyster rooms, returned home too frequently on the shoulders of policemen. Passepartout wishing, above all things, to be able to respect his master, ventured some mild remarks, which were badly received, and he left. In the meantime, he learned that Phileas Fogg, Esq., was hunting for a servant. He made some inquiry about this gentleman. A person whose existence was so regular, who never slept in a strange bed, who did not travel, who was never absent, not even for a day, could not but suit him. He presented himself, and was accepted under the circumstances that we already know.

At half-past eleven, Passepartout found himself alone in the

Saville Row mansion. He immediately commenced its inspection, going over it from cellar to garret. This clean, well-ordered, austere, Puritan house, well organised for servants, pleased him. It produced the effect upon him of a fine snail-shell, but one lighted and heated by gas, for carburetted hydrogen answered both purposes here. Passepartout found without difficulty, in the second story, the room designed for him. It suited him. Electric bells and speaking-tubes put it in communication with the lower stories. On the mantel an electric clock corresponded with the one in Phileas Fogg's bed-chamber, both beating the same second at the same instant. "That suits me, that suits me!" said Passepartout.

He observed also in his room a notice fastened above the clock. It was the programme for the daily service. It comprised—from eight o'clock in the morning, the regular hour at which Phileas Fogg rose, until half-past eleven, the hour at which he left his house to breakfast at the Reform Club—all the details of the service, the tea and toast at twenty-three minutes after eight, the shaving-water at thirty-seven minutes after nine, the toilet at twenty minutes before ten, etc. Then from half-past eleven in the morning until midnight, the hour at which the methodical gentleman retired—everything was noted down, foreseen, and regulated. Passepartout took a pleasure in contemplating this programme, and impressing upon his mind its various directions.

As to the gentleman's wardrobe, it was in very good taste, and wonderfully complete. Each pair of pantaloons, coat or vest, bore a regular number, which was also entered upon a register, indicating the date at which, according to the season, these garments were to be worn in their turn. The same rule applied to his shoes.

In short, in this house in Saville Row—which, in the time of the illustrious but dissipated Sheridan, must have been the temple of disorder—its comfortable furniture indicated a delightful ease. There was no study, there were no books, which would have been of no use to Mr. Fogg, since the Reform Club placed at his disposal two libraries, the one devoted to literature, the other to law and politics. In his bed-chamber there was a medium-sized safe, whose construction protected it from fire as well as from burglars. There were no weapons in the house, neither for the chase, nor for war. Everything there denoted the most peaceful habits.

After having minutely examined the dwelling, Passepartout rubbed his hands, his broad face brightened, and he repeated cheerfully: "This suits me! This is the place for me! Mr. Fogg and I will understand each other perfectly. A home-body, and so methodical! A genuine automaton! Well, I am not sorry to serve an automaton!"

CHAPTER 3

In which a conversation takes place which may cost Phileas Fogg dearly

Phileas Fogg had left his house in Saville Row at half-past eleven, and after putting his right foot before his left foot five hundred and seventy-five times, and his left foot before his right foot five hundred and seventy-six times, he arrived at the Reform Club, a spacious and lofty building in Pall Mall, which cost not less than three millions to build.

Phileas Fogg repaired immediately to the dining-room, whose nine windows opened upon a fine garden with trees already gilded by autumn. There, he took his seat at his regular table where the plate was awaiting him. His breakfast consisted of a side-dish, a boiled fish with Reading sauce of first quality, a scarlet slice of roast beef garnished with mushrooms, a rhubarb and gooseberry tart, and a bit of Chester cheese, the whole washed down with a few cups of that excellent tea, specially gathered for the stores of the Reform Club.

At forty-seven minutes past noon, this gentleman rose and turned his steps towards the large hall, a sumptuous apartment, adorned with paintings in elegant frames. There, a servant handed him *The Times* uncut, the tiresome cutting of which he managed with a steadiness of hand which denoted great practice in this difficult operation. The reading of this journal occupied Phileas Fogg until a quarter before four, and that of the *Standard*, which succeeded it, lasted until dinner. This repast passed off in the same way as the breakfast, with the addition of "Royal British Sauce."

At twenty minutes before six, the gentleman reappeared in the large hall, and was absorbed in the reading of the *Morning Chronicle.*

Half an hour later, various members of the Reform Club entered and came near the fireplace, in which a coal fire was burning. They were the usual partners of Phileas Fogg; like himself, passionate players of whist—the engineer, Andrew Stuart; the bankers, John Sullivan and Samuel Fallentin; the brewer, Thomas Flanagan; Gauthier Ralph, one of the directors of the Bank of England—rich and respected personages, even in this Club, counting among his members the *élite* of trade and finance.

"Well, Ralph," asked Thomas Flanagan, "how about that robbery?"

"Why," replied Andrew Stuart, "the bank will lose the money."

"I hope, on the contrary," said Gauthier Ralph, "that we will put our hands on the robber. Detectives, very skilful fellows, have been sent to America and the Continent, to all the principal ports of embarkation and debarkation, and it will be difficult for this fellow to escape."

"But you have the description of the robber?" asked Andrew Stuart.

"In the first place, he is not a robber," replied Gauthier Ralph seriously.

"How, is he not a robber, this fellow who has abstracted fifty-five thousand pounds in bank-notes?"

"No," replied Gauthier Ralph.

"Is he, then, a manufacturer" said John Sullivan.

"The *Morning Chronicle* assures us that he is a gentleman."

The party that made this reply was no other than Phileas Fogg, whose head then emerged from the mass of papers heaped around him. At the same time, he greeted his colleagues, who returned his salutation. The matter under discussion, and which the various journals of the United Kingdom were discussing ardently, had occurred three days before, on the 29th of September. A package of bank-notes, making the enormous sum of fifty-five thousand pounds, had been taken from the counter of the principal cashier of the Bank of England. The Under-Governor, Gauthier Ralph, only replied to anyone who was astonished that such a robbery could have been so easily accomplished, that at this very moment the cashier was occupied with registering a receipt of three shillings and sixpence, and that he could not have his eyes everywhere.

But it is proper to be remarked here—which makes the robbery less mysterious—that this admirable establishment, the Bank of England, seems to care very much for the dignity of the public. There are neither guards nor gratings; gold, silver, and bank-notes being freely exposed, and, so to speak, at the mercy of the first comer. They would not suspect the honour of anyone passing by. One of the best observers of English customs relates the following: He had the curiosity to examine closely, in one of the rooms of the bank, where he was one day, an ingot of gold, weighing seven to eight pounds, which was lying exposed on the cashier's table; he picked up this ingot, examined it, passed it to his neighbour, and he to another, so that the ingot, passing from hand to hand, went as far as the end of a dark entry, and did not return to its place for half an hour, and the cashier had not once raised his head.

But on the twenty-ninth of September, matters did not turn out quite in this way. The package of bank-notes did not return, and when the magnificent dock, hung above the "drawing office" announced at five o'clock the closing of the office, the Bank of England had only to pass fifty-five thousand pounds to the account of profit and loss.

The robbery being duly known, agents, detectives, selected

from the most skilful, were sent to the principal ports—Liverpool, Glasgow, Havre, Suez, Brindisi, New York, etc., with the promise, in case of success, of a reward of two thousand pounds and five per cent of the amount recovered. Whilst waiting for the information which the investigation, commenced immediately, ought to furnish, the detectives were charged with watching carefully all arriving and departing travellers.

As the *Morning Chronicle* said, there was good reason for supposing that the robber was not a member of any of the robber bands of England. During this day, the twenty-ninth of September, a well-dressed gentleman, of good manners, of a distinguished air, had been noticed going in and out of the paying room, the scene of the robbery. The investigation allowed a pretty accurate description of the gentleman to be made out, which was at once sent to all the detectives of the United Kingdom and of the Continent. Some hopeful minds, and Gauthier Ralph was one of the number, believed that they had good reason to expect that the robber would not escape.

As may be supposed, this affair was the talk of all London and throughout England.

It was discussed, and sides were taken vehemently for or against the probabilities of success of the city police. It will not be surprising, then, to hear the members of the Reform Club treating the same subject, all the more that one of the Under-Governors of the Bank was among them.

Honourable Gauthier Ralph was not willing to doubt the result of the search, considering that the reward offered ought to sharpen peculiarly the zeal and intelligence of the agents. But his colleague, Andrew Stuart, was far from sharing this confidence. The discussion continued then between the gentlemen, who were seated at a whist table, Stuart having Flanagan as a partner, and Fallentin Phileas Fogg. During the playing the parties did not speak, but between the rubbers the interrupted conversation was fully revived.

"I maintain," said Andrew Stuart, "that the chances are in favour of the robber, who must be a skilful fellow!"

"Well," replied Ralph, "there is not a single country where he can take refuge."

"Pshaw!"

"Where do you suppose he might go?"

"I don't know about that," replied Andrew Stuart, "but after all, the world is big enough."

"It was formerly," said Phileas Fogg in a low tone. Then he added: "It is your turn to cut, sir," presenting the cards to Thomas Flanagan.

The discussion was suspended during the rubber. But Andrew Stuart soon resumed it, saying:

"How, formerly? Has the world grown smaller perchance?"

"Without doubt," replied Gauthier Ralph. "I am of the opinion of Mr. Fogg. The world has grown smaller, since we can go round it now ten times quicker than one hundred years ago. And, in the case with which we are now occupied, this is what will render the search more rapid."

"And will render more easy, also, the flight of the robber."

"It is your turn to play, Mr. Stuart," said Phileas Fogg.

But the incredulous Stuart was not convinced, and when the hand was finished, he replied: "It must be confessed, Mr. Ralph, that you have found a funny way of saying that the world has grown smaller! Because the tour of it is now made in three months—"

"In eighty days only," said Phileas Fogg.

"Yes, gentlemen," added John Sullivan, "eighty days, since the section between Rothal and Allahabad, on the Great Indian Peninsular Railway, has been opened. Here is the calculation made by the *Morning Chronicle*:

From London to Suez via Mont Cenis and Brindisi, by rail and steamers	7 days
From Suez to Bombay, steamer	13 days
From Bombay to Calcutta, rail	3 days
From Calcutta to Hong-Kong (China) steamer	13 days
From Hong-Kong to Yokohama (Japan) steamer	6 days
From Yokohama to San Francisco, steamer	22 days
From San Francisco to New York, rail	7 days
From New York to London, steamer and rail	9 days
	80 days"

"Yes, eighty days!" exclaimed Andrew Stuart, who, by inattention, made a wrong deal, "but not including bad weather, contrary winds, shipwrecks, running off the track, etc."

"Everything included," replied Phileas Fogg, continuing to play, for this time the discussion no longer respected the game.

"Even if the Hindus or the Indians tear up the rails!" exclaimed Andrew Stuart, "if they stop the trains, plunder the cars, and scalp the passengers!"

"All included," replied Phileas Fogg, who, throwing down his cards, added: "Two trumps."

Andrew Stuart, whose turn it was to deal, gathered up the cards, saying:

"Theoretically, you are right, Mr. Fogg, but practically—"

"Practically also, Mr. Stuart."

"I would like very much to see you do it."

"It depends only upon you. Let us start together."

"Heaven preserve me!" exclaimed Stuart, abut I would willingly wager four thousand pounds that such a journey, made under these conditions, is impossible."

"On the contrary, quite possible," replied Mr. Fogg.

"Well, make it, then!"

"The tour of the world in eighty days?"

"Yes!"

"I am willing."

"When?"

"At once. Only I warn you that I shall do it at your expense."

"It is folly!" cried Stuart, who was beginning to be vexed at the persistence of his partner. "Stop! let us play rather."

"Deal again, then," replied Phileas Fogg, "for there is a false deal."

Andrew Stuart took up the cards again with a feverish hand; then suddenly, placing them upon the table, he said:

"Well, Mr. Fogg, yes, and I bet four thousand pounds!"

"My dear Stuart," said Fallentin, "compose yourself It is not serious."

"When I say—'I bet,'" replied Andrew Stuart, "it is always serious."

"So be it," said Mr. Fogg, and then, turning to his companions, continued: "I have twenty thousand pounds deposited at Baring Brothers. I will willingly risk them—"

"Twenty thousand pounds!" cried John Sullivan. "Twenty thousand pounds, which an unforeseen delay may make you lose."

"The unforeseen does not exist," replied Phileas Fogg quietly.

"But, Mr. Fogg, this period of eighty days is calculated only as a minimum of time?"

"A minimum well employed suffices for everything."

"But in order not to exceed it, you must jump mathematically from the trains into the steamers, and from the steamers upon the trains!"

"I will jump mathematically."

"That is a joke."

"A good Englishman never jokes when so serious a matter as a wager is in question," replied Phileas Fogg. "I bet twenty thousand pounds against who will that I will make the tour of the world in eighty days or less—that is, nineteen hundred and twenty hours, or one hundred and fifteen thousand two hundred minutes. Do you accept?"

"We accept," replied Messrs. Stuart, Fallentin, Sullivan, Flanagan, and Ralph, after having consulted.

"Very well," said Mr. Fogg. he Dover train starts at eight forty-five. I shall take it."

"This very evening?" asked Stuart.

"This very evening," replied Phileas Fogg. Then he added, consulting a pocket almanac, "since to-day is Wednesday, the second of October, I ought to be back in London, in this very saloon of the Reform Club, on Saturday, the twenty-first of December, at eight forty-five in the evening, in default of which the twenty thousand pounds at present deposited to my credit with Baring Brothers will belong to you, gentlemen, in fast and by right. Here is a cheque of like amount."

A memorandum of the wager was made and signed on the spot by the six parties in interest. Phileas Fogg had remained cool. He had certainly not bet to win, and had risked only these twenty thousand pounds—the half of his fortune—because he foresaw that he might have to expend the other half to carry out this difficult, not to say impracticable, project. As for his opponents, they seemed affected, not on account of the stake, but because they had a sort of scruple against a contest under these conditions.

Seven o'clock then struck. They offered to Mr. Fogg to stop playing, so that he could make his preparations for departure.

"I am always ready," replied this tranquil gentleman, and dealing the cards, he said: "Diamonds are trumps. It is your turn to play, Mr. Stuart."

CHAPTER 4

In which Phileas Fogg surprises Passepartout, his Servant, beyond measure

At twenty-five minutes after seven, Phileas Fogg having gained twenty guineas at whist, took leave of his honourable colleagues, and left the Reform. Club. At ten minutes of eight, he opened the door of his house and entered.

Passepartout, who had conscientiously studied his programme, was quite surprised at seeing Mr. Fogg guilty of the inexactness of appearing at this unusual hour. According to the notice, the occupant of Saville Row ought not to return before midnight precisely.

Phileas Fogg first went to his bedroom. Then he called "Passepartout!"

Passepartout could not reply, for this call could not be addressed to him, as it was not the hour.

"Passepartout," Mr. Fogg called again without raising his voice much.

Passepartout presented himself

"It is the second time that I have called you," said Mr. Fogg.

"But it is not midnight," replied Passepartout, with his watch in his hand.

"I know it," continued Phileas Fogg, "and I do not find fault with you. We leave in ten minutes for Dover and Calais."

A sort of faint grimace appeared on the round face of the French-man. It was evident that he had not fully understood.

"Monsieur is going to leave home?" he asked.

"Yes," replied Phileas Fogg. "We are going to make the tour of the world."

Passepartout, with his eyes wide open, his eyebrows raised, his arms extended, and his body collapsed, presented all the symptoms of an astonishment amounting to stupor.

"The tour of the world!" he murmured.

"In eighty days," replied Mr. Fogg. "So we have not a moment to lose."

"But the trunks?" said Passepartout, who was unconsciously swinging his head from right to left.

"No trunks necessary. Only a carpet-bag. In it two woollen shirts and three pairs of stockings. The same for you. We will purchase on the way. You may bring down my mackintosh and travelling cloak, also stout shoes, although we shall walk but little or not at all. Go."

Passepartout would have liked to make reply. He could not. He left Mr. Fogg's room, went up to his own, fell back into a chair, and making use of a common phrase in his country, he said: "Well, well, that's pretty tough. I who wanted to remain quiet!"

And mechanically he made his preparations for departure. The tour of the world in eighty days! Was he doing business with a madman? No. It was a joke, perhaps. They were going to Dover. Good. To Calais. Let it be so. After all, it could not cross the grain of the good fellow very much, who had not trod the soil of his native country for five years. Perhaps they would go as far as Paris, and, indeed, it would give him pleasure to see the great capital again. But, surely, a gentleman so careful of his steps would stop there. Yes, doubtless; but it was not less true that he was starting out, that he was leaving home, this gentleman who, until this time, had been such a home-body!

By eight o'clock, Passepartout had put in order the modest bag which contained his wardrobe and that of his master; then, his mind still disturbed, he left his room, the door of which he closed carefully, and he rejoined Mr. Fogg.

Mr. Fogg was ready. He carried under his arm *Bradshaw's Continental Railway Steam Transit and General Guide*, which was to furnish him all the necessary directions for his journey. He took the bag from Passepartout's hands, opened it, and slipped into it a heavy package of those fine bank-notes which are current in all countries.

"You have forgotten nothing.?" he asked.

"Nothing, monsieur."

"My mackintosh and cloak?"

"Here they are."

"Good; take this bag," and Mr. Fogg handed it to Passepartout. "And take good care of it," he added, "there are twenty thousand pounds in it."

The bag nearly slipped out of Passepartout's hands, as if the twenty thousand pounds had been in gold, and weighed very heavy.

The master and servant then descended, and the street door was double-locked. At the end of Saville Row there was a carriage stand. Phileas Fogg and his servant got into a cab, which was rapidly driven towards Charing Cross Station, at which one of the branches of the South Eastern Railway touches. At twenty minutes after eight the cab stopped before the gate of the station. Passepartout jumped out. His master followed him, and paid the driver. At this moment a poor beggar woman, holding a child in her arms, her bare feet all muddy, her head covered with a wretched bonnet, from which hung a tattered feather, and a ragged shawl over her other torn garments, approached Mr. Fogg, and asked him for help.

Mr. Fogg drew from his pocket the twenty guineas which he had just won at whist, and giving them to the woman, said:

"Here, my good woman, I'm glad to have met you." Then he passed on.

Passepartout had something like a sensation of moisture about his eyes. His master had made an impression upon his heart.

Mr. Fogg and he went immediately into the large sitting-room of the station. There Phileas Fogg gave Passepartout the order to get two first-class tickets for Paris. Then returning, he noticed his five colleagues of the Reform Club.

"Gentlemen, I am going," he said, "and the various vises put upon a passport which I take for that purpose will enable you on my return, to verify my journey."

"Oh! Mr. Fogg," replied Gauthier Ralph, "that is useless. We will depend upon your honour as a gentleman."

"It is better so," said Mr. Fogg.

"You do not forget that you ought to be back—" remarked Andrew Stuart.

"In eighty days," replied Mr. Fogg. "Saturday, December 21, 1872, at quarter before nine p.m. *Au revoir*, gentlemen."

At forty minutes after eight, Phileas Fogg and his servant took their seats in the same compartment. At eight forty-five the whistle sounded, and the train started.

The night was dark. A fine rain was falling. Phileas Fogg, leaning back in his corner, did not speak. Passepartout, still stupefied, mechanically hugged up the bag with the bank-notes.

But the train had not passed Sydenham, when Passepartout uttered a real cry of despair!

"What is the matter" asked Mr. Fogg.

"Why—in—in my haste—my disturbed state of mind, I forgot— —"

"Forgot what?"

"To turn off the gas in my room."

"Very well, young man," replied Mr. Fogg coldly, "it will burn at your expense."

Chapter 5

In which a new Security appears on the London Exchange

Phileas Fogg, in leaving London, doubtless did not suspect the great excitement which his departure was going to create. The news of the wager spread first in the Reform Club, and produced quite a stir among the members of the honourable circle. Then from the Club it went into the papers, through the medium of the reporters, and from the papers to the public of London and the entire United Kingdom. The question of "the tour of the world" was commented upon, discussed, dissected, with as much passion and warmth as if it were a new Alabama affair. Some took sides with Phileas Fogg, others—and they soon formed a considerable majority—declared against him. To accomplish this tour of the world otherwise than in theory and upon paper, in this minimum of time, with the means of communication employed at present, it was not only impossible, it was visionary. *The Times*, the *Standard*, the *Evening Star*, the *Morning Chronicle*, and twenty other papers of large circulation, declared against Mr. Fogg. The *Daily Telegraph* alone sustained him to a certain extent. Phileas Fogg was generally treated as a maniac, as a fool, and his colleagues were blamed for having taken up this wager, which impeached the soundness of the mental faculties of its originator. Extremely passionate, but very logical, articles appeared upon the subject. The interest felt in England for everything concerning geography is well known. So there was not a reader, to whatever class he belonged, who did not devour the columns devoted to Phileas Fogg.

During the first few days, a few bold spirits, principally ladies, were in favour of him, especially after the *Illustrated London News* had published his picture, copied from his photograph deposited in the archives of the Reform Club. Certain gentlemen dared to say, "Humph! why not, after all? More extraordinary things have been seen!" These were particularly the readers of the *Daily Telegraph* But it was soon felt that this journal commenced to be weaker in its support.

In fact, a long article appeared on the seventh of October, in the *Bulletin* of the Royal Geographical Society. It treated the question from all points of view, and demonstrated clearly the folly of the enterprise. According to this article, everything was against the traveller, the obstacles of man and the obstacles of nature. To succeed in this project, it was necessary to admit a miraculous agreement of the hours of arrival and departure, an agreement which did not exist, and which could not exist. The arrival of trains at a fixed hour could be counted upon strictly, and in Europe, where relatively short distances are in question; but when three days are employed to cross India, and seven days to cross the United States, could the elements of such a problem be established to a nicety? The accidents to machinery, running of trains off the track, collisions, bad weather, and the accumulations of snows, were they not all against Phileas Fogg? Would he not find himself in winter on the steamers at the mercy of the winds or of the fogs? Is it then so rare that the best steamers of the ocean lines experience delays of two or three days? But one delay was sufficient to break irreparably the chain of communication. If Phileas Fogg missed only by a few hours the departure of a steamer, he would be compelled to wait for the next steamer, and in this way his journey would be irrevocably compromised. The article made a great sensation. Nearly all the papers copied it, and the stock in Phileas Fogg went down in a marked degree.

During the first few days which followed the departure of the gentleman, important business transactions had been made on the strength of his undertaking. The world of betters in England is a more intelligent and elevated world than that of gamblers. To bet is according to the English temperament; so that not only the various members of the Reform Club made heavy bets for or against Phileas Fogg, but the mass of the public entered into the movement. Phileas Fogg was entered like a racehorse in a sort of stud book. A bond was issued, which was immediately quoted upon the London Exchange. "Phileas Fogg" was "bid" or "asked" firm or above par, and enormous transactions were made. But five days after his departure, after the appearance of the article in the *Bulletin* of the Geographical Society, the offerings commenced to come in plentifully. "Phileas Fogg" declined. It was offered in bundles. Taken first at five, then at ten, it was finally taken only at twenty, at fifty, at one hundred!

Only one adherent remained steadfast to him. It was the old paralytic, Lord Albemarle. This honourable gentleman, confined to his armchair, would have given his fortune to be able to make the tour of the world, even in ten years. He bet five thousand pounds in favour of Phileas Fogg, and even when the folly as well as the uselessness of the project was demonstrated to him, he contented himself with replying: "If the thing is feasible, it is well that an Englishman should be the first to do it."

The adherents of Phileas Fogg became fewer and fewer; everybody, and not without reason, was putting himself against him; bets were taken at one hundred and fifty and two hundred against one, when, seven days after his departure, an entirely unexpected incident caused them not to be taken at all.

At nine o'clock in the evening of this day, the Commissioner of the Metropolitan Police received a telegraphic dispatch in the following words:

"SUEZ TO LONDON.

"Cowan, Commissioner of Police, Central Office, Scotland Square: I have the bank robber, Phileas Fogg. Send without delay warrant of arrest to Bombay, British India.

"FIX, *Detective*."

The effect of this dispatch was immediate. The honourable gentleman disappeared to make room for the banknote robber. His photograph, deposited at the Reform Club with those of his colleagues, was examined. It reproduced, feature by feature, the man whose description had been furnished by the commission of inquiry. They recalled how mysterious Phileas Fogg's life had been, his isolation, his sudden departure; and it appeared evident that this person, under the pretext of a journey round the world, and supporting it by a senseless bet, had had no other aim than to mislead the agents of the English police.

CHAPTER 6

In which the Agent, Fix, shows a very proper impatience

These are the circumstances under which the dispatch concerning Mr. Phileas Fogg had been sent:

On Wednesday, the ninth of October, there was expected at Suez, at eleven o'clock a m., the iron steamer *Mongolia*, of the Peninsular and Oriental Company, sharp built, with a spar deck, of two thousand eight hundred tons burden, and nominally of five hundred horse-power. The *Mongolia* made regular trips from Brindisi to Bombay by the Suez Canal. It was one of the fastest sailers of the line, and always exceeded the regular rate of speed, that is, ten miles an hour between Brindisi and Suez, and nine and fifty-three hundredths miles between Suez and Bombay.

Whilst waiting for the arrival of the *Mongolia*, two men were walking up and down the wharf, in the midst of the crowd of natives and foreigners who come together in this town, no longer a small one, to which the great work of M. Lesseps assures a great future.

One of these men was the Consular agent of the United Kingdom, settled at Suez, who, in spite of the doleful prognostications of the British Government, and the sinister predictions of Stephenson, the engineer, saw English ships passing through this canal every day, thus cutting off one-half the old route from England to the East Indies around the Cape of Good Hope.

The other was a small, spare man, of a quiet, intelligent, nervous face, who was contracting his eyebrows with remarkabe persistence. Under his long eyelashes there shone very bright eyes, but whose brilliancy he could suppress at will. At this moment he showed some signs of impatience, going, coming, unable to remain in one spot.

The name of this man was Fix, and he was one of the detectives, or agents of the English police, that had been sent to the various seaports after the robbery committed upon the Bank of England. This Fix was to watch, with the greatest care, all travellers taking the Suez route, and if one of them seemed suspicious to him, to follow him up whilst waiting for a warrant of arrest Just two days before Fix had received from the Commissioner of the Metropolitan Police the description of the supposed robber. It was that of the distinguished and well-dressed gentleman who had been noticed in the paying-room of the bank. The detective, evidently much excited by the large reward promised in case of success, was waiting then with an impatience easy to understand, the arrival of the *Mongolia*

"And you say, Consul," he asked for the tenth time, "this vessel cannot be behind time?"

"No, Mr. Fix," replied the Consul. "She was signalled yesterday off Port Said, and the one hundred and sixty kilometres of the canal are of no moment for such a vessel I repeat to you that the *Mongolia* has always obtained the reward of twenty-five pounds given by the Government for every gain of twenty-four hours over the regulation time."

"This steamer comes directly from Brindisi?" asked Fix.

"Directly from Brindisi, where it took on the India mail; from Brindisi, which it left on Saturday, at five o'clock p.m. So have patience; it cannot be behind-hand in arriving. But really I do not see how, with the description you have received, you could recognise your man, if he is on board the *Mongolia*"

"Consul," replied Fix, awe feel these people rather than know them. You must have a scent for them, and the scent is like a special sense, in which are united hearing, sight, and smell. I have in my life arrested more than one of these gentlemen, and, provided that my robber is on board, I will venture that he will not slip from my hands."

"I hope so, Mr. Fix, for it is a very heavy robbery."

"A magnificent robbery," replied the enthusiastic detective. "Fifty-five thousand pounds! We don't often have such windfalls! The robbers are becoming mean fellows. The race of Jack Sheppard is dying out! They are hung now for a few shillings!"

"Mr. Fix," replied the Consul, "you speak in such a way that I earnestly wish you to succeed; but I repeat to you that, from the circumstances in which you find yourself, I fear that it will be difficult. Do you not know that, according to the description you have received, this robber resembles an honest man exactly?"

"Consul," replied the detective dogmatically, "great robbers always resemble honest people. You understand that those who have rogues' faces have but one course to take to remain honest, otherwise they would be arrested. Honest physiognomies are the very ones that must be unmasked. It is a difficult task, I admit; and it is not a trade so much as an art."

It is seen that the aforesaid Fix was not wanting in a certain amount of self-conceit.

In the meantime the wharf was becoming lively little by little. Sailors of various nationalities, merchants, shipbrokers, porters, and fellahs, were coming together in large numbers. The arrival of the steamer was evidently near. The weather was quite fine, but the atmosphere was cold from the east wind. A few minarets towered above the town in the pale rays of the sun. Towards the south, a jetty of about two thousand yards long extended like an arm into the Suez roadstead. Several fishing and coasting vessels were tossing upon the surface of the Red Sea, some of which preserved in their style the elegant shape of the ancient galley.

Moving among this crowd, Fix, from the habit of his profession, was carefully examining the passers-by with a rapid glance.

It was then half-past ten.

"But this steamer will never arrive!" he exclaimed on hearing the port clock strike.

"She cannot be far off," replied the Consul.

"How long will she stop at Suez" asked Fix.

"Four hours. Time enough to take in coal. From Suez to Aden, at the other end of the Red Sea, is reckoned thirteen hundred and ten miles, and it is necessary to lay in fuel."

"And from Suez this vessel goes directly to Bombay?"

"Directly, without breaking bulk."

"Well, then," said Fix, "if the robber has taken this route and this vessel, it must be in his plan to disembark at Suez, in order to reach by another route the Dutch or French possessions of Asia He must know very well that he would not be safe in India, which is an English country."

"Unless he is a very shrewd man," replied the Consul.

"You know that an English criminal is always better concealed in London than he would be abroad."

After this idea, which gave the detective much food for reflection, the Consul returned to his office, situated at a short distance. The detective remained alone, affected by a certain nervous impatience, having the rather singular presentiment that his robber was to be found aboard the *Mongolia*—and truly, if this rascal had left England with the intention of reaching the New World, the East India route, being watched less, or more difficult to watch than that of the Atlantic, ought to have had his preference.

Fix was not long left to his reflections. Sharp whistles announced the arrival of the steamer. The entire horde of porters and fellahs rushed towards the wharf in a bustle, somewhat inconveniencing the limbs and the clothing of the passengers. A dozen boats put off from the shore to meet the *Mongolia* Soon was seen the enormous hull of the *Mongolia* passing between the shores of the canal, and eleven o'clock was striking when the seamer came to anchor in the roadstead, while the escaping of the steam made a great noise. There was quite a number of passengers aboard. Some remained on the spar-deck, contemplating the picturesque panorama of the town; but the most of them came ashore in the boats which had gone to hail the *Mongolia.*

Fix was examining carefully all those that landed, when one of them approached him, after having vigorously pushed back the fellahs who overwhelmed him with their offers of service, and asked him very politely if he could show him the office of the English consular agent. And at the same time this passenger presented a passport upon which he doubtless desired to have the British *visé*. Fix instinctively took the passport, and at a glance read the description in it. An involuntary movement almost escaped him. The sheet trembled in his hand. The description contained in the passport was identical with that which he had received from the Commissioner of the Metropolitan Police.

"This passport is not yours?" he said to the passenger.

"No," replied the latter, "it is my master's passport."

"And your master?"

"Remained on board."

"But," continued the detective, "he must present himself in person at the Consul office to establish his identity."

"What, is that necessary?"

"Indispensable."

"And where is the office?"

"There at the corner of the square," replied the detective, pointing out a house two hundred paces off.

"Then I must go for my master, who will not be pleased to have his plans deranged!"

Thereupon the passenger bowed to Fix and returned aboard the steamer.

CHAPTER 7

Which shows once more the uselessness of Passports in Police Matters

The detective left the wharf and turned quickly towards the Consul's office. Immediately upon his pressing demand he was ushered into the presence of that official.

"Consul," he said, without any other preamble, "I have strong reasons for believing that our man has taken passage aboard the *Mongolia,*" and Fix related what had passed between the servant and himself with reference to the passport.

"Well Mr. Fix," replied the Consul, "I would not be sorry to see the face of this rogue. But perhaps he will not present himself at my office if he is what you suppose. A robber does not like to leave behind him the tricks of his passage, and besides the formality of passports is no longer obligatory."

"Consul," replied the detective, "if he is a shrewd man, as we think, he will come."

"To have his passport *viséd*?"

"Yes. Passports never serve but to incommode honest people and to aid the flight of rogues. I warrant you that his will be all regular, but I hope certainly that you will not *visé it*"

"And why not? If his passport is regular I have no sight to refuse my *visé*."

"But, Consul, I must retain this man until I have received from London a warrant of arrest."

"Ah, Mr. Fix, that is your business," replied the Consul, "but I—I cannot—"

The Consul did not finish his phrase. At this moment there was a knock at the door of his private office, and the office boy brought in two foreigners, one of whom was the very servant who had been talking with the detective. They were, indeed, the master and servant. The master presented his passport, asking the Consul briefly to be kind enough to vise it. The latter took the passport and read it carefully, while Fix, in one corner of the room, was observing or rather devouring the stranger with his eyes.

When the Consul had finished reading, he asked:

"You are Phileas Fogg, Esq.?"

"Yes, sir," replied the gentleman.

"And this man is your servant.?"

"Yes, a Frenchman named Passepartout."

"You come from London.?"

"Yes."

"And you are going?"

"To Bombay."

"Well, sir, you know that this formality of the *visé* is useless, and that we no longer demand the presentation of the passport?"

"I know it, sir," replied Phileas Fogg, "but I wish to prove by your *visé* my trip to Suez."

"Very well, sir."

And the Consul having signed and dated the passport, affixed his seal, Mr. Fogg settled the fee, and having bowed coldly, he went out, followed by his servant.

"Well?" asked the detective.

"Well," replied the Consul, "he has the appearance of a perfectly honest man!"

"Possibly," replied Fix; "but that is not the question with us. Do you find, Consul, that this phlegmatic gentleman resembles, feature for feature, the robber whose description I have received?"

"I agree with you, but you know that all descriptions—"

"I shall have a clear conscience about it, replied Fix. "The servant appears to me less of a riddle than the master. Moreover, he is a Frenchman, who cannot keep from talking. I will see you soon again, Consul."

The detective then went out, intent upon the search for Passepartout.

In the meantime Mr. Fogg, after leaving the Consul's house,

had gone towards the wharf. There he gave some orders to his servant; then he got into a boat, returned on board the *Mongolia*, and went into his cabin. He then took out his memorandum book, in which were the following notes:

"Left London, Wednesday, October 2, 8.45 p.m.

"Arrived at Paris, Thursday, October 3, 7.20 am.

"Left Paris, Thursday, 8.40 am.

"Arrived at Turin, via Mont Cenis, Friday, October 4, 6.35 am.

"Left Turin, Friday, 7.27 a.m.

"Arrived at Brindisi, Saturday, October 5, 4 p.m.

"Set sail on the *Mongolia*, Saturday, 5 p.m.

"Arrived at Suez, Wednesday, October 9, 11 a.m.

"Total of hours consumed, 158 1-2; or in days, 6 1-2 days."

Mr. Fogg wrote down these dates in a guide-book arranged by columns, which indicated, from the 2nd of October to the 21st of December—the month, the day of the month, the day of the week, the stipulated and actual arrivals at each principal point, Paris, Brindisi, Suez, Bombay, Calcutta, Singapore, Hong-Kong, Yokohama, San Francisco, New York, Liverpool, London, and which allowed him to figure the gain made or the loss experienced at each place on the route. In this methodical book he thus kept an account of everything, and Mr. Fogg knew always whether he was ahead of time or behind.

He noted down then this day, Wednesday, October 9, his arrival at Suez, which agreeing with the stipulated arrival, neither made a gain or a loss. Then he had his breakfast served up in his cabin. As to seeing the town, he did not even think of it, being of that race of Englishmen who have their servants visit the countries they pass through.

CHAPTER 8

In which Passepartout perhaps talks a little more than is proper

Fix had in a few moments rejoined Passepartout on the wharf, who was loitering and looking about, not believing that he was obliged not to see anything.

"Well, my friend," said Fix, coming up to him, "is your passport *viséd*?"

"Ah! it is you, monsieur," replied the Frenchman. "Much obliged. It is all in order."

"And you are looking at the country?"

"Yes, but we go so quickly that it seems to me as if I am travelling in a dream. And so we are in Suez?"

"Yes, in Suez."

"In Egypt?"

"You are quite right, in Egypt."

"And in Africa?"

"Yes, in Africa?"

"In Africa?" repeated Passepartout. "I cannot believe it. Just fancy, sir, that I imagined we would not go farther than Paris, and I saw this famous capital again between twenty minutes after seven and twenty minutes of nine in the morning, between the northern station and the Lyons station, through the windows of a cab in a driving rain! I regret it! I would have so much liked to see again Pere Lachaise and the Circus of the Champs-Elysees!"

"You are then in a great hurry?" asked the detective.

"No, I am not, but my master is. By the bye, I must buy some shirts and shoes! We came away without trunks, with a carpet-bag only."

"I am going to take you to a shop where you will find everything you want."

"Monsieur," replied Passepartout, "you are really very kind."

And both started off. Passepartout talked incessantly.

"Above all," he said, "I must take care not to miss the steamer!"

"You have the time," replied Fix, "it is only noon!"

Passepartout pulled out his large watch.

"Noon. Pshaw! It is eight minutes of ten!"

"Your watch is slow!" replied Fix.

"My watch! A family watch that has come down from my great-grandfather! It don't vary five minutes in the year. It is a genuine chronometer."

"I see what is the matter," replied Fix. "You have kept London time, which is about two hours slower than Suez. You must be careful to set your watch at noon in each country."

"What! I touch my watch!" cried Passepartout. "Never."

"Well, then, it will not agree with the sun."

"So much the worse for the sun, monsieur! The sun will be wrong then!"

And the good fellow put his watch back in his fob with a magnificent gesture.

A few moments after Fix said to him: "You left London very hurriedly then.?"

"I should think so! Last Wednesday, at eight o'clock in the evening, contrary to all his habits, Monsieur Fogg returned from his Club, and in three-quarters of an hour afterwards we were off."

"But where is your master going, then?"

"Right straight ahead! He is making the tour of the world!"

"The tour of the world!" cried Fix.

"Yes, in eighty days! On a wager, he says; but, between ourselves, I do not believe it. There is no common sense in it. There must be something else."

"This Mr. Fogg is an original genius?"

"I should think so."

"Is he rich?"

"Evidently, and he carries such a fine sum with him in fresh money on the route! And he doesn't spare his money on the route! Oh! but he has promised a splendid reward to the engineer of the *Mongolia,* if we arrive at Bombay considerably in advance!"

"And you have known him for a long time, this master of yours?"

"I," replied Passepartout, "I entered his service the very day of our departure."

The effect which these answers naturally produced upon the mind of the detective, already strained with excitement, may easily be imagined

This hurried departure from London so short a time after the robbery, this large sum carried away, this haste to arrive in distant countries, this pretext of an eccentric wager, all could have no other effect than to confirm Fix in his ideas. He kept the Frenchman talking, and learned to a certainty that this fellow did not know his master at all, that he lived isolated in London, that he was called rich without the source of his fortune being known, that he was a mysterious man, etc. But at the same time Fix was certain that Phileas Fogg would not get off at Suez, but he was really going to Bombay.

"Is Bombay far from here?" asked Passepartout.

"Pretty far," replied the detective. "It will take you ten days more by sea"

"And where do you locate Bombay?"

"In India"

"In Asia?"

"Of course."

"The deuce! What I was going to tell you—there is one thing that bothers me—it is my burner."

"What burner.?"

"My gas-burner, which I forgot to turn off, and which is burning at my expense. Now, I have calculated that it will cost me two shillings each twenty-four hours, exactly sixpence more than I earn, and you understand that, however little our journey may be prolonged—"

Did Fix understand the matter of the gas? It is improbable. He did not listen any longer, and was coming to a determination. The Frenchman and he had arrived at the shop. Fix left his companion there making his purchases, recommending him not to miss the departure of the *Mongolia*, and he returned in great haste to the Consul's office. Fix had regained his coolness completely, now he was fully convinced.

"Monsieur," said he to the Consul, "I have my man. He is passing himself off as an oddity, who wishes to make the tour of the world in eighty days."

"Then he is a rogue," replied the Consul, "and he counts on returning to London after having deceived all the police of the two continents."

"We will see," replied Fix.

"But are you not mistaken?" asked the Consul once more.

"I am-not mistaken."

"Why, then, has this robber insisted upon having his stopping at Suez confirmed by a *visé?*"

"Why? I do not know, Consul," replied the detective; "but listen to me." And in a few words he related the salient points of his conversation with the servant of the said Fogg.

'"Indeed," said the Consul, "all the presumptions are against this man. And what are you going to do?"

Send a dispatch to London with the urgent request to send to me at once at Bombay a warrant of arrest, set sail upon the *Mongolia*, follow my robber to the Indies, and there, on British soil, accost him politely, with the warrant in one hand, and the other hand upon his shoulder."

Having coolly uttered these words, the detective took leave of the Consul, and repaired to the telegraph office. Thence he dispatched to the Commissioner of the Metropolitan Police, as we have already seen. A quarter of a hour later Fix, with his light baggage in his hand, and besides well supplied with money, went on board the *Mongolia*, and soon the swift steamer was threading its way under full head of steam on the waters of the Red Sea.

Chapter 9

In which the Red Sea and the Indian Ocean show themselves Propitious to Phileas Fogg's designs

The distance between Suez and Aden is exactly thirteen hundred and ten miles, and the time-table of the company allows its steamer a period of one hundred and thirty-eight hours to make the distance. The *Mongolia* whose fires were well kept up, moved along rapidly enough to anticipate her stipulated arrival. Nearly all the passengers who came aboard at Brindisi had India for their destination. Some were going to Bombay, others to Calcutta, but via Bombay, for since a railway crosses the entire breadth of the Indian peninsula, it is no longer necessary to double the island of Ceylon.

Among these passengers of the *Mongolia*, there were several officials of the Civil Service and army officers of every grade. Of the latter, some belonged to the British Army, properly so-called, the others commanded the native Sepoy troops, all receiving high salaries, since the Government has taken the place of the powers and charge of the old East India Company; sub-lieutenants receiving £280; brigadiers, £2400; and generals, £4000. The emoluments of officials in the Civil Service are still higher: Simple assistants in the first rank get £480; judges, £2400; the president judges, £10,000; governors, £12,000; and the governor-general more than £24,000.

There was good living on board the *Mongolia*, in this company of officials, to which were added some young Englishmen, who, with a million in their pockets, were going to establish commercial houses abroad. The purser, the confidential man of the company, the equal of the captain on board the ship, did things up elegantly. At the breakfast, at the lunch at two o'clock, at the dinner at half-past five, at the supper at eight o'clock, the tables groaned under the dishes of fresh meat and the relishes, furnished by the refrigerator, and the pantries of the steamer. The ladies, of whom there were a few, changed their toilet twice a day. There was music, and there was dancing also when the sea allowed it.

But the Red Sea is very capricious and too frequently rough, like all long, narrow bodies of water. When the wind blew either from the coast of Asia, or from the coast of Africa, the *Mongolia*, being very long and sharp built, and struck amidships, rolled fearfully. The ladies then disappeared; the pianos were silent; songs and dances ceased at once. And yet, notwithstanding the squall and the agitated waters, the steamer, driven by its powerful engines, pursued its course without delay to the straits of Bab-el-Mandeb.

What was Phileas Fogg doing all this time? It might be supposed that, always uneasy and anxious, his mind would be occupied with the changes of the wind interfering with the progress of the vessel, the irregular movements of the squall threatening an accident to the,engine, and in short, all the possible injuries, which, compelling the *Mongolia* to put into some port, would have interrupted his journey.

By no means, or, at least, if this gentleman thought of these probabilities, he did not let it appear as if he did. He was the same impassible man, the imperturbable member of the Reform Club, whom no incident or accident could surprise. He did not appear more affected than the ship's chronometers. He was seldom seen upon the deck. He troubled himself very little about looking at this Red Sea, so fruitful in recollections, the spot where first historic scenes of mankind were enacted. He did not recognise the curious towns scattered upon its shores, and whose picturesque outlines stood out sometimes against the horizon. He did not even dream of the dangers of the Gulf of Arabia, of which the ancient historians, Strabo, Arrius, Artemidorus, and others, always spoke with dread, and upon which the navigators never ventured in former times without having consecrated their voyage by propitiatory sacrifices.

What was this queer fellow, imprisoned upon the *Mongolia* doing? At first he took his four meals a day, the rolling and pitching of the ship not putting out of order his mechanism, so wonderfully organised. Then he played at whist. For he found companions as devoted to it as himself: a collector of taxes, who was going to his post at Goa; a minister, the Rev. Decimus Smith, returning to Bombay; and a brigadier-general of the British Army, who was rejoining his corps at Benares. These three passengers had the same passion for whist as Mr. Fogg, and they played for entire hours, not less quietly than he.

As for Passepartout, sea-sickness had taken no hold on him. He occupied a forward cabin, and ate conscientiously. It must be said that the voyage made under these circumstances was decidedly not unpleasant to him. He rather liked his share of it. Well fed and well lodged, he was seeing the country, and besides, he asserted to himself that all this whim would end at Bombay. The next day after leaving Suez it was not without a certain pleasure that he met on deck the obliging person whom he had addressed on landing in Egypt.

"I am not mistaken," he said on approaching him with his most amiable smile; "you are the very gentleman that so kindly served as my guide in Suez?"

"Indeed," replied the detective, "I recognise you! You are the servant of that odd Englishman—"

"Just so, Monsieur—?"

"Fix."

"Monsieur Fix," replied Passepartout. "Delighted to meet you again on board this vessel. And where are you going?"

"Why, to the same place as yourself, Bombay."

"That is first rate! Have you already made this trip?"

"Several times," replied Fix. "I am an agent of the Peninsular Company."

"Then you know India?"

"Why—yes," replied Fix, who did not wish to commit himself too far.

"And this India is a curious place?"

"Very curious! Mosques, minarets, temples, fahirs, pagodas, tigers, serpents, dancing girls! But it is to be hoped that you will have time to visit the country?"

"I hope so, Monsieur Fix. You understand very well that it is not permitted to a man of sound mind to pass his life in jumping from a steamer into a railway car and from a railway car into a steamer, under the pretext of making the tour of the world in eighty days! No. All these gymnastics will cease at Bombay, don't doubt it."

"And Mr. Fogg is well?" asked Fox in a most natural tone.

"Very well, Monsieur Fix, and I am too. I eat like an ogre that has been fasting. It is the sea air."

"I never see your master on deck."

"Never. He is not inquisitive."

"Do you know, Mr. Passepartout, that this pretended tour in eighty days might very well be the cover for some secret mission—a diplomatic mission, for example!"

"Upon my word, Monsieur Fix, I don't know anything about it, I confess, and really I wouldn't give a half-crown to know."

After this meeting, Passepartout and Fix frequently talked together. The detective thought he ought to have close relations with the servant of this gentleman Fogg. There might be an occasion when he could serve him. He frequently offered him, in the barroom of the *Mongolia*, a few glasses of whisky or pale ale, which the good fellow accepted without reluctance, and returned even so as not to be behind him—finding this Fix to be a very honest gentleman.

In the meantime the steamer was rapidly getting on. On the 13th they sighted Mocha, which appeared in its enclosure of ruined walls, above which were hanging green date trees. At a distance, in the mountains, there were seen immense fields of coffee trees. Passepartout was delighted to behold this celebrated place, and he found, with its circular walls and a dismantled fort in the shape of a handle, it looked like an enormous cup and saucer.

During the following night the *Mongolia* passed through the Straits of Bab-el-Mandeb, the Arabic name of which signifies "The Gate of Tears," and the next day, the 14th, she put in at Steamer Point, to the north-west of Aden harbour. There she was to lay in coal again. This obtaining fuel for steamers at such distances from the centres of production is a very serious matter. It amounts to an annual expense for the Peninsular Company of eight hundred thousand pounds. It has been necessary, indeed, to establish depots in several ports, and in these distant seas coal reaches as high as from three to four pounds per ton.

The *Mongolia* had still sixteen hundred and fifty miles to make before reaching Bombay, and she had to remain four hours at Steamer Point, to lay in her coal. But this delay could not in any way be prejudicial to Phileas Fogg's programme. It was foreseen. Besides, the *Mongolia* instead of not arriving at Aden until the morning of the 15th, put in there the evening of the 14th, a gain of fifteen hours.

Mr. Fogg and his servant landed. The gentleman wished to have his passport *viséd* Fix followed him without being noticed. The formality of the *visé* through with, Phileas Fogg returned on board to resume his interrupted play. Passepartout, according to his custom, loitered about in the midst of the population of Somalis, Banyans, Parsees, Jews, Arabs, Europeans, making up the twenty-five thousand inhabitants of Aden. He admired the fortifications which make of this town the Gibraltar of the Indian Ocean, and some splendid cisterns, at which the English engineers were still working, two thousand years after the engineers of King Solomon. "Very singular, *very* singular" said Passepartout to himself on returning aboard. "I see that it is not useless travel, if we wish to see anything new."

At six o'clock p.m. the *Mongolia* was ploughing the waters of the Aden harbour, and soon reached the Indian Ocean. She had one hundred and sixty-eight hours to make the distance between Aden and Bombay. The Indian Ocean was favourable to her, the wind kept in the north-west, and the sails come to the aid of the steam. The ship well balanced, rolled less. The ladies, in fresh toilets, reappeared upon the deck. The singing and dancing recommenced. Their voyage was then progressing under the most favourable circumstances. Passepartout was delighted with the agreeable companion whom chance had procured for him in the person of Fix.

On Sunday, the 20th of October, towards noon, they sighted the Indian coast. Two hours later, the pilot came aboard the *Mongolia* The outlines of the hills blended with the sky. Soon the rows of palm trees which abound in the place came into distinct view. The steamer entered the harbour formed by the islands of Salcette, Colaba, Elephanta, Butcher, and at half-past four she put in at the wharves of Bombay. Phileas Fogg was then finishing the thirty-third rubber of the day, and his partner and himself, thanks to a bold manoeuvre, having made thirteen tricks, wound up this fine trip by a splendid victory. The *Mongolia* was not due at Bombay until the 22nd of October. She arrived on the 20th. This was a gain of two days, then, since his departure from London, and Phileas Fogg methodically noted it down in his memorandum-book in the column of gains.

Chapter 10

In which Passepartout is only too happy to get off with the loss of his shoes

No one is ignorant of the fact that India, this great reversed triangle whose base is to the north and its apex to the south, comprises a superficial area of fourteen hundred thousand square miles, over which is unequally scattered a population of one hundred and eighty millions of inhabitants. The British Government exercises a real dominion over a certain portion of this vast country. It maintains a Governor-General at Calcutta, Governors at Madras, Bombay, and Bengal, and a Lieutenant-Governor at Agra.

But British India, properly so-called, counts only a superficial area of seven hundred thousand square miles, and a population of one hundred to one hundred and ten millions of inhabitants. It is sufficient to say that a prominent part of the territory is still free from the authority of the Queen; and, indeed, with some of the rajahs of the interior, fierce and terrible, Hindu independence is still absolute. Since 1756—the period at which was founded the first English establishment on the spot to-day occupied by the City of Madras—until the year in which broke out the great Sepoy insurrection, the celebrated East India Company was all-powerful. It annexed little by little the various provinces, bought from the rajahs at the price of annual rents, which it paid in part or not at all; it named its Governor-General and all its civil or military employees; but now it no longer exists, and the British possessions in India are directly under the Crown. Thus the aspect, the manners, and the distinctions of race of the peninsula are being changed every day. Formerly they travelled by all the old means of conveyance, on foot, on horseback, in carts, in small vehicles drawn by men, in palanquins, on men's backs, in coaches, etc. Now, steamboats traverse with great rapidity the Indus and the Ganges, and a railway crossing the entire breadth of India, and branching in various directions, puts Bombay at only three days from Calcutta.

The route of this railway does not follow a straight line across India The air-line distance is only one thousand to eleven hundred miles, and trains, going at only an average rapidity, would not take three days to make it; but this distance is increased at least one-third by the arc described by the railway rising to Allahabad, in the northern part of the peninsula In short, these are the principal points of the route of the Great Indian Peninsular Railway. Leaving the island of Bombay, it crosses Salcette, touches the main land opposite Tannah, crosses the chain of the Western Ghauts, runs to the north-east as far as Burhampour, goes through the nearly independent territory of Bundelkund, rises as far as Allahabad, turns towards the east, meets the Ganges at Benares, turns slightly aside, and descending again to the south-east by Burdidan and the French town of Chandernagor, it reaches the end of the route at Calcutta.

It was at half-past four p.m. that the passengers of the *Mongolia* had landed in Bombay, and the train for Calcutta would leave at precisely eight o'clock. Mr. Fogg then took leave of his partners, left the steamer, gave his servant directions for some purchases, recommended him expressly to be at the station before eight o'clock, and with his regular step which beat the second like the pendulum of an astronomical clock, he turned his steps towards the passport office. He did not think of looking at any of the wonders of Bombay, neither the city hall, nor the magnificent library, nor the forts, nor the docks, nor the cotton market, nor the shops, nor the mosques, nor the synagogues, nor the Armenian churches, nor the splendid pagoda of Malebar Hill, adorned with two polygonal towers. He would not contemplate either the masterpieces of Elephanta, or its mysterious hypogea, concealed in the southeast of the harbour, or the Kanherian grottoes of the Islands of Salcette, those splendid remains of Buddhist architecture! No, nothing of that for him. After leaving the passport office, Phileas Fogg quietly returned to the station, and there had dinner served. Among other dishes, the landlord thought he ought to recommend to him a certain giblet of "native rabbit," of which he spoke in the highest terms. Phileas Fogg accepted the giblet and tasted it conscientiously; but in spite of the spiced sauce, he found it detestable. He rang for the landlord.

"Sir," he said, looking at him steadily, "is that rabbit.?"

"Yes, my lord," replied the rogue boldly, "the rabbit of the jungles."

"And that rabbit did not mew when it was killed?"

"Mew! oh, my lord! a rabbit! I swear to you—"

"Landlord," replied Mr. Fogg coolly, "don't swear, and recollect this: in former times, in India, cats were considered sacred animals. That was a good time."

"For the cats, my lord?"

"And perhaps also for the travellers!"

After this observation Mr. Fogg went on quietly with his dinner.

A few minutes after Mr. Fogg, the detective Fix also landed from the *Mongolia*, and hastened to the Commissioner of Police in Bombay. He made himself known in his capacity as detective, the mission with which he was charged, his position towards the robber. Had a warrant of arrest been received from London? They had received nothing. And, in fact, the warrant, leaving after Fogg, could not have arrived yet.

Fix was very much out of countenance. He wished to obtain from the Commissioner an order for the arrest of this gentleman Fogg. The director refused. The affair concerned the metropolitan government, and it alone could legally deliver a warrant. This strictness of principles, this rigorous observance of legality is easily explained with the English manners, which, in the matter of personal liberty, does not allow anything arbitrary. Fix did not persist, and understood that he would have to be resigned to waiting for his warrant. But he resolved not to lose sight of his mysterious rogue whilst he remained in Bombay. He did not doubt that Phileas Fogg would stop there—and as we know, it was also Passepartout's conviction—which would give the warrant of arrest the time to arrive.

But after the last orders which his master had given him on leaving the *Mongolia,* Passepartout had understood very well that it would be the same with Bombay as with Suez and Paris, that the journey would not stop here, that it would be continued at least as far as Calcutta, and perhaps farther. And he began to ask himself if, after all, this bet of Mr. Fogg was not really serious, and if fatality was not dragging him, he who wished to live at rest, to accomplish the tour of the world in eighty days! Whilst waiting, and after having obtained some shirts and shoes, he took a walk through the streets of Bombay. There was a great crowd of people there, and among them Europeans of all nationalities. Persians with pointed caps, Bunyas with round turbans, Sindes, with square caps, Armenians in long robes, Parsees in black mitres. A festival was just being held by the Parsees, the direct descendants of the followers of Zoroaster, who are the most industrious, the most civilised, the most intelligent, the most austere of the Hindus—a race to which now belong the rich native merchants of Bombay. Upon this day they were celebrating a sort of religious carnival, with processions and amusements, in which figured dancing girls dressed in rosecoloured gauze embroidered with gold and silver, who danced wonderfully and with perfect decency to the sound of viols and tamtams.

It is superfluous to insist here whether Passepartout looked at these curious ceremonies, whether his eyes and ears were stretched wide open to see and hear, whether his entire appearance was that of the freshest greenhorn that can be imagined. Unfortunately for himself and his master, whose journey he ran the risk of interrupting, his curiosity dragged him farther than was proper.

In fact, after having looked at this Parsee carnival, Passepartout turned towards the station, when passing the splendid pagoda on Malebar Hill, he took the unfortunate notion to visit its interior. He was ignorant of two things: First, that the entrance into certain Hindu pagodas is formally forbidden to Christians, and next, that the believers themselves cannot enter there without having left their shoes at the door. It must be remarked here that the British Government, for sound political reasons, respecting and causing to be respected in its most insignificant details the religion of the country, punishes severely whoever violates its practices. Passepartout having gone in, without thinking of doing wrong, like a simple traveller, was admiring in the interior the dazzling glare of the Brahmim ornamentation, when he was suddenly thrown down on the sacred floor. Three priests, with furious looks, rushed upon him, tore off his shoes and stockings, and commenced to beat him, uttering savage cries. The Frenchman, vigorous and agile, rose again quickly. With a blow of his fist and a kick he upset two of his adversaries, very much hampered by their long robes, and rushing out of the pagoda with all the quickness of his legs, he had soon distanced the third Hindu, who had followed him closely, by mingling with the crowd.

At five minutes of eight, just a few minutes before the leaving of the train, hatless and barefoot, having lost in the scuffle the bundle containing his purchases, Passepartout arrived at the railway station. Fix was on the wharf. Having followed Mr. Fogg to the station, he understood that the rogue was going to leave Bombay. His mind was immediately made up to accompany him to Calcutta, and farther, if it was necessary. Passepartout did not see Fix, who was standing in a dark place, but Fix heard him tell his adventures in a few words to his master.

"I hope it will not happen to you again," was all Phileas Fogg replied, taking a seat in one of the cars of the train. The poor fellow, barefoot and quite discomfited, followed his master without saying a word.

Fix was going to get in another car, when a thought stopped him, and suddenly modified his plan of departure. "No, I will remain," he said to himself "A transgression committed upon Indian territory. I have my man."

At this moment the locomotive gave a vigorous whistle, and the train disappeared in the darkness.

Chapter 11

In which Phileas Fogg buys a Conveyance at a Fabulous Price

The train had started to time. It carried a certain number of travellers, some officers, civil officials, and opium and indigo merchants, whose business called them to the eastern part of the peninsula.

Passepartout occupied the same compartment as his master. A third traveller was in the opposite corner.

It was the brigadier-general, Sir Francis Cromarty, one of the partners of Mr. Fogg during the trip from Suez to Bombay, who was rejoining his troops, stationed near Benares.

Sir Francis Cromarty, tall, fair, about fifty years old, who had distinguished himself highly during the last revolt of the

Sepoys, had truly deserved to be called a native. From his youth he had lived in India, and had only been occasionally in the country of his birth. He was a well-posted man, who would have been glad to give information as to the manners, the history, the organisation of this Indian country, if Phileas Fogg had been the man to ask for such things. But this gentleman was not asking anything. He was not travelling, he was describing a circumference. He was a heavy body, traversing an orbit around the terrestrial globe, according to the laws of rational mechanics. At this moment he was going over in his mind the calculations of the hours consumed since his departure from London, and he would have rubbed his hands, if it had been in his nature to make a useless movement.

Sir Francis Cromarty had recognised the originality of his travelling companion, although he had only studied him with his cards in his hand, and between two rubbers. He was ready to ask whether a human heart beat beneath this cold exterior, whether Phileas Fogg had a soul alive to the beauties of nature and to moral aspirations. That was the question for him. Of all the oddities the general had met, none were to be compared to this product of the exact sciences. Phileas Fogg had not kept secret from Sir Francis Cromarty his plan for a tour around the world, nor the conditions under which he was carrying it out. The general saw in this bet only an eccentricity without a useful aim, and which was wanting necessarily in the *transire benefaciendo* which ought to guide every reasonable man. In the manner in which this singular gentleman was moving on, he would evidently be doing nothing, either for himself or for others.

An hour after having left Bombay, the train, crossing the viaducts, had left behind the Island of Salcette and reached the main-land. At the station Callyan, it left to the right the branch which, via Kandallah and Pounah descends towards the south-east of India, and reaches the station Panwell. At this point, it became entangled in the defiles of the Western Ghaut mountains, with bases of trappe and basalt, whose highest summits are covered with thick woods.

From time to time, Sir Francis Cromarty and Phileas Fogg

exchanged a few words, and at this moment the general, recommencing a conversation which frequently lagged, said:

"A few years ago, Mr. Fogg, you would have experienced at this point a delay which would have probably interrupted your journey."

"Why so, Sir Francis?"

"Because the railway stopped at the base of these mountains, which had to be crossed in a palanquin or on a pony's back as r as the station of Kandallah, on the opposite slope."

"That delay would not have deranged my programme," replied Mr. Fogg. "I would have foreseen the probability of certain obstacles."

"But, Mr. Fogg," replied the general, "you are in danger of having a bad business on your hands with this young man's adventure."

Passepartout, with his feet wrapped up in his cloak, was sleeping soundly, and did not dream that they were talking about him.

"The British Government is extremely severe, and rightly, for this kind of trespass," replied Sir Francis Cromarty. "It insists, above all things, that the religious customs of the Hindus shall be respected, and if your servant had been taken—"

"Yes, *if* he had been taken, Sir Francis," replied Mr. Fogg, "he would have been sentenced, he would have undergone his punishment, and then he would have quietly returned to Europe. I do not see how this matter could have delayed his master!"

And, thereupon, the conversation stopped again. During the night, the train crossed the Ghauts, passed on to Nassik, and the next day, the 21st of October, it was hurrying across a comparatively flat country, formed by the Khandeish territory. The country, well cultivated, was strewn with small villages, above which the minaret of the pagoda took the place of the steeple of the European church. Numerous small streams, principally tributaries of the Godavery, irrigated this fertile country.

Passepartout having waked up, looked around, and could not believe that he was crossing the country of the Hindus in a train of the Great Peninsular Railway. It appeared improbable to him. And yet there was nothing more real! The locomotive, guided by the arm of an English engineer and heated with English coal, was puffing out its smoke over plantations of cotton trees, coffee, nutmeg, clove, and red pepper. The steam twisted itself into spirals about groups of palms, between which appeared picturesque bungalows, a few viharis (a sort of abandoned monasteries), and wonderful temples enriched by the inexhaustible ornament of Indian architecture. Then immense reaches of country stretched out of sight, jungles, in which were not wanting snakes and tigers whom the noise of the train did not frighten, and finally forests cut through by the route of the road, still the haunt of elephants, which, with a pensive eye, looked at the train as it passed so rapidly.

During the morning, beyond the station of Malligaum, the travellers traversed that fatal territory, which was so frequently drenched with blood by the sectaries of the goddess Kali. Not far off rose Ellora and its splendid pagodas, and the celebrated Aurungabad, the capital of the ferocious Aureng-Zeb, now simply the principal place of one of the provinces detached from the kingdom of Nizam. It was over this country that Feringhea, the chief of the Thugs, the king of stranglers, exercised his dominion. These assassins, united in the association that could not be reached, strangled in honour of the goddess of death, victims of every age, without ever shedding blood, and there was a time when the ground could not be dug up anywhere in this neighbourhood without finding a corpse. The British Government has been able, in great part, to prevent these murders, but the horrible organisation exists yet, and carries on its operations.

At half-past twelve, the train stopped at the station at Burhampour, and Passepartout was able to obtain for gold a pair of Indian slippers, ornamented with false pearls, which he put on with an evident show of vanity. The travellers took a hasty breakfast, and started again for Assurghur, after having for a moment stopped upon the shore of the Tapty, a small river emptying into the Gulf of Cambay, near Surat.

It is opportune to mention the thoughts with which

Passepartout was busied. Until his arrival at Bombay, he had thought that matters would go no farther. But now that he was hurrying at full speed across India. his mind had undergone a change. His natural feelings came back to him with a rush. He felt again the fancied ideas of youth, he took seriously his master's plans, he believed in the reality of the bet, and consequently in this tour of the world, and in this maximum of time which could not be exceeded. Already he was disturbed at the possible delays, the accidents which might occur upon the route. He felt interested in the wager, and trembled at the thought that he might have compromised it the evening before by his unpardonable foolishness, so that, much less phlegmatic than Mr. Fogg, he was much more uneasy. He counted and recounted the days that had passed, cursed the stopping of the train, accused it of slowness, and blamed Mr. Fogg *in petto* for not having promised a reward to the engineer. The good fellow did not know that what was possible upon a steamer was not on a railway train, whose speed is regulated.

Towards evening they entered the defiles of the mountains of Sutpour, which separate the territory of Khandeish from that of Bundelcund.

The next day, the 22nd of October, Passepartout, having consulted his watch, replied to a question of Sir Francis Cromarty that it was three o'clock in the morning. In fact, this famous watch, always regulated by the meridian of Greenwich, which is nearly seventy-seven degrees west, ought to be and was four hours slow.

Sir Francis then corrected the hour given by Passepartout, and added the same remark that the latter had already heard from Fix. He tried to make him understand that he ought to regulate his watch on each new meridian, and that since he was constantly going towards the east, that is, in the face of the sun, the days were shorter by as many times four minutes as he had crossed degrees. It was useless. Whether the stubborn fellow had understood the remarks of the general or not, he persisted in not putting his watch ahead, which he kept always at London time. An innocent madness at any rate, which could hurt no one.

At eight o'clock in the morning, and fifteen miles before they reached Rothal, the train stopped in the midst of an immense opening, on the edge of which were some bungalows and workmen's huts. The conductor of the train passed along the cars calling out, "The passengers will get out here!"

Phileas Fogg looked at Sir Francis Cromarty, who appeared not to understand this stop in the midst of a forest of tamarinds and acacias. Passepartout, not less surprised? rushed on to the track and returned almost immediately, crying, "Monsieur, no more railway!"

"What do you mean?" asked Sir Francis Cromarty.

"I mean that the train goes no farther."

The brigadier-general immediately got out of the car. Phileas Fogg, in no hurry, followed him. Both spoke to the conductor.

"Where are we?" asked Sir Francis Cromarty.

"At the hamlet of Kholby," replied the conductor.

"We stop here?"

"Without doubt. The railway is not finished—"

"How! It is not finished?"

"No! There is still a section of fifty miles to construct between this point and Allahabad, where the track commences again."

"But the papers have announced the opening of the entire line."

"But, generally, the papers were mistaken."

"And you give tickets from Bombay to Calcutta!" replied Sir Francis Cromarty, who was beginning to be excited.

"Of course," replied the conductor; "but travellers know very well that they have to be otherwise transported from Kholby to Allahabad."

Sir Francis Cromarty was furious. Passepartout would have willingly knocked the conductor down, who could not help himself He did not dare look at his master.

"Sir Francis," said Mr. Fogg simply, "we will go, if you will be kind enough to see about some way of reaching Allahabad."

"Mr. Fogg, this is a delay absolutely prejudicial to your interests!"

"No, Sir Francis, it was provided for."

"What, did you know that the railway—"

"By no means, but I knew that some obstacle or other would occur sooner or later upon my route. Now, nothing is interfered with. I have gained two days which I can afford to lose. A steamer leaves Calcutta for Hong-Kong at noon on the 25th. This is only the 23rd, and we shall arrive at Calcutta in time."

Nothing could be said in reply to such complete certainty.

It was only too true that the finished portion of the railway stopped at this point. The newspapers are like certain watches which have a mania of getting ahead of time, and they had announced the finishing of the line prematurely. The most of the passengers knew of this break in the line, and descending from the train, they examined the vehicles of all sorts in the village, four-wheeled palkigharis, carts drawn by zebus, a sort of ox with humps, travelling cars resembling walking pagodas, palanquins, ponies, etc. Mr. Fogg and Sir Francis Cromarty, after having hunted through the entire village, returned without having found anything.

"I shall go on foot," said Mr. Fogg.

Passepartout, who had then rejoined his master, made a significant grimace, looking down at his magnificent but delicate slippers. Very fortunate, he had also been hunting for something, and hesitating a little, he said:

"Monsieur, I believe I have found a means of conveyance."

"What?"

"An elephant belonging to an Indian living a hundred steps from here."

"Let us go to see the elephant," replied Mr. Fogg. Five minutes later, Phileas Fogg, Sir Francis Cromarty, and Passepartout arrived at a hut which was against an enclosure of high palisades. In the hut there was an Indian, and in the enclosure an elephant. Upon their demand, the Indian took Mr. Fogg and his two companions into the enclosure.

They found there a half-tamed animal, which his owner was raising, not to hire out, but as a beast of combat. To this end he had commenced to modify the naturally mild character of the animal in a manner to lead him gradually to that paroxysm of rage called "mutsh" in the Hindu language, and that by feeding him for three months with sugar and butter. This treatment may not seem the proper one to obtain such a result, but it is none the less employed with success by their keepers.

Kiouni, the animal's name, could, like all his fellows, go rapidly on a long march, and in default of other conveyance, Phileas Fogg determined to employ him. But elephants are very expensive in India, where they are beginning to get scarce. The males, which alone are fit for circus feats, are very much sought for. These animals are rarely reproduced when they are reduced to the tame state, so that they can be obtained only by hunting. So they are the object of extreme care, and when Mr. Fogg asked the Indian if he would hire him his elephant he flatly refused.

Fogg persisted, and offered an excessive price for the animal, ten pounds per hour. Refused. Twenty pounds. Still refused. Forty pounds. Refused again. Passepartout jumped at every advance in price. But the Indian would not be tempted. The sum was a handsome one, however. Admitting the elephant to be employed fifteen hours to reach Allahabad, it was six hundred pounds earned for his owner.

Phileas Fogg, without being at all excited, proposed then to the Indian to buy his animal, and offered him at first one thousand pounds. The Indian would not sell! Perhaps the rogue scented a large transaction.

Sir Francis Cromarty took Mr. Fogg aside and begged him to reflect before going further. Phileas Fogg replied to his companion that he was not in the habit of acting without reflection, that a bet of twenty thousand pounds was at stake, that this elephant was necessary to him, and that, should he pay twenty times his value, he would have this elephant.

Mr. Fogg went again for the Indian, whose small eyes, lit up with greed, showed that with him it was only a question of price. Phileas Fogg offered successively twelve hundred, fifteen hundred, eighteen hundred, and finally two thousand pounds. Passepartout, so rosy ordinarily, was pale with emotion.

At two thousand pounds the Indian gave up.

"By my slippers," cried Passepartout, "here is a magnificent price for elephant meat!"

The business concluded, all that was necessary was to find a guide. That was easier. A young Parsee, with an intelligent face, offered his services. Mr. Fogg accepted him, and offered him a large reward to sharpen his wits. The elephant was brought out and equipped without delay. The Parsee understood perfectly the business of "mahout," or elephant-driver. He covered with a sort of saddle cloth the back of the elephant, and put on each flank two kinds of rather uncomfortable howdahs.

Phileas Fogg paid the Indian in bank-notes taken from the famous carpet bag. It seemed as if they were taken from Passepartout's very vitals. Then Mr. Fogg offered to Sir Francis Cromarty to convey him to Allahabad. The general accepted; one passenger more was not enough to tire this enormous animal. Some provisions were bought at Kholby. Sir Francis Cromarty took a seat in one of the howdahs, Phileas Fogg in the other. Passepartout got astride the animal, between his master and the brigadier-general. The Parsee perched upon the elephant's neck, and at nine o'clock the animal, leaving the village, penetrated the thick forest of palm trees.

CHAPTER 12

In which Phileas Fogg and his Companions venture through the Forests of India, and what follows

The guide, in order to shorten the distance to be gone over, left to his right the line of the road, the construction of which was still in process. This line, very crooked, owing to the capricious ramifications of the Vindhia mountains, did not follow the shortest route, which it was Phileas Foggs interest to take. The Parsee, very familiar with the roads and paths of the country, thought to gain twenty miles by cutting through the forest, and they submitted to him.

Phileas Fogg and Sir Francis Cromarty, plunged to their necks in their howdahs, were much shaken up by the rough trot of the elephant, whom his mahout urged into a rapid gait. But they bore it with the peculiar British apathy, talking very little, and scarcely seeing each other.

As for Passepartout, perched upon the animal's back, and directly subjected to the swaying from side to side, he took care, upon his master's recommendation, not to keep his tongue between his teeth, as it would have been cut short off. The good fellow, at one time thrown forward on the elephant's neck, at another thrown back upon his rump, was making leaps like a clown on a spring-board But he joked and laughed in the midst of his somersaults, and from time to time he would take from his bag a lump of sugar, which the intelligent Kiouni took with the end of his trunk, without interrupting for an instant his regular trot.

After two hours' march the guide stopped the elephant, and gave him an hour's rest. The animal devoured branches of trees and shrubs, first having quenched his thirst at a neighbouring pond. Sir Francis Cromarty did not complain of this halt. He was worn out. Mr. Fogg appeared as if he had just got out of bed.

"But he is made of iron!" said the brigadier-general, looking at him with admiration.

"Of wrought iron," replied Passepartout, who was busy preparing a hasty breakfast.

At noon the guide gave the signal for starting. The country soon assumed a very wild aspect. To the large forests there succeeded copses of tamarinds and dwarf palms, then vast, arid plains, bristling with scanty shrubs, and strewn with large blocks of syenites. All this part of upper Bundelcund, very little visited by travellers, is inhabited by a fanatical population, hardened in the most terrible practices of the Hindu religion. The government of the British could not have been regularly established over a territory subject to the influence of the rajahs, whom it would have been difficult to reach in their inaccessible retreats in the Vindhias.

They were descending the last declivities of the Vindhias. Kiouni had resumed his rapid gait. Towards noon, the guide went round the village of Kallenger, situated on the Cani, one of the tributaries of the Ganges. He always avoided inhabited places, feeling himself safer, in those desert open stretches of country which mark the first depressions of the basin of the great river. Allahabad was not twelve miles to the north-east. Halt was made under a clump of banana trees, whose fruit, as healthy as bread, "as succulent as cream," travellers say, was very much appreciated.

At two o'clock, the guide entered the shelter of a thick forest, which he had to traverse for a space of several miles. He preferred to travel thus under cover of the woods. At all events, up to this moment there had been no unpleasant meeting, and it seemed a if the journey would be accomplished without accident, when the elephant, showing some signs of uneasiness, suddenly stopped.

It was then four o'clock.

"What is the matter?" asked Sir Francis Cromarty, raising his head above his howdah.

"I do not know, officer," replied the Parsee, listening to a confused murmur which came through the thick branches.

A few moments after, this murmur became more defined. It might have been called a concert, still very distant, of human voices and brass instruments.

Passepartout was all eyes, all ears. Mr. Fogg waited patiently, without uttering a word.

The Parsee jumped down, fastened the elephant to a tree, and plunged into the thickest of the undergrowth. A few minutes later he returned, saying:

"A Brahmin procession coming this way. If it is possible, let us avoid being seen."

The guide unfastened the elephant, and led him into a thicket, recommending the travellers not to descend. He held himself ready to mount the elephant quickly, should flight become necessary. But he thought that the troop of the faithful would pass without noticing him, for the thickness of the foliage entirely concealed him.

The discordant noise of voices and instruments approached. Monotonous chants were mingled with the sound of the drums and cymbals. Soon the head of the procession appeared from under the trees, at fifty paces from the spot occupied by Mr. Fogg and his companions. Through the branches they readily distinguished the curious personnel of this religious ceremony.

In the first line were the priests, with mitres upon their heads and attired in long robes adorned with gold and silver lace. They were surrounded by men, women, and children, who were singing a sort of funeral psalmody, interrupted at regular intervals by the beating of tom-toms and cymbals. Behind them on a car with large wheels, whose spokes and felloes represented serpents intertwined, appeared a hideous statue, drawn by two pairs of richly caparisoned zebus. This statue had four arms, its body coloured with dark red, its eyes haggard, its hair tangled, its tongue hanging out, its lips coloured with henna and betel. Its neck was encircled by a collar of skulls, around its waist a girdle of human hands. It was erect upon a prostrate giant, whose head was missing.

Sir Francis Cromarty recognised this statue.

"The goddess Kali," he murmured; "the goddess of love."

"Of death, I grant, but of love, never!" said Passepartout. The ugly old woman."

The Parsee made him a sign to keep quiet.

Around the statue there was a group of old fakirs, jumping and tossing themselves about convulsively. Smeared with bands of ochre, covered with cross-like cuts, whence their blood escaped drop by drop—stupid fanatics, who, in the great Hindu ceremonies, precipitated themselves under the wheels of the car of Juggernaut.

Behind them, some Brahmins in all the magnificence of their Oriental costume, were dragging a woman who could hardly hold herself erect.

This woman was young, and as fair as a European. Her head, her neck, her shoulders, her ears, her arms, her hands, and her toes were loaded down with jewels, necklaces, bracelets, ear-rings and finger-rings. A tunic, embroidered with gold, covered with a light muslin, displayed the outlines of her form.

Behind this young woman—a violent contrast for the eyes—were guards, armed with naked sabres fastened to their girdles and long damascened pistols, carrying a corpse upon a palanquin.

It was the body of an old man, dressed in the rich garments of a rajah, having, as in life, his turban embroidered with pearls, his robe woven of silk and gold, his sash of cashmere ornamented with diamonds, and his magnificent arms as an Indian prince.

Then, musicians and a rearguard of fanatics, whose cries sometimes drowned the deafening noise of the instruments, closed up the *cortège.*

Sir Francis Cromarty looked at all this pomp with a singularly sad air, and turning to the guide, he said:

"A suttee!"

The Parsee made an affirmative sign and put his fingers on his lips. The long procession came out from the trees, and soon the last of it disappeared in the depths of the forest.

Little by little the chanting died out. There were still the sounds of distant cries, and finally a profound silence succeeded all this tumult.

Phileas Fogg had heard the word uttered by Sir Francis Cromarty, and as soon as the procession had disappeared, he asked:

"What is a suttee?"

"A suttee, Mr. Fogg," replied the brigadier-general, "is a human sacrifice, but a voluntary sacrifice. The woman that you have just seen will be burned to-morrow in the early part of the day."

Oh, the villains!" cried Passepartout, who could not prevent this cry of indignation.

"And this corpse?" asked Mr. Fogg.

"It is that of the prince, her husband," replied the guide, "an independent rajah of Bundelcund."

"How," replied Phileas Fogg, without his voice betraying the least emotion, "do these barbarous customs still exist in India, and have not the British been able to extirpate them?"

"In the largest part of India," replied Sir Francis Cromarty, "these sacrifices do not come to pass; but we have no influence over these wild countries, and particularly over this territory of Bundelcund. All the northern slope of the Vindhias is the scene of murders and incessant robberies."

"The unfortunate woman," murmured Passepartout, "burned alive!"

"Yes," replied the general, "burned, and if she was not, you would not believe to what a miserable condition she would be reduced by her near relatives. They would shave her hair; they would scarcely feed her with a few handfuls of rice; they would repulse her; she would be considered as an unclean creature, and would die in some corner like a sick dog. So that the prospect of this frightful existence frequently drives these unfortunates to the sacrifice much more than love or religious fanaticism. Sometimes, however, the sacrifice is really voluntary, and the energetic intervention of the government is necessary to prevent it. Some years ago, I was living at Bombay, when a young widow came to the Governor to ask his authority for her to be burned with the body of her husband. As you may think, the Governor refused. Then the widow left the city, took refuge with an independent rajah, and there she accomplished the sacrifice."

During the narrative of the general, the guide shook his head, and when he was through, said:

"The sacrifice which takes place to-morrow is not voluntary."

"How do you know?"

"It is a story which everybody in Bundelcund knows," replied the guide.

"But this unfortunate did not seem to make any resistance," remarked Sir Francis Cromarty.

"Because she was intoxicated with the fumes of hemp and opium."

"But where are they taking her?"

"To the pagoda of Pillaji, two miles from here. There she will pass the night in waiting for the sacrifice."

"And this sacrifice will take place—?"

"At the first appearance of day."

After this answer, the guide brought the elephant out of the dense thicket, and jumped on his neck. But at the moment that he was going to start him off by a peculiar whistle, Mr. Fogg stopped him and addressing Sir Francis Cromarty, said, "If we could save this woman!"

"Save this woman, Mr. Fogg." cried the brigadier-general.

"I have still twelve hours to spare. I can devote them to her."

"Why, you are a man of heart!" said Sir Francis Cromarty.

"Sometimes," replied Phileas Fogg simply, "when I have time."

Chapter 13

In which Passepartout proves again that Fortune smiles upon the Bold

The design was bold, full of difficulties, perhaps impracticable. Mr. Fogg was going to risk his life, or at least his liberty, and consequently the success of his plans, but he did not hesitate. He found, besides, a decided ally in Sir Francis Cromarty.

As to Passepartout, he was ready and could be depended upon. His master's idea excited him. He felt that there was a heart and soul under this icy covering. He almost loved Phileas Fogg.

Then there was the guide. What part would he take in the matter? Would he not be with the Indians? In default of his aid, it was at least necessary to be sure of his neutrality.

Sir Francis Cromarty put the question to him frankly.

"Officer," replied the guide, "I am a Parsee, and that woman is a Parsee. Make use of me."

"Very well, guide," replied Mr. Fogg.

"However, do you know," replied the Parsee, "that we not only risk our lives, but horrible punishments if we are taken. So see."

"That is seen," replied Mr. Fogg. "I think that we shall have to wait for night to act?"

"I think so too," replied the guide.

The brave Hindu then gave some details as to the victim. She was an Indian of celebrated beauty, of the Parsee race, the daughter of a rich merchant of Bombay. She had received in that city an absolutely English education, and from her manners and cultivation she would have been thought an European. Her name was Aouda.

An orphan, she was married against her will to this old rajah of Bundelcund. Three months after she was a widow. Knowing the fate that awaited her, she fled, was retaken immediately, and the relatives of the rajah, who had an interest in her death, devoted her to this sacrifice from which it seemed that she could not escape.

This narrative could only strengthen Mr. Fogg and his companions in their generous resolution. It was decided that the guide should turn the elephant towards the pagoda of Pillaji, which he should approach as near as possible.

A half-hour afterwards a halt was made under a thick clump of trees, five hundred paces from the pagoda, which they could not see, but they heard distinctly the yellings of the fanatics.

The means of reaching the victim were then discussed. The guide was acquainted with the pagoda, in which he asserted that the young woman was imprisoned. Could they enter by one of the doors, when the whole band was plunged in the sleep of drunkenness, or would they have to make a hole through the wall? This could be decided only at the moment and the place. But there could be no doubt hat the abduction must be accomplished this very night, and not when, daylight arrived, the victim would be led to the sacrifice. Then no human intervention could save her.

Mr. Fogg and his companions awaited for night. As soon as the shadows fell, towards six o'clock in the evening, they determined to make a reconnaissance around the pagoda. The last cries of the fakirs had died out. According to their customs, these Indians were plunged in the heavy intoxication of "bang," liquid opium mixed with an infusion of hemp, and it would perhaps be possible to slip in between them to the temple.

The Parsee guiding, Mr. Fogg, Sir Francis Cromarty, and Passepartout advanced noiselessly through the forest. After ten minutes' creeping under the branches, they arrived on the edge of a small river, and there by the light of iron torches at the end of which was burning pitch, they saw a pile of wood. It was the funeral pile, made of costly sandal wood, and already saturated with perfumed oil. On its upper part the embalmed body of the rajah was resting, which was to be burned at the same time as his widow. At one hundred paces from this pile rose the pagoda, whose minarets in the darkness pierced the tops of the trees.

"Come!" said the guide in a low voice.

Soon the guide stopped at the end of a clearing, lit up by a few torches. The ground was covered with groups of sleepers, heavy with drunkenness.

In the background, among the trees, the temple of Pillaji stood out indistinctly. But to the great disappointment of the guide, the guards of the rajah, lighted by smoky torches, were watching at the doors, and pacing up and down with drawn sabres. Phileas Fogg and Sir Francis Cromarty understood as well as himself that they could attempt nothing on this side. They stopped and talked in a low tone.

"Let us wait," said the brigadier-general, "it is not eight o'clock yet, and it is possible that these guards may succumb to sleep."

"That is possible, indeed," replied the Parsee.

Phileas Fogg and his companions stretched themselves out at the foot of a tree and waited.

They waited thus until midnight. The situation did not change. The same watching outside. It was evident that they could not count on the drowsiness of the guards.

After a final conversation, the guide said he was ready to start. Mr. Fogg, Sir Francis, and Passepartout followed him. They made a pretty long detour, so as to reach the pagoda by the rear.

About a half-hour past midnight they arrived at the foot of the walls, without having met anyone. No watch had been established on this side, but windows and doors were entirely wanting.

But it was not sufficient to reach the foot of the walls, it was necessary to make an opening there. For this operation Phileas Fogg and his companions had nothing at all but their pocket-knives. Fortunately, the temple walls were composed of a mixture of bricks and wood, which could not be difficult to make a hole through. The first brick once taken out, the others would easily follow.

They went at it, making as little noise as possible. The Parsee, from one side, and Passepartout, from the other, worked to unfasten the bricks, so as to get an opening two feet wide.

The work was progressing, but—unfortunate mischance—some guards showed themselves at the rear of the pagoda, and established themselves there so as to hinder an approach.

It would be difficult to describe the disappointment of these four men, stopped in their work.

"What can we do but leave?" asked the general in a low voice.

"We can only leave," replied the guide.

"Wait," said Fogg. "It will do if I-reach Allahabad to-morrow before noon."

"But what hope have you?" replied Sir Francis Cromarty. "It will soon be daylight, and—"

"The chance which escapes us now may return at the last moment."

The general would have liked to read Phileas Fogg's eyes.

What was this cold-blooded Englishman counting on? Would he, at the moment of the sacrifice, rush towards the young woman, and openly tear her from her murderers?

That would have been madness, and how could it be admitted

that this man was mad to this degree? Nevertheless, Sir Francis Cromarty consented to wait until the *dénouement* of this terrible scene. However, the guide did not leave his companions at the spot where they had hid, and he took them back to the foreground of the clearing. There, sheltered by a clump of trees, they could watch the sleeping groups.

In the meantime Passepartout, perched upon the lower branches of a tree, was meditating an idea which had first crossed his mind like a flash, and which finally embedded itself in his brain.

He had commenced by saying to himself, "What madness!" and now he repeated, "Why not, after all? It is a chance, perhaps the only one, and with such brutes—"

At all events, Passepartout did not put his thought into any other shape, but he was not slow in sliding down, with the ease of a snake, on the lower branches of the tree, the end of which bent towards the ground.

The hours were passing, and soon a few less sombre shades announced the approach of day. But the darkness was still great.

It was the time fixed. It was like a resurrection in this slumbering crowd. The groups wakened up. The beating of tom-toms sounded, songs and cries burst out anew. The hour had come in which the unfortunate was to die.

The doors of the pagoda were now opened. A more intense light came from the interior. Mr. Fogg and Sir Francis could see the victim, all lighted up, whom two priests were dragging to the outside. It seemed to them that, shaking off the drowsiness of intoxication by the highest instinct of self-preservation, the unfortunate woman was trying to escape from her executioners. Sir Francis's heart throbbed violently and with a convulsive movement seizing Phileas Fogg's hand, he felt that it held an open knife.

At this moment the crowd was agitated. The young woman had fallen again into the stupor produced by the fumes of the hemp. She passed between the fakirs, who escorted her with their religious cries.

Phileas Fogg and his companions followed her, mingling with the rear ranks of the crowd.

Two minutes after they arrived at the edge of the river, and stopped less than fifty paces from the funeral pile, upon which was lying the rajah's body. In the semi-obscurity they saw the victim, motionless, stretched near her husband's corpse.

Then a torch was brought, and the wood, impregnated with oil soon took fire.

At this moment, Sir Francis Cromarty and the guide held back Phileas Fogg, who in a impulse of generous madness, was going to rush towards the pile.

But Phileas Fogg had already pushed them back, when the scene changed suddenly. A cry of terror arose. The whole crowd, frightened, cast themselves upon the ground.

The old rajah was not dead, then; he was seen suddenly rising upright, like a phantom, raising the young woman in his arms, descending from the pile in the midst of the clouds of smoke which gave him a spectral appearance.

The fakirs, the priests, overwhelmed with a sudden fear, were prostrate, their faces to the ground, not daring to raise their eyes, and look at such a miracle!

The inanimate victim was held by the vigorous arms carrying her, without seeming to be much of a weight. Mr. Fogg and Sir Francis had remained standing. The Parsee had bowed his head, and Passepartout, without doubt, was not less stupefied.

The resuscitated man came near the spot where Mr. Fogg and Sir Francis Cromarty were, and said shortly:

"Let us be off!"

It was Passepartout himself who had slipped to the pile in the midst of the thick smoke! It was Passepartout who, profiting by the great darkness still prevailing, had rescued the young woman from death! It was Passepartout who, playing his part with the boldest good luck, passed out in the midst of the general fright.

An instant after the four disappeared in the woods, and the elephant took them onwards with a rapid trot. But cries, shouts, and even a ball, piercing Phileas Fogg's hat, apprised them that the stratagem had been discovered.

Indeed, on the burning pile still lay the body of the old rajah.

The priests, recovered from their fright, learned that the abduction had taken place.

They immediately rushed into the forest. The guards followed them. Shots were fired; but the abductors fled rapidly, and, in a few moments, they were out of range of balls or arrows.

CHAPTER 14

In which Phileas Fogg descends the entire splendid Valley of the Ganges without ever thinking of looking at it

The bold abduction had succeeded. An hour after Passepartout was still laughing at his success. Sir Francis Cromarty grasped the hand of the brave fellow. His master said to him, "Good," which in that gentleman's mouth was equivalent to high praise. To which Passepartout replied that all the honour of the affair belonged to his master. As for himself he had only had a "droll" idea, and he laughed in thinking that for a few moments he, Passepartout, the former gymnast, the ex-sergeant of firemen, had been the widower of a charming woman, and old embalmed rajah!

As for the young Indian widow, she had no knowledge of what had passed. Wrapped up in travelling cloaks, she was resting in one of the howdahs.

Meanwhile the elephant, guided with the greatest certainty by the Parsee, moved on rapidly through the still dark forest. One hour after having left the pagoda of Pillaji, he shot across an immense plain. At seven o'clock they halted. The young woman was still in a state of complete prostration. The guide made her drink a few swallows of water and brandy, but the stupefying influence which overwhelmed her continued for some time longer. Sir Francis Cromarty, who knew the effects of intoxication produced by inhalation of the fumes of hemp, had no uneasiness on her account.

But if the restoration of the young woman was not a question in the general's mind, he was not less assured for the future. He did not hesitate to say to Phileas Fogg that if Mrs. Aouda remained in India, she would inevitably fall again into 'the hands of her executioners. These fanatics were scattered throughout the entire peninsula, and notwithstanding the English police, they would certainly be able to recapture their victim, whether at Madras, at Bombay, or at Calcutta. And in support of this remark, Sir Francis quoted a fact of the same nature which had recently transpired. According to his view, the young woman would really not be safe until after leaving India.

Phileas Fogg replied that he would note these remarks and think them over.

Towards ten o'clock the guide announced the station of Allahabad. The interrupted line of the railway recommenced there, whence trains traverse, in less than a day and a night, the distance separating Allahabad from Calcutta.

Phileas Fogg ought then to arrive in time to take a steamer which would not leave until the next day, October 25, at noon, for Honk-Kong.

The young woman was placed in a waiting-room of the station. Passepartout was directed to purchase for her various articles of dress, such as a robe, shawl, furs, etc., whatever he would find. His master opened an unlimited credit for him.

Passepartout went out immediately and ran through the streets of the city. Allahabad, that is, the "City of God," is one of the most venerated of India, on account of its being built at the junction of two sacred rivers, the Ganges and the Jumna, whose waters attract pilgrims from the whole peninsula It is said also that, according to the legends of the Ramayana, the Ganges takes its source in heaven, whence, thanks to Brahma, it descends upon the earth.

In making his purchases, Passepartout had soon seen the city, at one time defended by a magnificent fort, which had become a State prison. There are no more commerce and no more manufactures in this city, formerly a manufacturing and commercial point. Passepartout, who vainly sought a variety shop, such as there was in Regent Street, a few steps off from Farmer & Co., found only at a second-hand dealer's, an old whimsical Jew, the objects which he needed—a dress of Scotch stuff, a large mantle, and a magnificent otter-skin, pelisse, for which he did not hesitate to pay seventy-five pounds. Then, quite triumphant, he returned to the station.

Mrs. Aouda commenced to revive. The influence to which the priests of Pillaji had subjected her, disappeared by degrees, and her beautiful eyes resumed all their Indian softness.

When the poet-king, Ucaf Uddaul celebrates the charms of the Queen of Ahemhnagara, he thus expressed himself:

"Her shining tresses, regularly divided into two parts, encircle the harmonious outlines of her delicate and white cheeks, brilliant with their flow and freshness. Her ebony eyebrows have the form and strength of the bow of Kama, god of love; and under her long silken lashes, in the black pupil of her large limpid eyes, there float, as in the sacred lakes of the Himalaya, the purest reflections of the celestial light. Fine, regular, and white, her teeth shine out between her smiling lips, like dewdrops in the half-closed bosom of the pomegranate blossom. Her ears, types of the symmetric curves, her rosy hands, her little feet, curved and tender as lotus buds, shine with the splendour of the finest pearls of Ceylon, the most beautiful diamonds of Golconda Her delicate and supple waist, which a hand can clasp, heightens the elegant outline of her rounded figure, and the wealth of her bosom, where youth in its prime displays its most perfect treasures and under the silken folds of her tunic she seems to have been modelled in pure silver by the divine hand of Vicvarcarma, the immortal sculptor."

But, without all this poetic amplification, it is sufficient to say that Mrs. Aouda, the widow of the Rajah of Bundelcund, was a charming woman in the entire European acceptation of the phrase. She spoke English with great purity, and the guide had not exaggerated in asserting that this young Parsee woman had been transformed by education.

Meanwhile the train was about to leave Allahabad. The Parsee was waiting. Mr. Fogg paid him the compensation agreed upon, without exceeding it a farthing. This astonished Passepartout a little, who knew everything that his master owed to the devotion of the guide. The Parsee, in fact, had risked his life voluntarily in the affair at Pillaji; and if, later, the Hindus should learn it, he would hardly escape their vengeance.

The question of Kiouni also remained. What would be done with an elephant bought so dearly?

But Phileas Fogg had already taken a resolution upon this point.

"Parsee," he said to the guide, "you have been serviceable and devoted. I have paid for your service, but not for your devotion. Do you wish this elephant? It is yours."

The eyes of the guide sparkled.

"Your honour is giving me a fortune!" he cried.

"Accept, guide," replied Mr. Fogg, "and I will be yet your debtor."

"Good!" cried Passepartout. "Take him, friend! Kiouni is a brave and courageous animal."

And going to the brave, he gave him some lumps of sugar, saying:

"Here, Kiouni, here, here."

The elephant uttered some grunts of satisfaction. Then taking Passepartout by the waist, and encircling him with his trunk, he raised him as high as his head. Passepartout, not at all frightened, caressed the animal, who replaced him gently on the ground, and to the shaking of the honest Kiouni's trunk there answered a vigorous shaking of the good fellow's hand.

A few moments after, Phileas Fogg, Sir Francis Cromarty, and Passepartout, seated in a comfortable car, the best seat in which Mrs. Aouda occupied, were running at full speed towards Benares.

Eighty miles at the most separate this place from Allahabad, and they were passed over in two hours.

During this passage the young woman completely revived; the drowsy fumes of the "bang" disappeared.

What was her astonishment to find herself on this railway, in this compartment, clothed in European habiliments, in the midst of travellers entirely unknown to her.

At first, her companions gave her the greatest care, and revived her with a few drops of liquor; then the brigadier-general told the story. He dwelt upon the devotion of Phileas Fogg, who had not hesitated to stake his life to save her, and upon the *dénouement* of the adventure, due to the bold imagination of Passepartout.

Mr. Fogg let him go on without saying a word.

Passepartout, quite ashamed, repeated that "it was not worth while."

Mrs. Aouda thanked her deliverers profusely, by her tears more than by her words. Her beautiful eyes, rather than her lips, were the interpreters of her gratitude. Then, her thoughts carrying her back to the scenes of the suttee, seeing again the Indian country where so many dangers still awaited her, she shuddered with terror.

Phileas Fogg understood what was passing in Mrs.Aouda's mind, and, to reassure her, offered, very coolly, to take her to Hong-Kong, where she might remain until this affair had died out.

Mrs. Aouda accepted the offer gratefully. At Hong-Kong there resided one of her relatives, a Parsee like herself, and one of the principal merchants of that city, which is entirely English, though occupying a point on the Chinese coast

At half-past twelve noon the train stopped at the Benares station. The Brahmin legends assert that this place occupies the site of the ancient Casi, which was formerly suspended in space, between the zenith and the nadir, like Mohammed's tomb. But at this more material period, Benares, the Athens of India, in the saying of the Orientals, was prosaically resting on the earth, and Passepartout could for an instant see its brick houses, its clay huts, which gave it a very desolate appearance, without any local colour.

Here was where Sir Francis Cromarty was going to stop. The troops which he was rejoining were camping a few miles to the north of the city. The brigadier-general then made his adieux to Phileas Fogg, wishing him all possible success, and expressing the wish that he would recommence the journey in a less original but more profitable manner. Mr. Fogg pressed lightly his companion's fingers. The parting greetings of Mrs. Aouda were more demonstrative. She would never forget what she owed Sir Francis Cromarty. As for Passepartout, he was honoured with a hearty shake of the hand by the general. Quite affected, he asked where and when he could be of service to him. Then they parted.

Leaving Benares, the railway followed in part the Valley of the Ganges. Through the windows of the car, the weather being quite clear, appeared the varied country of Behar, mountains covered with verdure, fields of barley, corn, and wheat, jungles full of green alligators, villages well kept, forests yet green. A few elephants, and zebus with large humps, came to bathe in the waters of the sacred river, and also, notwithstanding the advanced season, and the already cold temperature, bands of Hindus of both sexes, who were piously performing their holy ablutions. These faithful ones, the bitter enemies of Buddhism, are fervent sectaries of the Brahmin religion, which is incarnate in these three persons: Vishnu, the solar deity; Shiva, the divine personification of the natural forces; and Brahma, the supreme master of priests and legislators. But in what light would Brahma, Shiva, and Vishnu regard this India, now "Britonised," when some steamboat passes, puffing and disturbing the consecrated waters of the Ganges, frightening the gulls flying over its surface, the turtles swarming on its banks, and the faithful stretched along its shores.

All this panorama passed like a flash, and frequently a cloud of steam concealed its details from them. The travellers could scarcely see the fort of Chunar, twenty miles to the south-east of Benares, the old stronghold of the rajahs of Behar, Ghazepour, and its large rose-water manufactories; the tomb of Lord Cornwallis rising on the left bank of the Ganges; the fortified town of Buxar; Patna the great manufacturing and commercial city, where the principal opium market in India is held; Monghir, a more than European town, as English as Manchester or Birmingham, famous for its iron foundries, its manufactories of cutlery, and whose high chimneys cover with a black smoke the heavens of Brahma—a real fist-blow in the country of dreams!

Then night came, and in the midst of the howlings of the tigers, the bears, and the wolves, which fled before the locomotive, the train passed on at full speed, and they saw nothing of the wonders of Bengal, or Golconda, or Gour in ruins, or Mourshedabad, the former capital, or Burdwan, or Hougly, or Chandernager, that French point in the Indian territory, on which Passepartout would have been proud to see his native flag floating.

Finally, at seven o'clock a.m., Calcutta was reached. The steamer to leave for Hong-Kong did not weigh anchor until noon. Phileas Fogg had then five hours before him.

According to his journal, this gentleman should arrive in the capital of India, October 25, twenty-three days after leaving London, and he arrived there on the stipulated day. He was neither behind nor ahead of time. Unfortunately, the two days gained by him between London and Bombay had been lost, we know how, in this trip across the Indian peninsula, but it is to be supposed that Phileas Fogg did not regret them.

Chapter 15

In which the Bag with the Bank-notes is relieved of a few Thousand Pounds more

The train had stopped at the station. Passepartout first got out of the car, and was followed by Mr. Fogg, who aided his young companion to descend. Phileas Fogg counted on going directly to the Hong-Kong steamer, in order to fix Mrs. Aouda there comfortably, whom he did not wish to leave as long as she was in this country, so dangerous for her.

At the moment that Mr. Fogg was going out of the station a policeman approached him and said:

"Mr. Phileas Fogg?"

"I am he."

"Is this man your servant?" added the policeman, pointing to Passepartout.

"Yes."

"You will both be so kind as to follow me."

Mr. Fogg made no movement indicating any surprise. This agent was a representative of the law, and for every Englishman the law is sacred. Passepartout, with his French habits, wanted to discuss the matter, but the policeman touched him with his stick, and Phileas Fogg made him a sign to obey.

"This young lady can accompany us?" asked Mr. Fogg.

"She can,"replied the policeman.

The policeman conducted Mr. Fogg, Mrs. Aouda, and Passepartout to a palkighari, a sort of four-wheeled vehicle with four seats, drawn by two horses. They started. No one spoke during the twenty minutes' ride.

The vehicle first crossed the "black town," with its narrow streets, its huts in which grovelled a miscellaneous population, dirty and ragged; then they passed through the European town, adorned with brick houses, shaded by coconut trees, bristling with masts, through which, notwithstanding the early hour, were driving handsomely-dressed gentlemen, in elegant turn-outs.

The palkighari stopped before a dwelling of plain appearance, but which was not used for private purposes. The policeman let his prisoners out, for they could, indeed, be called thus, and he led them into a room with grated windows, saying to them:

"At half-past eight you will appear before Judge Obadiah."

Then he left, and dosed the door.

"See! we are prisoners!" cried Passepartout, dropping into a chair.

Mrs. Aouda, addressing Mr. Fogg immediately, said in a voice whose emotion she sought in vain to disguise:

"Sir, you must leave me! It is on my account that you are pursued! It is because you have rescued me!"

Phileas Fogg contented himself with saying that that would not be possible. Pursued on account of this suttee affair. Inadmissible! How would the complainants dare present themselves? There was a mistake. Mr. Fogg added that, in any event he would not abandon the young woman, and that he would take her to Hong-Kong.

"But the steamer leaves at noon!" remarked Passepartout.

"Before noon we will be on board," was the simple reply of the impassible gentleman.

This was so flatly asserted that Passepartout could not help saying to himself:

"*Parbleu!* that is certain! before noon we will be on board!" But he was not at all reassured.

At half-past eight the door of the room was opened. The policeman reappeared, and he led.the prisoners into the next room. It was a court-room, and quite a large crowd, composed of Europeans and natives, already occupied the rear of the room.

Mr. Fogg, Mrs. Aouda, and Passepartout were seated on a bench in front of the seats reserved for the magistrate and the clerk.

This magistrate,Judge Obadiah, entered almost immediately, followed by the clerk. He was a large, fat man. He took down a wig hung on a nail and hastily put it on his head.

"The first case," he said.

But putting his hand to his head, he said:

"Humph! this is not my wig!"

"That's a fact, Mr. Obadiah, it is mine," replied the clerk.

"My dear Mr. Oysterpuff, how do you think that a judge can give a wise sentence with a clerk's wig?"

An exchange of wigs had been made. During these preliminaries Passepartout was boiling over with impatience, for the hands appeared to him to move terribly fast over the face of the large clock in the court-room.

"The first case,' said Judge Obadiah again.

"Phileas Fogg?" said Clerk Oysterpuff.

"Here I am," replied Mr. Fogg.

"Passepartout?"

"Present!" replied Passepartout.

"Good!" said Judge Obadiah. "For two days, prisoners, you have been looked for upon the arrival of all the trains from Bombay."

"But of what are we accused?" cried Passepartout impatiently.

"You shall know now," replied the judge.

"Sir," said Mr. Fogg then, "I am an English citizen, and have the right—"

"Have you been treated disrespectfully?" asked Mr. Obadiah.

"Not at all."

"Very well, let the complainants come in."

Upon the order of the judge a door was opened, and three Hindu priests were led in by a tip-staff.

"Well, well!" murmured Passepartout, "they are the rascals who were going to burn our young lady!"

The priest stood up before the judge, and the clerk read in a loud voice a complaint of sacrilege, preferred against Mr. Fogg and his servant, accused of having violated a place consecrated by the Brahmin religion.

"You have heard the charge?" the judge asked Phileas Fogg.

"Yes, sir," replied Mr. Fogg, consulting his watch, "and I confess it."

"Ah! You confess?"

"I confess and expect these three priests to confess in their turn what they were going to do at the pagoda of Pillaji."

The priests looked at each other. They did not seem to understand the words of the accused.

"Truly!" cried Passepartout impetuously, "at the pagoda of Pillaji, where they were going to burn their victim!"

More stupefaction of the priests, and profound astonishment of Judge Obadiah.

"What victim!" he answered. "Burn whom? In the heart of the city of Bombay?"

"Bombay?" cried Passepartout.

"Certainly. We are not speaking of the pagoda of Pillaji, but of the pagoda of Malebar in Bombay."

"And as a proof here are the desecrator's shoes," added the clerk, putting a pair on his desk.

"My shoes!" cried Passepartout, who, surprised at the last charge, could not prevent this involuntary exclamation.

The confusion in the minds of the master and servant may be imagined. They had forgotten the incident of the pagoda of Bombay, and that was the very thing which had brought them before the magistrate in Calcutta.

In fact, Fix understood the advantage that he might get from this unfortunate affair. Delaying his departure twelve hours, he had taken counsel with the priests of Malebar Hill, and had promised them large damages, knowing very well that the British Government was very severe upon this kind of trespass; then by the following train he had sent them forward on the track of the perpetrator. But in consequence of the time employed in the deliverance of the young widow, Fix and the Hindus arrived at Calcutta before Phileas Fogg and his servant, whom the authorities, warned by telegraph, were to arrest as they got out of the train. The disappointment of Fix may be judged of, when he learned that Phileas Fogg had not yet arrived in the capital of India. He was compelled to think that his robber, stopping at one of the stations of the Peninsular Railway, had taken refuge in the northern provinces. For twenty-four hours, in the greatest uneasiness, Fix watched for him at the station. What was his joy then when, this very morning, he saw him get out of the car accompanied, it is true, by a young woman whose presence he could not explain. He immediately sent a policeman after him; and this is how Mr. Fogg, Passepartout, and the widow of the rajah of Bundelcund were taken before Judge Obadiah.

And if Passepartout had been less preoccupied with his

affair, he would have perceived in a corner of the room the detective, who followed the discussion with an interest easy to understand, for at Calcutta, as at Bombay, and as at Suez, the warrant of arrest, was still not at hand!

But Judge Obadiah had taken a note of the confession escaped from Passepartout who would have given all he possessed to recall his imprudent words.

"The facts are admitted?" said the judge.

"Admitted," replied Mr. Fogg coldly.

"Inasmuch," continued the judge, "as the English law intends to protect equally and rigorously all the religions of the people of India, the trespass being admitted by this man Passepartout, convicted of having violated with sacrilegious feet the pavement of the pagoda of Malebar Hill in Bombay, on the 20th day of October, I sentence the said Passepartout to fifteen days' imprisonment, and a fine of three hundred pounds."

"Three hundred pounds!" cried Passepartout, who was really only alive to the fine.

"Silence!" said the tip-staff in a shrill voice.

"And," added Judge Obadiah, "inasmuch as it is not materially proved that there was not a connivance between the servant and the master, the latter of whom ought to be held responsible for the acts and gestures of a servant in his employ, I detain the said Phileas Fogg and sentence him to eight days' imprisonment and one hundred and fifty pounds fine. Clerk, call another case!"

Fix, in his corner, experienced an unspeakable satisfaction. Phileas Fogg, detained eight days in Calcutta! It would be more than time enough for the warrant to arrive.

Passepartout was crushed. This sentence would ruin his master. A wager of twenty thousand pounds lost, and all because, in the height of folly, he had gone into that cursed pagoda!

Phileas Fogg, as much master of himself as if this sentence did not concern him, did not even knit his eyebrows. But at the moment that the clerk was calling another case, he rose, and said:

"I offer bail."

"It is your right," replied the judge.

Fix felt a cold shudder down his back, but he recovered himself again, when he heard the judge, "in consideration of the fact of Phileas Fogg and his servant both being strangers," fix the bail for each at the enormous sum of one thousand pounds.

It would cost Mr. Fogg two thousand pounds, unless he would be cleared from his sentence.

"I will pay it," said that gentleman.

And he took from the bag which Passepartout carried a bundle of bank-notes, which he placed on the clerk's desk.

"This sum will be returned to you on coming out of prison," said the judge. "In the meantime, you are free under bail."

"Come," said Phileas Fogg to his servant.

"But they should at least return me my shoes," cried Passepartout, with an angry movement.

They returned him his shoes.

"These are dear!" he murmured; "more than a thousand pounds apiece! Without counting that they pinch me!"

Passepartout, with a very pitiful look, followed Mr. Fogg, who had offered his arm to the young woman. Fix still hoped that his robber would not decide to surrender this sum of two thousand pounds, and that he would serve out his eight days in prison. He put himself, then, on Fogg's tracks.

Mr. Fogg took a carriage, into which Mrs. Aouda, Passepartout, and he got immediately. Fix ran behind the carriage, which soon stopped on one of the wharves of the city.

Half a mile out in the harbour the *Rangoon* was anchored, her sailing flag hoisted-to the top of the mast. Eleven o'clock struck. Mr. Fogg was one hour ahead. Fix saw him get out of the carriage, and embark in a boat with Mrs. Aouda and his servant. The detective stamped his foot.

"The rascal!" he cried. "He is going off! Two thousand pounds sacrificed! Prodigal as a robber! Ah! I will follow him to the end of the world, if it is necessary; but, at the rate at which he is going, all the stolen money will be gone!"

The detective had good reason for making this remark. In

fact, since he left London, what with travelling expenses, rewards, the elephant purchase, bail, and fines, Phileas Fogg had already scattered more than five thousand pounds on his route, and the percentage of the sum recovered, promised to the detectives, was constantly diminishing.

Chapter 16

In which Fix has not the Appearance of knowing anything about the Matters concerning which They talk to Him

The *Rangoon,* one of the vessels employed by the Peninsular and Oriental Company in the Chinese and Japanese seas, was an iron screw steamer, of seventeen hundred and seventy tons, and nominally of four hundred horse-power. She was equally swift, but not so comfortable as the *Mongolia* Mrs. Aouda was not as well fixed in her as Phileas Fogg would have desired. But, after all, it was only a distance of three thousand five hundred miles, and the young woman did not show herself a troublesome passenger.

During the first few days of the passage Mrs. Aouda became better acquainted with Phileas Fogg. On every occasion she showed him the liveliest gratitude. The phlegmatic gentleman listened to her, at least in appearance, with the most extreme indifference, not one tone of his voice or gesture betraying in him the slightest emotion. He saw that she was wanting in nothing. At certain hours he came regularly, if not to talk with her, at least to listen to her. He fulfilled towards her the duties of the strictest politeness, but with the grace and startling effects of an automaton whose movements have been put together for that purpose. Mrs. Aouda did not know what to think of him, but Passepartout had explained to her a little the eccentric character of his master. He had told her what sort of a wager was taking him round the world. Mrs. Aouda had smiled! but, after all, she owed her life to him, and her deliverer could not lose, because she saw him through her gratitude.

Mrs. Aouda confirmed the narrative of the guide in reference to her affecting history. She belonged, in fact, to the race which occupies the first rank among the natives. Several Parsee merchants have made large fortunes in India in the cotton trade. One of them, Sir James Jejeebhoy, was raised to the nobility by the British Government, and Mrs. Aouda was a relative of this rich person, who lived in Bombay. It was indeed a cousin of Sir Jejeebhoy, the honourable Jejeeh, whom she counted on joining at Hong-Kong. Would she find a refuge with him and assistance? She could not say so positively. To which Mr. Fogg replied that she should not be uneasy, and everything would be mathematically arranged. That was the phrase he used.

Did the young woman understand this horrible adverb? We do not know. However, her large eyes were fixed upon those of Mr. Fogg—her large eyes "clear as the sacred lakes of the Himalaya!" But the intractable Fogg, as reserved as ever, did not seem to be the man to throw himself into this lake.

The first part of the *Rangoon's* voyage was accomplished under excellent conditions. The weather was moderate. All the lower portion of the immense Bay of Bengal was favourable to the steamer's progress. The *Rangoon* soon sighted the great Andaman, the principal one of the group of islands, which is distinguished by navigators at a great distance by the picturesque Saddle Peak mountain, two thousand four hundred feet high.

They kept pretty close to the coast. The savage Papuans of the island did not show themselves. They are beings in the lowest grade of humanity, but they have been wrongfully called cannibals.

The panoramic development of this island was superb.

Immense forests of palm-trees, arecas, bamboo, nutmeg-trees, teak-wood, giant mimosas, and tree-like ferns covered the country in the fore-ground, and in the background there stood out in relief the graceful outline of the mountains. Along the shore there swarmed by thousands those precious swallows whose edible nests form a dish much sought for in the Celestial Empire. But all this varied spectacle offered to the eyes by the Andaman group passed quickly, and the *Rangoon* swiftly pursued her way towards the Straits of Malacca, which were to give her access to the Chinese seas.

During this trip what was detective Fix doing, so unluckily dragged into a voyage round the world? On leaving Calcutta, after-having left instructions to forward the warrant to him at Hong-Kong, if it should arrive, he succeeded in getting aboard the *Rangoon* without being perceived by Passepartout, and he hoped that he might conceal his presence until the arrival of the steamer. In fact, it would have been difficult for him to explain how he was on board, without awaking the suspicions of Passepartout, who thought he was in Bombay. But he was led to renew his acquaintance with the good fellow by the very logic of circumstances. How? We will see.

All the hopes, all the desires of the detective were now concentrated on a single point in the world, Hong-Kong—for the steamer would stop too short a time in Singapore for him to operate in that city. The arrest of the robber must then be made in Hong-Kong, or he would escape irrecoverably.

In fact, Hong-Kong was still English soil, but the last he would find on the road. Beyond China and Japan, America would offer a pretty certain refuge to Mr. Fogg. At Hong-Kong, if he should finally find there the warrant of arrest, which was evidently running after him, Fix would arrest Fogg, and put him in the hands of the local police. No difficulty there. But after Hong-Kong a simple warrant of arrest would not be sufficient. An extradition order would be necessary. Thence delays and obstacles of every kind, of which the rogue would take advantage to escape finally. If he failed at Hong-Kong, it would be, if not impossible, at least very difficult to attempt it again with any chance of success.

"Then," repeated Fix during the long hours that he passed in his cabin, "then, either the warrant will be at Hong-Kong and I will arrest my man, or it will not be there, and this time I must, at all hazards, delay his departure! I have failed at Bombay, I have failed at Calcutta! If I miss at Hong-Kong, I shall lose my reputation! Cost what it may, I *must* succeed. But what means shall I employ to delay, if it is necessary, the departure of this accursed Fogg?"

As a last resort, Fix had decided to tell everything to Passepartout; to let him know who the master was that he was serving, and whose accomplice he certainly was not. Passepartout, enlightened by this revelation, fearing to be compromised, would without doubt take sides with him, Fix But it was a very hazardous means, which could only be employed in default of any other. One word from Passepartout to his master would have been sufficient to compromise the affair irrevocably.

The detective was then extremely embarrassed when the presence of Mrs. Aouda on board of the *Rangoon*, in company with Phileas Fogg, opened new perspectives to him.

Who was this woman? What combination of circumstances had made her Fogg's companion? The meeting had evidently taken place between Bombay and Calcutta. But at what point of the peninsula? Was it chance which had brought together Phileas Fogg and the young traveller? Had not his journey across India, on the contrary, been undertaken by this gentleman with the aim of joining this charming person? For she was charming! Fix had had a good view of-her in the audience-hall of the Calcutta tribunal.

It may be comprehended to what a point the detective would be entangled. He asked himself if there was not a criminal abduction in this affair. Yes! that must be it! This idea once fastened in the mind of Fix, and he recognised all the advantage that he could get from this circumstance. Whether this young woman was married or not, there was an abduction, and it was possible to put the ravisher in such embarrassment in Hong-Kong that he could not extricate himself by paying money.

But it was not necessary to await the arrival of the *Rangoon* at Hong-Kong. This Fogg had the detestable habit of jumping from one vessel into another, and before the affair was entered upon he might be far enough off.

The important thing was to warn the English authorities, and to signal the *Rangoon* before her arrival. Now, nothing would be easier to accomplish, as the steamer would put in at Singapore, which is connected with the Chinese coast by a telegraph line.

But, before acting, and to be more certain, Fix determined to question Passepartout. He knew it was not very difficult to start the young man talking, and he decided to throw off the incognito that he had maintained until that time. Now there was no time to lose. It was October 30, and the next day the *Rangoon* would drop anchor at Singapore.

This very day, October 30, Fix, leaving his cabin, went upon deck, with the intention of meeting Passepartout first, with signs of the greatest surprise. Passepartout was walking in the forward part of the vessel, when the detective rushed towards him, exclaiming:

"Is this you, on the *Rangoon*?"

"Monsieur Fix aboard!" replied Passepartout, very much surprised, recognised his old acquaintance of the *Mongolia*.

"What! I left you at Bombay, and I meet you again on the route to Hong-Kong! Are you making also the tour of the world?"

"No, no," replied Fix. "I expect to stop at Hong-Kong at least for a few days."

"Ah!" said Passepartout, who seemed astonished for a moment. "But why have I not seen you aboard since we left Calcutta?"

"Indeed, I was sick—a little sea-sickness—I remained lying down in my cabin—I did not get along as well in the Bay of Bengal as in the Indian Ocean. And your master, Phileas Fogg?"

"Is in perfect health, and as punctual as his diary! Not one day behind! Ah! Monsieur Fix, you do not know it, but we have a young lady with us also."

"A young lady!" replied the detective, who acted exactly as if he did not understand what his companion was saying.

But Passepartout soon gave him the thread of the whole story. He related the incident of the pagoda in Bombay, the purchase of the elephant at the cost of two thousand pounds, the suttee affair, the abduction of Aouda, the sentence of the Calcutta court, and their freedom under bail. Fix, who knew the last portion of these incidents, seemed not to know any of them, and Passepartout gave himself up to the pleasure of telling his adventures to a hearer who showed so much interest.

"But," asked Fix, at the end of the story, "does your master intend to take this young woman to Europe?"

"Not at all, Monsieur Fix; not at all! We are simply going to put her in charge of one of her relatives, a rich merchant of Hong-Kong."

"Nothing to be done there," said the detective to himself, concealing his disappointment. "Take a glass of gin, Mr. Passepartout."

"With pleasure, Monsieur Fix. It is the least that we should drink to our meeting aboard the *Rangoon*."

Chapter 17

In which one thing and another is talked about during the Trip from Singapore to Hong-Kong

After this day, Passepartout and the detective met frequently, but the latter maintained a very great reserve towards his companion, and he did not try to make him talk. Once or twice only he had a glimpse of Mr. Fogg, who was glad to remain in the grand saloon of the Rangoon, either keeping company with Mrs. Aouda, or playing at whist, according to his invariable habit.

As for Passepartout, he thought very seriously over the singular chance which had once more put Fix on his master's route. And, in fact, it was a little surprising. This gentleman, very amiable and very complacent, certainly, whom they met first at Suez, who embarked upon the *Mongolia,* who landed at Bombay, where he said that he would stop, whom they meet again on the *Rangoon, en route* for Hong-Kong—in a word, followng step by step the route marked out by Mr. Fogg—he was worth the trouble of being thought about. There was at least a singular coincidence in it all. What interest had Fix in it? Passepartout was ready to bet his slippers—he had carefully preserved them—that Fix would leave Hong-Kong at the same time as they, and probably on the same steamer.

If Passepartout had thought for a century, he would never have guessed the detective's mission. He would never have imagined that Phileas Fogg was being "followed," after the fashion of a robber, around the terrestrial globe. But as it is in human nature to give an explanation for everything, Passepartout, suddenly enlightened, interpreted in this way the permanent presence of Fix, and, indeed, his interpretation was very plausible. According to him Fix was, and could be, only a detective sent upon Mr. Fogg's tracks by his colleagues of the Reform Club, to prove that this tour around the world was accomplished regularly, according to the time agreed upon.

"That is plain! that is plain!" repeated the honest fellow to himself, quite proud of his clear sightedness. "He is a spy whom these gentlemen have put upon our heels. This is undignified! To have Mr. Fogg, a man so honourable and just, tracked by a detective! Ah! gentlemen of the Reform Club, this will cost you dearly!"

Passepartout delighted with his discovery, resolved, however, to say nothing of it to his master, feeling that he would be justly wounded at this mistrust which his opponents showed. But he promised himself to banter Fix, as opportunity offered, with covert allusions, and without committing himself.

On Wednesday, October 30, in the afternoon, the *Rangoon* entered the Straits of Malacca, separating the peninsula of that name from Sumatra Mountainous, craggy, and very picturesque islets concealed from the passenger the view of this large island.

At four o'clock the next morning, the *Rangoon*, having gained a half-day on its timetable, put in at Singapore, to take in a new supply of coal.

Phileas Fogg noted this gain in the proper column, and this time he landed, accompanying Mrs. Aouda, who had expressed a desire to walk about for a few hours.

Fix, to whom every act of Fogg seemed suspicious, followed him without letting himself be noticed. Passepartout, who was going to make his ordinary purchases, laughed *in petto* seeing Fix's manoeuvre.

The Island of Singapore is neither large nor of an imposing aspect. It is wanting in mountains, that is to say, in profiles. However, it is charming, even in its meagreness. It is a park laid out with fine roads. An elegant carriage, drawn by handsome horses, such as have been imported from New Holland, took Mrs. Aouda and Phileas Fogg into the midst of massive groups of palm trees, the brilliant foliage, and close trees, the cloves of which are formed from the very bud of the half-opened flower. There pepper plants replaced the thorny hedges of European countries; sage-trees, and large ferns with their superb branches, varied the aspect of this tropical region; and nutmeg-trees with shining leaves impregnated the air with a penetrating odour. Bands of monkeys, lively and grimacing, were not wanting in the woods, nor perhaps tigers in the jungles. Should anyone be astonished to learn that in this island, comparatively so small, these terrible carnivorous animals were not destroyed to the very last one, we may reply that they come from Malacca, swimming across the straits.

After having driven about the country for two hours, Mrs.

Aouda and her companion—who looked a little without seeing anything—returned into the town, a vast collection of heavy, flat-looking houses, surrounded by delightful gardens, in which grow mangoes, pineapples, and all the best fruits in the world.

At ten o'clock they returned to the steamer, having been followed, without suspecting it, by the detective, who had also gone to the expense of a carriage.

Passepartout was waiting for them on the deck of the *Rangoon*. The good fellow had bought a few dozen of mangoes, as large as ordinary apples—dark brown outside, brilliant red inside—and whose white pulp, melting in the mouth, gives the true gourmand an unexcelled enjoyment. Passepartout was only too happy to offer them to Mrs. Aouda, who thanked him very gracefully.

At eleven o'clock the *Rangoon*, having obtained a full supply of coal, slipped from her moorings, and a few hours later the passengers lost sight of the high mountains of Malacca, whose forests shelter the most beautiful tigers in the world.

About thirteen hundred miles separate Singapore from the Island of Hong-Kong, a small British territory, detached from the Chinese coast. It was Phileas Fogg's interest to accomplish this in six days at the most, in order to take at Hong-Kong the steamer leaving on the 6th of November for Yokohama, one of the principal ports of Japan.

The *Rangoon* was heavily laden. Many passengers had come aboard at Singapore—Hindus, Ceylonese, Chinamen, Malays, and Portuguese—mostly second class.

The weather, which had been quite fine until this time, changed with the last quarter of the moon. The sea was high. The wind sometimes blew a gale, but fortunately from the south-east, which favoured the movement of the steamer. When it was practicable, the captain had the sails unfurled. The *Rangoon*, brig-rigged, sailed frequently with its two top-sails and foresail, and its speed increased under the double impetus of steam and sail. The vessel thus made her way over a short and sometimes fatiguing sea, along the shores of Anam and Cochin China.

But the passengers would have to blame the *Rangoon* rather than the ocean for their sickness and fatigue.

In fact, the ships of the Peninsular Company, in the China service, are seriously defective in their construction. The proportion of their draught, when loaded, to their depth of hold, has been badly calculated, and consequently they stand the sea but poorly. Their bulk, closed, impenetrable to the water, is insufficient. They are "drowned," to use a maritime expression, and, in consequence, it does not take many waves thrown upon the deck to slacken their speed. These ships are then very inferior—if not in motive power and steam escapes—to the models of the French mail steamers, such as the *Imperattice* and *Cambodge.* Whilst, according to the calculations of the engineers, the latter can take on a weight of water equal to their own before sinking, the vessels of the Peninsular Company, the *Golcanda,* the *Corea,* and finally the *Rangoon,* could not take on the sixth of their weight without going to the bottom.

Great precautions had to be taken then in bad weather. It was sometimes necessary to sail under a small head of steam. This loss of time did not seem to affect Phileas Fogg at all, but Passepartout was much put out about it. He blamed the captain, the engineer, and the company, and set to old Nick all those who had anything to do. with the transportation of the passengers. Perhaps, also, the thought of the gas-burner still burning at his expense in the house in Saville Row had a large share in his impatience.

"Are you in a very great hurry to arrive at Hong-Kong?" the detective asked him one day.

"In a very great hurry!" replied Passepartout.

"You think that Mr. Fogg is in a hurry to take the Yokohama steamer?"

"In a dreadful hurry."

"Then you believe now in this singular voyage around the world?"

"Absolutely. And you, Monsieur Fix?"

"I? I don't believe in it."

"You're a sly fellow," replied Passepartout, winking at him.

This expression left the detective in a reverie. The epithet disturbed him without his knowing very well why. Had the Frenchman guessed his purpose? He did not know what to think. But how had Passepartout been able to discover his capacity as a detective, the secret of which he alone knew. And yet, in speaking thus to him Passepartout certainly had an afterthought.

It happened another day that the good fellow went further. It was too much for him; he could no longer hold his tongue.

"Let us see, Monsieur Fix," he asked his companion, in a roguish tone, "when we have arrived at Hong-Kong, shall we be so unfortunate as to leave you there?"

"Oh!" replied Fix, quite embarrassed, "I do not know! Perhaps—"

"Ah!" said Passepartout, "if you accompany us, I would be so happy! Let us see! An agent of the Peninsular Company could not stop on the route! You were only going to Bombay, and now you will soon be in China. America is not far off, and from America to Europe is only a step!"

Fix looked attentively at his companion, who showed the pleasantest face in the world, and he decided to laugh with him. But the latter who was in humour, asked him if his business brought him in much?

"Yes and no," replied Fix without frowning. "There are fortunate and unfortunate business enterprises. But you understand of course that I don't travel at my own expense!"

"Oh! I am very sure of that," replied Passepartout, laughing still louder.

The conversation finished, Fix returned to his cabin, and sat down to think. He was evidently suspected. In one way or another the Frenchman had recognised his capacity as a detective. But had he warned his master? What role would he play in all this? Was he an accomplice or not? Had they got wind of the matter, and was it consequently all up? The detective passed some perplexing hours there, at one time believing everything lost; at one time hoping that Fogg was ignorant of the situation; and, finally, not knowing what course to pursue.

Meanwhile his brain became calmer, and he resolved to act

frankly with Passepartout. If matters were not in the proper shape to arrest Fogg at Hong-Kong, and if Fogg was then prepared to leave finally the English territory, he (Fix) would tell Passepartout everything. Either the servant was the accomplice of his master, and the latter knew everything, and in this case the affair was definitely compromised, or the servant had no part in the robbery, and then his interest would be to abandon the robber.

Such was the respective situation of these two men, and above them Phileas Fogg was hovering in his majestic indifference. he was accomplishing rationally his orbit around the world, without being troubled by the asteroids gravitating around him.

And yet, in the vicinity, there was—according to the expression of astronomers—a disturbing star which ought to have produced a certain agitation in this gentleman's heart. But no! The charm of Mrs. Aouda did not act, to the great surprise of Passepartout, and the disturbances, if they existed, would have been more difficult to calculate that those of Uranus, which led to the discovery of Neptune.

Yes ! it was a surprise every day for Passepartout, who read in the eyes of the young woman so much gratitude to his master. Phileas Fogg had decidedly heart enough for heroic actions, but for love, none at all! As for the thoughts which the chances of the journey might have produced in him, there was not a trace. But Passepartout was living in a continual trance. One day, leaning on the railing of the engine-room, he was looking at the powerful engine which sometimes moved very violently, when, with the pitching of the vessel the screw would fly out of the water. The steam then escaped from the valves, which provoked the anger of the worthy fellow.

"These valves are not charged enough!" he cried. "We are not going! Oh, these Englishmen! If we were only in an American vessel, we would blow up, perhaps, but we would go more swiftly!"

CHAPTER 18

In which Phileas Fogg, Passepartout, and Fix each goes about His own business

During the last few days of the voyage the weather was pretty bad. The wind became very boisterous. Remaining in the north-west quarter, it impeded the progress of the steamer. The *Rangoon*, too unsteady already, rolled heavily, and the passengers quite lost their temper over the long, tiresome waves which the wind raised at a distance.

During the days of the 3rd and 4th of November it was a sort of tempest. The squall struck the sea with violence. The *Rangoon* had to go slowly for half a day, keeping herself in motion with only ten revolutions of the screw, so as to lean with the waves. All the sails had been reefed, and there was still too much rigging whistling in the squall.

The rapidity of the steamer, it may be imagined, was very much diminished, and it was estimated that she would arrive at Hong-Kong twenty hours behind time, and perhaps more, if the tempest did not cease.

Phileas Fogg looked intently at this spectacle of a raging sea, which seemed to struggle directly against him, with his customary impassibility. His brow did not darken an instant, and yet a delay of twenty hours might seriously interfere with his voyage, by making him miss the departure of the Yokohama steamer. But this man without nerves felt neither impatience nor annoyance. It seemed truly as if this tempest formed a part of his programme, and was foreseen. Mrs. Aouda, who talked with her companion about this mishap, found him as calm as in the past.

Fix did not look at these things in the same light. On the contrary, this tempest pleased him very much. His satisfaction would have known no bounds, if the *Rangoon* had been obliged to fly before the violent storm. All these delays suited him, for they would oblige this man Fogg to remain some days at Hong-Kong. Finally the skies with their squalls and tempests became his ally. He was a little sick, it is true, but what did that matter? He did not count his nausea, and when his body was writhing under the sea-sickness, his spirit was merry with the height of its satisfaction.

As for Passepartout, it may be guessed how ill concealed his anger was during this time of trial. Until then everything had moved on so well! Land and sea seemed to be devoted to his master. Steamers and railways obeyed him. Wind and steam combined to favour his journey. Had the hour of mistakes finally sounded? Passepartout, as if the twenty thousand pounds of the wager had to come out of his purse, was no longer happy. This tempest exasperated him, this squall put him in a rage, and he would have gladly whipped the disobedient sea! Poor fellow! Fix carefully concealed from him, his personal satisfaction, and it was well, for if Passepartout had guessed the secret delight of Fix, Fix would have been roughly used.

Passepartout remained on the *Rangoon's* deck during the entire continuance of the blow. He could not remain below; he climbed up in the masts; he astonished the crew, and helped at everything with the agility of a monkey. A hundred times he questioned the captain, the officers, the sailors, who could not help laughing at seeing him so much out of countenance. Passepartout wanted to know positively how long the storm would last. They sent him to the barometer, which would not decide to ascend. Passepartout shook the barometer, but nothing came of it, neither the shaking nor the insults that he heaped upon that irresponsible instrument.

Finally the tempest subsided. The sea became calmer on the 4th of November. The wind veered two points to the south and again became favourable.

Passepartout cleared up with the weather. The top-sails and lower sails could be unfurled, and the *Rangoon* resumed her route with marvellous swiftness.

But all the time lost could not be regained. They could only submit, and land was not signalled until the 6th at five o'clock a.m. The diary of Phileas Fogg put down the arrival of the steamer on the 5th, and she did not arrive until the 6th, which was a loss of twenty-four hours, and of course they would miss the Yokohama steamer.

At six o'clock the pilot came aboard the *Rangoon* and took his place on the bridge to guide the vessel through the channels into the port of Hong-Kong.

Passepartout was dying to ask this man whether the Yokohama steamer had left Hong-Kong. But he did not dare, preferring to preserve a little hope until the last moment. He had confided his anxiety to Fix, who—the cunning fox—tried to console him by saying that Mr. Fogg would be in time to take the next boat. This put Passepartout in a towering rage.

But if Passepartout did not venture to ask the pilot, Mr. Fogg, after consulting his *Bradshaw*, asked in his quiet manner of the said pilot if he knew when a vessel would leave Hong-Kong for Yokohama.

"To-morrow morning, at high tide," replied the pilot.

"Ah," said Mr. Fogg, without showing any astonishment.

Passepartout, who was present, would have liked to hug the pilot, whose neck Fix would have wrung with pleasure.

"What is the name of the steamer?" asked Fogg.

"The *Carnatic*," replied the pilot.

"Was she not to leave yesterday?"

"Yes, sir, but they had to repair one of her boilers, and her departure has been put off until to-morrow."

"Thank you," replied Mr. Fogg, who, with his automatic step, went down again into the saloon of the *Rangoon*.

Passepartout caught the pilot's hand, and, pressing it warmly, said:

"Pilot, you are a good fellow!"

The pilot doubtless never knew why his answers had procured him this friendly expression. A whistle blew, and he went again upon the bridge of the steamer and guided her through the flotilla of junks, tankas, fishing-boats, and vessels of all kinds which crowded the channels of Hong-Kong.

In an hour the *Rangoon* was at the wharf, and the passengers landed.

It must be confessed that in this circumstance chance had singularly served Phileas Fogg. Without the necessity of repairing the boilers, the *Carnatic* would have left on the 5th of November, and the passengers for Japan would have had to wait a week for the departure of the next steamer. Mr. Fogg, it is true, was twenty-four hours behind time, but this delay could not have any evil consequences for the rest of the journey.

In fact, the steamer which crosses the Pacific from Yokohama to San Francisco was in direct connection with the Hong-Kong steamer, and the former could not leave before the latter had arrived. Evidently they would be twenty-four hours behind time at Yokohama, but it would be easy to make them up during the voyage across the Pacific, lasting twenty-two days. Phileas Fogg found himself, then, within about twenty-four hours of the conditions of his programme thirty-five days after leaving London.

The *Carnatic* not leaving until five o'clock the next morning, Mr. Fogg had sixteen hours to attend to his business—that is, that which concerned Mrs. Aouda. On landing from the vessel, he offered his arm to the young woman and led her to a palanquin. He asked the men who carried it to point him out a hotel, and they named the Club Hotel. The palanquin started, followed by Passepartout, and twenty minutes after they arrived at their destination.

An apartment was secured for the young woman, and Phileas Fogg saw that she was made comfortable. Then he told Mrs. Aouda that he was going immediately to look for the relative in whose care he was to leave her at Hong-Kong. At the same time he ordered Passepartout to remain at the hotel until his return, so that the young woman should not be left alone.

The gentleman was shown the way to the Exchange. There, they would unquestionably know the personage, such as the honourable Jejeeh, who was reckoned among the richest merchants of the city.

The broker whom Mr. Fogg addressed did indeed know the Parsee merchant. But for two years he had not lived in China. Having made his fortune, he had gone to live in Europe—in Holland, it was believed, which was explained by the extensive correspondence which he had had with that country during his life as a merchant.

Phileas Fogg returned to the Club Hotel. He immediately asked permission to see Mrs. Aouda, and without any other preamble, told her that the honourable Jejeeh was no longer living in Hong-Kong, but probably was living in Holland.

Mrs. Aouda did not reply at first. Passing her hand over her forehead, she thought for a few moments, and then said in her sweet voice:

"What ought I to do, Mr. Fogg?"

"It is very simple," replied the gentleman. "Go on to Europe."

"But I cannot abuse—"

"You do not abuse, and your presence does not at all embarrass my programme. Passepartout!"

"Monsieur," replied Passepartout.

"Go to the *Carnatic* and engage three cabins."

Passepartout, delighted with continuing his voyage in the company of the young woman, who was very gracious to him, immediately left the Club Hotel.

Chapter 19

In which Passepartout takes a little too lively interest in his Master, and what follows

Hong-Kong is only a small island secured to England by the treaty of Nanking, after the war of 1842. In a few years, the colonising genius of Great Britain had established there an important city, and created the port Victoria. This island is situated at the mouth of the Canton River, and sixty miles only separate it from the Portuguese city of Macao, built on the other shore. Hong-Kong must necessarily vanquish Macao in a commercial struggle, and now the greatest part of the Chinese transportation is done through the English city. Docks, hospitals, wharves, warehouses, a Gothic cathedral, a Government House, macadamised streets, all would lead one to believe that one of the commercial cities of the counties of Kent or Surrey, traversing the terrestrial sphere, had found a place at this point in China nearly at its antipodes.

Passepartout, with his hands in his pockets, sauntered towards the port Victoria, looking at the palanquins, the curtained carriages still in favour in the Celestial Empire, and all the crowd of Chinese, Japanese, and Europeans hurrying along in the streets. In some things, it was like Bombay, Calcutta, or Singapore that the worthy fellow was finding again on his route. There is thus a track of English towns all around the world.

Passepartout arrived at Victoria port. There, at the mouth of Canton River, was a perfect swarm of the ships of all nations, English, French, American, Dutch, war and merchant vessels, Japanese or Chinese craft, junks, sempas, tankas, and even flower-boats, which formed so many parterres floating on the waters. Walking along, Passepartout noticed a certain number of natives dressed in yellow, all of quite advanced age. Having gone into a Chinese barber's to be shaved "à la Chinese," he learned from Figaro in the shop, who spoke pretty good English, that these ancient men were at least eighty years old, and that at this age they had the privilege of wearing yellow, the Imperial colour. Passepartout found this very funny, without knowing exactly why.

His beard shaved, he repaired to the wharf from which the *Carnatic* would leave, and there he perceived Fix walking up and down, at which he was not at all astonished. But the detective showed upon his face the marks of great disappointment.

"Good!" said Passepartout to himself; "that will be bad for the gentlemen of the Reform Club!"

And he accosted Fix with his merry smile, without seeming to notice the vexed air of his companion.

Now, the detective had good reason to fret about the infernal luck which was pursuing him. No warrant! It was evident that the warrant was running after him, and that it could reach him only if he stopped some days in this city. Now, Hong-Kong being the last British territory on the route, this Mr. Fogg would escape him finally, if he did not succeed in detaining him there.

"Well, Monsieur Fix, have you decided to come with us as far as America?" asked Passepartout.

"Yes," replied Fix between his closed teeth.

"Well then!" cried Passepartout, shouting with laughter. "I knew very well that you could not separate yourself from us. Come and engage your berth, come!"

And both entered the ticket office and engaged cabins for four persons. But the clerk told them that the repairs of the *Carnatic* being completed, the steamer would leave at eight o'clock in the evening, and not the next morning, as had been announced.

"Very good!" replied Passepartout, "that will suit my master. I am going to inform him."

At this moment Fix took an extreme step. He determined to tell Passepartout everything. It was the only means, perhaps, that he had of retaining Phileas Fogg for a few days in Hong-Kong.

Leaving the office, Fix offered to treat his companion in a tavern. Passepartout had the time. He accepted Fix's invitation.

A tavern opened on the quay. It had an inviting appearance. Both entered. It was a large room, finely decorated, at the back of which was stretched a camp-bed, furnished with cushions. Upon this bed were lying a number of sleepers.

Some thirty customers in the large room occupied small tables of plaited rushes. Some emptied pints of English beer, ale, or porter, others jugs of alcoholic liquors, gin, or brandy. Besides, the most of them were smoking long, red-clay pipes, stuffed with little balls of opium mixed with essence of rose. Then, from time to time, some smoker, overcome, would fall down under the table, and the waiters of the establishment, taking him by the head and feet, carried him on to the camp-bed, alongside of another. Twenty of these sots were thus laid side by side, in the last stage of brutishness.

Fix and Passepartout understood that they had entered a smoking-house haunted by those wretched, stupefied, lean, idiotic creatures, to whom mercantile England sells annually ten millions four hundred thousand pounds' worth of the fatal drug called opium. Sad millions are these, levied on one of the most destructive vices of human nature.

The Chinese Government has tried hard to remedy such an abuse by severe laws, but in vain. From the rich class, to whom the use of opium was at first formally reserved, it has descended to the lower classes, and its ravages can no longer be arrested. Opium is smoked everywhere and always in the Middle Empire. Men and women give themselves up to this deplorable passion, and when they are accustomed to inhaling the fumes they can no longer do without it, except by suffering terrible cramps in the stomach. A great smoker can smoke as many as eight pipes a day, but he dies in five years.

Now, it was in one of the numerous smoking-houses of this kind, which swarm even in Hong-Kong, that Fix and Passepartout had entered with the intention of refreshing themselves. Passepartout had no money, but he accepted willingly the "politeness" of his companion, ready to return it to him at the proper time and place.

They called for two bottles of port, to which the Frenchman did full justice, whilst Fix, more reserved, observed his companion with the closest attention. They talked of one thing and another, and especially of the excellent idea that Fix had of taking passage on the *Carnatic*. The bottles now being empty, Passepartout rose to inform his master that the steamer would leave several hours in advance of the time announced.

Fix detained him.

"One moment," he said.

"What do you wish, Monsieur Fix?"

"I have some serious matters to talk to you about."

"Serious matters?" cried Passepartout, emptying the few drops of wine remaining in the bottom of his glass. "Very well, we will talk about them to-morrow. I have not the time today."

"Remain," replied Fix. "It concerns your master."

Passepartout, at this phrase, looked attentively at his questioner.

The expression of Fix's face seemed singular to him. He took a seat again.

"What have you to say to me?" he asked.

Fix placed his hand upon his companion's arm, and lowering his voice, he asked him:

"You have guessed who I was."

"*Parbleu*?" said Passepartout, smiling.

"Then I am going to tell you everything."

"Now that I know everything, my friend. Ah! that's pretty tough! But go on. But first let me tell you that these gentlemen have put themselves to very useless expense."

"Useless," said Fix. "You speak confidently! It may be seen that you do not know the size of the sum!"

"But I do know it," said Passepartout. "Twenty thousand pounds!"

"Fifty-five thousand!" replied Fix, grasping the Frenchman's hand.

"What!" cried Passepartout, "Monsieur Fogg would have dared—fifty-five thousand pounds! Well, well! All the more reason that I should not lose an instant," he added, rising again.

"Fifty-five thousand pounds!" replied Fix, who forced Passepartout to sit down again, after having ordered a decanter of brandy— "and if I succeed, I get a reward of two thousand pounds. Do you wish five hundred of them on condition that you help me?"

"Help you!" cried Passepartout, whose eyes were opened very wide.

"Yes, help me to detain Mr. Fogg in Hong-Kong for a few days!"

"Phew!" said Passepartout, "what are you saying? How, not satisfied with having my master followed, with suspecting his faithfulness, do these gentlemen wish to throw new obstacles in his way. I am ashamed for them."

"Ah! what do you mean by that?" asked Fix.

"I mean that it is simple indelicacy. It is about the same as stripping Monsieur Fogg and putting his money in their pockets."

"Ah! that is the very thing we are coming to!"

"But it is a trap!" cried Passepartout—who was getting lively under the influence of the brandy with which Fix was plying him, and which he drank without noticing it—"a real trap! Gentlemen! Colleagues!"

Fix began to be puzzled.

"Colleagues!" cried Passepartout, "members of the Reform Club! You must know, Monsieur Fix, that my master is an honest man, and that, when he has made a bet, he intends to win it fairly."

"But who do you think I am?" asked Fix, fastening his look upon Passepartout.

"*Parbleu*! an agent of the members of the Reform Club with the mission to interfere with my master's journey, which is singularly humiliating. So, although it has been some time already since I guessed your business, I have taken good care not to disclose it to Monsieur Fogg."

"He knows nothing?" asked Fix quickly.

"Nothing," answered Passepartout, emptying his glass once more.

The agent passed his hand over his forehead. He hesitated before continuing the conversation. What ought he to do? The error of Passepartout seemed sincere, but it rendered his plan more difficult. It was evident that this young man was speaking with perfect good faith, and that he was not his master's accomplice—which Fix had feared.

"Well," he said to himself, "since he is not his accomplice, he will aid me."

The detective had the advantage a second time. Besides, he had no more time to wait At any cost Fogg must be arrested at Hong-Kong.

"Listen," said Fix, in an abrupt tone, "listen carefully to me. I am not what you think, that is, an agent of the members of the Reform Club—"

"Bah!" said Passepartout, looking at him in a jocose way.

"I am a police detective, charged with a mission by the Metropolitan Government."

"You—a detective!"

"Yes, and I will prove it," replied Fix. "Here is my commission."

And the agent, taking a paper from his pocket-book, showed his companion a commission signed by the Commissioner of the Central Police. Passepartout stunned, unable to articulate a word, looked at Fix.

"The bet of Mr. Fogg," continued Fix, "is only a pretext of which you are the dupes, you and his colleagues of the Reform Club, for he had an interest in assuring himself of your unconscious complicity."

"But why?" cried Passepartout.

"Listen. The 28th of September, ultimo, a robbery of fifty-five thousand pounds was committed at the Bank of England, by an individual whose description they were able to obtain. Now, look at this description, and it is feature for feature that of Mr. Fogg."

"Humbug!" cried Passepartout, striking the table with his clenched fist. "My master is the most honest man in the world!"

"How do you know?" replied Fix. "You are not even acquainted with him. You entered his service the day of his departure, and he left precipitately under a senseless pretext, without trunks, and carrying with him a large sum in banknotes! And you dare to maintain that he is an honest man?"

"Yes, yes!" repeated the poor fellow mechanically.

"Do you wish, then, to be arrested as his accomplice?"

Passepartout dropped his head in his hands. He could no longer be recognised. He did not look at the detective. Phileas Fogg, the deliverer of Aouda, the brave and generous man, a robber! And yet how many presumptions there were against him. Passepartout tried to force back the suspicions which would slip into his mind. He would never believe in his master's guilt.

"To conclude, what do you want of me?" said he to the detective by a strong effort.

"See here," replied Fix, "I have tracked Mr. Fogg to this point, but I have not yet received the warrant of arrest, for which I asked, from London. You must help me, then, to keep him in Hong-Kong—"

"I! Help you!"

"And I will share with you the reward of two thousand pounds promised by the Bank of England!"

"Never!" replied Passepartout, who wanted to rise, and fell back, feeling his reason and his strength at once escaping him.

"Monsieur Fix," he said, stammering, "even if everything you have told me should be true—if my master should be the robber whom you seek—which I deny—I have been—I am in his service—I have seen him kind and generous—betray him—never—no, not for all the gold in the world—I am from a village where they don't eat that kind of bread!"

"You refuse?"

"I refuse."

"Treat it as if I had said nothing," replied Fix, "and let's take a drink."

"All right, let's take a drink!"

Passepartout felt himself more and more overcome by intoxication. Fix, understanding that he must at all hazards separate him from his master, wanted to finish him. On the table were a few pipes filled with opium. Fix slipped one into Passepartout's hand, who took it, lifted it to his lips, lighted it, took a few puffs, and fell over, his head stupefied under the influence of the narcotic.

"At least," said Fix, seeing Passepartout out of the way, "Mr. Fogg will not be informed in time of the departure of the *Carnatic*, and if he leaves, he will be at least without this Frenchman !"

Then he left, after paying his bill.

CHAPTER 20

In which Fix comes in direct contact with Phileas Fogg

During this scene, which might perhaps seriously interfere with his future, Mr. Fogg, accompanying Mrs. Aouda, was taking a walk through the streets of the English town. Since Mrs. Aouda accepted his offer to take her to Europe, he had to think of all the details necessary for so long a journey. That an Englishman like him should make the tour of the world with a carpet-bag in his hand, might pass; but a lady could not undertake such a journey under the same conditions. Hence, the necessity of buying clothing and articles necessary for the voyage. Mr. Fogg acquitted himself of his task with the quiet characteristic of him, and he invariably replied to all the excuses and objections of the young woman, confused by so much kindness:

"It is in the interest of my journey; it is in my programme."

The purchases made, Mr. Fogg and the young woman returned to the hotel, and dined at the table d'hote which was sumptuously served. Then Mrs. Aouda, a little tired, went up into her room, after having shaken hands, English fashion, with her imperturbable deliverer.

He, Fogg, was absorbed all the evening in reading *The Times* and the *Illustrated London News*.

If he had been a man to be astonished at anything it would have been not to have seen his servant at the hour for retiring. But knowing that the Yokohama steamer was not to leave Hong-Kong before the next morning, he did not otherwise bother himself about it. The next morning Passepartout did not come at Mr. Fogg's ring.

What the honourable gentleman thought on learning that his servant had not returned to the hotel, no one could have said.

Mr. Fogg contented himself with taking his carpet-bag, calling for Mrs. Aouda, and sending for a palanquin.

It was then eight o'clock, and high tide, of which the *Carnatic* was to take advantage to go out through the passes, was put down at half-past nine.

When the palanquin arrived at the door of the hotel, Mr. Fogg and Mrs. Aouda got into the comfortable vehicle, and their baggage followed them on a wheelbarrow.

Half an hour later the travellers dismounted on the wharf, and there Mr. Fogg learned that the *Carnatic* had left the evening before.

Mr. Fogg, who counted on finding at the same time both the steamer and his servant, was compelled to do without both. But not a sign of disappointment appeared upon his face; and, when Mrs. Aouda looked at him with uneasiness, he contented himself with replying:

"It is an incident, madame, nothing more."

At this moment a person who had been watching him closely came up to him. It was the detective, Fix, who turned to him and said:

"Are you not like myself, sir, one of the passengers of the *Rangoon* who arrived yesterday"

"Yes, sir," replied Mr. Fogg coldly, "but I have not the honour—"

"Pardon me, but I thought I would find your servant here."

"Do you know where he is, sir?" asked the young woman quickly.

"What!" replied Fix, feigning surprise," is he not with you?"

"No," replied Mrs. Aouda. "He has not returned since yesterday. Has be perhaps embarked without us aboard the *Carnatic*?"

"Without you, madame?" replied Fix. "But, excuse my question, you expected then to leave by that steamer?"

"Yes, sir."

"I too, madame, and I am much disappointed. The *Carnatic*, having completed her repairs, left Hong-Kong twelve hours sooner without warning anyone, and we must now wait a week for another steamer!"

Fix felt his heart jump for joy in pronouncing these words, "a week." A week! Fogg detained a week at Hong-Kong! There would be time to receive the warrant of arrest. Chance would at last declare for the representative of the law.

It may be judged then what a stunning blow he received, when he heard Phileas Fogg say in his calm voice:

"But there are other vessels than the *Carnatic*, it seems to me, in the port of Hong-Kong."

And Mr. Fogg, offering his arm to Mrs. Aouda, turned towards the docks in search of a vessel leaving.

Fix, stupefied, followed. It might have been said that a thread attached him to this man.

However, chance seemed really to abandon him whom it had served so well up to that time. Phileas Fogg, for three hours, traversed the port in every direction, decided, if it was necessary, to charter a vessel to take him to Yokohama; but he saw only vessels loading or unloading, and which consequently could not set sail. Fix began to hope again.

But Mr. Fogg was not disconcerted, and he was going to continue his search if he had to go as far as Macao, when he was accosted by a sailor on the end of the pier.

"Your honour is looking for a boat.?" said the sailor to him taking off his hat.

"You have a boat ready to sail?" asked Mr. Fogg.

"Yes, your honour, a pilot-boat, No. 43, the best in the flotilla."

"She goes fast?"

"Between eight and nine knots an hour, nearly the latter. Will you look at her?"

"Yes."

"Your honour will be satisfied. Is it for an excursion?"

"No; for a voyage."

"A voyage?"

"You will undertake to convey me to Yokohama?"

The sailor, at these words, stood with arms extended and eyes starting from his head.

"Your honour is joking?" he said.

"No, I have missed the sailing of the *Carnatic*, and I must be at Yokohama on the 14th, at the latest, to take the steamer for San Francisco."

"I regret it," replied the pilot, abut it is impossible."

"I offer you one hundred pounds per day, and a reward of two hundred pounds if I arrive in time."

"You are in earnest?" asked the pilot.

"Very much in earnest," replied Mr. Fogg.

The pilot withdrew to one side. He looked at the sea, evidently struggling between the desire to gain an enormous sum and the fear of venturing so far. Fix was in mortal suspense.

During this time, Mr. Fogg had returned to Mrs. Aouda.

"You will not be afraid, madame?" he asked.

"With you—no; Mr. Fogg," replied the young woman.

The pilot had come toward the gentleman again, and was twisting his hat in his hands.

"Well, pilot.?" said Mr. Fogg.

"Well, your honour," replied the pilot, "I can risk neither my men, nor myself, nor yourself in so long a voyage on a boat of scarcely twenty tons at this time of the year. Besides, we would not arrive in time, for it is sixteen hundred and fifty miles from Hong-Kong to Yokohama."

"Only sixteen hundred," said Mr. Fogg.

"It is the same thing."

Fix took a good long breath.

"But," added the pilot, "there might perhaps be a means to arrange it otherwise."

Fix did not breathe any more.

"How?" asked Phileas Fogg.

"By going to Nagasaki, the southern extremity of Japan, eleven hundred miles, or only to Shanghai, eight hundred miles from Hong-Kong. In this last journey, we would not be at any distance from the Chinese coast, which would be a great advantage, all the more so that the currents run to the north."

"Pilot," replied Phileas Fogg, "I must take the American mail steamer at Yokohama, and not at Shanghai or Nagasaki."

"Why not?" replied the pilot. "The San Francisco steamer

does not start from Yokohama She stops there and at Nagasaki, but her port of departure is Shanghai."

"You are certain of what you are saying?"

"Certain."

"And when does the steamer leave Shanghai?"

"On the 11th, at seven o'clock in the evening. We have then four days before us. Four days, that is ninety-six hours, and with an average of eight knots, if we have good luck, if the wind keeps to the south-east, if the sea is calm, we can make the eight hundred miles which separate us from Shanghai."

"And you can leave—"

"In an hour, time enough to buy my provisions and hoist sail."

"It is a bargain—you are the master of the boat?"

"Yes, John Bunsby, master of the *Tankadere*."

"Do you wish some earnest money?"

"If it does not inconvenience your honour."

"Here are two hundred pounds on account—sir," added Phileas Fogg, turning toward Fix, "if you wish to take advantage—"

"Sir," answered Fix resolutely, "I was going to ask this favour of you."

"Well, in half an hour we will be on board."

"But this poor fellow—" said Mrs. Aouda, whom Passepartout's disappearance worried very much.

"I am going to do all I can to find him," replied Phileas Fogg.

And while Fix, nervous, feverish, angry, repaired to the pilot boat, the two others went to the police station at Hong-Kong. Phileas Fogg gave there Passepartout's description, and left a sufficient sum to find him. The same formality was carried out at the French consular agent's, and the palanquin having stopped at the hotel where the baggage had been taken, took the travellers back to the outer pier.

Three o'clock struck. The pilot-boat, No. 43, her crew on board, and her provisions stowed away, was ready to set sail.

She was a charming little schooner of twenty tons—this *Tankadere*—with a sharp cut-water, very graceful shape, and long water lines. She might have been called a racing yacht.

Her shining copper sheathing, her galvanised iron work, her deck white as ivory, showed that Master John Bunsby knew how to keep her in good condition. Her two masts leaned a little to the rear. She carried brigantine-foresail, storm jib, and standing jib, and could rig up splendidly for a rear wind. She ought to sail wonderfully well, and in fact she had won several prizes in pilot-boat matches.

The crew of the *Tankadere* were composed of the master, John Bunsby, and four men. They were of that class of hardy sailors who, in all weathers, ventured out in search of vessels, and are thoroughly acquainted with these seasons.John Bunsby, a man about forty-five years, vigorous, well sunburnt, of a lively expression, of an energetic face, self-reliant, well posted in his business, would have inspired confidence in the most timorous.

Phileas Fogg and Mrs. Aouda went on board. Fix was already there. They went down by steps in the rear of the schooner into a square cabin, whose walls bulged out in the form of cots, above a circular divan. In the middle there was a table lighted by a hanging lamp. It was small, but neat.

"I regret having nothing better to offer you," said Mr. Fogg to Fix, who bowed without replying.

The detective felt somewhat humiliated by thus taking advantage of Mr. Fogg's kindnesses.

"Surely," he thought, "he is a very polite rogue, but he is a rogue!"

At ten minutes after three the sails were hoisted. The English flag was flying at the gaff of the schooner. The passengers were seated on deck. Mr. Fogg and Mrs. Aouda cast a last look at the wharf, in hopes of seeing Passepartout.

Fix was not without apprehension, for chance might have brought to this place the unfortunate young man whom he had treated with such indignity, and then an explanation would have taken place, from which the detective would not have got out to advantage. But the Frenchman did not show himself, and doubtless the stupefying narcotic still held him under its influence.

Finally, Master John Bunsby gave the order to start, and the *Tankadere*, taking the wind under her brigantine-foresail and standing jib, flew out in the sea bounding.

CHAPTER 21

In which the Master of the "Tankadere" runs great risk of losing a Reward of Two Hundred Pounds

This voyage of eight hundred miles, undertaken in a craft of twenty tons, and especially in that season of the year, was venturesome. The Chinese seas are generally rough, exposed to terrible blows, principally during the equinoxes, and this was in the first days of November.

It would have very evidently been to the advantage of the pilot to take his passengers so far as Yokohama, as he was paid so much per day. But it would have been great imprudence on his part to attempt such a voyage under such conditions, and it was a bold act, if not a rash one, to go as far as Shanghai. But John Bunsby had confidence in his *Tankadere,* which rode the waves he a gull, and perhaps he was not wrong.

During the latter hours of this day the *Tankadere* sailed through the capricious channels of Hong-Kong, and, in all her movements, from whatever quarter the wind came, she behaved handsomely.

"I do not need, pilot," said Phileas Fogg, the moment the schooner touched the open sea, "to recommend to you all possible diligence."

"Your honour may depend upon me," replied John Bunsby. "In the matter of sails, we are carrying all that the wind will allow us to carry. Our poles would add nothing, and would only interfere with the sailing of our craft."

"It is your trade, and not mine, pilot, and I trust to you."

Phileas Fogg, his body erect and legs wide apart, standing straight as a sailor, looked at the surging sea without staggering. The young woman seated aft, felt quite affected looking at the ocean, already darkened by the twilight, which she was braving upon so frail a craft. Above her head were unfurled the white sails, looking in space like immense wings. The schooner, impelled by the wind, seemed to fly through the air.

Night set in. The moon was entering her first quarter, and her scanty light was soon extinguished in the haze of the horizon. Clouds were rising from the east, and already covered a portion of the heavens.

The pilot had put his lights in position—an indispensable precaution to take in these seas, so much frequented by vessels bound landward. Collisions were not rare, and at the rate she was going, the schooner would be shattered by the least shock.

Fix was dreaming forward on the vessel. He kept himself apart, knowing Fogg naturally to be not much of a talker. Besides, he hated to speak to this man, whose accommodations he had accepted. He was thinking thus of the future. It appeared certain to him that Mr. Fogg would not stop at Yokohama, that he would immediately take the San Francisco steamer to reach America, whose vast extent would assure him impunity with security. It seemed to him that Phileas Fogg's plan could not be simpler.

Instead of embarking in England for the United States, like a common rogue, this Fogg had made the grand rounds, and traversed three-quarters of the globe, in order to gain more surely the American continent, where he would quietly consume the large sum stolen from the bank, after having thrown the police off his track. But, once upon the soil of the United States, what would Fix do? Abandon this man? No, a hundred times no! And until he had obtained an extradition order he would not leave him for an instant. It was his duty, and he would fulfil it to the end. In any event, one happy result had been obtained. Passepartout was no longer with his master; and, especially after the confidence Fix had reposed in him, it was important that the master and servant should never see each other again.

Phileas Fogg was constantly thinking of his servant, who had disappeared so singularly. After having thought over everything, it seemed not impossible to him that, in consequence of a misunderstanding, the poor fellow had set sail upon the *Carnatic* at the last moment. It was the opinion of Mrs. Aouda also, who regretted very much this good servant, to whom she owed so much. It might be that they would find him again at Yokohama, and if the *Carnatic* had taken him thither, it would be easy to find it out.

Towards ten o'clock the breeze began to freshen. Perhaps it would have been prudent to take in a reef, but the pilot, having carefully examined the state of the heavens, left the rigging as it was. Besides the *Tankadere* carried sail admirably, having a deep draft of water, and everything was prepared to go rapidly, in case of a gale.

At midnight Phileas Fogg and Mrs. Aouda descended into the cabin. Fix had preceded them, and was stretched on one of the cots. As for the pilot and his men, they remained on deck all night.

The next day, the 8th of November, at sunrise, the schooner had made more than one hundred miles. Her course, frequently checked, showed that her average speed was between eight and nine knots. The *Tankadere* carried full sail, and in this rig she obtained the maximum of speed. If the wind kept the same, the chances were in her favour.

The *Tankadere,* during the whole day, did not go far from the coast, whose currents were favourable to her, and which was five miles off at the most from her starboard quarter, and irregularly outlined appeared sometimes across the clearings. The wind coming from the land was, on that account, not quite so strong, a fortunate circumstance for the schooner, for vessels of a small tonnage suffer above all from the roll of the sea which interferes with their speed, "killing" them, to use the sailors' expression.

Towards noon the breeze abated a little and set in from the south-east. The pilot put up his poles; but at the end of two hours it was necessary to take them down, as the wind freshened up again.

Mr. Fogg and the young woman, very fortunately unaffected by sea-sickness, ate with a good appetite the preserves and the ship biscuit. Fix was invited to share their repast, and was compelled to accept, knowing very well that it is as necessary to ballast stomachs as vessels, but it vexed him! To travel at this man's expense, to be fed from his provisions, was rather against his grain. He ate, daintily, it is true, but finally he ate.

However, this repast finished, he took Mr. Fogg aside and said to him:

"Sir—"

This "sir" scorched his lips, and he controlled himself so as not to collar this "gentleman!"

"Sir, you have been very kind to offer me a passage on your vessel. But, although my resources do not permit me to expend as freely as you, I intend to pay my share—"

"Let us not speak of that, sir," replied Mr. Fogg.

"But, if I insist—"

"No, sir," repeated Fogg, in a tone which did not admit of reply. "That will enter into the general expenses."

Fix bowed; he had a stifling feeling, and going forward, he lay down, and did not say a word more during the day.

In the meantime they were moving on rapidly.John Bunsby had high hopes. He said to Mr. Fogg several times that they would arrive at Shanghai at the desired time. Mr. Fogg simply replied that he counted on it. The whole crew went to work in earnest. The reward enticed these good people. So there was not a sheet which was not conscientiously tightened! Not a sail which was not vigorously hoisted! Not a lurch for which the man at the helm could be blamed! They would not have manoeuvred more vigorously in a regatta of the Royal Yacht Club.

In the evening, the pilot marked on the log a distance of two hundred and twenty miles from Hong-Kong, and Phileas Fogg might hope that on arriving at Yokohama he would not have to note any delay in his journal. Thus, the first serious mischance that he had suffered since his departure from London would probably not affect his journey worth mentioning.

During the night, towards the early morning hours, the *Tankadere* entered, without difficulty the Straits of Fo Kien, which separate the large Island of Formosa from the Chinese coast, and she crossed the Tropic of Cancer. The sea was very rough in these straits, full of eddies formed by counter-currents. The schooner laboured heavily. The short waves broke her course. It became very difficult to stand up on the deck.

With daybreak the wind became fresher. There was the appearance of a squall in the heavens. Besides, the barometer announced a speedy change of the atmosphere; its daily movement was irregular, and the mercury oscillated capriciously. The sea was seen rising towards the south-east in long swells betokening a tempest. The evening before the sun had set in a red haze, amid the phosphorescent scintillations of the ocean.

The pilot examined the threatening aspect of the sky for a long time, and muttered between his teeth indistinctly. At a certain moment, finding himself near his passenger, he said in a low voice:

"Can I speak freely to your honour?"

"You can," replied Phileas Fogg.

"Well, we are going to have a squall."

"Will it come from the north or the south?" asked Mr. Fogg simply-

"From the south. See. A typhoon is coming up."

"Good for the typhoon from the south, since it will send us in the right direction," replied Mr. Fogg.

"If you take it so," replied the pilot, "I have nothing more to say."

John Bunsby's presentiments did not deceive him. At a less advanced season of the year, the typhoon, according to the expression of a celebrated meteorologist, would have passed off like a luminous cascade of electric flames, but in the winter equinox it was to be feared that it would burst with violence.

The pilot took his precautions in advance. He had all the schooner's sails reefed, and the yards brought on deck. The polemasts were dispensed with. All hands went forward. The hatches were carefully fastened. Not a drop of water could then enter the hull of the vessel. A single triangular sail, a foresail of strong canvas, was hoisted as a storm-jib, so as to hold the schooner to the wind behind. And they waited.

John Bunsby had begged his passengers to go down into the cabin; but in the narrow space, almost deprived of air, and knocked about by the waves, this imprisonment had in it nothing agreeable. Neither Mr. Fogg, nor Mrs. Aouda, nor even Fix was contented to leave the deck.

Towards eight o'clock the storm of rain and wind struck the deck. With nothing but her little bit of sail, the *Tankadere* was raised like a feather by the wind, the violence of which could not well be described in words. Compare her speed to quadruple that of a locomotive rushing along under full head of steam, and it would still be below the truth.

During the whole day the vessel ran on thus towards the north, carried by the tremendous waves, preserving, fortunately, a rapidity equal to theirs. Twenty times she was almost submerged by these mountains of water which rose upon her from the rear, but an adroit turn of the helm by the pilot warded off the catastrophe. The passengers were sometimes covered over by the showers of spray, which they received philosophically. Fix did not like it, doubtless, but the intrepid Aouda, with her eyes fixed upon her companion, whose coolness she could only admire, showed herself worthy of him, and braved the storm at his side. As for Phileas Fogg, it seemed as if this typhoon formed a part of his programme.

Up to this time the *Tankadere* had always held her course towards the north: but, towards evening, as might have been feared, the wind, shifting three-quarters, blew from the northwest. The schooner, now having her side to the waves, was terribly shaken. The sea struck her with a violence well calculated to terrify anyone who does not know how solidly every part of a vessel is fastened together.

With nightfall the tempest grew wilder. Seeing darkness come on, and with it the increase of the storm, John Bunsby felt great uneasiness. He asked himself if it would not be time to put in somewhere, and he consulted his crew.

His men consulted, John Bunsby approached Mr. Fogg, and said to him:

"I believe, your honour, that we would do well to make one of the ports of the coast."

"I believe so, also," replied Phileas Fogg.

"Ah!" said the pilot, "but which one?"

"I only know one," replied Mr. Fogg quietly.

"And that is—?"

"Shanghai!"

The pilot could not at first comprehend for a few moments what this answer meant; how much obstinacy and tenacity it comprised. Then he cried:

"Ah well, yes! your honour is right. On to Shanghai!"

And the direction of the *Tankadere* was unwaveringly kept to the north.

It was truly a terrible night! It was a miracle that the little craft did not capsize. Twice she was submerged, and everything would have been carried off the deck, if the fastening of the ropes had given way. Mrs. Aouda was worn out, but she did not utter a complaint. More than once Mr. Fogg had to rush towards her to protect her from the violence of the waves.

Daylight reappeared. The tempest was still raging with the greatest fury. However, the wind fell again into the south-east. It was a favourable change, and the *Tankadere* resumed her way on this high sea, whose waves then struck those produced by the new direction of the wind. Thence a shock of counter-rolling waves, which would have crushed a less solidly-built barque.

From time to time through the broken mist the coast could be perceived, but not a ship in sight. The *Tankadere* was the only one keeping the sea.

At noon there were some signs of a calm, which, with the sinking of the sun towards the horizon, were more distinct.

The short duration of the tempest was owing to its very violence. The passengers, completely worn out, could eat a little and take some rest.

The night was comparatively quiet. The pilot had the sails again hoisted at a low reef. The speed of the vessel was considerable. The next day, the 11th, at daydawn, the coast being sighted,John Bunsby was able to assert that they were not one hundred miles from Shanghai.

One hundred miles, and only this day left to make the

distance! That very evening Mr. Fogg ought to arrive at Shanghai, if he did not wish to miss the departure of the Yokohama steamer. Without this storm, during which he lost several hours, he would not, at this moment, have been thirty miles from port.

The breeze sensibly slackened, but fortunately the sea fell with it. The schooner was covered with canvas. Poles, staysails, counter-jibs, all were carried, and the sea foamed under her keel.

At noon, the *Tankadere* was not more than forty-five miles from Shanghai. She had six hours more to make that port before the departure of the steamer for Yokohama.

The fears of all were great; they wanted to arrive at any cost. All felt their hearts impatiently beating—Phileas Fogg doubtless excepted. The little schooner must keep up an average of nine knots, and the wind was constantly going down! It was an irregular breeze, with capricious puffs coming from the coast. They passed, and the sea became more smooth immediately after.

But the vessel was so light, and her high sails, of a fine material, caught the capricious breeze so well that, with the current in their favour, at six o'clock John Bunsby counted only ten miles to Shanghai River, for the city itself is situated at a distance of twelve miles at least above the mouth.

At seven o'clock they were still three miles from Shanghai. A formidable oath escaped from the pilot's lips. It was evident that the reward of two hundred pounds was going to slip from him. He looked at Mr. Fogg. Mr. Fogg was impassible, and yet his whole fortune was at stake at this moment.

At this moment, too, a long, black funnel, crowned with a wreath of smoke, appeared on the edge of the water. It was the American steamer going at the regular hour.

"Maledictions on her!" cried John Bunsby, who pushed back the rudder desperately.

"Signal her!" said Phileas Fogg simply.

A small brass cannon stood on the forward deck of the *Tankadere*. It served to make signals in hazy weather.

The cannon was loaded to the muzzle, but at the moment

that the pilot was going to apply a red-hot coal to the touch-hole, Mr. Fogg said:

"Hoist your flag."

The flag was hoisted half-mast. It was a signal of distress, and it was to be hoped that the American steamer, perceiving it, would change her course for a moment to assist the little craft.

"Fire!" said Mr. Fogg.

And the booming of the little cannon sounded through the air.

Chapter 22

In which Passepartout sees very well that, even at the Antipodes, it is Prudent to have some Money in One's pocket

The *Carnatic* having left Hong-Kong on the 6th of November, at half-past six p.m., turned under full head of steam towards the Japanese shores. She carried a full load of freight and passengers. Two cabins aft were unoccupied. They were the ones retained for Mr. Phileas Fogg.

The next morning the men in the forward part of the vessel saw, not without some surprise, a passenger, with half-stupefied eyes and disordered head, coming out of the second cabin, and with tottering steps taking a seat on deck.

This passenger was Passepartout himself. This is what happened:

Some minutes after Fix left the smoking-house two waiters raised Passepartout, who was in a deep sleep, and laid him on the bed reserved for the smokers. But, three hours later,

Passepartout, pursued even in his bad dreams by a fixed idea, woke again and struggled against the stupefing action of the narcotic. The thought of unaccomplished duty shook off his torpor. He left this drunkard's bed, reeling, supporting himself by the wall, falling and rising, but always and irresistibly urged on by a sort of instinct. He finally went out of the smoking-house, crying in a dream, "the *Carnatic!* the *Carnatic!*"

The steamer was there, steam up, ready to leave. Passepartout had only a few steps to go. He rushed upon the plank, crossed it, and fell unconscious on the forward deck at the moment that the *Carnatic* was slipping her moorings.

Some of the sailors, as men accustomed to these kind of scenes, took the poor fellow down into a second cabin, and Passepartout only waked the next morning, one hundred and fifty miles from the Chinese coast.

This is then why Passepartout found himself this morning on the *Carnatic's* deck, taking full draughts of the fresh sea-breezes. The pure air sobered him. He commenced to collect his idea, but he did not succeed without difficulty. But, finally, he recalled the scenes of the day before, the confidences of Fix, the smoking-house, etc.

"It is evident," he said to himself, "that I have been abominably drunk! What will Mr. Fogg say. In any event I have not missed the steamer, and this is the principal thing."

Then, thinking of Fix, he said to himself:

"As for him, I hope we are now rid of him, and that he has not dared, after what he proposed to me, to follow us on the *Carnatic.* A police detective on my master's heels, accused of the robbery committed upon the Bank of England! Pshaw! Mr. Fogg is as much a robber as I am a murderer!"

Ought Passepartout to tell these things to his master? Would it be proper to inform him of the part played by Fix in this affair? Would it not be better to wait until his return to London, to tell him that an agent of the Metropolitan police had followed him, and then have a laugh with him? Yes, doubtless. In any event, it was a matter to be looked into. The most pressing thing was to rejoin Mr. Fogg and beg him to pardon him for his inexcusable conduct.

Passepartout then rose. The sea was rough, and the ship rolled heavily. The worthy fellow—his legs not very steady yet—reached as well as he could the after-deck of the ship.

He saw no one on the deck that resembled either his master or Mrs. Aouda.

"Good," said he, "Mrs. Aouda is still abed at this hour. As for Mr. Fogg, he has probably found some whist-player, and according to his habit—"

So saying, Passepartout descended to the saloon. Mr. Fogg was not there. Passepartout had but one thing to do; to ask the purser which cabin Mr. Fogg occupied. The purser replied that he did not know any passenger of that name.

"Pardon me," said Passepartout, persisting. "The gentleman in question is tall, cold, non-communicative, accompanied by a young lady—"

"We have no young lady on board," replied the purser. "To convince you, here is the list of passengers. You can examine it n Passepartout looked over the list. His master's name did not appear. He felt bewildered. Then an idea struck him.

"Ah! but see! I am on the *Carnatic*?" he cried.

"Yes," replied the purser.

"*En route* for Yokohama?"

"Exactly so."

Passepartout had for a moment feared that he had mistaken the vessel! But though he was on the *Carnatic*, he was certain that his master was not there.

Passepartout dropped into an armchair. It was a thunderstroke for him. And suddenly there was a gleam of light. He recollected that the hour of departure for the *Carnatic* had been anticipated, that he was to notify his master, and that he had not done it! It was his fault, then, if Mr. Fogg and Mrs. Aouda had missed this steamer!

His fault, yes, but still more that of the traitor who, to separate him from his master, to keep the latter in Hong-Kong, had made him drunk! For at last he understood the detective's manoeuvre. And now Mr. Fogg, surely ruined, his bet lost, arrested, perhaps imprisoned! Passepartout at this thought tore his hair. Ah! if Fix ever fell into his hands, what a settlement of accounts there would be!

Finally, after the first moment of bewilderment, Passepartout recovered his coolness and studied the situation. It was not enviable. The Frenchman was on the road to Japan. Certain of arriving there, how was he to get away? His pocket was empty. Not a shilling, not a penny in it! However, his passage and meals on board were paid in advance. He had then five or six days to come to a decision. It could not be described how he ate and drank during the voyage. He ate for his master, for Mrs. Aouda, and for himself. He ate as if Japan, where he was going to land, was a desert country, bare of every eatable substance.

At high tide on the morning of the 13th, the *Carnatic* entered the port of Yokohama.

This place is an important stopping point in the Pacific, where all the mail and passenger steamers between North America, China, Japan, and the Malay Islands put in. Yokohama is situated on the bay of Jeddo, at a short distance from that immense city, the second capital of the Japanese Empire, formerly the residence of the Tycoon, at the time that civil emperor existed, and the rival of Miako, the large city in which the Mikado, the ecclesiastical emperor, the descendant of the gods, lives.

The *Carnatic* came alongside the wharf at Yokohama near the jetties of the port and the Custom House, in the midst of the numerous vessels belonging to all nations.

Passepartout set foot, without any enthusiasm, on this so curious soil of the Sons of the Sun. He had nothing better to do than to take chance for his guide, and to go at a venture through the streets of the city.

Passepartout found himself at first in an absolutely European city, with its low front houses, ornamented with verandas, under which showed elegant peristyles, and which covered with its streets, its squares, its docks, its warehouses, the entire space comprised between "Treaty Promontory" and the river. There, as at Hong-Kong, and as at Calcutta, there was a confused swarm of people of all races, Americans, English,

Chinese, Dutch, merchants ready to sell everything and to buy everything, in the midst of whom the Frenchman found himself as strange as if he had been cast into the Hottentot country.

Passepartout had, it is true, one resource; it was to make himself known at the French or English consular agents established at Yokohama; but he hated to tell his story, so intimately connected with that of his master, and before coming to that, he wished to exhaust all other chances.

Then, having gone through the European quarter of the city without chance having served him in anything, he entered the Japanese quarter, decided, if it was necessary, to push on to Jeddo.

This native portion of Yokohama is called Benten, from the name of the goddess of the sea, worshipped in the neighbouring islands. There were to be seen splendid avenues of firs and cedars; the sacred gates of a strange architecture; bridges half-hid in the midst of bamboos and reeds; temples sheltered under the immense and melancholy shade of aged cedars, retreats in the depths of which vegetated the priest of Buddhism and the sectaries of the religion of Confucius; interminable streets in which could have been gathered a whole crop of children, rose-tinted and red-cheeked, good little people that might have been cut out of some native screen, and which were playing in the midst of short-legged poodles, and yellowish, tailless cats, very indolent, and very affectionate.

In the streets there was a constant swarm, going and coming incessantly; priests passing in procession, beating their monotonous tambourines; patrolmen, Custom House or police officers, with pointed hats encrusted with lace, and carrying two sabres in their belts; soldiers dressed in blue cottonade, with white stripes, and armed with percussion muskets; guards of the Mikado, enveloped in their silken doublets, with hauberk and coat-of-mail, and a number of other military men of all ranks—for in Japan the profession of a soldier is as much esteemed as it is despised in China. Then, mendicant friars, pilgrims in long robes, simple civilians, with their glossy and jet-black hair, large heads, long bust, slender legs, short stature, and complexions from the dark shades of copper to dead white, but never yellow like that of the Chinese, from whom the Japanese differ essentially. Finally, between the carriages, the palanquins, the horses, the porters, the curtained wheelbarrows, the "norimons" with lace-covered sides, and the substantial "cangos," genuine bamboo litters, were seen moving some homely women, with tightly-drawn eyes, sunken chests, and teeth blackened according to the fashion of the time, taking short steps with their little feet, upon which were canvas shoes, straw sandals, or clogs of worked wood. They also wore with elegance the national garment, the "kiri mon," a sort of dressing-gown, crossed with a silk scarf, whose broad girdle expanded behind into an extravagant knot, which the modern Parisian ladies seem to have borrowed from the Japanese.

Passepartout walked for some hours in the midst of this checkered crowd, looking at the curious and rich shops; the bazaars, where are heaped up all the display of Japanese jewellery; the restaurants, adorned with streamers and banners, into which he was interdicted from entering; and those tea-houses in which are drank full cups of the warm, fragrant tea, with "saki"—a liquor extracted from fermented rice—and those comfortable smoking-houses, where very fine tobacco is smoked, and not opium, whose use is almost unknown in Japan.

Then Passepartout found himself in the fields, in the midst of immense rice fields. There were expanding, with flowers which threw out their last perfumes, dazzling camelias, not borne upon shrubs, but upon trees; and in the bamboo enclosures, cherry, plum, and apple trees, which the natives cultivate rather for their blossoms than for their fruit, and which grinning scarecrows protect from the peak of the sparrows, the pigeons, the crows, and other voracious birds. There was not a majestic cedar which did not shelter some large eagle; not a weeping willow which did not cover with its foliage some heron, sadly perched on one foot; while, finally, in all directions there were rooks, ducks, hawks, wild geese, and a large number of those cranes which the Japanese treat as "lords," and which symbolise for them long life and good fortune.

Wandering thus, Passepartout saw some violets among the grass, and said: "food! there is my supper."

But having smelt them, he found no odour in them.

The good fellow had certainly had the foresight to breakfast as heartily as possible before he left the *Carnatic;* but after walking around for a day he felt that his stomach was very empty. He had noticed that sheep, goats, or pigs were entirely wanting at the stalls of the native butchers; and as he knew that it is a sacrilege to kill beeves, kept only for the needs of agriculture, he concluded that meat was scarce in Japan. He was not mistaken; but in default of butcher's meat, his stomach would have accommodated itself well to quarters of deer or wild boar, some partridges or quails, some poultry or fish, with which the Japanese feed themselves almost exclusively, with the product of the rice fields. But he had to put a brave heart against ill luck, and postponed to the next day the care of providing for his nourishment.

Night came on. Passepartout returned to the native quarter, and wandered in the streets in the midst of the many-coloured lanterns, looking at the groups of dancers, executing their feats of agility, and the astrologers in the open air gathering the crowd around their telescopes. Then he saw again the harbour, relieved by the fires of the fishermen who were catching fish by the light of their torches.

Finally, the streets became empty. To the crowd succeeded the rounds of the patrolmen. These officers, in their magnificent costumes and in the midst of their suite, resembled ambassadors, and Passepartout repeated pleasantly, each time that he met some dazzling patrol:

"Good, good! Another Japanese embassy starting for Europe!"

Chapter 23

In which Passepartout's nose is lengthened enormously

The next day Passepartout, tired out and hungry, said to himself that he must eat at any cost, and the sooner the better. He had this resource, to sell his watch, but he would rather die of hunger. Now was the time, or never, for this good fellow to utilise the strong, if not melodious voice, with which nature had favoured him.

He knew a few French and English airs, and he determined to try them. The Japanese ought certainly to be lovers of music, since everything with them was done to the sound of the cymbals, the tom-tom, and drums, and they could not but appreciate the talents of a European amateur.

But, perhaps, he was a little early to organise a concert, and the dilettanti, unexpectedly wakened, would, perhaps, not have paid the singer in money with the Mikado's likeness.

Passepartout decided, then, to wait a few hours; but in sauntering along the thought came to him that he would look too well dressed for a wandering artist, and the idea struck him to exchange his clothing for A suit more in harmony with his position. This exchange would besides produce a sum which he could immediately apply to satisfying his appetite.

This resolution taken, it only remained to execute it. It was only after a long search that Passepartout found a native clothes dealer, to whom he told his want. The European garments pleased the man, and soon Passepartout came out wrapped in an old Japanese robe, and on his head a sort of one-sided turban, discoloured by the action of the weather. But in return, a few small pieces of money jingled in his pocket.

"Good," he thought. "I will fancy that we are in the carnival!"

Passepartout's first care, thus, "Japanesed," was to enter a teahouse of modest appearance, and there, with some remains of poultry and a few handfuls of rice, he breakfasted like a man for whom dinner would be still a problem to be solved. "Now," he said to himself, when he had taken hearty refreshment, "the question is not to lose my head. I have no longer the resource of selling this garment for another still more Japanese. I must then consider the means of getting away as promptly as possible from this country of the Sun, of which I will preserve but a sorry recollection."

Passepartout then thought of visiting the steamers about to set sail for America. He counted on offering himself in the capacity of cook or servant, asking only his passage and his meals as his entire compensation. Once at San Francisco, he would see how he would get out of his scrape. The important thing was to traverse these four thousand seven hundred miles of the Pacific stretching between Japan and the New World.

Passepartout, not being a man to let an idea languish, turned towards the port of Yokohama. But as he approached the docks, his plans, which had appeared so simple to him at the moment when he had the idea, seemed more and more difficult of execution. Why should they need a cook or servant aboard an American steamer, and what confidence would he inspire, muffled up in this manner? What recommendations would be of any service? What references could he give?

As he was thus reflecting, his eyes fell upon an immense placard which a sort of clown was carrying through the streets of Yokohama. This programme was thus worded in English:

ACROBATIC JAPANESE TROUPE
OF THE
HONOURABLE WILLIAM BATULCAR.
LAST REPRESENTATIONS,
BEFORE THEIR DEPARTURE FOR THE
UNITED STATES OF AMERICA,
OF THE
LONG NOSES! LONG NOSES!
UNDER THE DIRECT PROTECTION OF THE
GOD TINGOU!
GREAT ATTRACTION!

"The United States of America," cried Passepartout, "that's just what I want!"

He followed the man with his placard, and thus soon he reentered the Japanese quarters. A quarter of an hour later, he stopped before a large house surrounded by clusters of streamers, and whose exterior walls represented, without perspective, but in violent colours, a whole company of jugglers.

It was the Honorable Batulcar's establishment, who was a sort of American Barnum, director of a troupe of montebanks, jugglers, clowns, acrobats, equilibrists, gymnasts, which, according to the placard, was giving its last performance before leaving the empire of the Sun for the States of the Union.

Passepartout entered under the porch in front of the house, and asked for Mr. Batulcar. He appeared in person.

"What do you wish?" he said to Passepartout, taking him at first for a native.

"Do you need a servant?" asked Passepartout.

"A servant," cried the Barnum, stroking his thick grey beard hanging heavily under his chin. "I have two, obedient and faithful, who have never left me, and who serve me for nothing, on condition that I feed them. And here they are," he added, showing his two robust arms, furrowed with veins as large as the strings of a bass viol.

"So I can be of no good to you?"

"None."

"The devil! It would have suited me so well to leave with you."

"Ah, I see!" said the Honourable Batulcar. "You are as much a Japanese as I am a monkey! Why are your dressed in this way?"

"One dresses as one can."

"Very true. You are a Frenchman.?"

"Yes, a Parisian from Paris."

"Then you ought to know how to make grimaces?"

"Indeed," replied Passepartout, vexed at seeing his nationality call forth this question, "we Frenchmen know how to make grimaces, it is true, but not better than the Americans."

"Just so. Well, if I do not take you as a servant I can take you as a clown. You understand, my good fellow. In France they exhibit foreign clowns, and abroad, French clowns."

"Ah!"

"You are strong, are you not?"

"Particularly when I have been at the table."

"And you know how to sing?"

"Yes," replied Passepartout, who had formerly taken part in street concerts.

"But do you know how to sing on your head, with a top spinning on the sole of your left foot, and a sabre balanced on the sole of your right?"

"*Parbleu*?"replied Passepartout, who recalled the first exercises of his youth.

"Then, you see, all is right!" replied the Honourable Batulcar.

The engagement was concluded there and then.

At last Passepartout had found a position. He was engaged to do everything in the celebrated Japanese troupe. It was not very flattering, but within a week he would be on his way to San Francisco.

The performance, so noisily announced by the Honourable Batulcar, was to commence at three o'clock, and soon the formidable instruments of a Japanese orchestra, drums and tam-tams, sounded at the door. We understand very well that Passepartout could not have studied a part, but he was to give the support of his solid shoulders in the grand feat of the "human pyramid," executed by the-Long Noses of the god Tingou. This great attraction of the performance was to close the series.

Before three o'clock the spectators had crowded the large building. Europeans and natives, Chinese and Japanese, men, woman, and children, rushed upon the narrow benches and into the boxes opposite the stage. The musicians had entered, and the full orchestra, with gongs, tam-tams, bones, flutes, tambourines, and large drums went to work furiously.

The performance was what all these acrobatic exhibitions are. But it must be confessed that the Japanese are the best equilibrists in the world. One, with his fan and small bits of paper, executed the graceful trick of the butterflies and flowers. Another, with the odorous smoke of his pipe, traced rapidly in the air a series of bluish words, which formed a compliment addressed to the audience. The latter juggled with lit candles, which he blew out in succession as they passed before his lips, and which he lit again, one after the other, without interrupting for a single moment his wonderful jugglery. The former produced, by means of spinning-tops, the most improbable combinations. Under his hand these humming machines seemed to be gifted with a life of their own in their interminable whirling; they ran over pipe stems, over the edges of sabres, over wires as thin as hair, stretched from one side of the stage to the other; they went round large glass vases, they went up and down bamboo ladders, and scattered into all the corners, and produced harmonic effects of a strange character by combining their various tones. The jugglers tossed them up, and they turned in the air; they threw them like shuttlecocks with wooden battledores, and they kept on turning; they thrust them into their pockets, and when they brought them out they were still spinning—until the moment when a relaxed spring made them bud out into a Chinese tree!

It is useless to describe here the wonderful feats of the acrobats and gymnasts of the troupe. The turning on ladders, poles, balls barrels, etc., was executed with remarkable precision. But the principal attraction of the performance was the exhibition of the Long Noses, astonishing equilibrists, with whom Europe is not yet acquainted.

These Long Noses form a special company placed under the direct patronage of the god Tingou. Dressed like heroes of the Middle Ages, they bore a splendid pair of wings on their shoulders. But what distinguished them more particularly was a long nose with which their faces were ornamented, and, above all, the use they made of them. These noses were nothing less than bamboos, five, six, ten feet long; some straight, others curved; the latter smooth, the former with warts on them. It was on these appendages, fastened firmly, that all their balancing feats were performed. A dozen of these sectaries of the god Tingou lay upon their backs, and their comrades came, dressed like lightning rods, to make sport on their noses, jumping, leaping from one to the other, executing the most incredible somersaults.

To close, they had specially announced to the public the "human pyramid," in which fifty Long Noses were to represent,the Car of Juggernaut. But instead of forming this pyramid by taking their shoulders for a point of support, the artists of the Honourable Batulcar made it with their noses. Now, the one of them who usually formed the base of the car had left the troupe, and as all that was necessary was to be strong and agile, Passepartout was chosen to take his place.

The good fellow felt quite melancholy, when—sad recollection of his youth—he had put on this costume of the Middle Ages, adorned with parti-coloured wings, and when a nose six feet long had been put on his face. But this nose was to earn his bread for him, and he took his part.

Passepartout went upon the stage and took his place with those of his colleagues who were to form the base of the Car of Juggernaut. All stretched themselves on the floor, their noses turned towards the ceiling. A second section of equilibrists placed themselves upon these long appendages, a third formed a story above, then a fourth, and on these noses which only touched at the point, a human monument soon rose to the height of the cornices of the theatre.

Now, the applause was redoubled, and the instruments in the orchestra crashed like so much thunder, when the pyramid shook, the equilibrium was broken, one of the noses of the base was missing, and the monument fell like a house of cards.

It was Passepartout's fault, who, leaving his post, clearing the footlights, without the aid of his wings, and climbing up to the right-hand gallery, fell at the feet of a spectator, crying:

"Ah! my master! my master!"

"You here?"

"Myself!"

"Well, then, in that case, to the steamer, young man!"

Mr. Fogg, Mrs. Aouda, who accompanied him, and Passepartout rushed through the lobbies to the outside of the building. But there they found the Honourable Batulcar, furious, claiming damages for the "breakage." Phileas Fogg appeased his anger by throwing him a handful of bank-notes. Mr. Fogg and Mrs. Aouda set foot on the American steamer, followed by Passepartout with his wings on his back, and on his face the nose six feet long which he had not yet been able to tear off!

CHAPTER 24

During which is Accomplished the Voyage across the Pacific Ocean

What had happened in sight of Shanghai is understood. The signals made by the *Tankadere* had been observed by the Yokohama steamer. The captain, seeing a flag at halfmast, had turned his vessel towards the little schooner. A few minutes after, Phileas Fogg, paying for his passage at the price agreed upon, put in the pocket of John Bunsby, master, five hundred and fifty pounds. Then the honourable gentleman, Mrs. Aouda, and Fix ascended to the deck of the steamer, which immediately took its course for Nagasaki and Yokohama

Having arrived on the morning of the 14th of November, on time, Phileas Fogg, letting Fix go about his business, had gone aboard the *Carnatic*, and there he learned, to the great joy of Mrs. Aouda—and perhaps to his own, but he did not let it appear— that the Frenchman, Passepartout, had really arrived the day before at Yokohama.

Phileas Fogg, who was to start again the same evening for San Francisco, set immediately in search of his servant. He inquired in vain of the French and English consular agents, and after uselessly running through the streets of Yokohama, he despaired of finding Passepartout again, when chance, or perhaps a sort of presentiment, made him enter the theatre of the Honourable Batulcar. He would certainly not have recognised his servant under this eccentric mountebank dress; but the latter, lying on his back, saw his master in the gallery. He could not restrain a movement of his nose. Thence a breaking of the equilibrium and what followed.

This is what Passepartout learned from Mrs. Aouda's mouth, who told him then how the voyage had been made from Hong-Kong to Yokohama in company of a Mr. Fix, on the schooner *Tankadere*.

At the name of Fix, Passepartout did not change countenance. He thought that the time had not come to tell his master what had passed between the detective and himself£ Thus, in the story which Passepartout told of his adventures, he only accused and excused himself of having been overcome by the intoxication of opium in a smoking-house in Hong-Kong.

Mr. Fogg listened coldly to this narrative, without replying; then he opened for his servant a credit sufficient for him to procure on board more suitable garments. And, indeed, an hour had not passed, when the good fellow, having cut off his nose and shed his wings, had nothing more about him which recalled the sectary of the god Tingou.

The steamer making the voyage from Yokohama to San Francisco belonged to the Pacific Mail Steamship Company, and was named the *General Grant*. She was a large side-wheel steamer of two thousand five hundred tons, well equipped, and of great speed. An enormous walking-beam rose and fell successively above the deck; at one of its ends moved the piston-rod, and at the other the connecting-rod which, changing the movement in a straight line to a circular one, was applied directly to the shaft of the wheels. The General Grant was rigged as a three-masted schooner, and she had a large surface of sails, which aided her steam power materially. By making twelve knots the steamer would only need twenty-one days to cross the Pacific. Phileas Fogg then had good reasons for believing that, landed at San Francisco on the 2nd of December, he would be in New York on the 11th, and in

London on the 20th, thus gaining some hours on the fatal date of the 21st of December.

The passengers aboard the steamer were quite numerous—some Englishmen, many Americans, a genuine emigration of coolies to America, and a certain number of officers of the Indian army, who made use of their leave of absence by making the tour of the world.

During this voyage there was no nautical incident. The steamer, borne up on its large wheels, supported by its large amount of canvas, rolled but little. The Pacific Ocean justified its name sufficiently. Mr. Fogg was as calm and non-communicative as usual. His young companion felt herself more and more attached to this man by other ties than those of gratitude. This silent nature, so generous in short, made a greater impression upon her than she thought, and almost unknown to herself she allowed herself to have feelings which did not seem to affect in any way the enigmatic Fogg.

Besides, Mrs. Aouda was very much interested in the gentleman's plans. She was uneasy at the retarding circumstances which might prevent the success of the tour. She frequently talked with Passepartout, who readily detected the feelings of Mrs. Aouda's heart. This good fellow had the most implicit faith with regard to his master; he did not exhaust his praises of the honesty, the generosity, the devotion of Phileas Fogg; then he reassured MTS. Aouda as to the issue of the voyage, repeating that the most difficult part was done, that they had left the fantastic countries of China and Japan, that they were returning to civilised countries, and finally, that a train from San Francisco to New York, and a transatlantic steamer from New York to Liverpool, would be sufficient, doubtless, to finish this impossible tour of the world in the time agreed upon.

Nine days after leaving Yokohama, Phileas Fogg had traversed exactly the half of the terrestrial globe.

In fact, the *General Grant*, on the 23rd of November, passed the one hundred and eightieth meridian, upon which in the southern hemisphere are to be found the antipodes of London. It is true that of the eighty days at his disposal he had used fifty-two, and there only remained to him twenty-eight to be consumed. But we must notice that if the gentleman only found himself half-way round by the difference of meridians, he had really accomplished more than two-thirds of its entire course. Indeed, what forced detours from London to Aden, from Aden to Bombay, from Calcutta to Singapore, from Singapore to Yokohama! By following around the fiftieth parallel, which is that of London, the distance would have been but about twelve thousand miles, while Phileas Fogg was compelled, by the caprices of the means of locomotion, to travel over twenty-six thousand, of which he had already made about seventeen thousand five hundred, at this date, the 23rd of November. But now the route was a straight one, and Fix was no longer there to accumulate obstacles.

It happened also that on this 23rd of November, Passepartout made quite a joyful discovery. It will be recollected that the obstinate fellow had insisted on keeping London time with his famous family watch, deeming incorrect the time of the various countries that he traversed. Now this day, although he had neither put his watch forward or back, it agreed with the ship's chronometers.

The triumph of Passepartout may be comprehended. He would have liked to know what Fix would have said if he had been present.

"The rogue who told me a heap of stories about the meridians, the sun and the moon!" said Passepartout. "Pshaw! if one listened to that sort of people, we should have a nice sort of clocks and watches! I was very sure that one day or another, the sun would decide to regulate itself by my watch!"

Passepartout was ignorant of this: that if the face of his watch had been divided into twenty-four hours like the Italian clocks, he would have had no reason for triumph, for the hands of his watch, when it was nine o'clock in the morning on the vessel, would have indicated nine o'clock in the evening, that is, the twenty-first hour after midnight—a difference precisely equal to that which exists between London and the one hundred and eightieth meridian.

But if Fix had been capable of explaining this purely

physical effect, Passepartout, doubtless, would have been incapable, if not of understanding it, at least of admitting it. And in any event, if the impossible thing should occur that the detective would unexpectedly show himself aboard at this moment, it is probable that Passepartout would have spitefully talked with him on quite a different subject, and in quite a different manner.

Now, where was Fix at this moment?

He was actually on board the *General Grant*.

In fact, on arriving at Yokohama the detective, leaving Mr. Fogg, whom he thought he would see again during the day, had immediately gone to the English Consul's. There he finally found the warrant of arrest, which, running after him from Bombay, was already forty days old, which had been sent to him from Hong-Kong on the very *Carnatic* on board of which he was supposed to be. The detective's disappointment may be imagined! The warrant was useless! Mr. Fogg had left the English possessions! An order of extradition was now necessary to arrest him!

"Let it be so!" said Fix to himself, after the first moment of anger. "My warrant is no longer good here; it will be in England. This rogue has the appearance of returning to his native country believing that he has thrown the police off their guard. Well, I will follow him there. As for the money, Heaven grant there may be some left! But what with travelling, rewards, trials, fines, elephants, expenses of every kind, my man has already left more than five thousand pounds on his route. After all, the Bank is rich!"

His decision taken, he immediately went on board the *General Grant*, and was there when Mr. Fogg and Mrs. Aouda arrived. To his extreme surprise, he recognised Passepartout under his fantastic costume. He concealed himself immediately in his cabin, to avoid an explanation which might damage everything—and, thanks to the number of the passengers, he counted on not being seen by his enemy, when this very day he found himself face to face with him on the forward part of the ship.

Passepartout jumped at Fix's throat, without any other

explanation, and to the great delight of certain Americans who immediately bet for him, he gave the unfortunate detective a superb volley of blows, showing the great superiority of French over English boxing.

When Passepartout had finished he found himself calmer and comforted. Fix rose in pretty bad condition, and, looking at his adversary, he said to him coldly:

"Is it finished.?"

"Yes, for the moment."

"Then I want a word with you."

"But I—"

"In your master's interest."

Passepartout, as if conquered by this coolness, followed the detective, and they both sat down in the forward part of the steamer.

"You have thrashed me," said Fix. "Good; I expected it. Now, listen to me. Until the present I have been Mr. Fogg's adversary, but now I am with him."

"At last!" cried Passepartout, "you believe him to be an honest man?"

"No," replied Fix coldly. "I believe him to be a rogue. Sh! Don't stir, and let me talk. As long as Mr. Fogg was in the English possessions, I had an interest in retaining him whilst waiting for a warrant of arrest. I did everything I could for that. I sent against him the priests of Bombay, I made you drunk at Hong-Kong, I separated you from your master, I made him miss the Yokohama steamer."

Passepartout listened with clenched fists.

"No," continued Fix, "Mr. Fogg seems to be returning to England? Well, I will follow him there. But henceforth it shall be my aim to clear the obstacles from his path as zealously and carefully as before I took pains to accumulate them. You see my game is changed, and it is changed because my interest desires it. I add, that your interest is similar to mine, for you will only know in England whether you are in the service of a criminal or an honest man!"

Passepartout listened to Fix very attentively, and he was convinced that the latter spoke with entire good faith.

"Are we friends?" asked Fix.

"Friends, no," replied Passepartout; "allies, yes; and under this condition that, at the least appearance of treason, I will twist your neck."

"Agreed," said the detective quietly.

Eleven days after, on the 3rd of December, the *General Grant* entered the Bay of the Golden Gate, and arrived at San Francisco.

Mr. Fogg had neither gained nor lost a single day.

Chapter 25

In which a slight glimpse of San Francisco is had—a Political Meeting

It was seven o'clock in the morning, when Phileas Fogg, Mrs. Aouda, and Passepartout set foot on the American continent, if this name can be given to the floating wharf on which they landed. These wharves, rising and falling with the tide facilitate the loading and unloading of vessels. Clippers of all sizes were moored there, steamers of all nationalities, and those steamboats with several decks, which ply on the Sacramento and its tributaries. There were accumulated also the products of a commerce which extends to Mexico, Peru, Chile, Brazil, Europe, Asia, and all the islands of the Pacific Ocean.

Passepartout, in his joy at finally touching American soil, thought in landing he would execute a perilous leap in his finest style. But when he fell upon the wharf, the planks of which were worm-eaten, he almost fell through. Quite put out by the manner in which he had "set foot" on the new continent, the good fellow uttered a terrible cry, which sent flying an innumerable flock of cormorants and pelicans, the customary inhabitants of the movable wharves.

Mr. Fogg, as soon as he landed, ascertained the hour at which the first train left for New York. It was six o'clock in the evening. He had, then, an entire day to spend in the California capital. He ordered a carriage for Mrs. Aouda and himself Passepartout mounted the box, and the vehicle, at three dollars for the trip, turned towards the International Hotel.

From the elevated position that he occupied, Passepartout observed with curiosity the great American city, the broad streets, low, evenly-ranged houses, the Anglo-Saxon Gothic churches and temples, the immense docks, the palatial warehouses, some of wood and some of brick; the numerous vehicles in the streets, omnibuses and horse-cars, and on the crowded sidewalks not only Americans and Europeans, but also Chinese and Indians—the component parts of the population of more than two hundred thousand inhabitants.

Passepartout was quite surprised at all he saw. He was yet in the city of 1849, in the city of bandits, incendiaries, and assassins, running after the native gold, an immense concourse of all the outlaws, who gambled with gold-dust, a revolver in one hand and a knife in the other. But this "good time" had passed away. San Francisco presented the aspect of a large commercial city. The high tower of the City Hall overlooked all these streets and avenues, crossing each other at right angles, between which were spread out verdant squares, then a Chinese quarter, which seemed to have been imported from the Celestial Empire, in a toybox. No more sombreros, or red shirts after the fashion of the miners, or Indians with feathers; but silk hats and black clothes, worn by a large number of gentlemen of absorbing activity. Certain streets, among others Montgomery Street, The Regent Street of London, the Boulevard des Italiens of Paris, the Broadway of New York, the State Street of Chicago were lined with splendid stores, in whose windows were displayed the products of the entire world.

When Passepartout arrived at the International Hotel, it seemed to him that he had not left England.

The ground floor of the hotel was occupied by an immense bar, a sort of sideboard opened gratis to every passer-by. Dried beef, oyster soup, biscuit, and cheese were dealt out without the customer having to take out his purse. He only paid for his drink—ale, porter, or sherry, if he fancied refreshment. That appeared "very American" to Passepartout.

The hotel restaurant was comfortable. Mr. Fogg and Mrs. Aouda took seats at a table and were abundantly served in very small dishes by negroes of darkest hue.

After breakfast, Phileas Fogg, accompanied by Mrs. Aouda, left the hotel to go to the office of the English Consul to have his passport *viséd* there. On the pavement he found his servant, who asked him if it would not be prudent, before starting on the Pacific railroad, to buy a few dozen Enfield rifles or Colt's revolvers. Passepartout had heard so much talk of the Sioux and Pawnees stopping trains like ordinary Spanish brigands. Mr. Fogg replied that it was a useless precaution, but he left him free to act as he thought best. Then he went to the office of the Consul.

Phileas Fogg had not gone two hundred steps, when, "by the greatest accident," he met Fix, who manifested very great surprise. How! Mr. Fogg and he had taken together the voyage across the Pacific, and they had not met on board the vessel! At all events, Fix could only be honoured by seeing again the gentleman to whom he owed so much; and his business calling him to Europe, he would be delighted to continue his journey in such agreeable company.

Mr. Fogg replied that the honour would be his, and Fix—who made it a point not to lose sight of him—asked his permission to visit with him this curious city of San Francisco, which was granted.

Mrs. Aouda, Phileas Fogg, and Fix sauntered through the streets. They soon found themselves in Montgomery Street, where the crowd of people was enormous. On the sidewalks, in the middle of the street, on the horse-car rails, notwithstanding the incessant passage of the coaches and omnibuses, on the steps of the stores, in the windows of all the houses, and even up to the roofs, there was an innumerable crowd.

Men with placards circulated among the groups. Banners and streamers floated in the wind. There were shouts in every direction.

"Hurrah for Camerfield!"

"Hurrah for Mandiboy!"

It was a political meeting. At least so Fix thought, and he communicated his ideas to Mr. Fogg, adding:

"We will perhaps do well, sir, not to mingle in this crowd. Only hard blows will be got here."

"In fact," replied Phileas Fogg, "blows, if they are political, are not less blows."

Fix could not help smiling at this remark, and in order to see, without being caught in the crowd, Mrs. Aouda, Phileas Fogg, and he secured a place upon the upper landing of a flight of steps reaching to the top of a terrace, situated in the upper end of Montgomery Street. Before them, on the other side of the street, between the wharf of a coal merchant and the warehouse of a petroleum dealer, there was a large platform in the open air, towards which the various currents of the crowd seemed to be tending.

And now, why this meeting? What was the occasion of its being held? Phileas Fogg did not know at all. Was it for the nomination of some high military or civil official, a State Governor, or a Member of Congress? It might be supposed so, seeing the great excitement agitating the city.

At this moment there was quite a movement in the crowd. Every hand was thrown in the air. Some, tightly closed, seemed to rise and fall rapidly in the midst of the cries—an energetic manner, no doubt, of casting a vote. The crowd fell back. The banners wavered, disappeared for an instant, and reappeared in tatters. The surging of the crowd extended to the steps, whilst every head moved up and down on the surface like a sea suddenly agitated by a squall. The number of black hats diminished perceptibly, and the most of them seemed to have lost their normal height.

"It is evidently a meeting," said Fix; "and the question which has excited it must be a stirring one. I would not be astonished if they were still discussing the Alabama affair, although it has been settled."

"Perhaps," simply replied Mr. Fogg.

"In any event," replied Fix, "two champions are in each other's presence, the Hon. Mr. Camerfield and the Hon. Mr. Mandiboy."

Mrs. Aouda, leaning on Phileas Fogg's arm, looked with surprise at this noisy scene, and Fix was going to ask one of his neighbours the reason of this popular effervescence, when a more violent movement broke out. The hurrahs, interspersed with insults, redoubled. The staffs of the banners were transformed into offensive arms. Instead of hands, there were fists everywhere. From the top of carriages and omnibuses, blocked in their course, formidable blows were exchanged. Everything was made use of as projectiles. Boots and shoes described extended curves in the air, and it seemed even as if some revolvers mingled their national sounds with the loud cries of the crowd.

The crowd approached the night of stairs, and swept over on to the lower steps. One of the parties had evidently been repulsed without disinterested spectators knowing whether the advantage was with Mandiboy or Camerfield.

"I believe that it is prudent for us to retire," said Fix, who did not want his "man" to get hurt or mixed up in a bad business. "If this is an English question, and we are recognised, we will be treated roughly in this mixed crowd."

"An English citizen—" replied Phileas Fogg.

But the gentleman could not finish his sentence. Behind him, on the terrace above the stairs, there were frightful yells. They cried "Hip! hip! hurrah for Mandiboy!" It was a party of voters coming to the rescue, flanking the Camerfield party.

Mr. Fogg, Mrs. Aouda, and Fix found themselves between two-fires. It was too late to escape. This torrent of men, armed with loaded canes and bludgeons, was irresistible. Phileas Fogg and Fix, in protecting the young woman, were very roughly treated. Mr. Fogg, not less phlegmatic than usual, tried to defend himself with the natural weapons placed at the end of the arms of every Englishman, but in vain. A large rough fellow, with a red beard, flushed face, and broad shoulders, who seemed to be the chief of the band, raised his formidable fist to strike r. Fogg, and he would have damaged that gentleman very much, if Fix, throwing himself in the way, had not received the blow in his place. An enormous bump rose at once under the detective's silk hat, transformed into a simple cap.

"Yankee!" said Mr. Fogg, casting at his adversary a look of deep scorn.

Englishman!" replied the other. "We will see each other again."

"When you please."

"Your name?"

"Phileas Fogg. And yours?"

"Colonel Stamp Proctor."

Then the crowd passed on, throwing Fix down. He rose with his clothes torn, but without serious hurt. His travelling overcoat was torn in two unequal parts, and his pantaloons resembled those of certain Indians. But to sum up, Mrs. Aouda had been spared, and Fix alone had been harmed by the fist-blow.

"Thanks," said Mr. Fogg to the detective, as soon as they were out of the crowd.

"No thanks necessary;" replied Fix, "but come with me."

"Where?"

"To a tailor's."

In fact, this visit was opportune. The garments of Phileas Fogg and Fix were in tatters, as if these two gentlemen had fought for the Hon. Messrs. Camerfield and Mandiboy.

An hour afterwards they had respectable clothes and hats. Then they returned to the International Hotel.

Passepartout was waiting there for his master, armed with a half-dozen sharp-shooting, six-barrelled, breech-loading revolvers. When he perceived Fix in company with Mr. Fogg, his brow darkened. Mrs. Aouda, however, having told in a few words what had happened, Passepartout became calm again. Fix was evidently no longer an enemy but an ally. He was keeping his word.

Dinner over, a coach drove up to take the passengers and their baggage to the station. As they were getting into the coach Mr. Fogg said to Fix:

"Did you see Colonel Proctor again?"

"No," replied Fix.

"I shall return to America to find him again," said Mr. Fogg coldly. "It would not be proper for an English citizen to allow himself to be treated in this way."

The detective smiled and did not answer him. But it is seen that Mr. Fogg was one of those Englishmen, who, while they do not tolerate duelling at home, will fight abroad, when it is necessary to maintain their honour.

At a quarter before six the travellers reached the station and found the train ready to start.

At the moment that Mr. Fogg was going to get into the car, he called a porter and asked him:

"Was there not some disturbance in San Francisco today?"

"It was a political meeting, sir," replied the porter.

"But I thought I noticed a certain excitement in the streets."

"It was simply a meeting organised for an election."

"The election of a general-in-chief, doubtless?" asked Mr. Fogg.

"No, sir, of a Justice of the Peace."

Upon this reply, Phileas Fogg jumped aboard the car, and the train started at full speed.

Chapter 26

In which our Party takes the Express Train on the Pacific Railroad

"From Ocean to Ocean"—so say the Americans, and these four words ought to be the general name of the "Grand Trunk," which traverses the United States in their greatest breadth. But in reality, the Pacific Railroad is divided into two distinct parts; the Central Pacific from San Francisco to Ogden, and the Union Pacific from Ogden to Omaha At that point five distinct lines meet, which place Omaha in frequent communications with New York.

New York and San Francisco are therefore now united by an uninterrupted metal ribbon, measuring not less than three thousand seven hundred and eighty-six miles. Between Omaha and the Pacific, the railroad traverses a country still frequented by the Indians and wild animals—a vast extent of territory which the Mormons commenced to colonise about 1845, after they were driven out of Illinois.

Formerly, under the most favourable circumstances, it took six months to go from New York to San Francisco. Now it is done in seven days.

It was in 1862, notwithstanding the opposition of the Southern Congressmen, who wished a more southerly line, that the route of the railroad was fixed between the forty-first and the forty-second parallel. President Lincoln, of so lamented memory, himself fixed in the State of Nebraska, at the city of Omaha, the beginning of the new network. Work was commenced immediately, and prosecuted with that American activity, which is neither slow nor routine-like. The rapidity of the construction did not in any way injure its thoroughness. On the prairies the road progressed at the rate of a mile and a half per day. A locomotive, moving over the rails laid yesterday, carried the rails for the next day, and ran upon them in proportion as they were laid.

The Pacific Railroad throws off several branches on its route in the States of Iowa, Kansas, Colorado, and Oregon. Leaving Omaha, it takes the left bank of Platte River as far as the mouth of the North Fort follows the South Fork, crosses the Laramie Territory, and the Wahsatch Mountains, turns Salt Lake, arrives at Salt Lake City, the capital of the Mormons, buries itself in the Tuilla Valley, crosses the American Desert, the Cedar and Humboldt Mountains, Humboldt River, the Sierra Nevada, and redescends via Sacramento to the Pacific, its grade, even in crossing the Rocky Mountains, not exceeding one hundred and twelve feet to the mile.

Such was this long artery which the trains would pass over in seven days, and which would permit the Honourable Phileas Fogg—at least he hoped so—to take the Liverpool steamer, on the 11th, at New York.

The car occupied by Phileas Fogg was a sort of long omnibus, resting on two trucks, each with four wheels, whose ease of motion permits of going round short curves. There were no compartments inside; two rows of seats placed on each side, perpendicularly to the axle, and between which was reserved an aisle, leading to the dressing-rooms and others, with which each car is provided. Through the whole length of the train the cars communicated by platforms, and the passengers could move about from one end to the other of the train, which placed at their disposal palace, balcony, restaurant, and smoking-cars. All that is wanting is a theatre-car. But there will be one, some day.

On the platforms book and news dealers were constantly circulating, dealing out their merchandise; and vendors of liquors, eatables, and cigars were not wanting in customers.

The travellers left Oakland Station at six o'clock. It was already night, cold and dreary, with an overcast sky, threatening snow. The train did not move with great rapidity. Counting the stops, it did not run more than a speed which ought, however, to enable it to cross the United States in the fixed time.

They talked but little in the car. Sleep soon overcame the passengers. Passepartout sat near the detective, but he did not speak to him. Since the late events, their relations had become somewhat cold. No more sympathy or intimacy. Fix had not changed his manner, but Passepartout retained an extreme reserve, ready at the least suspicion to choke his old friend.

An hour after the starting of the train a fine snow commenced to fall, which fortunately could not delay the progress of the train. Through the windows nothing was seen but an immense white sheet, against which the clouds of steam from the locomotive looked greyish.

At eight o'clock a steward entered the car, and announced to the passengers that the hour for retiring had come. This was a sleeping-car, which in a few minutes was transformed into a dormitory. The backs of the seats unfolded, beds carefully packed away were unrolled by an ingenious system, berths were improvised in a few moments, and each passenger had soon at his disposal a comfortable bed, which thick curtains protected from all indiscreet looks. The sheets were clean and the pillows soft. Nothing more to be done but to lie down and sleep—which everyone did, as if he had been in the comfortable cabin of a steamer—while the train moved on under full head of steam across the State of California

In that portion of the country between San Francisco and Sacramento the ground is not very hilly. This portion of the railroad, under the name of the Central Pacific, originally had Sacramento for its starting-point, and went towards the east to meet that starting from Omaha From San Francisco to the capital of California the line ran directly to the north-east, along American River, which empties into San Pablo Bay. The one hundred and twenty miles included between these two important cities were accomplished in six hours, and towards midnight, while they were getting their first sleep, the travellers passed through Sacramento. They saw nothing of that large city, the seat of the state government of California, nor its fine wharves, its broad streets, its splendid hotels, its squares, nor its churches.

Leaving Sacramento, the train having passed Junction, Roclin, Auburn, and Colfax Stations, plunged into the Sierra Nevada It was seven o'clock in the morning when Cisco Station was passed. An hour afterwards the dormitory had become an ordinary car, and the passengers could get through the windows a glimpse of the picturesque views of this mountainous country. The route of the train followed the windings of the Sierra, here clinging to the sides of the mountains, there suspended above precipices, avoiding sharp angles by bold curves, plunging into narrow gorges from which there seemed to be no exit. The locomotive, flashing fire like a chased animal, its large smoke-pipe throwing out lurid lights, its sharp bell, its cow-catcher, extending out like a spur, mingled its shrieks and bellowings with the noise of the torrents and cascades, and twined its smoke in the dark branches of the firs.

There were few or no tunnels or bridges on the route. The railroad turned the flank of the mountains, not seeking in a straight line the shortest route from one point to another, and not doing violence to nature.

About nine o'clock the train entered the State of Nevada, through the Carson Valley, always following a north-easterly direction. At noon it left Reno, where the passengers had twenty minutes for breakfast.

From this point, the iron road, skirting Humboldt River, passed a few miles to the north. Then it bent to the east, and did not leave the stream until it reached the Humboldt range, where the river takes its source, nearly in the eastern end of the State of Nevada.

After breakfasting, Mr. Fogg, Mrs. Aouda, and their companions took their seats again in the car. Phileas Fogg, the young woman, Fix, and Passepartout, comfortably seated, looked at the varied country passing before their sight, vast prairies, mountains whose profiles were shown upon the horizon, and creeks tumbling down, a.foaming mass of water. Sometimes, a large herd of bison, gathering in the distance, appeared like a moving dam. These innumerable armies of grazing animals frequently oppose an insurmountable obstacle to the passage of trains. Thousands of these animals have been seen moving on for several hours in close ranks across the railroad. The locomotive is then forced to stop and wait until the path is clear again.

The same thing happened on this occasion. About three o'clock in the afternoon a herd of ten or twelve thousand blocked the rail-road. The engine, having slackened its speed, tried to plunge its spur into the flank of the immense column, but it had to stop before the impenetrable mass.

They saw these buffaloes, as the Americans improperly call them, moving with their steady gait, frequently bellowing terribly. They had a larger body than those of the bulls of

Europe, short legs and tail, a projecting saddle forming a muscular bump, horns separated at the base, their heads, necks, and shoulders covered with long, shaggy hair. The could not think of stopping this moving mass. When the bison have adopted a course, nothing could swerve them from it or modify it. They are a torrent of living flesh which no dam could hold.

The travellers, scattered on the platforms, looked at this curious spectacle. But Phileas Fogg, who ought to be the most in a hurry, had remained in his seat, and was waiting philosophically until it should please the buffaloes to open a passage. Passepartout was furious at the delay caused by this mass of animals. He wanted to fire all the revolvers at them.

"What a country!" he cried. "Mere cattle stop trains, and move along in procession without hurrying? as if they did not impede travel! *Parbleu!* I would like to know if Mr. Fogg had foreseen this mischance in his programme! And what an engineer, who does not dare to rush his engine through this impeding mass of beasts!"

The engineer had not attempted to overcome the obstacle, and he acted wisely. He would undoubtedly have crushed the first buffaloes he struck by the cow-catcher; but, powerful as it was, the engine would have soon been stopped, and the train thrown off the track and wrecked.

The best course, then, was to wait patiently, ready to make up the lost time by an increase of the speed of the train. The passage of the bison lasted three full hours, and the road was not clear again until nightfall. At this moment the last ranks of the herd crossed the rails, whilst the first were disappearing below the southern horizon.

It was then eight o'clock, when the train passed through the defiles of the Humboldt range, and half-past nine when it entered Utah Territory, the region of the Great Salt Lake, the curious Mormon country.

CHAPTER 27

In which Passepartout follows, with a Speed of Twenty Miles an Hour, a Course of Mormon History

During the night of the 5th to the 6th of December, the train went for fifty miles to the south-east, then it ran upwards about as far northerly, approaching the Great Salt Lake.

Passepartout, about nine o'clock in the morning, went on the platform to take the air. The weather was cold, the sky grey, but it had stopped snowing. The disc of the sun, enlarged by the mist, looked like an enormous piece of gold, and Passepartout was busy calculating its value in pounds sterling, when his attention was taken from this useful work by the appearance of a very strange personage.

This personage, who took the train at Elko Station, was tall, very brown, had a black moustache, black stockings, a black silk hat, black waistcoat, black pantaloons, white cravat, and black dog-skin gloves. He might have been taken for a clergyman. He went from one end of the train to the other, and on the door of each car fastened with wafers a written notice.

Passepartout approached and read on one of these notices that Elder William Hitch, taking advantage of his presence on train No. 48, would, from eleven to twelve o'clock, deliver an address on Mormonism in car No. 117—inviting to hear him all desirous of being instructed concerning the mysteries of the religion of the "Latter Day Saints."

"Certainly, I will go," said Passepartout to himself, who knew nothing of Mormonism but its custom of polygamy, the base of Mormon society.

The news spread rapidly through the train, which carried about one hundred passengers. Of this number thirty at most, attracted by the notice of the meeting, occupied at eleven o'clock the seats in car No.117. Passepartout was prominent in the front rank of the faithful. Neither his master nor Fix thought it worth while to take the trouble.

At the appointed hour Elder William Hitch rose, and in quite an irritated voice, as if he had been contradicted in advance, he cried:

"I tell you that Joe Smith is a martyr, that his brother Hiram is a martyr, and that the persecution by the United States Government of the prophets will also make a martyr of Brigham Young. Who dares to maintain the contrary."

No one ventured to contradict the missionary, whose excitement contrasted with his naturally calm physiognomy. But, without doubt, his anger was explained by the fact that Mormonism was now subjected to severe trials. The United States Government had, not without difficulty, just reduced these independent fanatics. It had made itself master of Utah, and had subjected it to the laws of the Union, after imprisoning Brigham Young, accused of rebellion and polygamy. Since that period, the disciples of the prophet redoubled their efforts, and whilst not coming to acts, resisted in words the demands of Congress.

We see that Elder William Hitch was trying to proselyte even on the trains.

And then he related, emphasising his narrative by his loud voice and the violence of his gestures, the history of Mormonism from *Bible* times: "How in Israel, a Mormon prophet of the tribe of Joseph, published the annals of the new religion and bequeathed them to his son Morom; how, many centuries later, a translation of this precious book, written in Egyptian characters, was made by Joseph Smith, Jr., a farmer in the State of Vermont, who revealed himself as a mythical prophet in 1825; how, finally, a celestial messenger appeared to him in an illuminated forest and gave him the annals of the Lord."

At this moment some of his hearers, not much interested in the retrospective narrative of the missionary, left the car; but William Hitch, continuing, related, "how Smith, Jr., with his father, his two brothers, and a few disciples, founded the religion of the Latter Day Saints—a religion which, adopted not only in America, but in England, in Scandinavia, and in Germany, counts among its faithful, artisans and also a number of people engaged in the liberal professions; how a colony was founded in Ohio; how a temple was built at a cost of two hundred thousand dollars, and a city built at Kirkland; how Smith became an enterprising banker, and received from a simple mummy showman a papyrus scroll containing a narrative written by Abraham and other celebrated Egyptians."

This narrative becoming a little long, the ranks of his hearers thinned out still more, and the audience only consisted of twenty persons.

But the Elder, undisturbed by this desertion, related the details of "how Joe Smith became bankrupt in 1837; how his ruined stockholders gave him a coat of tar and feathers; how he appeared again, more honourable and more honoured than ever, a few years after, at Independence, in Missouri, at the head of a flourishing community, which counted not less than three thousand disciples; and that then, pursued by the hatred of the Gentiles, he had to fly to the far West."

Ten hearers were still there, and among them the honest Passepartout, who listened with all his ears. Thus he learned "how, after long persecutions, Smith appeared in Illinois, and in 1839 founded, on the banks of the Mississippi, Nauvoo, the beautiful, whose population rose to twenty-five thousand souls; how Smith became the Mayor, Chief Justice, and General-in-Chief; how in 1843 he announced himself as candidate for the Presidency of the United States; and how, finally, he was drawn into an ambuscade at Carthage, thrown into prison, and assassinated by a band of masked men."

At this moment Passepartout was the only hearer in the car, and the elder, looking him in the face, fascinating him by his words, recalled to his mind that, two years after the assassination of Smith, his successor, the inspired prophet, Brigham Young, leaving Nauvoo, established himself on the banks of Salt Lake, and that there, in that splendid territory, in the midst of that fertile country, on the road which the emigrants take in crossing Utah to reach California, the new colony, thanks to the Mormon principles of polygamy, had increased enormously.

"And this," added William Hitch, "is why the jealousy of Congress has been aroused against us? why the United States soldiers have invaded the soil of Utah! why our chief, the prophet Brigham Young, has been imprisoned in defiance of all justice. Shall we give up to force? Never! Driven from Vermont, driven from Illinois, driven from Ohio, driven from Missouri, driven from Utah, we shall find some independent territory yet where we shall pitch our tents. And you, my brother," added the Elder, fixing his angry look on his single hearer, "will you plant yours in the shadow of our flag?"

"No," replied Passepartout bravely, flying in his turn, leaving the fanatic to preach in the desert.

But, during this discourse, the train had advanced rapidly, and about half-past twelve it touched the north-west corner of the Great Salt Lake. Thence could be embraced in a vast circumstance the aspect of this inland lake, which also bears the name of the Dead Sea, and into which empties an American Jordan. A beautiful lake, hemmed in by craggy rocks of broad surface, encrusted with white salt, a superb sheet of water which formerly covered a larger space; but in time its shores, rising by degrees, reduced its superficial area and increased its depth.

The Salt Lake, about seventy miles long, and thirty-five wide, is situated three thousand eight hundred feet above the level of the sea. Very different from Lake Asphaltite, whose depression is twelve hundred feet below the sea, it holds considerable salt in solution, and one-fourth the weight of the water is solid matter. Its specific gravity is 1170, that of distilled water being 1000. Fishes cannot live in it. Those that the Jordan, Weber, and other creeks carry into it soon perish; but it is not true that the density of its waters is such that a man cannot dive into it.

Around the lake the country was admirably tilled; for the Mormons understand agricultural pursuits; ranches and corrals for domestic animals; fields of wheat, corn, sorghum, luxuriant prairies, and everywhere hedges of wild roses, clumps of acacias and euphorbias, such would have been the appearance of this country six months later; but at this moment the ground was covered with a thin sheet of snow, descending lightly upon it.

At two o'clock the travellers got out at Ogden. The train stopping for six hours, Mr. Fogg, Mrs. Aouda, and their two companions had time to repair to the City of the Saints by the short branch from Ogden. Two hours were sufficient to visit this absolutely American town, and as such, built after the pattern of all the cities of the Union, vast checkerboards with long cold lines, "with the sombre sadness of right angles," according to Victor Hugo's expression. The founder of the City of the Saints could not escape from the need for symmetry which distinguishes the Anglo-Saxons. In this singular country, where the men are certainly not up to the level of their institutions, everything is done "squarely," cities, houses, and follies.

At three o'clock, the travellers were promenading through the streets of the town, built between the banks of the Jordan and the first rise of the Wahsatch Mountains. They noticed there few or no churches, but as monuments, the prophet's house, the court-house, and the arsenal; then houses of bluish bricks, with verandas and porches, surrounded by gardens bordered with acacias, palms, and locusts. A wall of clay and pebbles, built in 1853, surrounded the town. In the principal street, where the market is, were some hotels adorned with pavilions, and among others Salt Lake House.

Mr. Fogg and his companions did not find the town thickly peopled. The streets were almost deserted, save perhaps the part where the Temple was, which they reached only after having traversed several quarters surrounded by palisades. The women were pretty numerous, which was explained by the singular composition of Mormon households. It must not be supposed, however, that all Mormons are polygamists. They are free, but it is well to remark that all the females in Utah are anxious to be married; for, according to the religion of the country, the Mormon heaven does not admit to the possession of its beatitudes the unmarried of the feminine sex. These poor creatures neither seemed well off, nor happy. Some, the richer ones, doubtless, wore a short, low-cut, black silk dress, under a hood or a very modest shawl. The others were dressed in Indian fashion.

Passepartout, in his position as one convinced, did not regard without a certain fright these Mormon women, charged, in groups, with making a single Mormon happy. With his good sense, it was the husband whom he specially pitied. It seemed to him terrible to have to guide so many wives at once through the vicissitudes of life, conduct them, as it were, in a body to the Mormon paradise, with the prospect of finding them to all eternity in the company of the glorious Smith, who was to be the ornament of this place of delights. Certainly, he did not feel called, and he thought—perhaps he was mistaken—that the women of Salt Lake City cast rather embarrassing looks at his person. Very fortunately, his stay in the City of the Saints was not prolonged. At a few minutes past four the travellers were again at the station, and took their seats in the cars.

The whistle sounded; but at the moment that the driving-wheels of the locomotive, slipping upon the rails, commenced to impart some movement to the train, the cry, "Stop! stop!" was heard.

They do not stop trains just started. The gentleman who uttered the cry was evidently a Mormon behind time. He was breathless from running. Fortunately for him the station had neither gates nor barriers. He rushed, then, on the track, jumped upon the steps of the last car, and fell, out of breath, on one of the seats.

Passepartout, who had followed with emotion the incidents of this gymnastic feat, went to look at the tardy one, in whom he took a lively interest, when he learned that this citizen of Utah had thus taken flight in consequence of a household scene.

When the Mormon had recovered his breath, Passepartout ventured to ask him politely how many wives he had to himself—and from the manner in which he had just run away he would suppose that he had at least twenty of them.

"One, sir!" replied the Mormon, raising his arms heavenward. "One, and that was enough!"

CHAPTER 28

In which Passepartout could not Succeed in making anyone listen to Reason

The train leaving Great Salt Lake and the station at Ogden, rose for an hour towards the north, as far as Weber River, having accomplished about nine hundred miles from San Francisco. Leaving this point, it resumed the easterly direction across the rocky hills of the Wahsatch Mountains. It is in this part of the Territory, comprised between these mountains and the Rocky Mountains properly so called, that the American engineers were caught with the greatest difficulties. On this portion of the route the subsidy of the United States Government was raised to forty-eight thousand dollars per mile, whilst on the plains it was only sixteen thousand dollars; but the engineers, as has already been said, have not done violence to nature—they have played with her, going round the difficulties. To reach the great basin, only one tunnel, fourteen thousand feet long, was bored in the entire route of the railroad.

At Salt Lake the road had up to this time reached its greatest altitude. From this point its profile described a very long curve, descending towards Bitter Creek Valley, then re-ascending to the dividing ridge of the waters between the Atlantic and the Pacific. The creeks were numerous in this mountainous region. It was necessary to cross the Muddy, the Green, and others, on culverts. Passepartout became more impatient in proportion as he approached the end of his journey. Fix in his turn would have been very glad to get out of this rough country. He feared delays, he dreaded accidents, and was more in a hurry than Phileas Fogg himself to set foot upon English soil!

At ten o'clock at night the train stopped at Fort Bridger station, which it left almost immediately, and twenty miles farther on it entered Wyoming Territory—following the entire valley of the Bitter Creek, whence flow a portion of the streams forming the water system of Colorado.

The next day, the 7th of December, there was a stop of a quarter-hour at Green River station. The snow had fallen quite heavily through the night, but mingled with rain and half-melted it could not interfere with the progress of the train. But this bad weather kept Passepartout in constant uneasiness, for the accumulation of the snow clogging the car wheels would certainly endanger the journey.

"What an idea," he said to himself, "for my master to travel during the winter! Could he not wait for the fine season of the year to increase his chances.?"

But at this moment, while the good fellow was busy only with the condition of the sky and the lowering of the temperature, Mrs. Aouda was experiencing more serious fears, which proceeded from quite another cause.

Some of the passengers had got out of the cars, and were walking on the platform of the Green River station, waiting for the train to leave. The young woman, looking through the window pane, recognised among them Colonel Stamp Proctor, the American who had behaved so rudely to Phileas Fogg at the time of the political meeting in San Francisco. Mrs. Aouda, not wishing to be seen, drew back from the window.

This circumstance made a lively impression upon the young woman. She was attached to the man who, however coldly, gave her every day tokens of the most absolute devotion. She doubtless did not comprehend the entire depth of the sentiment which her deliverer inspired in her, and to this sentiment she gave as yet only the name of gratitude; but unknown to herself it was more than that. Her heart was therefore wrung at the sight of the rough fellow of whom Mr. Fogg would, sooner or later, demand satisfaction. Evidently it was chance alone that had brought Colonel Proctor into this train; but he was there, and Phileas Fogg must be prevented at any cost from seeing his adversary.

When the train had started again, Mrs. Aouda took advantage for a moment, when Mr. Fogg was sleeping, to post Fix and Passepartout as to the situation.

"That Proctor is on the train!" cried Fix. "Well, compose yourself, madame; before dealing with the gentleman—with Mr. Fogg—he will have to deal with me! It seems to me that in all this business I have received the greatest insults!"

"And moreover," added Passepartout, "I will take care of him, Colonel as he is."

"Mr. Fix," continued Mrs. Aouda, "Mr. Fogg will allow no one to avenge him. He has said that he will return to America to find this ruffian. If, then, he sees Colonel Proctor, we cannot prevent an encounter, which may lead to deplorable results. He must therefore not see him."

"You are right, madame," replied Fox; "an encounter might ruin everything. Conquerer or conquered, Mr. Fogg would be delayed, and—"

"And," added Passepartout, "that would win the bet of the gentlemen of the Reform Club. In four days we shall be in New York! Well, then, if my master does not leave his car for four days, we may hope that chance will not put him face to face with this cursed American, confound him! Now, we can easily prevent him— "

The conversation was interrupted. Mr. Fogg had waked up, and was looking at the country through the window pane obscured by the snow. But later, and without being heard by his master or Mrs. Aouda, Passepartout said to the detective:

"Would you truly fight for him?"

"I would do anything to take him back to Europe alive!" simply replied Fix, in a tone which indicated an unbroken will.

Passepartout felt a shudder over him, but his convictions as to the honesty of his master were not weakened.

And now, were there any means by which Mr. Fogg could be detained in this car, so as to prevent any encounter between him and the colonel? That could not be difficult, as the gentleman was naturally not excitable or inquisitive. At all events, the detective thought he had found this means, for a few moments later he said to Phileas Fogg: "These are long and slow hours that we pass thus on the railway."

"Indeed they are," replied the gentleman, "but they pass."

"On board the steamers," continued the detective, "you used to take a turn at whist?"

"Yes," replied Phileas Fogg, "but here it would be difficult. I have neither cards nor partners."

"Oh! as for the cards, we will find it easy to buy them. They are sold on all trains in America. As for partners, if perchance, madame—"

"Certainly, sir," replied the young woman quickly, "I understand whist. That is part of the English education."

"And I," continued Fix, "have some pretensions to playing a good game. Now, with us three and a dummy—"

"As you please, sir," replied Phileas Fogg, delighted at resuming his favourite game, even on the railroad.

Passepartout was dispatched in search of the steward, and he soon returned with two complete decks of cards, counters, and a shelf covered with cloth. Nothing was wanting. The game commenced. Mrs. Aouda understood whist well enough, and she even was complimented sometimes by the severe Phileas Fogg. As for the detective, he was simply an adept, and worthy of holding his head up with this gentleman.

"Now," said Passepartout to himself, "we will keep him. He will not budge any more!"

At eleven o'clock in the morning, the train had reached the dividing ridge of the waters of the two oceans. It was at Bridger Pass, at a height of seven thousand five hundred and twenty-four English feet above the level of the sea, one of the highest points touched by the profile of the route in this passage across the Rocky Mountains. After going about two hundred miles, the travellers finally found themselves on the vast plains extending as far as the Atlantic, and which nature made so propitious for laying a railroad.

On the slopes of the Atlantic basin already appeared the first streams, tributaries of the North Platte River. The entire northern and eastern horizon was covered by the immense semicircular curtain, which forms the southern portion of the Rocky Mountains, the highest being Laramie's Peak. Between this curve and the line of the road extended vast and plentifully watered plains. On the right of the road rose the first spurs of the mountainous mass, rounding off to the south as far as the sources of the Arkansas river, one of the large tributaries of the Mississippi.

At half-past twelve, the travellers caught sight for an-instant of Fort Halleck, which commands this country. A few hours more, and the crossing of the Rocky Mountains would be accomplished. It was to be hoped, then, that no accident would mark the passage of the train through this difficult region. The snow had stopped falling. The weather became cold and dry. Large birds, frightened by the locomotive, were flying in the distance. Not a deer, a bear, or a wolf, showed itself on the plain. It was the desert in all its barrenness.

After a very comfortable breakfast, served up in the car, Mr. Fogg and his partners had just resumed their interminable whist, when sharp whistles were heard. The train stopped.

Passepartout put his head out of the door, and saw nothing which could explain this stop. No station was in sight.

Mrs. Aouda and Fix feared for an instant that Mr. Fogg would think of going out on the track. But the gentleman contented himself with saying to his servant:

"See then what it is."

Passepartout rushed out of the car. About forty passengers had left their seats, and among them Colonel Stamp Proctor.

The train had stopped in front of a red signal which blocked the way. The engineer and conductor, having got out, discussed quite excitedly with a signalman, whom the stationmaster at Medicine Bow, the next station, had sent in advance of the train. Some of the passengers approached and took part in the discussion, among others the aforesaid Colonel Proctor, with his loud voice and imperious gestures.

Passepartout, having rejoined the group, heard the signalman say:

"No! there is no means of passing. The bridge at Medicine Bow is shaky and will not bear the weight of the train."

The bridge in question was a suspension bridge over the rapids, about a mile from the place where the train had stopped. According to the signalman, it threatened to fall, several of the wires having snapped, and it was impossible to risk its passage. He did not exaggerate in any way, then, in asserting that they could not pass over the bridge. And besides, with the careless habits of the Americans, we may say that when they are prudent, we would be very foolish not to be so.

Passepartout, not daring to go to inform his master, listened with set teeth, immovable as a statue.

"Ah, indeed!" cried Colonel Proctor, "we are not going, I imagine, to remain here, and take root in the snow!"

"Colonel," replied the conductor," we have telegraphed to Omaha for a train, but it is not probable that it will arrive at Medicine Bow before six hours."

"Six hours!" cried Passepartout.

"Without doubt," replied the conductor. "Besides, that time will be necessary for us to reach the station on foot."

"But it is only a mile from here," said one of the passengers.

"A mile, in fact, but on the other side of the river."

And cannot the river be crossed in a boat?" asked the colonel.

"Impossible. The creek is swollen with the rains. It is a torrent, and we will be compelled to make a detour of ten miles to the north to find a ford."

The colonel launched a volley of oaths, blaming the company and the conductor, and Passepartout, furious, was not far from joining with him. There was a material obstacle against which, this time, all his master's bank-notes, would be of no avail.

The disappointment was general among the passengers, who, without counting the delay, saw themselves obliged to foot it fifteen miles across the plain covered with snow. There was a hub-bub, exclamations, loud and deep, which would certainly have attracted Phileas Fogg's attention, if that gentleman had not been absorbed in his game.

But Passepartout found himself compelled to inform him, and, with drooping head, he turned towards the car, when the engineer of the train, a genuine Yankee, named Forster, raising his voice, said:

"Gentlemen, there might be a way of passing."

"On the bridge?" asked a passenger.

"On the bridge."

"With our train?" asked the colonel.

"With our train."

Passepartout stopped, and devoured the engineer's words.

"But the bridge threatens to fall!" continued the conductor.

"It don't matter," replied Forster. "I believe that by rushing the train over at its maximum of speed we would have some chances of passing."

"The devil!" exclaimed Passepartout.

But a certain number of the passengers were immediately carried away by the proposition. It pleased Colonel Proctor particularly. That hot-head found the thing very feasible. He recalled, even, that engineers had had the idea of passing rivers without bridges, with trains closely coupled, rushing at the height of their speed, etc. And finally, all those interested took sides with the engineer's views.

"We have fifty chances for passing," said one:

"Sixty," said another.

"Eighty! Ninety out of one hundred!"

Passepartout was perplexed, although he was willing to try anything to accomplish the passage of Medicine Creek, but the attempt seemed to him a little too "American."

"Besides," he thought, "there is a much simpler thing to do, and these people don't even think of it—Monsieur," he said to one of the passengers, "the way proposed by the engineer seems a little hazardous to me, but—"

"Eighty chances !" replied the passenger, turning his back to him.

"I know very well," replied Passepartout, addressing another gentleman, abut a simple reflection—"

"No reflection, it is useless!" replied the American addressed, shrugging his shoulders, "since the engineer assures us that we will pass!"

'Without doubt," continued Passepartout, "we will pass, but it would perhaps be more prudent—"

"What prudent!" cried Colonel Proctor, jumping at this word, heard by chance. "At full speed, you have been told! Don't you understand? At full speed!"

"I know—I understand," repeated Passepartout, whom no one would allow to finish his phrase; abut it would be, if not more prudent, since the word offends you, at least more natural—"

"Who? What? How? What is the matter with this fellow'" was heard from all directions.

The poor fellow did not know whom to address.

"Are you afraid?" Colonel Proctor asked him.

"I, afraid?" cried Passepartout. "Well, so be it! I will show these people that a Frenchman can be as American as they!"

"All aboard! All aboard!" cried the conductor.

"Yes, all aboard," replied Passepartout; "all aboard! and right away! But they can't prevent me from thinking that it would have been more natural for us to have gone over the bridge afoot, and then brought the train afterwards!"

But no one heard this sage reflection, and no one would have acknowledged its justness.

The passengers took their seats again in the cars. Passepartout resumed his, without saying anything of what had occurred. The players were entirely absorbed in their game.

The locomotive whistled vigorously. The engineer reversed his engine, and backed for about a mile—returned like a jumper who is going to take a leap.

Then, to a second whistle, they commenced to move forwards, the speed increased; it soon became frightful: but a single puffing was heard from the locomotive; the pistons worked twenty strokes to the second; the axles smoked in the journals. They felt, so to speak, that the entire train, moving at the rate of one hundred miles to the hour, did not bear upon the rails. The speed destroyed the weight.

And they passed! And it was like a flash of lightning. They saw nothing of the bridge. The train leaped, it might be said, from one bank to the other, and the engineer could not stop his train for five miles beyond the station.

But the train had scarcely crossed the river than the bridge, already about to fall, went down with a crash into the rapids of Medicine Bow.

Chapter 29

In which certain Incidents are Related, only to be met with on the Railroads of the United States

That same evening the train continued its course without obstructions, passed Fort Sanders, crossed the Cheyenne Pass and arrived at Evans Pass. At this point, the railroad reached the highest point - on the route, i.e. eight thousand and ninety-one feet above the level of the ocean. The travellers now only had to descend to the Atlantic over those boundless plains levelled by nature.

There was the branch from the "Grand Trunk" to Denver City, the principal town of Colorado. This territory is rich in gold and silver mines, and more than fifty thousand inhabitants have already settled there.

At this moment thirteen hundred and eighty-two miles had been made from San Francisco in three days and three nights. Four nights and four days, if nothing interfered, ought to be sufficient to reach New York. Phileas Fogg was then still within his time.

During the night they passed to the left of Camp Walbach. Lodge Pole Creek ran parallel to the road, following the straight boundary between the Territories of Wyoming and

Colorado. At eleven o'clock they entered Nebraska, passing near Sedgwick, and they touched at Julesburg, on the South Fork of the Platte River.

It was at this point that the Union Pacific Road was inaugurated on the 23rd of October, 1867, by its chief engineer, General G. M. Dodge. There stopped the two powerful locomotives, drawing the nine cars of invited guests, prominent among whom was the Vice-President of the road, Thomas C. Durant; three cheers were given; there the Sioux and Pawnees gave an imitation Indian battle; there the fireworks were set off; there, finally, was struck off by means of a portable printing press the first number of the *Railway Pioneer*. Thus was celebrated the inauguration of this great railroad, an instrument of progress and civilisation, thrown across the desert, and destined to bind together towns and cities not yet in existence. The whistle of the locomotive, more powerful than the lyre of Amphion, was soon to make them rise from the American soil.

At eight o'clock in the morning Fort M'Pherson was left behind. Three hundred and fifty-seven miles separate this point from Omaha The railroad followed, on its left bank the capricious windings of the South Fork of Platte River. At nine o'clock they arrived at the important town of North Platte, built between the two arms of the main stream, which join each other around it, forming a single artery—a large tributary—whose waters mingle with those of the Missouri a little above Omaha.

The one hundred and first meridian was passed.

Mr. Fogg and his partner had resumed their play. Neither of them complained of the length of the route—not even the dummy. Mr. Fix had won a few guineas at first, which he was in a fair way to lose, but he was not less deeply interested than Mr. Fogg. During this morning chance singularly favoured this gentleman. Trumps and honours were showered into his hands. At a certain moment, after having made a bold combination, he was about to play a spade, when behind the seat a voice was heard, saying:

"I should play a diamond."

Mr. Fogg, Mrs. Aouda, and Fix raised their heads. Colonel Proctor was near them.

Stamp Proctor and Phileas Fogg recognised each other at once.

"Ah, it is you, Englishman," cried the colonel; "it's you who are going to play a spade."

"And who plays it," replied Phileas Fogg coldly, laying down a ten of that colour.

"Well, it suits me to have it diamonds," replied Colonel Proctor, in an irritated voice.

And he made a motion as if to pick up the card played, adding:

"You don't understand anything of this game."

"Perhaps I will be more skillful at another," said Phileas Fogg,

"You have only to try it, son of John Bull!" replied the coarse fellow.

Mrs. Aouda became pale. All the blood went to her heart. She seized Phileas Fogg's arm, and he gently repulsed her. Passepartout was ready to throw himself on the colonel, who was looking at his adversary with the most insulting air. But Fix had risen, and going to Colonel Proctor, said to him:

"You forget that you have me to deal with; me whom you have not only insulted, but struck!"

"Mr. Fix," said Mr. Fogg, "I beg your pardon, but it concerns me alone. In insisting that I was wrong in playing a spade, the colonel has insulted me anew, and he shall give me satisfaction."

"When you will, and where you will," replied the American, "and with whatever weapon you please!"

Mrs. Aouda tried in vain to restrain Mr. Fogg. The detective uselessly endeavoured to take up the quarrel on his own account. Passepartout wanted to throw the colonel out of the door, but a sign from his master stopped him. Phileas Fogg went out of the car, and the American followed him on the platform.

"Sir," said Mr. Fogg to his adversary, "I am very much in a hurry to return to Europe, and any delay whatever would be very prejudicial to my interest."

"Well! what does that concern me?" replied Colonel Proctor.

"Sir," replied Mr. Fogg, very politely, "after our meeting in San Francisco, I formed the plan to come back to America to find you, as soon as I had completed the business which calls me to the Old World."

"Truly!"

"Will you appoint a meeting with me in six months?"

"Why not in six years?"

"I say six months," replied Mr. Fogg, "and I will be prompt to meet you."

"All evasions!" cried Stamp Proctor. "Immediately, or not at all."

"All right," replied Mr. Fogg. "You are going to New York?"

"No."

"To Chicago?"

"No."

"To Omaha?"

"It concerns you very little! Do you know Plum Creek station.?"

"No," replied Mr. Fogg.

"It is the next station. The train will be there in an hour. It will stop ten minutes. In ten minutes we can exchange a few shots with our revolvers."

"Let it be so," replied Mr. Fogg. "I will stop at Plum Creek."

"And I believe that you will remain there!" added the American, with unparalleled insolence.

"Who knows, sir?" replied Mr. Fogg, and he re-entered the car as coolly as usual.

That gentleman commenced to reassure Mrs. Aouda, saying to her that blusterers were never to be feared. Then he begged Fix to act as his second in the encounter which was going to take place. Fix could not refuse, and Phileas Fogg resumed quietly his interrupted game, playing a spade with perfect serenity.

At eleven o'clock the whistle of the locomotive announced that they were near Plum Creek station. Mr. Fogg rose, and followed by Fix, he went out on the platform. Passepartout accompanied him, carrying a pair of revolvers. Mrs. Aouda remained in the car, pale as death.

At this moment the door of the next car opened, and Colonel Proctor appeared likewise upon the platform, followed by his second, a Yankee of his own stamp. But at the moment that the two adversaries were going to step off the train, the conductor ran up to them and cried:

"You can't get off, gentlemen."

"Why not?" asked the colonel.

"We are twenty minutes behind time, and the train does not stop."

"But I am going to fight a duel with this gentleman."

"I regret it," replied the conductor, "but we are going to start again immediately. Hear the bell ringing!"

The bell was ringing, and the train moved on.

"I am really very sorry, gentlemen," said the conductor. "Under any other circumstances, I could have obliged you. But, after all, since you had not the time to fight here, who hinders you from fighting while the train is in motion?"

"Perhaps that will not suit the gentleman!" said Colonel Proctor, with a jeering air.

"That suits me perfectly" replied Phileas Fogg.

"Well, we are decidedly in America!" thought Passepartout, "and the conductor is a gentleman of the first order."

Having said this, he followed his master.

The two combatants and their seconds, preceded by the conductor, repaired to the rear of the train, passing through the cars. The last car was only occupied by about ten or a dozen passengers. The conductor asked them if they would be kind enough to vacate for a few moments for two gentlemen who had an affair of honour to settle.

Why not? The passengers were only too happy to be able to accommodate the two gentlemen, and they retired on the platforms.

The car, fifty feet long, accommodated itself very conveniently to the purpose. The two adversaries might march on each other in the aisle, and fire at their ease. There never was a duel easier to arrange. Mr. Fogg and Colonel Proctor, each furnished with two six-barrelled revolvers, entered the car. Their seconds, remaining outside, shut them in. At the first whistle of the locomotive, they were to commence firing. Then after a lapse of two minutes what remained of the two gentlemen would be taken out of the car. Truly, there could be nothing simpler. It was even so simple that Fix and Passepartout felt their hearts beating almost as if they would break.

They were waiting for the whistle agreed upon, when suddenly savage cries resounded. Reports accompanied them, but they did not come from the car reserved for the duellists. These reports continued, on the contrary, as far as the front and along the whole line of the train. Cries of fright made themselves heard from the inside of the cars.

Colonel Proctor and Mr. Fogg, with their revolvers in hand, went out of the car immediately, and rushed forward where the reports and cries resounded more noisily.

They understood that the train had been attacked by a band of Sioux.

It was not the first attempt of these daring Indians. More than once already they had stopped the trains. According to their habit, without waiting for the stopping of the train, rushing upon the steps to the number of a hundred, they had scaled the cars like a clown does a horse at full gallop.

These Sioux were provided with guns. Thence the reports, to which the passengers, nearly all armed, replied sharply by shots from their revolvers. At first the Indians rushed upon the engine. The engineer and firemen were half-stunned with blows from their muskets. A Sioux chief, wishing to stop the train, but not knowing how to manoeuvre the handle of the regulator, had opened wide the steam valve instead of closing it, and the locomotive, beyond control, ran on with frightful rapidity.

At the same time, the Sioux entered the cars, they ran like enraged monkeys over the roofs, they drove in the doors and fought hand to hand with the passengers. The trunks, broken open and robbed, were thrown out of the baggage car on the road. Cries and shots did not cease.

But the passengers defended themselves courageously. Some of the cars, barricaded, sustained a siege, like real moving forts, borne on at a speed of one hundred miles an hour.

From the commencement of the attack, Mrs. Aouda had behaved courageously. With revolver in hand, she defended herself heroically, firing through the broken panes when some savage presented himself. About twenty Sioux, mortally wounded, fell upon the track, and the car wheels crushed like worms those that slipped on to the rails from the top of the platforms.

Several passengers, severely wounded by bullets or clubs, lay upon the seats.

But an end must be put to this. This combat had lasted already for ten minutes, and could only end to the advantage of the Sioux, if the train was not stopped. In fact, Fort Kearney station was not two miles distant. There was a military post, but that passed, between Fort Kearney and the next station the Sioux would be masters of the train.

The conductor was fighting at Mr. Fogg's side, when a ball struck him and he fell. As he fell, he cried: "We are lost if the train is not stopped inside of five minutes!"

"It shall be stopped!" said Phileas Fogg, who was about to rush out of the car.

"Remain, Monsieur," Passepartout cried to him. "That is my business."

Phileas Fogg had not the time to stop the courageous young man, who, opening a door without being seen by the Indians, succeeded in slipping under the car. Whilst the struggle continued, and whilst the balls were crossing each other above his head, recovering his agility, his suppleness as a clown, he made his way under the cars. Clinging to the chains, assisting himself by the lever of the brakes and the edges of the window-sashes, climbing from one car to another with marvellous skill he thus reached the front of the train. He had not been seen; he could not have been.

There, suspended by one hand between the baggage car and the tender, with the other he loosened the couplings, but in consequence of the traction, he would never have been able to pull out the yoking-bar if a sudden jolt of the engine had not made the bar jump out, and the train, detached, was left farther and farther be, hind, while the locomotive flew on with new speed.

Carried on by the force acquired, the train still rolled on for a few minutes, but the brakes were manoeuvred from the inside of the cars, and the train finally stopped, less than one hundred paces from Kearney station.

The soldiers of the fort, attracted by the firing, ran hastily to the train. The Sioux did not wait for them, before the train stopped entirely the whole band had decamped.

But when the passengers counted each other on the platform of the station, they noticed that several were missing, and among others the courageous Frenchman, whose devotion had just saved them.

CHAPTER 30

In which Phileas Fogg simply does his duty

Three passengers, including Passepartout, had disappeared. Had they been killed in the fight? Were they taken prisoners by the Sioux? As yet it could not be told.

The wounded were quite numerous, but none mortally. The one most seriously was Colonel Proctor, who had fought bravely, and who fell struck by a ball in the groin. He was carried to the station with the other passengers, whose condition demanded immediate care.

Mrs. Aouda was safe. Phileas Fogg, who had not spared himself, had not a scratch. Fix was wounded in the arm—but it was an unimportant wound. But Passepartout was missing, and tears flowed from the young woman's eyes.

Meanwhile, all the passengers had left the train. The wheels of the cars were stained with blood. To the hubs and spokes hung ragged pieces of flesh As far as the eye could reach long red trails were seen on the white plain. The last Indians were then disappearing in the south, along the banks of Republican River.

Mr. Fogg, with folded arms, stood motionless. He had a serious decision to make. Mrs. Aouda, near him, looked at him without uttering a word. He understood her look. If his servant was a prisoner ought he not to risk everything to rescue him from the Indians?

"I will find him dead or alive," he said simply, to Mrs. Aouda.

"Ah! Mr. Fogg—Mr. Fogg!" cried the young woman, seizing her companion's hands and covering them with tears.

"Alive!" added Mr. Fogg, "if we do not lose a minute!"

With this resolution Phileas Fogg sacrificed himself entirely. He had just pronounced his ruin. A single day's delay would make him miss the steamer from New York. His bet would be irrevocably lost. But in the face of the thought, "It is my duty!" he did not hesitate.

The captain commanding Fort Kearney was there. His soldiers—about a hundred men—had put themselves on the defensive in the event of the Sioux making a direct attack upon the station.

"Sir," said Mr. Fogg to the captain, "three passengers have disappeared."

"Killed?" asked the captain.

"Killed or prisoners," replied Mr. Fogg. "That is an uncertainty which we must bring to an end. It is your intention to pursue the Sioux?"

"It is a grave matter, sir," said the captain. "These Indians may fly beyond the Arkansas! I could not abandon the fort entrusted to me."

"Sir," replied Phileas Fogg, "it is a question of the life of three men."

"Doubtless—but can I risk the life of fifty to save three?"

"I do not know whether you can, but you ought."

"Sir," replied the captain, and one here has the right to tell me what my duty is."

"Let it be so!" said Phileas Fogg coldly, "I will go alone!"

"You, sir!" cried Fix, who approached, "go alone in pursuit of the Indians!"

"Do you wish me then to allow to perish the unfortunate man to whom every one of us that is living owes his life? I shall go."

"Well, no, you shall not go alone!" cried the captain, moved in spite of himself. "No! You are a brave heart! Thirty volunteers!" he added, turning to his soldiers.

The whole company advanced in a body. The captain had to select from these brave fellows. Thirty soldiers were picked out, and an old sergeant put at their head.

"Thanks, Captain!" said Mr. Fogg.

"You will permit me to accompany you?" Fix asked the gentleman.

"You will do as you please," replied Phileas Fogg. "But if you wish to do me a service, you will remain by Mrs. Aouda In case anything should happen to me—"

A sudden paleness overcast the detective's face. To separate himself from the man whom he had followed step by step and with so much persistence! To let him venture so much in the desert. Fix looked closely at the gentleman, and whatever he may have thought, in spite of his prejudices, in spite of his inward struggle, he dropped his eyes before that quiet, frank look.

"I will remain," he said.

A few moments after, Mr. Fogg pressed the young woman's hand: then, having placed in her care his precious travelling bag, he set out with the sergeant and his little band.

But before starting, he said to the soldiers:

"My friends, there are five thousand dollars for you if you save the prisoners!"

It was then a few minutes past noon.

Mrs. Aouda retired into a sitting-room of the station, and there, alone, she waited, thinking of Phileas Fogg, his simple and grand generosity, his quiet courage. Mr. Fogg had sacrificed his fortune, and now he was staking his life—and all this without hesitation, from a sense of duty, without words. Phileas Fogg was a hero in her eyes.

The detective (Fix) was not thinking thus, and he could not restrain his agitation. He walked feverishly up and down the platform of the station, one moment vanquished, he became himself again. Fogg having gone, he comprehended his foolishness in letting him go. What! Had he consented to be separated from the man that he had just been following around the world! His natural disposition got the upper hand; he criminated and accused himself; he treated himself as if he had been the director of the Metropolitan police reproving an agent caught at a very green trick.

"I have been a silly fellow!" he thought. "The other fellow would have told him who I was! He was gone; he will not return! Where can I capture him now? But how have I (Fix) so allowed myself to be fascinated, when I have a warrant for his arrest in my pocket! I am decidedly only an ass!"

Thus reasoned the detective, while the hours slipped on too slowly for his liking. He did not know what to do. Sometimes, he felt like telling Mrs. Aouda everything. But he understood how he would be received by the young woman. What course should he take? He was tempted to go in pursuit of this Fogg across the immense white plains. It did not seem impossible for him to find him. The footprints of the detachment were still imprinted upon the snow! But, under a fresh covering, every track would soon be effaced.

Fix was discouraged. He felt an almost insurmountable desire to abandon the party. This very occasion of leaving Kearney station and of prosecuting the journey, so fruitful of mishaps, was opened to him.

About two o'clock in the afternoon, while the snow was falling in large flakes, long whistles were heard coming from the east. An enormous shadow, preceded by a lurid light, slowly advanced, considerably increased by the mist, which gave it a fantastic appearance.

But no train was expected yet from the east. The help asked for by telegraph could not arrive so soon, and the train from Omaha to San Francisco would not pass until the next day. They were soon enlightened.

This locomotive, moving under a small head of steam, and

whistling very loud, was the one which, after being detached from the train, had continued its course with such frightful speed, carrying the unconscious fireman and engineer. It had run on for several miles; then the fire had gone down for want of fuel; the steam had slackened, and an hour afterwards, relaxing its speed by degrees, the engine finally stopped twenty miles beyond Kearney station.

Neither the engineer nor the fireman was dead, and after a very long swoon they revived.

The engine had stopped. When he saw himself in the desert, and the locomotive without cars attached to it, the engineer understood what had happened. e could not guess how the locomotive had been detached from the train, but he did not doubt that the train, left behind, was in distress.

The engineer did not hesitate as to what he ought to do. To continue his course in the direction of Omaha was prudent, to return towards the train, which the Indians were perhaps yet robbing, was dangerous. No matter! Coal and wood were thrown into the furnace, the fire started up again, the head of steam increased again, and about two o'clock in the afternoon the engine returned, running backwards to Kearney station. This was the whistling they heard in the mist.

It was a great satisfaction for the travellers, when they saw the locomotive put at the head of the train. They were going to be able to continue their journey so unfortunately interrupted.

On the arrival of the engine, Mrs. Aouda came out of the station, and addressing the conductor, she asked:

"You are going to start?"

"This very instant, madame."

"But the prisoners—our unfortunate companions— "

"I cannot interrupt the trip," replied the conductor. "We are already three hours behind time."

"And when will the next train coming from San Francisco pass?"

"To-morrow evening, madame."

"To-morrow evening! But it will be too late. We must wait—"

"Impossible," replied the conductor. "If you are going, get aboard the car."

"I will not go," replied the young woman.

Fix heard this conversation. A few moments before, when every means of locomotion failed him, he had decided to quit Kearney, and now that the train was there, ready to continue its course, and he only had to seat himself in the car, an irresistible force fixed him to the ground. The platform of the station burned his feet, and he could not tear himself away from it. The conflict within himself recommenced. His anger at his want of success choked him. He was going to struggle on to the end.

Meanwhile the passengers and some of the wounded—among others Colonel Proctor, whose condition was very serious—had taken seats in the cars. The buzzing of the overheated boiler was heard; the steam escaped through the valves; the engineer whistled, the train started, and soon disappeared, mingling its white smoke with the whirling of the snow.

The detective Fix had remained.

Some hours passed. The weather was very bad, the cold very keen. Fix, seated on a bench in the station, was motionless. It might have been supposed that he was sleeping. Notwithstanding the storm, Mrs. Aouda left every moment the room which had been placed at her disposal. She went to the end of the platform, trying to look through the tempest of snow, wishing to pierce the mist which narrowed the horizon around her, listening if she could hear any sound. But there was nothing. She went in then, chilled through, to return a few moments later, and always in vain.

Evening came. The little detachment had not returned. Where was it at this moment? Had it been able to overtake the Indians? Had there been a fight, or were these soldiers, lost in the mist, wandering at a venture? The captain of Fort Kearney was very uneasy, although he did not wish to let his uneasiness appear.

Night came; the snow fell less heavily, but the intensity of the cold increased. The most intrepid glance would not have looked at this vast, obscure space without terror. An absolute silence prevailed over the plain. Neither the flight of a bird nor the passage of a wild beast disturbed the unbroken quiet.

During the whole night, Mrs. Aouda, her mind full of dark presentiments, her heart filled with anguish, wandered on the border of the prairie. Her imagination carried her afar off and showed her a thousand dangers. What she suffered during those long hours could not be expressed.

Fix, still immovable in the same spot, did not sleep. At a certain moment, a man approached and spoke to him, but the detective sent him away, after replying to him by a negative sign.

Thus the night passed. At dawn, the half-concealed disc of the sun rose from a misty horizon. Still the eye might reach as far as two miles. Phileas Fogg and the detachment had gone to the south. The south was entirely deserted. It was then seven o'clock in the morning.

The captain, extremely anxious, did not know what course to take. Ought he to send a second detachment to help the first? Ought he to sacrifice fresh men with so few chances of saving those who were sacrificed at first? But his hesitation did not last, and with a gesture calling one of his lieutenants, he gave him the order to throw out a reconnaissance to the south, when shots were heard. Was it a signal? The soldiers rushed out of the fort, and half a mile distant they perceived a small band returning in good order.

Phileas Fogg marched at the head, and near him Passepartout and the two passengers, rescued from the hands of the Sioux.

There was a fight ten miles south of Fort Kearney. Passepartout and his two companions were already struggling against their captors, and the Frenchman had knocked down three of them with his fist, when his master and the soldiers rushed to their rescue.

All—the deliverers and the delivered—were received with cries of joy, and Phileas Fogg divided among the soldiers the reward he had promised them, whilst Passepartout repeated to himself, not without reason:

"I must confess that I am certainly costing my master very dearly."

Fix, without uttering a word, looked at Mr. Fogg, and it

would have been difficult to analyse the impression struggling within him. As for Mrs. Aouda, she took the gentleman's hand, and pressed it in hers, without being able to utter a word!

In the meantime Passepartout, upon his arrival, was looking for the train at the station, He thought he would find it there, ready to start for Omaha, and he hoped they could still make up the lost time.

"The train, the train!" he cried.

"Gone," replied Fix.

"And when will the next train pass?" asked Phileas Fogg.

"Not until this evening."

"Ah!" simply replied the impassible gentleman.

Chapter 31

In which the Detective Fix takes seriously in charge Phileas Fogg's Interests

Phileas Fogg found himself twenty hours behind time. Passepartout, the involuntary cause of this delay, was desperate. He had certainly ruined his master!

At this moment the detective approached Mr. Fogg, and looking closely in his face, asked:

"Very seriously, sir, you are in a hurry?"

"Very seriously," replied Phileas Fogg.

"I insist," continued Fix. "It is very much to your interest to be in New York on the 11th, before nine o'clock in the evening, the time of departure of the Liverpool steamer."

"I have a very great interest."

"And if your journey had not been interrupted by this Indian attack you would have arrived in New York on the morning of the 11th."

"Yes, twelve hours before the departure of the steamer."

"Well, you are now twenty hours behind time. The difference between twenty and twelve is eight. Eight hours are to be made up. Do you wish to try to do it?"

"On foot?" asked Mr. Fogg.

"No, on a sledge," replied Fix, "on a sledge with sails. A man has proposed this means of conveyance to me."

It was the man who had spoken to the detective during the night and whose offer he had refused.

Phileas Fogg did not reply to Fix; but Fix having shown him the man in question, who was walking up and down before the station, the gentleman went to him. An instant after, Phileas Fogg and this American, named Mudge, entered a hut built at the foot of Fort Kearney.

There Mr. Fogg examined a very singular vehicle, a sort of frame laid on two long beams, a little raised in front, like the runners of a sledge, and upon which five or six persons could be seated. On the front of the frame was fastened a very high mast, to which an immense brigantine sail was attached. The mast, firmly held by metallic fastenings, held an iron stay, which served to hoist a large jib-sail. At the rear a sort of rudder allowed the apparatus to be steered.

As could be seen, it was a sledge sloop-rigged. During the winter, on the icy plains, when the trains are blocked up by the snow, these vehicles make extremely rapid trips from one station to another. They carry a tremendous press of sail, far more than a cutter, and, with the wind behind, they glide over the surface of the prairie with a speed equal to, if not greater than, that of an express train.

In a few moments, the bargain was concluded between Mr. Fogg and the owner of this land craft. The wind was good. It blew with a strong breeze from the west. The snow had hardened, and Mudge was certain that he could take Mr. Fogg in a few hours to Omaha. There the trains are frequent, and the routes leading to Chicago and New York numerous. It was not impossible to make up the time lost. There should be no hesitation in making the attempt.

Mr. Fogg, not wishing to expose Mrs. Aouda to the discomforts of a trip in the open air, with the cold rendered more unbearable by the speed, proposed to her to remain under Passepartout's care at Kearney station. The honest fellow would undertake to bring her to Europe by a better route and under more acceptable conditions.

Mrs. Aouda refused to be separated from Mr. Fogg, and Passepartout felt very happy at this determination. Indeed, nothing in the world would have induced him to leave his master, since Fix was to accompany him.

As to what the detective then thought, it would be difficult to say. Had his convictions been shaken by Phileas Fogg's return, or rather did he consider him a very shrewd rogue, who, having accomplished his tour of the world, believed that he would be entirely safe in England? Perhaps Fix's opinion concerning Phileas Fogg was really modified. But he was none the less decided to do his duty, and more impatient than all of them to hasten with all his might the return to England.

At eight o'clock the sledge was ready to start. The travellers—we were tempted to say the passengers—took their places, and wrapped themselves closely in their travelling cloaks. The two immense sails were hoisted, and, under the pressure of the wind, the vehicle slipped over the hardened snow with a speed of forty miles an hours.

The distance between Fort Kearney and Omaha is, in a straight line—in a bee-line, as the Americans say—two hundred miles at the most. If the wind continued, this distance could be accomplished in five hours. If no accident happened, the sledge ought to reach Omaha at one o'clock in the afternoon.

What a journey! The travellers, huddled up against each other, could not speak. The cold, increased by the speed, cut off their words. The sledge glided as lightly over the surface of the plain as a vessel over the surface of the water—with the swell at least. When the breeze came, skimming the earth, it seemed as if the sledge was lifted from the ground by its sails, which were like huge wings. Mudge, at the rudder kept the straight line, and with a turn of the tiller he corrected the lurches which the apparatus had a tendency to make. All sail was carried. The jib had been arranged so that it no longer was screened by the brigantine. A top-mast was hoisted, and another jib stretched to the wind added its force to that of the other sails. It could not be exactly estimated, but certainly the speed of the sledge could not be less than forty miles an hour.

"If nothing breaks," said Mudge, "we shall arrive!"

It was Mudge's interest to arrive at the time agreed upon, for Mr. Fogg, adhering to his plan, had stimulated him by the promise of a handsome reward.

The prairie, which the sledge was crossing in a straight line, was as flat as a sea It might have been called a frozen pond. The railroad which ran through this section, ascended from south-west to north-west by Grand Island, Columbus, an important Nebraska town, Schuyler, Fremont, then Omaha During its entire course, it followed the right bank of Platte River. The sledge shortening this route, took the chord of the arc described by the railroad. Mudge did not fear being stopped by the Platte River, at the short bend in front of Fremont, as it was frozen over. The way was then entirely free of obstructions, and Phileas Fogg had only two things to fear: an accident to the apparatus, a change or a calm of the wind.

But the breeze did not abate. On the contrary, it blew so hard that it bent the mast, which the iron fastenings kept firm. These metal fastenings, like the chords of an instrument, resounded as if a violin-bow had produced their vibrations. The sledge slid along in the midst of a plaintive harmony, of a very peculiar intensity.

"These chords give the fifth and the octave," said Mr. Fogg.

And these were the only words he uttered during this trip. Mrs. Aouda carefully wrapped in furs and cloaks, was preserved as much as possible from the attacks of the cold.

Passepartout, his face red as the solar disc when it sets in the midst, drew in the biting air. With the depth of unshaken confidence that he possessed, he was ready to hope again. Instead of arriving in New York in the morning, they would arrive there in the evening, but there might be some chances that it would be before the departure of the Liverpool steamer.

Passepartout even experienced a strong desire to grasp the hand of his ally Fix. He did not forget that it was the detective himself who had procured the sledge with sails, and consequently the only means there was to reach Omaha in good time. But by some unknown presentiment, he kept himself in his accustomed reserve.

At all events, one thing which Passepartout would never forget, was the sacrifice which Mr. Fogg had unhesitatingly made to rescue him from the hands of the Sioux. As for that, Mr. Fogg had risked his fortune and his life—No! his servant would not forget him!

Whilst each one of the travellers allowed himself to wander off in such various reflections the sledge flew over the immense carpet of snow. If it passed over creeks, tributaries, or sub-tributaries of Little Blue River, they did not perceive it. The fields and the streams disappeared under a uniform whiteness.

The plain was absolutely deserted. Comprised between the Union Pacific Road and the branch uniting Kearney to St. Joseph, it formed as it were a large uninhabited island. Not a village, not a station, not even a fort. From time to time they saw passing like a flash some grimacing tree, whose white skeleton was twisted about by the wind. Sometimes flocks of wild birds rose; sometimes, also, prairie wolves in large bands, gaunt, famished, urged by a ferocious demand of nature, vied with the sledge in swiftness. Then Passepartout, with revolver in hand, held himself ready to fire upon those that came nearest. If any accident had then stopped the sledge, the travellers, attacked by these ferocious carnivorous beasts, would have run the greatest risks. But the sledge kept on in its course; it was not long in getting ahead, and soon the whole howling band was left behind.

At noon, Mudge recognised by certain landmarks that he was crossing the frozen course of the Platte River. He said nothing, but he was sure that in twenty miles more he would reach Omaha.

And, indeed, one hour afterwards this skillful guide, abandoning the helm, hastened to the halyards of the sails and furled them, whilst the sledge, carried on by its irresistible force, accomplished another half-mile under bare ropes. Finally it stopped, and Mudge pointing out a mass of roofs white with snow, said: "We have arrived."

Arrived! Arrived indeed at the station which, by numerous trains, is in daily communication with the eastern part of the United States!

Passepartout and Fix jumped to the ground and shook their stiffened limbs. They helped Mr. Fogg and the young woman to descend from the sledge. Phileas Fogg settled generously with Mudge, whose hand Passepartout shook like a friend's and all hurried towards the depot in Omaha.

The Pacific Railroad, properly so called, has its terminus at this important city in Nebraska, placing the Mississippi base in connection with the great ocean. To go from Omaha to Chicago, the Chicago, Rock Island and Pacific road is taken, running directly to the east, and passing fifty stations.

A through train was ready to start. Phileas Fogg and his companions had only time to hurry into a car. They had seen nothing of Omaha; but Passepartout acknowledged to himself that it was not to be regretted, as they were not on a sight-seeing tour.

The train passed with very great speed into the State of Iowa, through Council Bluffs, Des Moines, and Iowa City. During the night it crossed the Mississippi at Davenport, and, entered Illinois at Rock Island. The next day the 10th, at four o'clock in the afternoon, they arrived at Chicago, already risen from its ruins, and sitting more proudly than ever on the shores of the beautiful Lake Michigan.

Nine hundred miles separated Chicago from New York. Trains are not wanting at Chicago. Mr. Fogg passed immediately from one to the other. The nimble locomotive of the Pittsburg, Fort Wayne, and Chicago Railway started at full speed, as if it understood that the honourable gentleman "had no time to lose." It traversed Indiana and Ohio, passing by populous cities and over wide expanses of agricultural land, with but few pauses; and, sixteen hours after leaving Chicago, the Ohio was reached.

At thirty-five minutes after nine, on the evening of the 11th, the train entered the great depot at Jersey City, the walls of which are washed by the Hudson River. From this station, the eastern terminus of a railroad system of great magnitude, fifty-one passenger and eighty-one freight trains depart every twenty-four hours, and an equal number arrive. Steamers and sailing vessels lined the miles of docks extending on both sides of the station, and the mighty river was filled with craft of all kinds engaged in the commerce of New York, which rose in front of the travellers as they emerged upon the broad, covered way running in front of the depot, where the gigantic ferry-boats of the railroad company receive and land their myriads of travellers, pausing not in their work day or night.

At thirty-five minutes after nine at night, the train stopped in the depot, near the very pier of the Cunard line of steamers, otherwise called the British and North American Royal Mail Steam Packet Company.

The *China*, bound for Liverpool, left thirty-five minutes before!

CHAPTER 32

In which Phileas Fogg engages in a Direct Struggle with Ill Luck

The *China*, in leaving, seemed to have carried away with her Phileas Fogg's last hope.

In fact, none of the other steamers in the direct service between America and Europe, neither the French Transatlantic steamers, nor the ships of the White Star line, nor those of the Inman Company, nor those of the Hamburg line, nor any others, could serve the gentleman's project.

The *Pereire*, of the French Atlantic Company, would not start until the 14th of December. And besides, like those of the Hamburg Company, she would not go directly to Liverpool or London, but to Havre, and this additional trip from Havre to Southampton, delaying Phileas Fogg, would have rendered his last efforts of no avail.

The gentleman posted himself thoroughly about all this by consulting his Bradshaw, which gave him, day by day, the movements of the trans-oceanic vessels.

Passepartout was annihilated. It killed him to miss the steamer by thirty-five minutes. It was his fault—he who, instead of aiding his master, had not ceased to scatter obstacles in his way! And when he reviewed in his mind all the incidents of the journey; when he calculated the sums spent, which were a pure loss, and for his own interest; when he thought that this enormous bet, added to the heavy expenses of this now useless journey, would completely ruin Mr. Fogg, he overwhelmed himself with opprobrium.

Mr. Fogg did not reproach him at all, and leaving the pier of the ocean steamers, he said only these words:

"We will consult to-morrow. Come."

Mr. Fogg, Mrs. Aouda, Fix, and Passepartout crossed the Hudson from Jersey City in the ferry-boat, and got into a carriage, which took them to the St. Nicholas Hotel, on Broadway. Rooms were put at their disposal, and the night passed—a very short one for Phileas Fogg, who slept soundly, but very long for Mrs. Aouda and her companions, whose agitation did not allow them to rest.

The next day was the 12th of December. From the 12th, at seven in the morning, to the 21st, at eight forty-five in the evening, there remained nine days, thirteen hours, and forty-five minutes. If, then, Phileas Fogg had left the night before in the *China* one of the best sailers of the Cunard line, he would have arrived at Liverpool, and then in London, in the desired time!

Phileas Fogg left the hotel alone, having recommended his servant to wait for him, and to notify Mrs. Aouda to hold herself in readiness at any moment.

Mr. Fogg repaired to the banks of the Hudson, and among the ships moored to the wharf, or anchored in the stream, he sought with care those which were about to leave. Several vessels had their signals for departure up and were preparing to put to sea at the morning high tide, for in this immense and admirable port, there is not a day when a hundred vessels do not set sail for every quarter of the globe; but the most of them were sailing vessels, and they would not suit Phileas Fogg.

This gentleman was seeming to fail in his last attempt, when he perceived, moored in front of the Battery, at a cable's length at most, a merchantman, with screw, of one outlines, whose smokestack, emitting clouds of smoke, indicated that she was preparing to sail.

Phileas Fogg hailed a boat, got in it, and with a few strokes of the oar, he found himself at the ladder of the *Henrietta*, an iron-hulled steamer, with her upper parts of wood.

The captain of the *Henrietta* was on board. Phileas Fogg went up on deck and asked for the captain, who presented himself immediately.

He was a man fifty years old, a sort of sea wolf, a grumbler who would not be very accommodating. His large eyes, his complexion oxydised copper, his red hair, his large chest and shoulders, indicating nothing of the appearance of a man of the world.

"The captain?" asked Mr. Fogg.

"I am he."

"I am Phileas Fogg, of London."

"And I am Andrew Speedy, of Cardiff."

"You are going to start?"

"In an hour."

"You are loaded for—?"

"Bordeaux."

"And your cargo?"

"Gravel in the hold. I have no eight. I sail in ballast."

"You have passengers?"

"No passengers. Never have passengers. A merchandise that's in the way and reasons."

"Your vessel sails swiftly?"

"Between eleven and twelve knots. The *Henrietta* is well known."

"Do you wish to convey me to Liverpool, myself and three persons?"

"To Liverpool? Why not to China?"

"I said Liverpool."

"No!"

"No?"

"No. I am setting out for Bordeaux, and I shall go to Bordeaux."

"It doesn't matter what price?"

"It don't matter what price!"

The captain spoke in a tone which did not admit of a reply.

"But the owners of the *Henrietta*—" replied Phileas Fogg.

"The owners of the *Henrietta* are myself," replied the captain. "The vessel belongs to me."

"I will freight it for you."

"No."

"No?"

"I will buy it from you."

Phileas Fogg did not change countenance. But the situation was serious. It was not at New York as at Hong-Kong, nor with the captain of the *Henrietta* as with the captain of the *Tankadere*. Until the present the gentleman's money had always overcome obstacles. This time the money failed.

But the means of crossing the Atlantic in a vessel must be found, unless they went across in a balloon, which would have been very venturesome, and which, besides, was not practicable.

Phileas Fogg, however, appeared to have an idea, for he said to the captain:

"Well, will you take me to Bordeaux?"

"No, even if you would pay me two hundred dollars."

"I offer you two thousand."

"For each person?"

"For each person."

"And there are four of you?"

"Four."

Captain Speedy commenced to scratch his forehead as if he would tear the skin off. Eight thousand dollars to be made without changing his course; it was well worth the trouble of putting aside his decided antipathy for every kind of passenger. Passengers at two thousand dollars apiece, besides, are no longer passengers, but valuable merchandise.

"I leave at nine o'clock," said Captain Speedy simply, "and you and yours will be there?"

"At nine o'clock we will be on board!" simply replied Mr. Fogg.

It was half-past eight. To land from the *Henrietta*, get in a carriage, repair to the St. Nicholas Hotel, and take back with him, Mrs. Aouda, Passepartout, and even the inseparable Fix, to whom he graciously offered a passage, this was all done by the gentleman with the quiet which never deserted him under any circumstances.

At the moment that the *Henrietta* was ready to sail, all four were aboard.

When Passepartout learned what this last voyage would cost he uttered one of those prolonged "Oh's!" which run through all the spaces of the descending chromatic scale!

As for Detective Fix, he said to himself that the Bank of England would not come out whole from this affair. In fact, by the time of their arrival, and admitting that this Mr. Fogg would not throw a few handfuls besides into the sea, more than seven thousand pounds would be missing from the bank-notes in the travelling bag!

Chapter 33

In which Phileas Fogg shows Himself equal to Circumstances

An hour afterwards the steamer *Henrietta* passed the lightboat which marks the entrance of the Hudson, turned Sandy Hook point, and put to sea. During the day she skirted Long Island, in the offing of the Fire Island Light, and rapidly ran towards the east.

At noon the next day, the 13th of December, a man went upon the bridge to take charge of the vessel. It would certainly be supposed that this man was Captain Speedy! Not at all. It was Phileas Fogg.

As for Captain Speedy, he was very snugly locked up in his cabin, and was howling at a rate that denoted an anger very pardonable, which amounted to a paroxysm.

What had happened was very simple. Phileas Fogg wanted to go to Liverpool; the captain would not take him there. Then Phileas Fogg had agreed to take passage for Bordeaux, and during the thirty hours that he had been on board, he had manoeuvred so well with his bank-notes, that the crew, sailors, and firemen—an occasional crew, on bad terms with the captain—belonged to him. And this is why Phileas Fogg commanded in the place of Captain Speedy, while the captain was shut up in his cabin, and why, finally, the *Henrietta* was steering her course toward Liverpool. It was very clear, seeing Mr. Fogg's manoeuvre, that he had been a sailor.

Now, how the adventure would come out, would be known later. Mrs. Aouda's uneasiness did not cease, although she said nothing. Fix was stunned at first-Passepartout found the thing simply splendid.

"Between eleven and twelve knots," Captain Speedy had said, and the *Henrietta* did indeed maintain this average of speed.

If then—how many "ifs" yet?—if the sea did not become too rough, if the wind did not rise in the east, if no mishap occurred to the vessel, no accident to the engine, the *Henrietta* in the nine days, counting from the 12th of December to the 21st, could accomplish the three thousand miles separating New York from Liverpool. It is true that once arrived, the *Henrietta* affair on top of the Bank affair might take the gentleman a little farther than he would like.

During the first few days they went along under excellent conditions. The wind was not too rough; the wind seemed stationary in the north-east; the sails were hoisted, and with them the *Henrietta* sailed like a genuine transatlantic steamer.

Passepartout was delighted. The last exploit of his master, the consequences of which he preferred not to consider, filled him with enthusiasm. The crew had never seen a gayer, more agile fellow. He made a thousand friendships with the sailors and astonished them by his acrobatic feats. He lavished upon them the best names and the most attractive drinks. He thought that they manoeuvred like gentlemen, and that the firemen coaled up like heroes. His good humour was very communicative, and impressed itself upon all. He had forgotten the past, with its annoyances and its perils. He thought only of the end, so nearly reached, and sometimes he boiled over with impatience, as if he had been heated by the furnace of the *Henrietta* Frequently, also, the worthy fellow revolved around Fix; he looked at him with a distrustful eye, but he did not speak to him, for there no longer existed any intimacy between these two old friends.

Besides, Fix, it must be confessed, did not understand this thing at all. The conquest of the *Henrietta,* the purchase of her crew, and Fogg manoeuvring like an accomplished seaman—this combination of things confused him. He did not know what to think. But, after all, a man who commenced by stealing fifty-five thousand pounds could finish by stealing a vessel. And Fix was naturally led to believe that the *Henrietta,* directed by Fogg, was not going to Liverpool at all, but into some quarter of the world where the robber, become a pirate, would quietly place himself in safety! This hypothesis, it must be confessed, could not be more plausible, and the detective commenced to regret very seriously having entered upon this affair.

As for Captain Speedy, he continued to howl in his cabin, and Passepartout, whose duty it was to provide his meals, did it only with the greatest precautions, although he was so strong. Mr. Fogg had no longer the appearance of even suspecting that there was a captain on board.

On the 13th they passed the edge of the Banks of Newfoundland Those are bad latitudes. During the winter, especially, the fogs are frequent there, the blows dreadful. Since the day before, the barometer, suddenly fallen, indicated an approaching change in the atmosphere. In fact, during the night the temperature varied, the cold became keener, and at the same time the wind shifted into the south-east.

This was a misfortune. Mr. Fogg, in order not to be driven out of his course, had to reef his sails and increase his steam. But the progress of the ship was slackened, owing to the condition of the sea, whose long waves broke against her stern. She was violently tossed about, and to the detriment of her speed. The breeze increased by degrees to a hurricane, and it was already a probable event that the *Henrietta* might not be able to hold herself upright against the waves. Now, if she had to fly before the storm, the unknown, with all its bad chances, threatened them.

Passepartout's face darkened at the same time as the sky, and for two days the good fellow was in mortal dread. But Phileas Fogg was a bold sailor, who knew how to keep head against the sea, and he kept on his course, without even putting the vessel under a small head of steam. The *Henrietta,* whenever she could rise with the wave, passed over it, but her deck was swept from end to end. Sometimes, too, when a mountain wave raised the stern out of the water, the screw came out of the water, beating the air with its blades, but the ship still moved right on.

Still the wind did not become as severe as might have been feared. It was not one of those hurricanes which sweep on with a velocity of ninety miles an hour. It continued quite fresh, but unfortunately it blew obstinately from the south-east, and did not allow the sails to be hoisted. And yet, as we will see, it would have been very useful if they could have come to the aid of the steam!

The 16th of December was the seventy-fifth day that had elapsed since leaving London. The *Henrietta* had not yet seen seriously delayed. The half of the voyage was nearly accomplished, and the worst localities had been passed. In summer, success would have been certain. In winter they were at the mercy of the bad weather. Passepartout did not speak. Secretly he hoped, and if the wind failed them he counted at least upon the steam.

Now, on this day, the engineer ascended to the deck, met Mr. Fogg, and talked very earnestly with him.

Without knowing why—by a presentiment, doubtless—Passepartout felt a sort of vague uneasiness. He would have given one of his ears to have heard with the other what was said. But he could catch a few words, these among others, uttered by his master:

"You are certain of what you say?"

"I am certain, sir," replied the engineer. "Do not forget that, since our departure, all our furnaces have been going, and although we had enough coal to go under a small head of steam from New York to Bordeaux, we have not enough for a full head of steam from New York to Liverpool!"

"I will take the matter under consideration," replied Mr. Fogg. Passepartout understood. A mortal fear took possession of him.

The coal was about to give out.

"Ah! if my master wards that off," he said to himself, "he will certainly be a famous man!"

And having met Fix, he could not help posting him as to the situation.

"Then," replied the detective, with set teeth, "you believe that we are going to Liverpool.?"

"I do, indeed!"

"Idiot!" replied the detective, shrugging his shoulders as he turned away.

Passepartout was on the point of sharply resenting the epithet, whose true signification he could not understand; but he said to himself that the unfortunate Fix must be very much disappointed, and humiliated in his self-esteem, having so awkwardly followed a false scent around the world, and he refrained from condemning him.

And now what course was Phileas Fogg going to take? It was difficult to guess. But it appeared that the phlegmatic gentleman decided upon one, for that evening he sent for the engineer and said to him:

"Keep up your fires and continue on your course until the complete exhaustion of the fuel."

A few moments after, the smoke stack of the *Henrietta* was vomiting torrents of smoke.

The vessel continued, then, to sail under full steam; but, as he had announced, two days later, the 18th, the engineer informed him that the coal would give out during the day.

"Don't let the fires go out," replied Mr. Fogg. "On the contrary, let the valves be charged."

About noon of this day, having taken observations and calculated the position of the vessel, Phileas Fogg sent for Passepartout and ordered him to go for Captain Speedy. This good fellow felt as if he had been commanded to unchain a tiger, and he descended into the poop, saying to himself:

"Positively I shall find a madman!"

In fact, a few minutes later a bomb came on the poop-deck, in the midst of cries and oaths. This bomb was Captain Speedy. It was evident that it was going to burst.

"Where are we?" were the first words he uttered in the midst of his choking anger, and certainly if the worthy man had been apoplectic, he would never have recovered from it.

"Where are we?" he repeated, his face purple.

"Seven hundred and seventy miles from Liverpool," replied Mr. Fogg, with imperturbable calmness.

"Pirate!" cried Andrew Speedy.

"I have sent for you, sir—"

"Sea-skimmer!"

—"Sir," continued Phileas Fogg, "to ask you to sell me your ship."

"No! by all the devils, no!"

"I shall be obliged to burn her."

"To burn my ship!"

"At least her upper portions, for we are out of fuel."

"Burn my ship !" cried Captain Speedy, who could no longer pronounce his syllables. "A ship that is worth fifty thousand dollars!"

"Here are sixty thousand!" replied Phileas Fogg, offering him a roll of bank-notes.

This produced a powerful effect upon Andrew Speedy. No American is without emotion at the sight of sixty thousand dollars. The captain forgot in an instant his anger, his imprisonment, all his grievances from his passenger. His ship was twenty years old. It might be quite a bargain! The bomb could not explode. Mr. Fogg had withdrawn the fuse.

"And the iron hull will be left me," he said in a singularly softened tone.

"The iron hull and the engine, sir. It is a bargain?"

"A bargain."

And Andrew Speedy, snatching the roll of bank-notes, counted them and slipped them into his pocket.

During this scene, Passepartout was white as a sheet. As for Fix he narrowly escaped an apoplectic fit. Nearly twenty thousand pounds spent, and yet this Fogg was going to relinquish to the seller the hull and the engine, that is, nearly the entire value of the vessel! It is true that the sum stolen from the bank amounted to fifty-five thousand pounds!

When Andrew Speedy had pocketed his money, Mr. Fogg said to him:

"Sir, don't let all this astonish you. Know that I lose twenty thousand pounds if I am not in London on the 21st of December, at a quarter before nine in the evening. Now, I had missed the steamer from New York, and as you refused to take me to Liverpool—"

"And I have done well, by all the imps of the lower regions," cried Andrew Speedy, "since I make by it at least forty thousand dollars."

Then he added, more calmly:

"Do you know one thing, Captain—!"

"Fogg."

"Well, Captain Fogg, there is something of the Yankee in you."

And having paid his passenger what he thought to be a compliment, he went away, when Phileas Fogg said to him:

"Now this ship belongs to me?"

"Certainly, from the keel to the truck of the masts, all the wood, understand."

"Very well. Cut away the inside arrangements and fire up with the debris."

It may be judged how much of this dry wood was necessary to maintain the steam at sufficient pressure. This day, the poop-deck, the cabins, the bunks, and the spare deck all went.

The next day, the 19th of December, they burned the masts, the rafts, and the spars. They cut down the masts, and delivered them to the axe. The crew displayed an incredible zeal. Passepartout, hewing, cutting, sawing, did the work of ten men. It was a perfect fury of demolition.

The next day, the 20th, the railings, the armour, all of the ship above water, the greater part of the deck, were consumed. The *Henrietta* was now a vessel cut down like a pontoon.

But on this day they sighted the coast of Ireland and Fastnet Light.

However at ten o'clock in the evening the ship was only passing Queenstown. Phileas Fogg had only twenty-four hours to reach London. Now, this was the time the *Henrietta* needed to reach Liverpool, even under full headway. And the steam was about to fail the bold gentleman!

"Sir," said Captain Speedy to him then, who had come to be interested in his projects, "I really pity you. Everything is against you. We are yet only in front of Queenstown."

"Ah!" said Mr. Fogg, "that is Queenstown, the place where we perceive the light?"

"Yes."

"Can we enter the harbour?"

"Not for three hours. Only at high tide."

"Let us wait," Phileas Fogg replied calmly, without letting it be seen on his face that, by a last inspiration, he was going to try to conquer once more his contrary fate!

Queenstown is a port on the coast of Ireland, at which the transatlantic steamers coming from the United States deposit their mail-bag. These letters are carried to Dublin by express trains always ready to start. From Dublin they arrive in Liverpool by very swift vessels, thus gaining twelve hours over the most rapid sailers of the ocean companies.

These twelve hours which the America couriers gained, Phileas Fogg intended to gain too. Instead of arriving by the *Henrietta* in the evening of the next day, at Liverpool, he would be there by noon, and, consequently, he would have time enough to reach London before a quarter of nine in the evening.

Towards one o'clock in the morning, the *Henrietta* entered Queenstown harbour at high tide, and Phileas Fogg, having received a vigorous shake of the hand from Captain Speedy, left him on the levelled hulk of his vessel, still worth the half of what he had sold it for!

The passengers landed immediately. Fix at this moment, had a fierce desire to arrest Mr. Fogg. He did not do it, however. Why? What conflict was going on within him? Had he changed his mind with reference to Mr. Fogg? Did he finally perceive that he was mistaken? Fix, however, did not leave Mr. Fogg. With him, Mrs. Aouda, and Passepartout, who did not take time to breathe, he jumped into a train a Queenstown at half-past one in the morning, arrived at Dublin at break of day, and immediately embarked on one of those steamers—regular steel spindles, all engine—which, disdaining to rise with the waves, invariably pass right through them.

At twenty minutes before noon, the 21st of December, Phileas Fogg finally landed on the quay at Liverpool. He was now only six hours from London.

But at this moment Fix approached him, put his hand on his shoulder, and, showing his warrant, said:

"You are really Phileas Fogg?"

"Yes, sir."

"I arrest you in the name of the Queen."

Chapter 34

Which gives Passepartout the opportunity of letting out some atrocious, but perhaps Unpublished, Words

Phileas Fogg was in prison. He had been shut up in the Custom House in Liverpool, and was to pass the night there, awaiting his transfer to London.

At the moment of his arrest, Passepartout wished to rush upon the detective. Some policemen held him back. Mrs. Aouda, frightened by the brutality of the act, and knowing nothing about it, could not understand it. Passepartout explained the situation to her. Mr. Fogg, this honest and courageous gentleman, to whom she owed her life, was arrested as a robber. The young woman protested against such an allegation, her heart rose with indignation, and tears flowed from her eyes when she saw that she could not do anything, or attempt anything to save her deliverer.

As for Fix, he had arrested the gentleman because his duty commanded him to, whether he was guilty or not. The courts would decide the question.

But then a thought came to Passepartout—the terrible thought that he was certainly the cause of all this misfortune! Indeed, why had he concealed this adventure from Mr. Fogg? When Fix had revealed both his capacity as a detective and the mission into which he was charged, why had he decided not to warn his master? The latter, informed, would without doubt have given Fix proofs of his innocence; he would have demonstrated to him his error; at any rate, he would not have conveyed at his expense and on his tracks this unfortunate detective, whose first care was to arrest him the moment he set foot on the soil of the United Kingdom. Thinking of his faults and his imprudence, the poor fellow was overwhelmed with remorse. He wept, so that it was painful to look at him. He felt like blowing his brains out.

Mrs. Aouda and he remained, notwithstanding the cold, under the porch of the Custom House. Neither of them wished to leave the place. They wanted to see Mr. Fogg once more.

As for that gentleman, he was really ruined, and at the very moment that he was about to reach his end. This arrest would ruin him irrecoverably. Having arrived at Liverpool at twenty minutes before twelve, noon, on the 21st of December, he had until quarter of nine in the evening to appear at the Reform Club—that is, nine hours and five minutes, and he only needed six to reach London. At this moment, anyone entering the Custom House would have found Mr. Fogg seated motionless, on a wooden bench, without anger, imperturbable. He could not have been said to be resigned, but this blow had not been able to move him, in appearance at least. Was he fostering within himself one of those secret spells of anger, terrible because they are pent up, and which breaks out only at the last moment with irresistible force? We do not know. But Phileas Fogg was there, calm, waiting for—what? Did he cherish some hope? Did he still believe in success, when the door of his prison was dosed upon him?

However that may be, Mr. Fogg carefully put his watch on the table, and watched the hands move. Not a word escaped from his lips, but his look had a singular fixedness.

In any event, the situation was terrible, and for anyone that could read his thoughts, they ran thus:

An honest man, Phileas Fogg, was ruined.

A dishonest man, he was caught.

Did he think of escaping? Did he think of looking to see whether there was a practicable outlet from his prison? Did he think of flying? We would be tempted to believe so; for, once he took the tour of the room. But the door was securely locked and the windows had iron bars. He sat down again, and took from his pocket-book the diary of his journey. On the line which bore these words;

"December 21st, Saturday, Liverpool," he added:

"Eightieth day, 11.40 am.," and he waited.

The Custom House dock struck one. Mr. Fogg observed that his watch was two hours fast by this clock.

Two hours! Admitting that he should jump aboard an express train at this moment he could still arrive in London and at the Reform Club before quarter of nine in the evening. A light frown passed over his forehead.

At thirty-three minutes after two o'clock a noise sounded outside, a bustle from the opening of doors. The voice of Passepartout was heard, and also that of Fix.

Phileas Fogg's look brightened up a moment.

The door opened, and he saw Mrs. Aouda, Passepartout, Fix, rushing towards him.

Fix was out of breath, his hair all disordered, and he could not speak.

"Sir," he stammered, "sir—pardon—an unfortunate resemblance—robber arrested three days ago—you—free—!"

Phileas Fogg was free! He went to the detective, looked him well in the face, and with the only rapid movement that he ever had made or ever would make in his life, he drew both his arms back, and then, with the precision of an automaton, he struck the unfortunate detective with both his fists.

"Well Sir" cried Passepartout, who, allowing himself an atrocious flow of words, quite worthy of a Frenchman, added: "Zounds! this is what might be called a fine application of English fists!"

Fix, prostrate, did not utter a word. He only got what he deserved. But Mr. Fogg, Mrs. Aouda, and Passepartout immediately left the Custom House. They jumped into a carriage and in a few minutes arrived at the depot.

Phileas Fogg asked if there was an express train ready to start for London.

It was forty minutes past two. The express left thirty-five minutes before.

Phileas Fogg then ordered a special train.

There were several locomotives of great speed with steam up; but, owing to the exigencies of the service, the special train could not leave the depot before three o'clock.

At three o'clock, Phileas Fogg, after saying a few words to

the engineer about a certain reward to be won, moved on in the direction of London, in the company of the young woman and his faithful servant.

The distance which separates Liverpool from London must be accomplished in five hours and a half—a very feasible thing when the road is clear on the whole route. But there were compulsory delays, and when the gentleman arrived at the depot all the clocks in London were striking ten minutes of nine.

Phileas Fogg, after having accomplished this tour of the world, arrived, five minutes behind time!

He had lost his bet.

Chapter 35

In which Passepartout does not have repeated to Him twice the Order His Master gives Him

The next day the residents of Saville Row would have been much surprised if they had been told that Phileas Fogg had returned to his dwelling. The doors and windows were all closed. No change had taken place outside.

After leaving the depot Phileas Fogg gave Passepartout an order to buy some provisions, and he had gone into his house.

This gentleman received with his habitual impassibility the blow which struck him. Ruined! and by the fault of that awkward detective! After moving on with steady step during this long trip, overturning a thousand obstacles, braving a thousand dangers, and having still found time to do some good on his route, to fail before a brutal act, which he could not foresee, and against which he was defenceless—that was terrible! He had left only an insignificant remnant of the large sum which he had taken away with him when he started on his journey. His fortune now only consisted of the twenty thousand pounds deposited at Baring Brothers, and those twenty thousand pounds he owed to his colleagues of the Reform Club. Having incurred so many expenses, if he had won the bet he would not have been enriched; and it is probable that he had not sought to enrich himself, being of that class of men who bet for the sake of honour—but this bet lost would ruin him entirely. The gentleman's decision was taken. He knew what remained for him to do.

A room in the house in Saville Row was set apart for Mrs. Aouda. The young woman was desperate. From certain words which Mr.Fogg let drop, she understood that he contemplated some fatal design.

It is known, indeed, to what lamentable extremities these Englishmen are carried sometimes under the pressure of a fixed area. Thus, Passepartout, without seeming to do so, was closely watching his master.

But first the good fellow descended to his room and turned off the burner which had been burning for eighty days. He found in the letter-box a note from the gas company, and the thought that it was more than time to stop the expenses for which he was responsible.

The night passed. Mr. Fogg had retired; but had he slept? As for Mrs. Aouda, she could not take a single moment's rest. Passepartout had watched, like a dog, at his master's door.

The next morning Mr. Fogg sent for him, and ordered him very briefly to prepare Mrs. Aouda's breakfast. As for himself, he would be satisfied with a cup of tea and a piece of toast. Mrs. Aouda would be kind enough to excuse him from breakfast and dinner, for all his time would be devoted to arranging his affairs. He would not come down. He would only ask Mrs. Aouda's permission to have a few moment's conversation with her in the evening.

Passepartout, having been given the programme for the day, had nothing to do but to conform to it. He looked at his master, still so impassible, and he could not make up his mind to quit his room. His heart was full, and his conscience weighed down with remorse, for he accused himself more than ever for this irreparable disaster. Yes! if he had warned Mr. Fogg, if he had disclosed to him the plans of the detective Fix, Mr. Fogg would not have dragged the detective Fix with him as far as Liverpool, and then . . .

Passepartout could not hold in any longer.

"My master! Monsieur Fogg!" he cried, "curse me. It is through my fault that — "

"I blame no one," replied Phileas Fogg in the calmest tone. "Go."

Passepartout left the room and went to find the young woman, to whom he made known his master's intentions.

"Madame," he added, "I can do nothing by myself, nothing at all. I have no influence over my master's mind. You, perhaps—"

"What influence would I have," replied Mrs. Aouda "Mr.Fogg is subject to none. Has he ever understood that my gratitude for him was overflowing? Has he ever read my heart? My friend, you must not leave him a single instant. You say that he has shown a desire to speak to me this evening?"

"Yes, madame. It is no doubt with reference to making your position in England comfortable."

"Let us wait," replied the young woman, who was quite pensive.

Thus during this day, Sunday, the house in Saville Row was as if uninhabited, and for the first time since he lived there, Phileas Fogg did not go to his club, when the Parliament House clock struck half-past eleven.

And why should this gentleman have presented himself at the Reform Club? His colleagues no longer expected him. Since Phileas Fogg did not appear in the saloon of the Reform Club the evening of the day before, on this fatal date, Saturday, December 21st, at quarter before nine, his bet was lost. It was not even necessary that he should go to his banker's to draw this sum of twenty thousand pounds. His opponents had in their hands a cheque signed by him, and it only needed a simple writing to go to Baring Brothers in order that the twenty thousand pounds might be carried to their credit.

Mr. Fogg had then nothing to take him out, and he did not go out. He remained in his room, putting his affairs in order. Passepartout was continually going up and down stairs. The hours did not move for this poor fellow. He listened at the door of his master's room, and in doing so, did not think he committed the least indiscretion. He looked through the keyhole, and imagined that he had this right. Passepartout feared at every moment some catastrophe. Sometimes he thought of Fix, but a change had taken place in his mind. He no longer blamed the detective. Fix had been deceived, like everybody else, with respect to Phileas Fogg, and in following him and arresting him he had only done his duty, while he . . . This thought overwhelmed him, and he considered himself the most wretched of human beings.

When, finally, Passepartout would be too unhappy to be alone, he would knock at Mrs. Aouda's door, enter her room, and sit down in a corner without saying a word, and look at the young woman with a pensive air.

About half-past seven in the evening, Mr. Fogg sent to ask Mrs. Aouda if she could receive him, and in a few moments after the young woman and he were alone in the room.

Phileas Fogg took a chair and sat down near the fireplace opposite Mrs. Aouda. His face reflected no emotion. Fogg returned was exactly the Fogg who had gone away. The same calmness, the same impassibility.

He remained without speaking for five minutes. Then, raising his eyes to Mrs. Aouda, he said:

"Madame, will you pardon me for having brought you to England?"

"I, Mr. Fogg!" replied Mrs. Aouda, suppressing the throbbings of her heart.

"Be kind enough to allow me to finish," continued Mr. Fogg. "When I thought of taking you so far away from that country, become so dangerous for you, I was rich, and I counted on placing a portion of my fortune at your disposal. Your life would have been happy and free. Now, I am ruined."

"I know it, Mr. Fogg," replied the young woman, "and I in turn will ask you—Will you pardon me for having followed you, and— who knows? for having perhaps assisted in your ruin by delaying you?"

"Madame, you could not remain in India, and your safety was only assured by removing you so far that those fanatics could not retake you."

"So, Mr. Fogg," replied Mrs. Aouda, "not satisfied with rescuing me from a horrible death, you believe you were obliged to assure my position abroad?"

"Yes, madame, replied Fogg, "but events have turned against me. However, I ask your permission to dispose of the little I have left in your favour."

"But you, Mr. Fogg, what will become of you?" asked Mrs. Aouda.

"I, madame," replied the gentleman coldly, "I do not need anything."

"But how, sir, do you look upon the fate that awaits you.?"

"As I ought to look at it," replied Mr. Fogg.

"In any event," continued Mrs. Aouda, "want could not reach such-a man as you. Your friends—"

"I have no friends, madame."

"Your relatives—"

"I have no relatives now."

"I pity you, then, Mr. Fogg, for solitude is a sad thing. What! have you not one heart into which to pour your troubles? They say, however, that with two, misery itself is bearable!"

"They say so, madame."

"Mr. Fogg," then said Mrs. Aouda, rising and holding out her hand to the gentleman, ado you wish at once a relative and a friend? Will you have me for your wife?"

Mr. Fogg, at this, rose in his turn. There seemed to be an unusual reaction in his eyes, a trembling of his lips. Mrs. Aouda looked at him. The sincerity, rectitude, firmness, and sweetness of this soft look of a noble woman, who dared everything to save him to whom she owed everything, first astonished him, then penetrated him. He closed his eyes for an instant, as if to prevent this look from penetrating deeper. When he opened them again, he simply said:

"I love you. Yes, in truth, by everything most sacred in the world, I love you, and I am entirely yours!"

"Ah!" cried Mrs. Aouda, pressing his hand to her heart.

He rang for Passepartout. He came immediately. Mr. Fogg was still holding Mrs. Aouda's hand in his. Passepartout understood, and his broad face shone like the sun in the zenith of tropical regions.

Mr. Fogg asked him if he would be too late to notify Rev. Samuel Wilson, of Mary-le-Bone Parish.

Passepartout gave his most genial smile.

"Never too late," he said.

It was then five minutes after eight.

"It will be for to-morrow, Monday," he said.

"For to-morrow, Monday?" asked Mr. Fogg, looking at the young woman.

"For to-morrow, Monday!" replied Mrs. Aouda

Passepartout went out, running as hard as he could.

Chapter 36

In which "Phileas Fogg" is again at a Premium in the Market

It is time to tell here what a change of opinion was produced in the United Kingdom when they learned of the arrest of the true robber of the bank, a certain James Strand, which took place in Edinburgh on the 17th of December.

Three days before, Phileas Fogg was a criminal whom the police were pursuing to the utmost, and now he was the most honest gentleman, accomplishing mathematically his eccentric tour round the world.

What an effect, what an excitement in the papers! All the betters for or against, who had already forgotten this affair, revived as if by magic. All the transactions became of value. All the engagements were renewed, and it must be said that betting was resumed with new energy. The name of Phileas Fogg was again at a premium on the market.

The five colleagues of the gentleman, at the Reform Club, passed these three days in some uneasiness. Would this Phileas Fogg, whom they had forgotten, reappear before their eyes? Where was he at this moment? On the 17th of December—the day that James Strand was arrested—it was seventy-six days since Phileas Fogg started, and no news from him! Was be dead? Had he given up the effort, or was he continuing his course as agreed upon? And would he appear on Saturday, the 21st of December, at a quarter before nine in the evening, the very impersonation of exactness, on the threshold of the saloon of the Reform Club?

We must give up the effort to depict the anxiety in which for three days all of London society lived. They sent dispatches to America, to Asia, to get news of Phileas Fogg. They sent morning and evening to watch the house in Saville Row. Nothing there. The police themselves did not know what had become of the detective Fix, who had so unfortunately thrown himself on a false scent. This did not prevent bets from being entered into anew on a larger scale. Phileas Fogg, like a racehorse, was coming to the last turn. He was quoted no longer at one hundred, but at twenty, ten, five; and the old paralytic Lord Albemarle bet even in his favour.

So that on Saturday evening there was a crowd in Pall Mall and in the neighbouring streets. It might have been supposed that there was an immense crowd of brokers permanently established around the Reform Club. Circulation was impeded. They discussed, disputed, and cried the prices of "Phileas Fogg," like they did those of English Consuls. The policemen had much difficulty in keeping the crowd back, and in proportion as the hour approached at which Phileas Fogg ought to arrive, the excitement took incredible proportions.

This evening, the five colleagues of the gentleman were assembled in the grand saloon of the Reform Club. The two bankers, John Sullivan and Samuel Fallentin, the engineer Andrew Stuart, Gauthier Ralph, the director of the Bank of England, and the brewer, Thomas Flanagan, all waited with anxiety.

At the moment that the clock in the grand saloon indicated twenty-five minutes past eight, Andrew Stuart, rising, said:

"Gentlemen, in twenty minutes the time agreed upon between Mr. Phileas Fogg and ourselves will have expired."

"At what hour did the last train arrive from Liverpool asked Thomas Flanagan.

"At twenty-three minutes after seven," replied Gauthier Ralph, "and the next train does not arrive until ten minutes after twelve, midnight."

"Well, gentlemen," continued Andrew Stuart, "if Phileas Fogg had arrived in the train at twenty-three minutes after seven, he would already be here. We can then consider we have won the bet."

"Let us wait before deciding," replied Samuel Fallentin. "You know that our colleague is an oddity of the first order. His exactness in everything is well known. He never arrives too late or too soon, and he will appear here at the very last minute, or I shall be very much surprised."

"And I," said Andrew Stuart, who was, as always, very nervous, "would not believe it was he if I saw him."

"In fact," replied Thomas Flanagan, "Phileas Fogg's project was a senseless one. However exact he might be, he could not prevent the occurrence of inevitable delays, and a delay of but two or three days would be sufficient to compromise the tour."

"You will notice besides," added John Sullivan "that we have received no news from our colleague, and yet telegraph lines were not wanting upon his route."

"Gentlemen, he has lost," replied Andrew Stuart, "he has lost a hundred times! You know, besides, that the *China*—the only steamer from New York that he could take for Liverpool to be of any use to him—arrived yesterday. Now, here is the list of passengers, published by the *Shipping Gazette*, and the name of Phileas Fogg is not among them. Admitting the most favourable chances, our colleague has scarcely reached America! I calculate twenty days, at least, as the time that he will be behind, and old Lord Albermarle will be minus his five thousand pounds!"

"It is evident," replied Gauthier Ralph, "and to-morrow we have only to present to Baring Brothers Mr. Fogg's cheque."

At this moment, the clock in the saloon struck forty minutes after eight.

"Five minutes yet," said Andrew Stuart.

The five colleagues looked at each other. It may be believed that their hearts beat a little more rapidly, for, even for good players, it was a great risk. But they did not betray themselves, for at Samuel Fallentin's suggestion, they seated themselves at a card table.

"I would not give my part of four thousand pounds in the bet," said Andrew Stuart, seating himself, "even if I was offered three thousand nine hundred and ninety-nine!"

At this moment the hands noted forty-two minutes after eight.

The players took up their cards, but their eyes were constantly fixed upon the clock. It may be asserted that notwithstanding their security, the minutes had never seemed so long to them!

"Forty-three minutes after eight," said Thomas Flanagan, cutting the cards which Gauthier Ralph presented to him.

Then there was a moment's silence. The immense saloon of the Club was quiet. But outside they heard the hubbub of the crowd, above which were sometimes heard loud cries. The pendulum of the clock was beating the seconds with mathematical regularity, and every player could count them as they struck his ear.

"Forty-four minutes after eight," said John Sullivan, in a voice in which was heard an involuntary emotion.

One more minute and the bet would be won. Andrew Stuart and his colleagues played no longer. They had abandoned their cards! They were counting the seconds!

At the fortieth second, nothing. At the fiftieth still nothing!

At the fifty-fifth, there was a roaring like that of thunder outside, shouts, hurrahs, and even curses kept up in one prolonged roll.

The players rose.

At the fifty-seventh second, the door of the saloon opened, and the pendulum had not beat the sixtieth second, when Phileas Fogg appeared, followed by an excited crowd, who had forced an entrance into the Club, and in his calm voice he said:

"Gentlemen, here I am!"

Chapter 37

In which it is Proved that Phileas Fogg has gained nothing by making this Tour of the World, unless it be Happiness

Yes! Phileas Fogg in person.

It will be remembered that at five minutes after eight in the evening, about twenty-five hours after the arrival of the travellers in London, Passepartout was charged by his master to inform Rev. Samuel Wilson in reference to a certain marriage which was to take place the next day.

Passepartout went, delighted. He repaired with rapid steps to the residence of Rev. Samuel Wilson, who had not come home. Of course Passepartout waited, but he waited full twenty minutes at east. In short, it was thirty-five minutes past eight when he left the clergyman's house. But in what a condition! His hair disordered, hatless, running, running as has never been seen in the memory of man, upsetting passers-by, rushing along the sidewalks like a water-spout.

In three minutes, he had returned to the house in Saville Row, and fell out of breath, in Mr. Fogg's room.

He could not speak.

"What is the matter?" asked Mr. Fogg.

"Master"—stammered Passepartout—"Marriage—impossible!"

"Impossible-?"

"Impossible—to-morrow."

"Why?"

"Because to-morrow is—Sunday."

"Monday," replied Mr. Fogg.

"No—to-day—Saturday."

"Saturday? Impossible!"

"Yes, yes, yes!" cried Passepartout. "You have made a mistake of one day. We arrived twenty-four hours in advance—but there are not ten minutes left!"

Passepartout seized his master by the collar, and dragged him along with irresistible force!

Phileas Fogg, thus taken, without having time to reflect, left the room, went out of his house, jumped into a cab, promised one hundred pounds to the driver, and, after running over two dogs and running into five carriages, arrived at the Reform Club.

The clock indicated quarter of nine when he appeared in the grand saloon.

Phileas Fogg had accomplished this tour of the world in eighty days!

Phileas Fogg had won his bet of twenty thousand pounds!

And now, how could so exact and cautious a man have made the mistake of a day? How did he think that it was the evening of Saturday, December 21st, when it was only Friday, December 20th, only seventy-nine days after his departure.

This is the reason for this mistake. It is very simple.

Phileas Fogg had, without suspecting it, gained a day on his journey—only because he had made the tour of the world going to the *east*, and on the contrary, he would have lost a day going in the contrary direction, that is, towards the *west.*

Indeed, journeying towards the east, Phileas Fogg was going towards the sun, and consequently the days became as many times four minutes less for him, as he crossed degrees in that direction. Now there are three hundred and sixty degrees in the earth's circumference, and these three hundred and sixty degrees, multiplied by four minutes, give precisely twenty-four hours—that is to say, the day unconsciously gained. In other words, while Phileas Fogg, travelling towards the east, saw the sun pass the meridian *eighty* times, his colleagues, remaining in London, saw it pass only *seventy-nine* times. Therefore this very day, which was Saturday, and not Sunday, as Mr. Fogg thought, his friends were waiting for him in the saloon of the Reform Club.

And Passepartout's famous watch, which had always kept London time, would have shown this, if it had indicated days, as well as the minutes and hours!

Phileas Fogg then had won the twenty thousand pounds. But as he had spent in his journey about nineteen thousand, the pecuniary result was small. However, as has been said, the eccentric gentleman had sought in his bet to gain the victory and not to make money. And even the thousand pounds remaining he divided between Passepartout and the unfortunate Fix, against whom he could not cherish a grudge. Only for the sake of exactness, he retained from his servant the cost of the gas burned through his fault for nineteen hundred and twenty hours.

This very evening Mr. Fogg, as impassible and as phlegmatic as ever, said to Mrs. Aouda:

"This marriage is still agreeable to you?"

"Mr. Fogg," replied Mrs. Aouda, "it is for me to ask you that question. You were ruined; now you are rich—"

"Pardon me, madame; my fortune belongs to you. If you had not thought of the marriage, my servant would not have gone to the house of Rev. Samuel Wilson. I would not have been apprised of my mistake, and—"

"Dear Mr. Fogg—" said the young woman.

"Dear Aouda," replied Phileas Fogg.

It is readily understood that the marriage took place forty-eight hours later, and Passepartout, superb, resplendent, dazzling, was present as the young woman's witness. Had he not saved her, and did they not owe him that honour?

At daylight the next morning, Passepartout knocked noisily at his master's door.

The door opened, and the impassible gentleman appeared.

"What is the matter, Passepartout?"

"What's the matter, sir! I have just found out this moment—

"What?"

"That we could make the tour of the world in seventy-eight days."

"Doubtless," replied Mr. Fogg, "by not crossing India But if I had not crossed India, I would not have saved Mrs. Aouda, she would not be my wife, and—"

And Mr. Fogg quietly shut the door.

Thus Phileas Fogg won his bet. In eighty days he had accomplished the tour around the world!

To do this he had employed every means of conveyance, steamers, railways, carriages, yachts, merchant vessels, sledges, elephants. The eccentric gentleman had displayed in this affair his wonderful qualities of coolness and exactness.

But what then? What had he gained by leaving home? What had he brought back from his journey?

Nothing, do you say? Nothing, perhaps, but a charming woman, who—improbable as it may appear—made him the happiest of men!

Truly, would you not, for less than that, make the tour of the world?